WILLIAM MORRIS was a staggeringly talented man. He was architect, sculptor, author, musician, artist and translator extraordinary; he designed fabrics, glass, and furniture, musical instruments and, undoubtedly, many a labor-saving device around the house. For he believed in the wholeness of life, he admired the simplicity of an earlier day and deplored the industrial revolution of which he saw only the beginning.

In his writing he attempted to hark back to a simpler, wiser time, to values that seemed to be disappearing from his own world.

THE WELL AT THE WORLD'S END, his literary masterwork, is a commentary on life. The Well itself is a chimera, a test, indeed, the final deadly test for those few who find it. But it is the Journey that matters, the Road to the Well, the quest that encounters all the diversions of life itself and gets there despite the adventures, the threats, the dangers and the temptations. The Well is a grand tale, fully worthy of one of the nineteenth century's most creative artists.

Also by William Morris
published by Ballantine Books:

WATER OF THE WONDROUS ISLE

THE WOOD BEYOND THE WORLD

THE SUNDERING FLOOD

The Well
at the
World's End

a tale by

William Morris

Introduction by
Lin Carter

A Del Rey Book

BALLANTINE BOOKS • NEW YORK

A Del Rey Book
Published by Ballantine Books

ISBN 0-345-27239-0

Manufactured in the United States of America

First Ballantine Books Edition: July 1970
Third Printing: August 1973

First Revised Edition: July 1975
Second Printing: May 1977

Contents

BOOK ONE: THE ROAD UNTO LOVE

BOOK TWO: THE ROAD UNTO TROUBLE

BOOK THREE: THE ROAD TO THE WELL AT THE
WORLD'S END

BOOK FOUR: THE ROAD HOME

About THE WELL AT THE WORLD'S END, *and William Morris*

Utterbol, and the Way Thither

AND so the four sons of the King drew straws to see which of them would rule the little kingdom after their father, and which would ride to the north or the east or the west in quest of adventure. And so the youngest of the four princes set forth on his destrier, Falcon, and departed from the little kingdom of Upmeads in quest of Utterbol which lieth beyond the Wood Perilous, the Castle of Abundance, the Burg of the Four Friths, and the Vale of the Tower, to the place of the miraculous Well . . .

And thus begins *The Well at the World's End,* one of the first and one of the finest novels of heroic fantasy ever written.

Scholars and historians of fantasy, such as my friend L. Sprague de Camp, agree that it was the English novelist, poet, and artisan William Morris (1834–96) who founded the genre of the heroic fantasy laid in imaginary Medieval lands or worlds where magic works. His first novel in this genre, *The Wood Beyond The World* (1895), has already been revived in our Adult Fantasy Series. It was the first of all such tales of adventurous wanderings through the marvelous landscapes of worlds which have somehow managed to avoid the wear and tear of ever having actually existed. But far better, and nearly twice as long, is this present book, which is Morris' masterpiece.

The Well at the World's End was the second of his fantasy novels, published in 1896. At approximately 228,000 words, it is one of the longest fantasy novels ever written—probably the longest novel in this field before Professor Tolkien wrote *The Lord of the Rings*—and so lengthy that Ballantine previously published it in two volumes, which were combined for this edition.

Now, when de Camp or I say that William Morris

founded the heroic fantasy novel we are of course aware that earlier examples can be found. Even without going all the way back to the Late Middle Ages and such prose romances as *Palmerin of England, Amadis of Gaul,* or *Felixmarte of Hyrcania,* it is possible to find forerunners of Morris. One of them was George MacDonald, whose "faerie romance," *Lilith,* appeared in 1895, the same year as Morris' first great fantasy, *The Wood Beyond The World.* MacDonald also wrote a novel of fantasy, appropriately titled *Phantastes,* published in 1858 when William Morris was twenty-four. And then there was George Meredith, who wrote an Oriental extravaganza called *The Shaving of Shagpat,* published in 1855. And that Prince of Eccentrics, William Beckford, whose astonishing *Vathek* was published in English translation nearly three-quarters of a century earlier, in 1786. (Publication of the French original was preceded by the translation, oddly enough.)

These four famous fantasies came before William Morris, yet we still consider Morris the founder of the genre. There are two reasons for this seemingly contradictory claim. In the first place, Oriental tales like *Vathek* and *The Shaving of Shagpat* are set—not in completely imaginary worlds of their authors' invention, as are the romances of William Morris—but in "literary" versions of the actual Middle East: in exotic Arabian Nights landscapes, real but romanticized. Then again, such novels as *Lilith* and *Phantastes* are set in Dreamland: we are not expected to take their imagined landscapes seriously; over and over MacDonald reiterates that his heroes are wandering through a waking dream. Thus, if we accept MacDonald as the founder of the heroic fantasy laid in invented worlds, we would also have to admit *Alice's Adventures in Wonderland* (1865) to the fold, as well. And, obviously, that would never do. The key element in the imaginary-world romance is that the reader is to assume that the worldscape of the story is *a real place*: that the hero of such a story is in very real danger from the various monsters and magicians he encounters; in a word, you can get *killed* on the road to Utterbol. Not so, in MacDonald's dreamscapes.

The second reason why we consider Morris to be "the man who invented fantasy" is that the tradition of this genre descends from his romances in a direct line. No one ever tried to write another *Vathek* or *Shagpat,* and only a few books (such as the *Perelandra* trilogy of C. S. Lewis and David Lindsay's brilliant and astounding novel *A*

Voyage to Arcturus) show to any extent the influence of *Lilith* and *Phantastes*. But the genre of the heroic fantasy laid in an imaginary world descends from William Morris to Lord Dunsany and E. R. Eddison, and from thence to whole generations of writers such as James Branch Cabell, Fletcher Pratt (*The Blue Star*), Robert E. Howard, J. R. R. Tolkien, L. Sprague de Camp (*The Tritonian Ring* and *The Goblin Tower*), Fritz Leiber, Jack Vance, Jane Gaskell, Lloyd Alexander, and my own (as yet incomplete and unpublished) fantasy epic, *Khymyrium*.

No one—to my knowledge, anyway—has ever tried to explain just why Morris began making up the worlds in which he set his tales. It is especially puzzling when you consider that many of his works prior to that first great fantasy, *The Wood Beyond The World*, were set in actual historical or at least legendary settings. Such as his *Sigurd the Volsung*, laid against the scenery of the ancient Rhineland; or his book-length poem *The Life and Death of Jason*, which unfolds in settings borrowed from Greek mythology; or his first novel, *The House of the Wulfings*, published six years before *Wood* and depicting the struggle of the noble but primitive Germanic warriors against the advanced but decadent Roman legions.

Perhaps Morris found his storytelling talents uncomfortably restricted by the necessity of making his tales conform to known historical events or landscapes, and yearned for the completer freedom of the fantasy novelist. If so, his motive was the same as that which impelled the brilliant American novelist James Branch Cabell to turn aside from tales of cavaliers and Elizabethan heroes to his invented quasi-Medieval province of Poictesme and other realms—Antan, Cockaigne, Hell, and Paradise—whose attachments to Reality are even more remote and tenuous.

Most likely, however, Morris was improvising his worlds to a slightly larger extent than that found in the Medieval prose romances whose form and style he was imitating in these novels. He was nostalgically hearkening back to the sort of adventure story set in dim landscapes whose geography is at best, vague and imprecise. As, for example, in the early thirteenth century *Parzival* of Wolfram von Eschenbach, when Gahmuret in Book II journeys overland from Dolet (Toledo) to Waleis (Wales), somehow managing the trip without crossing the English Channel, no one is particularly surprised: that is the way things happen in romances!

The authors of Medieval romance mingled real and made-up geography with a fine contempt for consistency. In the Arthurian romances, the wandering knights appear equally at home in actual places like Scotland, Winchester, or Brittany, as they do in Sarras or Belacane or Avalon, which of course do not and never did exist. In the great *Amadis*, the Knight of the Green Sword finds actual realms such as Greece or France somehow contiguous to purely imaginary places such as the Firm Island or the land of Urganda the Unknown. And the knightly adventurers of *Orlando Furioso* are as likely to be found in Cathay or Tartary as they are in the mysterious kingdom of Prester John or the strange valleys of the Moon. What William Morris did was to go these early romancers one better, and make up a whole world insead of merely parts of one. In so doing, the fantasy novel was born.

This novel, *The Well at the World's End*, was first published by Longmans, Green and Co. in London in 1896. It has been out of print now, insofar as I have been able to discover, for slightly less than a half-century. As you will perhaps agree as you turn the page and set forth on the way to Utterbol and the wondrous Well, it is high time so marvelous a story was revived and once again made available to all of the many thousands of fantasy enthusiasts who have yet to venture in the magic worlds of William Morris, the man who invented fantasy.

—LIN CARTER
Hollis, Long Island, New York

BOOK ONE
The Road
Unto Love

CHAPTER 1
The Sundering of the Ways

Long ago there was a little land, over which ruled a regulus or kinglet, who was called King Peter, though his kingdom was but little. He had four sons whose names were Blaise, Hugh, Gregory and Ralph: of these Ralph was the youngest, whereas he was but of twenty winters and one; and Blaise was the oldest and had seen thirty winters.

Now it came to this at last, that to these young men the kingdom of their father seemed strait; and they longed to see the ways of other men, and to strive for life. For though they were king's sons, they had but little world's wealth; save and except good meat and drink, and enough or too much thereof; house-room of the best; friends to be merry with, and maidens to kiss, and these also as good as might be; freedom withal to come and go as they would; the heavens above them, the earth to bear them up, and the meadows and acres, the woods and fair streams, and the little hills of Upmeads, for that was the name of their country and the kingdom of King Peter.

1

So having nought but this little they longed for much; and that the more because, king's sons as they were, they had but scant dominion save over their horses and dogs: for the men of that country were stubborn and sturdy vavassors, and might not away with masterful doings, but were like to pay back a blow with a blow, and a foul word with a buffet. So that, all things considered, it was little wonder if King Peter's sons found themselves straitened in their little land: wherein was no great merchant city; no mighty castle, or noble abbey of monks: nought but fair little halls of yeomen, with here and there a franklin's court or a shield-knight's manor-house; with many a goodly church, and whiles a house of good canons, who knew not the road to Rome, nor how to find the door of the Chancellor's house.

So these young men wearied their father and mother a long while with telling them of their weariness, and their longing to be gone: till at last on a fair and hot afternoon of June King Peter rose up from the carpet which the Prior of St. John's by the Bridge had given him (for he had been sleeping thereon amidst the grass of his orchard after his dinner) and he went into the hall of his house, which was called the High House of Upmeads, and sent for his four sons to come to him. And they came and stood before his high-seat and he said:

"Sons, ye have long wearied me with words concerning your longing for travel on the roads; now if ye verily wish to be gone, tell me when would ye take your departure if ye had your choice?"

They looked at one another, and the three younger ones nodded at Blaise the eldest: so he began, and said: "Saving the love and honour that we have for thee, and also for our mother, we would be gone at once, even with the noon's meat still in our bellies. But thou art the lord in this land, and thou must rule. Have I said well, brethren?" And they all said "Yea, yea." Then said the king; "Good! now is the sun high and hot; yet if ye ride softly ye may come to some good harbour before nightfall without foundering your horses. So come ye in an hour's space to the Four-want-way, and there and then will I order your departure."

The young men were full of joy when they heard his word;

and they departed and went this way and that, gathering such small matters as each deemed that he needed, and which he might lightly carry with him; then they armed themselves, and would bid the squires bring them their horses; but men told them that the said squires had gone their ways already to the Want-way by the king's commandment: so thither they went at once a-foot all four in company, laughing and talking together merrily.

It must be told that this Want-way aforesaid was but four furlongs from the House, which lay in an ingle of the river called Upmeads Water amongst very fair meadows at the end of the upland tillage; and the land sloped gently up toward the hill-country and the unseen mountains on the north; but to the south was a low ridge which ran along the water, as it wound along from west to east. Beyond the said ridge, at a place whence you could see the higher hills to the south, that stretched mainly east and west also, there was presently an end of the Kingdom of Upmeads, though the neighbours on that side were peaceable and friendly, and were wont to send gifts to King Peter. But toward the north beyond the Want-way King Peter was lord over a good stretch of land, and that of the best; yet was he never a rich man, for he had no freedom to tax and tail his folk, nor forsooth would he have used it if he had; for he was no ill man, but kindly and of measure. On these northern marches there was war at whiles, whereas they ended in a great forest well furnished of trees; and this wood was debateable, and King Peter and his sons rode therein at their peril: but great plenty was therein of all wild deer, as hart, and buck, and roe, and swine, and bears and wolves withal. The lord on the other side thereof was a mightier man than King Pete, albeit he was a bishop, and a baron of Holy Church. To say sooth he was a close-fist and a manslayer; though he did his manslaying through his vicars, the knights and men-at-arms who held their manors of him, or whom he waged.

In that forest had King Peter's father died in battle, and his eldest son also; therefore, being a man of peace, he rode therein but seldom, though his sons, the three eldest of them, had both ridden therein and ran therefrom valiantly. As for

3

Ralph the youngest, his father would not have him ride the Wood Debateable as yet.

So came those young men to the Want-ways, and found their father sitting there on a heap of stones, and over against him eight horses, four destriers, and four hackneys, and four squires withal. So they came and stood before their father, waiting for his word, and wondering what it would be.

Now spake King Peter: "Fair sons, ye would go on all adventure to seek a wider land, and a more stirring life than ye may get of me at home: so be it! But I have bethought me, that, since I am growing old and past the age of getting children, one of you, my sons, must abide at home to cherish me and your mother, and to lead our carles in war if trouble falleth upon us. Now I know not how to choose by mine own wit which of you shall ride and which abide. For so it is that ye are diverse of your conditions; but the evil conditions which one of you lacks the other hath, and the valiancy which one hath, the other lacks. Blaise is wise and prudent, but no great man of his hands. Hugh is a stout rider and lifter, but headstrong and foolhardy, and over bounteous a skinker; and Gregory is courteous and many worded, but sluggish in deed; though I will not call him a dastard. As for Ralph, he is fair to look on, and peradventure he may be as wise as Blaise, as valiant as Hugh, and as smooth-tongued as Gregory; but of all this we know little or nothing, whereas he is but young and untried. Yet may he do better than you others, and I deem that he will do so. All things considered, then, I say, I know not how to choose between you, my sons; so let luck choose for me, and ye shall draw cuts for your roads; and he that draweth longest shall go north, and the next longest shall go east, and the third straw shall send the drawer west; but as to him who draweth the shortest cut, he shall go no whither but back again to my house, there to abide with me the chances and changes of life; and it is most like that this one shall sit in my chair when I am gone, and be called King of Upmeads.

"Now, my sons, doth this ordinance please you? For if so be it doth not, then may ye all abide at home, and eat of my meat, and drink of my cup, but little chided either for sloth or misdoing, even as it hath been aforetime."

The young men looked at one another, and Blaise answered and said: "Sir, as for me I say we will do after your commandment, to take what road luck may show us, or to turn back home again." They all yeasaid this one after the other; and then King Peter said: "Now before I draw the cuts, I shall tell you that I have appointed the squires to go with each one of you. Richard the Red shall go with Blaise; for though he be somewhat stricken in years, and wise, yet is he a fierce carle and a doughty, and knoweth well all feats of arms.

"Lancelot Longtongue shall be squire to Hugh; for he is good of seeming and can compass all courtesy, and knoweth logic (though it be of the law and not of the schools), yet is he a proper man of his hands; as needs must he be who followeth Hugh; for where is Hugh, there is trouble and debate.

"Clement the Black shall serve Gregory: for he is a careful carle, and speaketh one word to every ten deeds that he doeth; whether they be done with point and edge, or with the hammer in the smithy.

"Lastly, I have none left to follow thee, Ralph, save Nicholas Long-shanks; but though he hath more words than I have, yet hath he more wisdom, and is a man lettered and far-travelled, and loveth our house right well.

"How say ye, sons, is this to your liking?"

They all said "yea." Then quoth the king; "Nicholas, bring hither the straws ready dight, and I will give them my sons to draw."

So each young man came up in turn and drew; and King Peter laid the straws together and looked at them, and said:

"Thus it is, Hugh goeth north with Lancelot; Gregory westward with Clement." He stayed a moment and then said: "Blaise fareth eastward and Richard with him. As for thee, Ralph my dear son, thou shalt back with me and abide in my house and I shall see thee day by day; and thou shalt help me to live my last years happily in all honour; and thy love shall be my hope, and thy valiancy my stay."

Therewith he arose and threw his arm about the young man's neck; but he shrank away a little from his father, and

5

his face grew troubled; and King Peter noted that, and his countenance fell, and he said:

"Nay nay, my son; grudge not thy brethren the chances of the road, and the ill-hap of the battle. Here at least for thee is the bounteous board and the full cup, and the love of kindred and well-willers, and the fellowship of the folk. O well is thee, my son, and happy shalt thou be!"

But the young man knit his brows and said no word in answer.

Then came forward those three brethren who were to fare at all adventure, and they stood before the old man saying nought. Then he laughed and said: "O ho, my sons! Here in Upmeads have ye all ye need without money, but when ye fare in the outlands ye need money; is it not a lack of yours that your pouches be bare? Abide, for I have seen to it."

Therewith he drew out of his pouch three little bags, and said; "Take ye each one of these; for therein is all that my treasury may shed as now. In each of these is there coined money, both white and red, and some deal of gold uncoined, and of rings and brooches a few, and by estimation there is in each bag the same value reckoned in lawful silver of Upmeads and the Wolds and the Overhill-Countries. Take up each what there is, and do the best ye may therewith."

Then each took his bag, and kissed and embraced his father; and they kissed Ralph and each other, and so got to horse and departed with their squires, going softly because of the hot sun. But Nicholas slowly mounted his hackney and led Ralph's war-horse with him home again to King Peter's House.

CHAPTER 2

Ralph Goeth Back Home to the High House

Ralph and King Peter walked slowly home together, and as they went King Peter fell to telling of how in his young days he rode in the Wood Debateable, and was belated there all alone, and happed upon men who were outlaws and wolfheads, and feared for his life; but they treated him kindly, and honoured him, and saw him safe on his way in the morning. So that never thereafter would he be art and part with those who hunted outlaws to slay them. "For," said he, "it is with these men as with others, that they make prey of folk; yet these for the more part prey on the rich, and the lawful prey on the poor. Otherwise it is with these wolfheads as with lords and knights and franklins, that as there be bad amongst them, so also there be good; and the good ones I happed on, and so may another man."

Hereto paid Ralph little heed at that time, since he had heard the tale and its morality before, and that more than once; and moreover his mind was set upon his own matters, and these was he pondering. Albeit perchance the words abode with him. So came they to the House, and Ralph's mother, who was a noble dame, and well-liking as for her years, which were but little over fifty, stood in the hall-door to see which of her sons should come back to her, and when she saw them coming together, she went up to them, and cast her arms about Ralph and kissed him and caressed him,— being exceeding glad that it was he and not one of the others who had returned to dwell with them; for he was her best-beloved, as was little marvel, seeing that he was by far the fairest and the most loving. But Ralph's face grew troubled again in his mother's arms, for he loved her exceeding well; and forsooth he loved the whole house and all that dwelt

7

there, down to the turnspit dogs in the chimney ingle, and the swallows that nested in the earthen bottles, which when he was little he had seen his mother put up in the eaves of the out-bowers: but now, love or no love, the spur was in his side, and he must needs hasten as fate would have him. However, when he had disentangled himself from his mother's caresses, he enforced himself to keep a cheerful countenance, and upheld it the whole evening through, and was by seeming merry at supper, and went to bed singing.

CHAPTER 3

Ralph Cometh to the Cheaping-Town

He slept in an upper chamber in a turret of the House, which chamber was his own, and none might meddle with it. There the next day he awoke in the dawning, and arose and clad himself, and took his war-gear and his sword and spear, and bore all away without doors to the side of the Ford in that ingle of the river, and laid it for a while in a little willow copse, so that no chance-comer might see it; then he went back to the stable of the House and took his destrier from the stall (it was a dapple-grey horse called Falcon, and was right good,) and brought him down to the said willow copse, and tied him to a tree till he had armed himself amongst the willows, whence he came forth presently as brisk-looking and likely a man-at-arms as you might see on a summer day. Then he clomb up into the saddle, and went his ways splashing across the ford, before the sun had arisen, while the throstle-cocks were yet amidst their first song.

Then he rode on a little trot south away; and by then the sun was up he was without the bounds of Upmeads; albeit in the land thereabout dwelt none who were not friends to King Peter and his sons: and that was well, for now were folk stirring and were abroad in the fields; as a band of carles going with their scythes to the hay-field; or a maiden with her milking-pails going to her kine, barefoot through the seeding grass; or a company of noisy little lads on their way to the nearest pool of the stream that they might bathe in the warm morning after the warm night. All these and more knew him and his armour and Falcon his horse, and gave him the sele of the day, and he was nowise troubled at meeting them; for besides that they thought it no wonder to meet one of the lords of Upmeads going armed about his errands, their own errands were close at home, and it was little likely that they should go that day so far as to Upmeads Water, seeing that it ran through the meadows a half-score miles to the north-ward.

So Ralph rode on, and came into the high road, that led one way back again into Upmeads, and crossed the Water by a fair bridge late builded between King Peter and a house of Canons on the north side, and the other way into a good cheaping-town hight Wulstead, beyond which Ralph knew little of the world which lay to the south, and seemed to him a wondrous place, full of fair things and marvellous adventures.

So he rode till he came into the town when the fair morning was still young, the first mass over, and maids gathered about the fountain amidst the market-place, and two or three dames sitting under the buttercross. Ralph rode straight up to the house of a man whom he knew, and had often given him guesting there, and he himself was not seldom seen in the High House of Upmeads. This man was a merchant, who went and came betwixt men's houses, and bought and sold many things needful and pleasant to folk, and King Peter dealt with him much and often. Now he stood in the door of his house, which was new and goodly, sniffing the sweet scents which the morning wind bore into the town; he was clad in a goodly long gown of grey welted with silver, of thin cloth meet for the summer-tide: for little he wrought with his hands, but much with his tongue; he was a man of forty summers, ruddy-faced and black-bearded, and he was called Clement Chapman.

When he saw Ralph he smiled kindly on him, and came and held his stirrup as he lighted down, and said: "Welcome, lord! Art thou come to give me a message, and eat and drink in a poor huckster's house, and thou armed so gallantly?"

Ralph laughed merrily, for he was hungry, and he said: "Yea, I will eat and drink with thee and kiss my gossip, and go my ways."

Therewith the carle led him into the house; and if it were goodly without, within it was better. For there was a fair chamber panelled with wainscot well carven, and a cupboard of no sorry vessels of silver and latten: the chairs and stools as fair as might be; no king's might be better: the windows were glazed, and there were flowers and knots and posies in them; and the bed was hung with goodly web from over sea such as the soldan useth. Also, whereas the chapman's warebowers were hard by the chamber, there was a pleasant mingled smell therefrom floating about. The table was set with meat and drink and vessel of pewter and earth, all fair and good; and thereby stood the chapman's wife, a very goodly woman of two-score years, who had held Ralph at the font when she was a slim damsel new wedded; for she was come of no mean kindred of the Kingdom of Upmeads: her name was Dame Katherine.

Now she kissed Ralph's cheek friendly, and said: "Welcome, gossip! thou art here in good time to break thy fast; and we will give thee a trim dinner thereafter, when thou hast been here and there in the town and done thine errand; and then shalt thou drink a cup and sing me a song, and so home again in the cool of the evening."

Ralph seemed a little troubled at her word, and he said: "Nay, gossip, though I thank thee for all these good things as though I had them, yet must I ride away south straightway after I have breakfasted, and said one word to the goodman. Goodman, how call ye the next town southward, and how far is it thither?"

Quoth Clement: "My son, what hast thou to do with riding south? As thou wottest, going hence south ye must presently ride the hill-country; and that is no safe journey for a lonely man, even if he be a doughty knight like to thee, lord."

Said Ralph, reddening withal: "I have an errand that way."

10

"An errand of King Peter's or thine own?" said Clement.

"Of King Peter's, if ye must wot," said Ralph.

Clement were no chapman had he not seen that the lad was lying; so he said:

"Fair lord, saving your worship, how would it be as to the speeding of King Peter's errand, if I brought thee before our mayor, and swore the peace against thee; so that I might keep thee in courteous prison till I had sent to thy father of thy whereabouts?"

The young man turned red with anger; but ere he could speak Dame Katherine said sharply: "Hold thy peace, Clement! What hast thou to meddle or make in the matter? If our young lord hath will to ride out and see the world, why should we let him? Yea, why should his father let him, if it come to that? Take my word for it that my gossip shall go through the world and come back to those that love him, as goodly as he went forth. And hold! here is for a token thereof."

Therewith she went to an ark that stood in the corner, and groped in the till thereof and brought out a little necklace of blue and green stones with gold knobs betwixt, like a pair of beads; albeit neither pope nor priest had blessed them; and tied to the necklace was a little box of gold with something hidden therein. This gaud she gave to Ralph, and said to him: "Gossip, wear this about thy neck, and let no man take it from thee, and I think it will be salvation to thee in peril, and good luck to thee in the time of questing; so that it shall be to thee as if thou hadst drunk of the WELL AT THE WORLD'S END."

"What is that water?" said Ralph, "and how may I find it?"

"I know not rightly," she said, "but if a body might come by it, I hear say it saveth from weariness and wounding and sickness; and it winneth love from all, and maybe life everlasting. Hast thou not heard tell of it, my husband?"

"Yea," said the chapman, "many times; and how that whoso hath drunk thereof hath the tongue that none may withstand, whether in buying or selling, or prevailing over the hearts of men in any wise. But as for its whereabouts, ye shall not find it in these parts. Men say that it is beyond the

11

Dry Tree; and that is afar, God wot! But now, lord Ralph, I rede thee go back again this evening with Andrew, my nephew, for company: forsooth, he will do little less gainful than riding with thee to Upmeads than if he abide in Wulstead; for he is idle. But, my lord, take it not amiss that I spake about the mayor and the tipstaves; for it was but a jest, as thou mayest well wot."

Ralph's face cleared at that word, and he stood smiling, weighing the chaplet in his hand; but Dame Katherine said:

"Dear gossip, do it on speedily; for it is a gift from me unto thee: and from a gossip even king's sons may take a gift."

Quoth Ralph: "But is it lawful to wear it? is there no wizardry within it?"

"Hearken to him!" she said, "and how like unto a man he speaketh; if there were a brawl in the street, he would strike in and ask no word thereof, not even which were the better side: whereas here is my falcon-chick frighted at a little gold box and a pair of Saracen beads."

"Well," quoth Ralph, "the first holy man I meet shall bless them for me."

"That shall he not," said the dame, "that shall he not. Who wotteth what shall betide to thee or me if he do so? Come, do them on, and then to table! For seest thou not that the goodman is wearying for meat? and even thine eyes will shine the brighter for a mouthful, king's son and gossip."

She took him by the hand and did the beads on his neck, and kissed and fondled him before he sat down, while the goodman looked on, grinning rather sheepishly, but said nought to them; and only called on his boy to lead the destrier to stable. So when they were set down, the chapman took up the word where it had been dropped, and said: "So, Lord Ralph, thou must needs take to adventures, being, as thou deemest, full grown. That is all one as the duck taketh to water despite of the hen that hath hatched her. Well, it was not to be thought that Upmeads would hold you lords much longer. Or what is gone with my lords your brethren?"

Said Ralph: "They have departed at all adventure, north, east, and west, each bearing our father's blessing and a bag of pennies. And to speak the truth, goodman, for I perceive I

12

am no doctor at lying, my father and mother would have me stay at home when my brethren were gone, and that liketh me not; therefore am I come out to seek my luck in the world: for Upmeads is good for a star-gazer, maybe, or a simpler, or a priest, or a worthy good carle of the fields, but not for a king's son with the blood running hot in his veins. Or what sayest thou, gossip?"

Quoth the dame: "I could weep for thy mother; but for thee nought at all. It is good that thou shouldest do thy will in the season of youth and the days of thy pleasure. Yea, and I deem that thou shalt come back again great and worshipful; and I am called somewhat foreseeing. Only look to it that thou keep the pretty thing that I have just given thee."

"Well," said the chapman, "this is fine talk about pleasure and the doing of one's will; nevertheless a whole skin is good wares, though it be not to be cheapened in any market of the world. Now, lord, go thou where thou wilt, whether I say go or abide; and forsooth I am no man of King Peter's, that I should stay thee. As for the name of the next town, it is called Higham-on-the-Way, and is a big town plenteous of victuals, with strong walls and a castle, and a very rich abbey of monks: and there is peace within its walls, because the father abbot wages a many men to guard him and his, and to uphold his rights against all comers; wherein he doth wisely, and also well. For much folk flocketh to his town and live well therein; and there is great recourse of chapmen thither. No better market is there betwixt this and Babylon. Well, Sir Ralph, I rede thee if thou comest unhurt to Higham-on-the-Way, go no further for this time, but take service with the lord abbot, and be one of his men of war; thou may'st then become his captain if thou shouldest live; which would be no bad adventure for one who cometh from Upmeads."

Ralph looked no brighter for this word, and he answered nought to it: but said presently:

"And what is to be looked for beyond Higham if one goeth further? Dost thou know the land any further?"

The carle smiled: "Yea forsooth, and down to the Wood Perilous, and beyond it, and the lands beyond the Wood; and far away through them. I say not that I have been to the Dry Tree; but I have spoken to one who hath heard of him who

13

hath seen it; though he might not come by a draught of the Well at the World's End."

Ralph's eyes flashed, and his cheeks reddened as he listened hereto; but he spake quietly:

"Master Clement, how far dost thou make it to Higham-on-the-Way?"

"A matter of forty miles," said the Chapman; "because, as thou wottest, if ye ride south from hence, ye shall presently bring your nose up against the big downs, and must needs climb them at once; and when ye are at the top of Bear Hill, and look south away ye shall see nought but downs on downs with never a road to call a road, and never a castle, or church, or homestead: nought but some shepherd's hut; or at the most the little house of a holy man with a little chapel thereby in some swelly of the chalk, where the water hath trickled into a pool; for otherwise the place is waterless." Therewith he took a long pull at the tankard by his side, and went on:

"Higham is beyond all that, and out into the fertile plain; and a little river hight Coldlake windeth about the meadows there; and it is a fair land; though look you the wool of the downs is good, good, good! I have foison of this year's fleeces with me. Ye shall raise none such in Upmeads."

Ralph sat silent a little, as if pondering, and then he started up and said: "Good master Clement, we have eaten thy meat and thank thee for that and other matters. Wilt thou now be kinder, and bid thy boy bring round Falcon our horse; for we have far to go, and must begone straight-away."

"Yea, lord," said Clement, "even so will I do." And he muttered under his breath; "Thou talkest big, my lad, with thy 'we'; but thou art pressed lest Nicholas be here presently to fetch thee back; and to say sooth I would his hand were on thy shoulder even now."

Then he spake aloud again, and said:

"I must now begone to my lads, and I will send one round with thy war-horse. But take my rede, my lord, and become the man of the Abbot of St. Mary's of Higham, and all will be well."

Therewith he edged himself out of the chamber, and the dame fell to making a mighty clatter with the vessel and

14

trenchers and cups on the board, while Ralph walked up and down the chamber his war-gear jingling upon him. Presently the dame left her table-clatter and came up to Ralph and looked kindly into his face and said: "Gossip, hast thou perchance any money?"

He flushed up red, and then his face fell; yet he spake gaily: "Yea, gossip, I have both white and red: there are three golden crowns in my pouch, and a little flock of silver pennies: forsooth I say not as many as would reach from here to Upmeads, if they were laid one after the other."

She smiled and patted his cheek, and said:

"Thou art no very prudent child, king's son. But it comes into my mind that my master did not mean thee to go away empty-handed; else had he not departed and left us twain together."

Therewith she went to the credence that stood in a corner, and opened a drawer therein and took out a little bag, and gave it into Ralph's hand, and said: "This is the gift of the gossip; and thou mayst take it without shame; all the more because if thy father had been a worser man, and a harder lord he would have had more to give thee. But now thou hast as much or more as any one of thy brethren."

He took the bag smiling and shame-faced, but she looked on him fondly and said:

"Now I know not whether I shall lay old Nicholas on thine heels when he cometh after thee, as come he will full surely; or whether I shall suffer the old sleuth-hound nose out thy slot of himself, as full surely he will set on to it."

"Thou mightest tell him," said Ralph, "that I am gone to take service with the Abbot of St. Mary's of Higham: hah?"

She laughed and said: "Wilt thou do so, lord, and follow the rede of that goodman of mine, who thinketh himself as wise as Solomon?"

Ralph smiled and answered her nothing.

"Well," she said, "I shall say what likes me when the hour is at hand. Lo, here! thine horse. Abide yet a moment of time, and then go whither thou needs must, like the wind of the summer day."

Therewith she went out of the chamber and came back again with a scrip which she gave to Ralph and said: "Herein is a flask of drink for the waterless country, and a little meat for the way. Fare thee well, gossip! Little did I look for it when I rose up this morning and nothing irked me save the dulness of our town, and the littleness of men's doings therein, that I should have to cut off a piece of my life from me this morning, and say, farewell gossip, as now again I do."

Therewith she kissed him on either cheek and embraced him; and it might be said of her and him that she let him go thereafter; for though as aforesaid he loved her, and praised her kindness, he scarce understood the eagerness of her love for him; whereas moreover she saw him not so often betwixt Upmeads and Wulstead: and belike she herself scarce understood it. Albeit she was a childless woman.

So when he had got to horse, she watched him riding a moment, and saw how he waved his hand to her as he turned the corner of the market-place, and how a knot of lads and lasses stood staring on him after she lost sight of him. Then she turned her back into the chamber and laid her head on the table and wept. Then came in the goodman quietly and stood by her and she heeded him not. He stood grinning curiously on her awhile, and then laid his hand on her shoulder, and said as she raised her face to him:

"Sweetheart, it availeth nought; when thou wert young and exceeding fair, he was but a little babe, and thou wert looking in those days to have babes of thine own; and then it was too soon: and now that he is such a beauteous young man, and a king's son withal, and thou art wedded to a careful carle of no weak heart, and thou thyself art more than two-score years old, it is too late. Yet thou didst well to give our lord the money. Lo! here is wherewithal to fill up the lack in thy chest; and here is a toy for thee in place of the pair of beads thou gavest him; and I bid thee look on it as if I had given him my share of the money and the beads."

She turned to Clement, and took the bag of money, and the chaplet which he held out to her, and she said: "God wot thou art no ill man, my husband, but would God I had a son like to him!"

She still wept somewhat; but the chapman said: "Let it rest there, sweetheart! let it rest there! It may be a year or twain before thou seest him again: and then belike he shall be come back with some woman whom he loves better than any other; and who knows but in a way he may deem himself our son. Meanwhile thou hast done well, sweetheart, so be glad."

Therewith he kissed her and went his ways to his merchandize, and she to the ordering of her house, grieved but not unhappy.

CHAPTER 4

Ralph Rideth the Downs

As for Ralph, he rode on with a merry heart, and presently came to an end of the plain country, and the great downs rose up before him with a white road winding up to the top of them. Just before the slopes began to rise was a little thorp beside a stream, and thereby a fair church and a little house of Canons: so Ralph rode toward the church to see if therein were an altar of St. Nicholas, who was his good lord and patron, that he might ask of him a blessing on his journey. But as he came up to the churchyard-gate he saw a great black horse tied thereto as if abiding some one; and as he lighted down from his saddle he saw a man coming hastily from out the church-door and striding swiftly toward the said gate. He was a big man, and armed; for he had a bright steel sallet on his head, which covered his face all save the end of his chin; and plates he had on his legs and arms. He wore a green coat over his armour, and thereon was wrought in gold an image of a tree leafless: he had a little steel axe about his neck, and a great sword hung by his side. Ralph stood looking on him with his hand on the latch of the gate, but when the man came thereto he tore it open roughly and shoved through at once, driving Ralph back, so that he well-nigh overset him, and so sprang to his horse and swung himself into the saddle, just as Ralph steadied himself and ruffled up to him, half drawing his sword from the scabbard the while. But the man-at-arms cried out, "Put it back, put it back! If thou must needs deal with every man that shoveth thee in his haste, thy life is like to be but short."

He was settling himself in his saddle as he spoke, and now he shook his rein, and rode off speedily toward the hill-road. But when he was so far off that Ralph might but see his face but as a piece of reddish colour, he reined up for a moment of time, and turning round in his saddle lifted up his sallet and left his face bare, and cried out as if to Ralph, "The first time!" And then let the head-piece fall again, and set spurs to his horse and gallopped away.

Ralph stood looking at him as he got smaller on the long white road, and wondering what this might mean, and how the unknown man should know him, if he did know him. But presently he let his wonder run off him, and went his ways into the church, wherein he found his good lord and friend St. Nicholas, and so said a paternoster before his altar, and besought his help, and made his offering; and then departed and gat to horse again, and rode softly the way to the downs, for the day was hot.

The way was steep and winding, with a hollow cup of the hills below it, and above it a bent so steep that Ralph could see but a few yards of it on his left hand; but when he came to the hill's brow and could look down on the said bent, he saw strange figures on the face thereof, done by cutting away the turf so that the chalk might show clear. A tree with leaves was done on that hill-side, and on either hand of it a beast like a bear ramping up against the tree; and these signs were very ancient. This hill-side carving could not be seen from the thorp beneath, which was called Netherton, because the bent looked westward down into the hollow of the hill abovesaid; but from nigher to Wulstead they were clear to see, and Ralph had often beheld them, but never so nigh: and that hill was called after them Bear Hill. At the top of it was an earth-work of the ancient folk, which also was called Bear Castle. And now Ralph rode over the hill's brow into it; for the walls had been beaten down in places long and long ago.

Now he rode up the wall, and at the topmost of it turned

and looked aback on the blue country which he had ridden through stretching many a league below, and tried if he could pick out Upmeads from amongst the diverse wealth of the summer land: but Upmeads Water was hidden, and he could see nothing to be sure of to tell him whereabouts the High House stood; yet he deemed that he could make out the Debateable Wood and the hills behind it well enough. Then he turned his horse about, and had the down-country before him; long lines of hills to wit, one rising behind the other like the waves of a somewhat quiet sea: no trees thereon, nor houses that he might see thence: nought but a green road that went waving up and down before him greener than the main face of the slopes.

He looked at it all for a minute or two as the south-west wind went past his ears, and played a strange tune on the innumerable stems of the bents and the hard-stalked blossoms, to which the bees sang counterpoint. Then the heart arose within him, and he drew the sword from the scabbard, and waved it about his head, and shook it toward the south, and cried out, "Now, welcome world, and be thou blessed from one end to the other, from the ocean sea to the uttermost mountains!"

A while he held the white steel in his fist, and then sheathed the blade, and rode down soberly over the turf bridge across the ancient fosse, and so came on to the green road made many ages before by an ancient people, and so trotted south along fair and softly.

Little is to be told of his journey through the downs: as he topped a low hill whereon were seven grave-mounds of the ancient folk in a row, he came on a shepherd lying amidst of his sheep: the man sprang to his feet when he heard horse-hoofs anigh him and saw the glint of steel, and he set his hand to a short spear which lay by him; but when he saw nought but Ralph, and heard how he gave him the sele of the day, he nodded his head in a friendly way, though he said nought in salutation; for the loneliness of the downs made the speech slow within him.

Again some two miles further on Ralph met a flock of sheep coming down a bent which the road climbed, and with them were three men, their drovers, and they drew nigh him as he was amidst of the sheep, so that he could scarce see the way. Each of these three had a weapon; one a pole-axe, another a long spear, and the third a flail jointed and bound with iron, and an anlace hanging at his girdle. So they stood in the way and hailed him when the sheep were gone past; and the man with the spear asked him whither away. "I am turned toward Higham-on-the-Way," quoth he; "and how many miles shall I ride ere I get there?"

Said one of them: "Little less than twenty, lord." Now it was past noon two hours, and the day was hot; so whereas the faces of the men looked kind and friendly, albeit somewhat rugged, he lighted down from his horse and sat down by the way-side, and drew his bottle of good wine from out of his wallet, and asked the men if they were in haste. "Nay, master," said he of the pole-axe, while all eyes turned to the bottle, "HE has gone by too long; and will neither meddle with us, nor may we deal with him."

"Well then," quoth Ralph, "there is time for bever. Have ye ought of a cup, that we may drink to each other?"

"Yea," said the carle with the anlace, "that have I." Therewith he drew from his pouch a ram's horn rimmed with silver, and held it up, and said as if he were speaking to it: "Now, Thirly, rejoice! for ye shall have lord's wine poured into thy maw."

Therewith he held it out toward Ralph, who laughed and filled it up, and filled for himself a little silver cup which he carried, and said: "To you, shepherds! Much wool and little cry!" And he drank withal.

"And I," quoth the man with the horn, "call this health; Much cry and little wool!"

"Well, well, how mean ye by that, Greasy Wat?" said the man with the spear, taking the horn as he spake; "that is but a poor wish for a lord that drinketh out of our cup."

Said Wat: "Why, neighbour, why! thy wit is none too hasty. The wool that a knight sheareth is war and battle; that is wounding and death; but the cry is the talk and boasting and minstrelsy that goeth before all this. Which is the best wish to wish him? the wounds and the death, or the fore-rumour and stir thereof which hurteth no man?"

Ralph laughed thereat, and was merry and blithe with them; but the spearman, who was an old man, said:

"For all Wat sayeth, lord, and his japes, ye must not misdeem of us that we shepherds of the Downs can do nought but run to ales and feasts, and that we are but pot-valiant: maybe thou thyself mayst live to see things go otherwise: and in that day may we have such as thee for captain. Now, fair lord, I drink to thy crown of valour, and thy good luck; and we thank thee for the wine and yet more for the blithe fellowship."

So Ralph filled up the ram's horn till Dame Katherine's good island wine was well-nigh spent; and at last he said:

"Now, my masters, I must to horse; but I pray you tell or we depart, what did ye mean when ye said that HE had gone past? Who is HE?"

The merry faces of the men changed at his word, and they looked in each other's faces, till at last the old spearman answered him:

"Fair lord, these things we have little will to talk about: for we be poor men with no master to fleece us, and no lord to help us: also we be folk unlearned and unlettered, and from our way of life, whereas we dwell in the wilderness, we seldom come within the doors of a church. But whereas we have drunk with thee, who seemest to be a man of lineage, and thou hast been blithe with us, we will tell thee that we have seen one riding south along the Greenway, clad in a coat as green as the way, with the leafless tree done on his breast. So nigh to him we were that we heard his cry as he sped along, as ye may hear the lapwing whining; for he said: 'POINT AND EDGE, POINT AND EDGE! THE RED WATER AMIDST OF THE HILLS!' In my lifetime such a man hath, to my knowledge, been seen thrice before; and after each sight of him followed evil days and the death of men. Moreover this is the Eve of St. John, and we deem the token the worse therefor. Or how deemest thou?"

Ralph stood silent awhile; for he was thinking of the big man whom he had met at the churchyard gate, and all this tale seemed wonderful to him. But at last he said:

"I cannot tell what there is in it; herein am I no help to you. To-day I am but little; though I may one day be great.

Yet this may I do for you; tomorrow will I let sing a mass in St. Mary's Church on your behoof. And hereafter, if I wax as my will is, and I come to be lord in these lands, I will look to it to do what a good lord should do for the shepherds of the Downs, so that they may live well, and die in good hope. So may the Mother of God help me at need!"

Said the old shepherd: "Thou hast sworn an oath, and it is a good oath, and well sworn. Now if thou dost as thou swearest, words can but little thanks, yet deeds may. Wherefore if ever thou comest back hither, and art in such need that a throng of men may help thee therein; then let light a great fire upon each corner of the topmost wall of Bear Castle, and call to mind this watch-word: 'SMITE ASIDE THE AXE, O BEAR-FATHER,' and then shalt thou see what shall betide thee for thy good-hap: farewell now, with the saints to aid!"

Ralph bade them live well and hail, and mounted his horse and rode off down the Greenway, and as he rode the shepherds waved their weapons to him in token of good-will.

CHAPTER 5

Ralph Cometh to Higham-on-the-Way

Nought more befell Ralph to tell of till he came to the end of the Downs and saw Higham lying below him overlooked by a white castle on a knoll, and with a river lapping it about and winding on through its fair green meadows even as Clement had told. From amidst its houses rose up three towers of churches above their leaden roofs, and high above all, long and great, the Abbey Church; and now was the low sun glittering on its gilded vanes and the wings of the angels high upon the battlements.

So Ralph rode down the slopes and was brisk about it, for it was drawing toward sunset, and he knew not at what hour

22

they shut their gates. The road was steep and winding, and it was the more part of an hour ere he came to the gate, which was open, and like to be yet, for many folk were thronging in, which throng also had hindered him soon after he came into the plain country. The gate was fair and strong, but Ralph saw no men-at-arms about it that evening. He rode into the street unquestioned, and therein was the throng great of people clad in fair and gay attire; and presently Ralph called to mind that this was St. John's Eve, so that he knew that there was some feast toward.

At last the throng was so thick that he was stayed by it; and therewithal a religious who was beside him and thrust up against his horse, turned to him and gave him good even, and said: "By thy weapons and gear thou art a stranger here in our burg, Sir Knight?"

"So it is," said Ralph.

"And whither away?" said the monk; "hast thou some kinsman or friend in the town?"

"Nay," said Ralph, "I seek a good hostelry where I may abide the night for my money."

The monk shook his head and said: "See ye the folk? It is holiday time, and midsummer after haysel. Ye shall scarce get lodging outside our house. But what then? Come thou thither straightway and have harbour of the best, and see our prior, who loveth young and brisk men-at-arms like to thee. Lo now! the throng openeth a little; I will walk by thy bridle and lead thee the shortest road thither."

Ralph gainsaid him not, and they bored through the throng of the street till they came into the market-square, which was very great and clean, paved with stones all over: tall and fair houses rose up on three sides of it, and on the fourth was the Great Church which made those houses seem but low: most of it was new-built; for the lord Abbot that then was, though he had not begun it, had taken the work up from his forerunner and had pushed it forward all he might; for he was very rich, and an open-handed man. Like dark gold it showed under the evening sun, and the painted and gilded imagery shone like jewels upon it.

"Yea," said the monk, as he noted Ralph's wonder at this

23

wonder; "a most goodly house it is, and happy shall they be that dwell there."

Therewith he led Ralph on, turning aside through the great square. Ralph saw that there were many folk therein, though it was too big to be thronged thick with them. Amidst of it was now a great pile of wood hung about with flowers, and hard by it a stage built up with hangings of rich cloth on one side thereof. He asked the monk what this might mean, and he told him the wood was for the Midsummer bale-fire, and the stage for the show that should come thereafter. So the brother led Ralph down a lane to the south of the great west door, and along the side of the minster and so came to the Abbey gate, and there was Ralph well greeted, and had all things given him which were due to a good knight; and then was he brought into the Guest-hall, a very fair chamber, which was now full of men of all degrees. He was shown to a seat on the daïs within two of the subprior's, and beside him sat an honourable lord, a vassal of St. Mary's. So was supper served well and abundantly: the meat and drink was of the best, and the vessel and all the plenishing was as good as might be; and the walls of that chamber were hung with noble arras-cloth picturing the Pilgrimage of the Soul of Man.

Every man there who spoke with Ralph, and they were many, was exceeding courteous to him; and he heard much talk about him of the wealth of the lands of St. Mary's at Higham, and how it was flourishing; and of the Abbot how mighty he was, so that he might do what he would, and that his will was to help and to give, and be blithe with all men: and folk told of turmoil and war in other lands, and praised the peace of Higham-on-the-Way.

Ralph listened to all this, and smiled, and said to himself that to another man this might well be the end of his journey for that time; but for him all this peace and well-being was not enough; for though it were a richer land than Upmeads, yet to the peace and the quiet he was well used, and he had come forth not for the winning of fatter peace, but to try what new thing his youth and his might and his high hope and his good hap might accomplish.

So when the supper was over, and the wine and spices had been brought, the Guest-hall began to thin somewhat, and the brother who had brought Ralph thither came to him and said:

"Fair lord, it were nowise ill if ye went forth, as others of our guests have done, to see the deeds of Midsummer Eve that shall be done in the great square in honour of Holy John; for our manner therein at Higham has been much thought of. Look my son!"

He pointed to the windows of the hall therewith, and lo! they grew yellow and bright with some fire without, as if a new fiery day had been born out of the dusk of the summer night; for the light that shone through the windows out-did the candle-light in the hall. Ralph started thereat and laid his right hand to the place of his sword, which indeed he had left with the chamberlain; but the monk laughed and said: "Fear nothing, lord; there is no foeman in Higham: come now, lest thou be belated of the show."

So he led Ralph forth, and into the square, where there was a space appointed for the brethren and their guests to see the plays; and the square was now so full of folk that it seemed like as if that there were no one man in the streets which were erewhile so thronged.

There were rows of men-at-arms in bright armour also to keep the folk in their places, like as hurdles pen the sheep up; howbeit they were nowise rough with folk, but humble and courteous. Many and many were the torches and cressets burning steadily in the calm air, so that, as aforesaid, night was turned into day. But on the scaffold aforesaid were standing bright and gay figures, whose names or what they were Ralph had no time to ask.

Now the bells began to clash from the great tower of the minster, and in a little while they had clashed themselves into order and rang clear and tuneably for a space; and while they were ringing, lo! those gay-clad people departed from the scaffold, and a canvas painted like a mountain-side, rocky and with caves therein, was drawn up at the back of it. Then came thereon one clad like a king holding a fair maiden by the hand, and with him was a dame richly clad and with a crown on her head. So these two kissed the maiden, and lamented over her, and went their ways, and the maiden left alone sat down upon a rock and covered up her face and

25

wept; and while Ralph wondered what this might mean, or what grieved the maiden, there came creeping, as it were from out of a cranny of the rocks, a worm huge-headed and covered over with scales that glittered in the torch-light. Then Ralph sprang up in his place, for he feared for the maiden that the worm would devour her: but the monk who sat by him pulled him down by the skirt, and laughed and said: "Sit still, lord! for the champion also has been provided."

Then Ralph sat down again somewhat abashed and looked on; yet was his heart in his mouth the while. And so while the maiden stood as one astonied before the worm, who gaped upon her with wide open mouth, there came forth from a cleft in the rocks a goodly knight who bore silver, a red cross; and he had his sword in his hand, and he fell upon the worm to smite him; and the worm ramped up against him, and there was battle betwixt them, while the maiden knelt anigh with her hands clasped together.

Then Ralph knew that this was a play of the fight of St. George with the worm; so he sat silent till the champion had smitten off the worm's head and had come to the maiden and kissed and embraced her, and shown her the grisly head. Then presently came many folk on to the scaffold, to wit, the king and queen who were the father and mother of the maiden, and a bishop clad in very fair vestments, and knights withal; and they stood about St. George and the maiden, and with them were minstrels who fell to playing upon harps and fiddles; while other some fell to singing a sweet song in honour of St. George, and the maiden delivered.

So when it was all done, the monk said: "This play is set forth by the men-at-arms of our lord Abbot, who have great devotion toward St. George, and he is their friend and their good lord. But hereafter will be other plays, of wild men and their feasting in the woods in the Golden Age of the world; and that is done by the scribes and the limners. And after that will be a pageant of St. Agnes ordered by the clothiers and the webbers, which be both many and deft in this good town. Albeit thou art a young man and hast ridden far to-day belike, and mayhappen thou wilt not be able to endure it: so it may be well to bring thee out of this throng straightway.

26

Moreover I have bethought me, that there is much of what is presently to come which we shall see better from the minster roof, or even it may be from the tower: wilt thou come then?"

Ralph had liefer have sat there and seen all the plays to the end, for they seemed to him exceeding fair, and like to ravish the soul from the body; howbeit, being shamefaced, he knew not how to gainsay the brother, who took him by the hand, and led him through the press to the west front of the minster, where on the north side was a little door in a nook. So they went up a stair therein a good way till they came into a gallery over the western door; and looking forth thence Ralph deemed that he could have seen a long way had daylight been, for it was higher than the tops of the highest houses.

So there they abode a space looking down on the square and its throng, and the bells, which had been ringing when they came up, now ceased a while. But presently there arose great shouts and clamour amongst the folk below, and they could see men with torches drawing near to the pile of wood, and then all of a sudden shot up from it a great spiring flame, and all the people shouted together, while the bells broke out again over their heads.

Then the brother pointed aloof with his finger and said: "Lo you! fair lord, how bale speaks to bale all along the headlands of the down-country, and below there in the thorps by the river!"

Forsooth Ralph saw fire after fire break out to the westward; and the brother said: "And if we stood over the high altar and looked east, ye would see more of such fires and many more; and all these bales are piled up and lighted by vassals and villeins of my lord Abbot: now to-night they are but mere Midsummer bale-fires; but doubt ye not that if there came war into the land each one of these bales would mean at least a half-score of stout men, archers and men-at-arms, all ready to serve their lord at all adventure. All this the tyrants round about, that hate holy Church and oppress the poor, know full well; therefore we live in peace in these lands."

Ralph hearkened, but said nought; for amidst all this

27

flashing of fire and flame, and the crying out of folk, and the measured clash of the bells so near him, his thought was confused, and he had no words ready to hand. But the monk turned from the parapet and looked him full in the face and said to him:

"Thou art a fair young man, and strong, and of gentle blood as I deem; and thou seemest to me to have the lucky look in thine eyes: now I tell thee that if thou wert to take service with my lord thou shouldest never rue it. Yea, why shouldest thou not wax in his service, and become his Captain of Captains, which is an office meet for kings?"

Ralph looked on him, but answered nought, for he could not gather his thoughts for an answer; and the brother said: "Think of it, I bid thee, fair young lord; and be sure that nowhere shalt thou have a better livelihood, not even wert thou a king's son; for the children of my lord Abbot are such that none dareth to do them any displeasure; neither is any overlord as good as is Holy Church."

"Yea," said Ralph, "doubtless thou sayest sooth; yet I wot not that I am come forth to seek a master."

Said the brother: "Nay, do but see the lord Abbot, as thou mayst do to-morrow, if thou wilt."

"I would have his blessing," said Ralph.

"No less shalt thou have," said the brother; "but look you down yonder; for I can see tokens that my lord is even now coming forth."

Ralph looked down and beheld the folk parting to right and left, and a lane made amidst the throng, guarded by men-at-arms mingled with the cross-bearers and brethren; and the sound of trumpets blared forth over the noises of the throng.

"If the lord Abbot cometh," said Ralph, "I were fain of his blessing to-night before I sleep: so go we down straightway that I may kneel before him with the rest."

"What!" said the monk, "Wilt thou, my lord, kneel amongst all these burgesses and vavassors when thou mightest see the Abbot in his own chamber face to face alone with him?"

"Father," said Ralph, "I am no great man, and I must needs depart betimes to-morrow; for I perceive that here are things too mighty and over-mastering for such as I be."

28

"Well," said the monk, "yet mayst thou come back again; so at present I will make no more words about it."

So they went down, and came out amidst the throng, above which the bale still flared high, making the summer night as light as day. The brother made way for Ralph, so that they stood in the front row of folk: they had not been there one minute ere they heard the sound of the brethren singing, and the Abbot came forth out of the lane that went down to the gate. Then all folk went down upon their knees, and thus abode him. Right so Ralph deemed that he felt some one pull his sleeve, but in such a throng that was nought of a wonder; howbeit, he turned and looked to his left, whence came the tug, and saw kneeling beside him a tall man-at-arms, who bore a sallet on his head in such wise that it covered all his face save the point of his chin. Then Ralph bethought him of the man of the leafless tree, and he looked to see what armoury the man bore on his coat; but he had nothing save a loose frock of white linen over his hauberk. Nevertheless, he heard a voice in his ear, which said, "The second time!" whereon he deemed that it was verily that same man: yet had he nought to do to lay hold on him, and he might not speak with him, for even therewith came the Abbot in garments all of gold, going a-foot under a canopy of baudekyn, with the precious mitre on his head, and the crozier borne before him, as if he had been a patriarch: for he was an exceeding mighty lord.

Ralph looked hard on him as he passed by, blessing the folk with upraised hand; and he saw that he was a tall spare man, clean-shaven, and thin-faced; but no old man, belike scarce of fifty winters. Ralph caught his eye, and he smiled on the goodly young man so kindly, that for a moment Ralph deemed that he would dwell in St. Mary's House for a little while; for, thought he, if my father, or Nicholas, hear of me therein, they must even let me alone to abide here.

Therewith the Abbot went forth to his place, and sat him down under a goodly cloth of estate, and folk stood up again; but when Ralph looked for the man in the sallet he could see nought of him. Now when the Abbot was set down, men made a clear ring round about the bale, and there came into the said ring twelve young men, each clad in nought save a goat-skin, and with garlands of leaves and flowers about their middles: they had with them a wheel done about with straw and hemp payed with pitch and brimstone. They set fire to the same, and then trundled it blazing round about the bale twelve times. Then came to them twelve damsels clad in such-like guise as the young men: then both bands, the young men and the maidens, drew near to the bale, which was now burning low, and stood about it, and joined hands, and so danced round it a while, and meantime the fiddles played an uncouth tune merrily: then they sundered, and each couple of men and maids leapt backward and forward over the fire; and when they had all leapt, came forward men with buckets of water which they cast over the dancers till it ran down them in streams. Then was all the throng mingled together, and folk trod the embers of the bale under foot, and scattered them hither and thither all over the square.

All this while men were going about with pitchers of wine and ale, and other good drinks; and every man drank freely what he would, and there was the greatest game and joyance.

But now was Ralph exceeding weary, and he said: "Father, mightest thou lead me out of this throng, and show me some lair where I may sleep in peace, I would thank thee blithely."

As he spake there sounded a great horn over the square, and the Abbot rose in his place and blessed all the people once more. Then said the monk:

"Come then, fair field-lord, now shalt thou have thy will of bed." And he laughed therewith, and drew Ralph out of the throng and brought him into the Abbey, and into a fair little chamber, on the wall whereof was pictured St. Christopher, and St. Julian the lord and friend of wayfarers. Then he brought Ralph the wine and spices, and gave him good-night, and went his ways.

As Ralph put the raiment from off him he said to himself: a long day forsooth, so long that I should have thought no day could have held all that has befallen me. So many strange things have I seen, that surely my dreams shall be full of them; for even now I seem to see them, though I waken.

So he lay down in his bed and slept, and dreamed that he was fishing with an angle in a deep of Upmeads Water; and he caught many fish; but after a while whatsoever he caught was but of gilded paper stuffed with wool, and at last the water itself was gone, and he was casting his angle on to a dry road. Therewith he awoke and saw that day was dawning, and heard the minster clock strike three, and heard the thrushes singing their first song in the Prior's garden. Then he turned about and slept, and dreamed no more till he woke up in the bright sunny morning.

CHAPTER 6

Ralph Goeth His Ways From the Abbey of St. Mary at Higham

It was the monk who had been his guide the day before who had now waked him, and he stood by the bedside holding a great bowl of milk in his hand, and as Ralph sat up, and rubbed his eyes, with all his youthful sloth upon him, the monk laughed and said:

"That is well, lord, that is well! I love to see a young man so sleepy in the morning; it is a sign of thriving; and I see thou art thriving heartily for the time when thou shalt come back to us to lead my lord's host in battle."

"Where be the bale-fires?" said Ralph, not yet fully awake.

"Where be they!" said the brother, "where be they! They be sunken to cold coals long ago, like many a man's desires and hopes, who hath not yet laid his head on the bosom of the mother, that is Holy Church. Come, my lord, arise, and drink the monk's wine of morning, and then if ye must need ride, ride betimes, and ride hard; for the Wood Perilous beginneth presently as ye wend your ways; and it were well for thee to reach the Burg of the Four Friths ere thou be benighted. For, son, there be untoward things in the wood; and though some of them be of those for whom Christ's

Cross was shapen, yet have they forgotten hell, and hope not for heaven, and their by-word is, 'Thou shalt lack ere I lack.' Furthermore there are worse wights in the wood than they be—God save us!—but against them have I a good hauberk, a neck-guard which I will give thee, son, in token that I look to see thee again at the lovely house of Mary our Mother."

Ralph had taken the bowl and was drinking, but he looked over the brim, and saw how the monk drew from his frock a pair of beads, as like to Dame Katherine's gift as one pea to another, save that at the end thereof was a little box shapen crosswise. Ralph emptied the bowl hastily, got out of bed, and sat on the bed naked, save that on his neck was Dame Katherine's gift. He reached out his hand and took the beads from the monk and reddened therewith, as was his wont when he had to begin a contest in words: but he said:

"I thank thee, father; yet God wot if these beads will lie sweetly alongside the collar which I bear on my neck as now, which is the gift of a dear friend."

The monk made up a solemn countenance and said: "Thou sayest sooth, my son; it is most like that my chaplet, which hath been blessed time was by the holy Richard, is no meet fellow for the gift of some light love of thine: or even," quoth he, noting Ralph's flush deepen, and his brow knit, "or even if it were the gift of a well-willer, yet belike it is a worldly gift; therefore, since thy journey is with peril, thou wert best do it off and let me keep it for thee till thou comest again."

Now as he spake he looked anxiously, nay, it may be said greedily, at the young man. But Ralph said nought; for in his heart he was determined not to chaffer away his gossip's gift for any shaveling's token. Yet he knew not how to set his youthful words against the father's wisdom; so he stood up, and got his shirt into his hand, and as he did it over his head he fell to singing to himself a song of eventide of the High House of Upmeads, the words whereof were somewhat like to these:

Art thou man, art thou maid, through the long grass a-going?
   For short shirt thou bearest, and no beard I see,

And the last wind ere moonrise about thee is blowing.
    Would'st thou meet with thy maiden or look'st thou for me?

Bright shineth the moon now, I see thy gown longer;
    And down by the hazels Joan meeteth her lad:
But hard is thy palm, lass, and scarcely were stronger
    Wat's grip than thine hand-kiss that maketh me glad.

And now as the candles shine on us and over,
    Full shapely thy feet are, but brown on the floor,
As the bare-footed mowers amidst of the clover
    When the gowk's note is broken and mid-June is o'er.

O hard are mine hand-palms because on the ridges
    I carried the reap-hook and smote for thy sake;
And in the hot noon-tide I beat off the midges
    As thou slep'st 'neath the linden o'er-loathe to awake.

And brown are my feet now because the sun burneth
    High up on the down-side amidst of the sheep,
And there in the hollow wherefrom the wind turneth,
    Thou lay'st in my lap while I sung thee to sleep.

O friend of the earth, O come nigher and nigher,
    Thou art sweet with the sun's kiss as meads of the May,
O'er the rocks of the waste, o'er the water and fire,
    Will I follow thee, love, till earth waneth away.

The monk hearkened to him with knitted brow, and as one
that liketh not the speech of his fellow, though it be not wise
to question it: then he went out of the chamber, but left the
pair of beads lying in the window. But Ralph clad himself in
haste, and when he was fully clad, went up to the window
and took the beads in his hand, and looked into them curiously and turned them over, but left them lying there. Then
he went forth also, and came into the forecourt of the house,
and found there a squire of the men-at-arms with his weapons and horse, who helped him to do on his war-gear.

So then, just as he was setting his foot in the stirrup, came
the Brother again, with his face once more grown smiling

and happy; and in his left hand he held the chaplet, but did not offer it to Ralph again, but nodded his head to him kindly, and said: "Now, lord, I can see by thy face that thou art set on beholding the fashion of this world, and most like it will give thee the rue."

Then came a word into Ralph's mouth, and he said: "Wilt thou tell me, father, whose work was the world's fashion?"

The monk reddened, but answered nought, and Ralph spake again:

"Forsooth, did the craftsman of it fumble over his work?"

Then the monk scowled, but presently he enforced himself to speak blithely, and said: "Such matters are over high for my speech or thine, lord; but I tell thee, who knoweth, that there are men in this House who have tried the world and found it wanting."

Ralph smiled, and said stammering:

"Father, did the world try them, and find them wanting perchance?"

Then he reddened, and said: "Are ye verily all such as this in this House? Who then is it who hath made so fair a lordship, and so goodly a governance for so many people? Know ye not at all of the world's ways?"

"Fair sir," said the monk sternly, "they that work for us work for the Lord and all his servants."

"Yea," said Ralph, "so it is; and will the Lord be content with the service of him whom the devil hath cast out because he hath found him a dastard?"

The monk frowned, yet smiled somewhat withal, and said: "Sir, thou art young, but thy wits are over old for me; but there are they in this House who may answer thee featly; men who have read the books of the wise men of the heathen, and the doctors of Holy Church, and are even now making books for the scribes to copy." Then his voice softened, and he said: "Dear lord, we should be right fain of thee here, but since thou must needs go, go with my blessing, and double blessing shalt thou have when thou comest back to us." Then Ralph remembered his promise to the shepherds and took a gold crown from his pouch, and said: "Father, I pray thee say a mass for the shepherd downsmen; and this is for the offering."

34

The monk praised the gift and the bidding, and kissed Ralph, who clomb into his saddle; and the brother hospitalier brought him his wallet with good meat and drink therein for the way. Then Ralph shook his rein, and rode out of the abbey-gate, smiling at the lay-brethren and the men-at-arms who hung about there.

But he sighed for pleasure when he found himself in the street again, and looked on the shops of the chapmen and the booths of the petty craftsmen, as shoe-smiths and glovers, and tinsmiths and coppersmiths, and horners and the like; and the folk that he met as he rode toward the southern gate seemed to him merry and in good case, and goodly to look on. And he thought it pleasant to gaze on the damsels in the street, who were fair and well clad: and there were a many of them about his way now, especially as he drew nigh the gate before the streets branched off: for folk were coming in from the countryside with victual and other wares for the town and the Abbey; and surely as he looked on some of the maidens he deemed that Hall-song of Upmeads a good one.

CHAPTER 7

The Maiden of Bourton Abbas

So went he through the gate, and many, both of men and maids gazed at him, for he was fair to look on, but none meddled with him.

There was a goodly fauburg outside the gate, and therein were fair houses, not a few, with gardens and orchards about them; and when these were past he rode through very excellent meadows lying along the water, which he crossed thrice, once by a goodly stone bridge and twice by fords; for the road was straight, and the river wound about much.

After a little while the road led him off the plain meads

into a country of little hills and dales, the hill-sides covered with vineyards and orchards, and the dales plenteous of corn-fields; and now amongst these dales Higham was hidden from him.

Through this tillage and vine-land he rode a good while, and thought he had never seen a goodlier land; and as he went he came on husbandmen and women of the country going about their business: yet were they not too busy to gaze on him, and most greeted him; and with some he gave and took a little speech.

These people also he deemed well before the world, for they were well clad and buxom, and made no great haste as they went, but looked about them as though they deemed the world worth looking at, and as if they had no fear either of a blow or a hard word for loitering.

So he rode till it was noon, and he was amidst a little thorp of grey stone houses, trim enough, in a valley wherein there was more of wild-wood trees and less of fruit-bearers than those behind him. In the thorp was a tavern with the sign of the Nicholas, so Ralph deemed it but right to enter a house which was under the guard of his master and friend: therefore he lighted down and went in. Therein he found a lad of fifteen winters, and a maiden spinning, they two alone, who hailed him and asked his pleasure, and he bade them bring him meat and drink, and look to his horse, for that he had a mind to rest a while. So they brought him bread and flesh, and good wine of the hill-side, in a little hall well arrayed as of its kind; and he sat down and the damsel served him at table, but the lad, who had gone to see to his horse, did not come back.

So when he had eaten and drunk, and the damsel was still there, he looked on her and saw that she was sad and drooping of aspect; and whereas she was a fair maiden, Ralph, now that he was full, fell to pitying her, and asked her what was amiss. "For," said he, "thou art fair and ailest nought; that is clear to see; neither dwellest thou in penury, but by seeming hast enough and to spare. Or art thou a servant in this house, and hath any one misused thee?"

She wept at his words, for indeed he spoke softly to her; then she said: "Young lord, thou art kind, and it is thy kindness that draweth the tears from me; else it were not well to weep before a young man: therefore I pray thee pardon me. As for me, I am no servant, nor has any one misused me: the folk round about are good and neighbourly; and this house and the croft, and a vineyard hard by, all that is mine own and my brother's; that is the lad who hath gone to tend thine horse. Yea, and we live in peace here for the most part; for this thorp, which is called Bourton Abbas, is a land of the Abbey of Higham; though it be the outermost of its lands and the Abbot is a good lord and a defence against tyrants. All is well with me if one thing were not."

"What is thy need then?" said Ralph, "if perchance I might amend it." And as he looked on her he deemed her yet fairer than he had done at first. But she stayed her weeping and sobbing and said: "Sir, I fear me that I have lost a dear friend." "How then," said he, "why fearest thou, and knowest not? doth thy friend lie sick between life and death?" "O Sir," she said, "it is the Wood which is the evil and disease."

"What wood is that?" said he.

She said: "The Wood Perilous, that lieth betwixt us and the Burg of the Four Friths, and all about the Burg. And, Sir, if ye be minded to ride to the Burg to-day, do it not, for through the wood must thou wend thereto; and ye are young and lovely. Therefore take my rede, and abide till the Chapmen wend thither from Higham, who ride many in company. For, look you, fair lord, ye have asked of my grief, and this it is and nought else; that my very earthly love and speech-friend rode five days ago toward the Burg of the Four Friths all alone through the Wood Perilous, and he has not come back, though we looked to see him in three days' wearing: but his horse has come back, and the reins and the saddle all bloody."

And she fell a-weeping with the telling of the tale. But Ralph said (for he knew not what to say): "Keep a good heart, maiden; maybe he is safe and sound; oft are young men fond to wander wide, even as I myself."

She looked at him hard and said: "If thou hast stolen thyself away from them that love thee, thou hast done amiss. Though thou art a lord, and so fair as I see thee, yet will I tell thee so much."

Ralph reddened and answered nought; but deemed the maiden both fair and sweet. But she said: "Whether thou hast done well or ill, do no worse; but abide till the Chapmen come from Higham, on their way to the Burg of the Four Friths. Here mayst thou lodge well and safely if thou wilt. Or if our hall be not dainty enough for thee, then go back to Higham: I warrant me the monks will give thee good guesting as long as thou wilt."

"Thou art kind, maiden," said Ralph, "but why should I tarry for an host? and what should I fear in the Wood, as evil as it may be? One man journeying with little wealth, and unknown, and he no weakling, but bearing good weapons, hath nought to dread of strong-thieves, who ever rob where it is easiest and gainfullest. And what worse may I meet than strong-thieves?"

"But thou mayest meet worse," she said; and therewith fell a-weeping again, and said amidst her tears: "O weary on my life! And why should I heed thee when nought heedeth me; neither the Saints of God's House, nor the Master of it; nor the father and the mother that were once so piteous kind to me? O if I might but drink a draught from the WELL AT THE WORLD'S END!"

He turned about on her hastily at that word; for he had risen to depart; being grieved at her grief and wishful to be away from it, since he might not amend it. But now he said eagerly:

"Where then is that Well? Know ye of it in this land?"

"At least I know the hearsay thereof," she said; "but as now thou shalt know no more from me thereof; lest thou wander the wider in seeking it. I would not have thy life spilt."

Ever as he looked on her he thought her still fairer; and now he looked long on her, saying nought, and she on him in likewise, and the blood rose to her cheeks and her brow, but she would not turn her from his gaze. At last he said: "Well then, I must depart, no more learned than I came: but yet am I less hungry and thirsty than I came; and have thou thanks therefor."

Therewith he took from his pouch a gold piece of Upmeads, which was good, and of the touch of the Eastern lings, and held it out to her. And she put out her open hand and he put the money in it; but thought it good to hold her hand a while, and she gainsayed him not.

Then he said: "Well then, I must needs depart with things left as they are: wilt thou bid thy brother bring hither my horse, for time presses."

"Yea," she said (and her hand was still in his), "Yet do thine utmost, yet shalt thou not get to the Burg before nightfall. O wilt thou not tarry?"

"Nay," he said, "my heart will not suffer it; lest I deem myself a dastard."

Then she reddened again, but as if she were wroth; and she drew her hand away from his and smote her palms together thrice and cried out: "Ho Hugh! bring hither the Knight's horse and be speedy!"

And she went hither and thither about the hall and into the buttery and back, putting away the victual and vessels from the board and making as if she heeded him not: and Ralph looked on her, and deemed that each way she moved was better than the last, so shapely of fashion she was; and again he bethought him of the Even-song of the High House at Upmeads, and how it befitted her; for she went barefoot after the manner of maidens who work afield, and her feet were tanned with the sun of hay harvest, but as shapely as might be; but she was clad goodly withal, in a green gown wrought with flowers.

So he watched her going to and fro; and at last he said: "Maiden, wilt thou come hither a little, before I depart?"

"Yea," she said; and came and stood before him: and he deemed that she was scarce so sad as she had been; and she stood with her hands joined and her eyes downcast. Then he said:

"Now I depart. Yet I would say this, that I am sorry of thy sorrow: and now since I shall never see thee more, small would be the harm if I were to kiss thy lips and thy face."

And therewith he took her hands in his and drew her to him, and put his arms about her and kissed her many times, and she nothing lothe by seeming; and he found her as sweet as May blossom.

Thereafter she smiled on him, yet scarce for gladness, and

39

said: "It is not all so sure that I shall not see thee again; yet shall I do to thee as thou hast done to me."

Therewith she took his face between her hands, and kissed him well-favouredly; so that the hour seemed good to him.

Then she took him by the hand and led him out-a-doors to his horse, whereby the lad had been standing a good while; and he when he saw his sister come out with the fair knight he scowled on them, and handled a knife which hung at his girdle; but Ralph heeded him nought. As for the damsel, she put her brother aside, and held the stirrup for Ralph; and when he was in the saddle she said to him:

"All luck go with thee! Forsooth I deem thee safer in the Wood than my words said. Verily I deem that if thou wert to meet a company of foemen, thou wouldest compel them to do thy bidding."

"Farewell to thee maiden," said Ralph, "and mayst thou find thy beloved whole and well, and that speedily. Farewell!"

She said no more; so he shook his rein and rode his ways; but looked over his shoulder presently and saw her standing yet barefoot on the dusty highway shading her eyes from the afternoon sun and looking after him, and he waved his hand to her and so went his ways between the houses of the Thorp.

CHAPTER 8

Ralph Cometh to the Wood Perilous. An Adventure Therein

Now when he was clear of the Thorp the road took him out of the dale; and when he was on the hill's brow he saw that the land was of other fashion from that which lay behind him. For the road went straight through a rough waste, no pasture, save for mountain sheep or goats, with a few bushes scattered about it; and beyond this the land rose

40

into a long ridge; and on the ridge was a wood thick with trees, and no break in them. So on he rode, and soon passed that waste, which was dry and parched, and the afternoon sun was hot on it; so he deemed it good to come under the shadow of the thick trees (which at the first were wholly beech trees), for it was now the hottest of the day. There was still a beaten way between the tree-boles, though not overwide, albeit, a highway, since it pierced the wood. So thereby he went at a soft pace for the saving of his horse, and thought but little of all he had been told of the perils of the way, and not a little of the fair maid whom he had left behind at the Thorp.

After a while the thick beech-wood gave out, and he came into a place where great oaks grew, fair and stately, as though some lord's wood-reeve had taken care that they should not grow over close together, and betwixt them the greensward was fine, unbroken, and flowery. Thereby as he rode he beheld deer, both buck and hart and roe, and other wild things, but for a long while no man.

The afternoon wore and still he rode the oak wood, and deemed it a goodly forest for the greatest king on earth. At last he came to where another road crossed the way he followed, and about the crossway was the ground clearer of trees, while beyond it the trees grew thicker, and there was some underwood of holly and thorn as the ground fell off as towards a little dale.

There Ralph drew rein, because he doubted in his mind which was his right road toward the Burg of the Four Friths; so he got off his horse and abode a little, if perchance any might come by; he looked about him, and noted on the road that crossed his, and the sward about it, the sign of many horses having gone by, and deemed that they had passed but a little while. So he lay on the ground to rest him and let his horse stray about and bite the grass; for the beast loved him and would come at his call or his whistle.

Ralph was drowsy when he lay down, and though he said to himself that he would nowise go to sleep, yet as oft happens, he had no defence to make against sleepiness, and presently his hands relaxed, his head fell aside, and he slept quietly. When he woke up in a little space of time, he knew at once that something had awaked him and that he had not had his sleep out; for in his ears was the trampling of horse-hoofs and the clashing of weapons and loud speech of men. So he leapt up hastily, and while he was yet scarce awake, took to whistling on his horse; but even therewith those men were upon him, and two came up to him and laid hold of him; and when he asked them what they would, they bade him hold his peace.

Now his eyes cleared, and he saw that those men were in goodly war-gear, and bore coats of plate, and cuir-bouilly, or of bright steel; they held long spears and were girt with good swords; there was a pennon with them, green, whereon was done a golden tower, embattled, amidst of four white ways; and the same token bore many of the men on their coats and sleeves. Unto this same pennon he was brought by the two men who had taken him, and under it, on a white horse, sat a Knight bravely armed at all points with the Tower and Four Ways on his green surcoat; and beside him was an ancient man-at-arms, with nought but an oak wreath on his bare head, and his white beard falling low over his coat: but behind these twain a tall young man, also on a white horse and very gaily clad, upheld the pennon. On one side of these three were five men, unarmed, clad in green coats, with a leafless tree done on them in gold: they were stout carles, bearded and fierce-faced: their hands were bound behind their backs and their feet tied together under their horses' bellies. The company of those about the Knight, Ralph deemed, would number ten score men.

So when those twain stayed Ralph before the Knight, he turned to the old man and said:

"It is of no avail asking this lither lad if he be of them or no: for no will be his answer. But what sayest thou, Oliver?"

The ancient man drew closer to Ralph and looked at him up and down and all about; for those two turned him about as if he had been a joint of flesh on the roasting-jack; and at last he said:

"His beard is sprouting, else might ye have taken him for a maid of theirs, one of those of whom we wot. But to say sooth I seem to know the fashion of his gear, even as Duke Jacob knew Joseph's tabard. So ask him whence he is, lord, nd if he lie, then I bid bind him and lead him away, that we nay have a true tale out of him; otherwise let him go and ake his chance; for we will not waste the bread of the Good Town on him."

The Knight looked hard on Ralph, and spake to him somewhat courteously:

"Whence art thou, fair Sir, and what is thy name? for we have many foes in the wildwood."

Ralph reddened as he answered: "I am of Upmeads beyond the down country; and I pray thee let me be gone on mine errands. It is meet that thou deal with thine own robbers and reivers, but not with me."

Then cried out one of the bounden men: "Thou liest, lad, we be no robbers." But he of the Knight's company who stood by him smote the man on the mouth and said: "Hold thy peace, runagate! Thou shalt give tongue to-morrow when the hangman hath thee under his hands."

The Knight took no heed of this; but turned to the ancient warrior and said: "Hath he spoken truth so far?"

"Yea, Sir Aymer," quoth Oliver; "And now meseems I know him better than he knoweth me."

Therewith he turned to Ralph and said: "How fareth Long Nicholas, my lord?"

Ralph reddened again: "He is well," said he.

Then said the Knight: "Is the young man of a worthy house, Oliver?"

But ere the elder could speak, Ralph brake in and said: "Old warrior, I bid thee not to tell out my name, as thou lovest Nicholas."

Old Oliver laughed and said: "Well, Nicholas and I have been friends in a way, as well as foes; and for the sake of the old days his name shall help thee, young lord." Then he said to his Knight: "Yea, Sir Aymer, he is of a goodly house and an ancient; but thou hearest how he adjureth me. Ye shall let his name alone."

The Knight looked silently on Ralph for a while; then he said: "Wilt thou wend with us to the Burg of the Four Friths, fair Sir? Wert thou not faring thither? Or what else lost thou in the Wood Perilous?"

Ralph turned it over in his mind; and though he saw no

cause why he should not join himself to their company, yet something in his heart forbade him to rise to the fly too eagerly; so he did but say: "I am seeking adventures, fair lord."

The Knight smiled: "Then mayst thou fill thy budget with them if thou goest with us," quoth he. Now Ralph did not know how he might gainsay so many men at arms in the long run, though he were scarce willing to go; so he made no haste to answer; and even therewith came a man running, through the wood up from the dale; a long, lean carle, meet for running, with brogues on his feet, and nought else but a shirt; the company parted before him to right and left to let him come to the Knight, as though he had been looked for; and when he was beside him, the Knight leaned down while the carle spake softly to him and all men drew out of ear-shot. And when the carle had given his message the Knight drew himself straight up in his saddle again and lifted up his hand and cried out:

"Oliver! Oliver! lead on the way thou wottest! Spur! spur, all men!"

Therewith he blew one blast from a horn which hung at his saddle-bow; the runner leapt up behind old Oliver, and the whole company went off at a smart trot somewhat south-east, slantwise of the cross-roads, where the wood was nought cumbered with undergrowth; and presently they were all gone to the last horse-tail, and no man took any more note of Ralph.

CHAPTER 9

Another Adventure in the Wood Perilous

Ralph left alone pondered a little; and thought that he would by no means go hastily to the Burg of the Four Friths. Said he to himself; This want-way is all unlike to the one

44

near our house at home: for belike adventures shall befall here: I will even abide here for an hour or two; but will have my horse by me and keep awake, lest something hap to me unawares.

Therewith he whistled for Falcon his horse, and the beast came to him, and whinnied for love of him, and Ralph smiled and tied him to a sapling anigh, and himself sat down on the grass, and pondered many things; as to what folk were about at Upmeads, and how his brethren were faring; and it was now about five hours after noon, and the sun's rays fell aslant through the boughs of the noble oaks, and the scent of the grass and bracken trodden by the horse-hoofs of that company went up into the warm summer air. A while he sat musing but awake, though the faint sound of a little stream in the dale below mingled with all the lesser noises of the forest did its best to soothe him to sleep again: and presently had its way with him; for he leaned his head back on the bracken, and in a minute or two was sleeping once more and dreaming some dream made up of masterless memories of past days.

When he awoke again he lay still a little while, wondering where in the world he was, but as the drowsiness left him, he arose and looked about, and saw that the sun was sinking low and gilding the oakboles red. He stood awhile and watched the gambols of three hares, who had drawn nigh him while he slept, and now noted him not; and a little way he saw through the trees a hart and two hinds going slowly from grass to grass, feeding in the cool eventide; but presently he saw them raise their heads and amble off down the slope of the little dale, and therewith he himself turned his face sharply toward the north-west, for he was fine-eared as well as sharp-eyed, and on a little wind which had just arisen came down to him the sound of horse-hoofs once more.

So he went up to Falcon and loosed him, and stood by him bridle in hand, and looked to it that his sword was handy to him: and he hearkened, and the sound drew nigher and nigher to him. Then lightly he got into the saddle and gathered the reins into his left hand, and sat peering up the trodden wood-glades, lest he should have to ride for his life suddenly. Therewith he heard voices talking roughly and a man whistling, and athwart the glade of the wood from the northwest, or thereabout, came new folk; and he saw at once that there went two men a-horseback and armed; so he drew his sword and abode them close to the want-ways. Presently they saw the shine of his war-gear, and then they came but a little nigher ere they drew rein, and sat on their horses looking toward him. Then Ralph saw that they were armed and clad as those of the company which had gone before. One of the armed men rode a horse-length after his fellow, and bore a long spear over his shoulder. But the other who rode first was girt with a sword, and had a little axe hanging about his neck, and with his right hand he seemed to be leading something, Ralph could not see what at first, as his left side was turned toward Ralph and the want-way.

Now, as Ralph looked, he saw that at the spearman's saddle-bow was hung a man's head, red-haired and red-bearded; for this man now drew a little nigher, and cried out to Ralph in a loud and merry voice: "Hail, knight! whither away now, that thou ridest the green-wood sword in hand?"

Ralph was just about to answer somewhat, when the first man moved a little nigher, and as he did so he turned so that Ralph could see what betid on his right hand; and lo! he was leading a woman by a rope tied about her neck (though her hands were loose), as though he were bringing a cow to market. When the man stayed his horse she came forward and stood within the slack of the rope by the horse's head, and Ralph could see her well, that though she was not to say naked, her raiment was but scanty, for she had nought to cover her save one short and strait little coat of linen, and shoes on her feet. Yet Ralph deemed her to be of some degree, whereas he caught the gleam of gold and gems on her hands, and there was a golden chaplet on her head. She stood now by the horse's head with her hands folded, looking on, as if what was tiding and to betide, were but a play done for her pleasure.

So when Ralph looked on her, he was silent a while; and the spearman cried out again: "'Ho, young man, wilt thou speak, or art thou dumb-foundered for fear of us?"

But Ralph knit his brows, and was first red and then pale; for he was both wroth, and doubtful how to go to work; but he said:

46

"I ride to seek adventures; and here meseemeth is one come to hand. Or what will ye with the woman?"

Said the man who had the woman in tow: "Trouble not thine head therewith; we lead her to her due doom. As for thee, be glad that thou art not her fellow; since forsooth thou seemest not to be one of them; so go thy ways in peace."

"No foot further will I go," said Ralph, "till ye loose the woman and let her go; or else tell me what her worst deed is."

The man laughed, and said: "That were a long tale to tell; and it is little like that thou shalt live to hear the ending thereof."

Therewith he wagged his head at the spearman, who suddenly let his spear fall into the rest, and spurred, and drave on at Ralph all he might. There and then had the tale ended, but Ralph, who was wary, though he were young, and had Falcon well in hand, turned his wrist and made the horse swerve, so that the man-at-arms missed his attaint, but could not draw rein speedily enough to stay his horse; and as he passed by all bowed over his horse's neck, Ralph gat his sword two-handed and rose in his stirrups and smote his mightiest; and the sword caught the foeman on the neck betwixt sallet and jack, and nought held before it, neither leather nor ring-mail, so that the man's head was nigh smitten off, and he fell clattering from his saddle: yet his stirrups held him, so that his horse went dragging him on earth as he gallopped over rough and smooth betwixt the trees of the forest. Then Ralph turned about to deal with his fellow, and even through the wrath and fury of the slaying saw him clear and bright against the trees as he sat handling his axe doubtfully, but the woman was fallen back again somewhat.

But even as Ralph raised his sword and pricked forward, the woman sprang as light as a leopard on to the saddle behind the foeman, and wound her arms about him and dragged him back just as he was raising his axe to smite her, and as Ralph rode forward she cried out to him, "Smite him, smite! O lovely creature of God!"

Therewith was Ralph beside them, and though he were loth to slay a man held in the arms of a woman, yet he feared lest the man should slay her with some knife-stroke

47

unless he made haste; so he thrust his sword through him, and the man died at once, and fell headlong off his horse, dragging down the woman with him.

Then Ralph lighted down from his horse, and the woman rose up to him, her white smock all bloody with the slain man. Nevertheless was she as calm and stately before him, as if she were sitting on the daïs of a fair hall; so she said to him:

"Young warrior, thou hast done well and knightly, and I shall look to it that thou have thy reward. And now I rede thee go not to the Burg of the Four Friths; for this tale of thee shall get about and they shall take thee, if it were out of the very Frith-stool, and there for thee should be the scourge and the gibbet; for they of that Burg be robbers and murderers merciless. Yet well it were that thou ride hence presently; for those be behind my tormentors whom thou hast slain, who will be as an host to thee, and thou mayst not deal with them. If thou follow my rede, thou wilt take the way that goeth hence east away, and then shalt thou come to Hampton under Scaur, where the folk are peaceable and friendly."

He looked at her hard as she spake, and noted that she spake but slowly, and turned red and white and red again as she looked at him. But whatever she did, and in spite of her poor attire, he deemed he had never seen woman so fair. Her hair was dark red, but her eyes grey, and light at whiles and yet at whiles deep; her lips betwixt thin and full, but yet when she spoke or smiled clad with all enticements; her chin round and so wrought as none was ever better wrought; her body strong and well-knit; tall she was, with fair and large arms, and limbs most goodly of fashion, of which but little was hidden, since her coat was but thin and scanty. But whatever may be said of her, no man would have deemed her aught save most lovely. Now her face grew calm and stately again as it was at the first, and she laid a hand on Ralph's shoulder, and smiled in his face and said:

"Surely thou art fair, though thy strokes be not light." Then she took his hand and caressed it, and said again: "Dost thou deem that thou hast done great things, fair child? Maybe. Yet some will say that thou hast but slain two butchers: and if thou wilt say that thou hast delivered me;

48

yet it may be that I should have delivered myself ere long. Nevertheless hold up thine heart, for I think that greater things await thee."

Then she turned about, and saw the dead man, how his feet yet hung in the stirrups as his fellow's had done, save that the horse of this one stood nigh still, only reaching his head down to crop a mouthful of grass; so she said: "Take him away, that I may mount on his horse."

So he drew the dead man's feet out of the stirrups, and dragged him away to where the bracken grew deep, and laid him down there, so to say hidden. Then he turned back to the lady, who was pacing up and down near the horse as the beast fed quietly on the cool grass. When Ralph came back she took the reins in her hand and put one foot in the stirrup as if she would mount at once; but suddenly lighted down again, and turning to Ralph, cast her arms about him, and kissed his face many times, blushing red as a rose meantime. Then lightly she gat her up into the saddle, and bestrode the beast, and smote his flanks with her heels, and went her ways riding speedily toward the south-east, so that she was soon out of sight.

But Ralph stood still looking the way she had gone and wondering at the adventure; and he pondered her words and held debate with himself whether he should take the road she bade him. And he said within himself: "Hitherto have I been safe and have got no scratch of a weapon upon me, and this is a place by seeming for all adventures; and little way moreover shall I make in the night if I must needs go to Hampton under Scaur, where dwell those peaceable people; and it is now growing dusk already. So I will abide the morning hereby; but I will be wary and let the wood cover me if I may."

Therewith he went and drew the body of the slain man down into a little hollow where the bracken was high and the brambles grew strong, so that it might not be lightly seen. Then he called to him Falcon, his horse, and looked about for cover anigh the want-way, and found a little thin coppice of hazel and sweet chestnut, just where two great oaks had been felled a half score years ago; and looking through the leaves thence, he could see the four ways clearly enough, though it would not be easy for anyone to see him thence.

Thither he betook him, and he did the rein off Falcon, but tethered him by a halter in the thickest of the copse, and sat down himself nigher to the outside thereof; he did off his helm and drew what meat he had from out his wallet and ate and drank in the beginning of the summer night; and then sat pondering awhile on what had befallen on this second day of his wandering. The moon shone out presently, little clouded, but he saw her not, for though he strove to wake awhile, slumber soon overcame him, and nothing waked him till the night was passing, nor did he see aught of that company of which the lady had spoken, and which in sooth came not.

CHAPTER 10

A Meeting and a Parting
in the Wood Perilous

When the first glimmer of dawn was in the sky he awoke in the fresh morning, and sat up and hearkened, for even as he woke he had heard something, since wariness had made him wakeful. Now he hears the sound of horse-hoofs on the hard road, and riseth to his feet and goeth to the very edge of the copse; looking thence he saw a rider who was just come to the very crossing of the roads. The new comer was much muffled in a wide cloak, but he seemed to be a man low of stature. He peered all round about him as if to see if the way were clear, and then alighted down from horseback and let the hood fall off his head, and seemed pondering which way were the best to take. By this time it was grown somewhat lighter and Ralph, looking hard, deemed that the rider was a woman; so he stepped forward lightly, and as he came on to the open sward about the way, the new comer saw him and put a foot into the stirrup to mount, but yet looked at him over the shoulder, and then presently left the saddle and came forward a few steps as if to meet Ralph, having cast the cloak to the ground.

Then Ralph saw that it was none other than the damsel of the hostelry of Bourton Abbas, and he came up to her and reached out his hand to her, and she took it in both hers and held it and said, smiling: "It is nought save mountains that shall never meet. Here have I followed on thy footsteps; yet knew I not where thou wouldst be in the forest. And now I am glad to have fallen in with thee; for I am going a long way."

Ralph looked on her and himseemed some pain or shame touched his heart, and he said: "I am a knight adventurous; I have nought to do save to seek adventures. Why should I not go with thee?"

She looked at him earnestly awhile and said: "Nay, it may not be; thou art a lord's son, and I a yeoman's daughter." She stopped, and he said nothing in answer.

"Furthermore," said she, "it is a long way, and I know not how long." Again he made no answer, and she said: "I am going to seek the WELL AT THE WORLD'S END, and to find it and live, or to find it not, and die."

He spake after a while: "Why should I not come with thee?"

It was growing light now, and he could see that she reddened and then turned pale and set her lips close.

Then she said: "Because thou willest it not: because thou hadst liefer make that journey with some one else."

He reddened in his turn, and said: "I know of no one else who shall go with me."

"Well," she said, "it is all one, I will not have thee go with me." "Yea, and why not?" said he. She said: "Wilt thou swear to me that nought hath happed to thee to change thee betwixt this and Bourton? If thou wilt, then come with me; if thou wilt not, then refrain thee. And this I say because I see and feel that there is some change in thee since yesterday, so that thou wouldst scarce be dealing truly in being my fellow in this quest: for they that take it up must be single-hearted, and think of nought save the quest and the fellow that is with them."

She looked on him sadly, and his many thoughts tongue-tied him a while; but at last he said: "Must thou verily go on this quest?" "Ah," she said, "now since I have seen thee and spoken with thee again, all need there is that I should follow it at once."

Then they both kept silence, and when she spoke again her voice was as if she were gay against her will. She said: "Here am I come to these want-ways, and there are three roads besides the one I came by, and I wot that this that goeth south will bring me to the Burg of the Four Friths; and so much I know of the folk of the said Burg that they would mock at me if I asked them of the way to the Well at the World's End. And as for the western way I deem that that will lead me back again to the peopled parts whereof I know; therefore I am minded to take the eastern way. What sayest thou, fair lord?"

Said Ralph: "I have heard of late that it leadeth presently to Hampton under the Scaur, where dwelleth a people of goodwill."

"Who told thee this tale?" said she. Ralph answered, reddening again, "I was told by one who seemed to know both of that folk, and of the Burg of the Four Friths, and she said that the folk of Hampton were a good folk, and that they of the Burg were evil."

The damsel smiled sadly when she heard him say 'She,' and when he had done she said: "And I have heard, and not from yesterday, that at Hampton dwelleth the Fellowship of the Dry Tree, and that those of the fellowship are robbers and reivers. Nevertheless they will perchance be little worse than the others; and the tale tells that the way to the Well at the World's End is by the Dry Tree; so thither will I at all adventure. And now will I say farewell to thee, for it is most like that I shall not see thee again."

"O, maiden!" said Ralph, "why wilt thou not go back to Bourton Abbas? There I might soon meet thee again, and yet, indeed, I also am like to go to Hampton. Shall I not see thee there?"

She shook her head and said: "Nay, since I must go so far, I shall not tarry; and, sooth to say, if I saw thee coming in at one gate I should go out by the other, for why should I dally with a grief that may not be amended. For indeed I wot that

52

thou shalt soon forget to wish to see me, either at Bourton Abbas or elsewhere; so I will say no more than once again farewell."

Then she came close to him and put her hands on his shoulders and kissed his mouth; and then she turned away swiftly, caught up her cloak, and gat lightly into the saddle, and so shook her reins and rode away east toward Hampton, and left Ralph standing there downcast and pondering many things. It was still so early in the summer morning, and he knew so little what to do, that presently he turned and walked back to his lair amongst the hazels, and there he lay down, and his thoughts by then were all gone back again to the lovely lady whom he had delivered, and he wondered if he should ever see her again, and, sooth to say, he sorely desired to see her. Amidst such thoughts he fell asleep again, for the night yet owed him something of rest, so young as he was and so hard as he had toiled, both body and mind, during the past day.

CHAPTER 11

Now Must Ralph Ride For It

When he awoke again the sun was shining through the hazel leaves, though it was yet early; he arose and looked to his horse, and led him out of the hazel copse and stood and looked about him; and lo! a man coming slowly through the wood on Ralph's right hand, and making as it seemed for the want-way; he saw Ralph presently, and stopped, and bent a bow which he held in his hand, and then came towards him warily, with the arrow nocked. But Ralph went to meet him with his sword in his sheath, and leading Falcon by the rein, and the man stopped and took the shaft from the string: he had no armour, but there was a little axe and a wood-knife in his girdle; he was clad in homespun, and looked like a carle of the country-side. Now he greeted Ralph, and Ralph gave him the sele of the day, and saw that the new-comer was both tall and strong, dark of skin and black-haired, but of a cheerful countenance. He spake frank and free to Ralph, and said: "Whither away, lord, out of the woodland hall, and the dwelling of deer and strong-thieves? I would that the deer would choose them a captain, and gather head and destroy the thieves—and some few others with them."

Said Ralph: "I may scarce tell thee till I know myself. Awhile ago I was minded for the Burg of the Four Friths; but now I am for Hampton under Scaur."

"Yea?" said the carle, "when the Devil drives, to hell must we."

"What meanest thou, good fellow?" said Ralph, "Is Hampton then so evil an abode?" And indeed it was in his mind that the adventure of the lady led captive bore some evil with it.

Said the carle: "If thou wert not a stranger in these parts I need not to answer thy question; but I will answer it presently, yet not till we have eaten, for I hunger, and have in this wallet both bread and cheese, and thou art welcome to a share thereof, if thou hungerest also, as is most like, whereas thou art young and fresh coloured."

"So it is," said Ralph, laughing, "and I also may help to spread this table in the wilderness, since there are yet some crumbs in my wallet. Let us sit down and fall to at once."

"By your leave, Sir Gentleman," said the carle, "we will go a few yards further on, where there is a woodland brook, whereof we may drink when my bottle faileth."

"Nay, I may better that," said Ralph, "for I have wherewithal." "Nevertheless," said the carle, "we will go thither, for here is it too open for so small a company as ours, since this want-way hath an ill name, and I shall lead thee whereas we shall be somewhat out of the way of murder-carles. So come on, if thou trusteth in me."

Ralph yeasaid him, and they went together a furlong from the want-way into a little hollow place wherethrough ran a clear stream betwixt thick-leaved alders. The carle led Ralph to the very lip of the water so that the bushes covered them; there they sat down and drew what they had from their wallets, and so fell to meat; and amidst of the meat the carle said:

"Fair Knight, as I suppose thou art one, I will ask thee if any need draweth thee to Hampton?"

Said Ralph: "The need of giving the go-by to the Burg of the Four Friths, since I hear tell that the folk thereof be robbers and murderers."

"Thou shalt find that out better, lord, by going thither; but I shall tell thee, that though men may slay and steal there time and time about, yet in regard to Hampton under Scaur, it is Heaven, wherein men sin not. And I am one who should know, for I have been long dwelling in Hell, that is Hampton; and now am I escaped thence, and am minded for the Burg, if perchance I may be deemed there a man good enough to ride in their host, whereby I might avenge me somewhat on them that have undone me: some of whom meseemeth must have put in thy mouth that word against the Burg. Is it not so?"

"Maybe," said Ralph, "for thou seemest to be a true man." No more he spake though he had half a mind to tell the carle all the tale of that adventure; but something held him back when he thought of that lady and her fairness. Yet again his heart misgave him of what might betide that other maiden at Hampton, and he was unquiet, deeming that he must needs follow her thither. The carle looked on him curiously and somewhat anxiously, but Ralph's eyes were set on something that was not there; or else maybe had he looked closely on the carle he might have deemed that longing to avenge him whereof he spoke did not change his face much; for in truth there was little wrath in it.

Now the carle said: "Thou hast a tale which thou deemest unmeet for my ears, as it well may be. Well, thou must speak, or refrain from speaking, what thou wilt; but thou art so fair a young knight, and so blithe with a poor man, and withal I deem that thou mayest help me to some gain and good, that I will tell thee a true tale: and first that the Burg is a good town under a good lord, who is no tyrant nor oppressor of peaceful men; and that thou mayest dwell there in peace as to the folk thereof, who be good folk, albeit they be no dastards to let themselves be cowed by murder-carles.

And next I will tell thee that the folk of the town of
Hampton be verily as harmless and innocent as sheep; but
that they be under evil lords who are not their true lords,
who lay heavy burdens on them and torment them even to
the destroying of their lives: and lastly I will tell thee that I
was one of those poor people, though not so much a sheep as
the more part of them, therefore have these tyrants robbed
me of my croft, and set another man in my house; and me
they would have slain had I not fled to the wood that it
might cover me. And happy it was for me that I had neither
wife, nor chick, nor child, else had they done as they did with
my brother, whose wife was too fair for him, since he dwelt
at Hampton; so that they took her away from him to make
sport for them of the Dry Tree, who dwell in the Castle of
the Scaur, who shall be thy masters if thou goest thither.

"This is my tale, and thine, I say, I ask not; but I deem
that thou shalt do ill if thou go not to the Burg either with
me or by thyself alone; either as a guest, or as a good knight
to take service in their host."

Now so it was that Ralph was wary; and this time he
looked closely at the carle, and found that he spake coldly
for a man with so much wrath in his heart; therefore he was
in doubt about the thing; moreover he called to mind the
words of the lady whom he had delivered, and her loveliness,
and the kisses she had given him, and he was loth to find her
a liar; and he was loth also to think that the maiden of
Bourton had betaken her to so evil a dwelling. So he said:

"Friend, I know not that I must needs be a partaker in the
strife betwixt Hampton and the Burg, or go either to one or
the other of these strongholds. Is there no other way out of
this wood save by Hampton or the Burg? or no other place
anigh, where I may rest in peace awhile, and then go on
mine own errands?"

Said the Carle: "There is a thorp that lieth somewhat west
of the Burg, which is called Apthorp; but it is an open place,
not fenced, and is debateable ground, whiles held by them of
the Burg, whiles by the Dry Tree; and if thou tarry there,
and they of the Dry Tree take thee, soon is thine errand
sped; and if they of the Burg take thee, then shalt thou be led
into the Burg in worse case than thou wouldest be if thou go

thereto uncompelled. What sayest thou, therefore? Who shall hurt thee in the Burg, a town which is under good and strong law, if thou be a true man, as thou seemest to be? And if thou art seeking adventures, as may well be, thou shalt soon find them there ready to hand. I rede thee come with me to the Burg; for, to say sooth, I shall find it somewhat easier to enter therein if I be in the company of thee, a knight and a lord."

So Ralph considered and thought that there lay indeed but little peril to him in the Burg, whereas both those men with whom he had striven were hushed for ever, and there was none else to tell the tale of the battle, save the lady, whose peril from them of the Burg was much greater than his; and also he thought that if anything untoward befel, he had some one to fall back on in old Oliver: yet on the other hand he had a hankering after Hampton under Scaur, where, to say sooth, he doubted not to see the lady again.

So betwixt one thing and the other, speech hung on his lips awhile, when suddenly the carle said: "Hist! thou hast left thy horse without the bushes, and he is whinnying" (which indeed he was), "there is now no time to lose. To horse straightway, for certainly there are folk at hand, and they may be foemen, and are most like to be."

Therewith they both arose and hastened to where Falcon stood just outside the alder bushes, and Ralph leapt a-horseback without more ado, and the carle waited no bidding to leap up behind him, and pointing to a glade of the wood which led toward the highway, cried out, "Spur that way, thither! they of the Dry Tree are abroad this morning. Spur! 'tis for life or death!"

Ralph shook the rein and Falcon leapt away without waiting for the spur, while the carle looked over his shoulder and said, "Yonder they come! they are three; and ever they ride well horsed. Nay, nay! They are four," quoth he, as a shout sounded behind them. "Spur, young lord! spur! And thine horse is a mettlesome beast. Yea, it will do, it will do."

Therewith came to Ralph's ears the sound of their horse-hoofs beating the turf, and he spurred indeed, and Falcon flew forth.

"Ah," cried the carle! "but take heed, for they see that thy

57

horse is good, and one of them, the last, hath a bent Turk bow in his hand, and is laying an arrow on it; as ever their wont is to shoot a-horseback: a turn of thy rein, as if thine horse were shying at a weasel on the road!"

Ralph stooped his head and made Falcon swerve, and heard therewith the twang of the bowstring and straightway the shaft flew past his ears. Falcon galloped on, and the carle cried out: "There is the highway toward the Burg! Do thy best, do thy best! Lo you again!"

For the second shaft flew from the Turkish bow, and the noise of the chase was loud behind them. Once again twanged the bow-string, but this time the arrow fell short, and the woodland man, turning himself about as well as he might, shook his clenched fist at the chase, crying out in a voice broken by the gallop: "Ha, thieves! I am Roger of the Rope-walk, I go to twist a rope for the necks of you!"

Then he spake to Ralph: "They are turning back: they are beaten, and withal they love not the open road: yet slacken not yet, young knight, unless thou lovest thine horse more than thy life; for they will follow on through the thicket on the way-side to see whether thou wert born a fool and hast learned nothing later."

"Yea," said Ralph, "and now I deem thou wilt tell me that to the Burg I needs must."

"Yea, forsooth," said the carle, "nor shall we be long, riding thus, ere we come to the Burg Gate."

"Yea, or even slower," said Ralph, drawing rein somewhat, "for now I deem the chase done: and after all is said, I have no will to slay Falcon, who is one of my friends, as thou perchance mayest come to be another."

Thereafter he went a hand-gallop till the wood began to thin, and there were fields of tillage about the highway; and presently Roger said: "Thou mayst breathe thy nag now, and ride single, for we are amidst friends; not even a score of the Dry Tree dare ride so nigh the Burg save by night and cloud."

So Ralph stayed his horse, and he and Roger lighted down, and Ralph looked about him and saw a stone tower builded on a little knoll amidst a wheatfield, and below it some simple houses thatched with straw; there were folk moreover working, or coming and going about the fields, who took little heed of the two when they saw them standing quiet by the horse's head; but each and all of these folk, so far as could be seen, had some weapon.

Then said Ralph: "Good fellow, is this the Burg of the Four Friths?" The carle laughed, and said: "Simple is the question, Sir Knight: yonder is a watch-tower of the Burg, whereunder husbandmen can live, because there be men-at-arms therein. And all round the outskirts of the Frank of the Burg are there such-like towers to the number of twenty-seven. For that, say folk, was the tale of the winters of the Fair Lady who erewhile began the building of the Burg, when she was first wedded to the Forest Lord, who before that building had dwelt, he and his fathers, in thatched halls of timber here and there about the clearings of the wild-wood. But now, knight, if thou wilt, thou mayest go on softly toward the Gate of the Burg, and if thou wilt I will walk beside thy rein, which fellowship, as aforesaid, shall be a gain to me."

Said Ralph: "I pray thee come with me, good fellow, and show me how easiest to enter this stronghold." So, when Falcon was well breathed, they went on, passing through goodly acres and wide meadows, with here and there a homestead on them, and here and there a carle's cot. Then came they to a thorp of the smallest on a rising ground, from the further end of which they could see the walls and towers of the Burg. Thereafter right up to the walls were no more houses or cornfields, nought but reaches of green meadows plenteously stored with sheep and kine, and with a little stream winding about them.

CHAPTER 12

Ralph Entereth Into the Burg of the Four Friths

When they came up to the wall they saw that it was well builded of good ashlar, and so high that they might not see the roofs of the town because of it; but there were tall towers on it, a many of them, strong and white. The road led up straight to the master-gate of the Burg, and there was a bailey before it strongly walled, and manned with weaponed men, and a captain going about amongst them. But they entered it along with men bringing wares into the town, and none heeded them much, till they came to the very gate, on the further side of a moat that was both deep and clean; but as now the bridge was down and the portcullis up, so that the market-people might pass in easily, for it was yet early in the day. But before the door on either side stood men-at-arms well weaponed, and on the right side was their captain, a tall man with bare grizzled head, but otherwise all-armed, who stopped every one whom he knew not, and asked their business.

As Ralph came riding up with Roger beside him, one of the guard laid his spear across and bade them stand, and the captain spake in a dry cold voice: "Whence comest thou, man-at-arms?" "From the Abbey of St. Mary at Higham," said Ralph. "Yea," said the captain, smiling grimly, "even so I might have deemed: thou wilt be one of the Lord Abbot's lily lads." "No I am not," quoth Ralph angrily. "Well, well," said the captain, "what is thy name?"

"Ralph Motherson," quoth Ralph, knitting his brow. Said the captain "And whither wilt thou?" Said Ralph, "On mine own errands." "Thou answerest not over freely," quoth the captain. Said Ralph, "Then is it even; for thou askest freely enough." "Well, well," said the captain, grinning in no unfriendly wise, "thou seemest a stout lad enough; and as to my asking, it is my craft as captain of the North Gate: but now tell me friendly, goest thou to any kinsman or friend in the Burg?"

Then Ralph's brow cleared and he said, "Nay, fair sir." "Well then," said the captain, "art thou but riding straight through to another gate, and so away again?" "Nay," said Ralph, "if I may, I would abide here the night over, or may-happen longer." "Therein thou shalt do well, young man," said the captain; "then I suppose thou wilt to some hostelry? tell me which one."

Said Ralph, "Nay, I wot not to which one, knowing not the town." But Roger close by him spake and said: "My lord shall go to the Flower de Luce, which is in the big square."

"Truly," said the captain, "he goes to a good harbour; and moreover, fair sir, to-morrow thou shalt see a goodly sight from thine inn; thou mayst do no better, lord. But thou, carle, who art thou, who knowest the inside of our Burg so well, though I know thee not, for as well as I know our craftsmen and vavassors?"

Then Roger's words hung on his lips awhile, and the knight bent his brow on him, till at last he said, "Sir Captain, I was minded to lie, and say that I am this young knight's serving-man." The captain broke in on him grimly, "Thou wert best not lie."

"Yea, sir," quoth Roger, "I deemed, as it was on my tongue's end, that thou wouldst find me out, so I have nought to do but tell thee the very sooth: this it is: I am a man made masterless by the thieves of the Dry Tree. From my land at Hampton under Scaur have I been driven, my chattels have been lifted, and my friends slain; and therefore by your leave would I ride in the host of the Burg, that I may pay back the harm which I had, according to the saw, 'better bale by breeding bale.' So, lord, I ask thee wilt thou lend me the sword and give me the loaf, that I may help both thee, and the Burg, and me?"

The captain looked at him closely and sharply, while the carle faced him with open simple eyes, and at last he said: "Well, carle, thou wert about to name thyself this young knight's serving-man; be thou even so whiles he abideth in

61

the Burg; and when he leaveth the Burg then come back to me here any day before noon, and may be I shall then put a sword in thy fist and horse between thy thighs. But," (and he wagged his head threateningly at Roger) "see that thou art at the Flower de Luce when thou art called for."

Roger held his peace and seemed somewhat abashed at this word, and the captain turned to Ralph and said courteously: "Young knight, if thou art seeking adventures, thou shalt find them in our host; and if thou be but half as wise as thou seemest bold, thou wilt not fail to gain honour and wealth both, in the service of the Burg; for we be overmuch beset with foemen that we should not welcome any wight and wary warrior, though he be an alien of blood and land. If thou thinkest well of this, then send me thy man here and give me word of thy mind, and I shall lead thee to the chiefs of the Port, and make the way easy for thee."

Ralph thanked him and rode through the gate into the street, and Roger still went beside his stirrup.

Presently Ralph turned to Roger and spake to him somewhat sourly, and said: "Thou hadst one lie in thy mouth and didst swallow it; but how shall I know that another did not come out thence? Withal thou must needs be my fellow here, will I, nill I; for thou it was that didst put that word into the captain's mouth that thou shouldst serve me while I abide in the Burg. So I will say here and now, that my mind misgives me concerning thee, whether thou be not of those very thieves and tyrants whom thou didst mis-say but a little while ago."

"Yea," said Roger, "thou art wise indeed to set me down as one of the Dry Tree; doubtless that is why I delivered thee from their ambush even now. And as for my service, thou mayst need it; for indeed I deem thee not so safe as thou deemest thyself in this Burg."

"What!" said Ralph, "Dost thou blow hot and cold? why even now, when we were in the wood, thou wert telling me that I had nought at all to fear in the Burg of the Four Friths, and that all was done there by reason and with justice. What is this new thing then which thou hast found out, or what is that I have to fear?"

Roger changed countenance thereat and seemed somewhat

confused, as one who has been caught unawares; but he gat his own face presently, and said: "Nay, Sir Knight, I will tell thee the truth right out. In the wood yonder thy danger was great that thou mightest run into the hands of them of the Dry Tree; therefore true it is that I spake somewhat beyond my warrant concerning the life of the folk of the Burg, as how could I help it? But surely whatever thy peril may be here, it is nought to that which awaited thee at Hampton."

"Nay, but what is the peril?" said Ralph. Quoth Roger, "If thou wilt become their man and enter into their host, there is none; for they will ask few questions of so good a man-at-arms, when they know that thou art theirs; but if thou naysay that, it may well be that they will be for turning the key on thee till thou tellest them what and whence thou art." Ralph answered nought, thinking in his mind that this was like enough; so he rode on soberly, till Roger said:

"Anyhow, thou mayst turn the cold shoulder on me if thou wilt. Yet were I thee, I would not, for so it is, both that I can help thee, as I deem, in time to come, and that I have helped thee somewhat in time past."

Now Ralph was young and could not abide the blame of thanklessness; so he said, "Nay, nay, fellow, go we on together to the Flower de Luce."

Roger nodded his head and grumbled somewhat, and they made no stay except that now and again Ralph drew rein to look at goodly things in the street, for there were many open booths therein, so that the whole street looked like a market. The houses were goodly of building, but not very tall, the ways wide and well-paved. Many folk were in the street, going up and down on their errands, and both men and women of them seemed to Ralph stout and strong, but not very fair of favour. Withal they seemed intent on their business, and payed little heed to Ralph and his fellow, though he was by his attire plainly a stranger.

Now Ralph sees a house more gaily adorned than most, and a sign hung out from it whereon was done an image of St. Loy, and underneath the same a booth on which was set out weapons and war-gear exceeding goodly; and two knaves of the armourer were standing by to serve folk, and crying their wares with "what d'ye lack?" from time to time. So he stayed and fell to looking wistfully at the gleam and glitter of those fair things, till one of the aforesaid knaves came to his side and said:

"Fair Sir, surely thou lackest somewhat; what have we here for thy needs?" So Ralph thought and called to mind that strong little steel axe of the man whom he had slain yesterday, and asked for the sight of such a weapon, if he might perchance cheapen it. And the lad brought a very goodly steel axe, gold-inlaid about the shaft, and gave him the price thereof, which Ralph deemed he might compass; so he brought round his scrip to his hand, that he might take out the money. But while his hand was yet in the bag, out comes the master-armourer, a tall and very stark carle, and said in courteous wise: "Sir Knight, thou art a stranger to me and I know thee not; so I must needs ask for a sight of thy license to buy weapons, under the seal of the Burg."

"Hear a wonder," said Ralph, "that a free man for his money shall not buy wares set out to be bought, unless he have the Burg-Reeve's hand and seal for it! Nay, take thy florins, master, and give me the axe and let the jest end there." "I jest not, young rider," quoth the armourer. "When we know thee for a liegeman of the Burg, thou shalt buy what thou wilt without question; but otherwise I have told thee the law, and how may I, the master of the craft, break the law? Be not wrath, fair sir, I will set aside thine axe for thee, till thou bring me the license, or bid me come see it, and thou shalt get the said license at the Town Hall straightway, when they may certify thee no foeman of the Burg."

Ralph saw that it availed nothing to bicker with the smith, and so went his way somewhat crestfallen, and that the more as he saw Roger grinning a little.

Now they come into the market-place, on one side whereof was the master church of the town, which was strongly built and with a tall tower to it, but was not very big, and but little adorned. Over against it they saw the sign of the Flower de Luce, a goodly house and great. Thitherward they turned; but in the face of the hostelry amidmost the place was a thing which Roger pointed at with a grin that spoke as well as words; and this was a high gallows-tree furnished with four forks or arms, each carved and wrought in the fashion of the very bough of a tree, from which dangled four nooses, and above them all was a board whereon was written in big letters THE DRY TREE. And at the foot of this gallows were divers folk laughing and talking.

So Ralph understood at once that those four men whom he had seen led away bound yesterday should be hanged thereon; so he stayed a franklin who was passing by, and said to him, "Sir, I am a stranger in the town, and I would know if justice shall be done on the four woodmen to-day." "Nay," said the man, "but to-morrow; they are even now before the judges."

Then said Roger in a surly voice, "Why art thou not there to look on?" "Because," quoth the man, "there is little to see there, and not much more to hearken. The thieves shall be speedily judged, and not questioned with torments, so that they may be the lustier to feel what the hangman shall work on them to-morrow; then forsooth the show shall be goodly. But far better had it been if we had had in our hands the great witch of these dastards, as we looked to have her; but now folk say that she has not been brought within gates, and it is to be feared that she hath slipped through our fingers once more."

Roger laughed, and said: "Simple are ye folk of the Burg, and know nought of her shifts. I tell thee it is not unlike that she is in the Burg even now, and hath in hand to take out of your prison the four whom ye have caught."

The franklin laughed scornfully in his turn and said: "If we be simple, thou art a fool merely: are we not stronger and more than the Dry Tree? How should she not be taken? How should she not be known if she were walking about these streets? Have we no eyes, fool-carle?" And he laughed again, for he was wroth.

Ralph hearkened, and a kind of fear seemed griping his heart, so he asked the franklin: "Tell me, sir, are ye two speaking of a woman who is Queen of these strong-thieves?" "Yea," said he, "or it might better be said that she is their goddess, their mawmet, their devil, the very heart and soul of their wickedness. But one day shall we have her body and soul, and then shall her body have but an evil day of it till she dieth in this world."

"Yea, forsooth, if she can die at all," quoth Roger.

The franklin looked sourly on him and said: "Good man, thou knowest much of her, meseemeth—Whence art thou?" Said Roger speedily: "From Hampton under Scaur; and her rebel I am, and her dastard, and her runaway. Therefore I know her forsooth."

"Well," the Franklin said "thou seemest a true man, and yet I would counsel thee to put a rein on thy tongue when thou art minded to talk of the Devil of the Dry Tree, or thou mayst come to harm in the Burg."

He walked away towards the gallows therewith; and Roger said, almost as if he were talking to himself; "A heavy-footed fool goeth yonder; but after this talk we were better hidden by the walls of the Flower-de-Luce." So therewith they went on toward the hostel.

But the market place was wide, and they were yet some minutes getting to the door, and ere they came there Ralph said, knitting his brows anxiously: "Is this woman fair or foul to look on?" "That is nought so easy to tell of," said Roger, "whiles she is foul, whiles very fair, whiles young and whiles old; whiles cruel and whiles kind. But note this, when she is the kindest then are her carles the cruellest; and she is the kinder to them because they are cruel."

Ralph pondered what he said, and wondered if this were verily the woman whom he had delivered, or some other. As if answering to his unspoken thought, Roger went on: "They speak but of one woman amongst them of the Dry Tree, but in sooth they have many others who are like unto her in one way or other; and this again is a reason why they may not lay hands on the very Queen of them all."

Therewithal they came unto the hostel, and found it fair enough within, the hall great and goodly for such a house, and with but three chapmen-carles therein. Straightway they called for meat, for it was now past noon, and the folk of the house served them when the grooms had taken charge of Falcon. And Roger served Ralph as if he were verily his man. Then Ralph went to his chamber aloft and rested a while, but came down into the hall a little before nones, and found Roger there walking up and down the hall floor, and no man else, so he said to him: "Though thou art not of the

Burg, thou knowest it; wilt thou not come abroad then, and show it me? for I have a mind to learn the ways of the folk here."

Said Roger, and smiled a little: "If thou commandest me as my lord, I will come; yet I were better pleased to abide behind; for I am weary with night-waking and sorrow; and have a burden of thought, one which I must bear to the end of the road; and if I put it down I shall have to go back and take it up again."

Ralph thought that he excused himself with more words than were needed; but he took little heed of it, but nodded to him friendly, and went out of the house afoot, but left his weapons and armour behind him by the rede of Roger.

CHAPTER 13

The Streets of the Burg
of the Four Friths

He went about the streets and found them all much like to the one which they had entered by the north gate; he saw no poor or wretched houses, and none very big as of great lords; they were well and stoutly builded, but as aforesaid not much adorned either with carven work or painting: there were folk enough in the streets, and now Ralph, as was like to be, looked specially at the women, and thought many of them little better-favoured than the men, being both dark and low; neither were they gaily clad, though their raiment, like the houses, was stout and well wrought. But here and there he came on a woman taller and whiter than the others, as though she were of another blood; all such of these as he saw were clad otherwise than the darker women: their heads uncoifed, uncovered save for some garland or silken band: their gowns yellow like wheat-straw, but gaily embroidered; sleeveless withal and short, scarce reaching to the ancles, and whiles so thin that they were rather clad with the embroidery than the cloth; shoes they had not, but sandals bound on their naked feet with white thongs, and each bore an iron ring about her right arm.

The more part of the men wore weapons at their sides and had staves in hand, and were clad in short jerkins brown or blue of colour, and looked ready for battle if any moment should call them thereto; but among them were men of different favour and stature from these, taller for the most part, unarmed, and clad in long gowns of fair colours with cloths of thin and gay-coloured web twisted about their heads. These he took for merchants, as they were oftenest standing in and about the booths and shops, whereof there were some in all the streets, though the market for victuals and such like he found over for that day, and but scantily peopled.

Out of one of these markets, which was the fish and fowl market, he came into a long street that led him down to a gate right over against that whereby he had entered the Burg; and as he came thereto he saw that there was a wide way clear of all houses inside of the wall, so that men-at-arms might go freely from one part to the other; and he had also noted that a wide way led from each ort out of the great place, and each ended not but in a gate. But as to any castle in the town, he saw none; and when he asked a burgher thereof, the carle laughed in his face, and said to him that the whole Burg, houses and all, was a castle, and that it would turn out to be none of the easiest to win. And forsooth Ralph himself was much of that mind.

Now he was just within the south gate when he held this talk, and there were many folk thereby already, and more flocking thereto; so he stood there to see what should betide; and anon he heard great blowing of horns and trumpets all along the wall, and, as he deemed, other horns answered from without; and so it was; for soon the withoutward horns grew louder, and the folk fell back on either side of the way, and next the gates were thrown wide open (which before had been shut save for a wicket) and thereafter came the first of a company of men-at-arms, foot-men, with bills some, and

68

some with bows, and all-armed knights and sergeants a-horseback.

So streamed in these weaponed men till Ralph saw that it was a great host that was entering the Burg; and his heart rose within him, so warrior-like they were of men and array, though no big men of their bodies; and many of them bore signs of battle about them, both in the battering of their armour and the rending of their raiment, and the clouts tied about the wounds on their bodies.

After a while among the warriors came herds of neat and flocks of sheep and strings of horses, of the spoil which the host had lifted; and then wains filled, some with weapons and war gear, and some with bales of goods and household stuff. Last came captives, some going afoot and some for weariness borne in wains; for all these war-taken thralls were women and women-children; of males there was not so much as a little lad. Of the women many seemed fair to Ralph despite their grief and travel; and as he looked on them he deemed that they must be of the kindred and nation of the fair white women he had seen in the streets; though they were not clad like those, but diversely.

So Ralph gazed on this pageant till all had passed, and he was weary with the heat and the dust and the confused clamour of shouting and laughter and talking; and whereas most of the folk followed after the host and their spoil, the streets of the town there about were soon left empty and peaceful. So he turned into a street narrower than most, that went east from the South Gate and was much shaded from the afternoon sun, and went slowly down it, meaning to come about the inside of the wall till he should hit the East Gate, and so into the Great Place when the folk should have gone their ways home.

He saw no folk in the street save here and there an old woman sitting at the door of her house, and maybe a young child with her. As he came to where the street turned somewhat, even such a carline was sitting on a clean white door-step on the sunny side, somewhat shaded by a tall rose-laurel tree in a great tub, and she sang as she sat spinning, and Ralph stayed to listen in his idle mood, and he heard how she sang in a dry, harsh voice:

Clashed sword on shield
In the harvest field;
And no man blames
The red red flames,
War's candle-wick
On roof and rick.
Now dead lies the yeoman
unwept and unknown
On the field he hath furrowed,
the ridge he hath sown:
And all in the middle
of wethers and neat
The maidens are driven
with blood on their feet;
For yet 'twixt the Burg-gate
and battle half-won
The dust-driven highway
creeps uphill and on,
And the smoke of the beacons
goes coiling aloft,
While the gathering horn bloweth
loud, louder and oft.

Throw wide the gates
For nought night waits;
Though the chase is dead
The moon's o'erhead
And we need the clear
Our spoil to share.
Shake the lots in the helm then
for brethren are we,
And the goods of my missing
are gainful to thee.
Lo! thine are the wethers,
and his are the kine;
And the colts of the marshland
unbroken are thine,
With the dapple-grey stallion
that trampled his groom;
And Giles hath the gold-blossomed

rose of the loom.
Lo! leaps out the last lot
and nought have I won,
But the maiden unmerry,
by battle undone.

Even as her song ended came one of those fair yellow-gowned damsels round the corner of the street, bearing in her hand a light basket full of flowers: and she lifted up her head and beheld Ralph there; then she went slowly and dropped her eyelids, and it was pleasant to Ralph to behold her; for she was as fair as need be. Her corn-coloured gown was dainty and thin, and but for its silver embroidery had hidden her limbs but little; the rosiness of her ancles showed amidst her white sandal-thongs, and there were silver rings and gold on her arms along with the iron ring.

Now she lifted up her eyes and looked shyly at Ralph, and he smiled at her well-pleased, and deemed it would be good to hear her voice; so he went up to her and greeted her, and she seemed to take his greeting well, though she glanced swiftly at the carline in the doorway.

Said Ralph: "Fair maiden, I am a stranger in this town, and have seen things I do not wholly understand; now wilt thou tell me before I ask the next question, who will be those war-taken thralls whom even now I saw brought into the Burg by the host? of what nation be they, and of what kindred?"

Straightway was the damsel all changed; she left her dainty tricks, and drew herself up straight and stiff. She looked at him in the eyes, flushing red, and with knit brows, a moment, and then passed by him with swift and firm feet as one both angry and ashamed.

But the carline who had beheld the two with a grin on her wrinkled face changed aspect also, and cried out fiercely after the damsel, and said: "What! dost thou flee from the fair young man, and he so kind and soft with thee, thou jade? Yea, I suppose thou dost fetch and carry for some mistress who is young and a fool, and who has not yet learned how to deal with the daughters of thine accursed folk. Ah! if I had but money to buy some one of you, and a good one, she

71

should do something else for me than showing her fairness to young men; and I would pay her for her long legs and her white skin, till she should curse her fate that she had not been born little and dark-skinned and free, and with heels un-bloodied with the blood of her back."

Thus she went on, though the damsel was long out of ear-shot of her curses; and Ralph tarried not to get away from her spiteful babble, which he now partly understood; and that all those yellow-clad damsels were thralls to the folk of the Burg; and belike were of the kindred of those captives late-taken whom he had seen amidst the host at its entering into the Burg.

So he wandered away thence thinking on what he should do till the sun was set, and he had come into the open space underneath the walls, and had gone along it till he came to the East Gate: there he looked around him a little and found people flowing back from the Great Place, whereto they had gathered to see the host mustered and the spoil blessed; then he went on still under the wall, and noted not that here and there a man turned about to look upon him curiously, for he was deep in thought, concerning the things which he had seen and heard of, and pondered much what might have befallen his brethren since they sundered at the Want-way nigh to the High House of Upmeads. Withal the chief thing that he desired was to get him away from the Burg, for he felt himself unfree therein; and he said to himself that if he were forced to dwell among this folk, that he had better never have stolen himself away from his father and mother; and whiles even he thought that he would do his best on the morrow to get him back home to Upmeads again. But then when he thought of how his life would go in his old home, there seemed to him a lack, and when he questioned himself as to what that lack was, straightway he seemed to see that Lady of the Wildwood standing before the men-at-arms in her scanty raiment the minute before his life was at adventure because of them. And in sooth he smiled to himself then with a beating heart, as he told himself that above all things he desired to see that Lady, whatever she might be, and that he would follow his adventure to the end until he met her.

Amidst these thoughts he came unto the North Gate,

whereby he had first entered the Burg, and by then it was as dark as the summer night would be; so he woke up from his dream, as it were, and took his way briskly back to the Flower de Luce.

CHAPTER 14

What Ralph Heard of the Matters of the Burg of the Four Friths

There was no candle in the hall when he entered, but it was not so dark therein but he might see Roger sitting on a stool near the chimney, and opposite to him on the settle sat two men; one very tall and big, the other small; Roger was looking away from these, and whistling; and it came into Ralph's mind that he would have him think that he had nought to do with them, whether that were so or not. But he turned round as Ralph came up the hall and rose and came up to him, and fell to talking with him and asking him how he liked the Burg; and ever he spake fast and loud, so that again it came on Ralph that he was playing a part.

Ralph heeded him little, but ever looked through the hall-dusk on those twain, who presently arose and went toward the hall door, but when they were but half-way across the floor a chamberlain came in suddenly, bearing candles in his hands, and the light fell on those guests and flashed back from a salade on the head of the big man, and Ralph saw that he was clad in a long white gaberdine, and he deemed that he was the very man whom he had seen last in the Great Place at Higham, nigh the church, and before that upon the road. As for the smaller man Ralph had no knowledge of him, for he could see but little of his face, whereas he was wrapped up in a cloak, for as warm as the evening was, and wore a slouch hat withal; but his eyes seemed great and wondrous bright.

But when they were gone Ralph asked Roger if he knew

73

aught of them, or if they had told him aught. "Nay," said Roger, "they came in here as I sat alone, and had their meat, and spake nought to me, and little to each other. I deem them not to be of the Burg. Nay, sooth to say, I doubt if they be true men."

As he spake came in a sort of the townsmen somewhat merry and noisy, and called for meat and drink and more lights; so that the board was brought and the hall was speedily astir. These men, while supper was being dight, fell to talking to Ralph and Roger, and asking them questions of whence and whither, but nowise uncourteously: to whom Roger answered with the tale which he had told Ralph, and Ralph told what he would, and that was but little.

But when the board was dight they bade them sit down with them and eat. Ralph sat down at once, and Roger would have served him, but Ralph bade him do it not, and constrained him to sit by his side, and they two sat a little apart from the townsmen.

So when they had eaten their fill, and wine was brought, and men were drinking kindly, Ralph began to ask Roger concerning those women whom he had seen in the street, and the captives whom he had seen brought in by the host, and if they were of one kindred, and generally how it was with them: and he spake somewhat softly as if he would not break into the talk of the townsmen: but Roger answered him in a loud voice so that all could hear:

"Yea, lord, I will tell thee the tale of them, which setteth forth well both the wise policy and the great mercy of the folk of the Burg and their rulers."

Said Ralph: "Are these women also of the Dry Tree? For I perceive them to be born of the foes of the Burg."

Now the townsmen had let their talk drop a while to listen to the talk of the aliens; and Roger answered still in a loud voice: "Nay, nay, it is not so. These queens are indeed war-taken thralls, but not from them of the Dry Tree, or they would have been slain at once, like as the carles of those accursed ones. But these are of the folk of the Wheat-wearers, even as those whom thou sawest brought to-day amidst the other spoil. And to this folk the Burg showeth mercy, and whenso the host goeth against them and overcometh (and that is well-nigh whenever they meet) these worthy lords slay no woman of them, but the men only, whether they be old or young or youngest. As for their women they are brought hither and sold at the market-cross to the highest bidder. And this honour they have, that such of them as be fair, and that is the more part of the younger ones, fetch no ill penny. Yet for my part I were loth to cheapen such wares: for they make but evil servants, being proud, and not abiding stripes lightly, or toiling the harder for them; and they be somewhat too handy with the knife if they deem themselves put upon. Speak I sooth, my masters?" quoth he, turning toward them of the town.

Said a burgher somewhat stricken in years, "Nought but sooth; peaceable men like to me eschew such servants; all the more because of this, that if one of these queens misbehave with the knife, or strayeth from her master's bed, the laws of the Burg meddle not therein. For the wise men say that such folk are no more within the law than kine be, and may not for their deeds be brought before leet or assize any more than kine. So that if the master punish her not for her misdoings, unpunished she needs must go; yea even if her deed be mere murder."

"That is sooth," said a somewhat younger man; "yet whiles it fareth ill with them at the hands of our women. To wit, my father's brother has even now come from the war to find his thrall all spoilt by his wife: and what remedy may he have against his wife? his money is gone, even as if she had houghed his horse or his best cow."

"Yea," said a third, "we were better without such cattle. A thrust with a sword and all the tale told, were the better way of dealing with them."

Said another; "Yet are the queens good websters, and, lacking them, figured cloth of silk would be far-fetched and dear-bought here."

A young man gaily clad, who had been eyeing the speakers disdainfully, spake next and said: "Fair sirs, ye are speaking like hypocrites, and as if your lawful wives were here to hearken to you; whereas ye know well how goodly these thralls be, and that many of them can be kind enough withal; and ye would think yourselves but ill bestead if ye might not

75

cheapen such jewels for your money. Which of you will go to the Cross next Saturday and there buy him a fairer wife than he can wed out of our lineages? and a wife withal of whose humours he need take no more account of than the dullness of his hound or the skittish temper of his mare, so long as the thong smarts, and the twigs sting."

One or two grinned as he spake, but some bent their brows at him, yet scarce in earnest, and the talk thereover dropped, nor did Ralph ask any more questions; for he was somewhat down-hearted, calling to mind the frank and free maidens of Upmead, and their friendly words and hearty kisses. And him seemed the world was worse than he had looked to find it.

Howsoever, the oldest and soberest of the guests, seeing that he was a stranger and of noble aspect, came unto him and sat by him, and fell to telling him tales of the wars of the men of the Burg with the Wheat-wearers; and how in time past, when the town was but little fenced, the Wheat-wearers had stormed their gates and taken the city, and had made a great slaughter; but yet had spared many of the fighting-men, although they had abided there as the masters of them, and held them enthralled for three generations of men: after which time the sons' sons of the old Burg-dwellers having grown very many again, and divers of them being trusted in sundry matters by the conquerors, who oppressed them but little, rose up against them as occasion served, in the winter season and the Yule feast, and slew their masters, save for a few who were hidden away.

"And thereafter," quoth he, "did we make the Burg strong and hard to win, as ye see it to-day; and we took for our captain the Forest Lord, who ere-while had dwelt in the clearings of the wildwood, and he wedded the Fair Lady who was the son's daughter of him who had been our lord ere the Wheat-wearers overcame us; and we grew safe and free and mighty again. And the son of the Forest Lord, he whom we call the War-smith, he it was who beheld the Burg too much given to pleasure, and delighting in the softness of life; and he took order to harden our hearts, and to cause all freemen to learn the craft of war and battle, and let the women and thralls and aliens see to other craftsmanship and to chaffer;

and even so is it done as he would; and ye shall find us hardy of heart enough, though belike not so joyous as might be. Yet at least we shall not be easy to overcome."

"So indeed it seemeth," said Ralph. "Yet will I ask of you first one question, and then another."

"Ask on," said the burgher.

Said Ralph: "How is it that ye, being so strong, should still suffer them of the Dry Tree, taking a man here and a man there, when ye might destroy them utterly?"

The Burgher reddened and cleared his throat and said: "Sir, it must be made clear to you that these evil beasts are no peril to the Burg of the Four Friths; all the harm they may do us, is as when a cur dog biteth a man in the calf of the leg; whereby the man shall be grieved indeed, but the dog slain. Such grief as that they have done us at whiles: but the grief is paid for thus, that the hunting and slaying of them keeps our men in good trim, and pleasures them; shortly to say it, they are the chief deer wherewith our wood is stocked."

He stopped awhile and then went on again and said: "To say sooth they be not very handy for crushing as a man crushes a wasp, because sorcery goes with them, and the wiles of one who is their Queen, the evilest woman who ever spat upon the blessed Host of the Altar: yet is she strong; a devouring sea of souls, God help us!" And he blessed himself therewith.

Said Ralph: "Yet a word on these Wheat-wearers; it seemeth that ye never fail to overcome them in battle?"

"But seldom at least," quoth the Burgher.

Said Ralph: "Then it were no great matter for you to gather a host overwhelming, and to take their towns and castles, and forbid them weapons, and make them your thralls to till the land for you which now they call theirs; so that ye might have of their gettings all save what were needful for them to live as thralls."

"I deem it were an easy thing," said the burgher.

Quoth Ralph: "Then why do ye not so?"

"It were but a poor game to play," said the burgher. "Such of their wealth as we have a mind to, we can have now at the cost of a battle or two, begun one hour and ended the

77

next: were we their masters sitting down amidst of their hatred, and amidst of their plotting, yea, and in the very place where that were the hottest and thickest, the battle would be to begin at every sun's uprising, nor would it be ended at any sunset. Hah! what sayest thou?"

Said Ralph: "This seemeth to me but the bare truth; yet it is little after the manner of such masterful men as ye be. But why then do ye slay all their carles that are taken; whereas ye bear away the women and make thralls of them at home, that is to say, foes in every house?"

"It may be," said the Burgher, "that this is not amongst the wisest of our dealings. Yet may we do no otherwise; for thus we swore to do by all the greatest oaths that we might swear, in the days when we first cast off their yoke, and yet were not over strong at the first; and now it hath so grown into a part of our manners, yea, and of our very hearts and minds, that the slaying of a Wheat-wearer is to us a lighter matter than the smiting of a rabbit or a fowmart. But now, look you, fair sir, my company ariseth from table; so I bid thee a good night. And I give thee a good rede along with the good wish, to wit, that thou ask not too many questions in this city concerning its foemen: for here is the stranger looked upon with doubt, if he neither will take the wages of the Burg for battle, nor hath aught to sell."

Ralph reddened at his word, and the other looked at him steadily as he spoke, so that Ralph deemed that he mistrusted him: he deemed moreover that three or four of the others looked hard at him as they went towards the door, while Roger stood somewhat smiling, and humming a snatch of an old song.

But when the other guests had left the hostelry, Roger left his singing, and turned to Ralph and said: "Master, meseems that they mistrust us, and now maybe is that peril that I spake of nigher than I deemed when we came into the Burg this morning. And now I would that we were well out of the Burg and in the merry greenwood again, and it repents me that I brought thee hither."

"Nay, good fellow," quoth Ralph, "heed it not: besides, it was me, not thee, that they seemed to doubt of. I will depart hence to-morrow morning no worser than I came, and leave thee to seek thy fortune here; and good luck go with thee."

Roger looked hard at him and said: "Not so, young lord; if thou goest I will go with thee, for thou hast won my heart, I know not how: and I would verily be thy servant, to follow thee whithersoever thou goest; for I think that great deeds will come of thee."

This word pleased Ralph, for he was young and lightly put faith in men's words, and loved to be well thought of, and was fain of good fellowship withal. So he said: "This is a good word of thine, and I thank thee for it; and look to it that in my adventures, and the reward of them thou shalt have thy due share. Lo here my hand on it!"

Roger took his hand, yet therewith his face seemed a little troubled, but he said nought. Then spoke Ralph: "True it is that I am not fain to take the wages of the Burg; for it seems to me that they be hard men, and cruel and joyless, and that their service shall be rather churlish than knightly. Howbeit, let night bring counsel, and we will see to this to-morrow; for now I am both sleepy and weary." Therewith he called the chamberlain, who bore a wax light before him to his chamber, and he did off his raiment and cast himself on his bed, and fell asleep straightway, before he knew where Roger was sleeping, whether it were in the hall or some place else.

CHAPTER 15

How Ralph Departed From the Burg of the Four Friths

Himseemed he had scarce been asleep a minute ere awoke with a sound of someone saying softly, "Master, master, awake!" So he sat up and answered softly in his turn: "Who is it? what is amiss, since the night is yet young?"

"I am thy fellow-farer, Roger," said the speaker, "and this thou hast to do, get on thy raiment speedily, and take thy weapons without noise, if thou wouldst not be in the prison of the Burg before sunrise."

Ralph did as he was bidden without more words; for already when he lay down his heart misgave him that he was in no safe place; he looked to his weapons and armour that they should not clash, and down they came into the hall and found the door on the latch; so out they went and Ralph saw that it was somewhat cloudy; the moon was set and it was dark, but Ralph knew by the scent that came in on the light wind, and a little stir of blended sounds, that it was hard on dawning; and even therewith he heard the challenge of the warders on the walls and their crying of the hour; and the chimes of the belfry rang clear and loud, and seeming close above him, two hours and a half after midnight. Roger spake not, and Ralph was man-at-arms enough to know that he must hold his peace; and though he longed sore to have his horse Falcon with him, yet he wotted that it availed not to ask of his horse, since he durst not ask of his life.

So they went on silently till they were out of the Great Place and came into a narrow street, and so into another which led them straight into the houseless space under the wall. Roger led right on as if he knew the way well, and in a twinkling were they come to a postern in the wall betwixt the East Gate and the South. By the said postern Ralph saw certain men standing; and on the earth near by, whereas he was keen-eyed, he saw more than one man lying moveless.

Spake Roger softly to the men who stood on their feet: "Is the rope twined?" "Nay, rope-twiner," said one of them. Then Roger turned and whispered to Ralph: "Friends. Get out thy sword!" Wherewithal the gate was opened, and they all passed out through the wall, and stood above the ditch in the angle-nook of a square tower. Then Ralph saw some of the men stoop and shoot out a broad plank over the ditch, which was deep but not wide thereabout, and straightway he followed the others over it, going last save Roger. By then they were on the other side he saw a glimmer of the dawn in the eastern heaven, but it was still more than dusk, and no man spoke again. They went on softly across the plain fields outside the wall, creeping from bush to bush, and from tree to tree, for here, if nowhere about the circuit of the Burg, were a few trees growing. Thus they came into a little wood and passed through it, and then Ralph could see that the men were six besides Roger; by the glimmer of the growing dawn he saw before them a space of meadows with high hedges about them, and a dim line that he took for the roof of a barn or grange, and beyond that a dark mass of trees.

Still they pressed on without speaking; a dog barked not far off and the cocks were crowing, and close by them in the meadow a cow lowed and went hustling over the bents and the long, unbitten buttercups. Day grew apace, and by then they were under the barn-gable which he had seen aloof he saw the other roofs of the grange and heard the bleating of sheep. And now he saw those six men clearly, and noted that one of them was very big and tall, and one small and slender, and it came into his mind that these two were none other than the twain whom he had come upon the last night sitting in the hall of the Flower de Luce.

Even therewith came a man to the gate of the sheep-cote by the grange, and caught sight of them, and had the wits to run back at once shouting out: "Hugh, Wat, Richard, and all ye, out with you, out a doors! Here be men! Ware the Dry Tree! Bows and bills! Bows and bills!"

With that those fellows of Ralph made no more ado, but set off running at their best toward the wood aforesaid, which crowned the slope leading up from the grange, and now took no care to go softly, nor heeded the clashing of their armour. Ralph ran with the best and entered the wood alongside the slim youth aforesaid, who stayed not at the wood's edge but went on running still: but Ralph stayed and turned to see what was toward, and beheld how that tall man was the last of their company, and ere he entered the wood turned about with a bent bow in his hand, and even as he nocked the shaft, the men from the Grange, who were seven in all, came running out from behind the barn-gable, crying out: "Ho thieves! ho ye of the Dry Tree, abide till we come! flee not from handy strokes." The tall man had the shaft to his ear in a twinkling, and loosed straightway, and nocked and loosed another shaft without staying to note how the first had sped. But Ralph saw that a man was before each of the shafts, and had fallen to earth, though he had no time to see aught else, for even therewith the tall man caught him by the hand, and crying out, "The third time!" ran on with him after the rest of their company; and whereas he was long-legged and Ralph lightfooted, they speedily came up with them, who were running still, but laughing as they ran, and jeering at the men of the Burgh; and the tall man shouted out to them: "Yea, lads, the counterfeit Dry Tree that they have raised in the Burg shall be dry enough this time." "Truly," said another, "till we come to water it with the blood of these wretches."

"Well, well, get on," said a third, "waste not your wind in talk; those carles will make but a short run of it to the walls, long as it was for us, creeping and creeping as we behoved to."

The long man laughed; "Thou sayest sooth," said he, "but thou art the longest winded of all in talking: get on, lads."

They laughed again at his word and sped on with less noise; while Ralph thought within himself that he was come into strange company, for now he knew well that the big man was even he whom he had first met at the churchyard gate of the thorp under Bear Hill. Yet he deemed that there was nought for it now but to go on.

Within a while they all slacked somewhat, and presently did but walk, though swiftly, through the paths of the thicket, which Ralph deemed full surely was part of that side of the Wood Perilous that lay south of the Burg of the Four Friths. And now Roger joined himself to him, and spake to him aloud and said: "So, fair master, thou art out of the peril of death for this bout."

"Art thou all so sure of that?" quoth Ralph, "or who are these that be with us? meseems they smell of the Dry Tree."

"Yea, or rebels and runaways therefrom," said Roger, with a dry grin. "But whosoever they may be, thou shalt see that they will suffer us to depart whither we will, if we like not their company. I will be thy warrant thereof."

"Moreover," said Ralph, "I have lost Falcon my horse; it is a sore miss of him."

"Maybe," quoth Roger, "but at least thou hast saved thy skin; and whereas there are many horses on the earth, there is but one skin of thine: be content; if thou wilt, thou shall win somewhat in exchange for thine horse."

Ralph smiled, but somewhat sourly, and even therewith he heard a shrill whistle a little aloof, and the men stayed and held their peace, for they were talking together freely again now. Then the big man put his fingers to his mouth and whistled again in answer, a third whistle answered him; and lo, presently, as their company hastened on, the voices of men, and anon they came into a little wood-lawn wherein standing about or lying on the grass beside their horses were more than a score of men well armed, but without any banner or token, and all in white armour with white Gaberdines thereover; and they had with them, as Ralph judged, some dozen of horses more than they needed for their own riding.

Great was the joy at this meeting, and there was embracing and kissing of friends: but Ralph noted that no man embraced that slender youth, and that he held him somewhat aloof from the others, and all seemed to do him reverence.

Now spake one of the runaways: "Well, lads, here be all we four well met again along with those twain who came to help us at our pinch, as their wont is, and Roger withal, good at need again, and a friend of his, as it seemeth, and whom we know not. See ye to that."

Then stood forth the big man and said: "He is a fair young knight, as ye may see; and he rideth seeking adventures, and Roger did us to wit that he was abiding in the Burg at his peril, and would have him away, even if it were somewhat against his will: and we were willing that it should be so, all the more as I have a guess concerning what he is; and a foreseeing man might think that luck should go with him." Therewith he turned to Ralph and said: "How say ye, fair sir, will ye take guesting with us a while and learn our ways?"

Said Ralph: "Certain I am that whither ye will have me go, thither must I; yet I deem that I have an errand that lies not your way. Therefore if I go with you, ye must so look upon it that I am in your fellowship as one compelled. To be short with you, I crave leave to depart and go mine own road."

As he spoke he saw the youth walking up and down in

short turns; but his face he could scarce see at all, what for his slouched hat, what for his cloak; and at last he saw him go up to the tall man and speak softly to him awhile. The tall man nodded his head, and as the youth drew right back nigh to the thicket, spake to Ralph again.

"Fair sir, we grant thine asking; and add this thereto that we give thee the man who has joined himself to thee, Roger of the Rope-walk to wit, to help thee on the road, so that thou mayst not turn thy face back to the Burg of the Four Friths, where thine errand, and thy life withal, were soon sped now, or run into any other trap which the Wood Perilous may have for thee. And yet if thou think better of it, thou mayst come with us straightway; for we have nought to do to tarry here any longer. And in any case, here is a good horse that we will give thee, since thou hast lost thy steed; and Roger who rideth with thee, he also is well horsed."

Ralph looked hard at the big man, who now had his salade thrown back from his face, to see if he gave any token of jeering or malice, but could see nought such: nay, his face was grave and serious, not ill-fashioned, though it were both long and broad like his body: his cheek-bones somewhat high, his eyes grey and middling great, and looking, as it were, far away.

Now deems Ralph that as for a trap of the Wood Perilous, he had already fallen into the trap; for he scarce needed to be told that these were men of the Dry Tree. He knew also that it was Roger who had led him into this trap, although he deemed it done with no malice against him. So he said to himself that if he went with Roger he but went a roundabout road to the Dry Tree; so that he was well nigh choosing to go on with their company. Yet again he thought that something might well befall which would free him from that fellowship if he went with Roger alone; whereas if he went with the others it was not that he might be, but that he was already of the fellowship of the Dry Tree, and most like would go straight thence to their stronghold. So he spake as soberly as the tall man had done.

"Since ye give me the choice, fair sir, I will depart hence with Roger alone, whom ye call my man, though to me he seemeth to be yours. Howbeit, he has led me to you once, and belike will do so once more."

"Yea," quoth the big man smiling no whit more than erst, "and that will make the fourth time. Depart then, fair sir, and take this word with thee that I wish thee good and not evil."

CHAPTER 16

Ralph Rideth the Wood
Perilous Again

Now Roger led up to Ralph a strong horse, red roan of hue, duly harnessed for war, and he himself had a good grey horse, and they mounted at once, and Ralph rode slowly away through the wood at his horse's will, for he was pondering all that had befallen him, and wondering what next should hap. Meanwhile those others had not loitered, but were a-horseback at once, and went their ways from Ralph through the wildwood.

Nought spake Ralph for a while till Roger came close up to him and said: "Whither shall we betake us, fair lord? hast thou an inkling of the road whereon lies thine errand?"

Now to Ralph this seemed but mockery, and he answered sharply: "I wot not, thou wilt lead whither thou wilt, even as thou hast trained me hitherward with lies and a forged tale. I suppose thou wilt lead me now by some roundabout road to the stronghold of the Dry Tree. It matters little, since thou durst not lead me back into the Burg. Yet now I come to think of it, it is evil to be alone with a found out traitor and liar; and I had belike have done better to go with their company."

"Nay nay," quoth Roger, "thou art angry, and I marvel not thereat; but let thy wrath run off thee if thou mayest; for indeed what I have told thee of myself and my griefs is not all mere lying. Neither was it any lie that thou wert in peril

85

of thy life amongst those tyrants of the Burg; thou with thy manly bearing, and free tongue, and bred, as I judge, to hate cruel deeds and injustice. Such freedom they cannot away with in that fellowship of hard men-at-arms; and soon hadst thou come to harm amongst them. And further, let alone that it is not ill to be sundered from yonder company, who mayhap will have rough work to do or ever they win home, I have nought to do to bring thee to Hampton under Scaur if thou hast no will to go thither: though certes I would lead thee some whither, whereof thou shalt ask me nought as now; yet will I say thereof this much, that there thou shalt be both safe and well at ease. Now lastly know this, that whatever I have done, I have done it to do thee good and not ill; and there is also another one, whom I will not name to thee, who wisheth thee better yet, by the token of those two strokes stricken by thee in the Wood Perilous before yesterday was a day."

Now when Ralph heard those last words, such strong and sweet hope and desire stirred in him to see that woman of the Want-ways of the Wood Perilous that he forgat all else, except that he must nowise fall to strife with Roger, lest they should sunder, and he should lose the help of him, which he now deemed would bring him to sight of her whom he had unwittingly come to long for more than aught else; so he spake to Roger quietly and humbly: "Well, faring-fellow, thou seest how I am little more than a lad, and have fallen into matters mighty and perilous, which I may not deal with of my own strength, at least until I get nigher to them so that I may look them in the eyes, and strike a stroke or two on them if they be at enmity with me. So I bid thee lead me whither thou wilt, and if thou be a traitor to me, on thine own head be it; in good sooth, since I know nought of this wood and since I might go astray and so come back to the Burg where be those whom thou hast now made my foemen, I am content to take thee on thy word, and to hope the best of thee, and ask no question of thee, save whitherward."

"Fair sir," said Roger, "away from this place at least; for we are as yet over nigh to the Burg to be safe: but as to elsewhither we may wend, thereof we may speak on the road as we have leisure."

Therewith he smote his horse with his heel and they went forward at a smart trot, for the horses were unwearied, and the wood thereabouts of beech and clear of underwood; and Roger seemed to know his way well, and made no fumbling over it.

Four hours or more gone, the wood thinned and the beeches failed, and they came to a country, still waste, of little low hills, stony for the more part, beset with scraggy thorn-bushes, and here and there some other berry-tree sown by the birds. Then said Roger: "Now I deem us well out of the peril of them of the Burg, who if they follow the chase as far as the sundering of us and the others, will heed our slot nothing, but will follow on that of the company: so we may breathe our horses a little, though their bait will be but small in this rough waste: therein we are better off than they, for lo you, saddle bags on my nag and meat and drink therein."

So they lighted down and let their horses graze what they could, while they ate and drank; amidst which Ralph again asked Roger of whither they were going. Said Roger: "I shall lead thee to a good harbour, and a noble house of a master of mine, wherein thou mayst dwell certain days, if thou hast a mind thereto, not without solace maybe."

"And this master," said Ralph, "is he of the Dry Tree?" Said Roger: "I scarce know how to answer thee without lying: but this I say, that whether he be or not, this is true; amongst those men I have friends and amongst them foes; but fate bindeth me to them for a while." Said Ralph reddening: "Be there any women amongst them?" "Yea, yea," quoth Roger, smiling a little, "doubt not thereof."

"And that Lady of the Dry Tree," quoth Ralph, reddening yet more, but holding up his head, "that woman whereof the Burgher spoke so bitterly, threatening her with torments and death if they might but lay hold of her; what wilt thou tell me concerning her?" "But little," said Roger, "save this, that thou desirest to see her, and that thou mayest have thy will thereon if thou wilt be guided by me."

Ralph hearkened as if he heeded little what Roger said; but presently he rose up and walked to and fro in short turns with knit brows as one pondering a hard matter. He spake nought, and Roger seemed to heed him nothing, though in sooth he looked at him askance from time to time, till at last he came and lay down again by Roger, and in a while he spake: "I wot not why ye of the Dry Tree want me, or what ye will do with me; and but for one thing I would even now ride away from thee at all adventure."

Roger said: "All this ye shall learn later on, and shalt find it but a simple matter; and meanwhile I tell thee again that all is for thy gain and thy pleasure. So now ride away if thou wilt; who hindereth thee? certes not I."

"Nay," said Ralph, "I will ride with thee first to that fair house; and afterwards we shall see what is to hap." "Yea," quoth Roger, "then let us to horse straightway, so that we may be there if not before dark night yet at least before bright morn; for it is yet far away."

CHAPTER 17

Ralph Cometh to the House of Abundance

Therewithal they gat to horse and rode away through that stony land, wherein was no river, but for water many pools in the bottoms, with little brooks running from them. But after a while they came upon a ridge somewhat high, on the further side whereof was a wide valley well-grassed and with few trees, and no habitation of man that they might see. But a wide river ran down the midst of it; and it was now four hours after noon. Quoth Roger: "The day wears and we shall by no means reach harbour before dark night, even if we do our best: art thou well used to the water, lord?" "Much as a mallard is," said Ralph. Said Roger: "That is well, for though there is a ford some mile and a half down stream, for that same reason it is the way whereby men mostly cross the water into the wildwood; and here again we are more like to meet foes than well-wishers; or at the least there will be question of who we are, and whence and whither; and we may stumble in our answers." Said Ralph: "There is no need to tarry, ride we down to the water."

So did they, and took the water, which was deep, but not swift. On the further side they clomb up a hill somewhat steep; at the crown they drew rein to give their horses breath, and Ralph turned in his saddle and looked down on to the valley, and as aforesaid he was clear-sighted and far-sighted; now he said: "Fellow-farer, I see the riding of folk down below there, and meseems they be spurring toward the water; and they have weapons: there! dost thou not see the gleam?"

"I will take thy word for it, fair sir," said Roger, "and will even spur, since they be the first men whom we have seen since we left the thickets." And therewith he went off at a hand gallop, and Ralph followed him without more ado.

They rode up hill and down dale of a grassy downland, till at last they saw a wood before them again, and soon drew rein under the boughs; for now were their horses somewhat wearied. Then said Ralph: "Here have we ridden a fair land, and seen neither house nor herd, neither sheep-cote nor shepherd. I wonder thereat."

Said Roger: "Thou wouldst wonder the less didst thou know the story of it." "What story?" said Ralph. Quoth Roger: "A story of war and wasting." "Yea?" said Ralph, "yet surely some bold knight or baron hath rights in the land, and might be free to build him a strong house and gather men to him to guard the shepherds and husbandmen from burners and lifters." "Sooth is that," said Roger; "but there are other things in the tale." "What things?" said Ralph. Quoth Roger: "Ill hap and sorrow and the Hand of Fate and great Sorcery." "And dastards withal?" said Ralph. "Even so," said Roger, "yet mingled with valiant men. Over long is the tale to tell as now, so low as the sun is; so now ride we on with little fear of foemen. For look you, this wood, like the thickets about the Burg of the Four Friths, hath an evil name, and few folk ride it uncompelled; therefore it is the safer for us. And yet I will say this to thee, that whereas awhile agone thou mightest have departed from me with little peril of aught save the stumbling on some of the riders of the Burg of the Four Friths, departing from me now will be a hard matter to thee; for the saints in Heaven only know whitherward thou shouldest come, if thou wert to guide thyself now. This a rough word, but a true one, so help me God and Saint Michael! What sayest thou; art thou content, or wilt thou cast hard words at me again?"

So it was that for all that had come and gone Ralph was light-hearted and happy; so he laughed and said: "Content were I, even if I were not compelled thereto. For my heart tells me of new things, and marvellous and joyous that I shall see ere long."

"And thine heart lieth not," said Roger, "for amidst of this wood is the house where we shall have guesting to-night, which will be to thee, belike, the door of life and many marvels. For thence have folk sought ere now to the WELL AT THE WORLD'S END."

Ralph turned to him sharply and said: "Many times in these few days have I heard that word. Dost thou know the meaning thereof? For as to me I know it not." Said Roger: "Thou mayest well be as wise as I am thereon: belike men seek to it for their much thriving, and oftenest find it not. Yet have I heard that they be the likeliest with whom all women are in love."

Ralph held his peace, but Roger noted that he reddened at the word.

Now they got on horseback again, for they had lighted down to breathe their beasts, and they rode on and on, and never was Roger at fault: long was the way and perforce they rested at whiles, so that night fell upon them in the wood, but the moon rose withal. So night being fairly come, they rested a good while, as it would be dawn before moonset. Then they rode on again, till now the summer night grew old and waned, but the wood hid the beginnings of dawn.

At last they came out of the close wood suddenly into an open plain, and now, as the twilight of the dawn was passing into early day, they saw that wide grassy meadows and tilled fields lay before them, with a little river running through the plain; and amidst the meadows, on a green mound, was a white castle, strong, and well built, though not of the biggest.

Roger pointed to it, and said, "Now we are come home," and cried on his wearied beast, who for his part seemed to

90

see the end of his journey. They splashed through a ford of the river and came to the gate of the castle as day drew on apace; Roger blew a blast on a great horn that hung on the gate, and Ralph looking round deemed he had never seen fairer building than in the castle, what he could see of it, and yet it was built from of old. They waited no long while before they were answered; but whereas Ralph looked to see armed gatewards peer from the battlements or the shot window, and a porter espying them through a lattice, it happened in no such way, but without more ado the wicket was opened to them by a tall old woman, gaunt and grey, who greeted them courteously: Roger lighted down and Ralph did in likewise, and they led their horses through the gate into the court of the castle; the old woman going before them till they came to the hall door, which she opened to them, and taking the reins of their horses led them away to the stable, while those twain entered the hall, which was as goodly as might be. Roger led Ralph up to a board on the dais, whereon there was meat and drink enow, and Ralph made his way-leader sit down by him, and they fell to. There was no serving-man to wait on them nor a carle of any kind did they see; the old woman only, coming back from the horses, served them at table. Ever as she went about she looked long on Ralph, and seemed as if she would have spoken to him, but as often, she glanced at Roger and forbore.

So when they were well nigh done with their meat Ralph spake to the carline and said: "Belike the lord or the lady of this house are abed and we shall not see them till the morrow?"

Ere the carline could speak Roger broke in and said: "There is neither lord nor lady in the castle as now, nor belike will there be to-morrow morning, or rather, before noon on this day; so now ye were better to let this dame lead thee to bed, and let the next hours take care of themselves."

"So be it," said Ralph, who was by this time heartily wearied, "shall we two lie in the same chamber?"

"Nay," said the carline shortly, "lodging for the master and lodging for the man are two different things."

Roger laughed and said nought, and Ralph gave him good

night, and followed the carline nothing loth, who led him to a fair chamber over the solar, as if he had been the very master of the castle, and he lay down in a very goodly bed, nor troubled himself as to where Roger lay, nor indeed of aught else, nor did he dream of Burg, or wood, or castle, or man, or woman; but lay still like the image of his father's father on the painted tomb in the choir of St. Laurence of Upmeads.

CHAPTER 18

Of Ralph in the Castle of Abundance

Broad lay the sun upon the plain amidst the wildwood when he awoke and sprang out of bed and looked out of the window (for the chamber was in the gable of the hall and there was nought of the castle beyond it). It was but little after noon of a fair June day, for Ralph had slumbered as it behoved a young man. The light wind bore into the chamber the sweet scents of the early summer, the chief of all of them being the savour of the new-cut grass, for about the wide meadows the carles and queens were awork at the beginning of hay harvest; and late as it was in the day, more than one blackbird was singing from the bushes of the castle pleasance. Ralph sighed for very pleasure of life before he had yet well remembered where he was or what had befallen of late; but as he stood at the window and gazed over the meadows, and the memory of all came back to him, he sighed once more for a lack of somewhat that came into his heart, and he smiled shamefacedly, though there was no one near, as his thought bade him wonder if amongst the haymaking women yonder there were any as fair as those yellow-clad thrall-women of the Burg; and as he turned from the window a new hope made his heart beat, for he deemed that he had been brought to that house that he might meet some one who should change his life and make him a new man.

So he did on his raiment and went his ways down to the hall, and looked about for Roger, but found him not, nor any one else save the carline, who presently came in from the buttery, and of whom he asked, where was Roger. Quoth she: "He has been gone these six hours, but hath left a word for thee, lord, to wit, that he beseeches thee to abide him here for two days at the least, and thereafter thou art free to go if thou wilt. But as for me" (and therewith she smiled on him as sweetly as her wrinkled old face might compass) "I say to thee, abide beyond those two days if Roger cometh not, and as long as thou art here I will make thee all the cheer I may. And who knoweth but thou mayest meet worthy adventures here. Such have ere now befallen good knights in this house or anigh it."

"I thank thee, mother," quoth Ralph, "and it is like that I may abide here beyond the two days if the adventure befall me not ere then. But at least I will bide the eating of my dinner here to-day."

"Well is thee, fair lord," said the carline. "If thou wilt but walk in the meadow but a little half hour all shall be ready for thee. Forsooth it had been dight before now, but that I waited thy coming forth from thy chamber, for I would not wake thee. And the saints be praised for the long sweet sleep that hath painted thy goodly cheeks." So saying she hurried off to the buttery, leaving Ralph laughing at her outspoken flattering words.

Then he got him out of the hall and the castle, for no door was shut, and there was no man to be seen within or about the house. So he walked to and fro the meadow and saw the neat-herds in the pasture, and the hay-making folk beyond them, and the sound of their voices came to him on the little airs that were breathing. He thought he would talk to some of these folk ere the world was much older, and also he noted between the river and the wood many cots of the husbandmen trimly builded and thatched, and amidst them a little church, white and delicate of fashion; but as now his face was set toward the river because of the hot day. He came to a pool a little below where a wooden foot-bridge crossed the water, and about the pool were willows growing, which had not been shrouded these eight years, and the water was clear as glass with a bottom of fine sand. There then he bathed him, and as he sported in the water he bethought him of the long smooth reaches of Upmeads Water, and the swimming low down amidst the long swinging weeds between the chuckle of the reed sparrows, when the sun was new risen in the July morning. When he stood on the grass again, what with the bright weather and fair little land, what with the freshness of the water, and his good rest, and the hope of adventure to come, he felt as if he had never been merrier in his life-days. Withal it was a weight off his heart that he had escaped from the turmoil of the wars of the Burg of the Four Friths, and the men of the Dry Tree, and the Wheat-wearers, with the thralldom and stripes and fire-raising, and the hard life of strife and gain of the walled town and strong place.

When he came back to the castle gate there was the carline in the wicket peering out to right and left, seeking him to bring him in to dinner. And when she saw him so joyous, with his lips smiling and his eyes dancing for mirth, she also became joyous, and said: "Verily, it is a pity of thee that there is never a fair damsel or so to look on thee and love thee here to-day. Far would many a maiden run to kiss thy mouth, fair lad. But now come to thy meat, that thou mayest grow the fairer and last the longer."

He laughed gaily and went into the hall with her, and now was it well dight with bankers and dorsars of goodly figured cloth, and on the walls a goodly halling of arras of the Story of Alexander. So he sat to table, and the meat and drink was of the best, and the carline served him, praising him ever with fulsome words as he ate, till he wished her away.

After dinner he rested awhile, and called to the carline and bade her bring him his sword and his basnet. "Wherefore?" said she. "Whither wilt thou?"

Said he, "I would walk abroad to drink the air."

"Wilt thou into the wildwood?" said she.

"Nay, mother," he said, "I will but walk about the meadow and look on the hay-making folk."

"For that," said the carline, "thou needest neither sword

nor helm. I was afeard that thou wert about departing, and thy departure would be a grief to my heart: in the deep wood thou mightest be so bestead as to need a sword in thy fist; but what shouldst thou do with it in this Plain of Abundance, where are nought but peaceful husbandmen and frank and kind maidens? and all these are as if they had drunk a draught of the WELL AT THE WORLD'S END."

Ralph started as she said the word, but held his peace awhile. Then he said: "And who is lord of this fair land?" "There is no lord, but a lady," said the carline. "How hight she?" said Ralph. "We call her the Lady of Abundance," said the old woman. Said Ralph: "Is she a good lady?" "She is my lady," said the carline, "and doeth good to me, and there is not a carle in the land but speaketh well of her—it may be over well." "Is she fair to look on?" said Ralph. "Of women-folk there is none fairer," said the carline; "as to men, that is another thing."

Ralph was silent awhile, then he said: "What is the Well at the World's End?"

"They talk of it here," said she, "many things too long to tell of now: but there is a book in this house that telleth of it; I know it well by the look of it though I may not read in it. I will seek it for thee to-morrow if thou wilt."

. "Have thou thanks, dame," said he; "and I pray thee forget it not; but now I will go forth."

"Yea," said the carline, "but abide a little."

Therewith she went into the buttery, and came back bearing with her a garland of roses of the garden, intermingled with green leaves, and she said: "The sun is yet hot and over hot, do this on thine head to shade thee from the burning. I knew that thou wouldst go abroad to-day, so I made this for thee in the morning; and when I was young I was called the garland-maker. It is better summer wear than thy basnet."

He thanked her and did it on smiling, but somewhat ruefully; for he said to himself: "This is over old a dame that I should wear a love-token from her." But when it was on his head, the old dame clapped her hands and cried: "O there, there! Now art thou like the image of St. Michael in the Choir of Our Lady of the Thorn: there is none so lovely as thou. I would my Lady could see thee thus; surely the

95

sight of thee should gladden her heart. And withal thou art not ill clad otherwise."

Indeed his raiment was goodly, for his surcoat was new, and it was of fine green cloth, and the coat-armour of Upmead was beaten on it, to wit, on a gold ground an apple-tree fruited, standing by a river-side.

Now he laughed somewhat uneasily at her words, and so went forth from the castle again, and made straight for the hay-making folk on the other side of the water; for all this side was being fed by beasts and sheep; but at the point where he crossed, the winding of the stream brought it near to the castle gate. So he came up with the country folk and greeted them, and they did as much by him in courteous words: they were goodly and well-shapen, both men and women, gay and joyous of demeanour and well clad as for folk who work afield. So Ralph went from one to another and gave them a word or two, and was well pleased to watch them at their work awhile; but yet he would fain speak somewhat more with one or other of them. At last under the shade of a tall elm-tree he saw an old man sitting heeding the outer raiment of the haymakers and their victual and bottles of drink; and he came up to him and gave him the sele of the day; and the old man blessed him and said: "Art thou dwelling in my lady's castle, fair lord?" "A while at least," said Ralph. Said the old man: "We thank thee for coming to see us; and meseemeth from the look of thee thou art worthy to dwell in my Lady's House."

"What sayest thou?" said Ralph. "Is she a good lady and a gracious?" "O yea, yea," said the carle. Said Ralph: "Thou meanest, I suppose, that she is fair to look on, and soft-spoken when she is pleased?"

"I mean far more than that," said the carle; "surely is she most heavenly fair, and her voice is like the music of heaven: but withal her deeds, and the kindness of her to us poor men and husbandmen, are no worse than should flow forth from that loveliness."

"Will you be her servants?" said Ralph, "or what are ye?" Said the carle: "We be yeomen and her vavassors; there is no thralldom in our land." "Do ye live in good peace for the more part?" said Ralph. Said the carle: "Time has been when cruel battles were fought in these wood-lawns, and many poor people were destroyed therein: but that was before the coming of the Lady of Abundance."

"And when was that?" said Ralph. "I wot not," said the old carle; "I was born in peace and suckled in peace; and in peace I fell to the loving of maidens, and I wedded in peace, and begat children in peace, and in peace they dwell about me, and in peace shall I depart."

"What then," said Ralph (and a grievous fear was born in his heart), "is not the Lady of Abundance young?" Said the carle: "I have seen her when I was young and also since I have been old, and ever was she fair and lovely, and slender handed, as straight as a spear, and as sweet as white clover, and gentle-voiced and kind, and dear to our souls."

"Yea," said Ralph, "and she doth not dwell in this castle always; where else then doth she dwell?" "I wot not," said the carle, "but it should be in heaven: for when she cometh to us all our joys increase in us by the half."

"Look you, father," said Ralph, "May it not have been more than one Lady of Abundance that thou hast seen in thy life-days; and that this one that now is, is the daughter's daughter of the one whom thou first sawest—how sayest thou?" The carle laughed: "Nay, nay," said he, "It is not so: never has there been another like to her in all ways, in body and voice, and heart and soul. It is as I say, she is the same as she was always." "And when," said Ralph, with a beating heart, "does she come hither? Is it at some set season?" "Nay, from time to time, at all seasons," said the carle; "and as fair she is when she goeth over the snow, as when her feet are set amidst the June daisies."

Now was Ralph so full of wonder that he scarce knew what to say; but he bethought him of that fair waste on the other side of the forest, the country through which that wide river flowed, so he said: "And that land north-away beyond the wildwood, canst thou tell me the tale of its wars, and if it were wasted in the same wars that tormented this land?" The carle shook his head: "As to the land beyond this wood," quoth he, "I know nought of it, for beyond the wood go we never: nay, most often we go but a little way into it, no further than we can see the glimmer of the open daylight through its trees,—the daylight of the land of Abundance—that is enough for us."

"Well," said Ralph, "I thank thee for the tale thou hast told me, and wish thee more years of peace."

"And to thee, young man," said the carle, "I wish a good wish indeed, to wit that thou mayest see the Lady of Abundance here before thou departest."

His words once more made Ralph's heart beat and his cheek flush, and he went back to the castle somewhat speedily; for he said to himself, after the folly of lovers, "Maybe she will be come even now, and I not there to meet her." Yet when he came to the castle-gate his heart misgave him, and he would not enter at once, but turned about to go round the wall by the north and west. In the castle he saw no soul save the old dame looking out of the window and nodding to him, but in the pasture all about were neatherds and shepherds, both men and women; and at the north-west corner, whereas the river drew quite close to the wall, he came upon two damsels of the field-folk fishing with an angle in a quiet pool of the stream. He greeted them, and they, who were young and goodly, returned his greeting, but were shamefaced at his gallant presence, as indeed was he at the thoughts of his heart mingled with the sight of their fairness. So he passed on at first without more words than his greeting. Yet presently he turned back again, for he longed to hear some word more concerning the Lady whose coming he abode. They stood smiling and blushing as he came up to them again, and heeded their angles little.

Said Ralph: "Fair maidens, do ye know at all when the Lady of the castle may be looked for?" They were slow to answer, but at last one said: "No, fair sir, such as we know nothing of the comings and goings of great folk."

Said Ralph, smiling on her for kindness, and pleasure of her fairness: "Is it not so that ye will be glad of her coming?"

But she answered never a word, only looked at him steadily, with her great grey eyes fixed in wonderment, while the other one looked down as if intent on her angling tools.

Ralph knew not how to ask another question, so he turned

about with a greeting word again, and this time went on steadily round about the wall.

And now in his heart waxed the desire of that Lady, once seen, as he deemed, in such strange wise; but he wondered within himself if the devil had not sown that longing within him: whereas it might be that this woman on whom he had set his heart was herself no real woman but a devil, and one of the goddesses of the ancient world, and his heart was sore and troubled by many doubts and hopes and fears; but he said to himself that when he saw her then could he judge between the good and the evil, and could do or forbear, and that the sight of her would cure all.

Thus thinking he walked swiftly, and was soon round at the castle gate again, and entered, and went into the hall, where was the old dame, busied about some household matter. Ralph nodded to her and hastened away, lest she should fall to talk with him; and he set himself now to go from chamber to chamber, that he might learn the castle, what it was. He came into the guard-chamber and found the walls thereof all hung with armour and weapons, clean and in good order, though there was never a man-at-arms there, nor any soul except the old woman. He went up a stair therefrom on to the battlements, and went into the towers of the wall, and found weapons both for hand, and for cast and shot in each one of them, and all ready as if for present battle; then he came down into the court again and went into a very goodly ambulatory over against the hall, and he entered a door therefrom, which was but on the latch, and went up a little stair into a chamber, which was the goodliest and the richest of all. Its roof was all done with gold and blue from over sea, and its pavement wrought delicately in Alexandrine work. On the dais was a throne of carven ivory, and above it a canopy of baudekin of the goodliest fashion, and there was a foot-carpet before it, wrought with beasts and the hunting of the deer. As for the walls of that chamber, they were hung with a marvellous halling of arras, wherein was wrought the greenwood, and there amidst in one place a pot-herb garden, and a green garth with goats therein, and in that garth a little thatched house. And amidst all this greenery were figured over and over again two women, whereof one old and the other young; and the old one was clad in grand attire, with gold chains and brooches and rings, and sat with her hands before her by the house door, or stood looking on as the young one worked, spinning or digging in the garth, or milking the goats outside of it, or what not; and this one was clad in sorry and scanty raiment.

What all this might mean Ralph knew not; but when he had looked long at the greenery and its images, he said to himself that if he who wrought that cloth had not done the young woman after the likeness of the Lady whom he had helped in the wildwood, then it must have been done from her twin sister.

Long he abode in that chamber looking at the arras, and wondering whether the sitter in the ivory throne would be any other than the thrall in the greenwood cot. He abode there so long that the dusk began to gather in the house, and he could see the images no more; for he was filled with the sweetness of desire when he looked on them.

Then he went back slowly to the hall, and found the carline, who had lighted the waxlights and made meat ready for him; and when she saw him she cried out joyously: "Ah, I knew that thou wouldst come back. Art thou well content with our little land?"

"I like it well, dame," said he; "but tell me, if thou canst, what is the meaning of the halling in the chamber with the ivory throne?"

Said the carline: "Thereof shall another tell thee, who can tell of it better than I; but it is nought to hide that yonder chamber is the chamber of estate of our Lady, and she sitteth there to hear the cases of folk and to give dooms."

The old woman crossed herself as she spoke, and Ralph wondered thereat, but asked no more questions, for he was scarce sorry that the carline would not tell him thereof, lest she should spoil the tale.

So passed the evening, and he went to bed and slept as a young man should, and the next day he was up betimes and went abroad and mingled with the carles and queens afield; but this time he spake not of the Lady, and heard nought to heed from any of that folk. So he went back to the castle and gat him a bow and arrows, and entered the thicket of the

100

wood nigh where he and Roger first came out of it. He had prayed a young man of the folk to go with him, but he was not over willing to go, though he would not say wherefore. So Ralph went himself by himself and wandered some way into the wood, and saw nought worse than himself. As he came back, making a circuit toward the open meadows, he happened on a herd of deer in a lonely place, half wood half meadow, and there he slew a hart with one shaft, for he was a deft bowman. Then he went and fetched a leash of carles, who went with him somewhat less than half willingly, and between them they broke up the hart and carried him home to the castle, where the carline met them. She smiled on Ralph and praised the venison, and said withal that the hunting was well done; "For, as fond and as fair as thou mayst be, it is not good that young men should have their minds set on one thing only." Therewith she led him in to his meat, and set him down and served him; and all the while of his dinner he was longing to ask her if she deemed that the Lady would come that day, since it was the last day of those which Roger had bidden him wait; but the words would not out of his mouth.

She looked at him and smiled, as though she had a guess of his thought, and at last she said to him: "Thy tongue is tied to-day. Hast thou, after all, seen something strange in the wood?" He shook his head for naysay. Said she: "Why, then, dost thou not ask more concerning the Well at the World's End?"

He laughed, and said: "Maybe because I think that thou canst not tell me thereof." "Well," she said, "if I cannot, yet the book may, and this evening, when the sun is down, thou shalt have it."

"I thank thee, mother," said he; "but this is now the last day that Roger bade me wait. Dost thou think that he will come back to-night?" and he reddened therewith. "Nay," she said, "I know not, and thou carest not whether he will come or not. Yet I know that thou wilt abide here till some one else come, whether that be early or late." Again he reddened, and said, in a coaxing way: "And wilt thou give me guesting, mother, for a few more summer days?"

"Yea," she said, "and till summer is over, if need be, and

the corn is cut and carried, and till the winter is come and the latter end of winter is gone." He smiled faintly, though his heart fell, and he said: "Nay, mother, and can it by any chance be so long a-coming?"

"O, fair boy," she said, "thou wilt make it long, howsoever short it be. And now I will give thee a rede, lest thou vex thyself sick and fret thy very heart. To-morrow go see if thou canst meet thy fate instead of abiding it. Do on thy war-gear and take thy sword and try the adventure of the wildwood; but go not over deep into it." Said he: "But how if the Lady come while I am away from this house?"

"Sooth to say," said the carline, "I deem not that she will, for the way is long betwixt us and her."

"Dost thou mean," said Ralph, standing up from the board, "that she will not come ever? I adjure thee not to beguile me with soft words, but tell me the very sooth." "There, there!" said she, "sit down, king's son; eat thy meat and drink thy wine; for to-morrow is a new day. She will come soon or late, if she be yet in the world. And now I will say no more to thee concerning this matter."

Therewith she went her ways from the hall, and when she came back with hand-basin and towel, she said no word to him, but only smiled kindly. He went out presently into the meadow (for it was yet but early afternoon) and came among the haymaking folk and spake with them, hoping that perchance some of them might speak again of the Lady of Abundance; but none of them did so, though the old carle he had spoken with was there, and there also were the two maidens whom he had seen fishing; and as for him, he was over faint-hearted to ask them any more questions concerning her.

Yet he abode with them long, and ate and drank amidst the hay with them till the moon shone brightly. Then he went back to the castle and found the carline in the hall, and she had the book with her and gave it to him, and he sat down in the shot-window under the waxlights and fell to reading of it.

CHAPTER 19

Ralph Readeth in a Book Concerning the Well at the World's End

Fairly written was that book, with many pictures therein, the meaning of which Ralph knew not; but amongst them was the image of the fair woman whom he had holpen at the want-ways of the wood, and but four days ago was that, yet it seemed long and long to him. The book told not much about the Well at the World's End, but much it told of a certain woman whom no man that saw her could forbear to love: of her it told that erewhile she dwelt lonely in the wildwood (though how she came there was not said) and how a king's son found her there and brought her to his father's kingdom and wedded her, whether others were lief or loth: and in a little while, when the fame of her had spread, he was put out of his kingdom and his father's house for the love of her, because other kings and lords hankered after her; whereof befel long and grievous war which she abode not to the end, but sought to her old place in the wildwood; and how she found there another woman a sorceress, who made her her thrall; and tormented her grievously with toil and stripes. And how again there came a knight to that place who was seeking the Well at the World's End, and bore her away with him; and how the said knight was slain on the way, and she was taken by tyrants and robbers of the folk: but these being entangled in her love fought amongst themselves and she escaped, and went seeking that Well, and found it at the long last, and drank thereof, and throve ever after: and how she liveth yet, and is become the servant of the Well to entangle the seekers in her love and keep them from drinking thereof; because there was no man that beheld her, but anon he was the thrall of her love, and might not pluck his heart away from her to do any of the deeds whereby men thrive and win the praise of the people.

Ralph read on and on till the short night waned, and the wax-lights failed one after the other, and the windows of the hall grew grey and daylight came, and the throstles burst out a-singing at once in the castle pleasaunce, and the sun came up over the wood, and the sound of men-folk bestirring themselves a-field came to his ears through the open windows; and at last he was done with the tale, and the carline came not near him though the sun had clomb high up the heavens. As for Ralph, what he had read was sweet poison to him; for if before he was somewhat tormented by love, now was his heart sick and sore with it. Though he knew not for certain whether this tale had to do with the Lady of the Forest, and though he knew not if the Lady who should come to the castle were even she, yet he needs must deem that so it was, and his heart was weary with love. and his manhood seemed changed.

CHAPTER 20

Ralph Meeteth a Man
in the Wood

But the morning began to wear as he sat deep in these thoughts and still the Carline came not to him; and he thought: "She leaveth me alone that I may do her bidding: so will I without tarrying." And he arose and did on his hauberk and basnet, and girt his sword to his side, and went forth, a-foot as before. He crossed the river by a wide ford and stepping stones somewhat below the pool wherein he had bathed on that first day; and already by then he had got so far, what with the fresh air of the beauteous morning, what with the cheerful tinkling of his sword and hauberk, he was somewhat amended of his trouble and heaviness of spirit. A little way across the river, but nigher to the wood, was a house or cot of that country-folk, and an old woman sat spinning in the door. So Ralph went up thither, and greeted her, and craved of her a draught of milk; so the goody turned about and cried out to one within, and there came forth one of the maidens whom Ralph had met fishing that other day, and the old woman bade her bring forth milk and bread. Then the carline looked hard at Ralph, and said: "Ah! I have heard tell of thee: thou art abiding the turn of the days up at the castle yonder, as others have done before thee. Well, well, belike thou shalt have thy wish, though whether it shall be to thy profit, who shall say?"

Thereat Ralph's heart fell again, and he said: "Sayest thou, mother, that there have been others abiding like me in the tower? I know not what thy words mean."

The carline laughed. "Well," said she, "here comes thy morning's bait borne by shapely hands enough; eat and drink first; and then will I tell thee my meaning."

Therewith came the maiden forth with the bowl and the loaf; and indeed she was fair enough, and shy and kind; but Ralph heeded her little, nor was his heart moved by her at all. She set a stool for him beside the door and he sat down and ate and drank, though his heart was troubled; and the maiden hung about, and seemed to find it no easy matter to keep her eyes off him.

Presently the carline, who had been watching the two, said: "Thou askest of the meaning of my words; well, deemest thou that I have had more men than one to love me?" "I know not, mother," said Ralph, who could scarce hold himself patient. "There now!" quoth the carline, "look at my damsel! (she is not my daughter, but my brother's,) there is a man, and a brisk lad too, whom she calleth her batchelor, and is as I verily deem well-pleased with him: yet lo you how she eyeth thee, thou fair man, and doth so with her raiment that thou mayst best see how shapely she is of limb and foot, and toyeth her right hand with her left wrist, and the like.—Well, as for me, I have had more lovers than one or two. And why have I had just so many and no more? Nay, thou needest not make any long answer to me. I am old now, and even before I was old I was not young: I am now

105

foul of favour, and even before I became foul, I was not so fair—well then?"

"Yea, what then?" said Ralph. "This then, fair young fool," said she: "the one whom thou lovest, long hath she lived, but she is not old to look on, nor foul; but fair—O how fair!"

Then Ralph forgot his fear, and his heart grew greedy and his eyes glistened, and he said, yet he spoke faintly: "Yea, is she fair?" "What! hast thou not seen her?" said the carline. Ralph called to mind the guise in which he had seen her and flushed bright red, as he answered: "Yea, I deem that I have: surely it was she." The carline laughed: "Well," said she; "however thou hast seen her, thou hast scarce seen her as I have." Said Ralph, "How was that?" Said she: "It is her way here in the summer-tide to bathe her in yonder pool up the water:" (and it was the same pool wherein Ralph had bathed) "And she hath me and my niece and two other women to hold up the silken cloth betwixt her body and the world; so that I have seen her as God made her; and I shall tell thee that when he was about that work he was minded to be a craftsmaster; for there is no blemish about her that she should hide her at all or anywhere. Her sides are sleek, and her thighs no rougher than her face, and her feet as dainty as her hands: yea, she is a pearl all over, withal she is as strong as a knight, and I warrant her hardier of heart than most knights. A happy man shalt thou be; for surely I deem thou hast not come hither to abide her without some token or warrant of her."

Ralph held down his head, and he could not meet the old woman's eyes as she spake thus; and the maiden took herself out of earshot at the first words of the carline hereof, and was halfway down to the river by now.

Ralph spake after a while and said: "Tell me, is she good, and a good woman?" The dame laughed scornfully and said: "Surely, surely; she is the saint of the Forest Land, and the guardian of all poor folk. Ask the carles else!"

Ralph held his peace, and rose to be gone and turning saw the damsel wading the shallow ford, and looking over her shoulder at him. He gave the dame good day, and departed light-foot but heavy hearted. Yet as he went, he kept saying to himself: "Did she not send that Roger to turn my ways hither? yet she cometh not. Surely she hath changed in these last days, or it may be in these last hours: yea, or this very hour."

Amidst such thoughts he came into the wood, and made his way by the paths and open places, going south and east of the House: Whereas the last day he had gone west and north. He went a soft pace, but wandered on without any stay till it was noon, and he had seen nought but the wild things of the wood, nor many of them. But at last he heard the tinkle of a little bell coming towards him: so he stood still and got the hilt of his sword ready to his hand; and the tinkle drew nearer, and he heard withal the trample of some riding-beast; so he went toward the sound, and presently in a clearer place of the wood came upon a man of religion, a clerk, riding on a hackney, to whose neck hung a horse-bell: the priest had saddle bags beside him and carried in his right hand a book in a bag. When he met Ralph he blessed him, and Ralph gave him the sele of the day, and asked him whither he would. Said the Priest: "I am for the Little Plain and the Land of Abundance; whence art thou, my son, and whither wilt thou?" "From that very land I come," said Ralph, "and as to whither, I seek adventures; but unless I see more than I have this forenoon, or thou canst tell me of them, back will I whence I came: yet to say sooth, I shall not be sorry for a fellow to help me back, for these woodland ways are somewhat blind."

Said the Priest: "I will bear thee company with a good will; and I know the road right well; for I am the Vicar appointed by the fathers of the Thorn to serve the church of the Little Plain, and the chapel of St. Anthony yonder in the wood, and to-day I go to the church of the good folk there."

So Ralph turned, and went along with him, walking by his bridle-rein. And as they went the priest said to him: "Art thou one of my lady's lords?" Ralph reddened as he sighed, and said: "I am no captain of hers." Then smiled the priest and said: "Then will I not ask thee of thine errand; for belike thou wouldest not tell me thereof."

Ralph said nought, but waxed shamefaced as he deemed
107

that the priest eyed him curiously. At last he said: "I will ask thee a question in turn, father." "Yea," said the priest. Said Ralph: "This lady of the land, the Lady of Abundance, is she a very woman?" "Holy Saints!" quoth the priest, blessing himself, "what meanest thou?" Said Ralph: "I mean, is she of those who outwardly have a woman's semblance, but within are of the race of the ancient devils, the gods of the Gentiles?"

Then the priest crossed himself again, and spake as solemnly as a judge on the bench: "Son, I pray that if thou art not in thy right mind, thou will come thereinto anon. Know this, that whatever else she may be, she is a right holy woman. Or hast thou perchance heard any evil tales concerning her?"

Now Ralph was confused at his word, and knew not what to say; for though in his mind he had been piecing together all that he had heard of the lady both for good and for evil, he had no clear tale to tell even to himself: so he answered nothing.

But the priest went on: "Son, I shall tell thee that such tales I have heard, but from whose mouth forsooth? I will tell thee; from a sort of idle jades, young women who would be thought fairer than they be, who are afraid of everything save a naked man, and who can lie easier than they can say their paternoster: from such as these come the stories; or from old crones who live in sour anger with themselves and all else, because they have lived no goodly life in their youth, and have not learned the loveliness of holy church. Now, son, shall the tales of such women, old and young, weigh in thy mind beside the word I tell thee of what I have seen and know concerning this most excellent of ladies? I trow not. And for my part I tell thee, that though she is verily as fair as Venus (God save us) yet is she as chaste as Agnes, as wise as Katherine, and as humble and meek as Dorothy. She bestoweth her goods plentifully to the church, and is merciful to poor men therewith; and so far as occasion may serve her she is constant at the Holy Office; neither doth she spare to confess her sins, and to do all penance which is bidden her, yea and more. For though I cannot say to my knowledge that she weareth a hair; yet once and again have I seen her wending this woodland toward the chapel of her friend St. Anthony by night and cloud, so that few might see her, obedient to the Scripture which sayeth,—'Let not thy right hand know what thy left hand doeth,' and she barefoot in her smock amidst the rugged wood, and so arrayed fairer than any queen in a golden gown. Yea, as fair as the woodwives of the ancient heathen."

Therewith the priest stayed his words, and seemed as if he were fallen into a dream; and he sighed heavily. But Ralph walked on by his bridle-rein dreamy no less; for the words that he had heard he heeded not, save as they made pictures for him of the ways of that woman of the forest.

So they went on soberly till the priest lifted up his head and looked about like one come out of slumber, and said in a firm voice: "I tell thee, my son, that thou mayest set thy love upon her without sin." And therewith suddenly he fell a-weeping; and Ralph was ill at ease of his weeping, and went along by him saying nought; till the priest plucked up heart again, and said, turning to Ralph, but not meeting his eye: "My son, I weep because men and women are so evil, and mis-say each other so sorely, even as they do by this holy woman." As he spake his tears brake out again, and Ralph strode on fast, so as to outgo him, thinking it unmannerly to seem as if he noted not his sorrow; yet withal unable to say aught to him thereof. Moreover it irked him to hear a grown man weeping for grief, even though it were but a priest.

Within a while the priest caught up with him, his tears all staunched, and fell to talk with him cheerfully concerning the wood, and the Little Land and the dwellers therein and the conditions of them, and he praised them much, save the women. Ralph answered him with good cheer in likewise; and thus they came to the cot of the old woman, and both she and the maiden were without the house, the old carline hithering and thithering on some errand, the maiden leaning against a tree as if pondering some matter. As they passed by, the priest blessed them in words, but his eyes scowled on them, whereat the carline grinned, but the damsel heeded him not, but looked wistfully on Ralph. The priest muttered somewhat as he passed, which Ralph caught not the meaning of, and fell moody again; and when he was a little past the ford he drew rein and said: "Now, son, I must to my cell hard by the church yonder: but yet I will say one word to thee ere we sunder; to wit, that to my mind the Holy Lady will love no one but the saints of heaven, save it be some man with whom all women are in love."

Therewith he turned away suddenly, and rode smartly towards his church; and Ralph deemed that he was weeping once more. As for Ralph, he went quietly home toward the castle, for the sun was setting now, and as he went he pondered all these things in his heart.

CHAPTER 21

Ralph Weareth Away Three Days Uneasily

He read again in the book that night, till he had gotten the whole tale into his head, and he specially noted this of it, that it told not whence that Lady came, nor what she was, nor aught else save that there she was in the wood by herself, and was found therein by the king's son: neither told the tale in what year of the world she was found there, though it told concerning all the war and miseries which she had bred, and which long endured. Again, he could not gather from that book why she had gone back to the lone place in the woods, whereas she might have wedded one of those warring barons who sorely desired her: nor why she had yielded herself to the witch of that place and endured with patience her thrall-dom, with stripes and torments of her body, like the worst of the thralls of the ancient heathen men. Lastly, he might not learn from the book where in the world was that lone place, or aught of the road to the Well at the World's End. But amidst all his thinking his heart came back to this: "When I meet her, she will tell me of it all; I need be no wiser than to learn how to meet her and to make her love me; then shall she show me the way to the Well at the World's End, and I shall drink thereof and never grow old, even as she endureth in youth, and she shall love me for ever, and I her for ever."

So he thought; but yet amidst these happy thoughts came in this evil one, that whereas all the men-folk spoke well of her and worshipped her, the women-folk feared her or hated her; even to the lecherous old woman who had praised the beauty of her body for his torment. So he thought till his head grew heavy, and he went and lay down in his bed and slept, and dreamed of the days of Upmead; and things forgotten in his waking time came between him and any memories of his present longing and the days thereof.

He awoke and arose betimes in the morning, and when he had breakfasted he bade the carline bring him his weapons. "Wilt thou again to the wood?" said she. "Didst thou not bid me fare thither yesterday?" said he. "Yea," she said; "but to-day I fear lest thou depart and come not back." He laughed and said: "Seest thou not, mother, that I go afoot, and I in hauberk and helm? I cannot run far or fast from thee. Also" (and here he broke off his speech a little) "where should I be but here?"

"Ah," she said, "but who knows what may happen?" Nevertheless she went and fetched his war-gear and looked at him fondly as he did it on, and went his ways from the hall.

Now he entered the wood more to the south than he had done yesterday, and went softly as before, and still was he turning over in his mind the thoughts of last night, and ever they came back. "Might I but see her! Would she but love me! O for a draught of the Well at the World's End, that the love might last long and long!"

So he went on a while betwixt the trees and the thickets, till it was a little past noon. But all on a sudden a panic fear took him, lest she should indeed come to the castle while he was away, and not finding him, depart again, who knows whither; and when this thought came upon him, he cried aloud, and hastened at his swiftest back again to the castle, and came there breathless and wearied, and ran to the old woman, and cried out to her; "Is she come? is she come?"

The carline laughed and said, "Nay, she is not, but thou art come: praise be to the saints! But what aileth thee? Nay, fear not, she shall come at last."

Then grew Ralph shamefaced and turned away from her, and miscalled himself for a fool and a dastard that could not abide the pleasure of his lady at the very place whereto she had let lead him. So he wore through the remnant of the day howso he might, without going out-adoors again; and the carline came and spake with him; but whatever he asked her about the lady, she would not tell aught of any import, so he refrained him from that talk, and made a show of hearkening when she spake of other matters; as tales concerning the folk of the land, and the Fathers of the Thorn, and so forth.

On the next morning he arose and said to himself, that whatever betid, he would bide in the castle and the Plain of Abundance till the lady came; and he went amongst the haymaking folk in the morning and ate his dinner with them, and strove to be of good cheer, and belike the carles and queens thought him merry company; but he was now wearying his heart with longing, and might not abide any great while in one place; so when, dinner over, they turned to their work again, he went back to the Castle, and read in that book, and looked at the pictures thereof, and kept turning his wonder and hope and fear over and over again in his mind, and making to himself stories of how he should meet the Lady and what she would say to him, and how he should answer her, till at last the night came, and he went to his bed, and slept for the very weariness of his longing.

When the new day came he arose and went into the hall, and found the carline there, who said to him, "Fair sir, wilt thou to the wood again to-day?" "Nay," said Ralph, "I must not, I dare not." "Well," she said, "thou mayest if thou wilt; why shouldst thou not go?" Said Ralph, reddening and stammering: "Because I fear to; thrice have I been away long from the castle and all has gone well; but the fourth time she will come and find me gone."

The carline laughed: "Well," she said, "I shall be here if thou goest; for I promise thee not to stir out of the house whiles thou art away." Said Ralph: "Nay, I will abide here." "Yea," she said, "I see: thou trustest me not. Well, no matter; and to-day it will be handy if thou abidest. For I have an errand to my brother in the flesh, who is one of the

112

brethren of the Thorn over yonder. If thou wilt give me leave, it will be to my pleasure and gain."

Ralph was glad when he heard this, deeming that if she left him alone there, he would be the less tempted to stray into the wood again. Besides, he deemed that the Lady might come that day when he was alone in the Castle, and that himseemed would make the meeting sweeter yet. So he yea-said the carline's asking joyously, and in an hour's time she went her ways and left him alone there.

Ralph said to himself, when he saw her depart, that he would have the more joy in the castle of his Lady if he were alone, and would wear away the day in better patience therefor. But in sooth the hours of that day were worse to wear than any day there had yet been. He went not without the house at all that day, for he deemed that the folk abroad would note of him that he was so changed and restless.

Whiles he read in that book, or turned the leaves over, not reading it; whiles he went into the Chamber of Estate, and pored over the woven pictures there wherein the Lady was figured. Whiles he wandered from chamber to chamber, not knowing what to do.

At last, a little after dark, back comes the carline again, and he met her at the door of the hall, for he was weary of his own company, and the ceaseless turning over and over of the same thoughts.

As for her, she was so joyous of him that she fairly threw her arms about him and kissed and clipped him, as though she had been his very mother. Whereof he had some shame, but not much, for he deemed that her goodwill to him was abundant, which indeed it was.

Now she looks on him and says: "Truly it does my heart good to see thee: but thou poor boy, thou art wearing thyself with thy longing, and thy doubting, and if thou wilt do after my rede, thou wilt certainly go into the wood to-morrow and see what may befall; and indeed and in sooth thou wilt leave behind thee a trusty friend."

He looked on her kindly, and smiled, and said, "In sooth, mother, I deem thou art but right; though it be hard for me to leave this house, to which in a way my Lady hath bidden

113

me. Yet I will do thy bidding herein." She thanked him, and he went to his bed and slept; for now that he had made up his mind to go, he was somewhat more at rest.

CHAPTER 22

An Adventure in the Wood

Ralph arrayed himself for departure next morning without more words; and when he was ready the carline said to him: "When thou wentest forth before, I was troubled at thy going and feared for thy returning: but now I fear not; for I know that thou wilt return; though it may be leading a fair woman by the hand. So go, and all luck go with thee." Ralph smiled at her words and went his ways, and came into the wood that lay due south from the Castle, and he went on and on and had no thought of turning back. He rested twice and still went on, till the fashion of the thickets and the woods changed about him; and at last when the sun was getting low, he saw light gleaming through a great wood of pines, which had long been dark before him against the tall boles, and soon he came to the very edge of the wood, and going heedfully, saw between the great stems of the outermost trees, a green strand, and beyond it a long smooth water, a little lake between green banks on either side. He came out of the pinewood on to the grass; but there were thornbushes a few about, so that moving warily from one to the other, he might perchance see without being seen. Warily he went forsooth, going along the green strand to the east and the head of that water, and saw how the bank sloped up gently from its ending toward the pine-wood, in front of whose close-set trees stood three great-boled tall oak-trees on a smooth piece of green sward. And now he saw that there were folk come before him on this green place, and keen-sighted as he was, could make out that three men were on the hither side of the oak-trees, and on the further side of them was a white horse. Thitherward then he made, stealing from bush to bush, since he deemed that he needed not be seen of men who might be foes, for at the first sight he had noted the gleam of weapons there. And now he had gone no long way before he saw the westering sun shine brightly from a naked sword, and then another sprang up to meet it, and he heard faintly the clash of steel, and saw withal that the third of the folk had long and light raiment and was a woman belike. Then he bettered his pace, and in a minute or two came so near that he could see the men clearly, that they were clad in knightly war-gear, and were laying on great strokes so that the still place rang with the clatter. As for the woman, he could see but little of her, because of the fighting men before her; and the shadow of the oak boughs fell on her withal.

Now as he went, hidden by the bushes, they hid the men also from him, and when he was come to the last bush, some fifty paces from them, and peered out from it, in that very nick of time the two knights were breathing them somewhat, and Ralph saw that one of them, the furthest from him, was a very big man with a blue surcoat whereon was beaten a great golden sun, and the other, whose back was towards Ralph, was clad in black over his armour. Even as he looked and doubted whether to show himself or not, he of the sun raised his sword aloft, and giving forth a great roar as of wrath and grief mingled together, rushed on his foe and smote so fiercely that he fell to the earth before him, and the big man fell upon him as he fell, and let knee and sword-pommel and fist follow the stroke, and there they wallowed on the earth together.

Straightway Ralph came forth from the bushes with his drawn sword in his hand, and even therewith what with the two knights being both low upon the earth, what with the woman herself coming from out the shadow of the oak boughs, and turning her toward Ralph, he saw her clearly, and stood staring and amazed—for lo! it was the Lady whom he had delivered at the want-ways. His heart well nigh stood still with joy, yet was he shamefaced also: for though now she was no longer clad in that scanty raiment, yet did he seem to see her body through that which covered it. But now her attire was but simple; a green gown, thin and short, and thereover a cote-hardy of black cloth with orphreys of gold and colours: but on her neck was a collar that seemed to him like to that which Dame Katherine had given him; and the long tresses of her hair, which he had erst seen floating loose about her, were wound as a garland around her head. She looked with a flushed and joyous face on Ralph, and seemed as if she heeded nought the battle of the knights, but saw him only: but he feared her, and his love for her and stood still, and durst not move forward to go to her.

Thus they abode for about the space of one minute: and meanwhile the big man rose up on one knee and steadied him with his sword for a moment of time, and the blade was bloody from the point half way up to the hilt; but the black knight lay still and made no sign of life. Then the Knight of the Sun rose up slowly and stood on his feet and faced the Lady and seemed not to see Ralph, for his back was towards him. He came slowly toward the Lady, scowling, and his face white as chalk; then he spake to her coldly and sternly, stretching out his bloody sword before her.

"I have done thy bidding, and slain my very earthly friend of friends for thy sake. Wherewith wilt thou reward me?"

Then once more Ralph heard the voice, which he remembered so sweet amidst peril and battle aforetime, as she said as coldly as the Knight: "I bade thee not: thine own heart bade thee to strive with him because thou deemedst that he loved me. Be content! thou hast slain him who stood in thy way, as thou deemedst. Thinkest thou that I rejoice at his slaying? O no! I grieve at it, for all that I had such good cause to hate him."

He said: "My own heart! my own heart! Half of my heart biddeth me slay thee, who hast made me slay him. What wilt thou give me?" She knit her brow and spake angrily: "Leave to depart," she said. Then after a while, and in a kinder voice: "And thus much of my love, that I pray thee not to sorrow for me, but to have a good heart, and live as a true knight should." He frowned: "Wilt thou not go with me?" said he. "Not uncompelled," she said: "if thou biddest me go with threats of hewing and mangling the body which thou

116

sayest thou lovest, needs must I go then. Yet scarce wilt thou do this."

"I have a mind to try it," said he; "If I set thee on thine horse and bound thine hands for thee, and linked thy feet together under the beast's belly; belike thou wouldest come. Shall I have slain my brother-in-arms for nought?"

"Thou hast the mind," said she, "hast thou the might?" "So I deem," said he, smiling grimly.

She looked at him proudly and said: "Yea, but I misdoubt me thereof." He still had his back to Ralph and was staring at the lady; she turned her head a little and made a sign to Ralph, just as the Knight of the Sun said: "Thou misdoubtest thee? Who shall help thee in the desert?"

"Look over thy left shoulder," she said. He turned, and saw Ralph drawing near, sword in hand, smiling, but somewhat pale. He drew aback from the Lady and, spinning round on his heel, faced Ralph, and cried out: "Hah! Hast thou raised up a devil against me, thou sorceress, to take from me my grief and my lust, and my life? Fair will the game be to fight with thy devil as I have fought with my friend! Yet now I know not whether I shall slay him or thee."

She spake not, but stood quietly looking on him, not unkindly, while a wind came up from the water and played with a few light locks of hair that hung down from that ruddy crown, and blew her raiment from her feet and wrapped it close round her limbs; and Ralph beheld her, and close as was the very death to him (for huge and most warrior-like was his foeman) yet longing for her melted the heart within him, and he felt the sweetness of life in his inmost soul as he had never felt it before.

Suddenly the Knight of the Sun turned about to the Lady again, and fell down on his knees before her, and clasped his hands as one praying, and said: "Now pardon me all my words, I pray thee; and let this young man depart unhurt, whether thou madest him, or hast but led him away from country and friends and all. Then do thou come with me, and make some semblance of loving me, and suffer me to love thee. And then shall all be well, for in a few days we will go back to thy people, and there will I be their lord or thy servant, or my brother's man, or what thou wilt. O wilt thou not let the summer days be sweet?"

But she spake, holding up her head proudly and speaking in a clear ringing voice: "I have said it, that uncompelled I will not go with thee at all." And therewithal she turned her face toward Ralph, as she might do on any chance-met courteous man, and he saw her smiling, but she said nought to him, and gave no token of knowing him. Then the Knight of the Sun sprang to his feet, and shook his sword above his head and ran furiously on Ralph, who leapt nimbly on one side (else had he been slain at once) and fetched a blow at the Sun-Knight, and smote him, and brake the mails on his left shoulder, so that the blood sprang, and fell on fiercely enough, smiting to right and left as the other gave back at his first onset. But all was for nought, for the Knight of the Sun, after his giving aback under that first stroke drew himself up stark and stiff, and pressing on through all Ralph's strokes, though they rent his mail here and there, ran within his sword, and smote him furiously with the sword-pommel on the side of the head, so that the young man of Upmeads could not stand up under the weight of the blow, but fell to the earth swooning, and the Knight of the Sun knelt on him, and drew out an anlace, short, thick and sharp, and cried out: "Now, Devil, let see whether thou wilt bleed black." Therewith he raised up his hand: but the weapon was stayed or ever it fell, for the Lady had glided up to them when she saw that Ralph was overcome, and now she stretched out her arm and caught hold of the Knight's hand and the anlace withal, and he groaned and cried out: "What now! thou art strong-armed as well as white-armed; (for she had rent the sleeve back from her right arm) and he laughed in the extremity of his wrath. But she was pale and her lips quivered as she said softly and sweetly: "Wilt thou verily slay this young man?"

"And why not?" said he, "since I have just slain the best friend that I ever had, though he was nought willing to fight with me, and only for this, that I saw thee toying with him; though forsooth thou hast said truly that thou hadst more reason to hate him than love him. Well, since thou wilt not have this youngling slain, I may deem at least that he is no

118

devil of thy making, else wouldst thou be glad of his slaying, so that he might be out of the path of thee; so a man he is, and a well-favoured one, and young; and valiant, as it seemeth: so I suppose that he is thy lover, or will be one day—well then—"

And he lifted his hand again, but again she stayed him, and said: "Look thou, I will buy him of thee: and, indeed, I owe him a life." "How is that?" said he. "Why wouldst thou know?" she said; "thou who, if thou hadst me in thine hands again, wouldst keep me away from all men. Yea, I know what thou wouldst say, thou wouldst keep me from sinning again." And she smiled, but bitterly. "Well, the tale is no long one: "five days ago I was taken by them of the Burg: and thou wottest what they would do with me; yea, even if they deemed me less than they do deem me: well, as two of their men-at-arms were leading me along by a halter, as a calf is led to the butcher, we fell in with this goodly lad, who slew them both in manly fashion, and I escaped for that time: though, forsooth, I must needs put my neck in the noose again in delivering four of our people, who would else have been tormented to death by the Burgers."

"Well," said the knight, "perchance thou hast more mercy than I looked for of thee; though I misdoubt thee that thou mayst yet pray me or some other to slay him for thee. Thou art merciful, my Queen, though not to me, and a churl were I if I were less merciful than thou. Therefore will I give his life to him, yet not to thee will I give him if I may help it—Lo you, Sweet! he is just opening his eyes."

Therewith he rose up from Ralph, who raised himself a little, and sat up dazed and feeble. The Knight of the Sun stood up over him beside the lady with his hands clasped on his sword-hilt, and said to Ralph: "Young man, canst thou hear my words?" Ralph smiled feebly and nodded a yea-say. "Dost thou love thy life then?" said the Knight. Ralph found speech and said faintly, "Yea." Said the Knight: "Where dost thou come from, where is thine home?" Said Ralph, "Upmeads." "Well then," quoth the big knight, "go back to Upmeads, and live." Ralph shook his head and knit his brows and said, "I will not." "Yea," said the Knight, "thou wilt not live? Then must I shape me to thy humour. Stand on thy feet and fight it out; for now I am cool I will not slay a swordless man."

Ralph staggered up to his feet, but was so feeble still, that he sank down again, and muttered: "I may not; I am sick and faint;" and therewith swooned away again. But the Knight stood a while leaning on his sword, and looking down on him not unkindly. Then he turned about to the Lady, but lo! she had left his side. She had glided away, and got to her horse, which was tethered on the other side of the oak-tree, and had loosed him and mounted him, and so sat in the saddle there, the reins gathered in her hands. She smiled on the knight as he stood astonished, and cried to him; "Now, lord, I warn thee, draw not a single foot nigher to me; for thou seest that I have Silverfax between my knees, and thou knowest how swift he is, and if I see thee move, he shall spring away with me. Thou wottest how well I know all the ways of the woodland, and I tell thee that the ways behind me to the Dry Tree be all safe and open, and that beyond the Gliding River I shall come on Roger of the Ropewalk and his men. And if thou thinkest to ride after me, and overtake me, cast the thought out of thy mind. For thy horse is strong but heavy, as is meet for so big a knight, and morever he is many yards away from me and Silverfax: so before thou art in the saddle, where shall I be? Yea," (for the Knight was handling his anlace) "thou mayst cast it, and peradventure mayst hit Silverfax and not me, and peradventure not; and I deem that it is my body alive that thou wouldest have back with thee. So now, wilt thou hearken?"

"Yea," quoth the knight, though for wrath he could scarce bring the word from his mouth.

"Hearken," she said, "this is the bargain to be struck between us: even now thou wouldst not refrain from slaying this young man, unless perchance he should swear to depart from us; and as for me, I would not go back with thee to Sunhome, where erst thou shamedst me. Now will I buy thy nay-say with mine, and if thou give the youngling his life, and suffer him to come his ways with us, then will I go home with thee and will ride with thee in all the love and duty that I owe thee; or if thou like this fashion of words better, I will give thee my body for his life. But if thou likest not the bargain, there is not another piece of goods for thee in the market, for then I will ride my ways to the Dry Tree, and thou shalt slay the poor youth, or make of him thy sworn friend, like as was Walter—which thou wilt."

So she spake, and Ralph yet lay on the grass and heard nought. But the Knight's face was dark and swollen with anger as he answered: "My sworn friend! yea, I understand thy gibe. I need not thy words to bring to my mind how I have slain one sworn friend for thy sake."

"Nay," she said, "not for my sake, for thine own folly's sake." He heeded her not, but went on: "And as for this one, I say again of him, if he be not thy devil, then thou meanest him for thy lover. And now I deem that I will verily slay him, ere he wake again; belike it were his better luck."

She said: "I wot not why thou hagglest over the price of that thou wouldest have. If thou have him along with thee, shall he not be in thy power—as I shall be? and thou mayst slay him—or me—when thou wilt."

"Yea," he said, grimly, "when thou art weary of him. O art thou not shameless amongst women! Yet must I needs pay thy price, though my honour and the welfare of my life go with it. Yet how if he have no will to fare with us?" She laughed and said: "Then shalt thou have him with thee as thy captive and thrall. Hast thou not conquered him in battle?" He stood silent a moment and then he said: "Thou sayest it; he shall come with me, will he, nill he, unarmed, and as a prisoner, and the spoil of my valiancy." And he laughed, not altogether in bitterness, but as if some joy were rising in his heart. "Now, my Queen," said he, "the bargain is struck betwixt us, and thou mayest light down off Silverfax; as for me, I will go fetch water from the lake, that we may wake up this valiant and mighty youth, this newfound jewel, and bring him to his wits again."

She answered nought, but rode her horse close to him and lighted down nimbly, while his greedy eyes devoured her beauty. Then he took her hand and drew her to him, and kissed her cheek, and she suffered it, but kissed him not again. Then he took off his helm, and went down to the lake to fetch up water therein.

CHAPTER 23

The Leechcraft of the Lady

Meanwhile she went to Ralph and stood by him, who now began to stir again; and she knelt down by him and kissed his face gently, and rose up hastily and stood a little aloof again.

Now Ralph sat up and looked about him, and when he saw the Lady he first blushed red, and then turned very pale; for the full life was in him again, and he knew her, and love drew strongly at his heart-strings. But she looked on him kindly and said to him: "How fares it with thee? I am sorry of thy hurt which thou hast had for me." He said: "Forsooth, Lady, a chance knock or two is no great matter for a lad of Upmeads. But oh! I have seen thee before." "Yea," she said, "twice before, fair knight." "How is that?" he said; "once I saw thee, the fairest thing in the world, and evil men would have led thee to slaughter; but not twice."

She smiled on him still more kindly, as if he were a dear friend, and said simply: "I was that lad in the cloak that ye saw in the Flower de Luce; and afterwards when ye, thou and Roger, fled away from the Burg of the Four Friths. I had come into the Burg with my captain of war at the peril of our lives to deliver four faithful friends of mine who were else doomed to an evil death."

He said nought, but gazed at her face, wondering at her valiancy and goodness. She took him by the hand now, and held it without speaking for a little while, and he sat there still looking up into her face, wondering at her sweetness and his happiness. Then she said, as she drew her hand away and spake in such a voice, and so looking at him, that every word was as a caress to him: "Thy soul is coming back to thee, my friend, and thou art well at ease: is it not so?"

"O yea," he said, "and I woke up happily e'en now; for

ne-dreamed that my gossip came to me and kissed me
:indly; and she is a fair woman, but not a young woman."

As he spoke the knight, who had come nearly noiselessly
·ver the grass, stood by them, holding his helm full of water,
.nd looking grimly upon them; but the Lady looked up at
aim with wide eyes wonderingly, and Ralph, beholding her,
leemed that all he had heard of her goodness was but the
·ery sooth. But the knight spake: "Young man, thou hast
·ought with me, thou knowest not wherefore, and grim was
my mood when thou madest thine onset, and still is, so that
aever but once wilt thou be nigher thy death than thou hast
·een this hour. But now I have given thee life because of the
asking of this lady; and therewith I give thee leave to come
hy ways with us: nay, rather I command thee to come, for
hou art my prisoner, to be kept or ransomed, or set free as I
vill. But my will is that thou shalt not have thine armour and
veapons; and there is a cause for this, which mayhappen I
vill tell thee hereafter. But now I bid thee drink of this
vater, and then do off thine helm and hauberk and give me
hy sword and dagger, and go with us peaceably; and be not
·vermuch ashamed, for I have overcome men who boasted
hemselves to be great warriors.

So Ralph drank of the water, and did off his helm, and
:ast water on his face, and arose, and said smiling: "Nay, my
naster, I am nought ashamed of my mishaps: and as to my
;oing with thee and the Lady, thou hast heard me say under
hy dagger that I would not forbear to follow her; so I scarce
aeed thy command thereto." The knight scowled on him and
:aid: "Hold thy peace, fool! Thou wert best not stir my
vrath again." "Nay," said Ralph, "thou hast my sword, and
nayst slay me if thou wilt; therefore be not word-valiant
vith me."

Said the Knight of the Sun: "Well, well, thou hast the
ight of it there. Only beware lest thou try me overmuch. But
aow must we set forth on our road; and here is work for
hee to do: a hundred yards within the thick wood in a
traight line from the oak-tree thou shalt find two horses,
nine and the knight's who fell before me; go thou and bring
hem hither; for I will not leave thee with my lady, lest I
aave to slay thee in the end, and maybe her also."

Ralph nodded cheerfully, and set off on his task, and was the readier therein because the Lady looked on him kindly and compassionately as he went by her. He found the horses speedily, a black horse that was of the Black Knight, and bay of the Knight of the Sun, and he came back with them lightly.

But when he came to the oak-tree again, lo, the knight and the Lady both kneeling over the body of the Black Knight and Ralph saw that the Knight of the Sun was sobbing and weeping sorely, so that he deemed that he was taking leave of his friend that lay dead there: but when Ralph had tied up those other two steeds by Silverfax and drawn near to those twain, the Knight of the Sun looked up at him, and spake in a cheerful voice: "Thou seemest to be no ill man, though thou hast come across my lady; so now I bid thee rejoice that there is a good knight more in the world than we deemed e'en now; for this my friend Walter the Black is alive still." "Yea," said the Lady, "and belike he shall live a long while yet."

So Ralph looked, and saw that they had stripped the knight of his hauberk and helm, and bared his body, and that the Lady was dressing a great and sore wound in his side: neither was he come to himself again: he was a young man, and very goodly to look on, dark haired and straight of feature, fair of face; and Ralph felt a grief at his heart as he beheld the Lady's hands dealing with his bare flesh, though nought the man knew of it belike.

As for the Knight of the Sun, he was no more grim and moody, but smiling and joyous, and he spake and said: "Young man, this shall stand thee in good stead that I have not slain my friend this bout. Sooth to say, it might else have gone hard with thee on the way to my house, or still more in my house. But now be of good heart, for unless of thine own folly thou run on the sword's point, thou mayst yet live and do well." Then he turned to the Lady and said: "Dame, for as good a leech as ye be, ye may not heal this man so that he may sit in his saddle within these ten days; and now what is to do in this matter?"

She looked on him with smiling lips and a strange light in her eyes, and said: "Yea, forsooth, what wilt thou do? Wilt

ou abide here by Walter thyself alone, and let me bring the
mp of Upmeads home to our house? Or wilt thou ride home
nd send folk with a litter to us? Or shall this youngling ride
t all adventure, and seek to Sunway through the blind
oodland? Which shall it be?"

The knight laughed outright, and said: "Yea, fair one, this
s much like to the tale of the carle at the ferry with the fox,
nd the goat, and the cabbage."

There was scarce a smile on her face as she said gently:
One thing is to be thought of, that Walter's soul is not yet so
ast in his body that either thou or some rough-handed leech
may be sure of healing him; it must be this hand, and the
earning which it hath learned which must deal with him for
while. And she stretched out her arm over the wounded
man, with the fingers pointing down the water, and reddened
ithal, as if she felt the hearts' greediness of the two men
ho were looking on her beauty.

The big knight sighed, and said: "Well, unless I am to kill
im over again, there is nothing for it but our abiding with
im for the next few hours at least. To-morrow is a new day,
nd fair is the woodland-hall of summer-tide; neither shall
ater fail us. But as to victual, I wot not save that we have
one."

The Lady laughed, and said to Ralph; "Who knoweth
hat thou mayst find if thou go to the black horse and look
nto the saddle-bags which I saw upon him awhile agone? For
ndeed we need somewhat, if it were but to keep the life in
he body of this wounded man."

Ralph sprang up and turned to the horse, and found the
addle-bags on him, and took from them bread and flesh, and
flask of good wine, and brought them to the Lady, who
aughed and said: "Thou art a good seeker and no ill finder."
Then she gave the wounded man to drink of the wine, so that
e stirred somewhat, and the colour came into his face a
ittle. Then she bade gather store of bracken for a bed for
he Black Knight, and Ralph bestirred himself therein, but
he Knight of the Sun sat looking at the Lady as she busied
erself with his friend, and gloom seemed gathering on him
gain.

But when the bracken was enough, the Lady made a bed

125

deftly and speedily; and between the three they laid th
wounded man thereon, who seemed coming to himself som
what, and spake a few words, but those nothing to the poin
Then the Lady took her gay embroidered cloak, which lay
the foot of the oak tree, and cast it over him and, as Ralp
deemed, eyed him lovingly, and belike the Knight of the Su
thought in likewise, for he scowled upon her; and for awhi
but little was the joyance by the ancient oak, unless it wer
with the Lady.

CHAPTER 24

Supper and Slumber in the Woodland Hall

But when all was done to make the wounded knight
easy as might be, the Lady turned to the other twain, an
said kindly: "Now, lords, it were good to get to table, sin
here is wherewithal." And she looked on them both fu
kindly as she spake the words, but nowise wantonly; even
the lady of a fair house might do by honoured guests. So th
hearts of both were cheered, and nothing loth they sat dow
by her on the grass and fell to meat. Yet was the Knight
the Sun a little moody for a while, but when he had eate
and drunken somewhat, he said: "It were well if someon
might come hereby, some hermit or holy man, to whom w
might give the care of Walter: then might we home
Sunway, and send folk with a litter to fetch him home soft
when the due time were."

"Yea," said the Lady, "that might happen forsooth, an
perchance it will; and if it were before nightfall it wer
better."

Ralph saw that as she spake she took hold of the tw
fingers of her left hand with her right forefinger, and let th
thumb meet it, so that it made a circle about them, and sh
spake something therewith in a low voice, but he heeded

little, save as he did all ways that her body moved. As for the Knight of the Sun, he was looking down on the grass as one pondering matters, and noted this not. But he said presently: "What hast thou to say of Walter now? Shall he live?" "Yea," she said, "maybe as long as either of you twain." The knight looked hard at Ralph, but said nothing, and Ralph heeded not his looks, for his eyes were busy devouring the Lady.

So they abode a little, and the more part of what talk there was came from the Lady, and she was chiefly asking Ralph of his home in Upmeads, and his brethren and kindred, and he told her all openly, and hid naught, while her voice ravished his very soul from him, and it seemed strange to him, that such an one should hold him in talk concerning these simple matters and familiar haps, and look on him so kindly and simply. Ever and anon would she go and look to the welfare of the wounded man, and come back from him (for they sat a little way aloof), and tell them how he did. And still the Knight of the Sun took little heed, and once again gloom settled down on him.

Amidst all this the sun was set, and the long water lay beneath the heavens like a sheet of bright, fairhued metal, and naught stirred it: till at last the Lady leaned forward to Ralph, and touched his shoulder (for he was sitting over against her, with his back to the water), and she said: "Sir Knight, Sir Knight, his wish is coming about, I believe verily." He turned his head to look over his shoulder, and, as if by chance-hap, his cheek met the outstretched hand she was pointing with: she drew it not away very speedily, and as sweet to him was the touch of it as if his face had been brushed past by a summer lily.

"Nay, look! something cometh," she cried; and he looked and saw a little boat making down the water toward the end anigh them. Then the Knight of the Sun seemed to awake at her word, and he leapt to his feet, and stood looking at the new comer.

It was but a little while ere the boat touched the shore, and a man stepped out of it on to the grass and made it fast to the bank, and then stood and looked about him as if

seeking something; and lo, it was a holy man, a hermit in th
habit of the Blackfriars.

Then the Knight of the Sun hastened down to the strand t
meet him, and when Ralph was thus left alone with th
Lady, though it were but for a little, his heart beat and h
longed sore to touch her with his hand, but durst not, and di
but hope that her hand would stray his way as it had e'e
now. But she arose and stood a little way from him, an
spake to him sweetly of the fairness of the evening, and th
wounded man, and the good hap of the friar's coming befor
nightfall; and his heart was wrung sore with the love of her.

So came the knight up from the strand, and the holy ma
with him, who greeted Ralph and the Lady and blessed then
and said: "Now, daughter, show me thy sick man; for I ai
somewhat of a leech, and this thy baron would have me hea
him, and I have a right good will thereto."

So he went to the Black Knight, and when he had looke
to his hurts, he turned to them and said: "Have ye perchanc
any meat in the wilderness?" "Yea," quoth the Knight of th
Sun; "there is enough for a day or more, and if we mus
needs abide here longer, I or this young man may well mak
shift to slay some deer, great or little, for our sustenance an
the healing of my friend."

"It is well," said the Friar; "my hermitage is no great wa
hence, in the thicket at the end of this water. But now is th
fever on this knight, and we may not move him ere mornin
at soonest; but to-morrow we may make a shift to bear hir
hence by boat: or, if not, then may I go and fetch from m
cell bread and other meat, and milk of my goats; and thu
shall we do well till we may bring him to my cell, and ther
shall ye leave him there; and afterwards I will lead him hom
to Sunway where thou dwellest, baron, when he is wel
enough healed; or, if he will not go thither, let him go hi
ways, and I myself will come to Sunway and let thee wot o
his welfare."

The knight yeasaid all this, and thereafter the Friar an
the Lady together tended the wounded knight, and gave hir
water to drink, and wine. And meanwhile Ralph and th
Knight of the Sun lay down on the grass and watched the ev

128

arkening, and Ralph marvelled at his happiness, and wondered what the morrow would bring forth.

But amidst his happy thoughts the Knight of the Sun spake to him and said: "Young knight, I have struck a bargain with er that thou shalt follow us home, if thou wilt: but to say oth, I think when the bargain was struck I was minded hen I had thee at Sunway to cast thee into my prison. But ow I will do otherwise, and if thou must needs follow after ine own perdition, as I have, thou shalt do so freely; therefore take again thine armour and weapons, and do what thou ilt with them. But if thou wilt do after my rede, get thee way to-morrow, or better, to-night, and desire our fellowip no more."

Ralph heard him, and the heart within him was divided. It as in his mind to speak debonairely to the knight; but again e felt as if he hated him, and the blythe words would not ome, and he answered doggedly: "I will not leave my Lady nce she biddeth me go with her. If thou wilt then, make the ost of it that thou art stronger than I, and a warrior more roven; set me before thy sword, and fight with me and slay e."

Then rose the wrath to the knight's lips, and he brake orth: "Then is there one other thing for thee to do, and that that thou take thy sword, which I have just given back to ee, and thrust her through therewith. That were better for ee and for me, and for him who lieth yonder."

Therewith he arose and strode up and down in the dusk, nd Ralph wondered at him, yet hated him now not so much, nce he deemed that the Lady would not love him, and that e was angered thereby. Yet about Ralph's heart there hung certain fear of what should be.

But presently the knight came and sat down by him again, nd again fell to speech with him, and said: "Thou knowest at I may not slay thee, and yet thou sayest, fight with me; this well done?" "Is it ill done?" said Ralph, "I wot not hy."

The knight was silent awhile, and then he said: "With hat words shall I beseech thee to depart while it is yet time? may well be that in days to come I shall be good to thee, nd help thee."

129

But Ralph said never a word. Then said the knight, a
sighed withal: "I now see this of thee, that thou mayst
depart; well, so let it be!" and he sighed heavily again. T
Ralph strove with himself, and said courteously: "Sir, I
sorry that I am a burden irksome to thee; and that, wh
know not, thou mayst not rid thyself of me by the str
hand, and that otherwise thou mayst not be rid of me. W
then is this woman to thee, that thou wouldst have me s
her, and yet art so fierce in thy love for her?" The Knight
the Sun laughed wrathfully thereat, and was on the point
answering him, when up came those two from the wound
man, and the Friar said: "The knight shall do well; but v
it is for him that the Lady of Abundance was here for
helping; for from her hands goeth all healing, as it was w
the holy men of old time. May the saints keep her from
harm; for meek and holy indeed she is, as oft we have he
it."

The Lady put her hand on his shoulder, as if to bid h
silence, and then set herself down on the grass beside t
Knight of the Sun, and fell to talking sweetly and blithely
the three men. The Friar answered her with many wor
and told her of the deer and fowl of the wood and the wa
that he was wont to see nigh to his hermitage; for of su
things she asked him, and at last he said: "Good sooth
should be shy to say in all places and before all men of
my dealings with God's creatures which live about me the
Wot ye what? E'en now I had no thought of coming hith
ward; but I was sitting amongst the trees pondering ma
things, when I began to drowse, and drowsing I heard
thornbushes speaking to me like men, and they bade me ta
my boat and go up the water to help a man who was
need; and that is how I came hither; benedicite."

So he spake; but the Knight of the Sun did but put ir
word here and there, and that most often a sour and snapp
word. As for Ralph, he also spake but little, and stray
somewhat in his answers; for he could not but deem that s
spake softlier and kinder to him than to the others; and
was dreamy with love and desire, and scarce knew what
was saying.

Thus they wore away some two hours, the Friar or t
130

Lady turning away at whiles to heed the wounded man, who was now talking wildly in his fever.

But at last the night was grown as dark as it would be, since cloud and storm came not, for the moon had sunk down: so the Lady said: "Now, lords, our candle hath gone out, and I for my part will to bed; so let us each find a meet chamber in the woodland hall; and I will lie near to thee, father, and the wounded friend, lest I be needed to help thee in the night; and thou, Baron of Sunway, lie thou betwixt me and the wood, to ward me from the wild deer and the wood-wights. But thou, Swain of Upmeads, wilt thou deem it hard to lie anear the horses, to watch them if they be scared by aught?"

"Yea," said the Knight of the Sun, "thou art Lady here forsooth; even as men say of thee, that thou swayest man and beast in the wildwood. But this time at least it is not so ill-marshalled of thee: I myself would have shown folk to chamber here in likewise."

Therewith he rose up, and walked to and fro for a little, and then went, and sat down on a root of the oak-tree, clasping his knees with his hands, but lay not down awhile. But the Lady made herself a bed of the bracken which was over from those that Ralph had gathered for the bed of the wounded Knight; and the Friar lay down on the grass nigh to her, and both were presently asleep.

Then Ralph got up quietly; and, shamefacedly for very love, passed close beside the sleeping woman as he went to his place by the horses, taking his weapons and wargear with him: and he said to himself as he laid him down, that it was good for him to be quite alone, that he might lie awake and think at his ease of all the loveliness and kindness of his Lady. Howbeit, he was a young man, and a sturdy, used to lying abroad in the fields or the woods, and it was his custom to sleep at once and sweetly when he lay down after the day's work had wearied him, and even so he did now, and was troubled by no dreams of what was past or to come.

BOOK TWO
The Road Unto Trouble

CHAPTER 1

Ralph Meets With Love in the Wilderness

He woke up while it was yet night, and knew that he had been awakened by a touch; but, like a good hunter and warrior, he forebore to start up or cry out till sleep had so much run off him that he could tell somewhat of what was toward. So now he saw the Lady bending over him, and she said in a kind and very low voice: "Rise up, young man, rise up, Ralph, and say no word, but come with me a little way into the wood ere dawn come, for I have a word for thee."

So he stood up and was ready to go with her, his heart beating hard for joy and wonder. "Nay," she whispered, "take thy sword and war-gear lest ill befall: do on thine hauberk; I will be thy squire." And she held his war-coat out for him to do on. "Now," she said, still softly, "hide thy curly hair with the helm, gird thy sword to thee, and come without a word."

Even so he did, and therewithal felt her hand take his (for it was dark as they stepped amidst the trees), and she led him into the Seventh Heaven, for he heard her voice, though it were but a whisper, as it were a caress and a laugh of joy in each word.

She led him along swiftly, fumbling nought with the paths betwixt the pine-tree boles, where it was as dark as dark might be. Every minute he looked to hear her say a word of why she had brought him thither, and that then she would depart from him; so he prayed that the silence and the holding of his hand might last a long while—for he might think of naught save her—and long it lasted forsooth, and still she spake no word, though whiles a little sweet chuckle, as of the garden warbler at his softest, came from her lips, and the ripple of her raiment as her swift feet drave it, sounded loud to his eager ears in the dark, windless wood.

At last, and it was more than half-an-hour of their walking thus, it grew lighter, and he could see the shape of her alongside of him; and still she held his hand and glided on swifter and swifter, as he thought; and soon he knew that outside the wood dawn was giving place to day, and even there, in the wood, it was scarce darker than twilight.

Yet a little further, and it grew lighter still, and he heard the throstles singing a little way off, and knew that they were on the edge of the pine-wood, and still her swift feet sped on till they came to a little grassy wood-lawn, with nought anear it on the side away from the wood save maples and thorn-bushes: it was broad daylight there, though the sun had not yet arisen.

There she let fall his hand and turned about to him and faced him flushed and eager, with her eyes exceeding bright and her lips half open and quivering. He stood beholding her, trembling, what for eagerness, what for fear of her words when he had told her of his desire. For he had now made up his mind to do no less. He put his helm from off his head and laid it down on the grass, and he noted therewith that she had come in her green gown only, and had left mantle and cote hardie behind.

Now he stood up again and was just going to speak, when lo! she put both her palms to her face, and her bosom heaved, and her shoulders were shaken with sobs, and she burst out a weeping, so that the tears ran through her fingers. Then he cast himself on the ground before her, and kissed her feet, and clasped her about the knees, and laid his cheek to her raiment, and fawned upon her, and cried out many an idle word of love, and still she wept a while and spake not. At last she reached her hand down to his face and fondled it, and he let his lips lie on the hand, and she suffered it a while, and then took him by the arm and raised him up and led him on swiftly as before; and he knew not what to do or say, and durst by no means stay her, and could frame no word to ask her wherefore.

So they sped across a waste not much beset with trees, he silent, she never wearying or slacking her pace or faltering as to the way, till they came into the thick wood again, and ever when he would have spoken she hushed him, with "Not yet! Not yet!" Until at last when the sun had been up for some three hours, she led him through a hazel copse, like a deep hedge, into a cleared grassy place where were great grey stones lying about, as if it had been the broken doom-ring of a forgotten folk. There she threw herself down on the grass and buried her face amidst the flowers, and was weeping and sobbing again and he bending over her, till she turned to him and drew him down to her and put her hands to his face, and laid her cheeks all wet with tears to his, and fell to kissing him long and sweetly, so that in his turn he was like to weep for the very sweetness of love.

Then at last she spake: "This is the first word, that now I have brought thee away from death; and so sweet it is to me that I can scarce bear it."

"Oh, sweet to me," he said, "for I have waited for thee many days." And he fell to kissing and clipping her, as one who might not be satisfied. At last she drew herself from him a little, and, turning on him a face smiling with love, she said: "Forbear it a little, till we talk together." "Yea," quoth he, "but may I hold thine hand awhile?" "No harm in that," she said, laughing, and she gave him her hand and spake:

"I spake it that I have brought thee from death, and thou hast asked me no word concerning what and how." "I will ask it now, then," said he, "since thou wilt have it so." She said: "Dost thou think that he would have let thee live?"

"Who," said he, "since thou lettest me live?"

"He, thy foeman, the Knight of the Sun," she said. "Why

didst thou not flee from him before? For he did not so much desire to slay thee, but that he would have had thee depart; but if thou wert once at his house, he would thrust a sword through thee, or at the least cast thee into his prison and let thee lie there till thy youth be gone—or so it seemed to me," she said, faltering as she looked on him.

Said Ralph: "How could I depart when thou wert with him? Didst thou not see me there? I was deeming that thou wouldst have me abide."

She looked upon him with such tender love that he made as if he would cast himself upon her; but she refrained him, and smiled and said: "Ah, yes, I saw thee, and thought not that thou wouldst sunder thyself from me; therefore had I care of thee." And she touched his cheek with her other hand; and he sighed and knit his brows somewhat, and said: "But who is this man that he should slay me? And why is he thy tyrant, that thou must flee from him?"

She laughed and said: "Fair creature, he is my husband."

Then Ralph flushed red, and his visage clouded, and he opened his mouth to speak; but she stayed him and said: "Yet is he not so much my husband but that or ever we were bedded he must needs curse me and drive me away from his house." And she smiled, but her face reddened so deeply that her grey eyes looked strange and light therein.

But Ralph leapt up, and half drew his sword, and cried out loud: "Would God I had slain him! Wherefore could I not slay him?" And he strode up and down the sward before her in his wrath. But she leaned forward to him and laughed and said: "Yet, O Champion, we will not go back to him, for he is stronger than thou, and hath vanquished thee. This is a desert place, but thou art loud, and maybe over loud. Come rest by me."

So he came and sat down by her, and took her hand again and kissed the wrist therof and fondled it and said: "Yea, but he desireth thee sorely; that was easy to see. It was my ill-luck that I slew him not."

She stroked his face again and said: "Long were the tale if I told thee all. After he had driven me out, and I had fled from him, he fell in with me again divers times, as was like to be; for his brother is the Captain of the Dry Tree; the tall

136

man whom thou hast seen with me: and every time this baron hath come on me he has prayed my love, as one who would die despaired if I granted it not, but O my love with the bright sword" (and she kissed his cheek therewith, and fondled his hand with both her hands), "each time I said him nay, I said him nay." And again her face burned with blushes.

"And his brother," said Ralph, "the big captain that I have come across these four times, doth he desire thee also?" She laughed and said: "But as others have, no more: he will not slay any man for my sake."

Said Ralph: "Didst thou wot that I was abiding thy coming at the Castle of Abundance?" "Yea," she said, "have I not told thee that I bade Roger lead thee thither?" Then she said softly: "That was after that first time we met; after I had ridden away on the horse of that butcher whom thou slayedst."

"But why camest thou so late?" said he; "Wouldst thou have come if I had abided there yet?" She said: "What else did I desire but to be with thee? But I set out alone looking not for any peril, since our riders had gone to the north against them of the Burg: but as I drew near to the Water of the Oak, I fell in with my husband and that other man; and this time all my naysays were of no avail, and whatsoever I might say he constrained me to go with them; but straightway they fell out together, and fought, even as thou sawest." And she looked at him sweetly, and as frankly as if he had been naught but her dearest brother.

But he said: "It was concerning thee that they fought: hast thou known the Black Knight for long?"

"Yea," she said, "I may not hide that he hath loved me: but he hath also betrayed me. It was through him that the Knight of the Sun drave me from him. Hearken, for this concerneth thee: he made a tale of me of true and false mingled, that I was a wise-wife and an enchantress, and my lord trowed in him, so that I was put to shame before all the house, and driven forth wrung with anguish, barefoot and bleeding."

He looked and saw pain and grief in her face, as it had been the shadow of that past time, and the fierceness of love in him so changed his face, that she arose and drew a little way from him, and stood there gazing at him. But he also rose and knelt before her, and reached up for her hands and took them in his and said: "Tell me truly, and beguile me not; for I am a young man, and without guile, and I love thee, and would have thee for my speech-friend, what woman soever may be in the world. Whatever thou hast been, what art thou now? Art thou good or evil? Wilt thou bless me or ban me? For it is the truth that I have heard tales and tales of thee: many were good, though it maybe strange; but some, they seemed to warn me of evil in thee. O look at me, and see if I love thee or not! and I may not help it. Say once for all, shall that be for my ruin or my bliss? If thou hast been evil, then be good this one time and tell me."

She neither reddened now, nor paled at his words, but her eyes filled with tears, and ran over, and she looked down on him as a woman looks on a man that she loves from the heart's root, and she said: "O my lord and love, may it be that thou shalt find me no worse to thee than the best of all those tales. Forsooth how shall I tell thee of myself, when, whatever I say, thou shalt believe every word I tell thee? But O my heart, how shouldest thou, so sweet and fair and good, be taken with the love of an evil thing? At the least I will say this, that whatsoever I have been, I am good to thee—I am good to thee, and will be true to thee."

He drew her down to him as he knelt there, and took his arms about her, and though she yet shrank from him a little and the eager flame of his love, he might not be gainsayed, and she gave herself to him and let her body glide into his arms, and loved him no less than he loved her. And there between them in the wilderness was all the joy of love that might be.

CHAPTER 2

They Break Their Fast
in the Wildwood

Now when it was hard on noon, and they had lain long in that grassy place, Ralph rose up and stood upon his feet, and made as one listening. But the Lady looked on him and said: "It is naught save a hart and his hind running in the wood; yet mayhappen we were best on the road, for it is yet long." "Yea," said Ralph, "and it may be that my master will gather folk and pursue us." "Nay, nay," she said, "that were to wrong him, to deem that he would gather folk to follow one man; if he come, he will be by himself alone. When he found us gone he doubtless cast himself on Silverfax, my horse, in trust of the beast following after my feet."

"Well," said Ralph, "and if he come alone, there is yet a sword betwixt him and thee."

She was standing up by him now with her hand on his shoulder, "Hear now the darling, the champion! how he trusteth well in his heart and his right hand. But nay, I have cared for thee well. Hearken, if thou wilt not take it amiss that I tell thee all I do, good or evil. I said a word in the ear of Silverfax or ever I departed, and now the good beast knows my mind, and will lead the fierce lord a little astray, but not too much, lest he follow us with his eager heart and be led by his own keen woodcraft. Indeed, I left the horse behind to that end, else hadst thou ridden the woodland ways with me, instead of my wearying thee by our going afoot; and thou with thy weapons and wargear."

He looked upon her tenderly, and said smiling: "And thou, my dear, art thou not a little wearied by what should weary a knight and one bred afield?" "Nay," she said, "seest thou not how I walk lightly clad, whereas I have left behind my mantle and cote-hardie?" Thereat she gathered up her gown into her girdle ready for the way, and smiled as she saw his eyes embrace the loveliness of her feet; and she spake as she moved them daintily on the flowery grass: "Sooth to say, Knight, I am no weakling dame, who cannot move her limbs save in the dance, or to back the white palfrey and ride the meadows, goshawk on wrist; I am both well-knit and light-foot as the Wood-wife and Goddess of yore agone. Many a toil hath gone to that, whereof I may tell thee presently; but now we were best on our way. Yet before we go, I will at least tell thee this, that in my knowing of these woods, there is no sorcery at all; for in the woods, though not in these woods, was I bred; and here also I am at home, as I may say."

Hand in hand then they went lightly through the hazel copse, and soon was the wood thick about them, but, as before, the Lady led unfalteringly through the thicket paths. Now Ralph spake and said: "It is good that thou lead me whither thou wilt; but this I may say, that it is clear to me that we are not on the way to the Castle of Abundance." "Even so," said she; "indeed had I come to thee there, as I was minded, I should presently have brought thee on the way which we are wending now, or one nigh to it; and that is that which leadeth to Hampton under Scaur, and the Fellowship of Champions who dwell on the rock."

Said Ralph: "It is well; yet will I tell thee the truth, that a little sojourn in that fair house had liked me better. Fain had I been to see thee sitting in thine ivory chair in thy chamber of dais with the walls hung round with thee woven in pictures—wilt thou not tell me in words the story of those pictures? and also concerning the book which I read, which was also of thee?"

"Ah," she said, "thou hast read in the book—well, I will tell thee the story very soon, and that the more since there are matters written wrong in the book." Therewith she hurried him on, and her feet seemed never tired, though now, to say sooth, he began to go somewhat heavily.

Then she stayed him, and laughed sweetly in his face, and said: "It is a long while now since the beginning of the June day, and meseems I know thy lack, and the slaking of it lieth somewhat nearer than Hampton under Scaur, which we shall not reach these two days if we go afoot all the way."

"My lack?" said he; "I lack nought now, that I may not have when I will." And he put his arms about her shoulders and strained her to his bosom. But she strove with him, and freed herself and laughed outright, and said: "Thou art a bold man, and rash, my knight, even unto me. Yet must I see to it that thou die not of hunger." He said merrily: "Yea, by St. Nicholas, true it is: a while ago I felt no hunger, and had forgotten that men eat; for I was troubled with much longing, and in doubt concerning my life; but now am I free and happy, and hungry therewithal."

"Look," she said, pointing up to the heavens, "it is now past two hours after noon; that is nigh two hours since we left the lawn amidst the hazels, and thou longest to eat, as is but right, so lovely as thou art and young; and I withal long to tell thee something of that whereof thou hast asked me; and lastly, it is the hottest of the day, yea, so hot, that even Diana, the Wood-wife of yore agone, might have fainted somewhat, if she had been going afoot as we twain have been, and little is the risk of our resting awhile. And hereby is a place where rest is good as regards the place, whatever the resters may be; it is a little aside the straightest way, but meseems we may borrow an hour or so of our journey, and hope to pay it back ere nightfall. Come, champion!"

Therewith she led north through a thicket of mingled trees till Ralph heard water running, and anon they came to a little space about a brook, grassy and clear of trees save a few big thorn-bushes, with a green ridge or bank on the other side. There she stayed him and said: "Do off thy war-gear, knight. There is naught to fear here, less than there was amidst the hazels." So did he, and she kneeled down and drank of the clear water, and washed her face and hands therein, and then came and kissed him and said: "Lovely imp of Upmeads, I have some bread of last night's meal in my scrip here, and under the bank I shall find some woodland meat withal; abide a little and the tale and the food shall come back to thee together." Therewith she stepped lightly into the stream, and stood therein a minute to let her naked feet feel the cold ripple (for she had stripped off her foot-gear as she first came to the water), and then went hither and thither gathering strawberries about the bank, while he watched her, blessing her, till he well nigh wept at the thought of his happiness.

Back she came in a little while with good store of strawberries in the lap of her gown, and they sat down on the green lip of the brook, and she drew the bread from her scrip and they ate together, and she made him drink from the hollow of her hands, and kissed him and wept over him for joy, and the eagerness of her love. So at last she sat down quietly beside him, and fell to speaking to him, as a tale is told in the ingle nook on an even of Yule-tide.

CHAPTER 3

The Lady Telleth Ralph of the Past Days of Her Life

"Now shalt thou hear of me somewhat more than the arras and the book could tell thee; and yet not all , for time would fail us therefor—and moreover my heart would fail me. I cannot tell where I was born nor of what lineage, nor of who were my father and mother; for this I have known not of myself, nor has any told me. But when I first remember anything, I was playing about a garden, wherein was a little house built of timber and thatched with reed, and the great trees of the forest were all about the garden save for a little croft which was grown over with high grass and another somewhat bigger, wherein were goats. There was a woman at the door of the house and she spinning, yet clad in glittering raiment, and with jewels on her neck and fingers; this was the first thing that I remember, but all as it were a matter of every day, and use and wont, as it goes with the memories of children. Of such matters I will not tell thee at large, for thou knowest how it will be. Now the woman, who as I came to know was neither old nor young in those days, but of middle age, I called mother; but now I know that she was not my mother. She was hard and stern with me, but never beat me in those days, save to make me do what I would not have done unbeaten; and as to meat I ate and drank what I could get, as she did, and indeed was well-fed with simple meats as thou mayest suppose from the aspect of me to-day. But as she was not fierce but rather sour to me in her daily wont in my youngest days so also she was never tender, or ever kissed me or caressed me, for as little as I was. And I loved her naught, nor did it ever come into my mind that I should love her, though I loved a white goat of ours and deemed it dear and lovely; and afterwards other things also that came to me from time to time, as a squirrel that I saved from a weasel, and a jackdaw that fell from a tall ash-tree nigh our house before he had learned how to fly, and a house-mouse that would run up and down my hand and arm, and other such-like things; and shortly I may say that the wild things, even to the conies and fawns loved me, and had but little fear of me, and made me happy, and I loved them.

"Further, as I grew up, the woman set me to do such work as I had strength for as needs was; for there was no man dwelt anigh us and seldom did I ever see man or woman there, and held no converse with any, save as I shall tell thee presently: though now and again a man or a woman passed by; what they were I knew not, nor their whence and whither, but by seeing them I came to know that there were other folk in the world besides us two. Nought else I knew save how to spin, and to tend our goats and milk them, and to set snares for birds and small deer: though when I had caught them, it irked me sore to kill them, and I had let them go again had I not feared the carline. Every day early I was put forth from the house and garth, and forbidden to go back thither till dusk. While the days were long and the grass was growing, I had to lead our goats to pasture in the wood-lawns, and must take with me rock and spindle, and spin so much of flax or hair as the woman gave me, or be beaten. But when the winter came and the snow was on the ground, then that watching and snaring of wild things was my business.

"At last one day of late summer when I, now of some fifteen summers, was pasturing the goats not far from the

143

house, the sky darkened, and there came up so great a storm of thunder and lightning, and huge drift of rain, that I was afraid, and being so near to the house, I hastened thither, driving the goats, and when I had tethered them in the shed of the croft, I crept trembling up to the house, and when I was at the door, heard the clack of the loom in the weaving-chamber, and deemed that the woman was weaving there, but when I looked, behold there was no one on the bench, though the shuttle was flying from side to side, and the shed opening and changing, and the sley coming home in due order. Therewithal I heard a sound as of one singing a song in a low voice, but the words I could not understand: then terror seized on my heart, but I stepped over the threshold, and as the door of the chamber was open, I looked aside and saw therein the woman sitting stark naked on the floor with a great open book before her, and it was from her mouth that the song was coming: grim she looked, and awful, for she was a big woman, black-haired and stern of aspect in her daily wont, speaking to me as few words as might be, and those harsh enough, yea harsher than when I was but little. I stood for one moment afraid beyond measure, though the woman did not look at me, and I hoped she had not seen me; then I ran back into the storm, though it was now wilder than ever, and ran and hid myself in the thicket of the wood, half-dead with fear, and wondering what would become of me. But finding that no one followed after me, I grew calmer, and the storm also drew off, and the sun shone out a little before his setting: so I sat and spun, with fear in my heart, till I had finished my tale of thread, and when dusk came, stole back again to the house, though my legs would scarce bear me over the threshold into the chamber.

"There sat the woman in her rich attire no otherwise than her wont, nor did she say aught to me; but looked at the yarn that I had spun, to see that I had done my task, and nodded sternly to me as her wont was, and I went to bed amongst my goats as I was used to do, but slept not till towards morning, and then images of dreadful things, and of miseries that I may not tell thee of, mingled with my sleep for long.

"So I awoke and ate my meat and drank of the goats' milk

with a heavy heart, and then went into the house; and when I came into the chamber the woman looked at me, and contrary to her wont spoke to me, and I shook with terror at her voice; though she said naught but this: 'Go fetch thy white goat and come back to me therewith.' I did so, and followed after her, sick with fear; and she led me through the wood into a lawn which I knew well, round which was a wall, as it were, of great yew trees, and amidst, a table of stone, made of four uprights and a great stone plank on the top of them; and this was the only thing in all the wood wherein I was used to wander which was of man's handiwork, save and except our house, and the sheds and fences about it.

"The woman stayed and leaned against this stonework and said to me: 'Go about now and gather dry sticks for a fire.' I durst do naught else, and said to myself that I should be whipped if I were tardy, though, forsooth, I thought she was going to kill me; and I brought her a bundle, and she said, 'Fetch more.' And when I had brought her seven bundles, she said: 'It is enough: stand over against me and hearken.' So I stood there quaking; for my fear, which had somewhat abated while I went to and fro after the wood, now came back upon me tenfold.

"She said: 'It were thy due that I should slay thee here and now, as thou slayest the partridges which thou takest in thy springes: but for certain causes I will not slay thee. Again, it were no more than thy earnings were I to torment thee till thou shouldst cry out for death to deliver thee from the anguish; and if thou wert a woman grown, even so would I deal with thee. But thou art yet but a child, therefore I will keep thee to see what shall befall betwixt us. Yet must I do somewhat to grieve thee, and moreover something must be slain and offered up here on this altar, lest all come to naught, both thou and I, and that which we have to do. Hold thy white goat now, which thou lovest more than aught else, that I may redden thee and me and this altar with the blood thereof.'

"I durst do naught but obey her, and I held the poor beast, that licked my hands and bleated for love of me: and now since my terror and the fear of death was lessened at her words, I wept sore for my dear friend.

"But the woman drew a strong sharp knife from her girdle and cut the beast's throat, and dipped her fingers in the blood and reddened both herself and me on the breast, and the hands, and the feet; and then she turned to the altar and smote blood upon the uprights, and the face of the stone plank. Then she bade me help her, and we laid the seven faggots on the alter, and laid the carcase of the goat upon them: and she made fire, but I saw not how, and set it to the wood, and when it began to blaze she stood before it with her arms outspread, and sang loud and hoarse to a strange tune; and though I knew not the words of her song, it filled me with dread, so that I cast myself down on the ground and hid my face in the grass.

"So she went on till the beast was all burned up and the fire became naught but red embers, and then she ceased her song and sank down upon the grass, and laid her head back and so fell asleep; but I durst not move from the place, but cowered in the grass there, I know not how long, till she arose and came to me, and smote me with her foot and cried: 'Rise up, fool! what harm hast thou? Go milk thy goats and lead them to pasture.' And therewith she strode away home, not heeding me.

"As for me, I arose and dealt with my goats as she bade me; and presently I was glad that I had not been slain, yet thenceforth was the joy of my life that I had had amongst my goats marred with fear, and the sounds of the woodland came to me mingled with terror; and I was sore afraid when I entered the house in the morning and the evening, and when I looked on the face of the woman; though she was no harder to me than heretofore, but maybe somewhat softer.

"So wore the autumn, and winter came, and I fared as I was wont, setting springes for fowl and small-deer. And for all the roughness of the season, at that time it pleased me better than the leafy days, because I had less memory then of the sharpness of my fear on that day of the altar. Now one day as I went under the snow-laden trees, I saw something bright and big lying on the ground, and drawing nearer I saw that it was some child of man: so I stopped and cried out, 'Awake and arise, lest death come on thee in this bitter cold,' But it stirred not; so I plucked up heart and came up to it,

146

and lo! a woman clad in fair raiment of scarlet and fur, and I knelt down by her to see if I might help her; but when I touched her I found her cold and stiff, and dead, though she had not been dead long, for no snow had fallen on her. It still wanted more than an hour of twilight, and I by no means durst go home till nightfall; so I sat on there and watched her, and put the hood from her face and the gloves from her hands, and I deemed her a goodly and lovely thing, and was sorry that she was not alive, and I wept for her, and for myself also, that I had lost her fellowship. So when I came back to the house at dark with the venison, I knew not whether to tell my mistress and tyrant concerning this matter; but she looked on me and said at once: 'Wert thou going to tell me of something that thou hast seen?' So I told her all, even as it was, and she said to me: 'Hast thou taken aught from the corpse?' 'Nay,' said I. 'Then must I hasten,' she said, 'and be before the wolves.' Therewith she took a brand from the fire, and bade me bear one also and lead her: so did I easily enough, for the moon was up, and what with moon and snow, it was well nigh as bright as the day. So when we came to the dead woman, my mistress kneeled down by her and undid the collar of her cloak, which I had not touched, and took something from her neck swiftly, and yet I, who was holding the torch, saw that it was a necklace of blue stones and green, with gold between—Yea, dear Champion, like unto thine as one peascod is to another," quoth she.

And therewith the distressfulness of her face which had worn Ralph's heart while she had been telling her tale changed, and she came, as it were, into her new life and the love of him again, and she kissed him and laid her cheek to his and he kissed her mouth. And then she fetched a sigh, and began with her story again.

"My mistress took the necklace and put it in her pouch, and said as to herself: 'Here, then, is another seeker who hath not found, unless one should dig a pit for her here when the thaw comes, and call it the Well at the World's End: belike it will be for her as helpful as the real one.' Then she turned to me and said: 'Do thou with the rest what thou wilt,' and therewith she went back hastily to the house. But as for me, I went back also, and found a pick and a mattock in the goat-house, and came back in the moonlight and scraped the snow away, and dug a pit, and buried the poor damsel there with all her gear.

"Wore the winter thence with naught that I need tell of, only I thought much of the words that my mistress had spoken. Spring came and went, and summer also, well nigh tidingless. But one day as I drave the goats from our house there came from the wood four men, a-horseback and weaponed, but so covered with their armour that I might see little of their faces. They rode past me to our house, and spake not to me, though they looked hard at me; but as they went past I heard one say: 'If she might but be our guide to the Well at the World's End!' I durst not tarry to speak with them, but as I looked over my shoulder I saw them talking to my mistress in the door; but meseemed she was clad but in poor homespun cloth instead of her rich apparel, and I am far-sighted and clear-sighted. After this the autumn and winter that followed it passed away tidingless.

CHAPTER 4

The Lady Tells of Her
Deliverance

"Now I had outgrown my old fear, and not much befell to quicken it: and ever I was as much out of the house as I could be. But about this time my mistress, from being kinder to me than before, began to grow harder, and ofttimes used me cruelly: but of her deeds to me, my friend, thou shalt ask me no more than I tell thee. On a day of May-tide I fared abroad with my goats, and went far with them, further from the house than I had been as yet. The day was the fairest of the year, and I rejoiced in it, and felt as if some exceeding great good were about to befall me; and the burden of fears seemed to have fallen from me. So I went till I came to a

148

little flowery dell, beset with blossoming whitethorns and with a fair stream running through it; a place somewhat like to this, save that the stream there was bigger. And the sun was hot about noontide, so I did off my raiment, which was rough and poor, and more meet for winter than May-tide, and I entered a pool of the clear water, and bathed me and sported therein, smelling the sweet scent of the whitethorns and hearkening to the song of the many birds; and when I came forth from the water, the air was so soft and sweet to me, and the flowery grass so kind to my feet, and the May-blooms fell upon my shoulders, that I was loth to do on my rough raiment hastily, and withal I looked to see no child of man in that wilderness: so I sported myself there a long while, and milked a goat and drank of the milk, and crowned myself with white-thorn and hare-bells; and held the blossoms in my hand, and felt that I also had some might in me, and that I should not be a thrall of that sorceress for ever. And that day, my friend, belike was the spring-tide of the life and the love that thou holdest in thy kind arms.

"But as I abode thus in that fair place, and had just taken my rock and spindle in hand that I might go on with my task and give as little occasion as I might for my mistress to chastise me, I looked up and saw a child of man coming down the side of the little dale towards me, so I sprang up, and ran to my raiment and cast them on me hastily, for I was ashamed; and when I saw that it was a woman, I thought at first that it was my mistress coming to seek me; and I thought within myself that if she smote me I would bear it no more, but let it be seen which of the twain was the mightier. But I looked again and saw that it was not she but a woman smaller and older. So I stood where I was and abode her coming, smiling and unafraid, and half-clad.

"She drew near and I saw that it was an old woman grey haired, uncomely of raiment, but with shining bright eyes in her wrinkled face. And she made an obeisance to me and said: 'I was passing through this lonely wilderness and I looked down into the little valley and saw these goats there and the lovely lady lying naked amongst them, and I said I am too old to be afraid of aught; for if she be a goddess come back again from yore agone, she can but make an end of a poor old carline, a gangrel body, who hath no joy of her life now. And if she be of the daughters of men, she will belike methink her of her mother, and be kind to me for her sake, and give me a piece of bread and a draught of her goats' milk.'

"I spake hastily, for I was ashamed of her words, though I only half understood them: 'I hear thee and deem that thou mockest me: I have never known a mother; I am but a poor thrall, a goatherd dwelling with a mistress in a nook of this wildwood: I have never a piece of bread; but as to the goats' milk, that thou shalt have at once.' So I called one of my goats to me, for I knew them all, and milked her into a wooden bowl that I carried slung about me, and gave the old woman to drink: and she kissed my hand and drank and spake again, but no longer in a whining voice, like a beggar bidding alms in the street, but frank and free.

" 'Damsel,' she said, 'now I see that thy soul goes with thy body, and that thou art kind and proud at once. And whatever thou art, it is no mock to say of thee, that thou art as fair as the fairest; and I think that this will follow thee, that henceforth no man who seeth thee once will forget thee ever, of cease to long for thee: of a surety this is they weird. Now I see that thou knowest no more of the world and its ways than one of the hinds that run in these woods. So if thou wilt, I will sit down by thee and tell thee much that shall avail thee; and thou in thy turn shalt tell me all the tale concerning thy dwelling and thy service, and the like.'

"I said, I may not, I durst not; I serve a mighty mistress, and she would slay me if she knew that I had spoken to thee; and woe's me! I fear that even now she will not fail to know it. Depart in peace."

" 'Nay,' she said, 'thou needest not tell me, for I have an inkling of her and her ways: but I will give thee wisdom, and not sell it thee at a price. Sit down then, fair child, on this flowery grass, and I will sit beside thee and tell thee of many things worth thine heeding.' So there we sat awhile, and in good sooth she told me much of the world which I had not yet seen, of its fairness and its foulness; of life and death, and desire and disappointment, and despair; so that when she had done, if I were wiser than erst, I was perchance little more

150

joyous; and yet I said to myself that come what would I would be a part of all that.

"But at last she said: 'Lo the day is waning, and thou hast two things to do; either to go home to thy mistress at once, or flee away from her by the way that I shall show thee; and if thou wilt be ruled by me, and canst bear thy thralldom yet a little while thou wilt not flee at once, but abide till thou hast seen me again. And since it is here that thou hast met me, here mayst thou meet me again; for the days are long now, and thou mayst easily win thy way hither before noon on any day.'

"So I tied my goatskin shoes to my feet, and drave my goats together, and we went up together out of the dale, and were in the wide-spreading plain of the waste; and the carline said: 'Dost thou know the quarters of the heaven by the sun?' 'Yea,' said I. 'Then,' quoth she, 'whenso thou desirest to depart and come into the world of folk that I have told thee of, set thy face a little north of west, and thou shalt fall in with something or somebody before long; but be speedy on that day as thou art light-footed, and make all the way thou canst before thy mistress comes to know of thy departure; for not lightly will any one let loose such a thrall as thou.'

"I thanked her, and she went her ways over the waste, I wotted not whither, and I drave my goats home as speedily as I might; the mistress meddled not with me by word or deed, though I was short of my due tale of yarn. The next day I longed sore to go to the dale and meet the carline but durst not, and the next day I fared in likeways; but the third day I longed so to go, that my feet must needs take me there, whatsoever might befall. And when I had been in the dale a little, thither came the carline, and sat down by me and fell to teaching me wisdom, and showed me letters and told me what they were, and I learned like a little lad in the chorister's school.

"Thereafter I mastered my fear of my mistress and went to that dale day by day, and learned of the carline; though at whiles I wondered when my mistress would let loose her fury upon me; for I called to mind the threat she had made to me on the day when she offered up my white goat. And I made up my mind to this, that if she fell upon me with deadly intent

151

I would do my best to slay her before she should slay me. But so it was, that now again she held her hand from my body, and scarce cast a word at me ever, but gloomed at me, and fared as if hatred of me had grown great in her heart.

"So the days went by, and my feet had worn a path through the wilderness to the Dale of Lore, and May had melted into June, and the latter days of June were come. And on Midsummer Day I went my ways to the dale according to my wont, when, as I as driving on my goats hastily I saw a bright thing coming over the heath toward me, and I went on my way to meet it, for I had no fear now, except what fear of my mistress lingered in my heart; nay, I looked that everything I saw of new should add some joy to my heart. So presently I saw that it was a weaponed man riding a white horse, and anon he had come up to me and drawn rein before me. I wondered exceedingly at beholding him and the heart leaped within me at his beauty; for though the carline had told me of the loveliness of the sons of men, that was but words and I knew not what they meant; and the others that I had seen were not young men or goodly, and those last, as I told thee, I could scarce see their faces.

"And this one was even fairer than the dead woman that I had buried, whose face was worn with toil and trouble, as now I called to mind. He was clad in bright shining armour with a gay surcoat of green, embroidered with flowers over it; he had a light sallet on his head, and the yellow locks of his hair flowed down from under, and fell on his shoulders: his face was as beardless as thine, dear friend, but not clear brown like to thine but white and red like a blossom."

Ralph spake and said: "Belike it was a woman?" and his voice sounded loud in the quiet place. She smiled on him and kissed his cheek, and said: "Nay, nay, dear Champion, it is not so. God rest his soul! many a year he has been dead."

Said Ralph: "Many a year! what meanest thou?" "Ah!" she said, "fear not! as I am now, so shall I be for thee many a year. Was not thy fear that I should vanish away or change into something unsightly and gruesome? Fear not, I say; am I not a woman, and thine own?" And again she flushed bright red, and her grey eyes lightened, and she looked at him all confused and shamefaced.

He took her face between his hands and kissed her over and over; then he let her go, and said: "I have no fear: go on with thy tale, for the words thereof are as thy kisses to me, and the embracing of thine hands and thy body: tell on, I pray thee." She took his hand in hers and spake, telling her tale as before.

"Friend, well-beloved for ever! This fair young knight looked on me, and as he looked, his face flushed as red as mine did even now. And I tell thee that my heart danced with joy as I looked on him, and he spake not for a little while, and then he said: 'Fair maiden, canst thou tell me of any who will tell me a word of the way to the Well at the World's End?' I said to him, 'Nay, I have heard the word once and no more, I know not the way: and I am sorry that I cannot do for thee that which thou wouldest.' And then I spake again, and told him that he should by no means stop at our house, and I told him what it was like, so that he might give it the go by. I said, 'Even if thou hast to turn back again, and fail to find the thing thou seekest, yet I beseech thee ride not into that trap.'

"He sat still on his saddle a while, staring at me and I at him; and then he thanked me, but with so bad a grace, that I wondered of him if he were angry; and then he shook his rein, and rode off briskly, and I looked after him a while, and then went on my way; but I had gone but a short while, when I heard horse-hoofs behind me, and I turned and looked, and lo! it was the knight coming back again. So I stayed and abided him; and when he came up to me, he leapt from his horse and stood before me and said: 'I must needs see thee once again.'

"I stood and trembled before him, and longed to touch him. And again he spake, breathlessly, as one who has been running: 'I must depart, for I have a thing to do that I must do; but I long sorely to touch thee, and kiss thee; yet unless thou freely willest it, I will refrain me.' Then I looked at him and said, 'I will it freely.' Then he came close up to me, and put his hand on my shoulder and kissed my cheek; but I kissed his lips, and then he took me in his arms, and kissed me and embraced me; and there in that place, and in a little while, we loved each other sorely.

153

"But in a while he said to me: 'I must depart, for I am as one whom the Avenger of Blood followeth; and now I will give thee this, not so much as a gift, but as a token that we have met in the wilderness, thou and I.' Therewith he put his hand to his neck, and took from it this necklace which thou seest here, and I saw that it was like that which my mistress took from the neck of the dead woman. And no less is it like to the one that thou wearest, Ralph.

"I took it in my hand and wept that I might not help him. And he said: 'It is little likely that we shall meet again; but by the token of this collar thou mayest wot that I ever long for thee till I die: for though I am a king's son, this is the dearest of my possessions.' I said: 'Thou art young, and I am young; mayhappen we shall meet again: but thou shalt know that I am but a thrall, a goatherd.' For I knew by what the old woman told me of somewhat of the mightiness of the kings of the world. 'Yea,' he said, and smiled most sweetly, 'that is easy to be seen: yet if I live, as I think not to do, thou shalt sit where great men shall kneel to thee; not as I kneel now for love, and that I may kiss thy knees and thy feet, but because they needs must worship thee.'

"Therewith he arose to his feet and leapt on his horse, and rode his ways speedily: and I went upon my way with my goats, and came down into the Dale of Lore, and found the old woman abiding me; and she came to me, and took me by the hands, and touched the collar (for I had done it about my neck), and said:

"'Dear child, thou needest not to tell me thy tale, for I have seen him. But if thou must needs wear this necklace, I must give thee a gift to go with it. But first sit down by the old carline awhile and talk with her; for meseemeth it will be but a few days ere thou shalt depart from this uttermost wilderness, and the woods before the mountains.

"So I sat down by her, and in spite of her word I told her all that had befallen betwixt me and the king's son: for my heart was too full that I might refrain me. She nodded her head from time to time, but said naught, till I had made an end: and then fell to telling me of many matters for my avail; but yet arose earlier than her wont was; and when we were about sundering on the path which I had trodden above the Dale, she said: 'Now must I give thee that gift to go along with the gift of the lover, the King's son; and I think thou wilt find it of avail before many days are gone by.' Therewith she took from her pouch a strong sharp knife, and drew it from the sheath, and flashed it in the afternoon sun, and gave it to me; and I took it and laid it in my bosom and thanked her; for I thought that I understood her meaning, and how it would avail me. Then I went driving my goats home speedily, so that the sun was barely set when I came to the garth; and a great horror rather than a fear of my mistress was on me; and lo! she stood in the door of the house gazing down the garth and the woodland beyond, as though she were looking for my coming: and when her eyes lighted on me, she scowled, and drew her lips back from her teeth and clenched her hands with fury, though there was nought in them; and she was a tall and strong woman, though now growing somewhat old: but as for me, I had unsheathed the carline's gift before I came to the garth, and now I held it behind my back in my left hand.

"I had stayed my feet some six paces from the threshold, and my heart beat quick, but the sick fear and cowering had left me, though the horror of her grew in my heart. My goats had all gone off quietly to their house, and there was nothing betwixt me and her. In clearing from my sleeve the arm of me which held the knife, the rough clasp which fastened my raiment together at the shoulder had given way, and the cloth had fallen and left my bosom bare, so that I knew that the collar was clearly to be seen. So we stood a moment, and I had no words, but she spake at last in a hard, snarling voice, such as she oftenest used to me, but worse.

" 'Now at last the time has come when thou art of no more use to me; for I can see thee what thou hast got for thyself. But know now that thou hast not yet drunk of the Well at the World's End, and that it will not avail thee to flee out of this wood; for as long as I live thou wilt not be able to get out of reach of my hand; and I shall live long: I shall live long. Come, then, and give thyself up to me, that I may deal with thee as I threatened when I slew thy friend the white goat; for, indeed, I knew then that it would come to this.'

"She had but twice or thrice spoken to me so many words

155

together as this; but I answered never a word, but stood watching her warily. And of a sudden she gave forth a dreadful screaming roar, wherewith all the wood rang again, and rushed at me; but my hand came from behind my back, and how it was I know not, but she touched me not till the blade had sunk into her breast, and she fell across my feet, her right hand clutching my raiment. So I loosed her fingers from the cloth, shuddering with horror the while, and drew myself away from her and stood a little aloof, wondering what should happen next. And indeed I scarce believed but she would presently rise up from the ground and clutch me in her hands, and begin the tormenting of me. But she moved no more, and the grass all about her was reddened with her blood; and at last I gathered heart to kneel down beside her, and found that she no more breathed than one of those conies or partridges which I had been used to slay for her.

"Then I stood and considered what I should do, and indeed I had been pondering this all the way from the Dale thereto, in case I should escape my mistress. So I soon made up my mind that I would not dwell in that house even for one night; lest my mistress should come to me though dead, and torment me. I went into the house while it was yet light, and looked about the chamber, and saw three great books there laid on the lectern, but durst not have taken them even had I been able to carry them; nor durst I even to look into them, for fear that some spell might get to work in them if they were opened; but I found a rye loaf whereof I had eaten somewhat in the morning, and another untouched, and hanging to a horn of the lectern I found the necklace which my mistress had taken from the dead woman. These I put into my scrip, and as to the necklace, I will tell thee how I bestowed it later on. Then I stepped out into the twilight which was fair and golden, and full fain I was of it. Then I drove the goats out of their house and went my way towards the Dale of Lore, and said to myself that the carline would teach me what further to do, and I came there before the summer dark had quite prevailed, and slept sweetly and softly amongst my goats after I had tethered them in the best of the pasture.

156

CHAPTER 5

Yet More of the Lady's Story

"Lo thou, beloved," she said, "thou hast seen me in the wildwood with little good quickened in me: doth not thine heart sink at the thought of thy love and thy life given over to the keeping of such an one?" He smiled in her face, and said: "Belike thou hast done worse than all thou hast told me: and these days past I have wondered often what there was in the stories which they of the Burg had against thee: yet sooth to say, they told little of what thou hast done: no more belike than being their foe." She sighed and said: "Well, hearken; yet shall I not tell thee every deed that I have been partaker in.

"I sat in the Dale that next day and was happy, though I longed to see that fair man again: sooth to say, since my mistress was dead, everything seemed fairer to me, yea even mine own face, as I saw it in the pools of the stream, though whiles I wondered when I should have another mistress, and how she would deal with me; and ever I said I would ask the carline when she came again to me. But all that day she came not: nor did I marvel thereat. But when seven days passed and still she came not, I fell to wondering what I should do: for my bread was all gone, and I durst not go back to the house to fetch meal; though there was store of it there. Howbeit, I drank of the milk of the goats, and made curds thereof with the woodland roots, and ate of the wood-berries like as thou hast done, friend, e'en now. And it was easier for me to find a livelihood in the woods than it had been for most folk, so well as I knew them. So wore the days, and she came not, and I began to think that I should see the wise carline no more, as indeed fell out at that time; and the days began to hang heavy on my hands, and I fell to

157

thinking of that way to the west and the peopled parts, whereof the carline had told me; and whiles I went out of the Dale and went away hither and thither through the woods, and so far, that thrice I slept away out of the Dale: but I knew that the peopled parts would be strange to me and I feared to face them all alone.

"Thus wore the days till July was on the wane, and on a morning early I awoke with unwonted sounds in mine ears; and when my eyes were fairly open I saw a man standing over me and a white horse cropping the grass hard by. And my heart was full and fain, and I sprang to my feet and showed him a smiling happy face, for I saw at once that it was that fair man come back again. But lo! his face was pale and worn, though he looked kindly on me, and he said: 'O my beloved, I have found thee, but I am faint with hunger and can speak but little.' And even therewith he sank down on the grass. But I bestirred myself, and gave him milk of my goats, and curds and berries, and the life came into him again, and I sat down by him and laid his head in my lap, and he slept a long while; and when he awoke (and it was towards sunset) he kissed my hands and my arms, and said to me: 'Fair child, perhaps thou wilt come with me now; and even if thou art a thrall thou mayest flee with me; for my horse is strong and fat, though I am weak, for he can make his dinner on the grass.'

"Then he laughed and I no less; but I fed him with my poor victual again, and as he ate I said: 'I am no mistress's thrall now; for the evening of the day whereon I saw thee I slew her, else had she slain me.' 'The saints be praised,' said he: 'Thou wilt come with me, then?' 'O yea,' said I. Then I felt shamefaced and I reddened; but I said: 'I have abided here many days for a wise woman who hath taught me many things; but withal I hoped that thou wouldst come also.'

"Then he put his arms about my shoulders and loved me much; but at last he said: "Yet is it now another thing than that which I looked for, when I talked of setting thee by me on the golden throne. For now am I a beaten man; I have failed of that I sought, and suffered shame and hunger and many ills. Yet ever I thought that I might find thee here or hereby.' Then a thought came into my mind, and I said:

158

'Else maybe thou hadst found what thou soughtest, and overcome the evil things.' 'Maybe,' he said; 'it is now but a little matter.' "

"As for me, I could have no guess at what were the better things he had meant for me, and my heart was full of joy, and all seemed better than well. And we talked together long till the day was gone. Then we kissed and embraced each other in the Dale of Lore, and the darkness of summer seemed but short for our delight."

CHAPTER 6

The Lady Tells Somewhat of Her Doings After She Left the Wilderness

Ralph stayed her speech now, and said: "When I asked of thee in the Land of Abundance, there were some who seemed to say that thou hast let more men love thee than one: and it was a torment to me to think that even so it might be. But now when thine own mouth telleth me of one of them it irks me little. Dost thou think it little-hearted in me?"

"O friend," she said, "I see that so it is with thee that thou wouldst find due cause for loving me, whatever thou foundest true of me. Or dost thou deem that I was another woman in those days? Nay, I was not: I can see myself still myself all along the way I have gone." She was silent a little, and then she said: "Fear not, I will give thee much cause to love me. But now I know thy mind the better, I shall tell thee less of what befell me after I left the wilderness; for whatever I did and whatever I endured, still it was always I myself that was there, and it is me that thou lovest. Moreover, my life in the wilderness is a stranger thing to tell thee of than my dealings with the folk, and with Kings and Barons and Knights. But hereafter thou shalt hear of me what tales thou wilt of these matters, as the days and the years pass over our heads.

"Now on the morrow we would not depart at once, because there we had some victual, and the king's son was not yet so well fed as he should be; so we abode in that fair place another day, and then we went our ways westward, according to the rede of the carline; and it was many days before we gat us out of the wilderness, and we were often hard put to it for victual; whiles I sat behind my knight a-horseback, whiles he led the beast while I rode alone, and not seldom I went afoot, and that nowise slowly, while he rode the white horse, for I was as light-foot then as now.

"And of the way we went I will tell thee nought as now, because sure it is that if we both live, thou and I shall tread that road together, but with our faces turned the other way; for it is the road from the Well at the World's End, where I myself have been, or else never had thine eyes fallen on me."

Ralph said, "Even so much I deemed by reading in the book; yet it was not told clearly that thou hadst been there."

"Yea," she said, because the said book was made not by my friends but my foes, and they would have men deem that my length of days and the endurance of my beauty and never-dying youth of my heart came from evil and devilish sources; and if thou wilt trust my word it is not so, for in the Well at the World's End is no evil, but only the Quenching of Sorrow, and Clearing of the Eyes that they may behold. And how good it is that they look on thee now. And moreover, the history of that book is partly false of intention and ill-will, and partly a confused medley of true and false, which has come of mere chance-hap.

"Hearken now," she said, "till I tell thee in few word what befell me before I came to drink the Water of the Well. After we had passed long deserts of wood and heath, and gone through lands exceeding evil and perilous, and despaired of life for the horror of those places, and seen no men, we came at last amongst a simple folk who dealt kindly with us, yea, and more. These folk seemed to me happy and of good wealth, though to my lord they seemed poor and lacking of the goods of the world. Forsooth, by that time we lacked more than they, for we were worn with cold and

160

hunger, and hard life: though for me, indeed, happy had been the days of my wayfaring, but my lord remembered the days of his riches and the kingdom of his father, and the worship of mighty men, and all that he had promised me on the happy day when I first beheld him: so belike he was scarce so happy as I was.

"It was springtime when we came to that folk; for we had worn through the autumn and winter in getting clear of the wilderness. Not that the way was long, as I found out afterwards, but that we went astray in the woodland, and at last came out of it into a dreadful stony waste which we strove to cross thrice, and thrice were driven back into the greenwood by thirst and hunger; but the fourth time, having gotten us store of victual by my woodcraft, we overpassed it and reached the peopled country.

"Yea, spring was on the earth, as we, my lord and I, came down from the desolate stony heaths, and went hand and hand across the plain, where men and women of that folk were feasting round about the simple roofs and woodland halls which they had raised there. Then they left their games and sports and ran to us, and we walked on quietly, though we knew not whether the meeting was to be for death or life. But that kind folk gathered round us, and asked us no story till they had fed us, and bathed us, and clad us after their fashion. And then, despite the nakedness and poverty wherein they had first seen us, they would have it that we were gods sent down to them from the world beyond the mountains by their fathers of old time; for of Holy Church, and the Blessed Trinity, and the Mother of God they knew no more than did I at that time, but were heathen, as the Gentiles of yore agone. And even when we put all that Godhood from us, and told them as we might and could what we were (for we had no heart to lie to such simple folk), their kindness abated nothing, and they bade us abide there, and were our loving friends and brethren.

"There in sooth had I been content to abide till eld came upon me, but my lord would not have it so, but longed for greater things for me. Though in sooth to me it seemed as if his promise of worship of me by the folk had been already fulfilled; for when we had abided there some while, and our

161

beauty, which had been marred by the travail of our way-faring, had come back to us in full, or it maybe increased somewhat, they did indeed deal with us with more love than would most men with the saints, were they to come back on the earth again; and their children would gather round about me and make me a partaker of their sports, and be loth to leave me; and the faces of their old folk would quicken and gladden when I drew nigh: and as for their young men, it seemed of them that they loved the very ground that my feet trod on, though it grieved me that I could not pleasure some of them in such wise as they desired. And all this was soft and full of delight for my soul: and I, whose body a little while ago had been driven to daily toil with evil words and stripes, and who had known not what words of thanks and praise might mean!

"But so it must be that we should depart, and the kind folk showed us how sore their hearts were of our departure, but they gainsaid us in nowise, but rather furthered us all they might, and we went our ways from them riding on horned neat (for they knew not of horses), and driving one for a sumpter beast before us; and they had given us bows and arrows for our defence, and that we might get us venison.

"It is not to be said that we did not encounter perils; but thereof I will tell thee naught as now. We came to other peoples, richer and mightier than these, and I saw castles, and abbies, and churches, and walled towns, and wondered at them exceedingly. And in these places folk knew of the kingdom of my lord and his father, and whereas they were not of his foes (who lay for the more part on the other side of his land), and my lord could give sure tokens of what he was, we were treated with honour and worship, and my lord began to be himself again, and to bear him as a mighty man. And here to me was some gain in that poverty and nakedness wherewith we came out of the mountains and the raiment of the simple folk; for had I been clad in my poor cloth and goat-skins of the House of the Sorcerer, and he in his brave attire and bright armour, they would have said, it is a thrall that he is assotted of, and would have made some story and pretence of taking me from him; but they deemed me a great lady indeed, and a king's daughter, according to the tale that

162

he told them. Forsooth many men that saw me desired me beyond measure, and assuredly some great proud man or other would have taken me from my lord, but that they feared the wrath of his father, who was a mighty man indeed.

"Yea, one while as we sojourned by a certain town but a little outside the walls, a certain young man, a great champion and exceeding masterful, came upon me with his squires as I was walking in the meadows, and bore me off, and would have taken me to his castle, but that my lord followed with a few of the burghers, and there was a battle fought, wherein my lord was hurt; but the young champion he slew; and I cannot say but I was sorry of his death, though glad of my deliverance.

"Again, on a time we guested in a great baron's house, who dealt so foully by us that he gave my lord a sleeping potion in his good-night cup, and came to me in the dead night and required me of my love; and I would not, and he threatened me sorely, and called me a thrall and a castaway that my lord had picked up off the road: but I gat a knife in my hand and was for warding myself when I saw that my lord might not wake: so the felon went away for that time. But on the morrow came two evil men into the hall whom he had suborned, and bore false witness that I was a thrall and a runaway. So that the baron would have held me there (being a mighty man) despite my lord and his wrath and his grief, had not a young knight of his house been, who swore that he would slay him unless he let us go; and whereas there were other knights and squires there present who murmured, the baron was in a way compelled. So we departed, and divers of the said knights and squires went with us to see us safe on the way.

"But this was nigh to the kingdom of my lord's father, and that felon baron I came across again, and he was ever after one of my worst foes.

"Moreover, that young champion who had first stood up in the hall rode with us still, when the others had turned back; and I soon saw of him that he found it hard to keep his eyes off me; and that also saw my lord, and it was a near thing that they did not draw sword thereover: yet was that knight no evil man, but good and true, and I was exceedingly sorry for him; but I could not help him in the only way he would take help of me.

"Lo you, my friend, the beginnings of evil in those long past days, and the seeds of ill-hap sown in the field of my new life even before the furrow was turned.

"Well, we came soon into my lord's country, and fair and rich and lovely was it in those days; free from trouble and unpeace, a happy abode for the tillers of the soil, and the fashioners of wares. The tidings had gone to the king that my lord was come back, and he came to meet him with a great company of knights and barons, arrayed in the noblest fashion that such folk use; so that I was bewildered with their glory, and besought my lord to let me fall back out of the way, and perchance he might find me again. But he bade me ride on his right hand, for that I was the half of his life and his soul, and that my friends were his friends and my foes his foes.

"Then there came to me an inkling of the things that should befall, and I saw that the sweet and clean happiness of my new days was marred, and had grown into something else, and I began to know the pain of strife and the grief of confusion: but whereas I had not been bred delicately, but had endured woes and griefs from my youngest days, I was not abashed, but hardened my heart to face all things, even as my lord strove to harden his heart: for, indeed, I said to myself that if I was to him as the half of his life, he was to me little less than the whole of my life.

"It is as if it had befallen yesterday, my friend, that I call to mind how we stood beside our horses in the midst of the ring of great men clad in gold and gleaming with steel, in the meadow without the gates, the peace and lowly goodliness whereof with its flocks and herds feeding, and husbandmen tending the earth and its increase, that great and noble array had changed so utterly. There we stood, and I knew that the eyes of all those lords and warriors were set upon me wondering. But the love of my lord and the late-learned knowledge of my beauty sustained me. Then the ring of men opened, and the king came forth towards us; a tall man and big, of fifty-five winters, goodly of body and like to my lord to

164

look upon. He cast his arms about my lord, and kissed him and embraced him, and then stood a little aloof from him and said: 'Well, son, hast thou found it, the Well at the World's End?'

" 'Yea,' said my lord, and therewith lifted my hand to his lips and kissed it, and I looked the king in his face, and his eyes were turned to me, but it was as if he were looking through me at something behind me.

"Then he said: 'It is good, son: come home now to thy mother and thy kindred.' Then my lord turned to me while the king took no heed, and no man in the ring of knights moved from his place, and he set me in the saddle, and turned about to mount, and there came a lord from the ring of men gloriously bedight, and he bowed lowly before my lord, and held his stirrup for him: but lightly he leapt up into the saddle, and took my reins and led me along with him, so that he and the king and I went on together, and all the baronage and their folk shouted and tossed sword and spear aloft and followed after us. And we left the meadow quiet and simple again, and rode through the gate of the king's chief city, wherein was his high house and his castle, the dwelling-place of his kindred from of old.

CHAPTER 7

The Lady Tells of the Strife and Trouble That Befell After Her Coming to the Country of the King's Son

"When we came to the King's House, my lord followed his father into the hall, where sat his mother amongst her damsels: she was a fair woman, and looked rather meek than high-hearted; my lord led me up to her, and she embraced and kissed him and caressed him long; then she turned about to me and would have spoken to me, but the king, who stood behind us, scowled on her, and she forebore; but she looked me on somewhat kindly, and yet as one who is afeard.

"Thus it went for the rest of the day, and my lord had me to sit beside him in the great hall when the banquet was holden, and I ate and drank with him and beheld all the pageants by his side, and none meddled with me either to help or to hinder, because they feared the king. Yet many eyes I saw that desired my beauty. And so when night came, he took me to his chamber and his bed, as if I were his bride new wedded, even as it had been with us on the grass of the wilderness and the bracken of the wildwood. And then, at last, he spake to me of our case, and bade me fear not, for that a band of his friends, all-armed, was keeping watch and ward in the cloister without. And when I left the chamber on the morrow's morn, there were they yet, all in bright armour, and amongst them the young knight who had delivered me from the felon baron, and he looked mournfully at me, so that I was sorry for his sorrow.

"And I knew now that the king was minded to slay me, else had he bidden thrust me from my lord's side.

"So wore certain days; and on the seventh night, when we were come into our chamber, which was a fair as any house outside of heaven, my lord spake to me in a soft voice, and bade me not do off my raiment. 'For,' said he, 'this night we must flee the town, or we shall be taken and cast into prison to-morrow; for thus hath my father determined.' I kissed him and clung to him, and he no less was good to me. And when it was the dead of night we escaped out of our window by a knotted rope which he had made ready, and beneath was the city wall; and that company of knights, amongst whom was the young knight abovesaid, had taken a postern thereby, and were abiding us armed and with good horses. So we came into the open country, and rode our ways with the mind to reach a hill-castle of one of those young barons, and to hold ourselves there in despite of the king. But the king had been as wary as we were privy, and no less speedy than we; and he was a mighty and deft warrior, and he himself followed us on the spur with certain of his best men-at-arms. And they came upon us as we rested in a woodside not far from our house of refuge: and the king stood by to see the battle with his sword in his sheath, but soon was it at an end, for though our friends fought valiantly, they were everyone slain or hurt, and but few escaped with bare life; but that young man who loved me so sorely crept up to me grievously hurt, and I did not forbear to kiss him once on the face, for I deemed I should soon die also, and his blood stained my sleeve and my wrist, but he died not as then, but lived to be a dear friend to me for long.

"So we, my lord and I, were led back to the city, and he was held in ward and I was cast into prison with chains and hunger and stripes. And the king would have had me lie there till I perished, that I might be forgotten utterly; but there were many of the king's knights who murmured at this, and would not forget me; so the king being constrained, had me brought forth to be judged by his bishops of sorcery for the beguiling of my lord. Long was the tale to me then, but I will not make it long for thee; as was like to be, I was brought in guilty of sorcery, and doomed to be burned in the Great Square in three days time.

"Nay, my friend, thou hast no need to look so troubled; for thou seest that I was not burned. This is the selfsame body that was tied to the stake in the market place of the king's city many a year ago.

"For the friends of my lord, young men for the most part, and many who had been fain to be my friends also, put on their armour, and took my lord out of the courteous prison wherein he was, and came to the Great Square whenas I stood naked in my smock bound amid the faggots; and I saw the sheriffs' men give back, and great noise and rumour rise up around me: and then all about me was a clear space for a moment and I heard the tramp of the many horse-hoofs, and the space was full of weaponed men shouting, and crying out, 'Life for our Lord's Lady!' Then a minute, and I was loose and in my lord's arms, and they brought me a horse and I mounted, lest the worst should come and we might have to flee. So I could see much of what went on; and I saw that all the unarmed folk and lookers-on were gone, but at our backs was a great crowd of folk with staves and bows who cried out, 'Life for the Lady!' But before us was naught but the sheriffs' sergeants and a company of knights and men-at-arms, about as many as we were, and the king in front of them, fully armed, his face hidden by his helm, and a royal surcoat over his hauberk beaten with his bearing, to wit, a silver tower on a blue sky bestarred with gold.

"And now I could see that despite the bills and bows behind us the king was going to fall on with his folk; and to say sooth I feared but little and my heart rose high within me, and I wished I had a sword in my hand to strike once for life and love. But lo! just as the king was raising his sword, and his trumpet was lifting the brass to his lips, came a sound of singing, and there was come the Bishop and the Abbot of St. Peter's and his monks with him, and cross bearers and readers and others of the religious: and the Bishop bore in his hand the Blessed Host (as now I know it was) under a golden canopy, and he stood between the two companies and faced the king, while his folk sang loud and sweet about him.

"Then the spears went up and from the rest, and swords were sheathed, and there went forth three ancient knights from out of the king's host and came up to him and spake with him. Then he gat him away unto his High House; and the three old knights came to our folk, and spake with the chiefs; but not with my lord, and I heard not what they said. But my lord came to me in all loving-kindness and brought me into the house of one of the Lineage, and into a fair chamber there, and kissed me, and made much of me; and brought me fair raiment and did it on me with his own hands, even as his wont was to be for my tire-maiden.

"Then in a little while came those chiefs of ours and said that truce had been hanselled them for this time, but on these terms, that my lord and I and all those who had been in arms, and whosoever would, that feared the king's wrath, should have leave to depart from his city so that they went and abode no nearer than fifty miles thereof till they should know his further pleasure. Albeit that whosoever would go home peaceably might abide in the city still and need not fear the king's wrath if he stirred no further: but that in any case the Sorceress should get her gone from those walls.

"So we rode out of the gates that very day before sunset; for it was now midsummer again, and it was three hours before noon that I was to have been burned; and we were a gallant company of men-at-arms and knights; yet did I bethink me of those who were slain on that other day when we were taken, and fain had I been that they were riding with us; but at least that fair young man was in our company, though still weak with his hurts: for the prison and the process had worn away wellnigh two months. True it is that I rejoiced to see him, for I had deemed him dead.

"Dear friend, I pray thy pardon if I weary thee with making so long a tale of my friends of the past days; but needs must I tell thee somewhat of them, lest thou love that which is not. Since truly it is myself that I would have thee to love, and none other.

"Many folk gathered to us as we rode our ways to a town which was my lord's own, and where all men were his friends, so that we came there with a great host and sat down there in no fear of what the king might do against us. There was I duly wedded to my lord by a Bishop of Holy Church, and made his Lady and Queen; for even so he would have it.

"And now began the sore troubles of that land, which had been once so peaceful and happy; the tale whereof I may one day tell thee; or rather many tales of what befell me therein; but not now; for the day weareth; and I still have certain things that I must needs tell thee.

"We waged war against each other, my lord and the king, and whiles one, and whiles the other overcame. Either side belike deemed that one battle or two would end the strife; but so it was not, but it endured year after year, till fighting became the chief business of all in the land.

"As for me, I had many tribulations. Thrice I fled from the stricken field with my lord to hide in some stronghold of the mountains. Once was I taken of the foemen in the town where I abode when my lord was away from me, and a huge slaughter of innocent folk was made, and I was cast into prison and chains, after I had seen my son that I had borne to my lord slain before mine eyes. At last we were driven clean out of the Kingdom of the Tower, and abode a long while, some two years, in the wilderness, living like outlaws and wolves' heads, and lifting the spoil for our livelihood.

169

Forsooth of all the years that I abode about the Land of Tower those were the happiest. For we robbed no poor folk and needy, but rewarded them rather, and drave the spoil from rich men and lords, and hard-hearted chapmen-folk: we ravished no maid of the tillers, we burned no cot, and taxed no husbandman's croft or acre, but defended them from their tyrants. Nevertheless we gat an ill name wide about through the kingdoms and cities; and were devils and witches to the boot of thieves and robbers in the mouths of these men; for when the rich man is hurt his wail goeth heavens high, and none may say he heareth not.

"Now it was at this time that I first fell in with the Champions of the Dry Tree; for they became our fellows and brothers in arms in the wildwood: for they had not as yet builded their stronghold of the Scaur, whereas thou and I shall be in two days time. Many a wild deed did our folk in their company, and many that had been better undone. Whiles indeed they went on journeys wherein we were not partakers, as when they went to the North and harried the lands of the Abbot of Higham, and rode as far even as over the Downs to Bear Castle and fought a battle there with the Captain of Higham: whereas we went never out of the Wood Perilous to the northward; and lifted little save in the lands of our own proper foemen, the friends of the king.

"Now I say not of the men of the Dry Tree that they were good and peaceable men, nor would mercy hold their hands every while that they were hard bestead and thrust into a corner. Yet I say now and once for all that their fierceness was and is but kindness and pity when set against the cruelty of the Burg of the Four Friths; men who have no friend to love, no broken foe to forgive, and can scarce be kind even to themselves: though forsooth they be wise men and caute-lous and well living before the world, and wealthy and holy."

She stayed her speech a while, and her eyes glittered in her flushed face and she set her teeth; and she was as one beside herself till Ralph kissed her feet, and caressed her, and she went on again.

"Dear friend, when thou knowest what these men are and have been thou wilt bless thy friend Roger for leading thee

170

forth from the Burg by night and cloud, whatever else may happen to thee.

"Well, we abode in the wildwood, friends and good fellows from the first; and that young man, though he loved me ever, was somewhat healed of the fever of love, and was my faithful friend, in such wise that neither I nor my lord had aught to find fault with in him. Meanwhile we began to grow strong, for many joined us therein who had fled from their tyrants of the good towns and the manors of the baronage, and at last in the third year naught would please my lord but we must enter into the Kingdom of the Tower, and raise his banner in the wealthy land, and the fair cities.

"Moreover, his father, the King of the Tower, died in his bed in these days, and no word of love or peace had passed between them since that morning when I was led out to be burned in the Great Square.

"So we came forth from the forest, we, and the Champions of the Dry Tree; and made the tale a short one. For the king, the mighty warrior and wise man, was dead: and his captains of war, some of them were dead, and some weary of strife; and those who had been eager in debate were falling to ask themselves wherefore they had fought and what was to do that they should still be fighting; and lo! when it came to be looked into, it was all a matter of the life and death of one woman, to wit me myself, and why should she not live, why should she not sit upon the throne with the man who loved her?

"Therefore when at last we came out from the twilight of the woods into the sunny fields of the Land of the Tower, there was no man to naysay us; nay, the gates of the strong places flew open before the wind of our banners, and the glittering of our spears drew the folk together toward the places of rejoicing. We entered the master City in triumph, with the houses hung with green boughs and the maidens casting flowers before our feet, and I sat a crowned Queen upon the throne high raised on the very place where erst I stood awaiting the coming of the torch to the faggots which were to consume me.

"There then began the reign of the Woman of the Waste; for so it was, that my lord left to my hands the real ruling of the kingdom, though he wore the crown and set the seal to parchments. As to them of the Dry Tree, though some few of them abode in the kingdom, and became great there, the more part of them went back to the wildwood and lived the old life of the Wood, as we had found them living it aforetime. But or ever they went, the leaders of them came before me, and kissed my feet, and with tears and prayers besought me, and bade me that if aught fell amiss to me there, I should come back to them and be their Lady and Queen; and whereas these wild men loved me well, and I deemed that I owed much to their love and their helping, I promised them and swore to them by the Water of the Well at the World's End that I would do no less than they prayed me: albeit I set no term or year for the day that I would come to them.

"And now my lord and I, we set ourselves to heal the wounds which war had made in the land: and hard was the work, and late the harvest; so used had men become to turmoil and trouble. Moreover, there were many, and chiefly the women who had lost husband, lover, son or brother, who laid all their griefs on my back; though forsooth how was I guilty of the old king's wrath against me, which was the cause of all? About this time my lord had the Castle of Abundance built up very fairly for me and him to dwell in at whiles; and indeed we had before that dwelt at a little manor house that was there, when we durst withdraw a little from the strife; but now he had it done as fair as ye saw it, and had those arras cloths made with the story of my sojourn in the wilderness, even as ye saw them. But the days and the years wore, and wealth came back to the mighty of the land, and fields flourished and the acres bore increase, and fair houses were builded in the towns; and the land was called happy again.

"But for me I was not so happy: and I looked back fondly to the days of the greenwood and the fellowship of the Dry Tree, and the days before that, of my flight with my lord. And moreover with the wearing of the years those murmurs against me and the blind causeless hatred began to grow again, and chiefly methinks because I was the king, and my lord the king's cloak: but therewith tales concerning me began to spring up, how that I was not only a sorceress, but even one foredoomed from of old and sent by the lords of hell to wreck that fair Land of the Tower and make it unhappy and desolate. And the tale grew and gathered form, till now, when the bloom of my beauty was gone, I heard hard and fierce words cried after me in the streets when I fared abroad, and that still chiefly by the women: for yet most men looked on me with pleasure. Also my counsellors and lords warned me often that I must be wary and of great forbearance if trouble were to be kept back.

"Now amidst these things as I was walking pensively in my garden one summer day, it was told me that a woman desired to see me, so I bade them bring her. And when she came I looked on her, and deemed that I had seen her aforetime: she was not old, but of middle age, of dark red hair, and brown eyes somewhat small: not a big woman, but well fashioned of body, and looking as if she had once been exceeding dainty and trim. She spake, and again I seemed to have heard her voice before: 'Hail, Queen,' she said, 'it does my heart good to see thee thus in thy glorious estate.' So I took her greeting; but those tales of my being but a sending of the Devil for the ruin of that land came into my mind, and I sent away the folk who were thereby before I said more to her. Then she spake again: 'Even so I guessed it would be that thou wouldst grow great amongst women.'

"But I said, 'What is this? and when have I known thee before-time?' She smiled and said naught; and my mind went back to those old days, and I trembled, and the flesh crept upon my bones, lest this should be the coming back in a new shape of my mistress whom I had slain. But the woman laughed, and said, as if she knew my thoughts: 'Nay, it is not so: the dead are dead; fear not: but hast thou forgotten the Dale of Lore?'

"'Nay,' said I, 'never; and art thou then the carline that learned me lore? But if the dead come not back, how do the old grow young again? for 'tis a score of years since we two sat in the Dale, and I longed for many things.'

"Said the woman: 'The dead may not drink of the Well at the World's End; yet the living may, even if they be old; and that blessed water giveth them new might and changeth their blood, and they are as young folk for a long while again after they have drunken.' 'And hast thou drunken?' said I.

" 'Yea,' she said; 'but I am minded for another draught.' I said: 'And wherefore hast thou come to me, and what shall I give to thee?' She said, 'I will take no gift of thee as now, for I need it not, though hereafter I may ask a gift of thee. But I am to ask this of thee, if thou wilt be my fellow-farer on the road thither?' 'Yea?' said I, 'and leave my love and my lord, and my kingship which he hath given me? for this I will tell thee, that all that here is done, is done by me.'

" 'Great is thy Kingship, Lady,' said the woman, and smiled withal. Then she sat silent a little, and said: 'When six months are worn, it will be springtide; I will come to thee in the spring days, and know what thy mind is then. But now I must depart.' Quoth I: 'Glad shall I be to talk with thee again; for though thou hast learned me much of wisdom, yet much more I need; yea, as much as the folk here deem I have already.' 'Thou shalt have no less,' said the woman. Then she kissed my hands and went her ways, and I sat musing still for a long while: because for all my gains, and my love that I had been loved withal, and the greatness that I had gotten, there was as it were a veil of unhappiness wrapped round about my heart.

"So wore the months, and ere the winter had come befell an evil thing, for my lord, who had loved me so, and taken me out of the wilderness, died, and was gathered to the fathers, and there was I left alone; for there was no fruit of my womb by him alive. My first-born had been slain by those wretches, and a second son that I bore had died of a pestilence that war and famine had brought upon the land. I will not wear thy soul with words about my grief and sorrow: but it is to be told that I sat now in a perilous place, and yet I might not step down from it and abide in that land, for then it was a sure thing, that some of my foes would have laid hand on me and brought me to judgment for being but myself, and I should have ended miserably. So I gat to me all the strength that I might, and whereas there were many who loved me still, some for my own sake, and some for the sake of my lord that was, I endured in good hope that all my days were not done. Yet I longed for the coming of the Teacher

174

of Lore; for now I made up my mind that I would go with her, and seek to the Well at the World's End for weal and woe.

"She came while April was yet young: and I need make no long tale of how we gat us away: for whereas she was wise in hidden lore, it was no hard matter for her to give me another semblance than mine own, so that I might have walked about the streets of our city from end to end, and none had known me. So I vanished away from my throne and my kingdom, and that name and fame of a witch-wife clove to me once and for all, and spread wide about the cities of folk and the kingdoms, and many are the tales that have arisen concerning me, and belike some of these thou hast heard told."

Ralph reddened and said: "My soul has been vexed by some inkling of them; but now it is at rest from them for ever."

"May it be so!" she said: "and now my tale is wearing thin for the present time.

"Back again went my feet over the ways they had trodden before, though the Teacher shortened the road much for us by her wisdom. Once again what need to tell thee of these ways when thine own eyes shall behold them as thou wendest them beside me? Be it enough to say that once again I came to that little house in the uttermost wilderness, and there once more was the garth and the goat-house, and the trees of the forest beyond it, and the wood-lawns and the streams and all the places and things that erst I deemed I must dwell amongst for ever."

Said Ralph: "And did the carline keep troth with thee? Was she not but luring thee thither to be her thrall? Or did the book that I read in the Castle of Abundance but lie concerning thee?"

"She held her troth to me in all wise," said the Lady, "and I was no thrall of hers, but as a sister, or it may be even as a daughter; for ever to my eyes was she the old carline who learned me lore in the Dale of the wildwood.

"But now a long while, years long, we abode in that House of the Sorceress ere we durst seek further to the Well at the World's End. And yet meseems though the years wore, they wore me no older; nay, in the first days at least I waxed stronger of body and fairer than I had been in the King's Palace in the Land of the Tower, as though some foretaste of the Well was there for us in the loneliness of the desert; although forsooth the abiding there amidst the scantiness of livelihood, and the nakedness, and the toil, and the torment of wind and weather were as a penance for the days and deeds of our past lives. What more is to say concerning our lives here, saving this, that in those days I learned yet more wisdom of the Teacher of Lore, and amidst that wisdom was much of that which ye call sorcery: as the foreseeing of things to come, and the sending of dreams or visions, and certain other matters. And I may tell thee that the holy man who came to us last even, I sent him the dream which came to him drowsing, and bade him come to the helping of Walter the Black: for I knew that I should take thy hand and flee with thee this morning e'en as I have done: and I would fain have a good leech to Walter lest he should die, although I owe him hatred rather than love. Now, my friend, tell me, is this an evil deed, and dost thou shrink from the Sorceress?"

He strained her to his bosom and kissed her mouth, and then he said: "Yet thou hast never sent a dream to me." She laughed and said: "What! hast thou never dreamed of me since we met at the want-way of the Wood Perilous?" "Never," said he. She stroked his cheek fondly, and said: "Young art thou, sweet friend, and sleepest well a-nights. It was enough that thou thoughtest of me in thy waking hours." Then she went on with her tale.

CHAPTER 8

The Lady Maketh an End
of Her Tale

"Well, my friend, after we had lived thus a long time, we set out one day to seek to the Well at the World's End, each of us signed and marked out for the quest by bearing suchlike beads as thou and I both bear upon our necks today. Once again of all that befell us on that quest I will tell thee naught as now: because to that Well have I to bring thee: though myself, belike, I need not its waters again."

Quoth Ralph: "And must thou lead me thy very self, mayest thou not abide in some safe place my going and returning? So many and sore as the toils and perils of the way may be." "What!" she said, "and how shall I be sundered from thee now I have found thee? Yea, and who shall lead thee, thou lovely boy? Shall it be a man to bewray thee, or a woman to bewray me? Yet need we not go tomorrow, my beloved, nor for many days: so sweet as we are to each other.

"But in those past days it was needs must we begin our quest before the burden of years was over heavy upon us. Shortly to say it, we found the Well, and drank of its waters after abundant toil and peril, as thou mayst well deem. Then the life and the soul came back to us, and the past years were as naught to us, and my youth was renewed in me, and I became as thou seest me to-day. But my fellow was as a woman of forty summers again, strong and fair as I had seen her when she came into the garden in the days of my Queenhood, and thus we returned to the House of the Sorceress, and rested there for a little from our travel and our joy.

"At last, and that was but some five years ago, the Teacher said to me: 'Sister, I have learned thee all that thine heart can take of me, and thou art strong in wisdom, and more-

177

over again shall it be with thee, as I told of thee long ago, that no man shall look on thee that shall not love thee. Now I will not seek to see thy life that is coming, nor what thine end shall be, for that should belike be grievous to both of us; but this I see of thee, that thou wilt now guide thy life not as I will, but as thou wilt; and since my way is not thy way, and that I see thou shalt not long abide alone, now shall we sunder; for I am minded to go to the most ancient parts of the world, and seek all the innermost of wisdom whiles I yet live; but with kings and champions and the cities of folk will I have no more to do: while thou shalt not be able to refrain from these. So now I bid thee farewell.'

"I wept at her words, but gainsaid them naught, for I wotted that she spake but the truth; so I kissed her, and we parted; she went her ways through the wildwood, and I abode at the House of the Sorceress, and waited on the wearing of the days.

"But scarce a month after her departure, as I stood by the threshold one morning amidst of the goats, I saw men come riding from out the wood; so I abode them, and they came to the gate of the garth and there lighted down from their horses, and they were three in company; and no one of them was young, and one was old, with white locks flowing down from under his helm: for they were all armed in knightly fashion, but they had naught but white gaberdines over their hauberks, with no coat-armour or token upon them. So they came through the garth-gate and I greeted them and asked them what they would; then the old man knelt down on the grass before me and said: 'If I were as young as I am old my heart would fail me in beholding thy beauty: but now I will ask thee somewhat: far away beyond the forest we heard rumours of a woman dwelling in the uttermost desert, who had drunk of the Well at the World's End, and was wise beyond measure. Now we have set ourselves to seek that woman, and if thou be she, we would ask a question of thy wisdom.'

"I answered that I was even such as they had heard of, and bade them ask.

"Said the old man:

"'Fifty years ago, when I was yet but a young man, there

178

was a fair woman who was Queen of the Land of the Tower and whom we loved sorely because we had dwelt together with her amidst tribulation in the desert and the wildwood: and we are not of her people, but a fellowship of free men and champions hight the Men of the Dry Tree: and we hoped that she would one day come back and dwell with us and be our Lady and Queen: and indeed trouble seemed drawing anigh her, so that we might help her and she might become our fellow again, when lo! she vanished away from the folk and none knew where she was gone. Therefore a band of us of the Dry Tree swore an oath together to seek her till we found her, that we might live and die together: but of that band of one score and one, am I the last one left that seeketh; for the rest are dead, or sick, or departed: and indeed I was the youngest of them. But for these two men, they are my sons whom I have bred in the knowledge of these things and in the hope of finding tidings of our Lady and Queen, if it were but the place where her body lieth. Thou art wise: knowest thou the resting place of her bones?"

"When I had heard the tale of the old man I was moved to my inmost heart, and I scarce knew what to say. But now this long while fear was dead in me, so I thought I would tell the very sooth: but I said first: 'Sir, what I will tell, I will tell without beseeching, so I pray thee stand up.' So did he, and I said: 'Geoffrey, what became of the white hind after the banners had left the wildwood'? He stared wild at me, and I deemed that tears began to come into his eyes; but I said again: 'What betid to dame Joyce's youngest born, the fair little maiden that we left sick of a fever when we rode to Up-castle?' Still he said naught but looked at me wondering: and said: 'Hast thou ever again seen that great old oak nigh the clearing by the water, the half of which fell away in the summer-storm of that last July?'

"Then verily the tears gushed out of his eyes, and he wept, for as old as he was; and when he could master himself he said: 'Who art thou? Who art thou? Art thou the daughter of my Lady, even as these are my sons?' But I said: 'Now will I answer thy first question, and tell thee that the Lady thou seekest is verily alive; and she has thriven, for she has drunk of the Well at the World's End, and has put from her the burden of the years. O Geoffrey, and dost thou not know me?' And I held out my hand to him, and I also was weeping, because of my thought of the years gone by; for this old man had been that swain who had nigh died for me when I fled with my husband from the old king; and he became one of the Dry Tree, and had followed me with kind service about the woods in the days when I was at my happiest.

"But now he fell on his knees before me not like a vassal but like a lover, and kissed my feet, and was beside himself for joy. And his sons, who were men of some forty summers, tall and warrior-like, kissed my hands and made obeisance before me.

"Now when we had come to ourselves again, old Geoffrey, who was now naught but glad, spake and said: 'It is told amongst us that when our host departed from the Land of the Tower, after thou hadst taken thy due seat upon the throne, that thou didst promise our chieftains how thou wouldst one day come back to the fellowship of the Dry Tree and dwell amongst us. Wilt thou now hold to thy promise?' I said: 'O Geoffrey, if thou art the last of those seekers, and thou wert but a boy when I dwelt with you of old, who of the Dry Tree is left to remember me?' He hung his head awhile then, and spake: 'Old are we grown, yet art thou fittest to be amongst young folk: unless mine eyes are beguiled by some semblance which will pass away presently.' 'Nay,' quoth I, 'it is not so; as I am now, so shall I be for many and many a day.' 'Well,' said Geoffrey, 'wherever thou mayst be, thou shalt be Queen of men.'

"'I list not to be Queen again,' said I. He laughed and said: 'I wot not how thou mayst help it.'

"I said: 'Tell me of the Dry Tree, how the champions have sped, and have they grown greater or less.' Said he: 'They are warriors and champions from father to son; therefore have they thriven not over well; yet they have left the thick of the wood, and built them a great castle above the little town hight Hampton; so that is now called Hampton under Scaur, for upon the height of the said Scaur is our castle builded: and there we hold us against the Burg of the Four

Friths which hath thriven greatly; there is none so great as the Burg in all the lands about.'

"I said: 'And the Land of the Tower, thriveth the folk thereof at all?' 'Nay,' he said, 'they have been rent to pieces by folly and war and greediness: in the Great City are but few people, grass grows in its streets; the merchants wend not the ways that lead thither. Naught thriveth there since thou stolest thyself away from them.'

" 'Nay,' I said, 'I fled from their malice, lest I should have been brought out to be burned once more; and there would have been none to rescue then.' 'Was it so?' said old Geoffrey; 'well it is all one now; their day is done.'

" 'Well,' I said, 'come into my house, and eat and drink therein and sleep here to-night, and to-morrow I shall tell thee what I will do.'

"Even so they did; and on the morrow early I spake to Geoffrey and said: 'What hath befallen the Land of Abundance, and the castle my lord built for me there; which we held as our refuge all through the War of the Tower, both before we joined us to you in the wildwood, and afterwards?' He said: 'It is at peace still; no one hath laid hand on it; there is a simple folk dwelling there in the clearing of the wood, which forgetteth thee not; though forsooth strange tales are told of thee there; and the old men deem that it is but a little since thou hast ceased to come and go there; and they are ready to worship thee as somewhat more than the Blessed Saints, were it not for the Fathers of the Thorn who are their masters.'

"I pondered this a while, and then said: 'Geoffrey, ye shall bring me hence away to the peopled parts, and on the way, or when we are come amongst the cities and the kingdoms, we will settle it whither I shall go. See thou! I were fain to be of the brotherhood of the Dry Tree; yet I deem it will scarce be that I shall go and dwell there straightway.'

"Therewith the old man seemed content; and indeed now that the first joy of our meeting, when his youth sprang up in him once more, was over, he found it hard to talk freely with me, and was downcast and shy before me, as if something had come betwixt us, which had made our lives cold to each other.

181

"So that day we left the House of the Sorceress, which I shall not see again, till I come there hand in hand with thee, beloved. When we came to the peopled parts, Geoffrey and his sons brought me to the Land of Abundance, and I found it all as he had said to me: and I took up my dwelling in the castle, and despised not those few folk of the land, but was kind to them: but though they praised my gifts, and honoured me as the saints are honoured, and though they loved me, yet it was with fear, so that I had little part with them. There I dwelt then; and the book which thou didst read there, part true and part false, and altogether of malice against me, I bought of a monk who came our way, and who at first was sore afeared when he found that he had come to my castle. As to the halling of the Chamber of Dais, I have told thee before how my lord, the King's Son, did do make it in memory of the wilderness wherein he found me, and the life of thralldom from which he brought me. There I dwelt till nigh upon these days in peace and quiet: not did I go to the Dry Tree for a long while, though many of them sought to me there at the Castle of Abundance; and, woe worth the while! there was oftenest but one end to their guesting, that of all gifts, they besought me but of one, which, alack! I might not give them: and that is the love that I have given to thee, beloved.—And, oh! my fear, that it will weigh too light with thee, to win me pardon of thee for all that thou must needs pardon me, ere thou canst give me all thy love, that I long for so sorely."

CHAPTER 9

They Go On Their Way
Once More

"Look now," she said, "I have held thee so long in talk, that the afternoon is waning; now is it time for us to be on the way again; not because I misdoubt me of thy foeman, but because I would take thee to a fairer dwelling of the desert, and one where I have erst abided; and moreover, there thou shalt not altogether die of hunger. See, is it not as if I had thought to meet thee here?"

"Yea, in good sooth," said he, "I wot that thou canst see the story of things before they fall."

She laughed and said: "But all this that hath befallen since I set out to meet thee at the Castle of Abundance I foresaw not, any more than I can foresee to-morrow. Only I knew that we must needs pass by the place whereto I shall now lead thee, and I made provision there. Lo! now the marvel slain: and in such wise shall perish other marvels which have been told of me; yet not all. Come now, let us to the way."

So they joined hands and left the pleasant place, and were again going speedily amidst the close pine woods awhile, where it was smooth underfoot and silent of noises withal.

Now Ralph said: "Beloved, thou hast told me of many things, but naught concerning how thou camest to be wedded to the Knight of the Sun, and of thy dealings with him."

Said she, reddening withal: "I will tell thee no more than this, unless thou compel me: that he would have me wed him, as it were against my will, till I ceased striving against him, and I went with him to Sunway, which is no great way from the Castle of Abundance, and there befell that treason of Walter the Black, who loved me and prayed for my love, and when I gainsaid him, swore by all that was holy, before my lord, that it was I who sought his love, and how I had told and taught him ways of witchcraft, whereby we might fulfill our love, so that the Baron should keep a wife for another man. And the Knight of the Sun, whose heart had been filled with many tales of my wisdom, true and false, believed his friend whom he loved, and still believeth him, though he burneth for the love of me now; whereas in those first days of the treason, he burned with love turned to hatred. So of this came that shaming and casting-forth of me. Whereof I will tell thee but this, that the brother of my lord, even the tall champion whom thou hast seen, came upon me presently, when I was cast forth; because he was coming to see the Knight of the Sun at his home; and he loved me, but not after the fashion of his brother, but was

183

kind and mild with me. So then I went with him to Hampton
and the Dry Tree, and great joy made the folk thereof of my
coming, whereas they remembered their asking of aforetime
that I would come to be a Queen over them, and there have
I dwelt ever since betwixt Hampton and the Castle of Abundance; and that tall champion has been ever as a brother
unto me."

Said Ralph, "And thou art their Queen there?" "Yea," she
said, "in a fashion; yet have they another who is mightier than
I, and might, if she durst, hang me over the battlements of
the Scaur, for she is a fierce and hard woman, and now no
longer young in years."

"Is it not so then," said Ralph, "that some of the ill deeds
that are told of thee are of her doing?

"It is even so," she said, "and whiles when she has spoken
the word I may not be against her openly, therefore I use my
wisdom which I have learned, to set free luckless wights from
her anger and malice. More by token the last time I did thus
was the very night of the day we parted, after thou hadst
escaped from the Burg."

"In what wise was that?" said Ralph. She said: "When I
rode away from thee on that happy day of my deliverance by
thee, my heart laughed for joy of the life thou hadst given
me, and of thee the giver, and I swore to myself that I would
set free the first captive or death-doomed creature that I
came across, in honour of my pleasure and delight: now
speedily I came to Hampton and the Scaur; for it is not very
far from the want-ways of the wood: and there I heard how
four of our folk had been led away by the men of the Burg,
therefore it was clear to me that I must set these men free if
I could; besides, it pleased me to think that I could walk
about the streets of the foemen safely, who had been but just
led thitherward to the slaughter. Thou knowest how I sped
therein. But when I came back again to our people, after
thou hadst ridden away from us with Roger, I heard these
tidings, that there was one new-come into our prison, a
woman to wit, who had been haled before our old Queen for
a spy and doomed by her, and should be taken forth and
slain, belike, in a day or two. So I said to myself that I was
not free of my vow as yet, because those friends of mine, I

should in any case have done my best to deliver them: therefore I deemed my oath bound me to set that woman free. So in the night-tide when all was quiet I went to the prison and brought her forth, and led her past all the gates and wards, which was an easy thing to me, so much as I had learned, and came with her into the fields betwixt the thorp of Hampton and the wood, when it was more daylight than dawn, so that I could see her clearly, and no word as yet had we spoken to each other. But then she said to me: 'Am I to be slain here or led to a crueller prison?' And I said: 'Neither one thing nor the other: for lo! I have set thee free, and I shall look to it that there shall be no pursuit of thee till thou hast had time to get clear away.' But she said: 'What thanks wilt thou have for this? Wherefore hast thou done it?' And I said, 'It is because of the gladness I have gotten.' Said she, 'And would that I might get gladness!' So I asked her what was amiss now that she was free. She said: 'I have lost one thing that I loved, and found another and lost it also.' So I said: 'Mightest thou not seek for the lost?' She said, 'It is in this wood, but when I shall find it I shall not have it.' 'It is love that thou art seeking,' said I. 'In what semblance is he?'

"What wilt thou, my friend? Straightway she fell to making a picture of thee in words; so that I knew that she had met thee, and belike after I had departed from thee, and my heart was sore thereat; for now I will tell thee the very truth, that she was a young woman and exceeding fair, as if she were of pearl all over, and as sweet as eglantine; and I feared her lest she should meet thee again in these wildwoods. And so I asked her what would she, and she said that she had a mind to seek to the Well at the World's End, which quencheth all sorrow; and I rejoiced thereat, thinking that she would be far away from thee, not thinking that thou and I must even meet to seek to it also. So I gave her the chaplet which my witch-mistress took from the dead woman's neck; and went with her into the wildwood, and taught her wisdom of the way and what she was to do. And again I say to thee that she was so sweet and yet with a kind of pity in her both of soul and body, and wise withal and quiet, that I feared her, though I loved her; yea and still do: for I deem her better than me, and meeter for thee and thy love than I be.—Dost thou know her?"

"Yea," said Ralph, "and fair and lovely she is in sooth. Yet hast thou naught to do to fear her. And true it is that I saw her and spake with her after thou hadst ridden away. For she came by the want-ways of the Wood Perilous in the dawn of the day after I had delivered thee; and in sooth she told me that she looked either for Death, or the Water of the Well to end her sorrow."

Then he smiled and said; "As for that which thou sayest, that she had been meeter for me than thou, I know not this word. For look you, beloved, she came, and passed, and is gone, but thou art there and shalt endure."

She stayed, and turned and faced him at that word; and love so consumed her, that all sportive words failed her; yea and it was as if mirth and light-heartedness were swallowed up in the fire of her love; and all thought of other folk departed from him as he felt her tears of love and joy upon his face, and she kissed and embraced him there in the wilderness.

CHAPTER 10

Of the Desert-House and the Chamber of Love in the Wilderness

Then in a while they grew sober and went on their ways, and the sun was westering behind them, and casting long shadows. And in a little while they were come out of the thick woods and were in a country of steep little valleys, grassy, besprinkled with trees and bushes, with hills of sandstone going up from them, which were often broken into cliffs rising sheer from the tree-beset bottoms: and they saw plenteous deer both great and small, and the wild things seemed to fear them but little. To Ralph it seemed an exceeding fair land, and he was as joyous as it was fair; but the Lady was pensive, and at last she said: "Thou deemest it fair, and so it is; yet is it the lonesomest of deserts. I deem indeed that it was once one of the fairest of lands, with castles and cots and homesteads all about, and fair people no few, busy with many matters amongst them. But now it is all passed away, and there is no token of a dwelling of man, save it might be that those mounds we see, as yonder, and yonder again, are tofts of house-walls long ago sunken into the earth of the valley. And now few even are the hunters or way-farers that wend through it."

Quoth Ralph: "Thou speakest as if there had been once histories and tales of this pleasant wilderness: tell me, has it anything to do with that land about the wide river which we went through, Roger and I, as we rode to the Castle of Abundance the other day? For he spoke of tales of deeds and mishaps concerning it." "Yea," she said, "so it is, and the little stream that runs yonder beneath those cliffs, is making its way towards that big river aforesaid, which is called the Swelling Flood. Now true it is also that there are many tales about of the wars and miseries that turned this land into a desert, and these may be true enough, and belike are true. But these said tales have become blended with the story of those aforesaid wars of the Land of the Tower; of which indeed this desert is verily a part, but was desert still in the days when I was Queen of the Land; so thou mayst well think that they who hold me to be the cause of all this loneliness (and belike Roger thought it was so) have scarce got hold of the very sooth of the matter."

"Even so I deemed," said Ralph: "and to-morrow we shall cross the big river, thou and I. Is there a ferry or a ford there whereas we shall come, or how shall we win over it?"

She was growing merrier again now, and laughed at this and said: "O fair boy! the crossing will be to-morrow and not to-day; let to-morrow cross its own rivers; for surely to-day is fair enough, and fairer shall it be when thou hast been fed and art sitting by me in rest and peace till to-morrow morning. So now hasten yet a little more; and we will keep the said little stream in sight as well as we may for the bushes."

So they sped on, till Ralph said: "Will thy feet never tire, beloved?" "O child," she said, "thou hast heard my story, and mayst well deem that they have wrought many a harder day's work than this day's. And moreover they shall soon rest; for look! yonder is our house for this even, and till to-morrow's sun is high: the house for me and thee and none else with us." And therewith she pointed to a place where the stream ran in a chain of pools and stickles, and a sheer cliff rose up some fifty paces beyond it, but betwixt the stream and the cliff was a smooth table of greensward, with three fair thorn bushes thereon, and it went down at each end to the level of the river's lip by a green slope, but amidmost, the little green plain was some ten feet above the stream, and was broken by a little undercliff, which went down sheer into the water. And Ralph saw in the face of the high cliff the mouth of a cave, however deep it might be.

"Come," said the Lady, "tarry not, for I know that hunger hath hold of thee, and look, how low the sun is growing!" Then she caught him by the hand, and fell to running with him to the edge of the stream, where at the end of the further slope it ran wide and shallow before it entered into a deep pool overhung with boughs of alder and thorn. She stepped daintily over a row of big stones laid in the rippling shallow; and staying herself in mid-stream on the biggest of them, and gathering up her gown, looked up stream with a happy face, and then looked over her shoulder to Ralph and said: "The year has been good to me these seasons, so that when I stayed here on my way to the Castle of Abundance, I found but few stones washed away, and crossed wellnigh dry-shod, but this stone my feet are standing on now, I brought down from under the cliff, and set it amid-most, and I said that when I brought thee hither I would stay thereon and talk with thee while I stood above the freshness of the water, as I am doing now."

Ralph looked on her and strove to answer her, but no words would come to his lips, because of the greatness of his longing; she looked on him fondly, and then stooped to look at the ripples that bubbled up about her shoes, and touched them at whiles; then she said: "See how they long for the water, these feet that have worn the waste so long, and know how kind it will run over them and lap about them: but ye must abide a little, waste-wearers, till we have done a thing or two. Come, love!" And she reached her hand out behind her to Ralph, not looking back, but when she felt his hand touch it, she stepped lightly over the other stones, and on to the grass with him, and led him quietly up the slope that went up to the table of greensward before the cave. But when they came on to the level grass she kissed him, and then turned toward the valley and spake solemnly: "May all blessings light on this House of the wilderness and this Hall of the Summer-tide, and the Chamber of Love that here is!"

Then was she silent a while, and Ralph brake not the silence. Then she turned to him with a face grown merry and smiling, and said: "Lo! how the poor lad yearneth for meat, as well he may, so long as the day hath been. Ah, beloved, thou must be patient a little. For belike our servants have not yet heard of the wedding of us. So we twain must feed each the other. Is that so much amiss?"

He laughed in her face for love, and took her by the wrist, but she drew her hand away and went into the cave, and came forth anon holding a copper kettle with an iron bow, and a bag of meal, which she laid at his feet; then she went into the cave again, and brought forth a flask of wine and a beaker; then she caught up the little cauldron, which was well-beaten, and thin and light, and ran down to the stream therewith, and came up thence presently, bearing it full of water on her head, going as straight and stately as the spear is seen on a day of tourney, moving over the barriers that hide the knight, before he lays it in the rest. She came up to him and set the water-kettle before him, and put her hands on his shoulders, and kissed his cheek, and then stepped back from him and smote her palms together, and said: "Yea, it is well! But there are yet more things to do before we rest. There is the dighting of the chamber, and the gathering of wood for the fire, and the mixing of the meal, and the kneading and the baking of cakes; and all that is my work, and there is the bringing of the quarry for the roast, and that is thine."

Then she ran into the cave and brought forth a bow and a quiver of arrows, and said: "Art thou somewhat of an archer?" Quoth he: "I shoot not ill." "And I," she said, "shoot well, all woodcraft comes handy to me. But this eve I must trust to thy skill for my supper. Go swiftly and come back speedily. Do off thine hauberk, and beat the bushes down in the valley, and bring me some small deer, as roe or hare or coney. And wash thee in the pool below the stepping-stones, as I shall do whiles thou art away, and by then thou comest back, all shall be ready, save the roasting of the venison."

So he did off his wargear, but thereafter tarried a little, looking at her, and she said: "What aileth thee not to go? the hunt's up." He said: "I would first go see the rock-hall that is for our chamber to-night; wilt thou not bring me in thither?" "Nay," she said, "for I must be busy about many matters; but thou mayst go by thyself, if thou wilt."

So he went and stooped down and entered the cave, and found it high and wide within, and clean and fresh and well-smelling, and the floor of fine white sand without a stain.

So he knelt down and kissed the floor, and said aloud: "God bless this floor of the rock-hall whereon my love shall lie to-night!" Then he arose and went out of the cave, and found the Lady at the entry stooping down to see what he would do; and she looked on him fondly and anxiously; but he turned a merry face to her, and caught her round the middle and strained her to his bosom, and then took the bow and arrows and ran down the slope and over the stream, into the thicket of the valley.

He went further than he had looked for, ere he found a prey to his mind, and then he smote a roe with a shaft and slew her, and broke up the carcase and dight it duly, and so went his ways back. When he came to the stream he looked up and saw a little fire glittering not far from the cave, but had no clear sight of the Lady, though he thought he saw her gown fluttering nigh one of the thorn-bushes. Then he did off his raiment and entered that pool of the stream, and was glad to bathe him in the same place where her body had been but of late; for he had noted that the stones of the little shore were still wet with her feet where she had gone up from the water.

But now, as he swam and sported in the sun-warmed pool

190

he deemed he heard the whinnying of a horse, but was not sure, so he held himself still to listen, and heard no more. Then he laughed and bethought him of Falcon his own steed, and dived down under the water; but as he came up, laughing still and gasping, he heard a noise of the clatter of horse hoofs, as if some one were riding swiftly up the further side of the grassy table, where it was stony, as he had noted when they passed by.

A deadly fear fell upon his heart as he thought of his love left all alone; so he gat him at once out of the water and cast his shirt over his head; but while his arms were yet entangled in the sleeves thereof, came to his ears a great and awful sound of a man's voice roaring out, though there were no shapen words in the roar. Then were his arms free through the sleeves, and he took up the bow and fell to bending it, and even therewith he heard a great wailing of a woman's voice, and she cried out, piteously: "Help me, O help, lovely creature of God!"

Yet must he needs finish bending the bow howsoever his heart died within him; or what help would there be of a naked and unarmed man? At last it was bent and an arrow nocked on the string, as he leapt over the river and up the slope.

But even as he came up to that pleasant place he saw all in a moment of time; that there stood Silverfax anigh the Cave's mouth, and the Lady lying on the earth anigh the horse; and betwixt her and him the Knight of the Sun stood up stark, his shining helm on his head, the last rays of the setting sun flashing in the broidered image of his armouries.

He turned at once upon Ralph, shaking his sword in the air (and there was blood upon the blade) and he cried out in terrible voice: "The witch is dead, the whore is dead! And thou, thief, who hast stolen her from me, and lain by her in the wilderness, now shalt thou die, thou!"

Scarce had he spoken than Ralph drew his bow to the arrow-head and loosed; there was but some twenty paces betwixt them, and the shaft, sped by that fell archer, smote the huge man through the eye into the brain, and he fell down along clattering, dead without a word more.

But Ralph gave forth a great wail of woe, and ran forward

and knelt by the Lady, who lay all huddled up face down upon the grass, and he lifted her up and laid her gently on her back. The blood was flowing fast from a great wound in her breast, and he tore off a piece of his shirt to staunch it, but she without knowledge of him breathed forth her last breath ere he could touch the hurt, and he still knelt by her, staring on her as if he knew not what was toward.

She had dight her what she could to welcome his return from the hunting, and had set a wreath of meadow-sweet on her red hair, and a garland of eglantine about her girdle-stead, and left her feet naked after the pool of the stream, and had turned the bezels of her finger-rings outward, for joy of that meeting.

After a while he rose up with a most bitter cry, and ran down the green slope and over the water, and hither and thither amongst the bushes like one mad, till he became so weary that he might scarce go or stand for weariness. Then he crept back again to that Chamber of Love, and sat down beside his new-won mate, calling to mind all the wasted words of the day gone by; for the summer night was come now, most fair and fragrant. But he withheld the sobbing passion of his heart and put forth his hand, and touched her, and she was still, and his hand felt her flesh that it was cold as marble. And he cried out aloud in the night and the wilderness, where there was none to hear him, and arose and went away from her, passing by Silverfax who was standing nearby, stretching out his head, and whinnying at whiles. And he sat on the edge of the green table, and there came into his mind despite himself thoughts of the pleasant fields of Upmeads, and his sports and pleasures there, and the even-song of the High House, and the folk of his fellowship and his love. And therewith his breast arose and his face was wryed, and he wept loud and long, and as if he should never make an end of it. But so weary was he, that at last he lay back and fell asleep, and woke not till the sun was high in the heavens. And so it was, that his slumber had been so heavy, that he knew not at first what had befallen; and one moment he felt glad, and the next as if he should never be glad again, though why he wotted not. Then he turned about and saw Silverfax cropping the grass nearby, and the Lady lying there like an image that could move no whit, though the world awoke about her. Then he remembered, yet scarce all, so that wild hopes swelled his heart, and he rose to his knees and turned to her, and called to mind that he should never see her alive again, and sobbing and wailing broke out from him, for he was young and strong, and sorrow dealt hardly with him.

But presently he arose to his feet and went hither and thither, and came upon the quenched coals of the cooking-fire: she had baked cakes for his eating, and he saw them lying thereby, and hunger constrained him, so he took and ate of them while the tears ran down his face and mingled with the bread he ate. And when he had eaten, he felt stronger and therefore was life more grievous to him, and when he thought what he should do, still one thing seemed more irksome than the other.

He went down to the water to drink, and passed by the body of the Knight of the Sun, and wrath was fierce in his heart against him who had overthrown his happiness. But when he had drunk and washed hands and face he came back again, and hardened his heart to do what he must needs do. He took up the body of the Lady and with grief that may not be told of, he drew it into the cave, and cut boughs of trees and laid them over her face and all her body, and then took great stones from the scree at that other end of the little plain, and heaped them upon her till she was utterly hidden by them. Then he came out on to the green place and looked on the body of his foe, and said to himself that all must be decent and in order about the place whereas lay his love. And he came and stood over the body and said: "I have naught to do to hate him now: if he hated me, it was but for a little while, and he knew naught of me. So let his bones be covered up from the wolf and the kite. Yet shall they not lie alongside of her. I will raise a cairn above him here on this fair little plain which he spoilt of all joy." Therewith he fell to, and straightened his body, and laid his huge limbs together and closed his eyes and folded his arms over his breast; and then he piled the stones above him, and went on casting them on the heap a long while after there was need thereof.

Ralph had taken his raiment from the stream-side and

done them on before this, and now he did on helm and hauberk, and girt his sword to his side. Then as he was about leaving the sorrowful place, he looked on Silverfax, who had not strayed from the little plain, and came up to him and did off saddle and bridle, and laid them within the cave, and bade the beast go whither he would. He yet lingered about the place, and looked all around him and found naught to help him, and could frame in his mind no intent of a deed then, nor any tale of a deed he should do thereafter. Yet belike in his mind were two thoughts, and though neither softened his grief save a little, he did not shrink from them as he did from all others; and these two were of his home at Upmeads, which was so familiar to him, and of the Well at the World's End, which was but a word.

CHAPTER 11

Ralph Cometh Out of the Wilderness

Long he stood letting these thoughts run through his mind, but at last when it was now midmorning, he stirred and gat him slowly down the green slope, and for very pity of himself the tears brake out from him as he crossed the stream and came into the bushy valley. There he stayed his feet a little, and said to himself: "And whither then am I going?" He thought of the Castle of Abundance and the Champions of the Dry Tree, of Higham, and the noble warriors who sat at the Lord Abbot's board, and of Upmeads and his own folk: but all seemed naught to him, and he thought: "And how can I go back and bear folk asking me curiously of my wayfarings, and whether I will do this, that, or the other thing." Withal he thought of that fair damsel and her sweet mouth in the hostelry at Bourton Abbas, and groaned when he thought of love and its ending, and he said within himself: "and now she is a wanderer about the earth as I am;" and he thought of her quest, and the chaplet of dame Katherine, his gossip, which he yet bore on his neck, and he deemed that he had naught to choose but to go forward and seek that he was doomed to; and now it seemed to him that there was that one thing to do and no other. And though this also seemed to him but weariness and grief, yet whereas he had ever lightly turned him to doing what work lay ready to hand; so now he knew that he must first of all get him out of that wilderness, that he might hear the talk of folk concerning the Well at the World's End, which he doubted not to hear again when he came into the parts inhabited.

So now, with his will or without it, his feet bore him on, and he followed up the stream which the Lady had said ran into the broad river called the Swelling Flood; "for," thought he, "when I come thereabout I shall presently find some castle or good town, and it is like that either I shall have some tidings of the folk thereof, or else they will compel me to do something, and that will irk me less than doing deeds of mine own will."

He went his ways till he came to where the wood and the trees ended, and the hills were lower and longer, well grassed with short grass, a down country fit for the feeding of sheep; and indeed some sheep he saw, and a shepherd or two, but far off. At last, after he had left the stream awhile, because it seemed to him to turn and wind round over much to the northward, he came upon a road running athwart the down country, so that he deemed that it must lead one way down to the Swelling Flood; so he followed it up, and after a while began to fall in with folk; and first two Companions armed and bearing long swords over their shoulders: he stopped as they met, and stared at them in the face, but answered not their greeting; and they had no will to meddle with him, seeing his inches and that he was well armed, and looked no craven: so they went on.

Next he came on two women who had with them an ass between two panniers, laden with country stuff; and they were sitting by the wayside, one old and the other young. He made no stay for them, and though he turned his face their way, took no heed of them more than if they were trees; though the damsel, who was well-liking and somewhat gaily

195

clad, stood up when she saw his face anigh, and drew her gown skirt about her and moved daintily, and sighed and looked after him as he went on, for she longed for him.

Yet again came two men a-horseback, merchants clad goodly, with three carles, their servants, riding behind them; and all these had weapons and gave little more heed to him than he to them. But a little after they were gone, he stopped and said within himself: "Maybe I had better have gone their way, and this road doubtless leadeth to some place of resort."

But even therewith he heard horsehoofs behind him, and anon came up a man a-horseback, armed with jack and sallet, a long spear in his hand, and budgets at his saddle-bow, who looked like some lord's man going a message. He nodded to Ralph, who gave him good-day; for seeing these folk and their ways had by now somewhat amended his mind; and now he turned not, but went on as before.

At last the way clomb a hill longer and higher than any he had yet crossed, and when he had come to the brow and looked down, he saw the big river close below running through the wide valley which he had crossed with Roger on that other day. Then he sat down on the green bank above the way, so heavy of heart that not one of the things he saw gave him any joy, and the world was naught to him. But within a while he came somewhat to himself, and, looking down toward the river, he saw that where the road met it, it was very wide, and shallow withal, for the waves rippled merrily and glittered in the afternoon sun, though there was no wind; moreover the road went up white from the water on the other side, so he saw clearly that this was the ford of a highway. The valley was peopled withal: on the other side of the river was a little thorp, and there were carts and sheds scattered about the hither side, and sheep and neat feeding in the meadows, and in short it was another world from the desert.

CHAPTER 12

Ralph Falleth in With Friends and Rideth to Whitwall

Ralph looks on to the ford and sees folk riding through the thorp aforesaid and down to the river, and they take the water and are many in company, some two score by his deeming, and he sees the sun glittering on their weapons.

Now he thought that he would abide their coming and see if he might join their company, since if he crossed the water he would be on the backward way: and it was but a little while ere the head of them came up over the hill, and were presently going past Ralph, who rose up to look on them, and be seen of them, but they took little heed of him. So he sees that though they all bore weapons, they were not all men-at-arms, nay, not more than a half score, but those proper men enough. Of the others, some half-dozen seemed by their attire to be merchants, and the rest their lads; and withal they had many sumpter horses and mules with them. They greeted him not, nor he them, nor did he heed them much till they were all gone by save three, and then he leapt into the road with a cry, for who should be riding there but Blaise, his eldest brother, and Richard the Red with him, both in good case by seeming; for Blaise was clad in a black coat welted with gold, and rode a good grey palfrey, and Richard was armed well and knightly.

They knew him at once, and drew rein, and Blaise lighted down from his horse and cast his arms about Ralph, and said: "O happy day! when two of the Upmeads kindred meet thus in an alien land! But what maketh thee here, Ralph? I thought of thee as merry and safe in Upmeads?"

Ralph said smiling, for his heart leapt up at the sight of his kindred: "Nay, must I not seek adventures like the rest? So I stole myself away from father and mother." "Ill done, little lord!" said Blaise, stroking Ralph's cheek.

Then up came Richard, and if Blaise were glad, Richard was twice glad, and quoth he: "Said I not, Lord Blaise, that this chick would be the hardest of all to keep under the coop? Welcome to the Highways, Lord Ralph! But where is thine horse? and whence and whither is it now? Hast thou met with some foil and been held to ransom?"

Ralph found it hard and grievous and dull work to answer; for now again his sorrow had taken hold of him: so he said: "Yea, Richard, I have had adventures, and have lost rather than won; but at least I am a free man, and have spent but little gold on my loss."

"That is well," said Richard, "but whence gat ye any gold for spending?" Ralph smiled, but sadly, for he called to mind the glad setting forth and the kind face of dame Katherine his gossip, and he said: "Clement Chapman deemed it not unmeet to stake somewhat on my luck, therefore I am no pauper."

"Well," said Blaise, "if thou hast no great errand elsewhere, thou mightest ride with us, brother. I have had good hap in these days, though scarce kingly or knightly, for I have been buying and selling: what matter? few know Upmeads and its kings to wite me with fouling a fair name. Richard, go fetch a horse hither for Lord Ralph's riding, and we will tarry no longer." So Richard trotted on, and while they abode him, Ralph asked after his brethren, and Blaise told him that he had seen or heard naught of them. Then Ralph asked of whither away, and Blaise told him to Whitwall, where was much recourse of merchants from many lands, and a noble market.

Back then cometh Richard leading a good horse while Ralph was pondering his matter, and thinking that at such a town he might well hear tidings concerning the Well at the World's End.

Now Ralph mounts, and they all ride away together. On the way, partly for brotherhood's sake, partly that he might not be questioned overmuch himself, Ralph asked Blaise to tell him more of his farings; and Blaise said, that when he had left Upmeads he had ridden with Richard up and down and round about, till he came to a rich town which had just been taken in war, and that the Companions who had conquered it were looking for chapmen to cheapen their booty, and that he was the first or nearly the first to come who had will and money to buy, and the Companions, who were eager to depart, had sold him thieves' penny-worths, so that his share of the Upmeads' treasure had gone far; and thence he had gone to another good town where he had the best of markets for his newly cheapened wares, and had brought more there, such as he deemed handy to sell, and so had gone on from town to town, and had ever thriven, and had got much wealth: and so at last having heard tell of Whitwall as better for chaffer than all he had yet seen, he and other chapmen had armed them, and waged men-at-arms to defend them, and so tried the adventure of the wildwoods, and come safe through.

Then at last came the question to Ralph concerning his adventures, and he enforced himself to speak, and told all as truly as he might, without telling of the Lady and her woeful ending.

Thus they gave and took in talk, and Ralph did what he might to seem like other folk, that he might nurse his grief in his own heart as far asunder from other men as might be.

So they rode on till it was even, and came to Whitwall before the shutting of the gates and rode into the street, and found it a fair and great town, well defensible, with high and new walls, and men-at-arms good store to garnish them.

Ralph rode with his brother to the hostel of the chapmen, and there they were well lodged.

CHAPTER 13

Richard Talketh With Ralph Concerning the Well at the World's End. Concerning Swevenham

On the morrow Blaise went to his chaffer and to visit the men of the Port at the Guildhall: he bade Ralph come with him, but he would not, but abode in the hall of the hostel and sat pondering sadly while men came and went; but he heard no word spoken of the Well at the World's End. In like wise passed the next day and the next, save that Richard was among those who came into the hall, and he talked long with Ralph at whiles; that is to say that he spake, and Ralph made semblance of listening.

Now as is aforesaid Richard was old and wise, and he loved Ralph much, more belike than Lord Blaise his proper master, whereas he had no mind for chaffer, or aught pertaining to it: so he took heed of Ralph and saw that he was sad and weary-hearted; so on the sixth day of their abiding at Whitwall, in the morning when all the chapmen were gone about their business, and he and Ralph were left alone in the Hall, he spake to Ralph and said: "This is no prison, lord." "Even so," quoth Ralph. "Nay, if thou doubtest it," said Richard, "let us go to the door and try if they have turned the key and shot the bolt on us." Ralph smiled faintly and stood up, and said: "I will go with thee if thou willest it, but sooth to say I shall be but a dull fellow of thine to-day." Said Richard: "Wouldst thou have been better yesterday, lord, or the day before?" "Nay," said Ralph. "Wilt thou be better to-morrow?" said Richard. Ralph shook his head. Said Richard: "Yea, but thou wilt be, or thou mayst call me a fool else." "Thou art kind, Richard," said Ralph; "and I will come with thee, and do what thou biddest me; but I must needs tell

200

thee that my heart is sick." "Yea," quoth Richard, "and thou needest not tell me so much, dear youngling; he who runs might read that in thee. But come forth."

So into the street they went, and Richard brought Ralph into the market-place, and showed him where was Blaise's booth (for he was thriving greatly) but Ralph would not go anigh it lest his brother should entangle him in talk; and they went into the Guildhall which was both great and fair, and the smell of the new-shaven oak (for the roof was not yet painted) brought back to Ralph's mind the days of his childhood when he was hanging about the building of the water-reeve's new house at Upmeads. Then they went into the Great Church and heard a Mass at the altar of St. Nicholas, Ralph's very friend; and the said church was great to the letter, and very goodly, and somewhat new also, since the blossom-tide of Whitwall was not many years old: and the altars of its chapels were beyond any thing for fairness that Ralph had seen save at Higham on the Way.

But when they came forth from the church, Ralph looked on Richard with a face that was both blank and weary, as who should say: "What is to do now?" And forsooth so woe-begone he looked, that Richard, despite his sorrow and trouble for him, could scarce withhold his laughter. But he said: "Well, foster son (for thou art pretty much that to me), since the good town pleasureth thee little, go we further afield."

So he led him out of the market-place, and brought him to the east gate of the town which hight Petergate Bar, and forth they went and out into the meadows under the walls, and stayed him at a little bridge over one of the streams, for it was a land of many waters; there they sat down in a nook, and spake Richard to Ralph, saying:

"Lord Ralph, ill it were if the Upmeads kindred came to naught, or even to little. Now as for my own master Blaise, he hath, so please you, the makings of a noble chapman, but not of a noble knight; though he sayeth that when he is right rich he will cast aside all chaffer; naught of which he will do. As for the others, my lord Gregory is no better, or indeed worse, save that he shall not be rich ever, having no mastery

201

over himself; while lord Hugh is like to be slain in some empty brawl, unless he come back speedily to Upmeads."

"Yea, yea," said Ralph, "what then? I came not hither to hear thee missay my mother's sons." But Richard went on: "As for thee, lord Ralph, of thee I looked for something; but now I cannot tell; for the heart in thee seemeth to be dead; and thou must look to it lest the body die also." "So be it!" said Ralph.

Said Richard: "I am old now, but I have been young, and many things have I seen and suffered, ere I came to Upmeads. Old am I, and I cannot feel certain hopes and griefs as a young man can; yet have I bought the knowledge of them dear enough, and have not forgotten. Whereby I wot well that thy drearihead is concerning a woman. Is it not so?" "Yea," quoth Ralph. Said Richard: "Now shalt thou tell me thereof, and so lighten thine heart a little." "I will not tell thee," said Ralph; "or, rather, to speak more truly, I cannot." "Yea," said Richard, "and though it were now an easier thing for me to tell thee of the griefs of my life than for thee to hearken to the tale, yet I believe thee. But mayhappen thou mayst tell me of one thing that thou desirest more than another." Said Ralph: "I desire to die." And the tears started in his eyes therewith. But Richard spake, smiling on him kindly: "That way is open for thee on any day of the week. Why hast thou not taken it already?" But Ralph answered naught. Richard said: "Is it not because thou hopest to desire something; if not to-day, then to-morrow, or the next day or the next?" Still Ralph spake no word; but he wept. Quoth Richard: "Maybe I may help thee to a hope, though thou mayest think my words wild. In the land and the thorp where I was born and bred there was talk now and again of a thing to be sought, which should cure sorrow, and make life blossom in the old, and uphold life in the young." "Yea," said Ralph, looking up from his tears, "and what was that? and why hast thou never told me thereof before?" "Nay," said Richard, "and why should I tell it to the merry lad I knew in Upmeads? but now thou art a man, and hast seen the face of sorrow, it is meet that thou shouldest hear of THE WELL AT THE WORLD'S END."

Ralph sprang to his feet as he said the word, and cried out

202

eagerly: "Old friend, and where then wert thou bred and born?" Richard laughed and said: "See, then, there is yet a deed and a day betwixt thee and death! But turn about and look straight over the meadows in a line with yonder willow-tree, and tell me what thou seest." Said Ralph: "The fair plain spreading wide, and a river running through it, and little hills beyond the water, and blue mountains beyond them, and snow yet lying on the tops of them, though the year is in young July." "Yea," quoth Richard; "and seest thou on the first of the little hills beyond the river, a great grey tower rising up and houses anigh it?" "Yea," said Ralph, "the tower I see, and the houses, for I am far-sighted; but the houses are small." "So it is," said Richard; "now yonder tower is of the Church of Swevenham, which is under the invocation of the Seven Sleepers of Ephesus; and the houses are the houses of the little town. And what has that to do with me? sayest thou: why this, that I was born and bred at Swevenham. And indeed I it was who brought my lord Blaise here to Whitwall, with tales of how good a place it was for chaffer, that I might see the little town and the great grey tower once more. Forsooth I lied not, for thy brother is happy here, whereas he is piling up the coins one upon the other. Forsooth thou shouldest go into his booth, fair lord; it is a goodly sight."

But Ralph was walking to and fro hastily, and he turned to Richard and said: "Well, well! but why dost thou not tell me more of the Well at the World's End?"

Said Richard: "I was going to tell thee somewhat which might be worth thy noting; or might not be worth it: hearken! When I dwelt at Swevenham over yonder, and was but of eighteen winters, who am now of three score and eight, three folk of our township, two young men and one young woman, set out thence to seek the said Well: and much lore they had concerning it, which they had learned of an old man, a nigh kinsman of one of them. This ancient carle I had never seen, for he dwelt in the mountains a way off, and these men were some five years older than I, so that I was a boy when they were men grown; and such things I heeded not, but rather sport and play; and above all, I longed for the play of war and battle. God wot I have had my bellyful of it since those days! Howbeit I mind me the setting forth of these three. They had a sumpter-ass with them for their livelihood on the waste; but they went afoot crowned with flowers, and the pipe and tabour playing before them, and much people brought them on the way. By St. Christopher! I can see it all as if it were yesterday. I was sorry of the departure of the damsel; for though I was a boy I had loved her, and she had suffered me to kiss her and toy with her; but it was soon over. Now I call to mind that they had prayed our priest, Sir Cyprian, to bless them on their departure, but he naysaid them; for he held that such a quest came of the inspiration of the devils, and was but a memory of the customs of the ancient gentiles and heathen. But as to me, I deemed it naught, and was sorry that my white-bosomed, sweet-breathed friend should walk away from me thus into the clouds."

"What came of it?" said Ralph, "did they come back, or any of them?" "I wot not," said Richard, "for I was weary of Swevenham after that, so I girt myself to a sword and laid a spear upon my shoulder and went my ways to the Castle of the Waste March, sixty miles from Swevenham town, and the Baron took me in and made me his man: and almost as little profit were in my telling thee again of my deeds there, as there was in my doing them: but the grey tower of Swevenham I have never seen again till this hour."

Said Ralph: "Now then it behoveth me to go to Swevenham straightway: wilt thou come with me? it seemeth to be but some four miles hence."

Richard held his peace and knit his brows as if pondering the matter, and Ralph abided till he spake: so he said: "Foster-son, so to call thee, thou knowest the manner of up-country carles, that tales flow forth from them the better if they come without over much digging and hoeing of the ground; that is, without questioning; so meseems better it will be if I go to Swevenham alone, and better if I be asked to go, than if I go of myself. Now to-morrow is Saturday, and high market in Whitwall; and I am not so old but that it is likeliest that there will be some of my fellows alive and on their legs in Swevenham: and if such there be, there will be one at the least in the market to-morrow, and I will be there to find him out: and then it will go hard if he bring me not to Swevenham as a well-beloved guest; and when I am there, and telling my tidings, and asking them of theirs, if there be any tales concerning the Well at the World's End working in their bellies, then shall I be the midwife to bring them to birth. Ha? Will it do?"

"Yea," said Ralph, "but how long wilt thou be?" Said Richard: "I shall come back speedily if I find the land barren; but if the field be in ear I shall tarry to harvest it. So keep thou thy soul in patience." "And what shall I do now?" said Ralph. "Wear away the hours," said Richard. And to begin with, come back within the gates with me and let us go look at thy brother's booth in the market-place: it is the nethermost of a goodly house which he is minded to dwell in; and he will marry a wife and sit down in Whitwall, so well he seemeth like to thrive; for they have already bidden him to the freedom of the city, and to a brother of the Faring-Knights, whereas he is not only a stirring man, but of good lineage also: for now he hideth not that he is of the Upmeads kindred."

CHAPTER 14

Ralph Falleth in With Another Old Friend

Ralph went with Richard now without more words, and they came into the market-place and unto Blaise's booth and house, which was no worse than the best in the place; and the painters and stainers were at work on the upper part of it to make it as bright and goodly as might be with red and blue and green and gold, and all fair colours, and already was there a sign hung out of the fruitful tree by the waterside. As for the booth, it was full within of many wares and far-fetched and dear-bought things; as pieces of good and fine cloth plumbed with the seal of the greatest of the cities;

and silk of Babylon, and spices of the hot burning islands, and wonders of the silversmith's and the goldsmith's fashioning, and fair-wrought weapons and armour of the best, and every thing that a rich chapman may deal in. And amidst of it all stood Blaise clad in fine black cloth welted with needle work, and a gold chain about his neck. He was talking with three honourable men of the Port, and they were doing him honour with kind words and the bidding of help. When he saw Ralph and Richard come in, he nodded to them, as to men whom he loved, but were beneath him in dignity, and left not talking with the great men. Richard grinned a little thereat, as also did Ralph in his heart; for he thought: "Here then is one of the Upmeads kin provided for, so that soon he may buy with his money two domains as big as Upmeads and call them his manors."

Now Ralph looks about him, and presently he sees a man come forward to meet him from the innermost of the booth, and lo! there was come Clement Chapman. His heart rose at the sight of him, and he thought of his kind gossip till he could scarce withhold his tears. But Clement came to him and cast his arms about him, and kissed him, and said: "Thou shalt pardon me for this, lord, for it is the kiss of the gossip which she bade me give thee, if I fell in with thee, as now I have, praised be the Saints! Yet it irks me that I shall see little more of thee at this time, for to-morrow early I must needs join myself to my company; for we are going south awhile to a good town some fifty miles hence. Nevertheless, if thou dwellest here some eight days I shall see thee again belike, since thereafter I get me eastward on a hard and long journey not without peril. How sayest thou?"

"I wot not," quoth Ralph looking at Richard. Said Richard: "Thou mayst wot well, master Clement, that my lord is anhungered of the praise of the folks, and is not like to abide in a mere merchant-town till the mould grow on his back." "Well, well," said Clement, "however that may be, I have now done my matters with this cloth-lord, Blaise, and he has my florins in his pouch: so will not ye twain come with me and drink a cup till he hath done his talk with these magnates?"

Ralph was nothing loth, for besides that he loved master

Clement, and that his being in company was like having a piece of his home anigh him, he hoped to hear some tidings concerning the Well at the World's End.

So he and Richard went with master Clement to the Christopher, a fair ale-house over against the Great Church, and sat down to good wine; and Ralph asked of Clement many things concerning dame Katherine his gossip, and Clement told him all, and that she was well, and had been to Upmeads, and had seen King Peter and the mother of Ralph; and how she had assuaged his mother's grief at his departure by forecasting fair days for her son. All this Ralph heard gladly, though he was somewhat shamefaced withal, and sat silent and thinking of many matters. But Richard took up the word and said: "Which way camest thou from Wulstead, master Clement?" "The nighest way I came," said Clement, "through the Woods Perilous." Said Richard: "And they of the Dry Tree, heardest thou aught of them?" "Yea, certes," quoth Clement, "for I fell in with their Bailiff, and paid him due scot for the passage of the Wood; he knoweth me withal, and we talked together." "And had he any tidings to tell thee of the champions?" said Richard. Said Clement, "Great tidings maybe, how that there was a rumour that they had lost their young Queen and Lady; and if that be true, it will go nigh to break their hearts, so sore as they loved her. And that will make them bitter and fierce, till their grief has been slaked by the blood of men. And that the more as their old Queen abideth still, and she herself is ever of that mind."

Ralph hearkened, and his heart was wounded that other men should speak of his beloved: but he heard how Richard said: "Hast thou ever known why that company of champions took the name of the Dry Tree?" "Why, who should know that, if thou knowest it not, Richard of Swevenham?" said Clement: "Is it not by the token of the Dry Tree that standeth in the lands on the hither side of the Wall of the World?" Richard nodded his head; but Ralph cried out: "O Master Clement, and hast thou seen it, the Wall of the World?" "Yea, afar off, my son," said he; "or what the folk with me called so; as to the Dry Tree, I have told thee at Wulstead that I have seen it not, though I have known men who have told me that they have seen it." "And must they

207

who find the Well at the World's End come by the Dry Tree?" "Yea, surely," said Clement. Quoth Richard: "And thus have some heard, who have gone on that quest, and they have heard of the Champions of Hampton, and have gone thither, being deceived by that name of the Dry Tree, and whiles have been slain by the champions, whiles have entered their company." "Yea," said Clement, "so it is that their first error hath ended their quest. But now, lord Ralph, I will tell thee one thing; to wit, that when I return hither after eight days wearing, I shall be wending east, as I said e'en now, and what will that mean save going somewhat nigher to the Wall of the World; for my way lieth beyond the mountains that ye see from hence, and beyond the mountains that lie the other side of those; and I bid thee come with us, and I will be thy warrant that so far thou shalt have no harm: but when thou hast come so far, and hast seen three very fair cities, besides towns and castles and thorps and strange men, and fair merchandize, God forbid that thou shouldest wend further, and so cast away thy young life for a gay-coloured cloud. Then will be the time to come back with me, that I may bring thee through the perils of the way to Wulstead, and Upmeads at the last, and the folk that love thee."

Richard held his peace at this word, but Ralph said: "I thank thee, Master Clement, for thy love and thy helping hand; and will promise thee to abide thee here eight days at the least; and meanwhile I will ponder the matter well."

CHAPTER 15

Ralph Dreams a Dream Or Sees a Vision

Therewithall they parted after more talk concerning small matters, and Ralph wore through the day, but Richard again did him to wit, that on the morrow he would find his old friends of Swevenham in the Market. And Ralph was come to life again more than he had been since that evil hour in the desert; though hard and hard he deemed it that he should never see his love again.

Now as befalleth young men, he was a good sleeper, and dreamed but seldom, save such light and empty dreams as he might laugh at, if perchance he remembered them by then his raiment was on him in the morning. But that night himseemed that he awoke in his chamber at Whitwall, and was lying on his bed, as he verily was, and the door of the chamber opened, and there entered quietly the Lady of the Woodland, dight even as he had seen her as she lay dead beside their cooking fire on that table of greensward in the wilderness, barefoot and garlanded about her brow and her girdlestead, but fair and fresh coloured as she was before the sword had pierced her side; and he thought that he rejoiced to see her, but no wild hope rose in his heart, and no sobbing passion blinded his eyes, nor did he stretch out hand to touch her, because he remembered that she was dead. But he thought she spake to him and said: "I know that thou wouldst have me speak, therefore I say that I am come to bid thee farewell, since there was no farewell between us in the wilderness, and I know that thou are about going on a long and hard and perilous journey: and I would that I could kiss thee and embrace thee, but I may not, for this is but the image of me as thou hast known me. Furthermore, as I loved thee when I saw thee first, for thy youth, and thy fairness, and thy kindness and thy valiancy, so now I rejoice that all this shall endure so long in thee, as it surely shall."

Then the voice ceased, but still the image stood before him awhile, and he wondered if she would speak again, and tell him aught of the way to the Well at the World's End; and she spake again: "Nay," she said, "I cannot, since we may not tread the way together hand in hand; and this is part of the loss that thou hast had of me; and oh! but it is hard and hard." And her face became sad and distressful, and she turned and departed as she had come.

Then he knew not if he awoke, or if it were a change in his dream; but the chamber became dark about him, and he lay there thinking of her, till, as it seemed, day began to dawn, and there was some little stir in the world without, and the new wind moved the casement. And again the door opened, and someone entered as before; and this also was a woman: green-clad she was and barefoot, yet he knew at once that it was not his love that was dead, but the damsel of the ale-house of Bourton, whom he had last seen by the wantways of the Wood Perilous, and he thought her wondrous fair, fairer than he had deemed. And the word came from her: "I am a sending of the woman whom thou hast loved, and I should not have been here save she had sent me." Then the words ended, while he looked at her and wondered if she also had died on the way to the Well at the World's End. And it came into his mind that he had never known her name upon the earth. Then again came the word: "So it is that I am not dead but alive in the world, though I am far away from this land; and it is good that thou shouldst go seek the Well at the World's End not all alone: and the seeker may find me: and whereas thou wouldst know my name, I hight Dorothea."

So fell the words again: and this image stood awhile as the other had done, and as the other had done, departed, and once more the chamber became dark, so that Ralph could not so much as see where was the window, and he knew no more till he woke in the early morn, and there was stir in the street and the voice of men, and the scent of fresh herbs and worts, and fruits; for it was market-day, and the country folk were early afoot, that they might array their wares timely in the market-place.

CHAPTER 16

Of the Tales of Swevenham

Old Richard was no worse than his word, and failed not to find old acquaintance of Swevenham in the Saturday's market: and Ralph saw naught of him till midweek afterwards.

And he was sitting in the chamber of the hostel when Richard came in to him. Forsooth Blaise had bidden him come dwell in his fair house, but Ralph would not, deeming that he might be hindered in his quest and be less free to go whereso he would, if he were dwelling with one who was so great with the magnates as was Blaise.

Now Ralph was reading in a book when Richard came in, but he stood up and greeted him; and Richard said smiling: "What have ye found in the book, lord?" Said Ralph: "It telleth of the deeds of Alexander." "Is there aught concerning the Well at the World's End therein?" said Richard. "I have not found aught thereof as yet," said Ralph; "but the book tells concerning the Dry Tree, and of kings sitting in their chairs in the mountains nearby."

"Well then," said Richard, "maybe thou wilt think me the better tale-teller." "Tell on then," quoth Richard. So they went and sat them down in a window, and Richard said:

"When I came to Swevenham with two old men that I had known young, the folk made much of me, and made me good cheer, whereof were over long to tell thee; but to speak shortly, I drew the talk round to the matter that we would wot of: for we spake of the Men of the Dry Tree, and an old man began to say, as master Clement the other day, that this name of theirs was but a token and an armoury which those champions have taken from the Tree itself, which Alexander the Champion saw in his wayfarings; and he said that this tree was on the hither side of the mountains called the Wall of the World, and no great way from the last of the towns whereto Clement will wend; for Clement told me the name thereof, to wit, Goldburg. Then another and an older man, one that I remember a stout carle ere I left Swevenham, said that this was not so, but that the Tree was on the further side of the Wall of the World, and that he who could lay his hand on the bole thereof was like enough to drink of the Well at the World's End. Thereafter another spake, and told a tale of how the champions at Hampton first took the Dry Tree for a token; and he said that the rumour ran, that a woman had brought the tidings thereof to those valiant men, and had fixed the name upon them, though wherefore none knew. So the talk went on.

211

"But there was a carline sitting in the ingle, and she knew me and I her. And indeed in days past, when I was restless and longing to depart, she might have held me at Swevenham, for she was one of the friends that I loved there: a word and a kiss had done it, or maybe the kiss without the word: but if I had the word, I had not the kiss of her. Well, when the talk began to fall, she spake and said to me:

" 'Now it is somewhat strange that the talk must needs fall on this seeking of that which shall not be found, whereas it was but the month before thou wert last at Swevenham, that Wat Miller and Simon Bowyer set off to seek the Well at the World's End, and took with them Alice of Queenhough, whom Simon loved as well as might be, and Wat somewhat more than well. Mindest thou not? There are more than I alive that remember it.'

" 'Yea,' said I, 'I remember it well.'

"For indeed, foster-son, these were the very three of whom I told thee, though I told thee not their names.

" 'Well,' said I; 'how sped they? Came they back, or any of them?' 'Nay,' she said, 'that were scarce to be looked for.' Said I: 'Have any other to thy knowledge gone on this said quest?'

" 'Yea,' she said, 'I will tell thee all about it, and then there will be an end of the story, for none knoweth better thereof than I. First there was that old man, the wizard, to whom folk from Swevenham and other places about were used to seek for his lore in hidden matters; and some months after those three had departed, folk who went to his abode amongst the mountains found him not; and soon the word was about that he also, for as feeble as he was, had gone to seek the Well at the World's End; though may-happen it was not so. Then the next spring after thy departure, Richard, comes home Arnold Wright from the wars, and asks after Alice; and when he heard what had befallen, he takes a scrip with a little meat for the road, lays his spear on his shoulder, and is gone seeking the lost, and the thing which they found not— that, I deem, was the end of him. Again the year after that, as I deem, three of our carles fell in with two knights riding east from Whitwall, and were questioned of them concerning the road to the said Well, and doubted not but that they were

212

on that quest. Furthermore (and some of you wot this well enough, and more belike know it not) two of our young men were faring by night and cloud on some errand, good or bad, it matters not, on the highway thirty miles east of Whitwall: it was after harvest, and the stubble-fields lay on either side of the way, and the moon was behind thin clouds, so that it was light on the way, as they told me; and they saw a woman wending before them afoot, and as they came up with her, the moon ran out, and they saw that the woman was fair, and that about her neck was a chaplet of gems that shone in the moon, and they had a longing both for the jewel and the woman: but before they laid hand on her they asked her of whence and whither, and she said: From ruin and wrack to the Well at the World's End, and therewith turned on them with a naked sword in her hand; so that they shrank from before her.

" 'Hearken once more: the next year came a knight to Swevenham, and guested in this same house, and he sat just where sitteth now yon yellow-headed swain, and the talk went on the same road as it hath gone to-night; and I told him all the tale as I have said it e'en now; and he asked many questions, but most of the Lady with the pair of beads. And on the morrow he departed and we saw him not again.

"Then she was silent, but the young man at whom she had pointed flushed red and stared at her wide-eyed, but said no word. But I spake: 'Well dame, but have none else gone from Swevenham, or what hath befallen them?'

"She said: 'Hearken yet! Twenty years agone a great sickness lay heavy upon us and the folk of Whitwall, and when it was at its worst, five of our young men, calling to mind all the tales concerning the Well at the World's End, went their ways to seek it, and swore that back would they never, save they found it and could bear its water to the folk of Swevenham; and I suppose they kept their oath; for we saw naught either of the water or of them. Well, I deem that this is the last that I have to tell thee, Richard, concerning this matter: and now is come the time for thee to tell tales of thyself.'

"Thus for that time dropped the talk of the Well at the World's End, Lord Ralph, and of the way thither. But I hung about the township yet a while, and yesterday as I stood on their stone bridge, and looked on the water, up comes that long lad with the yellow hair that the dame had pointed at, and says to me: 'Master Richard, saving thine age and thy dignity and mastery, I can join an end to the tale which the carline began on Sunday night.' 'Yea, forsooth?' said I, and how, my lad?' Said he: 'Thou hast a goodly knife there in thy girdle, give it to me, and I will tell thee.' 'Yea,' quoth I, 'if thy tale be knife-worthy.'

"Well, the end of it was that he told me thus: That by night and moon he came on one riding the highway, just about where the other woman had been seen, whose tale he had heard of. He deemed at first this rider to be a man, or a lad rather for smallness and slenderness, but coming close up he found it was a woman, and saw on her neck a chaplet of gems, and deemed it no great feat to take it of her: but he asked her of whence and whither, and she answered:

" 'From unrest to the Well at the World's End.'

"Then when he put out his hand to her, he saw a great anlace gleaming in her hand, wherefore he forbore her; and this was but five days ago.

"So I gave the lad my knife, and deemed there would be little else to hear in Swevenham for this bout; and at least I heard no more tales to tell till I came away this morning; so there is my poke turned inside out for thee. But this word further would I say to thee, that I have seen on thy neck also a pair of beads exceeding goodly. Tell me now whence came they."

"From my gossip, dame Katherine," said Ralph; "and it seems to me now, though at the time I heeded the gift little save for its kindness, that she thought something great might go with it; and there was a monk at Higham on the Way, who sorely longed to have it of me." "Well," said Richard, "that may well come to pass, that it shall lead thee to the Well at the World's End. But as to the tales of Swevenham, what deemest thou of them?" Said Ralph: "What are they, save a token that folk believe that there is such a thing on earth as the Well? Yet I have made up my mind already that I would so do as if I trowed in it. So I am no nearer to it than erst. Now is there naught for it save to abide Master

214

Clement's coming; and when he hath brought me to Gold-burg, then shall I see how the quest looks by the daylight of that same city." He spake so cheerfully that Richard looked at him askance, wondering what was toward with him, and if mayhappen anything lay underneath those words of his.

But in his heart Ralph was thinking of that last tale of the woman whom the young man had met such a little while ago; and it seemed to him that she must have been in Whitwall when he first came there; and he scarce knew whether he were sorry or not that he had missed her: for though it seemed to him that it would be little more than mere grief and pain, nay, that it would be wicked and evil to be led to the Well at the World's End by any other than her who was to have brought him there; yet he longed, or thought he longed to speak with her concerning that love of his heart, so early rewarded, so speedily beggared. For indeed he doubted not that the said woman was the damsel of Bourton Abbas, whose image had named herself Dorothea to him in that dream.

CHAPTER 17

Richard Bringeth Tidings of Departing

Fell the talk between them at that time, and three days wore, and on the morning of the fourth day came Richard to Ralph, and said to him: "Foster-son, I am sorry for the word I must say, but Clement Chapman came within the gates this morning early, and the company with which he is riding are alboun for the road, and will depart at noon to-day, so that there are but four hours wherein we twain may be together; and thereafter whatso may betide thee, it may well be, that I shall see thy face no more; so what thou wilt tell me must be told straightway. And now I will say this to thee, that of all things I were fain to ride with thee, but I may not, because it is Blaise whom I am bound to serve in all ways. And I deem, moreover, that troublous times may be at hand here in Whitwall. For there is an Earl hight Walter the Black, a fair young man outwardly, but false at heart and a tyrant, and he had some occasion against the good town, and it was looked for that he should send his herald here to defy the Port more than a half moon ago; but about that time he was hurt in a fray as we hear, and may not back a horse in battle yet. Albeit, fristed is not forgotten, as saith the saw; and when he is whole again, we may look for him at our gates; and whereas Blaise knows me for a deft man-at-arms or something more, it is not to be looked for that he will give me to thee for this quest. Nay, of thee also it will be looked for that thou shouldest do knightly service to the Port, and even so Blaise means it to be; therefore have I lied to him on thy behalf, and bidden Clement also to lie (which forsooth he may do better than I, since he wotteth not wholly whither thou art minded), and I have said thou wouldst go with Clement no further than Cheaping Knowe, which lieth close to the further side of these mountains, and will be back again in somewhat more than a half-moon's wearing. So now thou art warned hereof."

Ralph was moved by these words of Richard, and he spake: "Forsooth, old friend, I am sorry to depart from thee; yet though I shall presently be all alone amongst aliens, yet now is manhood rising again in me. So for that cause at least shall I be glad to be on the way; and as a token that I am more whole than I was, I will now tell thee the tale of my grief, if thou wilt hearken to it, which the other day I might not tell thee."

"I will hearken it gladly," said Richard. And therewith they sat down in a window, for they were within doors in the hostel, and Ralph told all that had befallen him as plainly and shortly as he might; and when he had done, Richard said:

"Thou has had much adventure in a short space, lord, and if thou mightest now refrain thy longing for that which is gone, and set it on that which is to come, thou mayest yet harden into a famous knight and a happy man." Said Ralph: "Yea? now tell me all thy thought."

Said Richard: "My thought is that this lady who was slain,

was scarce wholly of the race of Adam; but that at the least there was some blending in her of the blood of the fays. Or how deemest thou?"

"I wot not," said Ralph sadly; "to me she seemed but a woman, though she were fairer and wiser than other women." Said Richard: "Well, furthermore, if I heard thee aright, there is another woman in the tale who is also fairer and wiser than other women?"

"I would she were my sister!" said Ralph. "Yea," quoth Richard, "and dost thou bear in mind what she was like? I mean the fashion of her body." "Yea, verily," said Ralph.

Again said Richard: "Doth it seem to thee as if the Lady of the Dry Tree had some inkling that thou shouldst happen upon this other woman: whereas she showed her of the road to the Well at the World's End, and gave her that pair of beads, and meant that thou also shouldest go thither? And thou sayest that she praised her,—her beauty and wisdom. In what wise did she praise her? how came the words forth from her? was it sweetly?"

"Like honey and roses for sweetness," said Ralph. "Yea," said Richard, "and she might have praised her in such wise that the words had came forth like gall and vinegar. Now I will tell thee of my thought, since we be at point of sundering, though thou take it amiss and be wroth with me: to wit, that thou wouldst have lost the love of this lady as time wore, even had she not been slain: and she being, if no fay, yet wiser than other women, and foreseeing, knew that so it would be." Ralph brake in: "Nay, nay, it is not so, it is not so!" "Hearken, youngling!" quoth Richard; "I deem that it was thus. Her love for thee was so kind that she would have thee happy after the sundering: therefore she was minded that thou shouldest find the damsel, who as I deem loveth thee, and that thou shouldest love her truly."

"O nay, nay!" said Ralph, "all this guess of thine is naught, saying that she was kind indeed. Even as heaven is kind to them who have died martyrs, and enter into its bliss after many torments."

And therewith he fell a-weeping at the very thought of her great kindness: for indeed to this young man she had seemed great, and exalted far above him.

Richard looked at him a while; and then said: "Now, I pray thee be not wroth with me for the word I have spoken. But something more shall I say, which shall like thee better. To wit, when I came back from Swevenham on Wednesday I deemed it most like that the Well at the World's End was a tale, a coloured cloud only; or that at most if it were indeed on the earth, that thou shouldest never find it. But now is my mind changed by the hearing of thy tale, and I deem both that the Well verily is, and that thou thyself shalt find it; and that the wise Lady knew this, and set the greater store by thy youth and goodliness, as a richer and more glorious gift than it had been, were it as fleeting as such things mostly be. Now of this matter will I say no more; but I think that the words that I have said, and which now seem so vain to thee, shall come into thy mind on some later day, and avail thee somewhat; and that is why I have spoken them. But this again is another word, that I have got a right good horse for thee, and other gear, such as thou mayest need for the road, and that Clement's fellowship will meet in Petergate hard by the church, and I will be thy squire till thou comest thither, and ridest thence out a-gates. Now I suppose that thou will want to bid Blaise farewell: yet thou must look to it that he will not deem thy farewell of great moment, since he swimmeth in florins and goodly wares; and moreover deemeth that thou wilt soon be back here."

"Nevertheless," said Ralph, "I must needs cast my arms about my own mother's son before I depart: so go we now, as all this talk hath worn away more than an hour of those four that were left me."

CHAPTER 18

Ralph Departeth From Whitwall
With the Fellowship of
Clement Chapman

Therewithal they went together to Blaise's house, and when Blaise saw them, he said: "Well, Ralph, so thou must needs work at a little more idling before thou fallest to in earnest. Forsooth I deem that when thou comest back thou wilt find that we have cut thee out a goodly piece of work for thy sewing. For the good town is gathering a gallant host of men; and we shall look to thee to do well in the hard hand-play, whenso that befalleth. But now come and look at my house within, how fair it is, and thou wilt see that thou wilt have somewhat to fight for, whereas I am."

Therewith he led them up a stair into the great chamber, which was all newly dight and hung with rich arras of the Story of Hercules; and there was a goodly cupboard of silver vessel, and some gold, and the cupboard was of five shelves as was but meet for a king's son. So Ralph praised all, but was wishful to depart, for his heart was sore, and he blamed himself in a manner that he must needs lie to his brother.

But Blaise brought them to the upper chamber, and showed them the goodly beds with their cloths, and hangings, and all was as fair as might be. Then Blaise bade bring wine and made them drink; and he gave Ralph a purse of gold, and an anlace very fair of fashion, and brought him to the door thereafter; and Ralph cast his arms about him, and kissed him and strained him to his breast. But Blaise was somewhat moved thereat, and said to him: "Why lad, thou art sorry to depart from me for a little while, and what would it be, were it for long? But ever wert thou a kind and tender-hearted youngling, and we twain are alone in an alien land. Forsooth, I wot that thou hast, as it were, embraced

219

the Upmeads kindred, father, mother and all; and good is that! So now God and the Saints keep thee, and bear in mind the hosting of the good town, and the raising of the banner, that shall be no great while. Fare thee well, lad!"

So they parted, and Ralph went back to the hostel, and gathered his stuff together, and laid it on a sumpter horse, and armed him, and so went into Petergate to join himself to that company. There he found the chapmen, five of them in all, and their lads, and a score of men-at-arms, with whom was Clement, not clad like a merchant, but weaponed, and bearing a coat of proof and a bright sallet on his head.

They greeted each the other, and Ralph said: "Yea, master Clement, and be we riding to battle?" "Maybe," quoth Clement; "the way is long, and our goods worth the lifting, and there are some rough places that we must needs pass through. But if ye like not the journey, abide here in this town the onset of Walter the Black."

Therewith he laughed, and Ralph understanding the jape, laughed also; and said: "Well, master Clement, but tell me who be these that we shall meet." "Yea, and I will tell thee the whole tale of them," said Clement, "but abide till we are without the gates; I am busy man e'en now, for all is ready for the road, save what I must do. So now bid thy Upmeads squire farewell, and then to horse with thee!"

So Ralph cast his arms about Richard, and kissed him and said: "This is also a farewell to the House where I was born and bred." And as he spake the thought of the House and the garden, and the pleasant fields of Upmeads came into his heart so bitter-sweet, that it mingled with his sorrow, and well-nigh made him weep. But as for Richard he forebore words, for he was sad at heart for the sundering.

Then he gat to horse, and the whole company of them bestirred them, and they rode out a-gates. And master Clement it was that ordered them, riding up and down along the array.

But Ralph fell to speech with the chapmen and men-at-arms; and both of these were very courteous with him; for they rejoiced in his company, and especially the chapmen, who were somewhat timorous of the perils of the road.

CHAPTER 19

Master Clement Tells Ralph Concerning the Lands Whereunto They Were Riding

When they were gotten a mile or two from Whitwall, and all was going smoothly, Clement came up to Ralph and rode at his left hand, and fell to speech with him, and said: "Now, lord, will I tell thee more concerning our journey, and the folk that we are like to meet upon the road. And of the perils, whatso they may be, I told thee not before, because I knew thee desirous of seeking adventures east-away, and knew that my tales would not hinder thee."

"Yea," said Ralph, "and had not this goodly fellowship been, I had gone alone, or with any carle that I could have lightly hired."

Clement laughed and said: "Fair sir, thou wouldst have failed of hiring any one man to go with thee east-ward a many miles. For with less than a score of men well-armed the danger of death or captivity is over great, if ye ride the mountain ways unto Cheaping Knowe. Yea, and even if a poor man who hath nothing, wend that way alone, he may well fall among thieves, and be stolen himself body and bones, for lack of anything better to steal."

Hereat Ralph felt his heart rise, when he thought of battle and strife, and he made his horse to spring somewhat, and then he said: "It liketh me well, dear friend, that I ride not with thee for naught, but that I may earn my daily bread like another."

"Yea," said Clement, looking on him kindly, "I deem of all thy brethren thou hast the biggest share of the blood of Red Robert, who first won Upmeads. And now thou shalt know that this good town of Whitwall that lieth behind us is the last of the lands we shall come to wherein folk can any

221

courtesy, or are ruled by the customs of the manor, or by due lawful Earls and Kings, or the laws of the Lineage or the Port, or have any Guilds for their guiding, and helping. And though these folks whereunto we shall come, are, some of them, Christian men by name, and have amongst them priests and religious; yet are they wild men of manners, and many heathen customs abide amongst them; as swearing on the altars of devils, and eating horse-flesh at the High-tides, and spell-raising more than enough, and such like things, even to the reddening of the doom-rings with the blood of men and of women, yea, and of babes: from such things their priests cannot withhold them. As for their towns that we shall come to, I say not but we shall find crafts amongst them, and worthy good men therein, but they have little might against the tyrants who reign over the towns, and who are of no great kindred, nor of blood better than other folk, but merely masterful and wise men who have gained their place by cunning and the high hand. Thou shalt see castles and fair strong-houses about the country-side, but the great men who dwell therein are not the natural kindly lords of the land yielding service to Earls, Dukes, and Kings, and having under them vavassors and villeins, men of the manor; but their tillers and shepherds and workmen and servants be mere thralls, whom they may sell at any market, like their horses or oxen. Forsooth these great men have with them for the more part free men waged for their service, who will not hold their hands from aught that their master biddeth, not staying to ask if it be lawful or unlawful. And that the more because whoso is a free man there, house and head must he hold on the tenure of bow and sword, and his life is like to be short if he hath not sworn himself to the service of some tyrant of a castle or a town."

"Yea, master Clement," said Ralph, "these be no peaceful lands whereto thou art bringing us, or very pleasant to dwell in."

"Little for peace, but much for profit," said Clement; "for these lands be fruitful of wine and oil and wheat, and neat and sheep; withal metals and gems are dug up out of the mountains; and on the other hand, they make but little by craftsmanship, wherefore are they the eagerer for chaffer

222

with us merchants; whereas also there are many of them well able to pay for what they lack, if not in money, then in kind, which in a way is better. Yea, it is a goodly land for merchants."

"But I am no merchant," said Ralph.

"So it is," said Clement, "yet thou desireth something; and whither we are wending thou mayst hear tidings that shall please thee, or tidings that shall please me. To say sooth, these two may well be adverse to each other, for I would not have thee hear so much of tidings as shall lead thee on, but rather I would have thee return with me, and not throw thy young life away: for indeed I have an inkling of what thou seekest, and meseems that Death and the Devil shall be thy faring-fellows."

Ralph held his peace, and Clement said in a cheerfuller voice: "Moreover, there shall be strange and goodly things to see; and the men of these parts be mostly goodly of body, and the women goodlier yet, as we carles deem."

Ralph sighed, and answered not at once, but presently he said: "Master Clement, canst thou give me the order of our goings for these next days?" "Yea, certes," said Clement. "In three days' time we shall come to the entry of the mountains: two days thence we shall go without coming under any roof save the naked heavens; the day thereafter shall we come to the Mid-Mountain House, which is as it were an hostelry; but it was built and is upheld by the folks that dwell anigh, amongst whom be the folk of Cheaping Knowe; and that house is hallowed unto truce, and no man smiteth another therein; so that we oft come on the mountain strong-thieves there, and there we be blithe together and feast together in good fellowship. But when there be foemen in that house together, each man or each fellowship departing, hath grace of an hour before his foeman follow. Such are the customs of that house, and no man breaketh them ever. But when we depart thence we shall ride all day and sleep amidst the mountains, and if we be not beset that night or the morrow's morn thereof, safe and unfoughten shall we come to Cheaping Knowe. Doth that suffice thee as at this time?" "Yea master," quoth Ralph.

So therewith their talk dropped, for the moment; but Clement talked much with Ralph that day, and honoured him much, as did all that company.

CHAPTER 20

They Come to the Mid-Mountain Guest-House

On that night they slept in their tents which they had pitched on the field of a little thorp beside a water; and there they had meat and drink and all things as they needed them. And in likewise it befell them the next day; but the third evening they set up their tents on a little hillside by a road which led into a deep pass, even the entry of the mountains, a road which went betwixt exceeding high walls of rock. For the mountain sides went up steep from the plain. There they kept good watch and ward, and naught befell them to tell of.

The next morning they entered the pass, and rode through it up to the heaths, and rode all day by wild and stony ways and came at even to a grassy valley watered by a little stream, where they guested, watching their camp well; and again none meddled with them.

As they were departing the next morn Ralph asked of Clement if he yet looked for onset from the waylayers. Said Clement: "It is most like, lord; for we be a rich prey, and it is but seldom that such a company rideth this road. And albeit that the wild men know not to a day when we shall pass through their country, yet they know the time within a four and twenty hours or so. For we may not hide our journey from all men's hearing; and when the ear heareth, the tongue waggeth. But art thou yet anxious concerning this matter, son?" "Yea," said Ralph, "for I would fain look on these miscreants."

"It is like that ye shall see them," said Clement; "but I shall look on it as a token that they are about waylaying us if we come on none of them in the Mountain House. For they will be fearful lest their purpose leak out from unwary lips." Ralph wondered how it would be, and what might come of it, and rode on, pondering much.

The road was rough that day, and they went not above a foot-pace the more part of the time; and daylong they were going up and up, and it grew cold as the sun got low; though it was yet summer. At last at the top of a long stony ridge, which lay beneath a great spreading mountain, on the crest whereof the snow lay in plenty, Ralph saw a house, long and low, builded of great stones, both walls and roof: at sight thereof the men of the fellowship shouted for joy, and hastened on, and Clement spurred up the stony slopes all he might. But Ralph rode slowly, since he had naught to see to, save himself, so that he was presently left alone. Now he looks aside, and sees something bright-hued lying under a big stone where the last rays of the sun just caught some corner of it. So he goes thither, deeming that mayhappen one of the company had dropped something, pouch or clout, or what not, in his haste and hurry. He got off his horse to pick it up, and when he had laid hand on it found it to be a handsbreadth of fine green cloth embroidered with flowers. He held it in his hand a while wondering where he could have seen such like stuff before, that it should smite a pang into his heart, and suddenly called to mind the little hall at Bourton Abbas with the oaken benches and the rush-strewn floor, and this same flower-broidered green cloth dancing about the naked feet of a fair damsel, as she moved nimbly hither and thither dighting him his bever. But his thought stayed not there, but carried him into the days when he was abiding in desire of the love that he won at last, and lost so speedily. But as he stood pondering he heard Clement shouting to him from the garth-gate of that house. So he leapt on his horse and rode up the slope into the garth and lighted down by Clement; who fell to chiding him for tarrying, and said: "There is peril in loitering outside this garth alone; for those Sons of the Rope often lurk hard by for what they may easily pick up, and they be brisk and nimble lads." "What ailed thee?" said Ralph. "I stayed to look at a flower which called Upmeads to my mind."

"Yea lad, yea," quoth Clement, "and art thou so soft as that? But come thou into the House; it is as I deemed it might be; besides the House-warden and his wife there is no soul therein. Thou shalt yet look on Mick Hangman's sons, as thou desirest."

So they went into the House, and men had all that they might need. The warden was an old hoar man, and his wife well-stricken in years; and after supper was talk of this and that, and it fell much, as was like to be, on those strong-thieves, and Clement asked the warden what he had seen of them of late.

The old carle answered: "Nay, master Clement, much according to wont: a few beeves driven into our garth; a pack or two brought into the hall; and whiles one or two of them come in hither with empty hands for a sleep and a bellyful; and again a captive led in on the road to the market. Forsooth it is now a good few days ago three of them brought in a woman as goodly as mine eyes have ever seen; and she sat on the bench yonder, and seemed to heed little that she was a captive and had shackles on her feet after the custom of these men, though indeed her hands were unbound, so that she might eat her meat; and the carle thief told me that he took her but a little way from the garth, and that she made a stout defence with a sword before they might take her, but being taken, she made but little of it."

"Would he do her any hurt?" said Ralph. "Nay, surely," said the carle; "doth a man make a hole in a piece of cloth which he is taking to market? Nay, he was courteous to her after his fashion, and bade us give her the best of all we had."

"What like was she?" said Ralph. Said the carle: "She was somewhat tall, if I am to note such matters, grey-eyed and brown haired, and great abundance of it. Her lips very red; her cheeks tanned with the sun, but in such wise that her own white and red shone through the sun's painting, so that her face was as sweet as the best wheat-ear in a ten-acre field when the season hath been good. Her hands were not like those of a demoiselle who sitteth in a chamber to be looked at, but brown as of one who hath borne the sickle in the sun.

But when she stretched out her hand so that the wrist of her came forth from her sleeve it was as white as milk."

"Well, my man," said the carline, "thou hast a good memory for an old and outworn carle. Why dost thou not tell the young knight what she was clad withal; since save for their raiment all women of an age are much alike?"

"Nay, do thou do it," said the carle; "she was even as fair as I have said; so that there be few like her."

Said the dame: "Well, there is naught so much to be said for her raiment: her gown was green, of fine cloth enough; but not very new: welts of needle-work it had on it, and a wreath of needle-work flowers round the hem of the skirt; but a cantle was torn off from it; in the scuffle when she was taken, I suppose, so that it was somewhat ragged in one place. Furthermore—"

She had been looking at Ralph as she spoke, and now she broke off suddenly, and said, still looking at him hard; "Well, it is strange!" "What is strange?" said Clement. "O naught, naught," said the dame, "save that folk should make so much to do about this matter, when there are so many coming and going about the Midhouse of the Mountains."

But Ralph noted that she was still staring at him even after she had let the talk drop.

Waned the even, and folk began to go bedward, so that the hall grew thin of guests. Then came up the carline to Ralph and took him aside into a nook, and said to him: "Young knight, now will I tell thee what seemed to me strange e'en now; to wit, that the captive damsel should be bearing a necklace about her neck as like to thine as one lamb is to another: but I thought thou mightest be liever that I spake it not openly before all the other folk. So I held my peace."

"Dame," said he, "I thank thee: forsooth I fear sorely that this damsel is my sister; for ever we have worn the samelike pair of beads. And as for me I have come hither to find her, and evil will it be if I find her enthralled, and it may be past redemption."

And therewith he gave her a piece of the gold money of Upmeads.

"Yea," said she, "poor youth; that will be sooth indeed, for

227

thou art somewhat like unto her, yet far goodlier. But I grieve for thee, and know not what thou wilt do; whereas by this time most like she has been sold and bought and is dwelling in some lord's strong-house; some tyrant that needeth not money, and will not let his prey go for a prayer. Here, take thou thy gold again, for thou mayst well need it, and let me shear a lock of thy golden hair, and I shall be well apaid for my keeping silence concerning thy love. For I deem that it is even so, and that she is not thy sister, else hadst thou stayed at home, and prayed for her with book and priest and altar, and not gone seeking her a weary way."

Ralph reddened but said naught, and let her put scizzors amongst his curly locks, and take what of them she would. And then he went to his bed, and pondered these matters somewhat, and said to himself that it was by this damsel's means that he should find the Well at the World's End. Yet he said also, that, whether it were so or not, he was bound to seek her, and deliver her from thralldom, since he had kissed her so sweet and friendly, like a brother, for the sweetness and kindness of her, before he had fallen into the love that had brought him such joy and such grief. And therewith he took out that piece of her gown from his pouch, and it seemed dear to him. But it made him think sadly of what grief or pain she might even then be bearing, so that he longed to deliver her, and that longing was sweet to him. In such thoughts he fell asleep.

CHAPTER 21

A Battle in the Mountains

When it was morning they arose early and ate a morsel; and Clement gave freely to the Warden and his helpmate on behalf of the fellowship; and then they saddled their nags, and did on the loads and departed; and the way was evil otherwise, but it was down hill, and all waters ran east.

All day they rode, and at even when the sun had not quite set, they pitched their camp at the foot of a round knoll amidst a valley where was water and grass; and looking down thence, they had a sight of the fruitful plain, wherein lay Cheaping Knowe all goodly blue in the distance.

This was a fair place and a lovely, and great ease would they have had there, were it not that they must keep watch and ward with more pains than theretofore; for Clement deemed it as good as certain that the wild men would fall upon them that night.

But all was peaceful the night through, and in the morning they gat to the way speedily, riding with their armour on, and their bows bent: and three of the men-at-arms rode ahead to espy the way.

So it befell that they had not ridden two hours ere back came the fore-riders with the tidings that the pass next below them was thick with the Strong-thieves.

The fellowship were as then in such a place, that they were riding a high bare ridge, and could not be assailed to the advantage of the thieves if they abode where they were; whereas if they went forward, they must needs go down with the road into the dale that was beset by the wild men. Now they were three-score and two all told, but of these but a score of men-at-arms besides Ralph, and Clement, who was a stout fighter when need was. Of the others, some were but lads, and of the Chapmen were three old men, and more than one blencher besides. However, all men were armed, and they had many bows, and some of the chapmen's knaves were fell archers.

So they took counsel together, and to some it seemed better to abide the onset on their vantage ground. But to Clement and the older men-at-arms this seemed of no avail. For though they could see the plain country down below, they would have no succour of it; and Clement bade them think how the night would come at last, and that the longer they abode, the greater would be the gathering of the Strong-thieves; so that, all things considered, it were better to fall on at once and to try the adventure of the valley. And this after some talk they yea-said all, save a few who held their skins so dear that their wits wandered somewhat.

So these timorous ones they bade guard the sumpter beasts and their loads; and even so they did, and abode a little, while the men-at-arms and the bowmen went forward without more ado; and Ralph rode betwixt Clement and the captain of the men-at-arms.

Presently they were come close to the place where the way went down into the valley, cleaving through a clayey bent, so that the slippery sides of the cleft went up high to right and left; wherefore by goodhap there were no big stones anigh to roll down upon them. Moreover the way was short, and they rode six abreast down the pass and were soon through the hollow way. As he rode Ralph saw a few of the Strong-thieves at the nether end where the pass widened out, and they let fly some arrows at the chapmen which did no hurt, though some of the shafts rattled on the armour of the companions. But when Clement saw that folk, and heard the noise of their shouting he lifted up a great axe that he bore and cried, "St. Agnes for the Mercers!" and set spurs to his horse. So did they all, and came clattering and shouting down the steep road like a stone out of a sling, and drave right into the valley one and all, the wouldbe laggards following after; for they were afraid to be left behind.

The wild men, who, save for wide shields which they bore, were but evilly armed, mostly in skins of beasts, made no countenance of defence, but fled all they might towards the steep slopes of the valley, and then turned and fell to shooting; for the companions durst not pursue in haste lest they should be scattered, and overwhelmed by the multitude of foemen; but they drew up along the south side of the valley, and had the mastery of the road, so that this first bout was without blood-shedding. Albeit the thieves still shot in their weak bows from the hill-side, but scarce hurt a man. Then the bowmen of the fellowship fell to shooting at the wild men, while the men-at-arms breathed their horses, and the sumpter-beasts were gathered together behind them; for they had no dread of abiding there a while, whereas behind them the ground was broken into a steep shaly cliff, bushed here and there with tough bushes, so that no man could come up it save by climbing with hand and knee, and that not easily.

Now when the archers had shot a good while, and some of the thieves had fallen before them, and men were in good heart because of the flight of the wild men, Ralph, seeing that these still hung about the slopes, cried out: "Master Clement, and thou Captain, sure it will be ill-done to leave these men unbroken behind us, lest they follow us and hang about our hindermost, slaying us both men and horses."

"Even so," quoth the captain, who was a man of few words, "let us go. But do thou, Clement, abide by the stuff with the lads and bowmen."

Then he cried out aloud: "St. Christopher to aid!" and shook his rein, and all they who were clad in armour and well mounted spurred on with him against the strong-thieves. But these, when they saw the onset of the horsemen, but drew a little up the hill-side and stood fast, and some of the horses were hurt by their shot. So the captain bade draw rein and off horse, while Clement led his bowmen nigher, and they shot well together, and hindered the thieves from closing round the men-at-arms, or falling on the horses. So then the companions went forward stoutly on foot, and entered into the battle of the thieves, and there was the thrusting and the hewing great: for the foemen bore axes, and malls, and spears, and were little afraid, having the vantage-ground; and they were lithe and strong men, though not tall.

Ralph played manfully, and was hurt by a spear above the knee, but not grievously; so he heeded it not, but cleared a space all about him with great strokes of the Upmeads' blade; then as the wild men gave back there was one of them who stood his ground and let drive a stroke of a long-handled hammer at him, but Ralph ran in under the stroke and caught him by the throat and drew him out of the press. And even therewith the wild men broke up before the onset of the all-armed carles, and fled up the hill, and the men-at-arms followed them but a little, for their armour made them unspeedy; so that they took no more of those men, though they slew some, but turned about and gathered round Ralph and made merry over his catch, for they were joyous with the happy end of battle; and Clement, who had

231

left his bowmen when the Companions were mingled with the wild-men, was there amidst the nighest.

Said Ralph to him: "Well, have I got me a servant and thrall good cheap?" "Yea," said Clement, "if thou deem a polecat a likely hound." Said the Captain: "Put thy sword through him, knight." Quoth another: "Let him run up hill, and our bowmen shall shoot a match at him."

"Nay," said Ralph, "they have done well with their shooting, let them rest. As to my thrusting my sword through the man, Captain, I had done that before, had I been so minded. At any rate, I will ask him if he will serve me truly. Otherwise he seemeth a strong carle and a handy. How sayest thou, lad, did I take thee fairly?" "Yea," said the man, "thou art a strong lad."

He seemed to fear the swords about him but little, and forsooth he was a warrior-like man, and not ill-looking. He was of middle height, strong and well-knit, with black hair like a beast's mane for shagginess, and bright blue eyes. He was clad in a short coat of grey homespun, with an ox-skin habergeon laced up over it; he had neither helm nor hat, nor shoes, but hosen made of a woollen clout tied about his legs; his shield of wood and ox-hide lay on the ground a few paces off, and his hammer beside it, which he had dropped when Ralph first handled him, but a great ugly knife was still girt to him.

Now Ralph saith to him: "Which wilt thou—be slain, or serve me?" Said the carle, grinning, yet not foully: "Guess if I would not rather serve thee!" "Wilt thou serve me truly?" said Ralph. "Why not?" quoth the carle: "yet I warn thee that if thou beat me, save in hot blood, I shall put a knife into thee when I may."

"O," said one, "thrust him through now at once, lord Ralph." "Nay, I will not," said Ralph; "he hath warned me fairly. Maybe he will serve me truly. Master Clement, wilt thou lend me a horse for my man to ride?" "Yea," said Clement; "yet I misdoubt me of thy new squire." Then he turned to the men-at-arms and said: "No tarrying, my masters! To horse and away before they gather gain!"

So they mounted and rode away from that valley of the pass, and Ralph made his man ride beside him. But the man said to him, as soon as they were riding: "Take note that I

232

will not fight against my kindred." "None biddeth thee so," said Ralph; "but do thou take heed that if thou fight against us I will slay thee outright." Said the man: "A fair bargain!" "Well," said Ralph, "I will have thy knife of thee, lest it tempt thee, as is the wont of cold iron, and a maiden's body." "Nay, master," quoth the man, "leave me my knife, as thou art a good fellow. In two hours time we shall be past all peril of my people, and when we come down below I will slay thee as many as thou wilt, so it be out of the kindred. Forsooth down there evil they be, and unkinsome."

"So be it, lad," said Ralph, laughing, "keep thy knife; but hang this word of mine thereon, that if thou slay any man of this fellowship save me, I will rather flay thee alive than slay thee." Quoth the carle: "That is the bargain, then, and I yeasay it." "Good," said Ralph; "now tell me thy name." "Bull Shockhead," said the carle.

But now the fellowship took to riding so fast down the slopes of the mountains on a far better road, that talking together was not easy. They kept good watch, both behind and ahead, nor were they set upon again, though whiles they saw clumps of men on the hill-sides.

So after a while, when it was a little past noon, they came adown to the lower slopes of the mountains and the foot-hills, which were green and unstony; and thereon were to be seen cattle and neatherds and shepherds, and here and there the garth of a homestead, and fenced acres about it.

So now that they were come down into the peopled parts, they displayed the banners of their fellowships, to wit, the Agnes, the White Fleece, the Christopher, and the Ship and Nicholas, which last was the banner of the Faring-knights of Whitwall; but Ralph was glad to ride under the banner of St. Nicholas, his friend, and deemed that luck might the rather come to him thereby. But they displayed their banners now, because they knew that no man of the peopled parts would be so hardy as to fall upon the Chapmen, of whom they looked to have many matters for their use and pleasure.

So now that they felt themselves safe, they stayed them, and sat down by a fair little stream, and ate their dinner of such meat and drink as they had; and Ralph departed his share with his thrall, and the man was hungry and ate well;

so that Clement said mockingly: "Thou feedest thy thrall over well, lord, even for a king's son: is it so that thou art minded to fatten him and eat him?" Then some of the others took up the jest, and bade the carle refrain him of the meat, so that he might not fatten, and might live the longer. He hearkened to them, and knit his brows and looked fiercely from one to the other. But Ralph laughed aloud, and shook his finger at him and refrained him, and his wrath ran off him and he laughed, and shoved the victual into him doughtily, and sighed for pleasure when he had made an end and drunk a draught of wine.

CHAPTER 22

Ralph Talks With Bull Shockhead

When they rode on again, Ralph rode beside Bull, who was merry and blithe now he was full of meat and drink; and he spake anon: "So thou art a king's son, master? I deemed from the first that thou wert of lineage. For as for these churls of chapmen, and the sworders whom they wage, they know not the name of their mother's mother, nor have heard one word of the beginner of their kindred; and their deeds are like unto their kinlessness."

"And are thy deeds so good?" said Ralph. "Are they ill," said Bull, "when they are done against the foemen?" Said Ralph: "And are all men your foemen who pass through these mountains?" "All," said Bull, "but they be of the kindred or their known friends."

"Well, Bull," said Ralph, "I like thy deeds little, that thou shouldest ravish men and women from their good life, and sell them for a price into toil and weariness and stripes."

Said Bull: "How much worse do we than the chapmen by his debtor, and the lord of the manor by his villein?" Said Ralph: "Far worse, if ye did but know it, poor men!" Quoth

234

Bull: "But I neither know it, nor can know it, nay, not when thou sayest it; for it is not so. And look you, master, this life of a bought thrall is not such an exceeding evil life; for oft they be dealt with softly and friendly, and have other thralls to work for them under their whips."

Ralph laughed: "Which shall I make thee, friend Bull, the upper or the under?" Bull reddened, but said naught. Said Ralph: "Or where shall I sell thee, that I may make the best penny out of my good luck and valiancy?" Bull looked chopfallen: "Nay," said he in a wheedling voice, "thou wilt not sell me, thou? For I deem that thou wilt be a good master to me: and," he broke into sudden heat hereat, "if I have another master I shall surely slay him whate'er betide."

Ralph laughed again, and said: "Seest thou what an evil craft ye follow, when thou deemest it better to be slain with bitter torments (as thou shouldest be if thou slewest thy master) than to be sold to any master save one exceeding good?"

Bull held his peace hereat, but presently he said: "Well, be our craft good or evil, it is gainful; and whiles there is prey taken right good, which, for my part, I would not sell, once I had my hand thereon." "Yea, women?" said Ralph. "Even so," said Bull, "such an one was taken by my kinsman Bull Nosy but a little while agone, whom he took down to the market at Cheaping Knowe, as I had not done if I had once my arms about her. For she was as fair as a flower; and yet so well built, that she could bear as much as a strong man in some ways; and, saith Nosy, when she was taken, there was no weeping or screeching in her, but patience rather and quietness, and intent to bear all and live. . . . Master, may I ask thee a question?" "Ask on," said Ralph. Said Bull: "The pair of beads about thy neck, whence came they?" "They were the gift of a dear friend," said Ralph. "A woman?" quoth Bull. "Yea," said Ralph.

"Now is this strange," said Bull, "and I wot not what it may betoken, but this same woman had about her neck a pair of beads as like to thine as if they had been the very same: did this woman give thee the beads? For I will say this of thee, master, that thou art well nigh as likely a man as she is a woman."

Ralph sighed, for this talk of the woman and the beads brought all the story into his mind, so that it was as if he saw it adoing again: the Lady of the Wildwood led along to death before he delivered her, and their flight together from the Water of the Oak, and that murder of her in the desert. And betwixt the diverse deeds of the day this had of late become somewhat dim to him. Yet after his grief came joy that this man also had seen the damsel, whom his dream of the night had called Dorothea, and that he knew of her captors; wherefore by his means he might come on her and deliver her.

Now he spake aloud: "Nay, it was not she that gave them to me, but yet were I fain to find this woman that thou sawest; for I look to meet a friend whenas I meet her. So tell me, dost thou think that I may cheapen her of thy kinsman?"

Bull shook his head, and said: "It may be: or it may be that he hath already sold her to one who heedeth not treasure so much as fair flesh; and fair is hers beyond most. But, lord, I will do my best to find her for thee; as thou art a king's son and no ill master, I deem."

"Do that," quoth Ralph, "and I in turn will do what more I may for thee besides making thee free." And therewith he rode forward that he might get out of earshot, for Bull's tongue seemed like to be long. And presently he heard laughter behind him, as the carle began jesting and talking with the chapman lads.

CHAPTER 23

Of the Town of Cheaping Knowe

Now when it was evening they pitched their camp down in the plain fields amidst tall elmtrees, and had their banners still flying over the tents to warn all comers of what they were. But the next morning the chapmen and their folk were up betimes to rummage their loads, and to array their wares for the market; and they gat not to the road before mid-morning. Meantime of their riding Ralph had more talk with Bull, who said to him: "Fair lord, I rede thee when thou art in the market of Cheaping Knowe, bid master Clement bring thee to the thrall-merchant, and trust me that if such a fair image as that we were speaking of hath passed through his hands within these three months, he will remember it; and then thou shalt have at least some tale of what hath befallen her but a little while ago."

That seemed good rede to Ralph, and when they went on their way he rode beside Clement, and asked him many things concerning Cheaping Knowe; and at last about the thrall-market therein. And Clement said that, though he dealt not in such wares, he had often seen them sold, and knew the master of that market. And when Ralph asked if the said master would answer questions concerning the selling of men and of women, Clement smiled and said: "Yea, yea, he will answer; for as he lives by selling thralls, and every time a thrall is sold by him he maketh some gain by it, it is to his profit that they change masters as often as may be; and when thou askest of the woman whom thou art seeking, he will be deeming that there will be some new chaffer ahead. I will bring thee to him, and thou shalt ask him of what thou wilt, and belike he will tell thee quietly over the wine-cup."

Therewith was Ralph well content, and he grew eager to enter into the town.

They came to the gates a little before sunset, after they had passed through much fair country; but nigh to the walls it was bare of trees and thickets, whereas, said Clement, they had been cut down lest they should serve as cover to strong-thieves or folk assailing the town. The walls were strong and tall, and a great castle stood high up on a hill, about which the town was builded; so that if the town were taken there would yet be another town within it to be taken also. But the town within, save for the said castle, was scarce so fairly builded as the worst of the towns which Ralph had seen erst, though there were a many houses therein.

Much people was gathered about the gate to see the merchants enter with banners displayed; and Ralph deemed many of the folk fair, such as were goodly clad; for many had but foul clouts to cover their nakedness, and seemed needy and hunger-pinched. Withal there were many warriors amongst the throng, and most of these bore a token on their sleeves, to wit, a sword reddened with blood. And Clement, speaking softly in Ralph's ear, did him to wit that this was the token of the lord who had gotten the castle in those days, and was tyrant of the town; and how that he had so many men-at-arms ready to do his bidding that none in the town was safe from him if he deemed it more for his pleasure and profit to rob or maim, or torment or slay, than to suffer them to live peaceably. "But with us chapmen," said Clement, "he will not meddle, lest there be an end of chaffer in the town; and verily the market is good."

Thus they rode through the streets into the market place, which was wide and great, and the best houses of the town were therein, and so came to the hostel of the Merchants, called the Fleece, which was a big house, and goodly enough.

The next morning Clement and the other chapmen went up into the Castle, bearing with them gifts out of their wares for the lord, and Clement bade Ralph keep close till he came back, and especially to keep his war-caught thrall, Bull Shockhead, safe at home, lest he be taken from him, and to clothe him in the guise of the chapman lads, and to dock his hair; and even so Ralph did, though Bull were loath thereto.

About noon the chapmen came back again well pleased; and Clement gave Ralph a parchment from the lord, which bade all men help and let pass Ralph of Upmeads, as a sergeant of the chapmen's guard, and said withal that now he was free to go about the town if he listed, so that he were back at the hostel of the Fleece by nightfall.

So Ralph went in company with some of the sergeants and others, and looked at this and that about the town without hindrance, save that the guard would not suffer them to pass further than the bailey of the Castle. And for the said bailey, forsooth, they had but little stomach; for they saw thence, on the slopes of the Castle-hill, tokens of the cruel justice of the said lord; for there were men and women there, yea, and babes also, hanging on gibbets and thrust through with sharp pales, and when they asked of folk why these had suffered, they but looked at them as if astonished, and passed on without a word.

So they went thence, and found the master-church, and deemed it not much fairer than it was great; and it was nowise great, albeit it was strange and uncouth of fashion.

Then they came to great gardens within the town, and they were exceeding goodly, and had trees and flowers and fruits in them which Ralph had not seen hitherto, as lemons, and oranges, and pomegranates; and the waters were running through them in runnels of ashlar; and the weather was fair and hot; so they rested in those gardens till it was evening, and then gat them home to Fleece, where they had good entertainment.

CHAPTER 24

Ralph Heareth More Tidings of the Damsel

The second day, while the merchants saw to their chaffer, most of the men-at-arms, and Ralph with them, spent their time again in those goodly gardens; where, indeed, some of them made friends of fair women of the place; in which there was less risk than had been for aliens in some towns, whereas at Cheaping Knowe such women as were wedded according to law, or damsels in the care of their kindred, or slaves who were concubines, had not dared so much as to look on a man.

The third day time hung somewhat heavy on Ralph's hands, not but that the Companions were well at ease, but rather because himseemed that he was not stirring in the quest.

But the next day Clement bade him come see that thrall-merchant aforesaid, and brought him to a corner of the market-place, where was a throng looking on at the cheaping. They went through the throng, and beside a stone like a leaping-on stone saw a tall man, goodly of presence, black bearded, clad in scarlet; and this was the merchant; and by him were two of his knaves and certain weaponed men who had brought their wares to the cheaping. And some of these were arrayed like those foemen of the mountains. There was a half score and three of these chattels to be sold, who stood up one after other on the stone, that folk might cheapen them. The cheaping was long about, because they that had a mind to buy were careful to know what they were buying, like as if they had been cheapening a horse, and most of them before they bid their highest had the chattels away into the merchant's booth to strip them, lest they should buy damaged or unhandsome bodies; and this more especially if it were a woman, for the men were already well nigh naked. Of women four of them were young and goodly, and Ralph looked at them closely; but they were naught like to the woman of his quest.

Now this cheaping irked Ralph sorely, as was like to be, whereas, as hath been told, he came from a land where were no thralls, none but vavassors and good yeomen: yet he abode till all was done, hansel paid, and the thralls led off by their new masters. Then Clement led him up to the merchant, to whom he gave the sele of the day, and said: "Master, this is the young knight of whom I told thee, who deemeth that a woman who is his friend hath been brought to this market and sold there, and if he might, he would ransom her."

The merchant greeted Ralph courteously, and bade him and Clement come into his house, where they might speak more privily. So did they, and he treated them with honour, and set wine and spices before them, and bade Ralph say whatlike the woman was. Ralph did so, and wondered at himself how well and closely he could tell of her, like as a picture painted. And, moreover, he drew forth that piece of her gown which he had come on by the Mid-Mountain House.

So when he had done, the merchant, who was a man sober of aspect and somewhat slow of speech, said: "Sir, I believe surely that I have seen this damsel, but she is not with me now, nor have I sold her ever; but hither was she brought to be sold by a man of the mountain folk not very many days ago. And the man's name was Bull Nosy, or the longnosed man of the kindred of the Bull, for in such wise are named the men of that unhappy folk. Now this was the cause why I might not sell her, that she was so proud and stout that men feared her, what she might do if they had her away. And when some spake to see her body naked, she denied it utterly, saying that she would do a mischief to whomsoever tried it. So I spake to him who owned her, and asked him if he thought it good to take her a while and quell her with such pains as would spoil her but little, and then bring her to market when she was meeker. But he heeded my words little, and led her away, she riding on a horse and he going afoot beside her; for the mountain-men be no horsemen."

Said Ralph: "Dost thou know at all whither he will have led her?" Said the merchant: "By my deeming, he will have gone first of all to the town of Whiteness, whither thy Fellowship will betake them ere long: for he will be minded to meet there the Lord of Utterbol, who is for such like wares; and he will either give her to him as a gift, for which he will have a gift in return, or he will sell her to my lord at a price if he dare to chaffer with him. At least so will he do if he be wise. Now if the said lord hath her, it will be somewhat more than hard for thee to get her again, till he have altogether done with her; for money and goods are naught to him beside the doing of his will. But there is this for thy comfort, that whereas she is so fair a woman, she will be well with my lord. For I warrant me that she will not dare to be proud with him, as she was with the folk here."

"Yea," said Ralph, "and what is this lord of Utterbol that all folk, men and women, fear him so?" Said the merchant: "Fair sir, thou must pardon me if I say no more of him. Belike thou mayst fall in with him; and if thou dost, take heed that thou make not thyself great with him."

So Ralph thanked the merchant and departed with Clement, of whom presently he asked if he knew aught of this lord of Utterbol. Said Clement: "God forbid that I should ever meet him, save where I were many and he few. I have never seen him; but he is deemed by all men as the worst of the tyrants who vex these lands, and, maybe, the mightiest."

So was Ralph sore at heart for the damsel, and anon he

spake to Bull again of her, who deemed somewhat, that his kinsman had been minded at the first to sell her to the lord of Utterbol. And Ralph thinks his game a hard one, yet deems that if he could but find out where the damsel was, he might deliver her, what by sleight, what by boldness.

CHAPTER 25

The Fellowship Comes to Whiteness

Two days thereafter the chapmen having done with their matters in Cheaping Knowe, whereas they must needs keep some of their wares for other places, and especially for Goldburg, they dight them to be gone and rode out a-gates of a mid-morning with banners displayed.

It was some fifty miles thence to Whiteness, which lay close underneath the mountains, and was, as it were, the door of the passes whereby men rode to Goldburg. The land which they passed through was fair, both of tillage and pasture, with much cattle therein. Everywhere they saw men and women working afield, but no houses of worthy yeomen or vavassors, or cots of good husbandmen. Here and there was a castle or strong-house, and here and there long rows of ugly hovels, or whiles houses, big tall and long, but exceeding foul and ill-favoured, such as Ralph had not yet seen the like of. And when he asked of Clement concerning all this, he said: "It is as I have told thee, that here be no freemen who work afield, nay, nor villeins either. All those whom ye have seen working have been bought and sold like to those whom we saw standing on the Stone in the market of Cheaping Knowe, or else were born of such cattle, and each one of them can be bought and sold again, and they work not save under the whip. And as for those hovels and the long and foul houses, they are the stables wherein this kind of cattle is harboured."

Then Ralph's heart sank, and he said: "Master Clement, I prithee tell me; were it possible that the damsel whom I seek may be come to such a pass as one of these?" "Nay," quoth Clement, "that is little like to be; such goodly wares are kept for the adornment of great men's houses. True it is that whiles the house-thralls be sent into the fields for their punishment; yet not such as she, unless the master be wholly wearied of them, or if their wrath outrun their wits; for it is more to the master's profit to chastise them at home; so keep a good heart I bid thee, and maybe we shall have tidings at Whiteness."

So Ralph refrained his anxious heart, though forsooth his thought was much upon the damsel and of how she was faring.

It was not till the third day at sunset that they came to Whiteness; for on the last day of their riding they came amongst the confused hills that lay before the great mountains, which were now often hidden from their sight; but whenever they appeared through the openings of the near hills, they seemed very great and terrible; dark and bare and stony; and Clement said that they were little better than they looked from afar. As to Whiteness, they saw it a long way off, as it lay on a long ridge at the end of a valley: and so long was the ridge, that behind it was nothing green; naught but the huge and bare mountains. The westering sun fell upon its walls and its houses, so that it looked white indeed against those great cliffs and crags; though, said Clement, that these were yet a good way off. Now when, after a long ride from the hither end of the valley, they drew nigh to the town, Ralph saw that the walls and towers were not very high or strong, for so steep was the hill whereon the town stood, that it needed not. Here also was no great castle within the town as at Cheaping Knowe, and the town itself nothing so big, but long and straggling along the top of the ridge. Cheaping Knowe was all builded of stone; but the houses here were of timber for the most part, done over with pargeting and whitened well. Yet was the town more cheerful of aspect than Cheaping Knowe, and the folk who came thronging about the chapmen at the gates not so woe-begone, and goodly enough.

Of the lord of Whiteness, Clement told that he paid tribute to him of Cheaping Knowe, rather for love of peace than for fear of him; for he was no ill lord, and free men lived well under him.

So the chapmen lodged in the market-place; and in two days time Ralph got speech of the Deacon of the Chapmen of the Town; who told him two matters; first that the lord of Utterbol had not been in Whiteness these six months; and next that the wild man had verily brought the damsel into the market; but he had turned away thence suddenly with her, without bringing her to the stone, and that it was most like that he would have the lord of Utterbol buy her; who, since he would be deeming that he might easily bend her to his will, would give him the better penny for her. "At the last," quoth the Deacon, "the wild man led her away toward the mountain pass that goeth to Goldburg, the damsel and he alone, and she with her hands unbound and riding a little horse." Of these tidings Ralph deemed it good that all traces of her were not lost; but his heart misgave him when he thought that by this time she must surely be in the hands of the lord of Utterbol.

CHAPTER 26

They Ride the Mountains
Toward Goldburg

Five days the Fellowship abode at Whiteness, and or ever they departed Clement waged men-at-arms of the lord of the town, besides servants to look to the beasts amongst the mountains, so that what with one, what with another, they entered the gates of the mountains a goodly company of four score and ten.

Ralph asked of Bull if any of those whom he might meet in these mountains were of his kindred; and he answered, nay, unless perchance there might be some one or two going their peaceful errands there like Bull Nosy. So Ralph armed him with a good sword and a shield, and would have given him a steel hood also, but he would not bear it, saying that if sword and shield could not keep his head he had well earned a split skull.

Seven days they rode the mountains, and the way was toilsome and weary enough, for it was naught but a stony maze of the rocks where nothing living dwelt, and nothing grew, save now and again a little dwarf willow. Yet was there naught worse to meet save toil, because they were over strong for the wild men to meddle with them, whereas the kindreds thereabout were but feeble.

But as it drew towards evening on the seventh day Ralph had ridden a little ahead with Bull alone, if he might perchance have a sight of the ending of this grievous wilderness, as Clement said might be, since now the way was down-hill, and all waters ran east. So as they rode, and it was about sunset, they saw something lying by a big stone under a cliff; so they drew nigh, and saw a man lying on his back, and they deemed he was dead. So Bull went up to him, and leapt off his horse close by him and bent over him, but straightway cast up his arms and set up a long wailing whoop, and then another and another, so that they that were behind heard it and came up upon the spur. But Ralph leapt from his horse, and ran up to Bull and said: "What aileth thee to whoop and wail? Who is it?" But Bull turned about and shook his head at him, and said: "It is a man of my kindred, even he that was leading away thy she-friend; and belike she it was that slew him, or why is she not here: Ochone! ahoo! ahoo!" Therewith fire ran through Ralph's heart, and he bethought him of that other murder in the wilderness, and he fell to wringing his hands, and cried out: "Ah, and where is she, where is she? Is she also taken away from me for ever? O me unhappy!"

And he drew his sword therewith, and ran about amongst the rocks and the bushes seeking her body.

And therewith came up Clement, and others of the company, and wondered to see Bull kneeling down by the corpse, and to hear him crying out and wailing, and Ralph running about like one mad, and crying out now: "Oh! that I might find her! Mayhappen she is alive yet, and anigh here in some cleft of the rocks in this miserable wilderness. O my love that hast lain in mine arms, wouldst thou not have me find her alive? But if she be dead, then will I slay myself, for as young as I am, that I may find thee and her out of the world, since from the world both ye are gone."

Then Clement went up to Ralph, and would have a true tale out of him, and asked him what was amiss; but Ralph stared wild at him and answered not. But Bull cried out from where he knelt: "He is seeking the woman, and I would that he could find her; for then would I slay her on the howe of my kinsman: for she hath slain him; she hath slain him."

That word heard Ralph, and he ran at Bull with uplifted sword to slay him; but Clement tripped him and he fell, and his sword flew out of his hand. Then Clement and two of the others bound his hands with their girdles, till they might know what had befallen; for they deemed that a devil had entered into him, and feared that he would do a mischief to himself or some other.

And now was the whole Fellowship assembled, and stood in a ring round about Ralph and Bull, and the dead man; as for him, he had been dead some time, many days belike; but in that high and clear cold air, his carcase, whistled by the wind, had dried rather than rotted, and his face was clear to be seen with its great hooked nose and long black hair: and his skull was cloven.

Now Bull had done his wailing for his kinsman, and he seemed to wake up as from a dream, and looked about the ring of men and spake: "Here is a great to do, my masters! What will ye with me? Have ye heard, or is it your custom, that when a man cometh on the dead corpse of his brother, his own mother's son, he turneth it over with his foot, as if it were the carcase of a dog, and so goeth on his way? This I ask, that albeit I be but a war-taken thrall, I be suffered to lay my brother in earth and heap a howe over him in these mountains."

They all murmured a yeasay to this save Ralph. He had been sobered by his fall, and was standing up now betwixt Clement and the captain, who had unbound his hands, now that the others had come up; he hung his head, and was

246

ashamed of his fury by seeming. But when Bull had spoken, and the others had answered, Ralph said to Bull, wrathfully still, but like a man in his wits: "Why didst thou say that thou wouldest slay her?" "Hast thou found her?" said Bull. "Nay," quoth Ralph, sullenly. "Well, then," said Bull, "when thou dost find her, we will speak of it." Said Ralph: "Why didst thou say that she hath slain him?" "I was put out of my wits by the sight of him dead," said Bull; "But now I say mayhappen she hath slain him."

"And mayhappen not," said Clement; "look here to the cleaving of his skull right through this iron headpiece, which he will have bought at Cheaping Knowe (for I have seen suchlike in the armourers' booth there): it must have taken a strong man to do this."

"Yea," quoth the captain, "and a big sword to boot: this is the stroke of a strong man wielding a good weapon."

Said Bull: "Well, and will my master bid me forego vengeance for my brother's slaying, or that I bear him to purse? Then let him slay me now, for I am his thrall." Said Ralph: "Thou shalt do as thou wilt herein, and I also will do as I will. For if she slew him, the taking of her captive should be set against the slaying." "That is but right," said the captain; "but Sir Ralph, I bid thee take the word of an old man-at-arms for it, that she slew him not; neither she, nor any other woman."

Said Clement: "Well, let all this be. But tell me, lord Ralph, what thou wouldst do, since now thou art come to thyself again?" Said Ralph: "I would seek the wilderness hereabout, if perchance the damsel be thrust into some cleft or cavern, alive or dead."

"Well," said Clement, "this is my rede. Since Bull Shockhead would bury his brother, and lord Ralph would seek the damsel, and whereas there is water anigh, and the sun is well nigh set, let us pitch our tents and abide here till morning, and let night bring counsel unto some of us. How say ye, fellows?"

None naysaid it, and they fell to pitching the tents, and lighting the cooking-fires; but Bull at once betook him to digging a grave for his brother, whilst Ralph with the captain and four others went and sought all about the place, and

247

looked into all clefts of rocks, and found not the maiden, nor any token of her. They were long about it, and when they were come back again, and it was night, though the moon shone out, there was Bull Shockhead standing by the howe of his brother Bull Nosy, which was heaped up high over the place where they had found him.

So when Bull saw him, he turned to him and said: "King's son, I have done what needs was for this present. Now, wilt thou slay me for my fault, or shall I be thy man again, and serve thee truly unless the blood feud come between us?" Said Ralph: "Thou shalt serve me truly, and help me to find him who hath slain thy brother, and carried off the damsel; for even thus it hath been done meseemeth, since about here we have seen no signs of her alive or dead. But to-morrow we shall seek wider ere I ride on my way." "Yea," said Bull, "and I will be one in the search."

So then they gat them to their sleeping-berths, and Ralph, contrary to his wont, lay long awake, pondering these things; till at last he said to himself that this woman, whom he called Dorothea, was certainly alive, and wotted that he was seeking her. And then it seemed to him that he could behold her through the darkness of night, clad in the green flowered gown as he had first seen her, and she bewailing her captivity and the long tarrying of the deliverer as she went to and fro in a great chamber builded of marble and done about with gold and bright colours: and or ever he slept, he deemed this to be a vision of what then was, rather than a memory of what had been; and it was sweet to his very soul.

CHAPTER 27

Clement Tells of Goldburg

Now when it was morning he rose early and roused Bull and the captain, and they searched in divers places where they had not been the night before, and even a good way back about the road they had ridden yesterday, but found no tidings. And Ralph said to himself that this was naught but what he had looked for after that vision of the night.

So he rode with his fellows somewhat shamefaced that they had seen that sudden madness in him; but was presently of better cheer than he had been yet. He rode beside Clement; they went downhill speedily, and the wilderness began to better, and there was grass at whiles, and bushes here and there. A little after noon they came out of a pass cleft deep through the rocks by a swift stream which had once been far greater than then, and climbed up a steep ridge that lay across the road, and looking down from the top of it, beheld the open country again. But this was otherwise from what they had beheld from the mountain's brow above Cheaping Knowe. For thence the mountains beyond Whiteness, even those that they had just ridden, were clear to be seen like the wall of the plain country. But here, looking adown, the land below them seemed but a great spreading plain with no hills rising from it, save that far away they could see a certain break in it, and amidst that, something that was brighter than the face of the land elsewhere. Clement told Ralph that this was Goldburg and that it was built on a gathering of hills, not great, but going up steep from the plain. And the plain, said he, was not so wholly flat and even as it looked from up there, but swelled at whiles into downs and low hills. He told him that Goldburg was an exceeding fair town to behold; that the lord who had built it had brought from over the mountains masons and wood-wrights and artificers of all kinds, that they might make it as fair as might be, and that he spared on it neither wealth nor toil nor pains. For in sooth he deemed that he should find the Well at the World's End, and drink thereof, and live long and young and fair past all record; therefore had he builded this city, to be the house and home of his long-enduring joyance.

Now some said that he had found the Well, and drank thereof; others naysaid that; but all deemed that they knew how that Goldburg was not done building ere that lord was slain in a tumult, and that what was then undone was cobbled up after the uncomely fashion of the towns thereabout.

Clement said moreover that, this happy lord dead, things had not gone so well there as had been looked for. Forsooth it had been that lord's will and meaning that all folks in Goldburg should thrive, both those who wrought and those for whom they wrought. But it went not so, but there were many poor folk there, and few wealthy.

Again said Clement that though the tillers and toilers of Goldburg were not for the most part mere thralls and chattels, as in the lands beyond the mountains behind them, yet were they little more thriving for that cause; whereas they belonged not to a master, who must at worst feed them, and to no manor, whose acres they might till for their livelihood, and on whose pastures they might feed their cattle; nor had they any to help or sustain them against the oppressor and the violent man; so that they toiled and swinked and died with none heeding them, save they that had the work of their hands good cheap; and they forsooth heeded them less than their draught beasts whom they must needs buy with money, and whose bellies they must needs fill; whereas these poor wretches were slaves without a price, and if one died another took his place on the chance that thereby he might escape present death by hunger, for there was a great many of them.

CHAPTER 28

Now They Come to Goldburg

That night they slept yet amongst the mountains, or rather in the first of the hill country at their feet; but on the morrow they rode down into the lowlands, and thereby lost all sight of Goldburg, and it was yet afar off, so that they rode four days through lands well-tilled, but for the most part ill-housed, a country of little hills and hollows and rising grounds, before they came in sight of it again heaving up huge and bright under the sun. It was built partly on three hills, the buttresses of a long ridge which turned a wide river, and on the ridge itself, and partly on the flat shore of the river, on either side, hillward and plainward: but a great white wall girt it all about, which went right over the river as a bridge, and on the plain side it was exceeding high, so that its battlements might be somewhat evened with those of the hill-wall above. So that as they came up to the place they saw little of the town because of the enormity of the wall; scarce aught save a spire or a tall towering roof here and there.

So when they were come anigh the gate, they displayed their banners and rode right up to it; and people thronged the walls to see their riding. One by one they passed through the wicket of the gate: which gate itself was verily huge beyond measure, all built of great ashlar-stones; and when they were within, it was like a hall somewhat long and exceeding high, most fairly vaulted; midmost of the said hall they rode through a noble arch on their right hand, and lo another hall exceeding long, but lower than the first, with many glazen windows set in its townward wall; and when they looked through these, they saw the river running underneath; for this was naught but the lower bridge of the city; and they learned afterwards and saw, that above the vault of this long bridge rose up the castle, chamber on chamber, till its battlements were level with the highest towers of the wall on the hill top.

Thus they passed the bridge, and turning to the left at its ending, came into the Water-Street of Goldburg, where the river, with wide quays on either side thereof, ran betwixt the houses. As for these, beneath the dwellings went a fair arched passage like to the ambulatory of an abbey; and every house all along this street was a palace for its goodliness. The houses were built of white stones and red and grey; with shapely pillars to the cloister, and all about carvings of imagery and knots of flowers; goodly were the windows and all glazed, as fair as might be. On the river were great barges, and other craft such as were not sea-goers, river-ships that might get them through the bridges and furnished with masts that might be lowered and shipped.

Much people was gathered to see the chapmen enter, yet scarce so many as might be looked for in so goodly a town; yea, and many of the folk were clad foully, and were haggard of countenance, and cried on the chapmen for alms. Howbeit some were clad gaily and richly enough, and were fair of favour as any that Ralph had seen since he left Upmeads: and amongst these goodly folk were women not a few, whose gear and bearing called to Ralph's mind the women of the Wheatwearers whom he had seen erst in the Burg of the Four Friths, whereas they were somewhat wantonly clad in scanty and thin raiment. And of these, though they were not all thralls, were many who were in servitude: for, as Clement did Ralph to wit, though the tillers of the soil, and the herdsmen, in short the hewers of wood and drawers of water, were men masterless, yet rich men might and did buy both men and women for servants in their houses, and for their pleasure and profit in divers wise.

So they rode to their hostel in the market place, which lay a little back from the river in an ingle of the ridge and one of its buttresses; and all round the said market were houses as fair as the first they had seen: but above, on the hill-sides, save for the castle and palace of the Queen (for a woman ruled in Goldburg), were the houses but low, poorly built of post and pan, and thatched with straw, or reed, or shingle. But the great church was all along one side of the market place; and albeit this folk was somewhat wild and strange of faith for Christian men, yet was it dainty and delicate as might be, and its steeples and bell-towers were high and well builded, and adorned exceeding richly.

So they lighted down at their hostel, and never had Ralph seen such another, for the court within was very great and with a fair garden filled with flowers and orchard-trees, and amidst it was a fountain of fresh water, built in the goodliest fashion of many-coloured marble-stones. And the arched and pillared way about the said court was as fair as the cloister of a mitred abbey; and the hall for the guests was of like fashion, vaulted with marvellous cunning, and with a row of pillars amidmost.

There they abode in good entertainment; yet this noted Ralph, that as goodly as was the fashion of the building of that house, yet the hangings and beds, and stools, and chairs, and other plenishing were no richer or better than might be seen in the hostelry of any good town.

So they went bedward, and Ralph slept dreamlessly, as was mostly his wont.

CHAPTER 29

Of Goldburg and the Queen Thereof

On the morrow, when Ralph and Clement met in the hall, Clement spake and said: "Lord Ralph, as I told thee in Whitwall, we chapmen are now at the end of our outward journey, and in about twenty days time we shall turn back to the mountains; but, as I deem, thou wilt be minded to follow up thy quest of the damsel, and whatsoever else thou mayst be seeking. Now this thou mayst well do whiles we are here in Goldburg, and yet come back hither in time to fare back with us: and also, if thou wilt, thou mayst have fellows in thy quest, to wit some of those our men-at-arms, who love thee well. But now, when thou hast done thy best these days during, if thou hast then found naught, I counsel thee and beseech thee to come thy ways back with us, that we twain may wend to Upmeads together, where thou shalt live well, and better all the deeds of thy father. Meseemeth this will be more meet for thee than the casting away of thy life in seeking a woman, who maybe will be naught to thee when thou hast found her; or in chasing some castle in the clouds, that shall be never the nigher to thee, how far soever thou farest. For now I tell thee that I have known this while how thou art seeking the Well at the World's End; and who knoweth that there is any such thing on the earth? Come, then, thou art fair, and young, and strong; and if ye seek wealth thou shalt have it, and my furtherance to the utmost, if that be aught worth. Bethink thee, child, there are they that love thee in Upmeads and thereabout, were it but thy gossip, my wife, dame Katherine."

Said Ralph: "Master Clement, I thank thee for all that thou hast said, and thy behest, and thy deeds. Thy rede is good, and in all ways will I follow it save one; to wit, that if I have not found the damsel ere ye turn back, I must needs abide in this land searching for her. And I pray the pardon both of thee and of thy gossip, if I answer not your love as ye would, and perchance as I should. Yea, and of Upmeads also I crave pardon. But in doing as I do, my deed shall be but according to the duty bounden on me by mine oath, when Duke Osmond made me knight last year, in the church of St. Laurence of Upmeads."

Said Clement: "I see that there is something else in it than that; I see thee to be young, and that love and desire bind thee in closer bonds than thy knightly oath. Well, so it must be, and till thou hast her, there is but one woman in the world for thee."

"Nay, it is not so, Master Clement," said Ralph, "and I will tell thee this, so that thou mayst trow my naysay; since I departed from Upmeads, I have been taken in the toils of love, and desired a fair woman, and I have won her and death hath taken her. Trowest thou my word?"

"Yea," said Clement, "but to one of thy years love is not plucked up by the root, and it soon groweth again." Then said Ralph, sadly: "Now tell my gossip of this when thou comest home." Clement nodded yeasay, and Ralph spake again in a moment: "And now will I begin my search in Goldburg by praying thee to bring me to speech of merchants and others who may have seen or heard tidings of my damsel."

He looked at Clement anxiously as he spoke; and Clement smiled, for he said to himself that looking into Ralph's heart on this matter was like looking into a chamber through an open window. But he said: "Fear not but I will look to it; I am thy friend, and not thy schoolmaster."

Therewith he departed from Ralph, and within three days he had brought him to speech of all those who were like to know anything of the matter; and one and all they said that they had seen no such woman, and that as for the Lord of Utterbol, he had not been in Goldburg these three months. But one of the merchants said: "Master Clement, if this young knight is boun for Utterbol, he beareth his life in his hand, as thou knowest full well. Now I rede thee bring him to our Queen, who is good and compassionate, and if she may not help him otherwise, yet belike she may give him in writing to show to that tyrant, which may stand him in stead: for it does not do for any man to go against the will of our Lady and Queen; who will surely pay him back for his ill-will some day or other." Said Clement: "It is well thought of, and I will surely do as thou biddest."

So wore four days, and, that time during, Ralph was going to and fro asking questions of folk that he came across, as people new come to the city and hunters from the mountain-feet and the forests of the plain, and mariners and such like, concerning the damsel and the Lord of Utterbol; and Bull also went about seeking tidings: but whereas Ralph asked downright what he wanted to know, Bull was wary, and rather led men on to talk with him concerning those things than asked them of them in such wise that they saw the question. Albeit it was all one, and no tidings came to them; indeed, the name of the Lord of Utterbol (whom forsooth Bull named not) seemed to freeze the speech of men's tongues, and they commonly went away at once when it was spoken.

On the fifth day came Clement to Ralph and said: "Now will I bring thee to the Queen, and she is young, and so fair, and withal so wise, that it seems to me not all so sure but that the sight of her will make an end of thy quest once for all. So that meseems thou mayest abide here in a life far better than wandering amongst uncouth folk, perilous and cruel. Yea, so thou mayst have it if thou wilt, being so exceeding goodly, and wise, and well-spoken, and of high lineage."

Ralph heard and reddened, but gave him back no answer; and they went together to the High House of the Queen, which was like a piece of the Kingdom of Heaven for loveliness, so many pillars as there were of bright marble stone, and gilded, and the chapiters carved most excellently: not many hangings on the walls, for the walls themselves were carven, and painted with pictures in the most excellent manner; the floors withal were so dainty that they seemed as if they were made for none but the feet of the fairest of women. And all this was set amidst of gardens, the like of which they had never seen.

But they entered without more ado, and were brought by the pages to the Lady's innermost chamber; and if the rest of the house were goodly, this was goodlier, and a marvel, so that it seemed wrought rather by goldsmiths and jewellers than by masons and carvers. Yet indeed many had said with Clement that the Queen who sat there was the goodliest part thereof.

Now she spake to Clement and said: "Hail, merchant! Is this the young knight of whom thou tellest, he who seeketh his beloved that hath been borne away into thralldom by evil men?"

"Even so," said Clement. But Ralph spake: "Nay, Lady, the damsel whom I seek is not my beloved, but my friend. My beloved is dead."

The Queen looked on him smiling kindly, yet was her face somewhat troubled. She said: "Master chapman, thy time here is not over long for all that thou hast to do; so we give thee leave to depart with our thanks for bringing a friend to see us. But this knight hath no affairs to look to: so if he will abide with us for a little, it will be our pleasure."

So Clement made his obeisance and went his ways. But the Queen bade Ralph sit before her, and tell her of his griefs, and she looked so kindly and friendly upon him that the heart melted within him, and he might say no word, for the tears that brake out from him, and he wept before her; while she looked on him, the colour coming and going in her face, and her lips trembling, and let him weep on. But he thought not of her, but of himself and how kind she was to him. But after a while he mastered his passion and began, and told her all he had done and suffered. Long was the tale in the telling, for it was sweet to him to lay before her both his grief and his hope. She let him talk on, and whiles she listened to him, and whiles, not, but all the time she gazed on him, yet

256

sometimes askance, as if she were ashamed. As for him, he saw her face how fair and lovely she was, yet was there little longing in his heart for her, more than for one of the painted women on the wall, for as kind and as dear as he deemed her.

When he had done, she kept silence a while, but at last she enforced her, and spake: "Sad it is for the mother that bore thee that thou art not in her house, wherein all things would be kind and familiar to thee. Maybe thou art seeking for what is not. Or maybe thou shalt seek and shalt find, and there may be naught in what thou findest, whereof to give thee such gifts as are meet for thy faithfulness and valiancy. But in thine home shouldst thou have all gifts which thou mayest desire."

Then was she silent awhile, and then spake: "Yet must I needs say that I would that thine home were in Goldburg."

He smiled sadly and looked on her, but with no astonishment, and indeed he still scarce thought of her as he said: "Lady and Queen, thou art good to me beyond measure. Yet, look you! One home I had, and left it; another I looked to have, and I lost it; and now I have no home. Maybe in days to come I shall go back to mine old home; and whiles I wonder with what eyes it will look on me. For merry is that land, and dear; and I have become sorrowful."

"Fear not," she said; "I say again that in thine home shall all things look kindly on thee."

Once more she sat silent, and no word did his heart bid him speak. Then she sighed and said: "Fair lord, I bid thee come and go in this house as thou wilt; but whereas there are many folk who must needs see me, and many things are appointed for me to do, therefore I pray thee to come hither in three days' space, and meanwhile I will look to the matter of thy search, that I may speed thee on the way to Utterness, which is no great way from Utterbol, and is the last town whereof we know aught. And I will write a letter for thee to give to the lord of Utterbol, which he will heed, if he heedeth aught my good-will or enmity. I beseech thee come for it in three days wearing."

Therewith she arose and took his hand and led him to the

door, and he departed, blessing her goodness, and wondering at her courtesy and gentle speech.

For those three days he was still seeking tidings everywhere, till folk began to know of him far and wide, and to talk of him. And at the time appointed he went to the Queen's House and was brought to her chamber as before, and she was alone therein. She greeted him and smiled on him exceeding kindly, but he might not fail to note of her that she looked sad and her face was worn by sorrow. She bade him sit beside her, and said: "Hast thou any tidings of the woman whom thou seekest?" "Nay, nay," said he, "and now I am minded to carry on the search out-a-gates. I have some good friends who will go with me awhile. But thou, Lady, hast thou heard aught?"

"Naught of the damsel," she said. "But there is something else. As Clement told me, thou seekest the Well at the World's End, and through Utterness and by Utterbol is a way whereby folk seek thither. Mayst thou find it, and may it profit thee more than it did my kinsman of old, who first raised up Goldburg in the wilderness. Whereas for him was naught but strife and confusion, till he was slain in a quarrel, wherein to fail was to fail, and to win the day was to win shame and misery."

She looked on him sweetly and said: "Thou art nowise such as he; and if thou drink of the Well, thou wilt go back to Upmeads, and thy father and mother, and thine own folk and thine home. But now here is the letter which thou shalt give to the Lord of Utterbol if thou meet him; and mayhappen he is naught so evil a man as the tale of him runs."

She gave him the letter into his hands, and spake again: "And now I have this to say to thee, if anything go amiss with thee, and thou be nigh enough to seek to me, come hither, and then, in whatso plight thou mayst be, or whatsoever deed thou mayst have done, here will be the open door for thee and the welcome of a friend."

Her voice shook a little as she spake, and she was silent again, mastering her trouble. Then she said: "At last I must say this to thee, that there may no lie be between us. That damsel of whom thou spakest that she was but thy friend, and not thy love—O that I might be thy friend in such-wise!

258

But over clearly I see that it may not be so. For thy mind looketh on thy deeds to come, that they shall be shared by some other than me. Friend, it seemeth strange and strange to me that I have come on thee so suddenly, and loved thee so sorely, and that I must needs say farewell to thee in so short a while. Farewell, farewell!"

Therewith she arose, and once more she took his hand in hers, and led him to the door. And he was sorry and all amazed: for he had not thought so much of her before, that he might see that she loved him; and he thought but that she, being happy and great, was kind to him who was hapless and homeless. And he was bewildered by her words and sore ashamed that for all his grief for her he had no speech, and scarce a look for her; he knew not what to do or say.

So he left the Queen's House and the court thereof, as though the pavement were growing red hot beneath his feet.

CHAPTER 30

Ralph Hath Hope of Tidings Concerning the Well at the World's End

Now he goes to Clement, and tells him that he deems he has no need to abide their departure from Goldburg to say farewell and follow his quest further afield; since it is clear that in Goldburg he should have no more tidings. Clement laughed and said: "Not so fast, Lord Ralph; thou mayst yet hear a word or two." "What!" said Ralph, "hast thou heard of something new?" Said Clement: "There has been a man here seeking thee, who said that he wotted of a wise man who could tell thee much concerning the Well at the World's End. And when I asked him of the Damsel and the Lord of Utterbol, if he knew anything of her, he said yea, but that he would keep it for thy privy ear. So I bade him go and come again when thou shouldst be here. And I deem that he will not tarry long."

Now they were sitting on a bench outside the hall of the hostel, with the court between them and the gate; and Ralph said: "Tell me, didst thou deem the man good or bad?" Said Clement: "He was hard to look into: but at least he looked not a fierce or cruel man; nor indeed did he seem false or sly, though I take him for one who hath lost his manhood—but lo you! here he comes across the court."

So Ralph looked, and saw in sooth a man drawing nigh, who came straight up to them and lowted to them, and then stood before them waiting for their word: he was fat and somewhat short, white-faced and pink-cheeked, with yellow hair long and curling, and with a little thin red beard and blue eyes: altogether much unlike the fashion of men of those parts. He was clad gaily in an orange-tawny coat laced with silver, and broidered with colours.

Clement spake to him and said: "This is the young knight who is minded to seek further east to wot if it be mere lies which he hath heard of the Well at the World's End."

The new-comer lowted before them again, and said in a small voice, and as one who was shy and somewhat afeared: "Lords, I can tell many a tale concerning that Well, and them who have gone on the quest thereof. And the first thing I have to tell is that the way thereto is through Utterness, and that I can be a shower of the way and a leader to any worthy knight who listeth to seek thither; and moreover, I know of a sage who dwelleth not far from the town of Utterness, and who, if he will, can put a seeker of the Well on the right road."

He looked askance on Ralph, whose face flushed and whose eyes glittered at that word. But Clement said: "Yea, that seemeth fair to look to: but hark ye! Is it not so that the way to Utterness is perilous?" Said the man: "Thou mayst rather call it deadly, to any who is not furnished with a let-pass from the Lord of Utterbol, as I am. But with such a scroll a child or a woman may wend the road unharmed." "Where hast thou the said let-pass?" said Clement. "Here," quoth the new-comer; and therewith he drew a scroll from out of his pouch, and opened it before them, and they read it together, and sure enough it was a writing charging all men so let pass and aid Morfinn the Minstrel (of whose aspect it told closely), under pain of falling into the displeasure of Gandolf, Lord of Utterbol; and the date thereon was but three months old.

Said Clement: "This is good, this let-pass: see thou, Ralph, the seal of Utterbol, the Bear upon the Castle Wall. None would dare to counterfeit this seal, save one who was weary of life, and longed for torments."

Said Ralph, smiling: "Thou seest, Master Clement, that there must be a parting betwixt us, and that this man's coming furthers it: but were he or were he not, yet the parting had come. And wert thou not liefer that it should come in a way to pleasure and aid me, than that thou shouldst but leave me behind at Goldburg when thou departest: and I with naught done toward the achieving my quest, but merely dragging my deedless body about these streets; and at last, it may be, going on a perilous journey without guiding or safe-conduct?"

"Yea, lad," said Clement, "I wotted well that thou wouldst take thine own way, but fain had I been that it had been mine also." Then he pondered a while and said afterwards: "I suppose that thou wilt take thy servant Bull Shockhead with thee, for he is a stout man-at-arms, and I deem him trusty, though he be a wild man. But one man is of little avail to a traveller on a perilous road, so if thou wilt I will give leave and license to a half score of our sergeants to follow thee on the road; for, as thou wottest, I may easily wage others in their place. Or else wouldst thou ask the Queen of Goldburg to give thee a score of men-at-arms; she looked to me the other day as one who would deny thee few of thine askings."

Ralph blushed red, and said: "Nay, I will not ask her this." Then he was silent; the new-comer looked from one to the other, and said nothing. At last Ralph spake: "Look you, Clement, my friend, I wot well how thou wouldst make my goings safe, even if it were to thy loss, and I thank thee for it: but I deem I shall do no better than putting myself into this man's hands, since he has a let-pass for the lands of him of Utterbol: and meseemeth from all that I have heard, that a half score or a score, or for the matter of that an hundred men-at-arms would not be enough to fight a way to Utterbol, and their gathering together would draw folk upon them, who would not meddle with two men journeying together, even if they had no let-pass of this mighty man." Clement sighed and grunted, and then said: "Well, lord, maybe thou art right."

"Yea," said the guide, "he is as right as may be: I have not spoken before lest ye might have deemed me untrusty: but now I tell thee this, that never should a small band of men unknown win through the lands of the Lord of Utterbol, or the land debatable that lieth betwixt them and Goldburg."

Ralph nodded friendly at him as he spake; but Clement looked on him sternly; and the man beheld his scowling face innocently, and took no heed of it.

Then said Ralph: "As to Bull Shockhead, I will speak to him anon; but I will not take him with me; for indeed I fear lest his mountain-pride grow up over greenly at whiles and entangle me in some thicket of peril hard to win out of."

"Well," said Clement, "and when wilt thou depart?" "To-morrow," said Ralph, "if my faring-fellow be ready for me by then." "I am all ready," said the man: "if thou wilt ride out by the east gate about two hours before noon to-morrow, I will abide thee on a good horse with all that we may need for the journey: and now I ask leave." "Thou hast it," said Clement.

So the man departed, and those two being left alone, Master Clement said: "Well, I deemed that nothing else would come of it: and I fear that thy gossip will be ill-content with me; for great is the peril." "Yea," said Ralph, "and great the reward." Clement smiled and sighed, and said: "Well, lad, even so hath a many thought before thee, wise men as well as fools." Ralph looked at him and reddened, and departed from him a little, and went walking in the cloister there to and fro, and pondered these matters; and whatever he might do, still would that trim figure be before his eyes which he had looked on so gladly erewhile in the hostel of Bourton Abbas; and he said aloud to himself: "Surely she needeth me, and draweth me to her whether I will or no." So wore the day.

CHAPTER 31

The Beginning of the Road
To Utterbol

Early next morning Ralph arose and called Bull Shockhead to him and said: "So it is, Bull, that thou art my war-taken thrall." Bull nodded his head, but frowned therewithal. Said Ralph: "If I bid thee aught that is not beyond reason thou wilt do it, wilt thou not?" "Yea," said Bull, surlily. "Well," quoth Ralph, "I am going a journey east-away, and I may not have thee with me, therefore I bid thee take this gold and go free with my goodwill." Bull's face lighted up, and the eyes glittered in his face; but he said: "Yea, king's son, but why wilt thou not take me with thee?" Said Ralph: "It is a perilous journey, and thy being with me will cast thee into peril and make mine more. Moreover, I have an errand, as thou wottest, which is all mine own."

Bull pondered a little and then said: "King's son, I was thinking at first that our errands lay together, and it is so; but belike thou sayest true that there will be less peril to each of us if we sunder at this time. But now I will say this to thee, that henceforth thou shalt be as a brother to me, if thou wilt have it so, and if ever thou comest amongst our people, thou wilt be in no danger of them: nay, they shall do all the good they may to thee."

Then he took him by the hand and kissed him, and he set his hand to his gear and drew forth a little purse of some small beast's skin that was broidered in front with a pair of bull's horns: then he stooped down and plucked a long and tough bent from the grass at his feet (for they were talking in the garden of the hostel) and twisted it swiftly into a strange knot of many plies, and opening the purse laid it therein and said: "King's son, this is the token whereby it shall be known amongst our folk that I have made thee my brother: were the flames roaring about thee, or the swords clashing over thine head, if thou cry out, I am the brother of Bull Shockhead, all those of my kindred who are near will be thy friends and thy helpers. And now I say to thee farewell: but it is not altogether unlike that thou mayst hear of me again in the furthest East." So Ralph departed from him, and Clement went with Ralph to the Gate of Goldburg, and bade him farewell there; and or they parted he said: "Meseems I have with me now some deal of the foreseeing of Katherine my wife, and in my mind it is that we shall yet see thee at Wulstead and Upmeads, and thou no less famous than now thou art. This is my last word to thee." Therewith they parted, and Ralph rode his ways.

He came on his way-leader about a bowshot from the gate and they greeted each other: the said guide was clad no otherwise than yesterday: he had saddle-bags on his horse, which was a strong black roadster: but he was nowise armed, and bore but a satchel with a case of knives done on to it, and on the other side a fiddle in its case. So Ralph smiled on him and said: "Thou hast no weapon, then?" "What need for weapon?" said he; "since we are not of might for battle. This is my weapon," said he, touching his fiddle, "and withal it is my field and mine acre that raiseth flesh-meat and bread for me: yea, and whiles a little drink."

So they rode on together and the man was blithe and merry: and Ralph said to him: "Since we are fellows for a good while, as I suppose, what shall I call thee?" Said he, "Morfinn the Minstrel I hight, to serve thee, fair lord. Or some call me Morfinn the Unmanned. Wilt thou not now ask me concerning that privy word that I had for thy ears?" "Yea," said Ralph reddening, "hath it to do with a woman?" "Naught less," said Morfinn. "For I heard of thee asking many questions thereof in Goldburg, and I said to myself, now may I, who am bound for Utterness, do a good turn to this fair young lord, whose face bewrayeth his heart, and telleth all men that he is kind and bounteous; so that there is no doubt but he will reward me well at once for any help I may give him; and also it may be that he will do me a good turn hereafter in memory of this that I have done him."

"Speak, wilt thou not," said Ralph, "and tell me at once if

thou hast seen this woman? Be sure that I shall reward thee."
"Nay, nay, fair sir," said Morfinn; "a woman I have seen
brought captive to the House of Utterbol. See thou to it if it
be she whom thou seekest."

He smiled therewith, but now Ralph deemed him not so
debonnaire as he had at first, for there was mocking in the
smile; therefore he was wroth, but he refrained him and said:
"Sir Minstrel, I wot not why thou hast come with a tale in
thy mouth and it will not out of it: lo you, will this open the
doors of speech to thee" (and he reached his hand out to him
with two pieces of gold lying therein) "or shall this?" and
therewith he half drew his sword from his sheath.

Said Morfinn, grinning again: "Nay, I fear not the bare
steel in thine hands, Knight; for thou hast not fool written
plain in thy face; therefore thou wilt not slay thy way-leader,
or even anger him over much. And as to thy gold, the wages
shall be paid at the journey's end. I was but seeking about in
my mind how best to tell thee my tale so that thou mightest
believe my word, which is true. Thus it goes: As I left
Utterbol a month ago, I saw a damsel brought in captive
there, and she seemed to me so exceeding fair that I looked
hard on her, and asked one of the men-at-arms who is my
friend concerning the market whereat she was cheapened;
and he told me that she had not been bought, but taken out
of the hands of the wild men from the further mountains. Is
that aught like to your story, lord?" "Yea," said Ralph,
knitting his brows in eagerness. "Well," said Morfinn, "but
there are more fair women than one in the world, and belike
this is not thy friend: so now, as well as I may, I will tell
thee what-like she was, and if thou knowest her not, thou
mayst give me those two gold pieces and go back again. She
was tall rather than short, and slim rather than bigly made.
But many women are fashioned so: and doubtless she was
worn by travel, since she has at least come from over the
mountains: but that is little to tell her by: her hands, and her
feet also (for she was a horseback and barefoot) wrought
well beyond most women: yet so might it have been with
some: yet few, methinks, of women who have worked afield,
as I deem her to have done, would have hands and feet so
shapely: her face tanned with the sun, but with fair colour

shining through it; her hair brown, yet with a fair bright colour shining therein, and very abundant: her cheeks smooth, round and well wrought as any imager could do them: her chin round and cloven: her lips full and red, but firm-set as if she might be both valiant and wroth. Her eyes set wide apart, grey and deep: her whole face sweet of aspect, as though she might be exceeding kind to one that pleased her; yet high and proud of demeanour also, meseemed, as though she were come of great kindred. Is this aught like to thy friend?"

He spake all this slowly and smoothly and that mocking smile came into his face now and again. Ralph grew pale as he spoke and knitted his brows as one in great wrath and grief; and he was slow to answer; but at last he said "Yea," shortly and sharply.

Then said Morfinn: "And yet after all it might not be she: for there might be another or two even in these parts of whom all this might be said. But now I will tell thee of her raiment, though there may be but little help to thee therein, as she may have shifted it many times since thou hast seen her. Thus it was: she was clad outwardly in a green gown, short of skirt as of one wont to go afoot; somewhat straight in the sleeves as of one who hath household work to do, and there was broidery many coloured on the seams thereof, and a border of flower-work round the hem: and this I noted, that a cantle of the skirt had been rent away by some hap of the journey. Now what sayest thou, fair lord? Have I done well to bring thee this tale?"

"O yea, yea," said Ralph, and he might not contain himself; but set spurs to his horse and galloped on ahead for some furlong or so: and then drew rein and gat off his horse, and made as if he would see to his saddle-girths, for he might not refrain from weeping the sweet and bitter tears of desire and fear, so stirred the soul within him.

Morfinn rode on quietly, and by then he came up, Ralph was mounting again, and when he was in the saddle he turned away his head from his fellow and said in a husky voice: "Morfinn, I command thee, or if thou wilt I beseech thee, that thou speak not to me again of this woman whom I am seeking; for it moveth me over much." "That is well,

266

lord," said Morfinn, "I will do after thy command; and there be many other matters to speak of besides one fair woman."

Then they rode on soberly a while, and Ralph kept silence, as he rode pondering much; but the minstrel hummed snatches of rhyme as he rode the way.

But at last Ralph turned to him suddenly and said: "Tell me, way-leader, in what wise did they seem to be using that woman?" The minstrel chuckled: "Fair lord," said he, "if I had a mind for mocking I might say of thee that thou blowest both hot and cold, since it was but half an hour ago that thou badest me speak naught of her: but I deem that I know thy mind herein: so I will tell thee that they seemed to be using her courteously; as is no marvel; for who would wish to mar so fair an image? O, it will be well with her: I noted that the Lord seemed to think it good to ride beside her, and eye her all over. Yea, she shall have a merry life of it if she but do somewhat after the Lord's will."

Ralph looked askance at him fiercely, but the other heeded it naught: then said Ralph, "And how if she do not his will?" Said Morfinn, grinning: "Then hath my Lord a many servants to do his will." Ralph held his peace for a long while; at last he turned a cleared brow to Morfinn and said: "Dost thou tell of the Lord of Utterbol that he is a good lord and merciful to his folk and servants?"

"Fair sir," said the minstrel; "thou hast bidden me not speak of one woman, now will I pray thee not to speak of one man, and that is my Lord of Utterbol."

Ralph's heart fell at this word, and he asked no question as to wherefore.

So now they rode on both, rather more than soberly for a while: but the day was fair; the sun shone, the wind blew, and the sweet scents floated about them, and Ralph's heart cast off its burden somewhat and he fell to speech again; and the minstrel answered him gaily by seeming, noting many things as they rode along, as one that took delight in the fashion of the earth.

It was a fresh and bright morning of early autumn, the sheaves were on the acres, and the grapes were blackening to the vintage, and the beasts and birds at least were merry. But little merry were the husbandmen whom they met, either

267

carles or queans, and they were scantily and foully clad, and sullen-faced, if not hunger-pinched.

If they came across any somewhat joyous, it was here and there certain gangrel folk resting on the wayside grass, or coming out of woods and other passes by twos and threes, whiles with a child or two with them. These were of aspect like to the gipsies of our time and nation, and were armed all of them, and mostly well clad after their fashion. Sometimes when there were as many as four or five carles of them together, they would draw up amidst of the highway, but presently would turn aside at the sight either of Ralph's war-gear or of the minstrel's raiment. Forsooth, some of them seemed to know him, and nodded friendly to him as they passed by, but he gave them back no good day.

They had now ridden out of the lands of Goldburg, which were narrow on that side, and the day was wearing fast. This way the land was fair and rich, with no hills of any size. They crossed a big river twice by bridges, and small streams often, mostly by fords.

Some two hours before sunset they came upon a place where a byway joined the high road, and on the ingle stood a chapel of stone (whether of the heathen or Christian men Ralph wotted not, for it was uncouth of fashion), and by the door of the said chapel, on a tussock of grass, sat a knight all-armed save the head, and beside him a squire held his war-horse, and five other men-at-arms stood anigh bearing halberds and axes of strange fashion. The knight rose to his feet when he saw the wayfarers coming up the rising ground, and Ralph had his hand on his sword-hilt; but ere they met, the minstrel said,—

"Nay, nay, draw thy let-pass, not thy sword. This knight shalt bid thee to a courteous joust; but do thou nay-say it, for he is a mere felon, and shalt set his men-at-arms on thee, and then will rob thee and slay thee after, or cast thee into his prison."

So Ralph drew out his parchment which Morfinn had given into his keeping, and held it open in his hand, and when the knight called out on him in a rough voice as they drew anigh, he said: "Nay, sir, I may not stay me now, need driveth me on." Quoth the knight, smoothing out a knitted brow: "Fair sir, since thou art a friend of our lord, wilt thou not come home to my house, which is hard by, and rest awhile, and eat a morsel, and drink a cup, and sleep in a fair chamber thereafter?"

"Nay, sir," said Ralph, "for time presses;" and he passed on withal, and the knight made no step to stay him, but laughed a short laugh, like a swine snorting, and sat him down on the grass again. Ralph heeded him naught, but was glad that his let-pass was shown to be good for something; but he could see that the minstrel was nigh sick for fear and was shaking like an aspen leaf, and it was long ere he found his tongue again.

Forth then they rode till dusk, when the minstrel stayed Ralph at a place where a sort of hovels lay together about a house somewhat better builded, which Ralph took for a hostelry, though it had no sign nor bush. They entered the said house, wherein was an old woman to whom the minstrel spake a word or two in a tongue that Ralph knew not, and straightway she got them victual and drink nowise ill, and showed them to beds thereafter.

In spite of both victuals and drink the minstrel fell silent and moody; it might be from weariness, Ralph deemed; and he himself had no great lust for talk, so he went bedward, and made the bed pay for all.

CHAPTER 32

Ralph Happens on Evil Days

Early on the morrow they departed, and now in the morning light and the sun the minstrel seemed glad again, and talked abundantly, even though at whiles Ralph answered him little.

As they rode, the land began to get less fertile and less, till at last there was but tillage here and there in patches: of houses there were but few, and the rest was but dark heath-land and bog, with scraggy woods scattered about the coun-try-side.

Naught happened to tell of, save that once in the after-noon, as they were riding up to the skirts of one of the woods aforesaid, weaponed men came forth from it and drew up across the way; they were a dozen in all, and four were horsed. Ralph set his hand to his sword, but the minstrel cried out, "Nay, no weapons, no weapons! Pull out thy let-pass again and show it in thine hand, and then let us on."

So saying he drew a white kerchief from his hand, and tied it to the end of his riding staff, and so rode trembling by Ralph's side: therewith they rode on together towards those men, whom as they drew nearer they heard laughing and jeering at them, though in a tongue that Ralph knew not.

They came so close at last that the waylayers could see the parchment clearly, with the seal thereon, and then they made obeisance to it, as though it were the relic of a saint, and drew off quietly into the wood one by one. These were big men, and savage-looking, and their armour was utterly uncouth.

The minstrel was loud in his mirth when they were well past these men; but Ralph rode on silently, and was some-what soberly.

"Fair sir," quoth the minstrel, "I would wager that I know thy thought." "Yea," said Ralph, "what is it them?" Said the minstrel: "Thou art thinking what thou shalt do when thou meetest suchlike folk on thy way back; but fear not, for with that same seal thou shalt pass through the land again." Said Ralph: "Yea, something like that, forsooth, was my thought. But also I was pondering who should be my guide when I leave Utterbol." The minstrel looked at him askance; quoth he: "Thou mayst leave thinking of that awhile." Ralph looked hard at him, but could make naught of the look of his face; so he said: "Why dost thou say that?" Said Morfinn: "Because I know whither thou art bound, and have been wondering this long while that thou hast asked me not about the way to the WELL at the WORLD'S END: since I told thy friend the merchant that I could tell thee somewhat concerning it. But I suppose thou hast been thinking of something else?"

"Well," said Ralph, "tell me what thou hast to say of the Well." Said Morfinn: "This will I tell thee first: that if thou hast any doubt that such a place there is, thou mayst set that aside; for we of Utterness and Utterbol are sure thereof; and of all nations and peoples whereof we know, we deem that we are the nighest thereto. How sayest thou, is that not already something?" "Yea, verily," said Ralph.

"Now," said Morfinn, "the next thing to be said is that we are on the road thereto: but the third thing again is this, lord, that though few who seek it find it, yet we know that some have failed not of it, besides that lord of Goldburg, of whom I know that thou hast heard. Furthermore, there dwelleth a sage in the woods not right far from Utterbol, a hermit living by himself; and folk seek to him for divers lore, to be holpen by him in one way or other, and of him men say that he hath so much lore concerning the road to the Well (whether he hath been there himself they know not certainly), that if he will, he can put anyone on the road so surely that he will not fail to come there, but he be slain on the way, as I said to thee in Goldburg. True it is that the said sage is chary of his lore, and if he think any harm of the seeker, he will show him naught; but, fair sir, thou art so valiant and so goodly, and as meseemeth so good a knight per amours, that I deem it a certain thing that he will tell thee the uttermost of his knowledge."

Now again waxed Ralph eager concerning his quest; for true it is that since he had had that story of the damsel from the minstrel, she had stood in the way before the Well at the World's End. But now he said: "And canst thou bring me to the said sage, good minstrel?" "Without doubt," quoth Morfinn, "when we are once safe at Utterbol. From Utterbol ye may wend any road."

"Yea," said Ralph, "and there are perils yet a few on the way, is it not so?" "So it is," said the minstrel; "but to-morrow shall try all." Said Ralph: "And is there some special peril ahead to-morrow? And if it be so, what is it?" Said his fellow: "It would avail thee naught to know it. What then, doth that daunt thee?" "No," said Ralph, "by then it is nigh enough to hurt us, we shall be nigh enough to see it." "Well said!" quoth the minstrel; "but now we must mend our pace, or dark night shall overtake us amid these rough ways."

Wild as the land was, they came at even to a place where were a few houses of woodmen or hunters; and they got off their horses and knocked at the door of one of these, and a great black-haired carle opened to them, who, when he saw the knight's armour, would have clapped the door to again, had not Ralph by the minstrel's rede held out the parchment to him, who when he saw it became humble indeed, and gave them such guesting as he might, which was scant indeed of victual or drink, save wild-fowl from the heath. But they had wine with them from the last guest-house, whereof they bade the carle to drink; but he would not, and in all wise seemed to be in dread of them.

When it was morning early they rode their ways, and the carle seemed glad to be rid of them. After they had ridden a few miles the land bettered somewhat; there were islands of deep green pasture amidst the blackness of the heath, with cattle grazing on them, and here and there was a little tillage: the land was little better than level, only it swelled a little this way and that. It was a bright sunny day and the air very clear, and as they rode Ralph said: "Quite clear is the sky, and yet one cloud there is in the offing; but this is strange about it, though I have been watching it this half hour, and looking to see the rack come up from that quarter, yet it changes not at all. I never saw the like of this cloud."

Said the minstrel: "Yea, fair sir, and of this cloud I must tell thee that it will change no more till the bones of the earth are tumbled together. Forsooth this is no cloud, but the topmost head of the mountain ridge which men call the Wall of the World: and if ever thou come close up to the said Wall, that shall fear thee, I deem, however fearless thou be." "Is it nigh to Utterness?" said Ralph. "Nay," said the minstrel, "not so nigh; for as huge as it seemeth thence."

Said Ralph: "Do folk tell that the Well at the World's End lieth beyond it?" "Surely," said the minstrel.

Said Ralph, his face flushing: "Forsooth, that ancient lord of Goldburg came through those mountains, and why not I?" "Yea," said the minstrel, "why not?" And therewith he

272

looked uneasily on Ralph, who heeded his looks naught, for his mind was set on high matters.

On then they rode, and when trees or some dip in the land hid that mountain top from them, the way seemed long to Ralph.

Naught befell to tell of for some while; but at last, when it was drawing towards evening again, they had been riding through a thick pine-wood for a long while, and coming out of it they beheld before them a plain country fairly well grassed, but lo! on the field not far from the roadside a pavilion pitched and a banner on the top thereof, but the banner hung down about the staff, so that the bearing was not seen: and about this pavilion, which was great and rich of fashion, were many tents great and small, and there were horses tethered in the field, and men moving about the gleam of armour.

At this sight the minstrel drew rein and stared about him wildly; but Ralph said: "What is this, is it the peril aforesaid?" "Yea," quoth the minstrel, shivering with fear. "What aileth thee?" said Ralph; "have we not the let-pass, what then can befall us? If this be other than the Lord of Utterbol, he will see our let-pass and let us alone; or if it be he indeed, what harm shall he do to the bearers of his own pass? Come on then, or else (and therewith he half drew his sword) is this Lord of Utterbol but another name for the Devil in Hell?"

But the minstrel still stared wild and trembled; then he stammered out: "I thought I should bring thee to Utterness first, and that some other should lead thee thence, I did not look to see him. I dare not, I dare not! O look, look!"

As he spake the wind arose and ran along the wood-side, and beat back from it and stirred the canvas of the tents and raised the folds of the banner, and blew it out, so that the bearing was clear to see; yet Ralph deemed it naught dreadful, but an armoury fit for a baron, to wit, a black bear on a castle-wall on a field of gold.

But as Ralph sat on his horse gazing, himseemed that men were looking towards him, and a great horn was sounded hard by the pavilion; then Ralph looked toward the minstrel fiercely, and laughed and said: "I see now that thou art another traitor: so get thee gone; I have more to do than the slaying of thee." And therewith he turned his horse's head, and smote the spurs into the sides of him, and went a great gallop over the field on the right side of the road, away from the gay pavilion; but even therewith came a half-score of horsemen from the camp, as if they were awaiting him, and they spurred after him straightway.

The race was no long one, for Ralph's beast was wearied, and the other horses were fresh, and Ralph knew naught of the country before him, whereas those riders knew it well. Therefore it was but a few minutes till they came up with him, and he made no show of defence, but suffered them to lead him away, and he crossed the highway, where he saw no token of the minstrel.

So they brought him to the pavilion, and made him dismount and led him in. The dusk had fallen by now, but within it was all bright with candles. The pavilion was hung with rich silken cloth, and at the further end, on a carpet of the hunting, was an ivory chair, whereon sat a man, who was the only one sitting. He was clad in a gown of blue silk, broidered with roundels beaten with the Bear upon the Castle-wall.

Ralph deemed that this must be no other than the Lord of Utterbol, yet after all the tales he had heard of that lord, he seemed no such terrible man: he was short of stature, but broad across the shoulders, his hair long, strait, and dark brown of hue, and his beard scanty: he was straight-featured and smooth-faced, and had been no ill-looking man, save that his skin was sallow and for his eyes, which were brown, small, and somewhat bloodshot.

Beside him stood Morfinn bowed down with fear and not daring to look either at the Lord or at Ralph. Wherefore he knew for certain that when he had called him traitor even now, that it was no more than the very sooth, and that he had fallen into the trap; though how or why he wotted not clearly. Well then might his heart have fallen, but so it was, that when he looked into the face of this Lord, the terror of the lands, hatred of him so beset his heart that it swallowed up fear in him. Albeit he held himself well in hand, for his soul was waxing, and he deemed that he should yet do great

274

deeds, therefore he desired to live, whatsoever pains or shame of the passing day he might suffer.

Now this mighty lord spake, and his voice was harsh and squeaking, so that the sound of it was worse than the sight of his face; and he said: "Bring the man forth, that I may see him." So they brought up Ralph, till he was eye to eye with the Lord, who turned to Morfinn and said: "Is this thy catch, lucky man?" "Yea," quavered Morfinn, not lifting his eyes; "Will he do, lord?"

"Do?" said the lord, "How can I see him when he is all muffled up in steel? Ye fools! doff his wargear."

Speedily then had they stripped Ralph of hauberk, and helm, and arm and leg plates, so that he stood up in his jerkin and breeches, and the lord leaned forward to look on him as if he were cheapening a horse; and then turned to a man somewhat stricken in years, clad in scarlet, who stood on his other hand, and said to him: "Well, David the Sage, is this the sort of man? Is he goodly enough?"

Then the elder put on a pair of spectacles and eyed Ralph curiously a while, and then said: "There are no two words to be said about it; he is a goodly and well-fashioned a young man as was ever sold."

"Well," said the lord, turning towards Morfinn, "the catch is good, lucky man: David will give thee gold for it, and thou mayst go back west when thou wilt. And thou must be lucky again, moreover; because there are women needed for my house; and they must be goodly and meek, and not grievously marked with stripes, or branded, so that thou hadst best take them, luckily if thou mayst, and not buy them. Now go, for there are more than enough men under this woven roof, and we need no half-men to boot."

Said David, the old man, grinning: "He will hold him well paid if he go unscathed from before thee, lord: for he looked not to meet thee here, but thought to bring the young man to Utterness, that he might be kept there till thou camest."

The lord said, grimly: "He is not far wrong to fear me, maybe: but he shall go for this time. But if he bring me not those women within three months' wearing, and if there be but two uncomely ones amongst them, let him look to it. Give him his gold, David. Now take ye the new man, and let

275

him rest, and give him meat and drink. And look you, David, if he be not in condition when he cometh home to Utterbol, thou shalt pay for it in one way or other, if not in thine own person, since thou art old, and deft of service, then through those that be dear to thee. Go now!"

David smiled on Ralph and led him out unto a tent not far off, and there he made much of him, and bade bring meat and drink and all he needed. Withal he bade him not to try fleeing, lest he be slain; and he showed him how nigh the guards were and how many.

Glad was the old man when he saw the captive put a good face on matters, and that he was not down-hearted. In sooth that hatred of the tyrant mingled with hope sustained Ralph's heart. He had been minded when he was brought before the lord to have shown the letter of the Queen of Goldburg, and to defy him if he still held him captive. But when he had beheld him and his fellowship a while he thought better of it. For though they had abundance of rich plenishing, and gay raiment, and good weapons and armour, howbeit of strange and uncouth fashion, yet he deemed when he looked on them that they would scarce have the souls of men in their bodies, but that they were utterly vile through and through, like the shapes of an evil dream. Therefore he thought shame of it to show the Queen's letter to them, even as if he had shown them the very naked body of her, who had been so piteous kind to him. Also he had no mind to wear his heart on his sleeve, but would keep his own counsel, and let his foemen speak and show what was in their minds. For this cause he now made himself sweet, and was of good cheer with old David, deeming him to be a great men there; as indeed he was, being the chief counsellor of the Lord of Utterbol; though forsooth not so much his counsellor as that he durst counsel otherwise than as the Lord desired to go; unless he thought that it would bring his said Lord, and therefore himself, to very present peril and damage. In short, though this man had not been bought for money, he was little better than a thrall of the higher sort, as forsooth were all the Lord's men, saving the best and trustiest of his warriors: and these were men whom the Lord somewhat feared himself: though, on the other hand, he could not but know that they understood how the dread of the Lord of Utterbol was a shield to them, and that if it were to die out amongst men, their own skins were not worth many days' purchase.

So then David spake pleasantly with Ralph, and ate and drank with him, and saw that he was well bedded for the night, and left him in the first watch. But Ralph lay down in little more trouble than the night before, when, though he were being led friendly to Utterness, yet he had not been able to think what he should do when he came there: whereas now he thought: Who knoweth what shall betide? and for me there is nought to do save to lay hold of the occasion that another may give me. And at the worst I scarce deem that I am being led to the slaughter.

CHAPTER 33

Ralph is Brought on the Road
Towards Utterbol

But now when it was morning they struck the tents and laded them on wains, and went their ways the selfsame road that Ralph had been minded for yesterday; to wit the road to Utterness; but now must he ride it unarmed and guarded: other shame had he none. Indeed David, who stuck close to his side all day, was so sugary sweet with him, and praised and encouraged him so diligently, that Ralph began to have misgivings that all this kindness was but as the flower-garlands wherewith the heathen times men were wont to deck the slaughter-beasts for the blood-offering. Yea, and into his mind came certain tales of how there were heathen men yet in the world, who beguiled men and women, and offered them up to their devils, whom they called gods: but all this ran off him soon, when he bethought him how little wisdom there was in running to meet the evil, which might be on the way, and that way a rough and perilous one. So he plucked up heart, and spake freely and gaily with David and one or two others who rode anigh.

They were amidst of the company: the Lord went first after his fore-runners in a litter done about with precious cloths; and two score horsemen came next, fully armed after their manner. Then rode Ralph with David and a half dozen of the magnates: then came a sort of cooks and other serving men, but none without a weapon, and last another score of men-at-arms: so that he saw that fleeing was not to be thought of though he was not bound, and save for lack of weapons rode like a free man.

The day was clear as yesterday had been, wherefore again Ralph saw the distant mountain-top like a cloud; and he gazed at it long till David said: "I see that thou art gazing hard at the mountains, and perchance art longing to be beyond them, were it but to see what like the land is on the further side. If all tales be true thou art best this side thereof, whatever thy lot may be."

"Lieth death on the other side then?" quoth Ralph. "Yea," said David, "but that is not all, since he is not asleep elsewhere in the world: but men say that over there are things to be seen which might slay a strong man for pure fear, without stroke of sword or dint of axe."

"Yea," said Ralph, "but how was it then with him that builded Goldburg?"

"O," said David, "hast hou heard that tale? Well, they say of him, who certes went over those mountains, and drank of the Well at the World's End, that he was one of the lucky: yet for all his luck never had he drunk the draught had he not been helped by one who had learned many things, a woman to wit. For he was one of them with whom all women are in love; and thence indeed was his luck. . . . Moreover, when all is said, 'tis but a tale."

"Yea," quoth Ralph laughing, "even as the tales of the ghosts and bugs that abide the wayfarer on the other side of yonder white moveless cloud."

David laughed in his turn and said: "Thou hast me there; and whether or no, these tales are nothing to us, who shall never leave Utterbol again while we live, save in such a company as this." Then he held his peace, but presently spake

278

again: "Hast thou heard anything, then, of those tales of the Well at the World's End? I mean others beside that concerning the lord of Goldburg?"

"Yea, surely I have," said Ralph, nowise changing countenance. Said David: "Deemest thou aught of them? deemest thou that it may be true that a man may drink of the Well and recover his youth thereby?"

Ralph laughed and said: "Master, it is rather for me to ask thee hereof, than thou me, since thou dwellest so much nigher thereto than I have done heretofore."

David drew up close to him, and said softly: "Nigher? Yea, but belike not so much nigher."

"How meanest thou?" said Ralph.

Said David: "Is it so nigh that a man may leave home and come thereto in his life-time?"

"Yea," said Ralph, "in my tales it is."

Said the old man still softlier: "Had I deemed that true I had tried the adventure, whatever might lie beyond the mountains, but (and he sighed withal) I deem it untrue."

Therewith dropped the talk of that matter: and in sooth Ralph was loath to make many words thereof, lest his eagerness shine through, and all the story of him be known.

Anon it was noon, and the lord bade all men stay for meat: so his serving men busied them about his dinner, and David went with them. Then the men-at-arms bade Ralph sit among them and share their meat. So they sat down all by the wayside, and they spake kindly and friendly to Ralph, and especially their captain, a man somewhat low of stature, but long-armed like the Lord, a man of middle age, beardless and spare of body, but wiry and tough-looking, with hair of the hue of the dust of the sandstone quarry. This man fell a-talking with Ralph, and asked him of the manner of tilting and courteous jousting between knights in the countries of knighthood, till that talk dropped between them. Then Ralph looked round upon the land, which had now worsened again, and was little better than rough moorland, little fed, and not at all tilled, and he said: "This is but a sorry land for earth's increase."

"Well," said the captain, "I wot not; it beareth plover and whimbrel and conies and hares; yea, and men withal, some few. And whereas it beareth naught else, that cometh of my lord's will: for deemest thou that he should suffer a rich land betwixt him and Goldburg, that it might sustain an host big enough to deal with him?"

"But is not this his land?" said Ralph.

Said the captain: "Nay, and also yea. None shall dwell in it save as he willeth, and they shall pay him tribute, be it never so little. Yet some there are of them, who are to him as the hounds be to the hunter, and these same he even wageth, so that if aught rare and goodly cometh their way they shall bring it to his hands; as thou thyself knowest to thy cost."

"Yea," said Ralph smiling, "and is Morfinn the Unmanned one of these curs?" "Yea," said the captain, with a grin, "and one of the richest of them, in despite of his fiddle and minstrel's gear, and his lack of manhood: for he is one of the cunningest of men. But my Lord unmanned him for some good reason."

Ralph kept silence and while and then said: "Why doth the Goldburg folk suffer all this felony, robbery and confusion, so near their borders, and the land debateable?"

Said the captain, and again he grinned: "Passing for thy hard words, sir knight, why dost thou suffer me to lead thee along whither thou wouldest not?"

"Because I cannot help myself," said Ralph.

Said the captain: "Even so it is with the Goldburg folk: if they raise hand against some of these strong-thieves or man-stealers, he has but to send the war-arrow round about these deserts, as ye deem them, and he will presently have as rough a company of carles for his fellows as need be, say ten hundred of them. And the Goldburg folk are not very handy at a fray without their walls. Forsooth within them it is another matter, and beside not even our Lord of Utterbol would see Goldburg broken down, no, not for all that he might win there."

"Is it deemed a holy place in the land, then?" said Ralph.

"I wot not the meaning of holy," said the other: "but all we deem that when Goldburg shall fall, the world shall change, so that living therein shall be hard to them that have not drunk of the water of the Well at the World's End."

Ralph was silent a while and eyed the captain curiously: then he said: "Have the Goldburgers so drunk?" Said the captain: "Nay, nay; but the word goes that under each tower of Goldburg lieth a youth and a maiden that have drunk of the water, and might not die save by point and edge."

Then was Ralph silent again, for once more he fell pondering the matter if he had been led away to be offered as a blood offering to some of evil gods of the land. But as he pondered a flourish of trumpets was blown, and all men sprang up, and the captain said to Ralph: "Now hath our Lord done his dinner and we must to horse." Anon they were on the way again, and they rode long and saw little change in the aspect of the land, neither did that cloudlike token of the distant mountains grow any greater or clearer to Ralph's deeming.

CHAPTER 34

The Lord of Utterbol Will Wot of Ralph's Might and Minstrelsy

A little before sunset they made halt for the night, and Ralph was shown to a tent as erst, and had meat and drink good enough brought to him. But somewhat after he had done eating comes David to him and says: "Up, young man! and come to my lord, he asketh for thee."

"What will he want with me?" said Ralph.

"Yea, that is a proper question to ask!" quoth David; "as though the knife should ask the cutler, what wilt thou cut with me? Dost thou deem that I durst ask him of his will with thee?" "I am ready to go with thee," said Ralph.

So they went forth; but Ralph's heart fell and he sickened at the thought of seeing that man again. Nevertheless he set his face as brass, and thrust back both his fear and his hatred for a fitter occasion.

Soon they came into the pavilion of the Lord, who was

sitting there as yester eve, save that his gown was red, and done about with gold and turquoise and emerald. David brought Ralph nigh to his seat, but spake not. The mighty lord was sitting with his head drooping, and his arm hanging over his knee, with a heavy countenance as though he were brooding matters which pleased him naught. But in a while he sat up with a start, and turned about and saw David standing there with Ralph, and spake at once like a man waking up: "He that sold thee to me said that thou wert of avail for many things. Now tell me, what canst thou do?"

Ralph so hated him, that he was of half a mind to answer naught save by smiting him to slay him; but there was no weapon anigh, and life was sweet to him with all the tale that was lying ahead. So he answered coldly: "It is sooth, lord, that I can do more than one deed."

"Canst thou back a horse?" said the Lord. Said Ralph: "As well as many." Said the Lord: "Canst thou break a wild horse, and shoe him, and physic him?"

"Not worse than some," said Ralph.

"Can'st thou play with sword and spear?" said the Lord.

"Better than some few," said Ralph. "How shall I know that?" said the Lord. Said Ralph: "Try me, lord!" Indeed, he half hoped that if it came to that, he might escape in the hurley.

The Lord looked on him and said: "Well, it may be tried. But here is a cold and proud answerer, David. I misdoubt me whether it be worth while bringing him home."

David looked timidly on Ralph and said: "Thou hast paid the price for him, lord."

"Yea, that is true," said the Lord. "Thou! can'st thou play at the chess?" "Yea," said Ralph. "Can'st thou music?" said the other. "Yea," said Ralph, "when I am merry, or whiles indeed when I am sad."

The lord said: "Make thyself merry or sad, which thou wilt; but sing, or thou shalt be beaten. Ho! Bring ye the harp." Then they brought it as he bade.

But Ralph looked to right and left and saw no deliverance, and knew this for the first hour of his thralldom. Yet, as he thought of it all, he remembered that if he would do, he must needs bear and forbear; and his face cleared, and he looked round about again and let his eyes rest calmly on all eyes that he met till they came on the Lord's face again. Then he let his hand fall into the strings and they fell a-tinkling sweetly, like unto the song of the winter robin, and at last he lifted his voice and sang:

Still now is the stithy this morning unclouded,
Nought stirs in the thorp save the yellow-haired maid
A-peeling the withy last Candlemas shrouded
From the mere where the moorhen now swims unafraid.

For over the Ford now the grass and the clover
Fly off from the tines as the wind driveth on;
And soon round the Sword-howe the swathe shall lie over,
And to-morrow at even the mead shall be won.

But the Hall of the Garden amidst the hot morning,
It drew my feet thither; I stood at the door,
And felt my heart harden 'gainst wisdom and warning
As the sun and my footsteps came on to the floor.

When the sun lay behind me, there scarce in the dimness
I say what I sought for, yet trembled to find;
But it came forth to find me, until the sleek slimness
Of the summer-clad woman made summer o'er kind.

There we the once-sundered together were blended,
We strangers, unknown once, were hidden by naught.
I kissed and I wondered how doubt was all ended,
How friendly her excellent fairness was wrought.

Round the hall of the Garden the hot sun is burning,
But no master nor minstrel goes there in the shade,
It hath never a warden till comes the returning,
When the moon shall hang high and all winds shall be laid.

Waned the day and I hied me afield, and thereafter
I sat with the mighty when daylight was done,
But with great men beside me, midst high-hearted laughter,
I deemed me of all men the gainfullest one.

To wisdom I hearkened; for there the wise father
Cast the seed of his learning abroad o'er the hall,

Till men's faces darkened, but mine gladdened rather
With the thought of the knowledge I knew over all.

Sang minstrels the story, and with the song's welling
Men looked on each other and glad were they grown,
But mine was the glory of the tale and its telling
How the loved and the lover were naught but mine own.

When he was done all kept silence till they should know
whether the lord should praise the song or blame; and he said
naught for a good while, but sat as if pondering: but at last
he spake: "Thou art young, and would that we were young
also! Thy song is sweet, and it pleaseth me, who am a man of
war, and have seen enough and to spare of rough work, and
would any day rather see a fair woman than a band of
spears. But it shall please my lady wife less: for of love, and
fair women, and their lovers she hath seen enough; but of
war nothing save its shows and pomps; wherefore she desireth to hear thereof. Now sing of battle!"

Ralph thought awhile and began to smite the harp while he
conned over a song which he had learned one yule-tide from a
chieftain who had come to Upmeads from the far-away
Northland, and had abided there till spring was waning into
summer, and meanwhile he taught Ralph this song and many
things else, and his name was Sir Karr Wood-neb. This song
now Ralph sang loud and sweet, though he were now a thrall
in an alien land:

Leave we the cup!
For the moon is up,
And bright is the gleam
Of the rippling stream,
That runneth his road
To the old abode,
Where the walls are white
In the moon and the night;
The house of the neighbour that drave us away

When strife ended labour amidst of the hay,
And no road for our riding was left us but one
Where the hill's brow is hiding that earth's ways are done,
And the sound of the billows comes up at the last
Like the wind in the willows ere autumn is past.
But oft and again
Comes the ship from the main,
And we came once more
And no lading we bore
But the point and the edge,
And the ironed ledge,
And the bolt and the bow,
And the bane of the foe.
To the House 'neath the mountain we came in the morn,
Where welleth the fountain up over the corn,
And the stream is a-running fast on to the House
Of the neighbours uncunning who quake at the mouse,
As their slumber is broken; they know not for why;
Since yestreen was not token on earth or in sky.

Come, up, then up!
Leave board and cup,
And follow the gleam
Of the glittering stream
That leadeth the road
To the old abode,
High-walled and white
In the moon and the night;
Where low lies the neighbour that drave us away
Sleep-sunk from his labour amidst of the hay.
No road for our riding is left us save one,
Where the hills' brow is hiding the city undone,
And the wind in the willows is with us at last,
And the house of the billows is done and o'er-past.

Haste! mount and haste
Ere the short night waste,
For night and day,
Late turned away,
Draw nigh again

All kissing-fain;
And the morn and the moon
Shall be married full soon.
So ride we together with wealth-winning wand,
The steel o'er the leather, the ash in the hand.
Lo! white walls before us, and high are they built;
But the luck that outwore us now lies on their guilt;
Lo! the open gate biding the first of the sun,
And to peace are we riding when slaughter is done.

When Ralph had done singing, all folk fell to praising his song, whereas the Lord had praised the other one; but the Lord said, looking at Ralph askance meanwhile: "Yea, if that pleaseth me not, and I take but little keep of it, it shall please my wife to her heart's root; and that is the first thing. Hast thou others good store, new-comer?" "Yea, lord," said Ralph. "And canst thou tell tales of yore agone, and of the fays and such-like? All that she must have." "Some deal I can of that lore," said Ralph.

Then the Lord sat silent, and seemed to be pondering: at last he said, as if to himself: "Yet there is one thing: many a blencher can sing of battle; and it hath been seen, that a fair body of a man is whiles soft amidst the hard hand-play. Thou! Morfinn's luck! art thou of any use in the tilt-yard?" "Wilt thou try me, lord?" said Ralph, looking somewhat brisker. Said the Lord: "I deem that I may find a man or two for thee, though it is not much our manner here; but now go thou! David, take the lad away to his tent, and get him a flask of wine of the best to help out thy maundering with him."

Therewith they left the tent, and Ralph walked by David sadly and with hanging head at first; but in a while he called to mind that, whatever betid, his life was safe as yet; that every day he was drawing nigher to the Well at the World's End; and that it was most like that he shall fall in with that Dorothea of his dream somewhere on the way thereto. So he lifted up his head again, and was singing to himself as he stooped down to enter into his tent.

Next day naught happed to tell of save that they journeyed on; the day was cloudy, so that Ralph saw no sign of the distant mountains; ever the land was the same, but belike somewhat more beset with pinewoods; they saw no folk at all on the road. So at even Ralph slept in his tent, and none meddled with him, save that David came to talk with him or he slept, and was merry and blithe with him, and he brought with him Otter, the captain of the guard, who was good company.

Thus wore three days that were hazy and cloudy, and the Lord sent no more for Ralph, who on the road spake for the more part with Otter, and liked him not ill; howbeit it seemed of him that he would make no more of a man's life than of a rabbit's according as his lord might bid slay or let live.

The three hazy days past, it fell to rain for four days, so that Ralph could see little of the face of the land; but he noted that they went up at whiles, and never so much down as up, so that they were wending up hill on the whole.

On the ninth day of his captivity the rain ceased and it was sunny and warm but somewhat hazy, so that naught could be seen afar, but the land near-hand rose in long, low downs now, and was quite treeless, save where was a hollow here and there and a stream running through it, where grew a few willows, but alders more abundantly.

This day he rode by Otter, who said presently: "Well, youngling of the North, to-morrow we shall see a new game, thou and I, if the weather be fair." "Yea," said Ralph, "and what like shall it be?" Said Otter, "At mid-morn we shall come into a fair dale amidst the downs, where be some houses and a tower of the Lord's, so that that place is called the Dale of the Tower: there shall we abide a while to gather victual, a day or two, or three maybe: so my Lord will hold a tourney there: that is to say that I myself and some few others shall try thy manhood somewhat." "What?" said Ralph, "are the new colt's paces to be proven? And how if he fail?"

Quoth Otter, laughing: "Fail not, I rede thee, or my lord's love for thee shall be something less than nothing." "And then will he slay me?" said Ralph. Said Otter: "Nay I deem not, at least not at first: he will have thee home to Utterbol, to make the most of his bad bargain, and there shalt thou be a mere serving-thrall, either in the house or the field: where thou shalt be well-fed (save in times of scarcity), and belike well beaten withal." Said Ralph, somewhat downcast: "Yea, I am a thrall, who was once a knight. But how if thou fail before me?" Otter laughed again: "That is another matter; whatever I do my Lord will not lose me if he can help it; but as for the others who shall stand before thy valiancy, there will be some who will curse the day whereon my lord bought thee, if thou turnest out a good spear, as ye call it in your lands. Howsoever, that is not thy business; and I bid thee fear naught; for thou seemest to be a mettle lad."

So they talked, and that day wore like the others, but the haze did not clear off, and the sun went down red. In the evening David talked with Ralph in his tent, and said: "If to-morrow be clear, knight, thou shalt see a new sight when thou comest out from the canvas." Said Ralph: "I suppose thy meaning is that we shall see the mountains from hence?" "Yea," said David; "so hold up thine heart when that sight first cometh before thine eyes. As for us, we are used to the sight, and that from a place much nigher to the mountains: yet they who are soft-hearted amongst us are overcome at whiles, when there is storm and tempest, and evil tides at hand."

Said Ralph: "And how far then are we from Utterbol?" Said David: "After we have left Bull-mead in the Dale of the Tower, where to-morrow thou art to run with the spear, it is four days' ride to Utterness; and from Utterness ye may come (if my lord will) unto Utterbol in twelve hours. But tell me, knight, how deemest thou of thy tilting to-morrow?" Said Ralph: "Little should I think of it, if little lay upon it." "Yea," said David, "but art thou a good tilter?" Ralph laughed: quoth he, "That hangs on the goodness of him that tilteth against me: I have both overthrown, and been overthrown oft enough. Yet again, who shall judge me? for I must tell thee, that were I fairly judged, I should be deemed no ill spear, even when I came not uppermost: for in all these games are haps which no man may foresee."

"Well, then," said David, "all will go well with thee for his time: for my lord will judge thee, and if it be seen that thou hast spoken truly, and art more than a little deft at the play, he will be like to make the best of thee, since thou art already paid for." Ralph laughed: yet as though the jest pleased him but little; and they fell to talk of other matters. And so David departed, and Ralph slept.

CHAPTER 35

Ralph Cometh To the Vale of the Tower

But when it was morning Ralph awoke, and saw that the sun was shining brightly; so he cast his shirt on him, and went out at once, and turned his face eastward, and, scarce awake, said to himself that the clouds lay heavy in the eastward heavens after last night's haze: but presently his eyes cleared, and he saw that what he had taken for clouds was a huge wall of mountains, black and terrible, that rose up sharp and clear into the morning air; for there was neither cloud nor mist in all the heavens.

Now Ralph, though he were but little used to the sight of great mountains, yet felt his heart rather rise than fall at the sight of them; for he said: "Surely beyond them lieth some new thing for me, life or death: fair fame or the forgetting of all men." And it was long that he could not take his eyes off them.

As he looked, came up the Captain Otter, and said: "Well, Knight, thou hast seen them this morn, even if ye die ere nightfall." Said Ralph: "What deemest thou to lie beyond them?"

"Of us none knoweth surely," said Otter; "whiles I deem that if one were to get to the other side there would be a great plain like to this: whiles that there is naught save mountains beyond, and yet again mountains, like the waves of a huge stone sea. Or whiles I think that one would come to an end of the world, to a place where is naught but a ledge, and then below it a gulf filled with nothing but the howling of winds, and the depth of darkness. Moreover this is my thought, that all we of these parts should be milder men and of better conditions, if yonder terrible wall were away. It is as if we were thralls of the great mountains."

Said Ralph, "Is this then the Wall of the World?" "It may well be so," said Otter; "but this word is at whiles said of something else, which no man alive amongst us has yet seen. It is a part of the tale of the seekers for the Well at the World's End, whereof we said a word that other day."

"And the Dry Tree," said Ralph, "knowest thou thereof?" said Ralph. "Such a tree, much beworshipped," said Otter, "we have, not very far from Utterbol, on the hither side of the mountains. Yet I have heard old men say that it is but a toy, and an image of that which is verily anigh the Well at the World's End. But now haste thee to do on thy raiment, for we must needs get to horse in a little while." "Yet one more word," said Ralph; "thou sayest that none alive amongst you have seen the Wall of the World?" "None alive," quoth Otter; "forsooth what the dead may see, that is another question." Said Ralph: "But have ye not known of any who have sought to the Well from this land, which is so nigh thereunto?" "Such there have been," said Otter; "but if they found it, they found something beyond it, or came west again by some way else than by Utterbol; for they never came back again to us."

Therewith he turned on his heel, and went his ways, and up came David and one with him bringing victual; and David said: "Now, thou lucky one, here is come thy breakfast! for we shall presently be on our way. Cast on thy raiment, and eat and strengthen thyself for the day's work. Hast thou looked well on the mountains?" "Yea," said Ralph, "and the sight of them has made me as little downhearted as thou art. For thou art joyous of mood this morning." David nodded and smiled, and looked so merry that Ralph wondered what was toward. Then he went into his tent and clad himself, and ate his breakfast, and then gat to horse and rode betwixt two of the men-at-arms, he and Otter; for David was ridden forward to speak with the Lord. Otter talked ever gaily enough; but Ralph heeded him little a while, but had his eyes ever on the mountains, and could see that for all they were so dark, and filled up so much of the eastward heaven, they were so far away that he could see but little of them save that they were dark blue and huge, and one rising up behind the other.

Thus they rode the down country, till at last, two hours before noon, coming over the brow of a long down, they had before them a shallow dale, pleasanter than aught they had yet seen. It was well-grassed, and a little river ran through it, from which went narrow leats held up by hatches, so that the more part of the valley bottom was a water-meadow, wherein as now were grazing many kine and sheep. There were willows about the banks of the river, and in an ingle of it stood a grange or homestead, with many roofs half hidden by clumps of tall old elm trees. Other houses there were in the vale; two or three cots, to wit, on the slope of the hither down, and some half-dozen about the homestead; and above and beyond all these, on a mound somewhat away from the river and the grange, a great square tower, with barriers and bailey all dight ready for war, and with a banner of the Lord's hanging out. But between the tower and the river stood as now a great pavilion of snow-white cloth striped with gold and purple; and round about it were other tents, as though a little army were come into the vale.

So when they looked into that fair place, Otter the Captain rose in the stirrups and cast up his hand for joy, and cried out aloud: "Now, young knight, now we are come home: how likest thou my Lord's land?"

"It is a fair land," said Ralph; "but is there not come some one to bid thy Lord battle for it? or what mean the tents down yonder?"

Said Otter, laughing: "Nay, nay, it hath not come to that yet. Yonder is my Lord's lady-wife, who hath come to meet him, but in love, so to say, not in battle—not yet. Though I say not that the cup of love betwixt them be brim-full. But this it behoveth me not to speak of, though thou art to be my brother-in-arms, since we are to tilt together presently: for lo! yonder the tilt-yard, my lad."

Therewith he pointed to the broad green meadow: but Ralph said: "How canst thou, a free man, be brother-in-arms to a thrall?" "Nay, lad," quoth Otter, "let not that wasp sting

291

thee: for even such was I, time was. Nay, such am I now, but that a certain habit of keeping my wits in a fray maketh me of avail to my Lord, so that I am well looked to. Forsooth in my Lord's land the free men are of little account, since they must oftenest do as my Lord and my Lord's thralls bid them. Truly, brother, it is we who have the wits and the luck to rise above the whipping-post and the shackles that are the great men hereabouts. I say we, for I deem that thou wilt do no less, whereas thou hast the lucky look in thine eyes. So let to-day try it."

As he spake came many glittering figures from out of those tents, and therewithal arose the sound of horns and clashing of cymbals, and their own horns gave back the sound of welcome. Then Ralph saw a man in golden armour of strange, outlandish fashion, sitting on a great black horse beside the Lord's litter; and Otter said: "Lo! my Lord, armed and a-horseback to meet my lady: she looketh kinder on him thus; though in thine ear be it said, he is no great man of war; nor need he be, since he hath us for his shield and his hauberk."

Herewith were they come on to the causeway above the green meadows, and presently drew rein before the pavilion, and stood about in a half-ring facing a two score of gaily clad men-at-arms, who had come with the Lady and a rout of folk of the household. Then the Lord gat off his horse, and stood in his golden armour, and all the horns and other music struck up, and forth from the pavilion came the Lady with a half-score of her women clad gaily in silken gowns of green, and blue, and yellow, broidered all about with gold and silver, but with naked feet, and having iron rings on their arms, so that Ralph saw that they were thralls. Something told him that his damsel should be amongst these, so he gazed hard on them, but though they were goodly enough there was none of them like to her.

As to the Queen, she was clad all in fine linen and gold, with gold shoes on her feet: her arms came bare from out of the linen: great they were, and the hands not small; but the arms round and fair, and the hands shapely, and all very white and rosy: her hair was as yellow as any that can be seen, and it was plenteous, and shed all down about her. Her eyes were blue and set wide apart, her nose a little snubbed, her mouth wide, full-lipped and smiling. She was very tall, a full half-head taller than any of her women: yea, as tall as a man who is above the middle height of men.

Now she came forward hastily with long strides, and knelt adown before the Lord, but even as she kneeled looked round with a laughing face. The Lord stooped down to her and took her by both hands, and raised her up, and kissed her on the cheek (and he looked but little and of no presence beside her:) and he said: "Hail to thee, my Lady; thou art come far from thine home to meet me, and I thank thee therefor. Is it well with our House?"

She spake seeming carelessly and loud; but her voice was somewhat husky: "Yea, my Lord, all is well; few have done amiss, and the harvest is plenteous." As she spake the Lord looked with knit brows at the damsels behind her, as if he were seeking something; and the Lady followed his eyes, smiling a little and flushing as if with merriment.

But the Lord was silent a while, and then let his brow clear and said: "Yea, Lady, thou art thanked for coming to meet us; and timely is thy coming, since there is game and glee for thee at hand; I have cheapened a likely thrall of Morfinn the Unmanned, and he is a gift to thee; and he hath given out that he is no ill player with the spear after the fashion of them of the west; and we are going to prove his word here in this meadow presently."

The Lady's face grew glad, and she said, looking toward the ring of new comers: "Yea, Lord, and which of these is he, if he be here?"

The Lord turned a little to point out Ralph, but even therewith the Lady's eyes met Ralph's, who reddened for shame of being so shown to a great lady; but as for her she flushed bright red all over her face and even to her bosom, and trouble came into her eyes, and she looked adown. But the Lord said: "Yonder is the youngling, the swordless one in the green coat; a likely lad, if he hath not lied about his prowess; and he can sing thee a song withal, and tell a piteous tale of old, and do all that those who be reared in the lineages of the westlands deem meet and due for men of knightly blood. Dost thou like the looks of him, lady? wilt thou have him?"

The Lady still held her head down, and tormented the grass with her foot, and murmured somewhat; for she could not come to herself again as yet. So the Lord looked sharply on her and said: "Well, when this tilting is over, thou shalt tell me thy mind of him; for if he turn out a dastard I would not ask thee to take him."

Now the lady lifted up her face, and she was grown somewhat pale; but she forced her speech to come, and said: "It is well, Lord, but now come thou into my pavilion, for thy meat is ready, and it lacketh but a minute or so of noon." So he took her hand and led her in to the pavilion, and all men got off their horses, and fell to pitching the tents and getting their meat ready; but Otter drew Ralph apart into a nook of the homestead, and there they ate their meat together.

CHAPTER 36

The Talk of Two Women Concerning Ralph

But when dinner was done, came David and a man with him bringing Ralph's war gear, and bade him do it on, while the folk were fencing the lists, which they were doing with such stuff as they had at the Tower; and the Lord had been calling for Otter that he might command him what he should tell to the marshals of the lists and how all should be duly ordered, wherefore he went up unto the Tower whither the Lord had now gone. So Ralph did on his armour, which was not right meet for tilting, being over light for such work; and his shield in especial was but a target for a sergent, which he had brought at Cheaping Knowe; but he deemed that his deftness and much use should bear him well through.

Now, the Lady had abided in her pavilion when her Lord went abroad; anon after she sent all her women away, save one whom she loved, and to whom she was wont to tell the innermost of her mind; though forsooth she mishandled her at whiles; for she was hot of temper, and over-ready with her hands when she was angry; though she was nowise cruel. But the woman aforesaid, who was sly and sleek, and somewhat past her first youth, took both her caresses and her buffets with patience, for the sake of the gifts and largesse wherewith they were bought. So now she stood by the board in the pavilion with her head drooping humbly, yet smiling to herself and heedful of whatso might betide. But the Lady walked up and down the pavilion hastily, as one much moved.

At last she spake as she walked and said: "Agatha, didst thou see him when my Lord pointed him out?" "Yea," said the woman lifting her face a little.

"And what seemed he to thee?" said the Lady. "O my Lady," quoth Agatha, "what seemed he to thee?" The lady stood and turned and looked at her; she was slender and dark and sleek; and though her lips moved not, and her eyes did not change, a smile seemed to steal over her face whether she would or not. The Lady stamped her foot and lifted her hand and cried out. "What! dost thou deem thyself meet for him?" And she caught her by the folds over her bosom. But Agatha looked up into her face with a simple smile as of a child: "Dost thou deem him meet for thee, my Lady—he a thrall, and thou so great?" The Lady took her hand from her, but her face flamed with anger and she stamped on the ground again: "What dost thou mean?" she said; "am I not great enough to have what I want when it lieth close to my hand?" Agatha looked on her sweetly, and said in a soft voice: "Stretch out thine hand for it then." The Lady looked at her grimly, and said: "I understand thy jeer; thou meanest that he will not be moved by me, he being so fair, and I being but somewhat fair. Wilt thou have me beat thee? Nay, I will send thee to the White Pillar when we come home to Utterbol."

The woman smiled again, and said: "My Lady, when thou hast sent me to the White Pillar, or the Red, or the Black, my stripes will not mend the matter for thee, or quench the fear of thine heart that by this time, since he is a grown man, he loveth some other. Yet belike he will obey thee if

295

thou command, even to the lying in the same bed with thee; for he is a thrall." The Lady hung her head, but Agatha went on in her sweet clear voice: "The Lord will think little of it, and say nothing of it unless thou anger him otherwise; or unless, indeed, he be minded to pick a quarrel with thee, and hath baited a trap with this stripling. But that is all unlike: thou knowest why, and how that he loveth the little finger of that new-come thrall of his (whom ye left at home at Utterbol in his despite), better than all thy body, for all thy white skin and lovely limbs. Nay, now I think of it, I deem that he meaneth this gift to make an occasion for the staying of any quarrel with thee, that he may stop thy mouth from crying out at him—well, what wilt thou do? he is a mighty Lord."

The Lady looked up (for she had hung her head at first), her face all red with shame, yet smiling, though ruefully, and she said: "Well, thou art determined that if thou art punished it shall not be for naught. But thou knowest not my mind." "Yea, Lady," said Agatha, smiling in despite of herself, "that may well be."

Now the Lady turned from her, and went and sat upon a stool that was thereby, and said nothing a while; only covering her face with her hands and rocking herself to and fro, while Agatha stood looking at her. At last she said: "Hearken, Agatha, I must tell thee what lieth in mine heart, though thou hast been unkind to me and hast tried to hurt my soul. Now, thou art self-willed, and hot-blooded, and not unlovely, so that thou mayst have loved and been loved ere now. But thou art so wily and subtle that mayhappen thou wilt not understand what I mean, when I say that love of this young man hath suddenly entered into my heart, so that I long for him more this minute than I did the last, and the next minute shall long still more. And I long for him to love me, and not alone to pleasure me."

"Mayhappen it will so betide without any pushing the matter," said Agatha.

"Nay," said the Lady, "Nay; my heart tells me that it will not be so; for I have seen him, that he is of higher kind than we be; as if he were a god come down to us, who if he might not cast his love upon a goddess, would disdain to love an earthly woman, little-minded and in whom perfection is not."

Therewith the tears began to run from her eyes; but Agatha looked on her with a subtle smile and said: "O my Lady! and thou hast scarce seen him! And yet I will not say but that I understand this. But as to the matter of a goddess, I know not. Many would say that thou sitting on thine ivory chair in thy golden raiment, with thy fair bosom and white arms and yellow hair, wert not ill done for the image of a goddess; and this young man may well think so of thee. However that may be, there is something else I will say to thee; (and thou knowest that I speak the truth to thee—most often—though I be wily). This is the word, that although thou hast time and again treated me like the thrall I am, I deem thee no ill woman, but rather something overgood for Utterbol and the dark lord thereof."

Now sat the Lady shaken with sobs, and weeping without stint; but she looked up at that word and said: "Nay, nay, Agatha, it is not so. To-day hath this man's eyes been a candle to me, that I may see myself truly; and I know that though I am a queen and not uncomely, I am but coarse and little-minded. I rage in my household when the whim takes me, and I am hot-headed, and masterful, and slothful, and should belike be untrue if there were any force to drive me thereto. And I suffer my husband to go after other women, and this new thrall is especial, so that I may take my pleasure unstayed with other men whom I love not greatly. Yes, I am foolish, and empty-headed, and unclean. And all this he will see through my queenly state, and my golden gown, and my white skin withal."

Agatha looked on her curiously, but smiling no more. At last she said: "What is to do, then? or must I think of something for thee?"

"I know not, I know not," said the Lady between her sobs; "yet if I might be in such case that he might pity me; belike it might blind his eyes to the ill part of me. Yea," she said, rising up and falling walking to and fro swiftly, "if he might hurt me and wound me himself, and I so loving him"

Said Agatha coldly: "Yes, Lady, I am not wily for naught; and I both deem that I know what is in thine heart, and that it is good for something; and moreover that I may help thee somewhat therein. So in a few days thou shalt see whether I am worth something more than hard words and beating. Only thou must promise in all wise to obey me, though I be the thrall, and thou the Lady, and to leave all the whole matter in my hands."

Quoth the Lady: "That is easy to promise; for what may I do by myself?"

Then Agatha fell pondering a while, and said thereafter: "First, thou shalt get me speech with my Lord, and cause him to swear immunity to me, whatsoever I shall say or do herein." Said the Lady: "Easy is this. What more hast thou?"

Said Agatha: "It were better for thee not to go forth to see the jousting; because thou art not to be trusted that thou show not thy love openly when the youngling is in peril; and if thou put thy lord to shame openly before the people, he must needs thwart thy will, and be fierce and cruel, and then it will go hard with thy darling. So thou shalt not go from the pavilion till the night is dark, and thou mayst feign thyself sick meantime."

"Sick enough shall I be if I may not go forth to see how my love is faring in his peril: this at least is hard to me; but so be it! At least thou wilt come and tell me how he speedeth." "Oh yes," said Agatha, "if thou must have it so; but fear thou not, he shall do well enough."

Said the Lady: "Ah, but thou wottest how oft it goes with a chance stroke, that the point pierceth where it should not; nay, where by likelihead it could not."

"Nay," said Agatha, "what chance is there in this, when the youngling knoweth the whole manner of the play, and his foemen know naught thereof? It is as the chance betwixt Geoffrey the Minstrel and Black Anselm, when they play at chess together, that Anselm must needs be mated ere he hath time to think of his fourth move. I wot of these matters, my Lady. Now, further, I would have thy leave to marshal thy maids about the seat where thou shouldest be, and moreover there should be someone in thy seat, even if I sat in it myself." Said the Lady: "Yea, sit there if thou wilt."

"Woe's me!" said Agatha laughing, "why should I sit there? I am like to thee, am I not?" "Yea," said the Lady, "as the swan is like to the loon." "Yea, my Lady," said Agatha, "which is the swan and which the loon? Well, well, fear not; I shall set Joyce in thy seat by my Lord's leave; she is tall and fair, and forsooth somewhat like to thee." "Why wilt thou do this?" quoth the Lady; "Why should thralls sit in my seat?" Said Agatha: "O, the tale is long to tell; but I would confuse that young man's memory of thee somewhat, if his eyes fell on thee at all when ye met e'en now, which is to be doubted."

The Lady started up in sudden wrath, and cried out: "She had best not be too like to me then, and strive to draw his eyes to her, or I will have her marked for diversity betwixt us. Take heed, take heed!"

Agatha looked softly on her and said: "My Lady. ye fair-skinned, open-faced women should look to it not to show yourselves angry before men-folk. For open wrath marreth your beauty sorely. Leave scowls and fury to the dark-browed, who can use them without wrying their faces like a three months' baby with the colic. Now that is my last rede as now. For methinks I can hear the trumpets blowing for the arraying of the tourney. Wherefore I must go to see to matters, while thou hast but to be quiet. And to-night make much of my Lord, and bid him see me to-morrow, and give heed to what I shall say to him. But if I meet him without, now, as is most like, I shall bid him in to thee, that thou mayst tell him of Joyce, and her sitting in thy seat. Otherwise I will tell him as soon as he is set down in his place. Sooth to say, he is little like to quarrel with either thee or me for setting a fair woman other than thee by his side."

Therewith she lifted the tent lap and went out, stepping daintily, and her slender body swaying like a willow branch, and came at once face to face with the Lord of Utterbol, and bowed low and humbly before him, though her face, unseen of him, smiled mockingly. The Lord looked on her greedily, and let his hand and arm go over her shoulder, and about her side, and he drew her to him, and kissed her, and said: "What, Agatha! and why art thou not bringing forth thy mistress to us?" She raised her face to him, and murmured softly, as one afraid, but with a wheedling smile on her face and in her eyes: "Nay, my Lord, she will abide within

299

to-day, for she is ill at ease; if your grace goeth in, she will tell thee what she will have."

"Agatha," quoth he, "I will hear her, and I will do her pleasure if thou ask me so to do." Then Agatha cast down her eyes, and her speech was so low and sweet that it was as the cooing of a dove, as she said: "O my Lord, what is this word of thine?"

He kissed her again, and said: "Well, well, but dost thou ask it?" "O yea, yea, my Lord," said she.

"It is done then," said the Lord; and he let her go; for he had been stroking her arm and shoulder, and she hurried away, laughing inwardly, to the Lady's women. But he went into the pavilion after he had cast one look at her.

CHAPTER 37

How Ralph Justed With
the Aliens

Meanwhile Captain Otter had brought Ralph into the staked-out lists, which, being hastily pitched, were but slenderly done, and now the Upmeads stripling stood there beside a good horse which they had brought to him, and Otter had been speaking to him friendly. But Ralph saw the Lord come forth from the pavilion and take his seat on an ivory chair set on a turf ridge close to the stakes of the lists: for that place was used of custom for such games as they exercised in the lands of Utterbol. Then presently the Lady's women came out of their tents, and, being marshalled by Agatha, went into the Queen's pavilion, whence they came forth again presently like a bed of garden flowers moving, having in the midst of them a woman so fair, and clad so gloriously, that Ralph must needs look on her, though he were some way off, and take note of her beauty. She went and sat her down beside the Lord, and Ralph doubted not that it was the Queen, whom he had but glanced at when they first made stay before the pavilion. Sooth to say, Joyce being well nigh as tall as the Queen, and as white of skin, was otherwise a far fairer woman.

Now spake Otter to Ralph: "I must leave thee here, lad, and go to the other side, as I am to run against thee." Said Ralph: "Art thou to run first?" "Nay, but rather last," said Otter; "they will try thee first with one of the sergeants, and if he overcome thee, then all is done, and thou art in an evil plight. Otherwise will they find another and another, and at last it will be my turn. So keep thee well, lad."

Therewith he rode away, and there came to Ralph one of the sergeants, who brought him a spear, and bade him to horse. So Ralph mounted and took the spear in hand; and the sergeant said: "Thou art to run at whatsoever meeteth thee when thou hast heard the third blast of the horn. Art thou ready?" "Yea, yea," said Ralph; "but I see that the spear-head is not rebated, so that we are to play at sharps."

"Art thou afraid, youngling?" said the sergeant, who was old and crabbed, "if that be so, go and tell the Lord: but thou wilt find that he will not have his sport wholly spoiled, but will somehow make a bolt or a shaft out of thee."

Said Ralph: "I did but jest; I deem myself not so near my death to-day as I have been twice this summer or oftener." Said the sergeant, "It is ill jesting in matters wherein my Lord hath to do. Now thou hast heard my word: do after it."

Therewith he departed, and Ralph laughed and shook the spear aloft, and deemed it not over strong; but he said to himself that the spears of the others would be much the same.

Now the horn blew up thrice, and at the latest blast Ralph pricked forth, as one well used to the tilt, but held his horse well in hand; and he saw a man come driving against him with his spear in the rest, and deemed him right big; but this withal he saw, that the man was ill arrayed, and was pulling on his horse as one not willing to trust him to the rush; and indeed he came on so ill that it was clear that he would never strike Ralph's shield fairly. So he swerved as they met, so that his spear-point was never near to Ralph, who turned his horse toward him a little, and caught his foeman by the gear about his neck, and spurred on, so that he dragged him clean out of his saddle, and let him drop, and rode back quietly to his place, and got off his horse to see to his girths; and he heard great laughter rising up from the ring of men, and from the women also. But the Lord of Utterbol cried out: "Bring forth some one who doth not eat my meat for nothing: and set that wretch and dastard aside till the tilting be over, and then he shall pay a little for his wasted meat and drink."

Ralph got into his saddle again, and saw a very big man come forth at the other end of the lists, and wondered if he should be overthrown of him; but noted that his horse seemed not over good. Then the horn blew up and he spurred on, and his foeman met him fairly in the midmost of the lists: yet he laid his spear but ill, and as one who would thrust and foin with it rather than letting it drive all it might, so that Ralph turned the point with his shield that it glanced off, but he himself smote the other full on the shoulder, and the shaft brake, but the point had pierced the man's armour, and the truncheon stuck in the wound: yet since the spear was broken he kept his saddle. The Lord cried out, "Well, Black Anselm, this is better done; yet art thou a big man and a well-skilled to be beaten by a stripling."

So the man was helped away and Ralph went back to his place again.

Then another man was gotten to run against Ralph, and it went the same-like way: for Ralph smote him amidst of the shield, and the spear held, so that he fell floundering off his horse.

Six of the stoutest men of Utterbol did Ralph overthrow or hurt in this wise; and then he ran three courses with Otter, and in the first two each brake his spear fairly on the other; but in the third Otter smote not Ralph squarely, but Ralph smote full amidst of his shield, and so dight him that he well-nigh fell, and could not master his horse, but yet just barely kept his saddle.

Then the Lord cried out: "Now make we an end of it! We have no might against this youngling, man to man: or else would Otter have done it. This comes of learning a craft diligently."

So Ralph got off his horse, and did off his helm and awaited tidings; and anon comes to him the surly sergeant, and brought him a cup of wine, and said: "Youngling, thou art to drink this, and then go to my Lord; and I deem that thou art in favour with him. So if thou art not too great a man, thou mightest put in a word for poor Redhead, that first man that did so ill. For my Lord would have him set up, and head down and buttocks aloft, as a target for our bowmen. And it will be his luck if he be sped with the third shot, and last not out to the twentieth."

"Yea, certes," said Ralph, "I will do no less, even if it anger the Lord." "O thou wilt not anger him," said the man, "for I tell thee, thou art in favour. Yea, and for me also thou mightest say a word also, when thou becomest right great; for have I not brought thee a good bowl of wine?" "Doubt it not, man," said Ralph, "if I once get safe to Utterbol: weary on it and all its ways!" Said the sergeant: "That is an evil wish for one who shall do well at Utterbol. But come, tarry not."

So he brought Ralph to the Lord, who still sat in his chair beside that fair woman, and Ralph did obeysance to him; yet he had a sidelong glance also for that fair seeming-queen, and deemed her both proud-looking, and so white-skinned, that she was a wonder, like the queen of the fays: and it was just this that he had noted of the Queen as he stood before her earlier in the day when they first came into the vale; therefore he had no doubt of this damsel's queenship.

Now the Lord spake to him and said: "Well, youngling, thou hast done well, and better than thy behest: and since ye have been playing at sharps, I deem thou would'st not do ill in battle, if it came to that. So now I am like to make something other of thee than I was minded to at first: for I deem that thou art good enough to be a man. And if thou wilt now ask a boon of me, if it be not over great, I will grant it thee."

Ralph put one knee to the ground, and said: "Great Lord, I thank thee: but whereas I am in an alien land and seeking great things, I know of no gift which I may take for myself save leave to depart, which I deem thou wilt not grant me. Yet one thing thou mayst do for my asking if thou wilt. If

303

thou be still angry with the carle whom I first unhorsed, I pray thee pardon him his ill-luck."

"Ill-luck!" said the Lord, "Why, I saw him that he was downright afraid of thee. And if my men are to grow blenchers and soft-hearts what is to do then? But tell me, Otter, what is the name of this carle?" Said Otter, "Redhead he hight, Lord." Said the Lord: "And what like a man is he in a fray?" "Naught so ill, Lord," said Otter. "This time, like the rest of us, he knew not this gear. It were scarce good to miss him at the next pinch. It were enough if he had the thongs over his back a few dozen times; it will not be the first day of such cheer to him."

"Ha!" said the Lord, "and what for, Otter, what for?" "Because he was somewhat rough-handed, Lord," said Otter. "Then shall we need him and use him some day. Let him go scot free and do better another bout. There is thy boon granted for thee, knight; and another day thou mayst ask something more. And now shall David have a care of thee. And when we come to Utterbol we shall see what is to be done with thee."

Then Ralph rose up and thanked him, and David came forward, and led him to his tent. And he was wheedling in his ways to him, as if Ralph were now become one who might do him great good if so his will were.

But the Lord went back again into the Tower.

As to the Lady, she abode in her pavilion amidst many fears and desires, till Agatha entered and said: "My Lady, so far all has gone happily." Said the Lady: "I deemed from the noise and the cry that he was doing well. But tell me, how did he?" "'My Lady," quoth Agatha, "he knocked our folk about well-favouredly, and seemed to think little of it."

"And Joyce," said the Lady, "how did she?" "She looked a queen, every inch of her, and she is tall," said Agatha: "soothly some folk stared on her, but not many knew of her, since she is but new into our house. Though it is a matter of course that all save our new-come knight knew that it was not thou that sat there. And my Lord was well-pleased, and now he hath taken her by the hand and led her into the Tower."

The Lady reddened and scowled, and said: "And he . . .

did he come anigh her?" "O yea," said Agatha, "whereas he stood before my Lord a good while, and then kneeled to him to pray pardon for one of our men who had done ill in the tilting: yea, he was nigh enough to her to touch her had he dared, and to smell the fragrance of her raiment. And he seemed to think it good to look out of the corners of his eyes at her; though I do not say that she smiled on him." The Lady sprang up, her cheeks burning, and walked about angrily a while, striving for words, till at last she said: "When we come home to Utterbol, my lord will see his new thrall again, and will care for Joyce no whit: then will I have my will of her; and she shall learn, she, whether I am verily the least of women at Utterbol! Ha! what sayest thou? Now why wilt thou stand and smile on me?—Yea, I know what is in thy thought; and in very sooth it is good that the dear youngling hath not seen this new thrall, this Ursula. Forsooth, I tell thee that if I durst have her in my hands I would have a true tale out of her as to why she weareth ever that pair of beads about her neck."

"Now, our Lady," said Agatha, "thou art marring the fairness of thy face again. I bid thee be at peace, for all shall be well, and other than thou deemest. Tell me, then, didst thou get our Lord to swear immunity for me?" Said the Lady: "Yea, he swore on the edge of the sword that thou mightest say what thou wouldst, and neither he nor any other should lay hand on thee."

"Good," said Agatha; "then will I go to him to-morrow morning, when Joyce has gone from him. But now hold up thine heart, and keep close for these two days that we shall yet abide in Tower Dale: and trust me this very evening I shall begin to set tidings going that shall work and grow, and shall one day rejoice thine heart."

So fell the talk betwixt them.

CHAPTER 38

A Friend Gives Ralph Warning

On the morrow Ralph wandered about the Dale where he would, and none meddled with him. And as he walked east along the stream where the valley began to narrow, he saw a man sitting on the bank fishing with an angle, and when he drew near, the man turned about, and saw him. Then he lays down his angling rod and rises to his feet, and stands facing Ralph, looking sheepish, with his hands hanging down by his sides; and Ralph, who was thinking of other folk, wondered what he would. So he said: "Hail, good fellow! What wouldst thou?" Said the man: "I would thank thee." "What for?" said Ralph, but as he looked on him he saw that it was Redhead, whose pardon he had won of the Lord yesterday; so he held out his hand, and took Redhead's, and smiled friendly on him. Redhead looked him full in the face, and though he was both big and very rough-looking, he had not altogether the look of a rascal.

He said: "Fair lord, I would that I might do something for thine avail, and perchance I may: but it is hard to do good deeds in Hell, especially for one of its devils."

"Yea, is it so bad as that?" said Ralph. "For thee not yet," said Redhead, "but it may come to it. Hearken, lord, there is none anigh us that I can see, so I will say a word to thee at once. Later on it may be over late: Go thou not to Utterbol whatever may betide."

"Yea," said Ralph, "but how if I be taken thither?" Quoth Redhead: "I can see this, that thou art so favoured that thou mayst go whither thou wilt about the camp with none to hinder thee. Therefore it will be easy for thee to depart by night and cloud, or in the grey of morning, when thou comest to a good pass, whereof I will tell thee. And still I say, go thou not to Utterbol: for thou art over good to be made a devil of, like to us, and therefore thou shalt be tormented till thy life is spoilt, and by that road shalt thou be sent to heaven."

"But thou saidst even now," said Ralph, "that I was high in the Lord's grace." "Yea," said Redhead, "that may last till thou hast command to do some dastard's deed and nay-sayest it, as thou wilt: and then farewell to thee; for I know what my Lord meaneth for thee." "Yea," said Ralph, "and what is that?" Said Redhead; "He hath bought thee to give to his wife for a toy and a minion, and if she like thee, it will be well for a while: but on the first occasion that serveth him, and she wearieth of thee (for she is a woman like a weather-cock), he will lay hand on thee and take the manhood from thee, and let thee drift about Utterbol a mock for all men. For already at heart he hateth thee."

Ralph stood pondering this word, for somehow it chimed in with the thought already in his heart. Yet how should he not go to Utterbol with the Damsel abiding deliverance of him there: and yet again, if they met there and were espied on, would not that ruin everything for her as well as for him?

At last he said: "Good fellow, this may be true, but how shall I know it for true before I run the risk of fleeing away, instead of going on to Utterbol, whereas folk deem honour awaiteth me."

Said Redhead: "There is no honour at Utterbol save for such as are unworthy of honour. But thy risk is as I say, and I shall tell thee whence I had my tale, since I love thee for thy kindness to me, and thy manliness. It was told me yester-eve by a woman who is in the very privity of the Lady of Utterbol, and is well with the Lord also: and it jumpeth with mine own thought on the matter; so I bid thee beware: for what is in me to grieve would be sore grieved wert thou cast away."

"Well," said Ralph, "let us sit down here on the bank and then tell me more; but go on with thine angling the while, lest any should see us."

So they sat down, and Redhead did as Ralph bade; and he said: "Lord, I have bidden thee to flee; but this is an ill land to flee from, and indeed there is but one pass whereby ye may well get away from this company betwixt this and Utterbol; and we shall encamp hard by it on the second day of our faring hence. Yet I must tell thee that it is no road for a dastard; for it leadeth through the forest up into the mountains: yet such as it is, for a man bold and strong like thee, I bid thee take it: and I can see to it that leaving this company shall be easy to thee: only thou must make up thy mind speedily, since the time draws so nigh, and when thou art come to Utterbol with all this rout, and the house full, and some one or other dogging each footstep of thine, fleeing will be another matter. Now thus it is: on that same second night, not only is the wood at hand to cover thee, but I shall be chief warder of the side of the camp where thou lodgest, so that I can put thee on the road: and if I were better worth, I would say, take me with thee, but as it is, I will not burden thee with that prayer."

"Yea," said Ralph, "I have had one guide in this country-side and he bewrayed me. This is a matter of life and death, so I will speak out and say how am I to know but that thou also art going about to bewray me?"

Redhead lept up to his feet, and roared out: "What shall I say? what shall I say? By the soul of my father I am not bewraying thee. May all the curses of Utterbol be sevenfold heavier on me if I am thy traitor and dastard."

"Softly lad, softly," said Ralph, "lest some one should hear thee. Content thee, I must needs believe thee if thou makest so much noise about it."

Then Redhead sat him down again, and for all that he was so rough and sturdy a carle he fell a-weeping.

"Nay, nay," said Ralph, "this is worse in all wise than the other noise. I believe thee as well as a man can who is dealing with one who is not his close friend, and who therefore spareth truth to his friend because of many years use and wont. Come to thyself again and let us look at this matter square in the face, and speedily too, lest some un-friend or busybody come on us. There now! Now, in the first place dost thou know why I am come into this perilous and tyrannous land?"

Said Redhead: "I have heard it said that thou art on the quest of the Well at the World's End."

"And that is but the sooth," said Ralph. "Well then," quoth Redhead, "there is the greater cause for thy fleeing at the time and in the manner I have bidden thee. For there is a certain sage who dwelleth in the wildwood betwixt that place and the Great Mountains, and he hath so much lore concerning the Mountains, yea, and the Well itself, that if he will tell thee what he can tell, thou art in a fair way to end thy quest happily. What sayest thou then?"

Said Ralph, "I say that the Sage is good if I may find him. But there is another cause why I have come hither from Goldburg. "What is that?" said Redhead. "This," said Ralph, "to come to Utterbol." "Heaven help us!" quoth Redhead, "and wherefore?"

Ralph said: "Belike it is neither prudent nor wise to tell thee, but I do verily trust thee; so hearken! I go to Utterbol to deliver a friend from Utterbol; and this friend is a woman—hold a minute—and this woman, as I believe, hath been of late brought to Utterbol, having been taken out of the hands of one of the men of the mountains that lie beyond Cheaping Knowe."

Redhead stared astonished, and kept silence awhile; then he said: "Now all the more I say, flee! flee! flee! Doubtless the woman is there, whom thou seekest; for it would take none less fair and noble than that new-come thrall to draw to her one so fair and noble as thou art. But what availeth it? If thou go to Utterbol thou wilt destroy both her and thee. For know, that we can all see that the Lord hath set his love on this damsel; and what better can betide, if thou come to Utterbol, but that the Lord shall at once see that there is love betwixt you two, and then there will be an end of the story."

"How so?" quoth Ralph. Said Redhead: "At Utterbol all do the will of the Lord of Utterbol, and he is so lustful and cruel, and so false withal, that his will shall be to torment the damsel to death, and to geld and maim thee; so that none hereafter shall know how goodly and gallant thou hast been."

"Redhead," quoth Ralph much moved, "though thou art in no knightly service, thou mayst understand that it is good for a friend to die with a friend."

"Yea, forsooth," said Redhead, "If he may do no more to help than that! Wouldst thou not help the damsel? Now when thou comest back from the quest of the Well at the World's End, thou wilt be too mighty and glorious for the Lord of Utterbol to thrust thee aside like to an over eager dog; and thou mayst help her then. But now I say to thee, and swear to thee, that three days after thou hast met thy beloved in Utterbol she will be dead. I would that thou couldst ask someone else nearer to the Lord than I have been. The tale would be the same as mine."

Now soothly to say it, this was even what Ralph had feared would be, and he could scarce doubt Redhead's word. So he sat there pondering the matter a good while, and at last he said: "My friend, I will trust thee with another thing; I have a mind to flee to the wildwood, and yet come to Utterbol for the damsel's deliverance." "Yea," said Redhead, "and how wilt thou work in the matter?" Said Ralph; "How would it be if I came hither in other guise than mine own, so that I should not be known either by the damsel or her tyrants?"

Said Redhead: "There were peril in that; yet hope also. Yea, and in one way thou mightest do it; to wit, if thou wert to find that Sage, and tell him thy tale: if he be of good will to thee, he might then change not thy gear only, but thy skin also; for he hath exceeding great lore."

"Well," said Ralph, "Thou mayst look upon it as certain that on that aforesaid night, I will do my best to shake off this company of tyrant and thralls, unless I hear fresh tidings, so that I must needs change my purpose. But I will ask thee to give me some token that all holds together some little time beforehand." Quoth Redhead: "Even so shall it be; thou shalt see me at latest on the eve of the night of thy departure; but on the night before that if it be anywise possible."

"Now will I go away from thee," said Ralph, "and I thank thee heartily for thine help, and deem thee my friend. And if thou think better of fleeing with me, thou wilt gladden me the more." Redhead shook his head but spake not, and Ralph went his ways down the dale.

CHAPTER 39

The Lord of Utterbol Makes
Ralph a Free Man

He went to and fro that day and the next, and none
meddled with him; with Redhead he spake not again those
days, but had talk with Otter and David, who were blithe
enough with him. Agatha he saw not at all; nor the Lady,
and still deemed that the white-skinned woman whom he had
seen sitting by the Lord after the tilting was the Queen.

As for the Lady she abode in her pavilion, and whiles lay
in a heap on the floor weeping, or dull and blind with grief;
whiles she walked up and down mad wroth with whomsoever
came in her way, even to the dealing out of stripes and blows
to her women.

But on the eve before the day of departure Agatha came
into her, and chid her, and bade her be merry: "I have seen
the Lord and told him what I would, and found it no hard
matter to get him to yeasay our plot, which were hard to
carry out without his goodwill. Withal the seed that I have
sowed two days or more ago is bearing fruit; so that thou
mayst look to it that whatsoever plight we may be in, we
shall find a deliverer."

"I wot not thy meaning," quoth the Lady, "but I deem
thou wilt now tell me what thou art planning, and give me
some hope, lest I lay hands on myself."

Then Agatha told her without tarrying what she was about
doing for her, the tale of which will be seen hereafter; and
when she had done, the Lady mended her cheer, and bade
bring meat and drink, and was once more like a great and
proud Lady.

On the morn of departure, when Ralph arose, David came
to him and said: "My Lord is astir already, and would see
thee for thy good." So Ralph went with David, who brought

311

him to the Tower, and there they found the Lord sitting in a window, and Otter stood before him, and some others of his highest folk. But beside him sat Joyce, and it seemed that he thought it naught but good to hold her hand and play with the fingers thereof, though all those great men were by; and Ralph had no thought of her but that she was the Queen.

So Ralph made obeisance to the Lord and stood awaiting his word; and the Lord said: "We have been thinking of thee, young man, and have deemed thy lot to be somewhat of the hardest, if thou must needs be a thrall, since thou art both young and well-born, and so good a man of thine hands. Now, wilt thou be our man at Utterbol?"

Ralph delayed his answer a space and looked at Otter, who seemed to him to frame a Yea with his lips, as who should say, take it. So he said: "Lord, thou art good to me, yet mayst thou be better if thou wilt."

"Yea, man!" said the Lord knitting his brows; "What shall it be? say thy say, and be done with it."

"Lord," said Ralph, "I pray thee to give me my choice, whether I shall go with thee to Utterbol or forbear going?"

"Why, lo you!" said the Lord testily, and somewhat sourly; "thou hast the choice. Have I not told thee that thou art free?" Then Ralph knelt before him, and said: "Lord, I thank thee from a full heart, in that thou wilt suffer me to depart on mine errand, for it is a great one." The scowl deepened on the Lord's face, and he turned away from Ralph, and said presently: "Otter take the Knight away and let him have all his armour and weapons and a right good horse; and then let him do as he will, either ride with us, or depart if he will, and whither he will. And if he must needs ride into the desert, and cast himself away in the mountains, so be it. But whatever he hath a mind to, let none hinder him, but further him rather; hearest thou? take him with thee."

Then was Ralph overflowing with thanks, but the Lord heeded him naught, but looked askance at him and sourly. And he rose up withal, and led the damsel by the hand into another chamber; and she minced in her gait and leaned over to the Lord and spake softly in his ear and laughed, and he laughed in his turn and toyed with her neck and shoulders.

312

But the great men turned and went their ways from the Tower, and Ralph went with Otter and was full of glee, and as merry as a bird. But Otter looked on him, and said gruffly: "Yea now, thou art like a song-bird but newly let out of his cage. But I can see the string which is tied to thy leg, though thou feelest it not."

"Why, what now?" quoth Ralph, making as though he were astonished. "Hearken," said Otter: "there is none nigh us, so I will speak straight out; for I love thee since the justing when we tried our might together. If thou deemest that thou art verily free, ride off on the backward road when we go forward; I warrant me thou shalt presently meet with an adventure, and be brought in a captive for the second time." "How then," said Ralph, "hath not the Lord good will toward me?"

Said Otter: "I say not that he is now minded to do thee a mischief for cruelty's sake; but he is minded to get what he can out of thee. If he use thee not for the pleasuring of his wife (so long as her pleasure in thee lasteth) he will verily use thee for somewhat else. And to speak plainly, I now deem that he will make thee my mate, to use with me, or against me as occasion may serve; so thou shalt be another captain of his host." He laughed withal, and said again: "But if thou be not wary, thou wilt tumble off that giddy height, and find thyself a thrall once more, and maybe a gelding to boot." Now waxed Ralph angry and forgat his prudence, and said: "Yea, but how shall he use me when I am out of reach of his hand?" "Oho, young man," said Otter, "whither away then, to be out of his reach?"

"Why," quoth Ralph still angrily, "is thy Lord master of all the world?" "Nay," said the captain, "but of a piece there of. In short, betwixt Utterbol and Goldburg, and Utterbol and the mountains, and Utterbol and an hundred miles north, and an hundred miles south, there is no place where thou canst live, no place save the howling wilderness, and scarcely there either, where he may not lay hand on thee if he do but whistle. What, man! be not downhearted! come with us to Utterbol, since thou needs must. Be wise, and then the Lord shall have no occasion against thee; above all, beware of crossing him in any matter of a woman. Then who

313

knows" (and here he sunk his voice well nigh to a whisper) "but thou and I together may rule in Utterbol and make better days there."

Ralph was waxen master of himself by now, and was gotten wary indeed, so he made as if he liked Otter's counsel well, and became exceeding gay; for indeed the heart within him was verily glad at the thought of his escaping from thralldom; for more than ever now he was fast in his mind to flee at the time appointed by Rednead.

So Otter said: "Well, youngling, I am glad that thou takest it thus, for I deem that if thou wert to seek to depart, the Lord would make it an occasion against thee."

"Such an occasion shall he not have, fellow in arms," quoth Ralph. "But tell me, we ride presently, and I suppose are bound for Utterness by the shortest road?" "Yea," said Otter, "and anon we shall come to the great forest which lieth along our road all the way to Utterness and beyond it; for the town is, as it were, an island in the sea of woodland which covers all, right up to the feet of the Great Mountains, and does what it may to climb them whereso the great wall or its buttresses are anywise broken down toward our country; but the end of it lieth along our road, as I said, and we do but skirt it. A woeful wood it is, and save for the hunting of the beasts, which be there in great plenty, with wolves and bears, yea, and lions to boot, which come down from the mountains, there is no gain in it. No gain, though forsooth they say that some have found it gainful."

"How so?" said Ralph. Said Otter: "That way lieth the way to the Well at the World's End, if one might find it. If at any time we were clear of Utterbol, I have a mind for the adventure along with thee, lad, and so I deem hast thou from all the questions thou hast put to me thereabout."

Ralph mastered himself so that his face changed not, and he said: "Well, Captain, that may come to pass; but tell me, are there any tokens known whereby a man shall know that he is on the right path to the Well?"

"The report of folk goeth," said Otter, "concerning one token, where is the road and the pass through the Great Mountains, to wit, that on the black rock thereby is carven the image of a Fighting Man, or monstrous giant, of the days

314

long gone by. Of other signs I can tell thee naught; and few of men are alive that can. But there is a Sage dwelleth in the wood under the mountains to whom folk seek for his diverse lore; and he, if he will, say men, can set forth all the way, and its perils, and how to escape them. Well, knight, when the time comes, thou and I will go find him together, for he at least is not hard to find, and if he be gracious to us, then will we on our quest. But as now, see ye, they have struck our tents and the Queen's pavilion also; so to horse, is the word."

"Yea," quoth Ralph, looking curiously toward the place where the Queen's pavilion had stood; "is not yonder the Queen's litter taking the road?" "Yea, surely," said Otter.

"Then the litter will be empty," said Ralph. "Maybe, or maybe not," said Otter; "but now I must get me gone hastily to my folk; doubtless we shall meet upon the road to Utterbol."

So he turned and went his ways; and Ralph also ran to his horse, whereby was David already in the saddle, and so mounted, and the whole rout moved slowly from out of Vale Turris, Ralph going ever by David. The company was now a great one, for many wains were joined to them, laden with meal, and fleeces, and other household stuff, and withal there was a great herd of neat, and of sheep, and of goats, which the Lord's men had been gathering in the fruitful country these two days; but the Lord was tarrying still in the tower.

CHAPTER 40

They Ride Toward Utterness
From Out of Vale Turris

So they rode by a good highway, well beaten, past the Tower and over the ridge of the valley, and came full upon the terrible sight of the Great Mountains, and the sea of woodland lay before them, swelling and falling, and swelling again, till it broke grey against the dark blue of the mountain wall. They went as the way led, down hill, and when they were at the bottom, thence along their highway parted the tillage and fenced pastures from the rough edges of the woodland like as a ditch sunders field from field. They had the wildwood ever on their right hand, and but a little way from where they rode the wood thickened for the more part into dark and close thicket, the trees whereof were so tall that they hid the overshadowing mountains whenso they rode the bottoms, though when the way mounted on the ridges, and the trees gave back a little, they had sight of the woodland and the mountains. On the other hand at whiles the thicket came close up to the roadside.

Now David biddeth press on past the wains and the driven beasts, which were going very slowly. So did they, and at last were well nigh at the head of the Lord's company, but when Ralph would have pressed on still, David refrained him, and said that they must by no means outgo the Queen's people, or even mingle with them; so they rode on softly. But as the afternoon was drawing toward evening they heard great noise of horns behind them, and the sound of horses galloping. Then David drew Ralph to the side of the way, and everybody about, both before and behind them, drew up in wise at the wayside, and or ever Ralph could ask any question, came a band of men-at-arms at the gallop led by Otter, and after them the Lord on his black steed, and beside him on a white palfrey the woman whom Ralph had seen in the Tower, and whom he had taken for the Queen, her light raiment streaming out from her, and her yellow hair flying loose. They passed in a moment of time, and then David and Ralph and the rest rode on after them.

Then said Ralph: "The Queen rideth well and hardily." "Yea," said David, screwing his face into a grin, would he or no. Ralph beheld him, and it came into his mind that this was not the Queen whom he had looked on when they first came into Vale Turris, and he said: "What then! this woman is not the Queen?"

David spake not for a while, and then he answered: "Sir

Knight, there be matters whereof we servants of my Lord say little or nothing, and thou wert best to do the like." And no more would he say thereon.

CHAPTER 41

Redhead Keeps Tryst

They rode not above a dozen miles that day, and pitched their tents and pavilions in the fair meadows by the wayside looking into the thick of the forest. There this betid to tell of, that when Ralph got off his horse, and the horse-lads were gathered about the men-at-arms and high folk, who should take Ralph's horse but Redhead, who made a sign to him by lifting his eyebrows as if he were asking him somewhat; and Ralph took it as a question as to whether his purpose held to flee on the morrow night; so he nodded a yeasay, just so much as Redhead might note it; and naught else befell betwixt them.

When it was barely dawn after that night, Ralph awoke with the sound of great stir in the camp, and shouting of men and lowing and bleating of beasts; so he looked out, and saw that the wains and the flocks and herds were being got on to the road, so that they might make good way before the company of the camp took the road. But he heeded it little and went to sleep again.

When it was fully morning he arose, and found that the men were not hastening their departure, but were resting by the wood-side and disporting them about the meadow; so he wandered about amongst the men-at-arms and serving-men, and came across Redhead and hailed him; and there was no man very nigh to them; so Redhead looked about him warily, and then spake swiftly and softly: "Fail not to-night! fail not! For yesterday again was I told by one who wotteth surely, what abideth thee at Utterbol if thou go thither. I say if thou fail, thou shalt repent but once—all thy life long to wit."

Ralph nodded his head, and said: "Fear not, I will not fail thee." And therewith they turned away from each other lest they should be noted.

About two hours before noon they got to horse again, and,

being no more encumbered with the wains and the beasts, rode at a good pace. As on the day before the road led them along the edge of the wildwood, and whiles it even went close to the very thicket. Whiles again they mounted somewhat, and looked down on the thicket, leagues and leagues thereof, which yet seemed but a little space because of the hugeness of the mountain wall which brooded over it; but oftenest the forest hid all but the near trees.

Thus they rode some twenty miles, and made stay at sunset in a place that seemed rather a clearing of the wood than a meadow; for they had trees on their left hand at a furlong's distance, as well as on their right at a stone's throw.

Ralph saw not Redhead as he got off his horse, and David according to his wont went with him to his tent. But after they had supped together, and David had made much of Ralph, and had drank many cups to his health, he said to him: "The night is yet young, yea, but new-born; yet must I depart from thee, if I may, to meet a man who will sell me a noble horse good cheap; and I may well leave thee now, seeing that thou hast become a free man; so I bid thee goodnight."

Therewith he departed, and was scarce gone out ere Redhead cometh in, and saith in his wonted rough loud voice: "Here, knight, here is the bridle thou badest me get mended; will the cobbling serve?" Then seeing no one there, he fell to speaking softer and said: "I heard the old pimp call thee a free man e'en now: I fear me that thou art not so free as he would have thee think. Anyhow, were I thou, I would be freer in two hours space. Is it to be so?"

"Yea, yea," said Ralph. Redhead nodded: "Good is that," said he; "I say in two hours' time all will be quiet, and we are as near the thicket as may be; there is no moon, but the night is fair and the stars clear; so all that thou hast to do is to walk out of this tent, and turn at once to thy right hand: come out with me now quietly, and I will show thee."

They went out together and Redhead said softly: "Lo thou that doddered oak yonder; like a piece of a hay-rick it looks under the stars; if thou seest it, come in again at once."

Ralph turned and drew Redhead in, and said when they were in the tent again: "Yea, I saw it: what then?"

318

Said Redhead: "I shall be behind it abiding thee." "Must I go afoot?" said Ralph, "or how shall I get me a horse?" "I have a horse for thee," said Redhead, "not thine own, but a better one yet, that hath not been backed to-day. Now give me a cup of wine, and let me go."

Ralph filled for him and took a cup himself, and said: "I pledge thee, friend, and wish thee better luck; and I would have thee for my fellow in this quest."

"Nay," said Redhead, "it may not be: I will not burden thy luck with my ill-luck ... and moreover I am seeking something which I may gain at Utterbol, and if I have it, I may do my best to say good-night to that evil abode."

"Yea," said Ralph, "and I wish thee well therein." Said Redhead, stammering somewhat; "It is even that woman of the Queen's whereof I told thee. And now one last word, since I must not be over long in thy tent, lest some one come upon us. But, fair sir, if thy mind misgive thee for this turning aside from Utterbol; though it is not to be doubted that the damsel whom thou seekest hath been there, it is not all so sure that thou wouldst have found her there. For of late, what with my Lord and my Lady being both away, the place hath been scant of folk; and not only is the said damsel wise and wary, but there be others who have seen her besides my Lord, and who so hath seen her is like to love her; and such is she, that whoso loveth her is like to do her will. So I bid thee in all case be earnest in thy quest; and think that if thou die on the road thy damsel would have died for thee; and if thou drink of the Well and come back whole and safe, I know not why thou shouldest not go straight to Utterbol and have the damsel away with thee, whosoever gainsay it. For they (if there be any such) who have drunk of the Well at the World's End are well looked to in this land. Now one more word yet; when I come to Utterbol, if thy damsel be there still, fear not but I will have speech of her, and tell of thee, and what thou wert looking to, and how thou deemedst of her."

Therewith he turned and departed hastily.

But Ralph left alone was sorely moved with hope and fear, and a longing that grew in him to see the damsel. For though he was firmly set on departure, and on seeking the sage aforesaid, yet his heart was drawn this way and that: and it came into his mind how the damsel would fare when the evil Lord came home to Utterbol; and he could not choose but make stories of her meeting of the tyrant, and her fear and grief and shame, and the despair of her heart. So the minutes went slow to him, till he should be in some new place and doing somewhat toward bringing about the deliverance of her from thralldom, and the meeting of him and her.

BOOK THREE

The Road To The Well
At World's End.

CHAPTER I

An Adventure in the Wood
Under the Mountains

Now was the night worn to the time appointed, for it was
two hours after midnight, so he stepped out of his tent clad
in all his war gear, and went straight to the doddered oak,
and found Redhead there with but one horse, whereby Ralph
knew that he held to his purpose of going his ways to
Utterbol: so he took him by the shoulders and embraced
him, rough carle as he was, and Redhead kneeled to him one
moment of time and then arose and went off into the night.
But Ralph got a-horseback without delay and rode his ways
warily across the highway and into the wood, and there was
none to hinder him. Though it was dark but for the starlight,
there was a path, which the horse, and not Ralph, found, so
that he made some way even before the first glimmer of
dawn, all the more as the wood was not very thick after the
first mile, and there were clearings here and there.

So rode Ralph till the sun was at point to rise, and he was
about the midst of one of those clearings or wood-lawns, on

the further side whereof there was more thicket, as he deemed, then he had yet come to; so he drew rein and looked about him for a minute. Even therewith he deemed he heard a sound less harsh than the cry of the jay in the beech-trees, and shriller than the moaning of the morning breeze in the wood. So he falls to listening with both ears, and this time deems that he hears the voice of a woman: and therewith came into his mind that old and dear adventure of the Wood Perilous; for he was dreamy with the past eagerness of his deeds, and the long and lonely night. But yet he doubted somewhat of the voice when it had passed his ears, so he shook his rein, for he thought it not good to tarry.

Scarce then had his horse stepped out, ere there came a woman running out of the thicket before him and made toward him over the lawn. So he gat off his horse at once and went to meet her, leading his horse; and as he drew nigh he could see that she was in a sorry plight; she had gathered up her skirts to run the better, and her legs and feet were naked: the coif was gone from her head and her black hair streamed out behind her: her gown was rent about the shoulders and bosom, so that one sleeve hung tattered, as if by the handling of some one.

So she ran up to him crying out: "Help, knight, help us!" and sank down therewith at his feet panting and sobbing. He stooped down to her, and raised her up, and said in a kind voice: "What is amiss, fair damsel, that thou art in such a plight; and what may I for thine avail? Doth any pursue thee, that thou fleest thus?"

She stood sobbing awhile, and then took hold of his two hands and said: "O fair lord, come now and help my lady! for as for me, since I am with thee, I am safe."

"Yea," said he, "Shall I get to horse at once?" And therewith he made as if he would move away from her; but she still held his hands, and seemed to think it good so to do, and she spake not for a while but gazed earnestly into his face. She was a fair woman, dark and sleek and lithe . . . for in good sooth she was none other than Agatha, who is afore told of.

Now Ralph is somewhat abashed by her eagerness, and lets

his eyes fall before hers; and he cannot but note that despite the brambles and briars of the wood that she had run through, there were no scratches on her bare legs, and that her arm was unbruised where the sleeve had been rent off.

At last she spake, but somewhat slowly, as if she were thinking of what she had to say: "O knight, by thy knightly oath I charge thee come to my lady and help and rescue her: she and I have been taken by evil men, and I fear that they will put her to shame, and torment her, ere they carry her off; for they were about tying her to a tree when I escaped: for they heeded not me who am but the maid, when they had the mistress in their hands." "Yea," said he, "and who is thy mistress?" Said the damsel: "She is the Lady of the Burnt Rock; and I fear me that these men are of the Riders of Utterbol; and then will it go hard with her; for there is naught but hatred betwixt my lord her husband and the tyrant of Utterbol." Said Ralph: "And how many were they?" "O but three, fair sir, but three," she said; "and thou so fair and strong, like the war-god himself."

Ralph laughed: "Three to one is long odds," quoth he, "but I will come with thee when thou hast let go my hands so that I may mount my horse. But wilt thou not ride behind me, fair damsel; so wearied and spent as thou wilt be by thy flight."

She looked on him curiously, and laid a hand on his breast, and the hauberk rings tinkled beneath the broidered surcoat; then she said: "Nay, I had best go afoot before thee, so disarrayed as I am."

Then she let him go, but followed him still with her eyes as he gat him into the saddle. She walked on beside his horse's head; and Ralph marvelled of her that for all her haste she had been in, she went somewhat leisurely, picking her way daintily so as to tread the smooth, and keep her feet from the rough.

Thus they went on, into the thicket and through it, and the damsel put the thorns and briars aside daintily as she stepped, and went slower still till they came to a pleasant place of oak-trees with greensward beneath them; and then she stopped, and turning, faced Ralph, and spoke with another voice than heretofore, whereas there was naught rueful or whining therein, but somewhat both of glee and of mocking as it seemed. "Sir knight," she said, "I have a word or two for thy ears; and this is a pleasant place, and good for us to talk together, whereas it is neither too near to her, nor too far from her, so that I can easily find my way back to her. Now, lord, I pray thee light down and listen to me." And therewith she sat down on the grass by the bole of a great oak.

"But thy lady," said Ralph, "thy lady?" "O sir," she said; "My lady shall do well enough: she is not tied so fast, but she might loose herself if the need were pressing. Light down, dear lord, light down!"

But Ralph sat still on his horse, and knit his brows, and said: "What is this, damsel? hast thou been playing a play with me? Where is thy lady whom thou wouldst have me deliver? If this be but game and play, let me go my ways; for time presses, and I have a weighty errand on hand."

She rose up and came close to him, and laid a hand on his knee and looked wistfully into his face as she said: "Nay then, I can tell thee all the tale as thou sittest in thy saddle; for meseems short will be thy farewell when I have told it." And she sighed withal.

Then Ralph was ashamed to gainsay her, and she now become gentle and sweet and enticing, and sad withal; so he got off his horse and tied him to a tree, and went and stood by the damsel as she lay upon the grass, and said: "I prithee tell thy tale and let me depart if there be naught for me to do."

Then she said: "This is the first word, that as to the Red Rock, I lied; and my lady is the Queen of Utterbol, and I am her thrall, and it is I who have drawn thee hither from the camp."

The blood mounted to Ralph's brow for anger; when he called to mind how he had been led hither and thither on other folk's errands ever since he left Upmeads. But he said naught, and Agatha looked on him timidly and said: "I say I am her thrall, and I did it to serve her and because she bade me." Said Ralph roughly: "And Redhead, him whom I saved

324

from torments and death; dost thou know him? didst thou know him?"

"Yea," she said, "I had from him what he had learned concerning thee from the sergeants and others, and then I put words into his mouth." "Yea then," quoth Ralph, "then he also is a traitor!" "Nay, nay," she said, "he is a true man and loveth thee, and whatever he hath said to thee he troweth himself. Moreover, I tell thee here and now that all that he told thee of the affairs of Utterbol, and thine outlook there, is true and overtrue."

She sprang to her feet therewith, and stood before him and clasped her hands before him and said: "I know that thou seekest the Well at the World's End and the deliverance of the damsel whom the Lord ravished from the wild man: now I swear it by thy mouth, that if thou go to Utterbol thou art undone and shalt come to the foulest pass there, and moreover that so going thou shalt bring the uttermost shame and torments on the damsel."

Said Ralph: "Yea, but what is her case as now? tell me."

Quoth Agatha: "She is in no such evil case; for my lady hateth her not as yet, or but little; and, which is far more, my lord loveth her after his fashion, and withal as I deem feareth her; for though she hath utterly gainsaid his desire, he hath scarce so much as threatened her. A thing unheard of. Had it been another woman she had by this time known all the bitterness that leadeth unto death at Utterbol." Ralph paled and he scowled on her, then he said: "And how knowest thou all the privity of the Lord of Utterbol? who telleth thee of all this?" She smiled and spake daintily: "Many folk tell me that which I would know; and that is because whiles I conquer the tidings with my wits, and whiles buy it with my body. Anyhow what I tell thee is the very sooth concerning this damsel, and this it is: that whereas she is but in peril, she shall be in deadly peril, yea and that instant, if thou go to Utterbol, thou, who art her lover . . ." "Nay," said Ralph angrily, "I am not her lover, I am but her well-willer." "Well," quoth Agatha looking down and knitting her brows, "when thy good will towards her has become known, then shall she be thrown at once into the pit of my

325

lord's cruelty. Yea, to speak sooth, even as it is, for thy sake (for her I heed naught) I would that the lord might find her gone when he cometh back to Utterbol."

"Yea," said Ralph, reddening, "and is there any hope for her getting clear off?" "So I deem," said Agatha. She was silent awhile and then spake in a low voice: "It is said that each man that seeth her loveth her; yea, and will befriend her, even though she consent not to his desire. Maybe she hath fled from Utterbol."

Ralph stood silent awhile with a troubled face; and then he said: "Yet thou hast not told me the why and wherefore of this play of thine, and the beguiling me into fleeing from the camp. Tell it me that I may pardon thee and pass on."

She said: "By thine eyes I swear that this is sooth, and that there is naught else in it than this: My lady set her love, when first she set her eyes upon thee—as forsooth all women must: as for me, I had not seen thee (though I told my lady that I had) till within this hour that we met in the wood."

She sighed therewith, and with her right hand played with the rent raiment about her bosom. Then she said: "She deemed that if thou camest a mere thrall to Utterbol, though she might command thy body, yet she would not gain thy love; but that if perchance thou mightest see her in hard need, and evilly mishandled, and mightest deliver her, there might at least grow up pity in thee for her, and that love might come thereof, as oft hath happed aforetime; for my lady is a fair woman. Therefore I, who am my lady's servant and thrall, and who, I bid thee remember, had not seen thee, took upon me to make this adventure, like to a minstrel's tale done in the flesh. Also I spake to my lord and told him thereof; and though he jeered at my lady to me, he was content, because he would have her set her heart on thee utterly; since he feared her jealousy, and would fain be delivered of it, lest she should play some turn to his newly beloved damsel and do her a mischief. Therefore did he set thee free (in words) meaning, when he had thee safe at Utterbol again (as he nowise doubted to have thee) to do as he would with thee, according as occasion might serve. For at heart he hateth thee, as I could see well. So a little before thou didst leave the camp, we, the Queen and I, went privily into a place of the woods but a little way hence. There I disarrayed both my lady and myself so far as was needful for the playing out the play which was to have seemed to thee a real adventure. Then came I to thee as if by chance hap, that I might bring thee to her; and if thou hadst come, we had a story for thee, whereby thou mightest not for very knighthood forbear to succour her and bring her whither she would, which in the long run had been Utterbol, but for the present time was to have been a certain strong-house appertaining to Utterbol, and nigh unto it. This is all the tale, and now if thou wilt, thou mayst pardon me; or if thou wilt, thou mayst draw out thy sword and smite off my head. And forsooth I deem that were the better deed."

She knelt down before him and put her palms together, and looked up at him beseechingly. His face darkened as he beheld her thus, but it cleared at last, and he said: "Damsel, thou wouldst turn out but a sorry maker, and thy play is naught. For seest thou not that I should have found out all the guile at Utterbol, and owed thy lady hatred rather than love thereafter."

"Yea," she said, "but my lady might have had enough of thy love by then, and would belike have let thee alone to fall into the hands of the Lord. Lo now! I have delivered thee from this, so that thou art quit both of the Lord and the lady and me: and again I say that thou couldst scarce have missed, both thou and thy damsel, of a miserable ending at Utterbol."

"Yea," said Ralph, softly, and as if speaking to himself, "yet am I lonely and unholpen." Then he turned to Agatha and said: "The end of all this is that I pardon thee, and must depart forthwith; for when ye two come back to the camp, then presently will the hunt be up."

She rose from her knees, and stood before him humbly and said: "Nay, I shall requite thee thy pardon thus far, that I will fashion some tale for my lady which will keep us in the woods two days or three; for we have provided victual for our adventure."

Said Ralph: "I may at least thank thee for that, and will

trust in thee to do so much." Quoth she: "Then might I ask a reward of thee: since forsooth other reward awaiteth me at Utterbol."

"Thou shalt have it," said Ralph. She said: "The reward is that thou kiss me ere we part."

"It must needs be according to my word," said Ralph, "yet I must tell thee that my kiss will bear but little love with it."

She answered naught but laid her hands on his breast and put up her face to him, and he kissed her lips. Then she said: "Knight, thou hast kissed a thrall and a guileful woman, yet one that shall smart for thee; therefore grudge not the kiss nor repent thee of thy kindness."

"How shalt thou suffer?" said he. She looked on him steadfastly a moment, and said: "Farewell! may all good go with thee." Therewith she turned away and walked off slowly through the wood, and somewhat he pitied her, and sighed as he got into his saddle; but he said to himself: "How might I help her? Yet true it is that she may well be in an evil case: I may not help everyone." Then he shook his rein and rode his ways.

CHAPTER 2

Ralph Rides the Wood Under the Mountains

A long way now rode Ralph, and naught befell him but the fashion of the wood. And as he rode, the heart within him was lightened that he had escaped from all the confusion and the lying of those aliens, who knew him not, nor his kindred, and yet would all use him each for his own ends: and withal he was glad that he was riding all alone upon his quest, but free, unwounded, and well weaponed.

The wood was not very thick whereas he rode, so that he could see the whereabouts of the sun, and rode east as far as he could judge it. Some little victual he had with him, and he found woodland fruit ripening here and there, and eked out his bread therewith; neither did water fail him, for he rode a good way up along a woodland stream that cleft the thicket, coming down as he deemed from the mountains, and thereby he made the more way: but at last he deemed that he must needs leave it, as it turned overmuch to the north. The light was failing when he came into a woodlawn amidst of which was a pool of water, and all that day he had had no adventure with beast or man, since he had sundered from Agatha. So he lay down and slept there with his naked sword by his side, and awoke not till the sun was high in the heavens next morning. Then he arose at once and went on his way after he had washed him, and eaten a morsel.

After a little the thick of the wood gave out, and the land was no longer flat, as it had been, but was of dales and of hills, not blinded by trees. In this land he saw much deer, as hart and wild swine; and he happened also on a bear, who was about a honey tree, and had taken much comb from the wild bees. On him Ralph drew his sword and drave him exceeding loth from his purchase, so that the knight dined off the bear's thieving. Another time he came across a bent where on the south side grew vines well fruited, and the grapes a-ripening; and he ate well thereof before he went on his way.

Before nightfall he came on that same stream again, and it was now running straight from the east; so he slept that night on the bank thereof. On the morrow he rode up along it a great way, till again it seemed to be coming overmuch from the north; and then he left it, and made on east as near as he could guess it by the sun.

Now he passed through thickets at whiles not very great, and betwixt them rode hilly land grassed mostly with long coarse grass, and with whin and thorn-trees scattered about. Thence he saw again from time to time the huge wall of the mountains rising up into the air like a great black cloud that would swallow up the sky, and though the sight was terrible, yet it gladdened him, since he knew that he was on the right way. So far he rode, going on the whole up-hill, till at last there was a great pine-wood before him, so that he could see no ending to it either north or south.

It was now late in the afternoon, and Ralph pondered whether he should abide the night where he was and sleep the night there, or whether he should press on in hope of winning to some clear place before dark. So whereas he was in a place both rough and waterless, he deemed it better to go on, after he had rested his horse and let him bite the herbage a while. Then he rode his ways, and entered the wood and made the most of the way.

CHAPTER 3

Ralph Meeteth With Another Adventure in the Wood Under the Mountain

Soon the wood grew very thick of pine-trees, though there was no undergrowth, so that when the sun sank it grew dark very speedily; but he still rode on in the dusk, and there were but few wild things, and those mostly voiceless, in the wood, and it was without wind and very still. Now he thought he heard the sound of a horse going behind him or on one side, and he wondered whether the chace were up, and hastened what he might, till at last it grew black night, and he was constrained to abide. So he got off his horse, and leaned his back against a tree, and had the beast's reins over his arm; and now he listened again carefully, and was quite sure that he could hear the footsteps of some hard-footed beast going nowise far from him. He laughed inwardly, and said to himself: "If the chacer were to pass but three feet from my nose he should be none the wiser but if he hear me or my horse." And therewith he cast a lap of his cloak over the horse's head, lest he should whinny if he became aware of the other beast; and so there he stood abiding, and the noise grew greater till he could hear clearly the horse-hoofs drawing nigh, till they came very nigh, and then stopped.

Then came a man's voice that said: "Is there a man anigh in the wood?"

Ralph held his peace till he should know more; and the voice spake again in a little while: "If there be a man anigh let him be sure that I will do him no hurt; nay, I may do him good, for I have meat with me." Clear was the voice, and as sweet as the April blackbird sings. It spake again: "Naught answereth, yet meseemeth I know surely that a man is anigh; and I am aweary of the waste, and long for fellowship."

Ralph hearkened, and called to mind tales of way-farers entrapped by wood-wives and evil things; but he thought: "At least this is no sending of the Lord of Utterbol, and, St. Nicholas to aid, I have little fear of wood-wights. Withal I shall be but a dastard if I answer not one man, for fear of I know not what." So he spake in a loud and cheerful voice: "Yea, there is a man anigh, and I desire thy fellowship, if we might but meet. But how shall we see each other in the blackness of the wildwood night?"

The other laughed, and the laugh sounded merry and sweet, and the voice said: "Hast thou no flint and fire-steel?" "No," said Ralph. "But I have," said the voice, "and I am fain to see thee, for thy voice soundeth pleasant to me. Abide till I grope about for a stick or two."

Ralph laughed in turn, as he heard the new-comer moving about; then he heard the click of the steel on the flint, and saw the sparks showering down, so that a little piece of the wood grew green again to his eyes. Then a little clear flame sprang up, and therewith he saw the tree-stems clearly, and some twenty yards from him a horse, and a man stooping down over the fire, who sprang up now and cried out: "It is a knight-at-arms! Come hither, fellow of the waste; it is five days since I have spoken to a child of Adam; so come nigh and speak to me, and as a reward of thy speech thou shalt have both meat and firelight."

"That will be well paid," said Ralph laughing, and he stepped forward leading his horse, for now the wood was light all about, as the fire waxed and burned clear; so that

Ralph could see that the new-comer was clad in quaintly-fashioned armour after the fashion of that land, with a bright steel sallet on the head, and a long green surcoat over the body armour. Slender of make was the new-comer, not big nor tall of stature.

Ralph went up to him hastily, and merrily put his hand on his shoulder, and kissed him, saying: "The kiss of peace in the wilderness to thee!" And he found him smooth-faced and sweet-breathed.

But the new comer took his hand and led him to where the firelight was brightest and looked on him silently a while; and Ralph gave back the look. The strange-wrought sallet hid but little of the new comer's face, and as Ralph looked thereon a sudden joy came into his heart, and he cried out: "O, but I have kissed thy face before! O, my friend, my friend!"

Then spake the new-comer and said: "Yea, I am a woman, and I was thy friend for a little while at Bourton Abbas, and at the want-ways of the Wood Perilous."

Then Ralph cast his arms about her and kissed her again; but she withdrew her from him, and said: "Help me, my friend, that we may gather sticks to feed our fire, lest it die and the dark come again so that we see not each other's faces, and think that we have but met in a dream."

Then she busied herself with gathering the kindling; but presently she looked up at him, and said: "Let us make the wood shine wide about, for this is a feastful night."

So they gathered a heap of wood and made the fire great; and then Ralph did off his helm and hauberk and the damsel did the like, so that he could see the shapeliness of her uncovered head. Then they sat down before the fire, and the damsel drew meat and drink from her saddle-bags, and gave thereof to Ralph, who took it of her and her hand withal, and smiled on her and said: "Shall we be friends together as we were at Bourton Abbas and the want-ways of the Wood Perilous?" She shook her head and said: "If it might be! but it may not be. Not many days have worn since then; but they have brought about changed days." He looked on her wistfully and said: "But thou wert dear to me then."

"Yea," she said, "and thou to me; but other things have befallen, and there is change betwixt."

"Nay, what change?" said Ralph.

Even by the firelight he saw that she reddened as she answered: "I was a free woman then; now am I but a runaway thrall." Then Ralph laughed merrily, and said, "Then are we brought the nigher together, for I also am a runaway thrall."

She smiled and looked down: then she said: "Wilt thou tell me how that befell?"

"Yea," said he, "but I will ask thee first a question or two." She nodded a yeasay, and looked on him soberly, as a child waiting to say its task.

Said Ralph: "When we parted at the want-ways of the Wood Perilous thou saidst that thou wert minded for the Well at the World's End, and to try it for life or death. But thou hadst not then the necklace, which now I see thee bear, and which, seest thou! is like to that about my neck. Wilt thou tell me whence thou hadst it?"

She said: "Yea; it was given unto me by a lady, mighty as I deem, and certainly most lovely, who delivered me from an evil plight, and a peril past words, but whereof I will tell thee afterwards. And she it was who told me of the way to the Well at the World's End, and many matters concerning them that seek it, whereof thou shalt wot soon."

Said Ralph: "As to how thou wert made a thrall thou needest not to tell me; for I have learned that of those that had to do with taking thee to Utterbol. But tell me; here are met we two in the pathless wilds, as if it were on the deep sea, and we two seeking the same thing. Didst thou deem that we should meet, or that I should seek thee?"

Now was the fire burning somewhat low, but he saw that she looked on him steadily; yet withal her sweet voice trembled a little as she answered: "Kind friend, I had a hope that thou wert seeking me and wouldst find me: for indeed that fairest of women who gave me the beads spake to me of thee, and said that thou also wouldst turn thee to the quest of the Well at the World's End; and already had I deemed thine eyes lucky as well as lovely. But tell me, my friend, what has

333

befallen that lady that she is not with thee? For in such wise she spake of thee, that I deemed that naught would sunder you save death."

"It is death that hath sundered us," said Ralph.

Then she hung her head, and sat silent a while, neither did he speak till she had risen up and cast more wood upon the fire; and she stood before it with her back towards him. Then he spake to her in a cheerful voice and said: "Belike we shall be long together: tell me thy name; is it not Dorothy?" She turned about to him with a smiling face, and said: "Nay lord, nay: did I not tell thee my name before? They that held me at the font bid the priest call me Ursula, after the Friend of Maidens. But what is thy name?"

"I am Ralph of Upmeads," quoth he; and sat a while silent, pondering his dream and how it had betrayed him as to her name, when it had told him much that he yet deemed true.

She came and sat down by him again, and said to him: "Thy questions I have answered; but thou hast not yet told me the tale of thy captivity." Her voice sounded exceeding sweet to him, and he looked on her face and spake as kindly as he knew how, and said: "A short tale it is to-night at least: I came from Whitwall with a Company of Chapmen, and it was thee I was seeking and the Well at the World's End. All went well with me, till I came to Goldburg, and there I was betrayed by a felon, who had promised to lead me safe to Utterness, and tell me concerning the way unto the Well. But he sold me to the Lord of Utterbol, who would lead me to his house; which irked me not, at first, because I looked to find thee there. Thereafter, if for shame I may tell the tale, his lady and wife cast her love upon me, and I was entangled in the nets of guile: yet since I was told, and believed that it would be ill both for thee and for me if I met thee at Utterbol, I took occasion to flee away, I will tell thee how another while."

She had turned pale as she heard him, and now she said: "It is indeed God's mercy that thou camest not to Utterbol nor foundest me there, for then had both we been undone amidst the lusts of those two; or that thou camest not there to find me fled, else hadst thou been undone. My heart is sick to think of it, even as I sit by thy side."

Said Ralph: "Thy last word maketh me afraid and ashamed to ask thee a thing. But tell me first, is that Lord of Utterbol as evil as men's fear would make him? for no man is feared so much unless he is deemed evil."

She was silent a while, and then she said: "He is so evil that it might be deemed that he has been brought up out of hell."

Then Ralph looked sore troubled, and he said: "Dear friend, this is the thing hard for me to say. In what wise did they use thee at Utterbol? Did they deal with thee shamefully?" She answered him quietly: "Nay," she said, "fear not! no shame befell me, save that I was a thrall and not free to depart. Forsooth," she said, smiling, "I fled away timely before the tormentors should be ready. Forsooth it is an evil house and a mere piece of hell. But now we are out of it and free in the wildwood, so let us forget it; for indeed it is a grief to remember it. And now once more let us mend the fire, for thy face is growing dim to me, and that misliketh me. Afterwards before we lie down to sleep we will talk a little of the way, whitherward we shall turn our faces to-morrow."

So they cast on more wood, and pineapples, and sweet it was to Ralph to see her face come clear again from out the mirk of the wood. Then they sat down again together and she said: "We two are seeking the Well at the World's End; now which of us knows more of the way? who is to lead, and who to follow?" Said Ralph: "If thou know no more than I, it is little that thou knowest. Sooth it is that for many days past I have sought thee that thou mightest lead me."

She laughed sweetly, and said: "Yea, knight, and was it for that cause that thou soughtest me, and not for my deliverance?" He said soberly: "Yet in very deed I set myself to deliver thee." "Yea," she said, "then since I am delivered, I must needs deem of it as if it were through thy deed. And as I suppose thou lookest for a reward therefor, so thy reward shall be, that I will lead thee to the Well at the World's End. Is it enough?" "Nay," said Ralph. They held their peace a minute, then she said: "Maybe when we have drunk of that Water and are coming back, it will be for thee to lead. For true it is that I shall scarce know whither to wend; since amidst of my dreaming of the Well, and of ... other matters, my home that was is gone like a dream."

He looked at her, but scarce as if he were heeding all her words. Then he spoke: "Yea, thou shalt lead me. I have been led by one or another ever since I have left Upmeads." Now she looked on him somewhat ruefully, and said: "Thou wert not hearkening e'en now; so I say it again, that the time shall come when thou shalt lead me."

In Ralph's mind had sprung up again that journey from the Water of the Oak-tree; so he strove with himself to put the thought from him, and sighed and said: "Dost thou verily know much of the way?" She nodded yeasay. "Knowest thou of the Rock of the Fighting Man?" "Yea," she said. "And of the Sage that dwelleth in this same wood?" "Most surely," she said, "and to-morrow evening or the morrow after we shall find him; for I have been taught the way to his dwelling; and I wot that he is now called the Sage of Swevenham. Yet I must tell thee that there is some peril in seeking to him; whereas his dwelling is known of the Utterbol riders, who may follow us thither. And yet again I deem that he will find some remedy thereto."

Said Ralph: "Whence didst thou learn all this, my friend?" And his face grew troubled again; but she said simply: "She taught it to me who spake to me in the wood by Hampton under Scaur."

She made as if she noted not the trouble in his face, but said: "Put thy trust in this, that here and with me thou art even now nigher to the Well at the World's End than any other creature on the earth. Yea, even if the Sage of Swevenham be dead or gone hence, yet have I tokens to find the Rock of the Fighting Man, and the way through the mountains, though I say not but that he may make it all clearer. But now I see thee drooping with the grief of days bygone; and I deem also that thou art weary with the toil of the way. So I rede thee lie down here in the wilderness and sleep, and forget grief till to-morrow is a new day."

"Would it were come," said he, "that I might see thy face the clearer; yet I am indeed weary."

So he went and fetched his saddle and lay down with his head thereon; and was presently asleep. But she, who had again cast wood on the fire, sat by his head watching him with a drawn sword beside her, till the dawn of the woodland began to glimmer through the trees: then she also laid herself down and slept.

CHAPTER 4

They Ride the Wood Under the Mountains

When Ralph woke on the morrow it was broad day as far as the trees would have it so. He rose at once, and looked about for his fellow, but saw her not, and for some moments of time he thought he had but dreamed of her; but he saw that the fire had been quickened from its embers, and close by lay the hauberk and strange-fashioned helm, and the sword of the damsel, and presently he saw her coming through the trees barefoot, with the green-sleeved silken surcoat hanging below the knees and her hair floating loose about her. She stepped lightly up to Ralph with a cheerful smiling countenance and a ruddy colour in her cheeks, but her eyes moist as if she could scarce keep back the tears for joy of the morning's meeting. He thought her fairer than erst, and made as if he would put his arms about her, but she held a little aloof from him, blushing yet more. Then she said in her sweet clear voice: "Hail fellow-farer! now begins the day's work. I have been down yonder, and have found a bright woodland pool, to wash the night off me, and if thou wilt do in likewise and come back to me, I will dight our breakfast meantime, and will we speedily to the road." He did as she bade him, thinking of her all the while till he came back to her fresh and gay. Then he looked to their horses and gave them fodder gathered from the pool-side, and so turned to Ursula and found her with the meat ready dight; so they ate and were glad.

When they had broken their fast Ralph went to saddle the horses, and coming back found Ursula binding up her long hair, and she smiled on him and said: "Now we are for the road I must be an armed knight again: forsooth I unbound my hair e'en now and let my surcoat hang loose about me in token that thou wottest my secret. Soothly, my friend, it irks me that now we have met after a long while, I must needs be clad thus graceless. But need drave me to it, and withal the occasion that was given to me to steal this gay armour from a lad at Utterbol, the nephew of the lord; who like his eme was half my lover, half my tyrant. Of all which I will tell thee hereafter, and what wise I must needs steer betwixt stripes and kisses these last days. But now let us arm and to horse. Yet first lo you, here are some tools that in thine hands shall keep us from sheer famine: as for me I am no archer; and forsooth no man-at-arms save in seeming."

Therewith she showed him a short Turk bow and a quiver of arrows, which he took well pleased. So then they armed each the other, and as she handled Ralph's wargear she said: "How well-wrought and trusty is this hauberk of thine, my friend; my coat is but a toy to it, with its gold and silver rings and its gemmed collar: and thy plates be thick and wide and well-wrought, whereas mine are little more than adornments to my arms and legs."

He looked on her lovingly and loved her shapely hands amidst the dark grey mail, and said: "That is well, dear friend, for since my breast is a shield for thee it behoves it to be well covered." She looked at him, and her lips trembled, and she put out her hand as if to touch his cheek, but drew it back again and said: "Come now, let us to horse, dear fellow in arms."

So they mounted and went their ways through a close pine-wood, where the ground was covered with the pine-tree needles, and all was still and windless. So as they rode said Ursula: "I seek tokens of the way to the Sage of Sweven-

338

ham. Hast thou seen a water yesterday?" "Yea," said Ralph, "I rode far along it, but left it because I deemed that it turned north overmuch." "Thou wert right," she said, "besides that thy turning from it hath brought us together; for it would have brought thee to Utterbol at last. But now have we to hit upon another that runneth straight down from the hills: not the Great Mountains, but the high ground whereon is the Sage's dwelling. I know not whether the ride be long or short; but the stream is to lead us."

On they rode through the wood, wherein was little change for hours, and as they rested Ursula gave forth a deep breath, as one who has cast off a load of care. And Ralph said: "Why sighest thou, fellow-farer?" "O," she said, "it is for pleasure, and a thought that I had: for a while ago I was a thrall, living amongst fears that sickened the heart; and then a little while I was a lonely wanderer, and now ... Therefore I was thinking that if ever I come back to mine own land and my home, the scent of a pine-wood shall make me happy."

Ralph looked on her eagerly, but said naught for a while; but at last he spoke: "Tell me, friend," said he, "if we be met by strong-thieves on the way, what shall we do then?"

"It is not like to befall," she said, "for men fear the wood, therefore is there little prey for thieves therein: but if we chance on them, the token of Utterbol on mine armour shall make them meek enough." Then she fell silent a while, and spoke again: "True it is that we may be followed by the Utterbol riders; for though they also fear the wood, they fear it not so much as they fear their Lord. Howbeit, we be well ahead, and it is little like that we shall be overtaken before we have met the Sage; and then belike he shall provide."

"Yea," said Ralph, "but what if the chase come up with us: shall we suffer us to be taken alive?" She looked on him solemnly, laid her hand on the beads about her neck, and answered: "By this token we must live as long as we may, whatsoever may befall; for at the worst may some road of escape be opened to us. Yet O, how far easier it were to die than to be led back to Utterbol!"

A while they rode in silence, both of them: but at last

spake Ralph, but slowly and in a dull and stern voice: "Maybe it were good that thou told me somewhat of the horrors and evil days of Utterbol?" "Maybe," she said, "but I will not tell thee of them. Forsooth there are some things which a man may not easily tell to a man, be he never so much his friend as thou art to me. But bethink thee" (and she smiled somewhat) "that this gear belieth me, and that I am but a woman; and some things there be which a woman may not tell to a man, nay, not even when he hath held her long in his arms." And therewith she flushed exceedingly. But he said in a kind voice: "I am sorry that I asked thee, and will ask thee no more thereof." She smiled on him friendly, and they spake of other matters as they rode on.

But after a while Ralph said: "If it were no misease to thee to tell me how thou didst fall into the hands of the men of Utterbol, I were fain to hear the tale."

She laughed outright, and said: "Why wilt thou be forever harping on the time of my captivity, friend? And thou who knowest the story somewhat already? Howbeit, I may tell thee thereof without heart-burning, though it be a felon tale."

He said, somewhat shame-facedly: "Take it not ill that I am fain to hear of thee and thy life-days, since we are become fellow-farers."

"Well," she said, "this befell outside Utterbol, so I will tell thee.

"After I had stood in the thrall-market at Cheaping Knowe, and not been sold, the wild man led me away toward the mountains that are above Goldburg; and as we drew near to them on a day, he said to me that he was glad to the heart-root that none had cheapened me at the said market; and when I asked him wherefore, he fell a weeping as he rode beside me, and said: 'Yet would God that I had never taken thee.' I asked what ailed him, though indeed I deemed that I knew. He said: 'This aileth me, that though thou art not of the blood wherein I am bound to wed, I love thee sorely, and would have thee to wife; and now I deem that thou wilt not love me again.' I said that he guessed aright, but that if he would do friendly with me, I would be no less than a friend to him. 'That availeth little,' quoth he; 'I would have thee be mine of thine own will.' I said that might not be, that I could love but one man alone. 'Is he alive?' said he. 'Goodsooth, I hope so,' said I, 'but if he be dead, then is desire of men dead within me.'

"So we spake, and he was downcast and heavy of mood; but thenceforward was he no worse to me than a brother. And he proffered it to lead me back, if I would, and put me safely on the way to Whitwall; but, as thou wottest, I had need to go forward, and no need to go back.

"Thus we entered into the mountains of Goldburg; but one morning, when he arose, he was heavier of mood than his wont, and was restless withal, and could be steadfast neither in staying nor going, nor aught else. So I asked what ailed him, and he said: 'My end draweth nigh; I have seen my fetch, and am fey. My grave abideth me in these mountains.' 'Thou hast been dreaming ugly dreams,' said I, 'such things are of no import.' And I spoke lightly, and strove to comfort him. He changed not his mood for all that; but said: 'This is ill for thee also; for thou wilt be worser without me than with me in these lands.' Even so I deemed, and withal I was sorry for him, for though he were uncouth and ungainly, he was no ill man. So against my will I tumbled into the same-like mood as his, and we both fared along drearily. But about sunset, as we came round a corner of the cliffs of those mountains, or ever we were ware we happed upon a half-score of weaponed men, who were dighting a camp under a big rock thereby: but four there were with them who were still a-horseback; so that when Bull Nosy (for that was his name) strove to flee away with me, it was of no avail; for the said horsemen took us, and brought us before an evil-looking man, who, to speak shortly, was he whom thou hast seen, to wit, the Lord of Utterbol: he took no heed of Bull Nosy, but looked on me closely, and handled me as a man doth with a horse at a cheaping, so that I went nigh to smiting him, whereas I had a knife in my bosom, but the chaplet refrained me. To make a short tale of it, he bade Bull sell me to him, which Bull utterly naysaid, standing stiff and stark before the Lord, and scowling on him. But the

Lord laughed in his face and said: 'So be it, for I will take her without a price, and thank thee for sparing my gold.' Then said Bull: 'If thou take her as a thrall, thou wert best take me also; else shall I follow thee as a free man and slay thee when I may. Many are the days of the year, and on some one of them will betide the occasion for the knife.'

"Thereat the Lord waxed very pale, and spake not, but looked at that man of his who stood by Bull with a great sword in his fist, and lifted up his hand twice, and let it fall twice, whereat that man stepped back one pace, and swung his sword, and smote Bull, and clave his skull.

"Then the colour came into the Lord's face again, and he said: 'Now, vassals, let us dine and be merry, for at least we have found something in the mountains.' So they fell to and ate and drank, and victual was given to me also, but I had no will to eat, for my soul was sick and my heart was heavy, foreboding the uttermost evil. Withal I was sorry for Bull Nosy, for he was no ill man and had become my friend.

"So they abode there that night, leaving Bull lying like a dog unburied in the wilderness; and on the morrow they took the road to Utterbol, and went swiftly, having no baggage, and staying but for victual, and for rest every night. The Lord had me brought to him on that first evening of our journey, and he saw me privily and spake to me, bidding me do shameful things, and I would not; wherefore he threatened me grievously; and, I being alone with him, bade him beware lest I should slay him or myself. Thereat he turned pale, as he had done before Bull Nosy, yet sent for none to slay me, but only bade me back to my keepers. And so I came to Utterbol unscathed."

"And at Utterbol," said Ralph, "what befell thee there?" Ursula smiled on him, and held up her finger; yet she answered: "Utterbol is a very great house in a fair land, and there are sundry roofs and many fair chambers. There was I brought to a goodly chamber amidst a garden; and women servants were given me who led me to the bath and clad me in dainty raiment, and gave me to eat and to drink, and all that I needed. That is all my tale for this time."

342

CHAPTER 5

They Come on the Sage
of Swevenham

Night was at hand before they came to the stream that they sought. They found it cleaving the pine-wood, which held on till the very bank of it, and was thick again on the further side in a few yards' space. The stream was high-banked and ran deep and strong. Said Ursula as they came up to it: "We may not cross it, but it matters not; and it is to-morrow that we must ride up along it."

So they abode there, and made a fire by the waterside, and watched there, turn and turn about, till it was broad day. Naught befell to tell of, save that twice in the night Ralph deemed that he heard a lion roar.

They got to horse speedily when they were both awake, and rode up the stream, and began to go up hill, and by noon were come into a rough and shaggy upland, whence from time to time they could see the huge wall of the mountains, which yet seemed to Ralph scarce nigher, if at all, than when he had beheld it ere he had come to Vale Turris. The way was rough day-long, and now and again they found it hard to keep the stream in sight, as especially when it cleft a hill, and ran between sheer cliffs with no low shore on either side.

They made way but slowly, so that at last Ralph lost patience somewhat, and said that he had but little hope of falling in with the Sage that day or any day. But Ursula was of good cheer, and mocked him merrily but sweetly, till his heart was lightened again. Withal she bade him seek some venison, since they were drawing out the time, and she knew not how long it would be ere they came to the Sage's dwelling. Therefore he betook him to the Turk bow, and shot a leash of heath-fowl, and they supped on the meat merrily in the wilderness.

But if they were merry, they were soon weary; for they journeyed on after sunset that night, since the moon was up, and there was no thick wood to turn dusk into dark for them. Their resting-place was a smooth piece of greensward betwixt the water and a half circle of steep bent that well nigh locked it about.

There then they abode, and in the stillness of the night heard a thundering sound coming down the wind to them, which they deemed was the roaring of distant waters; and when they went to the lip of the river they saw flocks of foam floating by, wherefore they thought themselves to be near some great mountain-neck whereover the water was falling from some high place. But with no to-do they lay down upon the greensward this second night of their fellow-ship, and waked later than on the day before; for so weary had they been, that they had kept but ill watch in the dark night, and none at all after dawn began to glimmer.

Now Ralph sat up and saw Ursula still sleeping; then he rose to his feet and looked about him, and saw their two horses cropping the grass under the bent, and beside them a man, tall and white bearded, leaning on his staff. Ralph caught up his sword and went toward the man, and the sun gleamed from the blade just as the hoary-one turned to him; he lifted up his staff as if in greeting to Ralph, and came toward him, and even therewith Ursula awoke and arose, and saw the greybeard at once; and she cried out: "Take heed to thy sword, fellow-farer, for, praised be the saints, this is the Sage of Swevenham!"

So they stood there together till the Sage came up to them and kissed them both, and said: "I am glad that ye are come at last; for I looked for you no later than this. So now mount your horses and come with me straightway; because life is short to them who have not yet drunk of the Well at the World's End. Moreover if ye chance to come on the riders of Utterbol, it shall go hard with you unless I be at hand."

Ralph saw of him that though he was an old hoar man to look on, yet he was strong and sturdy, tall, and of goodly presence, with ruddy cheeks, and red lips and bright eyes, and that the skin of his face and hands was nowise wrinkled: but about his neck was a pair of beads like unto his own gossip's gift.

So now they mounted at once, and with no more words he led them about the bent, and they came in a little while into the wood again, but this time it was of beech, with here and there an open place sprinkled about with hollies and thorns; and they rode down the wide slope of a long hill, and up again on the other side.

Thus they went for an hour, and the elder spake not again, though it might have been deemed by his eyes that he was eager and fain. They also held their peace; for the hope and fear of their hearts kept them from words.

They came to the hill-top, and found a plain land, though the close wood still held on a while; but soon they rode into a clearing of some twelve acres, where were fenced crofts with goats therein, and three garths of tillage, wherein the wheatshocks were yet standing, and there were coleworts and other pot-herbs also. But at the further end, whereas the wood closed in again, was a little house builded of timber, strong and goodly, and thatched with wheat-straw; and beside it was a bubbling spring which ran in a brook athwart the said clearing; over the house-door was a carven rood, and a bow and short spear were leaned against the wall of the porch.

Ralph looked at all closely, and wondered whether this were perchance the cot wherein the Lady of Abundance had dwelt with the evil witch. But the elder looked on him, and said: "I know thy thought, and it is not so; that house is far away hence; yet shalt thou come thereto. Now, children, welcome to the house of him who hath found what ye seek, but hath put aside the gifts which ye shall gain; and who belike shall remember what ye shall forget."

Therewith he brought them into the house, and into a chamber, the plenishing whereof was both scanty and rude. There he bade them sit, and brought them victual, to wit, cheese and goats' milk and bread, and they fell to speech concerning the woodland ways, and the seasons, and other unweighty matters. But as for the old man he spoke but few words, and as one unused to speech, albeit he was courteous and debonair. But when they had eaten and drunk he spake to them and said:

"Ye have sought to me because ye would find the Well at the World's End, and would have lore of me concerning the road thereto; but before I tell you what ye would, let me know what ye know thereof already."

Quoth Ralph: "For me, little enough I know, save that I must come to the Rock of the Fighting Man, and that thou knowest the way thither."

"And thou, damsel," quoth the long-hoary, "what knowest thou? Must I tell thee of the way through the mountains and the Wall of the World, and the Winter Valley, and the Folk Innocent, and the Cot on the Way, and the Forest of Strange Things and the Dry Tree?"

"Nay," she said, "of all this I wot somewhat, but it may be not enough."

Said the Sage: "Even so it was with me, when a many years ago I dwelt nigh to Swevenham, and folk sought to me for lore, and I told them what I knew; but maybe it was not enough, for they never came back; but died belike or ever they had seen the Well. And then I myself, when I was gotten very old, fared thither a-seeking it, and I found it; for I was one of those who bore the chaplet of the seekers. And now I know all, and can teach all. But tell me, damsel, whence hadst thou this lore?"

Said Ursula: "I had it of a very fair woman who, as it seemeth, was Lady and Queen of the Champions of Hampton under the Scaur, not far from mine own land."

"Yea," quoth the Sage, "and what hath befallen her? . . . Nay, nay," said he, "I need not ask; for I can see by your faces that she is dead. Therefore hath she been slain, or otherwise she had not been dead. So I ask you if ye were her friends?"

Quoth Ursula; "Surely she was my friend, since she befriended me; and this man I deem was altogether her friend."

Ralph hung his head, and the Sage gazed on him, but said naught. Then he took a hand of each of them in his hands,

346

and held them a while silently, and Ralph was still downcast and sad, but Ursula looked on him fondly.

Then spake the Sage: "So it is, Knight, that now I seem to understand what manner of man thou art, and I know what is between you two; whereof I will say naught, but will let the tree grow according to its seed. Moreover, I wot now that my friend of past years would have me make you both wise in the lore of the Well at the World's End; and when I have done this, I can do no more, but let your good hap prevail if so it may. Abide a little, therefore."

Then he went unto an ark, and took thence a book wrapped in a piece of precious web of silk and gold, and bound in cuir-bouilly wrought in strange devices. Then said he: "This book was mine heritage at Swevenham or ever I became wise, and it came from my father's grandsire: and my father bade me look on it as the dearest of possessions; but I heeded it naught till my youth had waned, and my manhood was full of weariness and grief. Then I turned to it, and read in it, and became wise, and the folk sought to me, and afterwards that befell which was foredoomed. Now herein amongst other matters is written of that which ye desire to know, and I will read the same to you and expound it. Yet were it not well to read in this book under a roof, nay, though it be as humble and innocent as this. Moreover, it is not meet that ye should hearken to this wisdom of old times clad as ye are; thou, knight, in the raiment of the manslayer, with the rod of wrath hanging at thy side; and thou, maiden, attired in the garments of the tyrant, which were won of him by lying and guile."

Then he went to another ark, and took from it two bundles, which he gave, the one to Ralph, the other to Ursula, and said: "Thou, maiden, go thou into the inner chamber here and doff thy worldly raiment, and don that which thou wilt find wrapped in this cloth; and thou, knight, take this other and get thee into the thicket which is behind the house, and there do the like, and abide there till we come to thee."

So Ralph took the bundle, and came out into the thicket and unarmed him, and did on the raiment which he found in the cloth, which was but a long gown of white linen, much like to an alb, broidered about the wrists and the hems and collar with apparels of gold and silk, girt with a red silk girdle. There he abode a little, wondering at all these things and all that had befallen him since he had left Upmeads.

Anon the two others came to him, and Ursula was clad in the same-like raiment and the elder had the book in his hand. He smiled on Ralph and nodded friendly to him. As to Ursula, she flushed as red as a rose when she set eyes on him, for she said to herself that he was as one of the angels which she had seen painted in the choir of St. Mary's at Higham.

CHAPTER 6

Those Two Are Learned Lore by the Sage of Swevenham

Now the Sage led them through the wood till they came to a grassy lawn amidst of which was a table of stone, which it seemed to Ralph must be like to that whereon the witch-wife had offered up the goat to her devils as the Lady of Abundance had told him; and he changed countenance as the thought came into his mind. But the Sage looked on him and shook his head and spake softly: "In these wastes and wilds are many such-like places, where of old time the ancient folks did worship to the Gods of the Earth as they imagined them: and whereas the lore in this book cometh of such folk, this is no ill place for the reading thereof. But if ye fear the book and its writers, who are dead long ago, there is yet time to go back and seek the Well without my helping; and I say not but that ye may find it even thus. But if ye fear not, then sit ye down on the grass, and I will lay the book on this most ancient table, and read in it, and do ye hearken heedfully."

So they sat down side by side, and Ralph would have taken Ursula's hand to caress it, but she drew it away from him;

howbeit she found it hard to keep her eyes from off him. The Elder looked on them soberly, but nowise in anger, and presently began reading in the book. What he read shall be seen hereafter in the process of this tale; for the more part thereof had but to do with the way to the Well at the World's End, all things concerning which were told out fully, both great and small. Long was this a-reading, and when the Sage had done, he bade now one, now the other answer him questions as to what he had read; and if they answered amiss he read that part again, and yet again, as children are taught in the school. Until at last when he asked any question Ralph or the maiden answered it rightly at once; and by this time the sun was about to set. So he bade them home to his house that they might eat and sleep there.

"But to-morrow," said he, "I shall give you your last lesson from this book, and thereafter ye shall go your ways to the Rock of the Fighting Man, and I look not for it that ye shall come to any harm on the way; but whereas I seem to-day to have seen the foes of Utterbol seeking you, I will lead you forth a little."

So they went home to the house, and he made them the most cheer that he might, and spake to them in friendly and pleasant mood, so that they were merry.

When it was morning they went again to the ancient altar, and again they learned lore from the Elder, till they were waxen wise in the matters of the Well at the World's End, and long they sat and hearkened him till it was evening again, and once more they slept in the house of the Sage of Swevenham.

CHAPTER 7

An Adventure by the Way

When morrow dawned they arose betimes and did on their worldly raiment; and when they had eaten a morsel they made them ready for the road, and the elder gave them victual for the way in their saddle-bags, saying: "This shall suffice for the passing days, and when it is gone ye have learned what to do."

Therewithall they gat to horse; but Ralph would have the Elder ride his nag, while he went afoot by the side of Ursula. So the Sage took his bidding, but smiled therewith, and said: "Thou art a King's son and a friendly young man, else had I said nay to this; for it needeth not, whereas I am stronger than thou, so hath my draught of the Well dealt with me."

Thus then they went their ways; but Ralph noted of Ursula that she was silent and shy with him, and it irked him so much, that at last he said to her: "My friend, doth aught ail me with thee? Wilt thou not tell me, so that I may amend it? For thou are grown of few words with me and turnest thee from me, and seemest as if thou heedest me little. Thou art as a fair spring morning gone cold and overcast in the afternoon. What is it then? we are going a long journey together, and belike shall find little help or comfort save in each other; and ill will it be if we fall asunder in heart, though we be nigh in body."

She laughed and reddened therewithal; and then her countenance fell and she looked piteously on him and said: "If I seemed to thee as thou sayest, I am sorry; for I meant not to be thus with thee as thou deemest. But so it is that I was thinking of this long journey, and of thee and me together in

350

it, and how we shall be with each other if we come back again alive, with all things done that we had to do."

She stayed her speech awhile, and seemed to find it hard to give forth the word that was in her; but at last she said: "Friend, thou must pardon me; but that which thou sawest in me, I also seemed to see in thee, that thou wert grown shy and cold with me; but now I know it is not so, since thou hast seen me wrongly; but that I have seen thee wrongly, as thou hast me."

Therewith she reached her hand to him, and he took it and kissed it and caressed it while she looked fondly at him, and they fared on sweetly and happily together. But as this was a-saying and a-doing betwixt them, and a while after, they had heeded the Elder little or not at all, though he rode on the right hand of Ralph. And for his part the old man said naught to them and made as if he heard them not, when they spake thuswise together.

Now they rode the wood on somewhat level ground for a while; then the trees began to thin, and the ground grew broken; and at last it was very rugged, with high hills and deep valleys, and all the land populous of wild beasts, so that about sunset they heard thrice the roar of a lion. But ever the Sage led them by winding ways that he knew, round the feet of the hills, along stream-sides for the most part, and by passes over the mountain-necks when they needs must, which was twice in the day.

Dusk fell on them in a little valley, through which ran a stream bushed about its edges, and which for the rest was grassy and pleasant, with big sweet-chestnut trees scattered about it.

"Now," quoth the Elder; "two things we have to beware of in this valley, the lions first; which, though belike they will not fall upon weaponed men, may well make an onslaught on your horses, if they wind them; and the loss of the beasts were sore to you as now. But the second thing is the chase from Utterbol. As to the lions, if ye build up a big fire, and keep somewhat aloof from the stream and its bushes, and tether you horses anigh the fire, ye will have no harm of them."

"Yea," said Ralph, "but if the riders of Utterbol are anigh us, shall we light a candle for them to show them the way?" Said the Sage: "Were ye by yourselves, I would bid you journey night-long, and run all risk rather than the risk of falling into their hands. But whereas I am your guide, I bid you kindle your fire under yonder big tree, and leave me to deal with the men of Utterbol; only whatso I bid you, that do ye straightway."

"So be it," said Ralph, "I have been bewrayed so oft of late, that I must needs trust thee, or all help shall fail me. Let us to work." So they fell to and built up a big bale and kindled it, and their horses they tethered to the tree; and by then they had done this, dark night had fallen upon them. So they cooked their victual at the fire (for Ralph had shot a hare by the way) and the Sage went down to the stream and fetched them water in a lethern budget: "For," said he, "I know the beasts of the wood and they me, and there is peace betwixt us." There then they sat to meat unarmed, for the Sage had said to them: "Doff your armour; ye shall not come to handystrokes with the Utterbol Riders."

So they ate their meat in the wilderness, and were nowise ungleeful, for to those twain the world seemed fair, and they hoped for great things. But though they were glad, they were weary enough, for the way had been both rugged and long; so they lay them down to sleep while the night was yet young. But or ever Ralph closed his eyes he saw the Sage standing up with his cloak wrapped about his head, and making strange signs with his right hand; so that he deemed that he would ward them by wizardry. So therewith he turned about on the grass and was asleep at once.

After a while he started and sat up, half awake at first; for he felt some one touch him; and his halfdreams went back to past days, and he cried out: "Hah Roger! is it thou? What is toward?" But therewith he woke up fully, and knew that it was the Sage that had touched him, and withal he saw hard by Ursula, sitting up also.

There was still a flickering flame playing about the red embers of their fire, for they had made it very big; and the moon had arisen and was shining bright in a cloudless sky.

The Sage spake softly but quickly: "Lie down together, ye two, and I shall cast my cloak over you, and look to it that ye stir not from out of it, nor speak one word till I bid you, whate'er may befall: for the riders of Utterbol are upon us."

They did as he bade them, but Ralph got somewhat of an eye-shot out of a corner of the cloak, and he could see that the Sage went and stood up against the tree-trunk holding a horse by the bridle, one on each side of him. Even therewith Ralph heard the clatter of horse-hoofs over the stones about the stream, and a man's voice cried out: "They will have heard us; so spur over the grass to the fire and the big tree: for then they cannot escape us." Then came the thump of horse-hoofs on the turf, and in half a minute they were amidst of a rout of men a-horseback, more than a score, whose armour and weapons gleamed in the moonlight: yet when these riders were gotten there, they were silent, till one said in a quavering voice as if afeard: "Otter, Otter! what is this? A minute ago and we could see the fire, and the tree, and men and horses about them: and now, lo you! there is naught save two great grey stones lying on the grass, and a man's bare bones leaning up against the tree, and a ruckle of old horse-bones on either side of him. Where are we then?"

Then spake another; and Ralph knew the voice for Otter's: "I wot not, lord; naught else is changed save the fire and the horses and the men: yonder are the hills, yonder overhead is the moon, with the little light cloud dogging her; even that is scarce changed. Belike the fire was an earth-fire, and for the rest we saw wrong in the moonlight."

Spake the first man again, and his voice quavered yet more: "Nay nay, Otter, it is not so. Lo you the skeleton and the bones and the grey stones! And the fire, here this minute, there the next. O Otter, this is an evil place of an evil deed! Let us go seek elsewhere; let us depart, lest a worse thing befall us." And so with no more ado he turned his horse and smote his spurs into him and galloped off by the way he had come, and the others followed, nothing loth; only Otter tarried a little, and looked around him and laughed and said: "There goes my Lord's nephew; like my Lord he is not over bold, save in dealing with a shackled man. Well, for my part if those others have sunk into the earth, or gone up into the air, they are welcome to their wizardry, and I am glad of it. For I know not how I should have done to have seen my mate that out-tilted me made a gelded wretch of; and it would have irked me to see that fair woman in the hands of the tormentors, though forsooth I have oft seen such sights. Well, it is good; but better were it to ride with my mate than serve the Devil and his Nephew."

Therewith he turned rein and galloped off after the others, and in a little while the sound of them had died off utterly into the night, and they heard but the voices of the wild things, and the wimbrel laughing from the hill-sides. Then came the Sage and drew the cloak from those two, and laughed on them and said: "Now may ye sleep soundly, when I have mended our fire; for ye will see no more of Utterbol for this time, and it yet lacks three hours of dawn: sleep ye then and dream of each other." Then they arose and thanked the Sage with whole hearts and praised his wisdom. But while the old man mended the fire Ralph went up to Ursula and took her hand, and said: "Welcome to life, fellow-farer!" and he gazed earnestly into her eyes, as though he would have her fall into his arms: but whereas she rather shrank from him, though she looked on him lovingly, if somewhat shyly, he but kissed her hand, and laid him down again, when he had seen her lying in her place. And therewith they fell asleep and slept sweetly.

CHAPTER 8
They Come to the Sea of Molten Rocks

When they woke again the sun was high above their heads, and they saw the Sage dighting their breakfast. So they arose and washed the night off them in the stream and ate hastily,

354

and got to horse on a fair forenoon; then they rode the mountain neck east from that valley; and it was a long slope of stony and barren mountain nigh waterless.

And on the way Ursula told Ralph how the man who was scared by the wizardry last night was verily the nephew of the Lord from whom she had stolen her armour by wheedling and a seeming promise. "But," said she, "his love lay not so deep but that he would have avenged him for my guile on my very body had he taken us." Ralph reddened and scowled at her word, and the Sage led them into the other talk.

So long was that fell, that they were nigh benighted ere they gained the topmost, or came to any pass. When they had come to a place where there was a little pool in a hollow of the rocks they made stay there, and slept safe, but ill-lodged, and on the morrow were on their way betimes, and went toiling up the neck another four hours, and came to a long rocky ridge or crest that ran athwart it; and when they had come to the brow thereof, then were they face to face with the Great Mountains, which now looked so huge that they seemed to fill all the world save the ground whereon they stood. Cloudless was the day, and the air clean and sweet, and every nook and cranny was clear to behold from where they stood: there were great jutting nesses with straight-walled burgs at their top-most, and pyramids and pinnacles that no hand of man had fashioned, and awful clefts like long streets in the city of the giants who wrought the world, and high above all the undying snow that looked as if the sky had come down on to the mountains and they were upholding it as a roof.

But clear as was the fashion of the mountains, they were yet a long way off: for betwixt them and the ridge whereon those fellows stood, stretched a vast plain, houseless and treeless, and, as they beheld it thence grey and ungrassed (though indeed it was not wholly so) like a huge river or firth of the sea it seemed, and such indeed it had been once, to wit a flood of molten rock in the old days when the earth was a-burning.

Now as they stood and beheld it, the Sage spake: "Lo ye, my children, the castle and its outwork, and its dyke that wardeth the land of the Well at the World's End. Now from to-morrow, when we enter into the great sea of the rock molten in the ancient earth-fires, there is no least peril of pursuit for you. Yet amidst that sea should ye perish belike, were it not for the wisdom gathered by a few; and they are dead now save for the Book, and for me, who read it unto you. Now ye would not turn back were I to bid you, and I will not bid you. Yet since the journey shall be yet with grievous toil and much peril, and shall try the very hearts within you, were ye as wise as Solomon and as mighty as Alexander, I will say this much unto you; that if ye love not the earth and the world with all your souls, and will not strive all ye may to be frank and happy therein, your toil and peril aforesaid shall win you no blessing but a curse. Therefore I bid you be no tyrants or builders of cities for merchants and usurers and warriors and thralls, like the fool who built Goldberg to be for a tomb to him: or like the thrall-masters of the Burg of the Four Friths, who even now, it may be, are pierced by their own staff or overwhelmed by their own wall. But rather I bid you to live in peace and patience without fear or hatred, and to succour the oppressed and love the lovely, and to be the friends of men, so that when ye are dead at last, men may say of you, they brought down Heaven to the Earth for a little while. What say ye, children?"

Then said Ralph: "Father, I will say the sooth about mine intent, though ye may deem it little-minded. When I have accomplished this quest, I would get me home again to the little land of Upmeads, to see my father and my mother, and to guard its meadows from waste and its houses from fire-raising: to hold war aloof and walk in free fields, and see my children growing up about me, and lie at last beside my fathers in the choir of St. Laurence. The dead would I love and remember; the living would I love and cherish; and Earth shall be the well beloved house of my Fathers, and Heaven the highest hall thereof."

"It is well," said the Sage, "all this shalt thou do and be no little-heart, though thou do no more. And thou, maiden?"

She looked on Ralph and said: "I lost, and then I found, and then I lost again. Maybe I shall find the lost once more. And for the rest, in all that this man will do, I will help, living or dead, for I know naught better to do."

"Again it is well," said the Sage, "and the lost which was verily thine shalt thou find again, and good days and their ending shall betide thee. Ye shall have no shame in your lives and no fear in your deaths. Wherefore now lieth the road free before you."

Then was he silent a while, neither spake the others aught, but stood gazing on the dark grey plain, and the blue wall that rose beyond it, till at last the Sage lifted up his hand and said: "Look yonder, children, to where I point, and ye shall see how there thrusteth out a ness from the mountain-wall, and the end of it stands like a bastion above the lava-sea, and on its sides and its head are streaks ruddy and tawny, where the earth-fires have burnt not so long ago: see ye?"

Ralph looked and said: "Yea, father, I see it, and its rifts and its ridges, and its crannies."

Quoth the Sage: "Behind that ness shall ye come to the Rock of the Fighting Man, which is the very Gate of the Mountains; and I will not turn again nor bid you farewell till I have brought you thither. And now time presses; for I would have you come timely to that cavern, whereof I have taught you, before ye fall on the first days of winter, or ye shall be hard bestead. So now we will eat a morsel, and then use diligence that we may reach the beginning of the rock-sea before nightfall."

So did they, and the Sage led them down by a slant-way from off the ridge, which was toilsome but nowise perilous. So about sunset they came down into the plain, and found a belt of greensward, and waters therein betwixt the foot of the ridge and the edge of the rock-sea. And as for the said sea, though from afar it looked plain and unbroken, now that they were close to, and on a level with it, they saw that it rose up into cliffs, broken down in some places, and in others arising high into the air, an hundred foot, it might be. Sometimes it thrust out into the green shore below the fell, and otherwhile drew back from it as it had cooled ages ago.

So they came to a place where there was a high wall of rock round three sides of a grassy place by a stream-side, and there they made their resting-place, and the night went calmly and sweetly with them.

CHAPTER 9

They Come Forth From the Rock-Sea

On the morrow the Sage led them straight into the rock-sea whereas it seemed to them at first that he was but bringing them into a blind alley; but at the end of the bight the rock-wall was broken down into a long scree of black stones. There the Sage bade Ralph and Ursula dismount (as for him he had been going afoot ever since that first day) and they led the horses up the said scree, which was a hard business, as they were no mountain beasts. And when they were atop of the scree it was harder yet to get them down, for on that side it was steeper; but at last they brought it about, and came down into a little grassy plain or isle in the rock sea, which narrowed toward the eastern end, and the rocks on either side were smooth and glossy, as if the heat had gone out of them suddenly, when the earth-fires had ceased in the mountains.

Now the Sage showed them on a certain rock a sign cut, whereof they had learned in the book aforesaid, to wit, a sword crossed by a three-leaved bough; and they knew by the book that they should press on through the rock-sea nowhere, either going or returning, save where they should see this token.

Now when they came to the narrow end of the plain they found still a wide way between the rock-walls, that whiles widened out, and whiles drew in again. Whiles withal were screes across the path, and little waters that ran out of the

358

lava and into it again, and great blocks of fallen stone, sometimes as big as a husbandman's cot, that wind and weather had rent from the rocks; and all these things stayed them somewhat. But they went on merrily, albeit their road winded so much, that the Sage told them, when evening was, that for their diligence they had but come a few short miles as the crow flies.

Many wild things there were, both beast and fowl, in these islands and bridges of the rock-sea, hares and conies to wit, a many, and heathfowl, and here and there a red fox lurking about the crannies of the rock-wall. Ralph shot a brace of conies with his Turk bow, and whereas there were bushes growing in the chinks, and no lack of whin and ling, they had firing enough, and supped off this venison of the rocks.

So passed that day and two days more, and naught befell, save that on the midnight of the first day of their wending the rock-sea, Ralph awoke and saw the sky all ablaze with other light than that of the moon; so he arose and went hastily to the Sage, and took him by the shoulder, and bid him awake; "For meseems the sky is afire, and perchance the foe is upon us."

The Sage awoke and opened his eyes, and rose on his elbow and looked around sleepily; then he said laughing: "It is naught, fair lord, thou mayst lie down and sleep out the remnant of the night, and thou also, maiden: this is but an earth-fire breaking out on the flank of the mountains; it may be far away hence. Now ye see that he may not scale the rocks about us here without toil; but to-morrow night we may climb up somewhere and look on what is toward."

So Ralph lay down and Ursula also, but Ralph lay long awake watching the light above him, which grew fiercer and redder in the hours betwixt moonset and daybreak, when he fell asleep, and woke not again till the sun was high.

But on the next day as they went, the aspect of the rock-sea about them changed: for the rocks were not so smooth and shining and orderly, but rose up in confused heaps all clotted together by the burning, like to clinkers out of some monstrous forge of the earth-giants, so that their way was naught so clear as it had been, but was rather a maze of jagged stone. But the Sage led through it all untumbling, and moreover now and again they came on that carven token of the sword and the bough. Night fell, and as it grew dark they saw the glaring of the earth-fires again; and when they were rested, and had done their meat, the Sage said: "Come now with me, for hard by is there a place as it were a stair that goeth to the top of a great rock, let us climb it and look about us."

So did they, and the head of the rock was higher than the main face of the rock-sea, so that they could see afar. Thence they looked north and beheld afar off a very pillar of fire rising up from a ness of the mountain wall, and seeming as if it bore up a black roof of smoke; and the huge wall gleamed grey, because of its light, and it cast a ray of light across the rock-sea as the moon doth over the waters of the deep: withal there was the noise as of thunder in the air, but afar off: which thunder indeed they had heard oft, as they rode through the afternoon and evening.

Spake the Sage: "It is far away: yet if the wind were not blowing from us, we had smelt the smoke, and the sky had been darkened by it. Now it is naught so far from Utterbol, and it will be for a token to them there. For that ness is called the Candle of the Giants, and men deem that the kindling thereof forebodeth ill to the lord who sitteth on the throne in the red hall of Utterbol."

Ralph laid his hand on Ursula's shoulder and said: "May the Sage's saw be sooth!"

She put her hand upon the hand and said: "Three months ago I lay on my bed at Bourton Abbas, and all the while here was this huge manless waste lying under the bare heavens and threatened by the storehouse of the fires of the earth: and I had not seen it, nor thee either, O friend; and now it hath become a part of me for ever."

Then was Ralph exceeding glad of her words, and the Sage laughed inwardly when he beheld them thus.

So they came adown from the rock and lay down presently under the fiery heavens: and their souls were comforted by the sound of the horses cropping the grass so close to their ears, that it broke the voice of the earth-fires' thunder, that ever and anon rolled over the grey sea amidst which they lay.

On the morrow they still rode the lava like to clinkers, and it rose higher about them, till suddenly nigh sunset it ended at a turn of their winding road, and naught lay betwixt them and that mighty ness of the mountains, save a wide grassy plain, here and there swelling into low wide risings not to be called hills, and besprinkled with copses of bushes, and with trees neither great nor high. Then spake the Sage: "Here now will we rest, and by my will to-morrow also, that your beasts may graze their fill of the sweet grass of these unwarded meadows. which feedeth many a herd unowned of man, albeit they pay a quit-rent to wild things that be mightier than they. And now, children, we have passed over the mighty river that once ran molten betwixt these mountains and the hills yonder to the west, which we trod the other day; yet once more, if your hearts fail you, there is yet time to turn back; and no harm shall befall you, but I will be your fellow all the way home to Swevenham if ye will. But if ye still crave the water of the Well at the World's End, I will lead you over this green plain, and then go back home to mine hermitage, and abide there till ye come to me, or I die."

Ralph smiled and said: "Master, no such sorry story shall I bear back to Upmeads, that after many sorrows borne, and perils overcome, I came to the Gates of the Mountains, and turned back for fear of that which I had not proved."

So spake he; but Ursula laughed and said: "Yea, then should I deem thy friendship light if thou leftest me alone and unholpen in the uttermost wilderness; and thy manhood light to turn back from that which did not make a woman afraid."

Then the Sage looked kindly on them and said: "Yea, then is the last word spoken, and the world may yet grow merrier to me. Look you, some there be who may abuse the gifts of the Well for evil errands, and some who may use it for good deeds; but I am one who hath not dared to use it lest I should abuse it, I being along amongst weaklings and fools: but now if ye come back, who knows but that I may fear no

361

longer, but use my life, and grow to be a mighty man. Come now, let us dight our supper, and kindle as big a fire as we lightly may; since there is many a prowling beast about, as bear and lynx and lion; for they haunt this edge of the rock-sea whereto the harts and the wild bulls and the goats resort for the sweet grass, and the water that floweth forth from the lava."

So they cut good store of firing, whereas there was a plenty of bushes growing in the clefts of the rocks, and they made a big fire and tethered their horses anigh it when they lay down to rest; and in the night they heard the roaring of wild things round about them, and more than once or twice, awakening before day, they saw the shape of some terrible creature by the light of the moon mingled with the glare of the earth-fires, but none of these meddled with them, and naught befell them save the coming of the new day.

CHAPTER 10
They Come to the Gate of the Mountains

That day they herded their horses thereabout, and from time to time the Sage tried those two if they were perfect in the lore of the road; and he found that they had missed nothing.

They lay down in the self-same place again that night, and arose betimes on the morrow and went their ways over the plain as the Sage led, till it was as if the mountains and their terror hung over their very heads, and the hugeness and blackness of them were worse than a wall of fire had been. It was still a long way to them, so that it was not till noon of the third day from the rock-sea that they came to the very feet of that fire-scorched ness, and wonderful indeed it seemed to them that anything save the eagles could have aught to tell of what lay beyond it.

There were no foothills or downs betwixt the plain and the mountains, naught save a tumble of rocks that had fallen from the cliffs, piled up strangely, and making a maze through which the Sage led them surely; and at last they were clear even of this, and were underneath the flank of that ness, which was so huge that themseemed that there could scarce be any more mountain than that. Little of its huge height could they see, now they were close to it, for it went up sheer at first and then beetled over them till they could see no more of its side; as they wound about its flank, and they were long about it, the Sage cried out to those two and stretched out his hand, and behold! the side of the black cliff plain and smooth and shining as if it had been done by the hand of men or giants, and on this smooth space was carven in the living rock the image of a warrior in mail and helm of ancient fashion, and holding a sword in his right hand. From head to heel he seemed some sixty feet high, and the rock was so hard, that he was all clean and clear to see; and they deemed of him that his face was keen and stern of aspect.

So there they stood in an awful bight of the mountain, made by that ness, and the main wall from which it thrust out. But after they had gazed awhile and their hearts were in their mouths, the Sage turned on those twain and said: "Here then is the end of my journey with you; and ye wot all that I can tell you, and I can say no word more save to bid you cast all fear aside and thrive. Ye have yet for this day's journey certain hours of such daylight as the mountain pass will give you, which at the best is little better than twilight; therefore redeem ye the time."

But Ralph got off his horse, and Ursula did in likewise, and they both kissed and embraced the old man, for their hearts were full and fain. But he drew himself away from them, and turned about with no word more, and went his ways, and presently was hidden from their eyes by the rocky maze which lay about the mountain's foot. Then the twain mounted their horses again and set forth silently on the road, as they had been bidden.

In a little while the rocks of the pass closed about them, leaving but a way so narrow that they could see a glimmer of the stars above them as they rode the twilight; no sight they had of the measureless stony desert, yet in their hearts they saw it. They seemed to be wending a straight-walled prison without an end, so that they were glad when the dark night came on them.

Ralph found some shelter in the cleft of a rock above a mound where was little grass for the horses. He drew Ursula into it, and they sat down there on the stones together. So long they sat silent that a great gloom settled upon Ralph, and he scarce knew whether he were asleep or waking, alive or dead. But amidst of it fell a sweet voice on his ears, and familiar words asking him of what like were the fields of Upmeads, and the flowers; and of the fish of its water, and of the fashion of the building of his father's house; and of his brethren, and the mother that bore him. Then was it to him at first as if a sweet dream had come across the void of his gloom, and then at last the gloom and the dread and the deadness left him, and he knew that his friend and fellow was talking to him, and that he sat by her knee to knee, and the sweetness of her savoured in his nostrils as she leaned her face toward him, and he knew himself for what he was; and yet for memory of that past horror, and the sweetness of his friend and what not else, he fell a-weeping. But Ursula bestirred herself and brought out food from her wallet, and sat down beside him again, and he wiped the tears from his eyes and laughed, and chid himself for being as a child in the dark, and then they ate and drank together in that dusk nook of the wilderness. And now was he happy and his tongue was loosed, and he fell to telling her many things of Upmeads, and of the tale of his forefathers, and of his old loves and his friends, till life and death seemed to him as they had seemed of time past in the merry land of his birth. So there anon they fell asleep for weariness, and no dreams of terror beset their slumbers.

CHAPTER 11

They Come to the Vale of Sweet Chestnuts

When they went on their way next morning they found little change in the pass, and they rode the dread highway daylong, and it was still the same: so they rested a little before nightfall at a place where there was water running out of the rocks, but naught else for their avail. Ralph was merry and helpful and filled water from the runnel, and wrought what he might to make the lodging meet; and as they ate and rested he said to Ursula: "Last night it was thou that beguiled me of my gloom, yet thereafter till we slept it was my voice for the more part, and not thine, that was heard in the wilderness. Now to-night it shall be otherwise, and I will but ask a question of thee, and hearken to the sweetness of thy voice."

She laughed a little and very sweetly, and she said: "Forsooth, dear friend, I spoke to thee that I might hear thy voice for the more part, and not mine, that was heard in the desert; but when I heard thee, I deemed that the world was yet alive for us to come back to."

He was silent awhile, for his heart was pierced with the sweetness of her speech, and he had fain have spoken back as sweetly as a man might; yet he could not because he feared her somewhat, lest she should turn cold to him; therefore himseemed that he spoke roughly, as he said: "Nevertheless, my friend, I beseech thee to tell me of thine old home, even as last night I told thee of mine."

"Yea," she said, "with a good will." And straightway she fell to telling him of her ways when she was little, and of her father and mother, and of her sister that had died, and the brother whom Ralph had seen at Bourton Abbas: she told also of bachelors who had wooed her, and jested concerning them, yet kindly and without malice, and talked so sweetly and plainly, that the wilderness was become a familiar place to Ralph, and he took her hand in the dusk and said: "But, my friend, how was it with the man for whom thou wert weeping when I first fell in with thee at Bourton Abbas?"

She said: "I will tell thee plainly, as a friend may to a friend. Three hours had not worn from thy departure ere tidings came to me concerning him, that neither death nor wounding had befallen him; and that his masterless horse and bloodstained saddle were but a device to throw dust into our eyes, so that there might be no chase after him by the men of the Abbot's bailiff, and that he might lightly do as he would to wit, swear himself into the riders of the Burg of the Four Friths; for, in sooth, he was weary of me and mine. Yet further, I must needs tell thee that I know now, that when I wept before thee it was partly in despite, because I had found out in my heart (though I bade it not tell me so much) that I loved him but little."

"Yea," said Ralph, "and when didst thou come to that knowledge of thine heart?"

"Dear friend," she said, "mayhappen I may tell thee hereafter, but as now I will forbear." He laughed for joy of her, and in a little that talk fell down between them.

Despite the terror of the desert and the lonely ways, when Ralph laid him down on his stony bed, happiness wrapped his heart about. Albeit all this while he durst not kiss or caress her, save very measurely, for he deemed that she would not suffer it; nor as yet would he ask her wherefore, though he had it in his mind that he would not always forbear to ask her.

Many days they rode that pass of the mountains, though it was not always so evil and dreadful as at the first beginning: for now again the pass opened out into little valleys, wherein was foison of grass and sweet waters withal, and a few trees. In such places must they needs rest them, to refresh their horses as well as themselves, and to gather food, of venison, and wild-fruit and nuts. But abiding in such vales was very pleasant to them.

At last these said valleys came often and oftener, till it was so that all was pretty much one valley, whiles broken by a mountain neck, whiles straitened by a ness of the mountains that jutted into it, but never quite blind: yet was the said valley very high up, and as it were a trench of the great mountain. So they were glad that they had escaped from that strait prison betwixt the rock-walls, and were well at ease: and they failed never to find the tokens that led them on the way, even as they had learned of the Sage, so that they were not beguiled into any straying.

And now they had worn away thirty days since they had parted from the Sage, and the days began to shorten and the nights to lengthen apace; when on the forenoon of a day, after they had ridden a very rugged mountain-neck, they came down and down into a much wider valley into which a great reef of rocks thrust out from the high mountain, so that the northern half of the said vale was nigh cleft atwain by it; well grassed was the vale, and a fair river ran through it, and there were on either side the water great groves of tall and great sweet-chestnuts and walnut trees, whereon the nuts were now ripe. They rejoiced as they rode into it; for they remembered how the Sage had told them thereof, that their travel and toil should be stayed there awhile, and that there they should winter, because of the bread which they could make them of the chestnuts, and the plenty of walnuts, and that withal there was foison of vension.

So they found a ford of the river and crossed it, and went straight to the head of the rocky ness, being shown thither by the lore of the Sage, and they found in the face of the rock the mouth of a cavern, and beside it the token of the sword and the branch. Therefore they knew that they had come to their winter house, and they rejoiced thereat, and without more ado they got off their horses and went into the cavern. The entry thereof was low, so that they must needs creep into it, but within it was a rock-hall, high, clean and sweet-smelling.

There then they dight their dwelling, doing all they might to be done with their work before the winter was upon them. The day after they had come there they fell to on the ingathering of their chestnut harvest, and they dried them, and made them into meal; and the walnuts they gathered also. Withal they hunted the deer, both great and small; amongst which Ralph, not without some peril, slew two great bears, of which beasts, indeed, there was somewhat more than enough, as they came into the dale to feed upon the nuts and the berry-trees. So they soon had good store of peltries for their beds and their winter raiment, which Ursula fell to work on deftly, for she knew all the craft of needlework; and, shortly to tell it, they had enough and to spare of victual and raiment.

CHAPTER 12

Winter Amidst of the Mountains

In all this they had enough to be busy with, so that time hung not heavy on their hands, and the shadow of the Quest was nowise burdensome to them, since they wotted that they had to abide the wearing of the days till spring was come with fresh tidings. Their labour was nowise irksome to them, since Ralph was deft in all manner of sports and crafts, such as up-country folk follow, and though he were a king's son, he had made a doughty yeoman: and as for Ursula, she also was country-bred, of a lineage of field-folk, and knew all the manners of the fields.

Withal in whatsoever way it were, they loved each other dearly, and all kind of speech flowed freely betwixt them. Sooth to say, Ralph, taking heed of Ursula, deemed that she were fain to love him bodily, and he wotted well by now, that, whatever had befallen, he loved her, body and soul. Yet still was that fear of her naysay lurking in his heart, if he should kiss her, or caress her, as a man with a maid. Therefore he forbore, though desire of her tormented him grievously at whiles.

They wore their armour but little now, save when they were about some journey wherein was peril of wild beasts. Ursula had dight her some due woman's raiment betwixt her knight's surcoat and doe-skins which they had gotten, so that it was not unseemly of fashion. As for their horses, they but seldom backed them, but used them to draw stuff to their rock-house on sledges, which they made of tree-boughs; so that the beasts grew fat, feeding on the grass of the valley and the wild-oats withal, which grew at the upper end of the bight of the valley, toward the northern mountains, where the ground was sandy. No man they saw, nor any signs of man, no had they seen any save the Sage, since those riders of Utterbol had vanished before them into the night.

So wore autumn into winter, and the frost came, and the snow, with prodigious winds from out of the mountains: yet was not the weather so hard but that they might go forth most days, and come to no hurt if they were wary of the drifts; and forsooth needs must they go abroad to take venison for their livelihood.

So the winter wore also amidst sweet speech and friendliness betwixt the two, and they lived still as dear friends, and not as lovers.

Seldom they spoke of the Quest, for it seemed to them now a matter over great for speech. But now they were grown so familiar each to each that Ursula took heart to tell Ralph more of the tidings of Utterbol, for now the shame and grief of her bondage there was but as a story told of another, so far away seemed that time from this. But so grievous was her tale that Ralph grew grim thereover, and he said: "By St. Nicholas! it were a good deed, once we are past the mountains again, to ride to Utterbol and drag that swine and wittol from his hall and slay him, and give his folk a good day. But then there is thou, my friend, and how shall I draw thee into deadly strife?"

"Nay," she said, "whereso thou ridest thither will I, and one fate shall lie on us both. We will think thereof and ask the Sage of it when we return. Who knows what shall have

befallen then? Remember the lighting of the candle of Utterbol that we saw from the Rock-sea, and the boding thereof."
So Ralph was appeased for that time.

Oft also they spake of the little lands whence they came, and on a time amidst of such talk Ursula said: "But alas, friend, why do I speak of all this, when now save for my brother, who loveth me but after a fashion, to wit that I must in all wise do his bidding, lad as he is, I have no longer kith nor kin there, save again as all the folk of one stead are somewhat akin. I think, my dear, that I have no country, nor any house to welcome me."

Said Ralph: "All lands, any land that thou mayst come to, shall welcome thee, and I shall look to it that so it shall be." And in his heart he thought of the welcome of Upmeads, and of Ursula sitting on the dais of the hall of the High-House.

So wore the days till Candlemass, when the frost broke and the snows began to melt, and the waters came down from the mountains, so that the river rose over its banks and its waters covered the plain parts of the valley, and those two could go dryshod but a little way out of their cavern; no further than the green mound or toft which lay at the mouth thereof: but the waters were thronged with fowl, as mallard and teal and coots, and of these they took what they would. Whiles also they waded the shallows of the flood, and whiles poled a raft about it, and so had pleasure of the waters as before they had had of the snow. But when at last the very spring was come, and the grass began to grow after the showers had washed the plain of the waterborne mud, and the snowdrop had thrust up and blossomed, and the celandine had come, and then when the blackthorn bloomed and the Lent-lilies hid the grass betwixt the great chestnut-boles, when the sun shone betwixt the showers and the west wind blew, and the throstles and blackbirds ceased not their song betwixt dawn and dusk, then began Ralph to say to himself, that even if the Well at the World's End were not, and all that the Sage had told them was but a tale of Swevenham, yet were all better than well if Ursula were but to him a woman beloved rather than a friend. And whiles he was pensive and silent, even when she was by him, and she noted it and forbore somewhat the sweetness of her glances, and the caressing of her soft speech: though oft when he looked on her fondly, the blood would rise to her cheeks, and her bosom would heave with the thought of his desire, which quickened hers so sorely, that it became a pain and grief to her.

CHAPTER 13
Of Ursula and the Bear

It befell on a fair sunny morning of spring, that Ralph sat alone on the toft by the rock-house, for Ursula had gone down the meadow to disport her and to bathe in the river. Ralph was fitting the blade of a dagger to a long ashen shaft, to make him a strong spear; for with the waxing spring the bears were often in the meadows again; and the day before they had come across a family of the beasts in the sandy bight under the mountains; to wit a carle, and a quean with her cubs; the beasts had seen them but afar off, and whereas the men were two and the sun shone back from their weapons, they had forborne them; although they were fierce and proud in those wastes, and could not away with creatures that were not of their kind. So because of this Ralph had bidden Ursula not to fare abroad without her sword, which was sharp and strong, and she no weakling withal. He bethought him of this just as he had made an end of his spear-shaping, so therewith he looked aside and saw the said sword hanging to a bough of a little quicken-tree, which grew hard by the door. Fear came into his heart therewith, so he arose and strode down over the meadow hastily bearing his new spear, and girt with his sword. Now there was a grove of chestnuts betwixt him and the river, but on the other side of them naught but the green grass down to the water's edge.

Sure enough as he came under the trees he heard a shrill cry, and knew that it could be naught save Ursula; so he ran thitherward whence came the cry, shouting as he ran, and was scarce come out of the trees ere he saw Ursula indeed mother-naked, held in chase by a huge bear as big as a bullock: he shouted again and ran the faster; but even therewith whether she heard and saw him, and hoped for timely help, or whether she felt her legs failing her, she turned on the bear, and Ralph saw that she had a little axe in her hand wherewith she smote hardily at the beast; but he, after the fashion of his kind, having risen to his hind legs, fenced with his great paws like a boxer, and smote the axe out of her hand, and she cried out bitterly and swerved from him and fell a running again; but the bear tarried not, and would have caught her in a few turns; but even therewith was Ralph come up, who thrust the beast into the side with his long-headed spear, and not waiting to pull it out again, drew sword in a twinkling, and smote a fore-paw off him and then drave the sword in over the shoulder so happily that it reached his heart, and he fell over dead with a mighty thump.

Then Ralph looked around for Ursula; but she had already run back to the river-side and was casting her raiment on her; so he awaited her beside the slain bear, but with drawn sword, lest the other bear should come upon them; for this was the he-bear. Howbeit he saw naught save presently Ursula all clad and coming towards him speedily; so he turned toward her, and when they met he cast himself upon her without a word, and kissed her greedily; and she forbore not at all, but kissed and caressed him as if she could never be satisfied.

So at last they drew apart a little, and walked quietly toward the rock-house hand in hand. And on the way she told him that even as she came up on to the bank from the water she saw the bear coming down on her as fast as he could drive, and so she but caught up her axe, and ran for it: "Yet I had little hope, dear friend," she said, "but that thou shouldst be left alone in the wilderness." And therewith she turned on him and cast her arms about him again, all weeping for joy of their two lives.

Thus slowly they came before the door of their rock-house

and Ralph said: "Let us sit down here on the grass, and if thou art not over wearied with the flight and the battle, I will ask thee a question." She laid herself down on the grass with a sigh, yet it was as of one who sighs for pleasure and rest, and said, as he sat down beside her: "I am fain to rest my limbs and my body, but my heart is at rest; so ask on, dear friend."

The song of birds was all around them, and the scent of many blossoms went past on the wings of the west wind, and Ralph was silent a little as he looked at the loveliness of his friend; then he said: "This is the question; of what kind are thy kisses this morning, are they the kisses of a friend or a lover? Wilt thou not called me beloved and not friend? Shall not we two lie on the bridal bed this same night?"

She looked on him steadily, smiling, but for love and sweetness, not for shame and folly; then she said: "O, dear friend and dearest lover, three questions are these and not one; but I will answer all three as my heart biddeth me. And first, I will tell thee that my kisses are as thine; and if thine are aught but the kisses of love, then am I befooled. And next, I say that if thou wilt be my friend indeed, I will not spare to call thee beloved, or to be all thy friend. But as to thy third question; tell me, is there not time enough for that?"

She faltered as she spake, but he said: "Look, beloved, and see how fair the earth is to-day! What place and what season can be goodlier than this? And were it not well that we who love each other should have our full joy out of this sweet season, which as now is somewhat marred by our desire?"

"Ah, beloved!" she said, looking shyly at him, "is it so marred by that which marreth not us?"

"Hearken!" he said; "how much longer shall this fairness and peace, and our leisure and safety endure? Here and now the earth rejoiceth about us, and there is none to say us nay; but to-morrow it may all be otherwise. Bethink thee, dear, if but an hour ago the monster had slain thee, and rent thee ere we had lain in each other's arms!"

"Alas!" she said, "and had I lain in thine arms an hundred times, or an hundred times an hundred, should not the world be barren to me, wert thou gone from it, and that could never more be? But thou friend, thou well-beloved, fain were I to do thy will that thou mightest be the happier . . . and I withal. And if thou command it, be it so! Yet now should I tell thee all my thought, and it is on my mind, that for a many hundreds of years, yea, while our people were yet heathen, when a man should wed a maid all the folk knew of it, and were witnesses of the day and the hour thereof: now thou knowest that the time draws nigh when we may look for those messengers of the Innocent Folk, who come every spring to this cave to see if there be any whom they may speed on the way to the Well at the World's End. Therefore if thou wilt (and not otherwise) I would abide their coming if it be not over long delayed; so that there may be others to witness our wedding besides God, and those his creatures who dwell in the wilderness. Yet shall all be as thou wilt."

"How shall I not do after thy bidding?" said Ralph. "I will abide their coming: yet would that they were here to-day! And one thing I will pray of thee, that because of them thou wilt not forbear, or cause me to forbear, such kissing and caressing as is meet betwixt troth-plight lovers."

She laughed and said: "Nay, why should I torment thee . . . or me? We will not tarry for this." And therewith she took her arm about his neck and kissed him oft.

Then they said naught awhile, but sat listening happily to the song of the pairing birds. At last Ralph said: "What was it, beloved, that thou wert perchance to tell me concerning the thing that caused thine heart to see that thy betrothed, for whom thou wepst or seemedst to weep at the ale-house at Bourton Abbas, was of no avail to thee?"

She said: "It was the sight of thee; and I thought also how I might never be thine. For that I have sorrowed many a time since."

Said Ralph: "I am young and unmighty, yet lo! I heal thy sorrow as if I were an exceeding mighty man. And now I tell thee that I am minded to go back with thee to Upmeads straightway; for love will prevail."

"Nay," she said, "that word is but from the teeth outwards; for thou knowest, as I do, that the perils of the homeward road shall overcome us, despite of love, if we have not drunk of the Well at the World's End."

Again they were silent awhile, but anon she arose to her feet and said: "Now must I needs dight victual for us twain; but first" (and she smiled on him withal), "how is it that thou hast not asked me if the beast did me any hurt? Art thou grown careless of me, now the wedding is so nigh?"

He said: "Nay, but could I not see thee that thou wert not hurt? There was no mark of blood upon thee, nor any stain at all." Then she reddened, and said: "Ah, I forgot how keen-eyes thou art." And she stood silent a little while, as he looked on her and loved her sweetness. Then he said: "I am exceeding full of joy, but my body is uneasy; so I will now go and skin that troll who went so nigh to slay thee, and break up the carcase, if thou wilt promise to abide about the door of the house, and have thy sword and the spear ready to hand, and to don thine helm and hauberk to boot."

She laughed and said: "That were but strange attire for a cook-maid, Ralph, my friend; yet shall I do thy will, my lord and my love."

Then went Ralph into the cave, and brought forth the armour and did it on her, and kissed her, and so went his ways to the carcase of the bear, which lay some two furlongs from their dwelling; and when he came to the quarry he fell to work, and was some time about it, so huge as the beast was. Then he hung the skin and the carcase on a tree of the grove, and went down to the river and washed him, and then went lightly homewards.

CHAPTER 14

Now Come the Messengers of the Innocent Folk

But when he had come forth from the chestnut-grove, and could see the face of their house-rock clearly, he beheld new tidings; for there were folk before the door of the dwelling, and Ursula was standing amidst of them, for he could see the gleam of her armour; and with the men he could see also certain beasts of burden, and anon that these were oxen. So he hastened on to find what this might mean, and drew his sword as he went. But when he came up to the rock, he found there two young men and an elder, and they had with them five oxen, three for riding, and two sumpter beasts, laden: and Ursula and these men were talking together friendly; so that Ralph deemed that the new-comers must be the messengers of the Innocent Folk. They were goodly men all three, somewhat brown of skin, but well fashioned, and of smiling cheerful countenance, well knit, and tall. The elder had a long white beard, but his eye was bright, and his hand firm and smooth. They were all clad in white woollen raiment, and bore no armour, but each had an axe with a green stone blade, curiously tied to the heft, and each of the young men carried a strong bow and a quiver of arrows.

Ralph greeted the men, and bade them sit down on the toft and eat a morsel; they took his greeting kindly, and sat down, while Ursula went into the cave to fetch them matters for their victual, and there was already venison roasting at the fire on the toft, in the place where they were wont to cook their meat. So then came Ursula forth from the cave, and served the new-comers and Ralph of such things as she had, and they ate and drank together; and none said aught of their errand till they had done their meat, but they talked together pleasantly about the spring, and the blossoms of the plain and the mountain, and the wild things that dwelt thereabout.

But when the meal was over, the new-comers rose to their feet, and bowed before Ralph and Ursula, and the elder took up the word and said: "Ye fair people, have ye any errand in the wilderness, or are ye chance-comers who have strayed thus far, and know not how to return?"

"Father," said Ralph, "we have come a long way on an errand of life or death; for we seek the WELL at the WORLD'S END. And see ye the token thereof, the pair of beads which we bear, either of us, and the fashion whereof ye know."

Then the elder bowed to them again, and said: "It is well; then is this our errand with you, to be your way-leaders as far as the House of the Sorceress, where ye shall have other help. Will ye set out on the journey to-day? In one hour shall we be ready."

"Nay," said Ralph, "we will not depart till tomorrow morn, if it may be so. Therewith I bid you sit down and rest you, while ye hearken a word which I have to say to you."

So they sat down again, and Ralph arose and took Ursula by the hand, and stood with her before the elder, and said: "This maiden, who is my fellow-farer in the Quest, I desire to wed this same night, and she also desireth me: therefore I would have you as witnesses hereto. But first ye shall tell us if our wedding and the knowing each other carnally shall be to our hurt in the Quest; for if that be so, then shall we bridle our desires and perform our Quest in their despite."

The old man smiled upon them kindly, and said: "Nay, son, we hear not that it shall be the worse for you in any wise that ye shall become one flesh; and right joyful it is to us, not only that we have found folk who seek to the Well at the World's End, but also that there is such love as I perceive there is betwixt such goodly and holy folk as ye be. For hither we come year by year according to the behest that we made to the fairest woman of the world, when she came back to us from the Well at the World's End, and it is many and many a year ago since we found any seekers after the

Well dwelling here. Therefore have we the more joy in you
And we have brought hither matters good for you, a
raiment, and meal, and wine, on our sumpter-beasts; therefor
as ye have feasted us this morning, so shall we feast you thi
even. And if ye will, we shall build for you in the grov
yonder such a bower as we build for our own folk on th
night of the wedding."

Ralph yeasaid this, and thanked them. So then the elde
cried: "Up, my sons, and show your deftness to these dea
friends!" Then the young men arose, naught loth, and whe
they had hoppled their oxen and taken the burdens from of
them, they all went down the meadow together into th
chestnut grove, and they fell to and cut willow boughs, anc
such-like wood, and drave stakes and wove the twigs together; and Ralph and Ursula worked with them as they bade
and they were all very merry together: because for those two
wanderers it was a great delight to see the faces of th
children of men once more after so many months, and tc
hold converse with them; while for their part the young mer
marvelled at Ursula's beauty, and the pith and goodliness of
Ralph.

By then it was nigh evening they had made a very goodly
wattled bower, and roofed it with the skins that were in the
cave, and hung it about with garlands, and strewn flowers or
the floor thereof. And when all was done they went back tc
the toft before the rock-chamber, where the elder had
opened the loads, and had taken meal thence, and was
making cakes at the fire. And there was wine there in
well-hooped kegs, and wooden cups fairly carven, and
raiment of fine white wool for those twain, broidered in
strange but beauteous fashion with the feathers of bright-
hued birds.

So then were those twain arrayed for the bridal; and the
meat was dight and the cups filled, and they sat down on the
grassy toft a little before sunset, and feasted till the night was
come, and was grown all light with the moon; and then
Ralph rose up, and took Ursula's hand, and they stood before
the elder, and bade him and the young men bear witness that

378

they were wedded: then those twain kissed the newcomers and departed to their bridal bower hand in hand through the freshness of the night.

CHAPTER 15

They Come to the Land of the Innocent Folk

When it was morning they speedily gat them ready for the road, whereas they had little to take with them; so they departed joyously, howbeit both Ralph and Ursula felt rather love than loathing for their winter abode. The day was yet young when they went their ways. Their horses and all their gear were a great wonder to the young men, for they had seen no such beasts before: but the elder said that once in his young days he had led a man to the Well who was riding a horse and was clad in knightly array.

So they went by ways which were nowise dreadful, though they were void of men-folk, and in three days' time they were come out of the mountains, and in three more the said mountains were to behold but a cloud behind them, and the land was grown goodly, with fair valleys and little hills, though still they saw no men, and forsooth they went leisurely, for oxen are but slow-going nags. But when they were gone eight days from the Valley of Sweet-chestnuts, they came across a flock of uncouth-looking sheep on a green hill-side, and four folk shepherding them, two carles to wit, and two queans, like to their way-leaders, but scarce so goodly, and ruder of raiment. These men greeted them kindly, and yet with more worship than fellowship, and they marvelled exceedingly at their horses and weapons. Thence they passed on, and the next day came into a wide valley, well-grassed and watered, and wooded here and there; moreover there were cots scattered about it. There and thenceforth they met men a many, both carles and queans, and sheep and neat in plenty, and they passed by garths wherein the young corn was waxing, and vineyards on the hillsides, where the vines were beginning to grow green. The land seemed as goodly as might be, and all the folk they met were kind, if somewhat over reverent.

On the evening of that day they came into the town of that folk, which was but simple, wholly unfenced for war, and the houses but low, and not great. Yet was there naught of filth or famine, nor any poverty or misery; and the people were merry-faced and well-liking, and clad goodly after their fashion in white woollen cloth or frieze. All the people of the town were come forth to meet them, for runners had gone before them, and they stood on either side of the way murmuring greetings, and with their heads bent low in reverence.

Thus rode Ralph and Ursula up to the door of the Temple, or Mote-house, or Guest-house, for it was all these, a house great, and as fair as they knew how to make it. Before the door thereof were standing the elders of the Folk; and when they drew rein, the eldest and most reverend of these came forth and spake in a cheerful voice, yet solemnly: "Welcome and thrice welcome to the Seekers after length of days and happy times, and the loving-kindness of the Folks of the Earth!"

Then all the elders gathered about them, and bade them light down and be at rest amongst them, and they made much of them and brought them into the Mote-house, wherein were both women and men fair and stately, and the men took Ralph by the hand and the women Ursula, and brought them into chambers where they bathed them and did off their wayfaring raiment, and clad them in white woollen gowns of web exceeding fine, and fragrant withal. Then they crowned them with flowers, and led them back into the hall, whereas now was much folk gathered, and they set them down on a dais as though they had been kings, or rather gods; and when they beheld them there so fair and lovely, they cried out for joy of them, and bade them hail oft and oft.

There then were they feasted by that kind folk, and when

meat was done certain youths and maidens fell to singing songs very sweetly; and the words of the songs were simple and harmless, and concerning the fairness of the earth and the happy loves of the creatures that dwell therein.

Thereafter as the night aged, they were shown to a sleeping chamber, which albeit not richly decked, or plenished with precious things, was most dainty clean, and sweet smelling, and strewn with flowers, so that the night was sweet to them in a chamber of love.

CHAPTER 16

They Come to the House of the Sorceress

On the morrow the kind people delayed them little, though they sorrowed for their departure, and before noon were their old way-leaders ready for them; and the old man and his two grandsons (for such they were) were much honoured of the simple people for their way-leading of the Heavenly Folk; for so they called Ralph and Ursula. So they gat them to the way in suchlike guise as before, only they had with them five sumpter oxen instead of two; for the old man told them that not only was their way longer, but also they must needs pass through a terrible waste, wherein was naught for their avail, neither man, nor beast, nor herb. Even so they found it as he said; for after the first day's ride from the town they came to the edge of this same waste, and on the fourth day were deep in the heart of it: a desert it was, rather rocky and stony and sandy than mountainous, though they had hills to cross also: withal there was but little water there, and that foul and stinking. Long lasted this waste, and Ralph thought indeed that it had been hard to cross, had not their way-leaders been; therefore he made marks and signs by the wayside, and took note of the bearings of rocks and mounds against the day of return.

Twelve days they rode this waste, and on the thirteenth it began to mend somewhat, and there was a little grass, and sweet waters, and they saw ahead the swelling hills of a great woodland, albeit they had to struggle through marshland and low scrubby thicket for a day longer, or ever they got to the aforesaid trees, which at first were naught but pines; but these failed in a while, and they rode a grass waste nearly treeless, but somewhat well watered, where they gat them good store of venison. Thereafter they came on woods of oak and sweet-chestnut, with here and there a beech-wood.

Long and long they rode the woodland, but it was hard on May when they entered it, and it was pleasant therein, and what with one thing, what with another, they had abundant livelihood there. Yet was June at its full when at last they came within sight of the House of the Sorceress, on the hottest of a fair afternoon. And it was even as Ralph had seen it pictured in the arras of the hall of the Castle of Abundance; a little house built after the fashion of houses in his own land of the west; the thatch was trim, and the windows and doors were unbroken, and the garth was whole, and the goats feeding therein, and the wheat was tall and blossoming in the little closes, where as he had looked to see all broken down and wild, and as to the house, a mere grass-grown heap, or at the most a broken gable fast crumbling away.

Then waxed his heart sore with the memory of that passed time, and the sweetness of his short-lived love, though he refrained him all he might: yet forsooth Ursula looked on him anxiously, so much his face was changed by the thoughts of his heart.

But the elder of the way-leaders saw that he was moved, and deemed that he was wondering at that house so trim and orderly amidst the wildwood, so he said: "Here also do we after our behest to that marvellous and lovely Lady, that we suffer not this house to go to ruin: ever are some of our folk here, and every year about this season we send two or more to take the places of those who have dwelt in the House

382

year-long: so ever is there someone to keep all things trim. But as to strangers, I have never in my life seen any Seeker of the Well herein, save once, and that was an old hoar man like to me, save that he was feebler in all wise than I be."

Now Ralph heard him talking, yet noted his words but little; for it was with him as if all the grief of heart which he had penned back for so long a while swelled up within him and burst its bounds; and he turned toward Ursula and their eyes met, and she looked shy and anxious on him and he might no longer refrain himself, but put his hands to his face (for they had now drawn rein at the garth-gate) and brake out a weeping, and wept long for the friend whose feet had worn that path so often, and whose heart, though she were dead, had brought them thither for their thriving; and for love and sorrow of him Ursula wept also.

But the old man and his grandsons turned their heads away from his weeping, and got off their horses, and went up to the house-door, whereby were now standing a carle and a quean of their people. But Ralph slowly gat off his horse and stood by Ursula who was on the ground already, but would not touch her, for he was ashamed. But she looked on him kindly and said: "Dear friend, there is no need for shame; for though I be young, I know how grievous it is when the dead that we have loved come across our ways, and we may not speak to them, nor they to us. So I will but bid thee be comforted and abide in thy love for the living and the dead." His tears brake out again at that word, for he was but young, and for a while there was a lull in the strife that had beset his days. But after a little he looked up, and dashed the tears from his eyes and smiled on Ursula and said: "The tale she told me of this place, the sweetness of it came back upon me, and I might not forbear." She said: "O friend, thou art kind, and I love thee."

So then they joined hands and went through the garth together, and up to the door, where stood the wardens, who, when they saw them turning thither, came speedily down the path to them, and would have knelt in worship to them; but they would not suffer it, but embraced and kissed them, and thanked them many times for their welcome. The said wardens, both carle and quean, were goodly folk of middle age, stalwart, and kind of face.

So then they went into the house together, and entered into the self-same chamber, where of old the Lady of Abundance had sickened for fear of the Sorceress sitting naked at her spell-work.

Great joy they made together, and the wardens set meat and drink before the guests, and they ate and drank and were of good cheer. But the elder who had brought them from Chestnut-dale said: "Dear friends, I have told you that these two young men are my grand-children, and they are the sons of this man and woman whom ye see; for the man is my son. And so it is, that amongst us the care of the Quest of the Well at the World's End hath for long been the heritage of our blood, going with us from father to son. Therefore is it naught wonderful, though I have been sundry times at this house, and have learned about the place all that may be learned. For my father brought me hither when I was yet a boy; that time it was that I saw the last man of whom we know for sure that he drank of the Water of the Well, and he was that old hoar man like unto me, but, as I said, far weaker in all wise; but when he came back to us from the Well he was strong and stalwart, and a better man than I am now; and I heard him tell his name to my father, that he was called the Sage of Swevenham."

Ralph looked on Ursula and said: "Yea, father, and it was through him that we had our lore concerning the way hither; and it was he that bade us abide your coming in the rock-house of the Vale of Sweet-chestnuts."

"Then he is alive still," said the elder. Said Ralph: "Yea, and as fair and strong an old man as ye may lightly see." "Yea, yea," said the elder, "and yet fifty years ago his course seemed run."

Then said Ralph: "Tell me, father, have none of your own folk sought to the Well at the World's End?" "Nay, none," said the elder. Said Ralph: "That is strange, whereas ye are so nigh thereto, and have such abundant lore concerning the way."

"Son," said the elder, "true it is that the water of that Well shall cause a man to thrive in all ways, and to live through many generations of men, maybe, in honour and good-liking; but it may not keep any man alive for ever; for so have the Gods given us the gift of death lest we weary of life. Now our folk live well and hale, and without the sickness and pestilence, such as I have heard oft befall folk in other lands: even as I heard the Sage of Swevenham say, and I wondered at his words. Of strife and of war also we know naught: nor do we desire aught which we may not easily attain to. Therefore we live long, and we fear the Gods if we should strive to live longer, lest they should bring upon us war and sickness, and over-weening desire, and weariness of life. Moreover it is little that all of us should seek to the Well at the World's End; and those few that sought and drank should be stronger and wiser than the others, and should make themselves earthly gods, and, maybe, should torment the others of us and make their lives a very burden to be borne. Of such matters are there tales current amongst us that so it hath been of yore and in other lands; and ill it were if such times came back upon us."

Ralph hung his head and was silent; for the joy of the Quest seemed dying out as the old man's words dropped slowly from his mouth. But he smiled upon Ralph and went on: "But for you, guests, it is otherwise, for ye of the World beyond the Mountains are stronger and more godlike than we, as all tales tell; and ye wear away your lives desiring that which ye may scarce get; and ye set your hearts on high things, desiring to be masters of the very Gods. Therefore ye know sickness and sorrow, and oft ye die before your time, so that ye must depart and leave undone things which ye deem ye were born to do; which to all men is grievous. And because of all this ye desire healing and thriving, whether good come of it, or ill. Therefore ye do but right to seek to the Well at the World's End, that ye may the better accomplish that which behoveth you, and that ye may serve your fellows and deliver them from the thralldom of those that be strong and unwise and unkind, of whom we have heard strange tales."

Ralph reddened as he spake, and Ursula looked on him

385

anxiously, but that talk dropped for the present, and they fell to talking of lighter and more familiar matters.

Thereafter they wandered about the woods with the wardens and the way-leaders, and the elder brought them to the ancient altar in the wood whereon the Sorceress had offered up the goat; and the howe of the woman dight with the necklace of the Quest whom the Lady found dead in the snow; and the place nigh the house where the Sorceress used to torment her thrall that was afterwards the Lady of Abundance; yea, and they went further afield till they came to the Vale of Lore, and the Heath above it where they met, the King's Son and the Lady. All these and other places were now become as hallowed ground to the Innocent People, and to Ralph no less. In the house, moreover, was a fair ark wherein they kept matters which had belonged to the Lady, as her shoes and her smock, wrapped in goodly cloth amidst well-smelling herbs; and these things they worshipped as folk do with relics of the saints. In another ark also they showed the seekers a book wherein was written lore concerning the Well, and the way thereto. But of this book had the Sage forewarned Ralph and his mate, and had bidden them look to it that they should read in it, and no otherwhere than at that ancient altar in the wood, they two alone, and clad in suchlike gear as they wore when they hearkened to his reading by his hermitage. And so it was that they found the due raiment in the ark along with the book. Therefore day after day betimes in the morning they bore the said book to the altar and read therein, till they had learned much wisdom.

Thus they did for eight days, and on the ninth they rested and were merry with their hosts: but on the tenth day they mounted their horses and said farewell, and departed by the ways they had learned of, they two alone. And they had with them bread and meal, as much as they might bear, and water-skins moreover, that they might fill them at the last sweet water before they came to the waterless desert.

CHAPTER 17

They Come Through the
Woodland to the Thirsty Desert

So they ride their ways, and when they were come well into the wildwood past the house, and had spoken but few words to each other, Ralph put forth his hand, and stayed Ursula, and they gat off their horses under a great-limbed oak, and did off their armour, and sat down on the greensward there, and loved each other dearly, and wept for joy of their pain and travail and love. And afterwards, as they sat side by side leaning up against the great oak-bole, Ralph spake and said: "Now are we two once again all alone in the uttermost parts of the earth, and belike we are not very far from the Well at the World's End; and now I have bethought me that if we gain that which we seek for, and bear back our lives to our own people, the day may come when we are grown old, for as young as we may seem, that we shall be as lonely then as we are this hour, and that the folk round about us shall be to us as much and no more than these trees and the wild things that dwell amongst them."

She looked on him and laughed as one over-happy, and said: "Thou runnest forward swiftly to meet trouble, beloved! But I say that well will it be in those days if I love the folk then as well as now I love these trees and the wild things whose house they are."

And she rose up therewith and threw her arms about the oak-bole and kissed its ruggedness, while Ralph as he lay kissed the sleekness of her feet. And there came a robin hopping over the leaves anigh them, for in that wood most of the creatures, knowing not man, were tame to him, and feared the horses of those twain more than their riders. And now as Ursula knelt to embrace Ralph with one hand, she held out the other to the said robin who perched on her wrist, and sat there as a hooded falcon had done, and fell to whistling his sweet notes, as if he were a-talking to those new-comers: then Ursula gave him a song-reward of their broken meat, and he flew up and perched on her shoulder, and nestled up against her cheek, and she laughed happily and said: "Lo you, sweet, have not the wild things understood my words, and sent this fair messenger to foretell us all good?"

"It is good," said Ralph laughing, "yet the oak-tree hath not spoken yet, despite of all thy kissing: and lo there goes thy friend the robin, now thou hast no more meat to give him."

"He is flying towards the Well at the World's End," she said, "and biddeth us onward: let us to horse and hasten: for if thou wilt have the whole truth concerning my heart, it is this, that some chance-hap may yet take thee from me ere thou hast drunk of the waters of the Well."

"Yea," said Ralph, "and in the innermost of my heart lieth the fear that mayhappen there is no Well, and no healing in it if we find it, and that death, and the backward way may yet sunder us. This is the worst of my heart, and evil is my coward fear."

But she cast her arms about him and kissed and caressed him, and cried out: "Yea, then fair have been the days of our journeying, and fair this hour of the green oak! And bold and true thine heart that hath led thee thus far, and won thee thy desire of my love."

So then they armed them, and mounted their horses and set forward. They lived well while they were in the wood, but on the third day they came to where it thinned and at last died out into a stony waste like unto that which they had passed through before they came to the House of the Sorceress, save that this lay in ridges as the waves of a great sea; and these same ridges they were bidden to cross over at their highest, lest they should be bewildered in a maze of little hills and dales leading no whither.

So they entered on this desert, having filled their water-skins at a clear brook, whereat they rejoiced when they found that the face of the wilderness was covered with a salt

388

scurf, and that naught grew there save a sprinkling of small sage bushes.

Now on the second day of their riding this ugly waste, as they came up over the brow of one of these stony ridges, Ralph the far-sighted cried out suddenly: "Hold! for I see a man weaponed."

"Where is he?" quoth Ursula, "and what is he about?" Said Ralph: "He is up yonder on the swell of the next ridge, and by seeming is asleep leaning against a rock."

Then he bent the Turk bow and set an arrow on the string and they went on warily. When they were down at the foot of the ridge Ralph hailed the man with a lusty cry, but gat no answer of him; so they went on up the bent, till Ralph said: "Now I can see his face under his helm, and it is dark and the eyes are hollow: I will off horse and go up to him afoot, but do thou, beloved, sit still in thy saddle."

But when he had come nigher, he turned and cried out to her: "The man is dead, come anigh." So she went up to him and dismounted, and they both together stood over the man, who was lying up against a big stone like one at rest. How long he had lain there none knows but God; for in the saltness of the dry desert the flesh had dried on his bones without corrupting, and was as hardened leather. He was in full armour of a strange and ancient fashion, and his sword was girt to his side, neither was there any sign of a wound about him. Under a crag anigh him they found his horse, dead and dry like to himself; and a little way over the brow of the ridge another horse in like case; and close by him a woman whose raiment had not utterly perished, nor her hair; there were gold rings on her arms, and her shoes were done with gold: she had a knife stuck in her breast, with her hand still clutching the handle thereof; so that it seemed that she had herself given herself death.

Ralph and Ursula buried these two with the heaping of stones and went their ways; but some two miles thence they came upon another dead man-at-arms, and near him an old man unweaponed, and they heaped stones on them.

Thereabout night overtook them, and it was dark, so they lay down in the waste, and comforted each other, and slept two or three hours, but arose with the first glimmer of dawn, and mounted and rode forth onward, that they might the sooner be out of that deadly desert, for fear clung to their hearts.

This day, forsooth, they found so many dead folk, that they might not stay to bury them, lest they themselves should come to lie there lacking burial. So they made all the way they might, and rode on some hours by starlight after the night was come, for it was clear and cold. So that at last they were so utterly wearied that they lay down amongst those dead folk, and slept soundly.

On the morrow morn Ralph awoke and saw Ursula sleeping peacefully as he deemed, and he looked about on the dreary desert and its dead men and saw no end to it, though they lay on the top of one of those stony bents; and he said softly to himself: "Will it end at all then? Surely all this people of the days gone by were Seekers of the Well as we be; and have they belike turned back from somewhere further on, and might not escape the desert despite of all? Shall we turn now: shall we turn? surely we might get into the kindly wood from here."

So he spake; but Ursula sat up (for she was not asleep) and said: "The perils of the waste being abundant and exceeding hard to face, would not the Sage or his books have told us of the most deadly?" Said Ralph: "Yet here are all these dead, and we were not told of them, nevertheless we have seen the token on the rocks oft-times yesterday, so we are yet in the road, unless all this hath been but a snare and a betrayal."

She shook her head, and was silent a little; then she said: "Ralph, my lad, didst thou see this token (and she set hand to the beads about her neck) on any of those dead folk yesterday?" "Nay," said Ralph, "though sooth to say I looked for it." "And I in likewise," she said; "for indeed I had misgivings as the day grew old; but now I say, let us on in the faith of that token and the kindness of the Sage, and the love of the Innocent People; yea, and thy luck, O lad of the green fields far away, that hath brought thee unscathed so far from Upmeads."

390

So they mounted and rode forth, and saw more and more of the dead folk; and ever and anon they looked to them to note if they wore the beads like to them but saw none so dight. Then Ursula said: "Yea, why should the Sage and the books have told us aught of these dead bodies, that are but as the plenishing of the waste; like to the flowers that are cast down before the bier of a saint on a holy-day to be trodden under foot by the churls and the vicars of the close. Forsooth had they been alive now, with swords to smite withal, and hands to drag us into captivity, it had been another matter: but against these I feel bold."

Ralph sighed, and said: "Yea, but even if we die not in the waste, yet this is piteous; so many lives passed away, so many hopes slain."

"Yea," she said; "but do not folk die there in the world behind us? I have seen sights far worser than this at Utterbol, little while as I was there. Moreover I can note that this army of dead men has not come all in one day or one year, but in a long, long while, by one and two and three; for hast thou not noted that their raiment and wargear both, is of many fashions, and some much more perished than other, long as things last in this Dry Waste? I say that men die as in the world beyond, but here we see them as they lie dead, and have lain for so long."

He said: "I fear neither the Waste nor the dead men, if thou fearest not, beloved: but I lament for these poor souls."

"And I also," said she; "therefore let us on, that we may come to those whose grief we may heal."

CHAPTER 18

They Come to the Dry Tree

Presently as they rode they had before them one of the greatest of those land-waves, and they climbed it slowly, going afoot and leading their horses; but when they were but a little way from the brow they saw, over a gap thereof, something, as it were huge horns rising up into the air beyond the crest of the ridge. So they marvelled, and drew their swords, and held them still awhile, misdoubting if this were perchance some terrible monster of the waste; but whereas the thing moved not at all, they plucked up heart and fared on.

So came they to the brow and looked over it into a valley, about which on all sides went the ridge, save where it was broken down into a narrow pass on the further side, so that the said valley was like to one of those theatres of the ancient Roman Folk, whereof are some to be seen in certain lands. Neither did those desert benches lack their sitters; for all down the sides of the valley sat or lay children of men; some women, but most men-folk, of whom the more part were weaponed, and some with their drawn swords in their hands. Whatever semblance of moving was in them was when the eddying wind of the valley stirred the rags of their raiment, or the long hair of the women. But a very midmost of this dreary theatre rose up a huge and monstrous tree, whose topmost branches were even the horns which they had seen from below the hill's brow. Leafless was that tree and lacking of twigs, and its bole upheld but some fifty of great limbs, and as they looked on it, they doubted whether it were not made by men's hands rather than grown up out of the earth. All round about the roots of it was a pool of clear water, that cast back the image of the valley-side and the bright sky of the desert, as though it had been a mirror of burnished steel. The limbs of that tree were all behung with blazoned shields and knight's helms, and swords, and spears, and axes, and hauberks; and it rose up into the air some hundred feet above the flat of the valley.

For a while they looked down silently on to this marvel, then from both their lips at once came the cry THE DRY TREE. Then Ralph thrust his sword back into his sheath and said: "Meseems I must needs go down amongst them; there is naught to do us harm here; for all these are dead like the others that we saw."

Ursula turned to him with burning cheeks and sparkling eyes, and said eagerly: "Yea, yea, let us go down, else might we chance to miss something that we ought to wot of."

Therewith she also sheathed her sword, and they went both of them down together, and that easily; for as aforesaid the slope was as if it had been cut into steps for their feet. And as they passed by the dead folk, for whom they had often to turn aside, they noted that each of the dead leathery faces was drawn up in a grin, as though they had died in pain, and yet beguiled, so that all those visages looked somewhat alike, as though they had come from the workshop of one craftsman.

At last Ralph and Ursula stood on the level ground underneath the Tree, and they looked up at the branches, and down to the water at their feet; and now it seemed to them as though the Tree had verily growth in it, for they beheld its roots, that they went out from the mound or islet of earth into the water, and spread abroad therein, and seemed to waver about. So they walked around the Tree, and looked up at the shields that hung on its branches, but saw no blazon that they knew, though they were many and diverse; and the armour also and weapons were very diverse of fashion.

Now when they were come back again to the place where they had first stayed, Ralph said: "I thirst, and so belike dost thou; and here is water good and clear; let us drink then, and so spare our water-skins, for belike the dry desert is yet long." And therewith he knelt down that he might take of the water in the hollow of his hand. But Ursula drew him back, and cried out in terror: "O Ralph, do it not! Seest thou not this water, that although it be bright and clear, so that we may see all the pebbles at the bottom, yet nevertheless when the wind eddies about, and lifts the skirts of our raiment, it makes no ripple on the face of the pool, and doubtless it is heavy with venom; and moreover there is no sign of the way hereabout, as at other watering-steads; O forbear, Ralph!"

Then he rose up and drew back with her but slowly and unwillingly as she deemed; and they stood together a while gazing on these marvels. But lo amidst of this while, there came a crow wheeling over the valley of the dead, and he croaked over the Dry Tree, and let himself drop down to the edge of the pool, whereby he stalked about a little after the manner of his kind. Then he thrust his neb into the water and drank, and thereafter took wing again; but ere he was many feet off the ground he gave a grievous croak, and turning over in the air fell down stark dead close to the feet of those twain; and Ralph cried out but spake no word with meaning therein; then said Ursula: "Yea, thus are we saved from present death." Then she looked in Ralph's face, and turned pale and said hastily: "O my friend how is it with thee?" But she waited not for an answer, but turned her face to the bent whereby they had come down, and cried out in a loud, shrill voice: "O Ralph, Ralph! look up yonder to the ridge whereby we left our horses; look, look! there glitters a spear and stirreth! and lo a helm underneath the spear: tarry not, let us save our horses!"

Then Ralph let a cry out from his mouth, and set off running to the side of the slope, and fell to climbing it with great strides, not heeding Ursula; but she followed close after, and scrambled up with foot and hand and knee, till she stood beside him on the top, and he looked around wildly and cried out: "Where! where are they?"

"Nowhere," she said, "it was naught but my word to draw

thee from death; but praise to the saints that thou are come alive out of the accursed valley."

He seemed not to hearken, but turned about once, and beat the air with his hands, and then fell down on his back; and with a great wail she cast herself upon him, for she deemed at first that he was dead. But she took a little water from one of their skins, and cast it into his face, and took a flask of cordial from her pouch, and set it to his lips, and made him drink somewhat thereof. So in a while he came to himself and opened his eyes and smiled upon her, and she took his head in her hands and kissed his cheek, and he sat up and said feebly: "Shall we not go down into the valley? there is naught there to harm us."

"We have been down there already," she said, "and well it is that we are not both lying there now."

Then he got to his feet, and stretched himself, and yawned like one just awakened from long sleep. But she said: "Let us to horse and begone; it is early hours to slumber, for those that are seeking the Well at the World's End."

He smiled on her again and took her hand, and she led him to his horse, and helped him till he was in the saddle, and lightly she gat a-horseback, and they rode away swiftly from that evil place; and after a while Ralph was himself again, and remembered all that had happened till he fell down on the brow of the ridge. Then he praised Ursula's wisdom and valiancy till she bade him forbear lest he weary her. Albeit she drew up close to him and kissed his face sweetly.

CHAPTER 19

They Come Out of the Thirsty Desert

Past the Valley of the Dry Tree they saw but few dead men lying about, and soon they saw never another: and, though the land was still utterly barren, and all cast up into ridges as before, yet the salt slime grew less and less, and before nightfall of that day they had done with it: and the next day those stony waves were lower; and the next again the waste was but a swelling plain, and here and there they came on patches of dwarf willow, and other harsh and scanty herbage, whereof the horses might have a bait, which they sore needed, for now was their fodder done: but both men and horses were sore athirst; for, as carefully as they had hoarded their water, there was now but little left, which they durst not drink till they were driven perforce, lest they should yet die of drought.

They journeyed long that day, and whereas the moon was up at night-tide they lay not down till she was set; and their resting place was by some low bushes, whereabout was rough grass mingled with willow-herb, whereby Ralph judged that they drew nigh to water, so or ever they slept, they and the horses all but emptied the water-skins. They heard some sort of beasts roaring in the night, but they were too weary to watch, and might not make a fire.

When Ralph awoke in the morning he cried out that he could see the woodland; and Ursula arose at his cry and looked where he pointed, and sure enough there were trees on a rising ground some two miles ahead, and beyond them, not very far by seeming, they beheld the tops of great dark mountains. On either hand moreover, nigh on their right hand, far off on their left, ran a reef of rocks, so that their way seemed to be as between two walls. And these said reefs were nowise like those that they had seen of late, but black and, as to their matter, like to the great mountains by the rock of the Fighting Man: but as the reefs ran eastward they seemed to grow higher.

Now they mounted their horses at once and rode on; and the beasts were as eager as they were, and belike smelt the water. So when they had ridden but three miles, they saw a fair little river before them winding about exceedingly, but flowing eastward on the whole. So they spurred on with light hearts and presently were on the banks of the said river, and its waters were crystal-clear, though its sands were black: and the pink-blossomed willow-herb was growing abundantly on the sandy shores. Close to the water was a black rock, as big as a man, whereon was graven the sign of the way; so they knew that there was no evil in the water, wherefore they drank their fill and watered their horses abundantly, and on the further bank was there abundance of good grass. So when they had drunk their fill, for the pleasure of the cool water they waded the ford barefoot, and it was scarce above Ursula's knee. Then they had great joy to lie on the soft grass and eat their meat, while the horses tore eagerly at the herbage close to them. So when they had eaten, they rested awhile, but before they went further they despoiled them, one after other, and bathed in a pool of the river to wash the foul wilderness off them. Then again they rested and let the horses yet bite the grass, and departed not from that pleasant place till it was two hours after noon. As they were lying there Ralph said he could hear a great roar like the sound of many waters, but very far off: but to Ursula it seemed naught but the wind waxing in the boughs of the woodland anigh them.

CHAPTER 20

They Come to the Ocean Sea

Being come to the wood they went not very far into it that day, for they were minded to rest them after the weariness of the wilderness: they feasted on a hare which Ralph shot, and made a big fire to keep off evil beasts, but none came nigh them, though they heard the voices of certain beasts as the night grew still. To be short, they slept far into the morrow's morn, and then, being refreshed, and their horses also, they rode strongly all day, and found the wood to be not very great; for before sunset they were come to its outskirts, and the mountains lay before them. These were but little like to that huge wall they had passed through on their way to Chestnut-dale, being rather great hills than mountains, grass-grown, and at their feet somewhat wooded, and by seeming not over hard to pass over.

The next day they entered them by a pass marked with the token, which led them about by a winding way till they were on the side of the biggest fell of all; so there they rested that night in a fair little hollow or dell in the mountain-side. There in the stillness of the night both Ursula, as well as Ralph, heard that roaring of a great water, and they said to each other that it must be the voice of the Sea, and they rejoiced thereat, for they had learned by the Sage and his books that they must needs come to the verge of the Ocean-Sea, which girdles the earth about. So they arose betimes on the morrow, and set to work to climb the mountain, going mostly a-foot; and the way was long, but not craggy or exceeding steep, so that in five hours' time they were at the mountain-top, and coming over the brow beheld beneath them fair green slopes besprinkled with trees, and beyond them, some three or four miles away, the blue landless sea, and on either hand of them was the sea also, so that they were nigh-hand at the ending of a great ness, and there was naught beyond it; and naught to do if they missed the Well, but to turn back by the way they had come.

Now when they saw this they were exceedingly moved, and they looked on one another, and each saw that the other was pale, with glistening eyes, since they were to come to the very point of their doom, and that it should be seen whether there were no such thing as the Well in all the earth, but that they had been chasing a fair-hued cloud; or else their Quest should be achieved and they should have the world before them, and they happy and mighty, and of great worship amidst all men.

Little they tarried, but gat them down the steep of the mountain, and so lower and lower till they were come to ground nigh level; and then at last it was but thus, that without any great rock-wall or girdle of marvellous and strange land, there was an end of earth, with its grass and trees and streams, and a beginning of the ocean, which stretched away changeless, and it might be for ever. Where the land ended there was but a cliff of less than an hundred feet above the eddying of the sea; and on the very point of the ness was a low green toft with a square stone set atop of it, whereon as they drew nigh they saw the token graven, yea on each face thereof.

Then they went along the edge of the cliff a mile on each side of the said toft, and then finding naught else to note, naught save the grass and the sea, they came back to that place of the token, and sat down on the grass of the toft.

It was now evening, and the sun was setting beyond them, but they could behold a kind of stair cut in the side of the cliff, and on the first step whereof was the token done; wherefore they knew that they were bidden to go down by the said stair; but it seemed to lead no whither, save straight into the sea. And whiles it came into Ralph's mind that this

was naught but a mock, as if to bid the hapless seekers cast
themselves down from the earth, and be done with it for
ever. But in any case they might not try the adventure of
that stair by the failing light, and with the night long before
them. So when they had hoppled their horses, and left them
to graze at their will on the sweet grass of the meadow, they
laid them down behind the green toft, and, being forwearied,
it was no long time ere they twain slept fast at the uttermost
end of the world.

CHAPTER 21

Now They Drink of the Well at the World's End

Ralph awoke from some foolish morning dream of
Upmeads, wondering where he was, or what familiar voice
had cried out his name: then he raised himself on his elbow,
and saw Ursula standing before him with flushed face and
sparkling eyes, and she was looking out seaward, while she
called on his name. So he sprang up and strove with the slumber that still hung about him, and as his eyes cleared he
looked down, and saw that the sea, which last night had
washed the face of the cliff, had now ebbed far out, and left
bare betwixt the billows and the cliff some half mile of black
sand, with rocks of the like hue rising out of it here and there.
But just below the place where they stood, right up against
the cliff, was builded by man's hand of huge stones a garth of
pound, the wall whereof was some seven feet high, and the
pound within the wall of forty feet space endlong and over-
thwart; and the said pound was filled with the waters of a
spring that came forth from the face of the cliff as they
deemed, though from above they might not see the issue

thereof; but the water ran seaward from the pound by some way unseen, and made a wide stream through the black sand of the foreshore: but ever the great basin filled somewhat faster than it voided, so that it ran over the lip on all sides, making a thin veil over the huge ashlar-stones of the garth. The day was bright and fair with no wind, save light airs playing about from the westward ort, and all things gleamed and glittered in the sun.

Ralph stood still a moment, and then stretched abroad his arms, and with a great sob cast them round about the body of his beloved, and strained her to his bosom as he murmured about her, THE WELL AT THE WORLD'S END. But she wept for joy as she fawned upon him, and let her hands beat upon his body.

But when they were somewhat calmed of their ecstasy of joy, they made ready to go down by that rocky stair. And first they did off their armour and other gear, and when they were naked they did on the hallowed raiment which they had out of the ark in the House of the Sorceress; and so clad gat them down the rock-hewn stair, Ralph going first, lest there should be any broken place; but naught was amiss with those hard black stones, and they came safely to a level place of the rock, whence they could see the face of the cliff, and how the waters of the Well came gushing forth from a hollow therein in a great swelling wave as clear as glass; and the sun glistened in it and made a foam-bow about its edges. But above the issue of the waters the black rock had been smoothed by man's art, and thereon was graven the Sword and the Bough, and above it these words, to wit:

YE WHO HAVE COME A LONG WAY TO LOOK UPON ME, DRINK OF ME, IF YE DEEM THAT YE BE STRONG ENOUGH IN DESIRE TO BEAR LENGTH OF DAYS: OR ELSE DRINK NOT; BUT TELL YOUR FRIENDS AND THE KINDREDS OF THE EARTH HOW YE HAVE SEEN A GREAT MARVEL.

So they looked long and wondered; and Ursula said: "Deemest thou, my friend, that any have come thus far and forborne to drink?"

Said Ralph: "Surely not even the exceeding wise might remember the bitterness of his wisdom as he stood here."

Then he looked on her and his face grew bright beyond measure, and cried out: "O love, love! why tarry we? For yet I fear lest we be come too late, and thou die before mine eyes ere yet thou hast drunken."

"Yea," she said, "and I also fear for thee, though thy face is ruddy and thine eyes sparkle, and thou art as lovely as the Captain of the Lord's hosts."

Then she laughed, and her laughter was as silver bells rung tunably, and she said: "But where is the cup for the drinking?"

But Ralph looked on the face of the wall, and about the height of his hand saw square marks thereon, as though there were an ambrye; and amidst the square was a knop of latten, all green with the weather and the salt spray. So Ralph set his hand to the knop and drew strongly, and lo it was a door made of a squared stone hung on brazen hinges, and it opened easily to him, and within was a cup of goldsmith's work, with the sword and the bough done thereon; and round about the rim writ this posey: "THE STRONG OF HEART SHALL DRINK FROM ME." So Ralph took it and held it aloft so that its pure metal flashed in the sun, and he said: "This is for thee, Sweetling."

"Yea, and for thee," she said.

Now that level place, or bench-table went up to the very gushing and green bow of the water, so Ralph took Ursula's hand and led her along, she going a little after him, till he was close to the Well, and stood amidst the spray-bow thereof, so that he looked verily like one of the painted angels on the choir wall of St. Laurence of Upmeads. Then he reached forth his hand and thrust the cup into the water, holding it stoutly because the gush of the stream was strong, so that the water of the Well splashed all over him, wetting Ursula's face and breast withal: and he felt that the water was sweet without any saltness of the sea. But he turned to Ursula and reached out the full cup to her, and said: "Sweetling, call a health over the cup!"

She took it and said: "To thy life, beloved!" and drank withal, and her eyes looked out of the cup the while, like a child's when he drinketh. Then she gave him the cup again and said: "Drink, and tarry not, lest thou die and I live."

Then Ralph plunged the cup into the waters again, and he held the cup aloft, and cried out: "To the Earth, and the World of Manfolk!" and therewith he drank.

For a minute then they clung together within the spray-bow of the Well, and then she took his hand and led him back to the midst of the bench-table, and he put the cup into the ambrye, and shut it up again, and then they sat them down on the widest of the platform under the shadow of a jutting rock; for the sun was hot; and therewithal a sweet weariness began to steal over them, though there was speech betwixt them for a little, and Ralph said: "How is it with thee, beloved?"

"O well indeed," she said.

Quoth he: "And how tasteth to thee the water of the Well?"

Slowly she spake and sleepily: "It tasted good, and as if thy love were blended with it."

And she smiled in his face; but he said: "One thing I wonder over: how shall we wot if we have drunk aright? For whereas if we were sick or old and failing, or ill-liking, and were now presently healed of all this, and become strong and fair to look on, then should we know it for sure—but now, though, as I look on thee, I behold thee the fairest of all women, and on thy face is no token of toil and travail, and the weariness of the way; and though the heart-ache of loneliness and captivity, and the shame of Utterbol has left no mark upon thee—yet hast thou not always been sweet to my eyes, and as sweet as might be? And how then?" . . . But he broke off and looked on her and she smiled upon the love in his eyes, and his head fell back and he slept with a calm and smiling face. And she leaned over him to kiss his face, but even therewith her own eyes closed and she laid her head upon his breast, and slept as peacefully as he.

CHAPTER 22

Now They Have Drunk and Are Glad

Long they slept till the shadows were falling from the west, and the sea was flowing fast again over the sands beneath them, though there was still a great space bare betwixt the cliff and the sea. Then spake Ursula as if Ralph had but just left speaking; and she said: "Yea, dear lord, and I also say, that, lovely as thou art now, never hast thou been aught else but lovely to me. But tell me, hast thou had any scar of a hurt upon thy body? For if now that were gone, surely it should be a token of the renewal of thy life. But if it be not gone, then there may yet be another token."

Then he stood upon his feet, and she cried out: "O but thou art fair and mighty, who now shall dare gainsay thee? Who shall not long for thee?"

Said Ralph: "Look, love! how the sea comes over the sand like the creeping of a sly wood-snake! Shall we go hence and turn from the ocean-sea without wetting our bodies in its waters?"

"Let us go," she said.

So they went down on to the level sands, and along the edges of the sweet-water stream that flowed from the Well; and Ralph said: "Beloved, I will tell thee of that which thou hast asked me: when I was but a lad of sixteen winters there rode men a-lifting into Upmeads, and Nicholas Long-shanks, who is a wise man of war, gathered force and went against them, and I must needs ride beside him. Now we came to our above, and put the thieves to the road; but in the hurly I got a claw from the war-beast, for the stroke of a

404

sword sheared me off somewhat from my shoulder: belike thou hast seen the scar and loathed it."

"It is naught loathsome," she said, "for a lad to be a bold warrior, nor for a grown man to think lightly of the memory of death drawn near for the first time. Yea, I have noted it; but let me see now what has befallen with it."

As she spoke they were come to a salt pool in a rocky bight on their right hand, which the tide was filling speedily; and Ralph spake: "See now, this is the bath of the water of the ocean sea." So they were speedily naked and playing in the water: and Ursula took Ralph by the arm and looked to his shoulder and said: "O my lad of the pale edges, where is gone thy glory? There is no mark of the sword's pilgrimage on thy shoulder." "Nay, none?" quoth he.

"None, none!" she said, "Didst thou say the very sooth of thy hurt in the battle, O poor lad of mine?" "Yea, the sooth," said he. Then she laughed sweetly and merrily like the chuckle of a flute over the rippling waters, that rose higher and higher about them, and she turned her eyes askance and looked adown to her own sleek side, and laid her hand on it and laughed again. Then said Ralph: "What is toward, beloved? For thy laugh is rather of joy that of mirth alone."

She said: "O smooth-skinned warrior, O Lily and Rose of battle; here on my side yesterday was the token of the hart's tyne that gored me when I was a young maiden five years ago: look now and pity the maiden that lay on the grass of the forest, and the woodman a-passing by deemed her dead five years ago."

Ralph stooped down as the ripple washed away from her, then said: "In sooth here is no mark nor blemish, but the best handiwork of God, as when he first made a woman from the side of the Ancient Father of the field of Damask. But lo you, love, how swift the tide cometh up, and I long to see thy feet on the green grass, and I fear the sea, lest it stir the joy over strongly in our hearts and we be not able to escape from its waves."

So they went up from out of the water, and did on the hallowed raiment fragrant with strange herbs, and passed joyfully up the sand towards the cliff and its stair; and speedily withal, for so soon as they were clad again, the little ripple of the sea was nigh touching their feet. As they went, they noted that the waters of the Well flowed seaward from the black-walled pound by three arched openings in its outer face, and they beheld the mason's work, how goodly it was; for it was as if it had been cut out of the foot of a mountain, so well jointed were its stones, and its walls solid against any storm that might drive against it.

They climbed the stair, and sat them down on the green grass awhile watching the ocean coming in over the sand and the rocks, and Ralph said: "I will tell thee, sweetling, that I am grown eager for the road; though true it is that whiles I was down yonder amidst the ripple of the sea I longed for naught but thee, though thou wert beside me, and thy joyous words were as fire to the heart of my love. But now that I am on the green grass of the earth I called to mind a dream that came to me when we slept after the precious draught of the Well: for methought that I was standing before the porch of the Feast-hall of Upmeads and holding thine hand, and the ancient House spake to me with the voice of a man, greeting both thee and me, and praising thy goodliness and valiancy. Surely then it is calling me to deeds, and if it were but morning, as it is now drawing towards sunset, we would mount and be gone straightway."

"Surely," she said, "thou hast drunk of the Well, and the fear of thee has already entered into the hearts of thy foemen far away, even as the love of thee constraineth me as I lie by thy side; but since it is evening and sunset, let it be evening, and let the morning see to its own matters. So now let us be pilgrims again, and eat the meal of pilgrims, and see to our horses, and then wander about this lovely wilderness and its green meads, where no son of man heedeth the wild things, till the night come, bringing to us the rest and the sleep of them that have prevailed over many troubles."

Even so they did, and broke bread above the sea, and looked to their horses, and then went hand in hand about the goodly green bents betwixt the sea and the rough of the

406

mountain; and it was the fairest and softest of summer evenings; and the deer of that place, both little and great, had no fear of man, but the hart and hind came to Ursula's hand; and the thrushes perched upon her shoulder, and the hares gambolled together close to the feet of the twain; so that it seemed to them that they had come into the very Garden of God; and they forgat all the many miles of the waste and the mountain that lay before them, and they had no thought for the strife of foemen and the thwarting of kindred, that belike awaited them in their own land, but they thought of the love and happiness of the hour that was passing. So sweetly they wore through the last minutes of the day, and when it was as dark as it would be in that fair season, they lay down by the green knoll at the ending of the land, and were lulled to sleep by the bubbling of the Well at the World's End.

BOOK FOUR

The Road Home

◆

CHAPTER 1

Ralph and Ursula Come Back Again Through the Great Mountains

On the morrow morning they armed them and took to their horses and departed from that pleasant place and climbed the mountain without weariness, and made provision of meat and drink for the Dry Desert, and so entered it, and journeyed happily with naught evil befalling them till they came back to the House of the Sorceress; and of the Desert they made little, and the wood was pleasant to them after the drought of the Desert.

But at the said House they saw those kind people, and they saw in their eager eyes as in a glass how they had been bettered by their drinking of the Well, and the Elder said to them: "Dear friends, there is no need to ask you whether ye have achieved your quest; for ye, who before were lovely, are now become as the very Gods who rule the world. And now methinks we have to pray you but one thing, to wit that ye will not be overmuch of Gods, but will be kind and lowly with them that needs must worship you."

They laughed on him for kindness' sake, and kissed and embraced the old man, and they thanked them all for their helping, and they abode with them for a whole day in good-will and love, and thereafter the carle, who was the son of the Elder, with his wife, bade farewell to his kinsmen, and led Ralph and Ursula back through the wood and over the desert to the town of the Innocent Folk. The said Folk received them in all joy and triumph, and would have them abide there the winter over. But they prayed leave to depart, because their hearts were sore for their own land and their kindred. So they abode there but two days, and on the third day were led away by a half score of men gaily apparelled after their manner, and having with them many sumpter-beasts with provision for the road. With this fellowship they came safely and with little pain unto Chestnut Vale, where they abode but one night, though to Ralph and Ursula the place was sweet for the memory of their loving sojourn there.

They would have taken leave of the Innocent Folk in the said vale, but those others must needs go with them a little further, and would not leave them till they were come to the jaws of the pass which led to the Rock of the Fighting Man. Further than that indeed they would not, or durst not go; and those huge mountains they called the Wall of Strife, even as they on the other side called them the Wall of the World.

So the twain took leave of their friends there, and howbeit that they had drunk of the Well at the World's End, yet were their hearts grieved at the parting. The kind folk left with them abundant provision for the remnant of the road, and a sumpter-ox to bear it; so they were in no doubt of their livelihood. Moreover, though the turn of autumn was come again and winter was at hand, yet the weather was fair and calm, and their journey through the dreary pass was as light as it might be to any men.

CHAPTER 2

They Hear New Tidings
of Utterbol

It was on a fair evening of later autumn-tide that they won their way out of the Gates of the Mountains, and came under the rock of the Fighting Man. There they kissed and comforted each other in memory of the terror and loneliness wherewith they had entered the Mountains that other time; though, sooth to say, it was to them now like the reading of sorrow in a book.

But when they came out with joyful hearts into the green plain betwixt the mountains and the River of Lava, they looked westward, and beheld no great way off a little bower or cot, builded of boughs and rushes by a blackthorn copse; and as they rode toward it they saw a man come forth therefrom, and presently saw that he was hoary, a man with a long white beard. Then Ralph gave a glad cry, and set spurs to his horse and galloped over the plain; for he deemed that it could be none other than the Sage of Swevenham; and Ursula came pricking after him laughing for joy. The old man abode their coming, and Ralph leapt off his horse at once, and kissed and embraced him; but the Sage said: "There is no need to ask thee of tidings; for thine eyes and thine whole body tell me that thou hast drunk of the Well at the World's End. And that shall be better for thee belike than it has been for me; though for me also the world has not gone ill after my fashion since I drank of that water."

Then was Ursula come up, and she also lighted down and made much of the Sage. But he said: "Hail, daughter! It is sweet to see thee so, and to wot that thou art in the hands of a mighty man: for I know that Ralph thy man is minded for his Father's House, and the deeds that abide him there; and I think we may journey a little way together; for as for me, I

411

would go back to Swevenham to end my days there, whether they be long or short."

But Ralph said: "As for that, thou mayst go further than Swevenham, and as far as Upmeads, where there will be as many to love and cherish thee as at Swevenham."

The old man laughed a little, and reddened withal, but answered nothing.

Then they untrussed their sumpter-beast, and took meat and drink from his burden, and they ate and drank together, sitting on the green grass there; and the twain made great joy of the Sage, and told him the whole tale; and he told them that he had been abiding there since the spring-tide, lest they might have turned back without accomplishing their quest, and then may-happen he should have been at hand to comfort them, or the one of them left, if so it had befallen. "But," quoth he, "since ye have verily drunk of the Well at the World's End, ye have come back no later than I looked for you."

That night they slept in the bower there, and on the morrow betimes, the Sage drove together three or four milch goats that he pastured there, and went their ways over the plain, and so in due time entered into the lava-sea. But the first night that they lay there, though it was moonless and somewhat cloudy, they saw no glare of the distant earth-fires which they had looked for; and when on the morrow they questioned the Sage thereof, he said: "The Earth-fires ceased about the end of last year, as I have heard tell. But sooth it is that the fore-boding of the Giant's Candle was not for naught. For there hath verily been a change of masters at Utterbol."

"Yea," said Ralph, "for better or worse?"

Said the Sage: "It could scarce have been for worse; but if rumour runneth right it is much for the better. Hearken how I learned thereof. One fair even of late March, a little before I set off hither, as I was sitting before the door of my house, I saw the glint of steel through the wood, and presently rode up a sort of knights and men-at-arms, about a score; and at the head of them a man on a big red-roan horse, with his surcoat blazoned with a white bull on a green field: he was a man black-haired, but blue-eyed; not very big, but well knit and strong, and looked both doughty and knightly; and he wore a gold coronet about his basnet: so not knowing his blazonry, I wondered who it was that durst be so bold as to ride in the lands of the Lord of Utterbol. Now he rode up to me and craved a drink of milk, for he had seen my goats; so I milked two goats for him, and brought whey for the others, whereas I had no more goats in milk at that season. So the bull-knight spake to me about the woodland, and wherefore I dwelt there apart from others; somewhat rough in his speech he was, yet rather jolly than fierce; and he thanked me for the bever kindly enough, and said: "I deem that it will not avail to give thee money; but I shall give thee what may be of avail to thee. Ho, Gervaise! give me one of those scrolls!" So a squire hands him a parchment and he gave it me, and it was a safe-conduct to the bearer from the Lord of Utterbol; but whereas I saw that the seal bore not the Bear on the Castle-wall, but the Bull, and that the superscription was unknown to me, I held the said scroll in my hand and wondered; and the knight said to me: "Yea, look long at it; but so it is, though thou trow it not, that I am verily Lord of Utterbol, and that by conquest; so that belike I am mightier than he was, for that mighty runagate have I slain. And many there be who deem that no mishap, heathen though I be. Come thou to Utterbol and see for thyself if the days be not changed there; and thou shalt have a belly-full of meat and drink, and honour after thy deserving." So they rested a while, and then went their ways. To Utterbol I went not, but ere I departed to come hither two or three carles strayed my way, as whiles they will, who told me that this which the knight had said was naught but the sooth, and that great was the change of days at Utterbol, whereas all men there, both bond and free, were as merry as they deserved to be, or belike merrier."

Ralph pondered this tale, and was not so sure but that this new lord was not Bull Shockhead, his wartaken thrall; natheless he held his peace; but Ursula said: "I marvel not much at the tale, for sure I am, that had Gandolf of the Bear been slain when I was at Utterbol, neither man nor woman had stirred a finger to avenge him. But all feared him, I scarce know why; and, moreover, there was none to be master if he were gone."

Thereafter she told more tales of the miseries of Utterbol

than Ralph had yet heard, as though this tale of the end of that evil rule had set her free to utter them; and they fell to talking of others matters.

CHAPTER 3

They Winter With the Sage; and Thereafter Come Again to Vale Turris

Thus with no peril and little pain they came to the Sage's hermitage; and whereas the autumn was now wearing, and it was not to be looked for that they should cross even the mountains west of Goldburg, let alone those to the west of Cheaping Knowe, when winter had once set in, Ralph and Ursula took the Sage's bidding to abide the winter through with him, and set forth on their journey again when spring should be fairly come and the mountain ways be clear of snow.

So they dwelt there happily enough; for they helped the Sage in his husbandry, and he enforced him to make them cheer, and read in the ancient book to them, and learned them as much as it behoved them to hearken; and told them tales of past time.

Thereafter when May was at hand they set out on their road, and whereas the Sage knew the wood well, he made a long story short by bringing them to Vale Turris in four days' time. But when they rode down into the dale, they saw the plain meads below the Tower all bright with tents and booths, and much folk moving about amidst them; here and there amidst the roofs of cloth withal was showing the half finished frame of a timber house a-building. But now as they looked and wondered what might be toward, a half score of weaponed men rode up to them and bade them, but courteously, to come with them to see their Lord. The Sage drew forth his let-pass thereat; but the leader of the riders said, as he shook his head: "That is good for thee, father; but these two knights must

414

needs give an account of themselves: for my lord is minded to put down all lifting throughout his lands; therefore hath he made the meshes of his net small. But if these be thy friends it will be well. Therefore thou art free to come with them and bear witness to their good life."

Here it must be said that since they were on the road again Ursula had donned her wargear once more, and as she rode was to all men's eyes naught but a young and slender knight.

So without more ado they followed those men-at-arms, and saw how the banner of the Bull was now hung out from the Tower; and the sergeants brought them into the midst of the vale, where, about those tents and those half-finished framehouses (whereof they saw six) was a market toward and much concourse of folk. But the sergeants led through them and the lanes of the booths down to the side of the river, where on a green knoll, with some dozen of men-at-arms and captains about him, sat the new Lord of Utterbol.

Now as the others drew away from him to right and left, the Lord sat before Ralph with naught to hide him, and when their eyes met Ralph gave a cry as one astonished; and the Lord of Utterbol rose up to his feet and shouted, and then fell a laughing joyously, and then cried out: "Welcome, King's Son, and look on me! for though the feathers be fine 'tis the same bird. I am Lord of Utterbol and therewithal Bull Shockhead, whose might was less than thine on the bent of the mountain valley."

Therewith he caught hold of Ralph's hand, and sat himself down and drew Ralph down, and made him sit beside him.

"Thou seest I am become great?" said he. "Yea," said Ralph, "I give thee joy thereof!" Said the new Lord: "Perchance thou wilt be deeming that since I was once thy war-taken thrall I should give myself up to thee: but I tell thee I will not: for I have much to do here. Moreover I did not run away from thee, but thou rannest from me, lad."

Thereat in his turn Ralph fell a laughing, and when he might speak he said: "What needeth the lord of all these spears to beg off his service to the poor wandering knight?"

Then Bull put his arms about him, and said: "I am fain at the sight of thee, time was thou wert a kind lad and a good master; yet naught so merry as thou shouldest have been; but now I see that gladness plays all about thy face, and sparkles in thine eyes; and that is good. But these thy fellows? I have seen the old carle before: he was dwelling in the wildwood because he was overwise to live with other folk. But this young man, who may he be? Or else—yea, verily, it is a young woman. Yea, and now I deem that it is the thrall of my brother Bull Nosy. Therefore by heritage she is now mine."

Ralph heard the words but saw not the smiling face, so wroth he was; therefore the bare sword was in his fist in a twinkling. But ere he could smite Bull caught hold of his wrist, and said: "Master, master, thou art but a sorry lawyer, or thou wouldst have said: 'Thou art my thrall, and how shall a thrall have heritage?' Dost thou not see that I cannot own her till I be free, and that thou wilt not give me my freedom save for hers? There, now is all the matter of the service duly settled, and I am free and a Lord. And this damsel is free also, and —yea, is she not thy well-beloved, King's Son?"

Ralph was somewhat abashed, and said: "I crave thy pardon, Lord, for misdoubting thee: but think how feeble are we two lovers amongst the hosts of the aliens."

"It is well, it is well," said Bull, "and in very sooth I deem thee my friend; and this damsel was my brother's friend. Sit down, dear maiden, I bid thee; and thou also, O man overwise; and let us drink a cup, and then we will talk about what we may do for each other."

So they sat down all on the grass, and the Lord of Utterbol called for wine, and they drank together in the merry season of May; and the new Lord said: "Here be we friends come together, and it were pity of our lives if we must needs sunder speedily: howbeit, it is thou must rule herein, King's Son; for in my eyes thou art still greater than I, O my master. For I can see in thine eyes and thy gait, and in thine also, maiden, that ye have drunk of the Well at the World's End. Therefore I pray you gently and heartily that ye come home with me to Utterbol."

Ralph shook his head, and answered: "Lord of Utterbol, I bid thee all thanks for thy friendliness, but it may not be."

"But take note," said Bull, "that all is changed there, and it hath become a merry dwelling of men. We have cast down the Red Pillar, and the White and the Black also; and it is no longer a place of torment and fear, and cozening and murder; but the very thralls are happy and free-spoken. Now come ye, if it were but for a moon's wearing: I shall be there in eight days' time. Yea, Lord Ralph, thou would'st see old acquaintance there withal: for when I slew the tyrant, who forsooth owed me no less than his life for the murder of my brother, I made atonement to his widow, and wedded her: a fair woman as thou wottest, lord, and of good kindred, and of no ill conditions, as is well seen now that she lives happy days. Though I have heard say that while she was under the tyrant she was somewhat rough with her women when she was sad. Eh, fair sir! but is it not so that she cast sheep's eyes on thee, time was, in this same dale?"

Ralph reddened and answered naught; and Bull spake again, laughing: "Yea, so it is: she told me that much herself, and afterwards I heard more from her damsel Agatha, who told me the merry tale of that device they made to catch thee, and how thou brakest through the net. Forsooth, though this she told me not, I deem that she would have had the same gift of thee as her mistress would. Well, lad, lucky are they with whom all women are in love. So now I prithee trust so much in thy luck as to come with me to Utterbol."

Quoth Ralph: "Once again, Lord of Utterbol, we thank thee; but whereas thou hast said that thou hast much to do in this land; even so I have a land where deeds await me. For I stole myself away from my father and mother, and who knows what help they need of me against foemen, and evil days; and now I might give help to them were I once at home, and to the people of the land also, who are a stout-hearted and valiant and kindly folk."

The new Lord's face clouded somewhat, as he said: "If thine heart draweth thee to thy kindred, there is no more to say. As for me, what I did was for kindred's sake, and then what followed after was the work of need. Well, let it be! But since we must needs part hastily, this at least I bid you, that ye abide with me for to-night, and the banquet in the great pavilion. Howsoever ye may be busied, gainsay me not this; and to-morrow I shall further you on your way, and give you a score of spears to follow thee to Goldburg. Then as for Goldburg and Cheaping Knowe, see ye to it yourselves: but beyond Cheaping Knowe and the plain country, thy name is known, and the likeness of thee told in words; and no man in those mountains shall hurt or hinder thee, but all thou meetest shall aid and further thee. Moreover, at the feast to-night thou shalt see thy friend Otter, and he and I betwixt us shall tell thee how I came to Utterbol, and of the change of days, and how it betid. For he is now my right-hand man, as he was of the dead man. Forsooth, after the slaying I would have had him take the lordship of Utterbol, but he would not, so I must take it perforce or be slain, and let a new master reign there little better than the old. Well then, how sayest thou? Or wilt thou run from me without leave-taking, as thou didst ere-while at Goldburg?"

Ralph laughed at his word, and said that he would not be so churlish this time, but would take his bidding with a good heart; and thereafter they fell to talking of many things. But Ralph took note of Bull, that now his hair and beard were trim and his raiment goodly, for all his rough speech and his laughter and heart-whole gibes and mocking, his aspect and bearing was noble and knightly.

CHAPTER 4

A Feast in the Red Pavilion

So in a while they went with him to the Tower, and there was woman's raiment of the best gotten for Ursula, and afterwards at nightfall they went to the feast in the Red Pavilion of Utterbol, which awhile ago the now-slain Lord of Utterbol, had let make; and it was exceeding rich with broidery of pearl and gems: since forsooth gems and fair women were

hat the late lord had lusted for the most, and have them he
ould at the price of howsoever many tears and groans. But
at pavilion was yet in all wise as it was wont to be, saving
at the Bull had supplanted the Bear upon the Castle-wall.

Now the wayfarers were treated with all honour and were
t upon the high-seat, Ralph upon the right-hand of the Lord,
d Ursula upon his left, and the Sage of Swevenham out from
er. But on Ralph's right hand was at first a void place,
hereto after a while came Otter, the old Captain of the
uard. He came in hastily, and as though he had but just tak-
a his armour off: for his raiment was but such as the men-at-
m of that country were wont to wear under their war-gear,
d was somewhat stained and worn; whereas the other
nights and lords were arrayed grandly in silks and fine cloth
nbroidered and begemmed.

Otter was fain when he saw Ralph, and kissed and embraced
im, and said: "Forsooth, I saw by thy face, lad, that the world
ould be soft before thee; and now that I behold thee I know
lready that thou hast won thy quest; and the Gods only know
what honour thou shalt attain."

Ralph laughed for joy of him, and yet said soberly: "As to
onour, meseems I covet little world's goods, save that it may
e well with my folk at home." Nevertheless as the words were
ut of his mouth his thought went back to the tall man whom
e had first met at the churchyard gate of Netherton, and it
eemed to him that he wished his thriving, yea, and in a lesser
ay, he wished the same to Roger of the Rope-walk, whereas
e deemed that both of these, each in his own way, had been
ue to the lady whom he had lost.

Then Otter fell a-talking to him of the change of days at
tterbol, and how that it was the Lord's intent that a cheaping
wn should grow up in the Dale of the Tower, and that the
ilderness beyond it should be tilled and builded. "And," said
e, "if this be done, and the new lord live to see it, as he
ay, being but young of years, he may become exceedingly
ighty, and if he hold on in the way whereas he now is, he
all be well-beloved also."

So they spake of many things, and there was minstrelsy and

419

diverse joyance, till at last the Lord of Utterbol stood up an
said: "Now bring in the Bull, that we may speak some word
over him; for this is a great feast." Ralph wondered what bu
this might be whereof he spake; but the harps and fiddlers
and all instruments of music struck up a gay and gallant tune
and presently there came into the hall four men richly attired
who held up on spears a canopy of bawdekin, under whic
went a man-at-arms helmed, and clad in bright armour, wh
held in his hands a great golden cup fashioned like to a bul
and he bore it forth unto the dais, and gave it into the hand
of the Lord. Then straightway all the noise ceased, and th
glee and clatter of the hall, and there was dead silence. The
the Lord held the cup aloft and said in a loud voice:

"Hail, all ye folk! I swear by the Bull, and they that mad
him, that in three years' time or less I will have purged all th
lands of Utterbol of all strong-thieves and cruel tyrants, b
they big or little, till all be peace betwixt the mountains an
the mark of Goldburg; and the wilderness shall blossom lik
the rose. Or else shall I die in the pain."

Therewith he drank of the cup, and all men shouted. The
he sat him down and bade hand the cup to Otter; and Otte
took the cup and looked into the bowl and saw the wave o
wine, and laughed and cried out: "As for me, what shall
swear but that I will follow the Bull through thick and thir
through peace and unpeace, through grief and joy. This is m
oath-swearing."

And he drank mightily and sat down.

Then turned the Lord to Ralph and said: "And thou who ar
my master, wilt thou not tell thy friends and the Gods wha
thou wilt do?"

"No great matter, belike," said Ralph; "but if ye will it,
will speak out my mind thereon."

"We will it," said the Lord.

Then Ralph arose and took the cup and lifted it and spake
"This I swear, that I will go home to my kindred, yet on th
road will I not gainsay help to any that craveth it. So may al
Hallows help me!"

Therewith he drank: and Bull said: "This is well said, C
happy man! But now that men have drunk well, do ye thre

420

ad Otter come with me into the Tower, whereas the chambers
re dight for you, that I may make the most of this good day
herein I have met thee again."

So they went with him, and when they had sat down in the
oodliest chamber of the Tower, and they had been served
ith wine and spices, the new Lord said to Ralph: "And now,
y master, wilt thou not ask somewhat concerning me?"
Yea," said Ralph, "I will ask thee to tell the tale of how thou
amest into thy Lordship." Said the Lord, "This shall ye hear
f me with Otter to help me out. Hearken!"

CHAPTER 5

Bull Telleth of His Winning of
the Lordship of Utterbol

"When thou rannest away from me, and left me alone at
oldburg, I was grieved; then Clement Chapman offered to
ake me back with him to his own country, which, he did me
o wit, lieth hard by thine: but I would not go with him, since
had an inkling that I should find the slayer of my brother,
nd be avenged on him. So the Chapmen departed from
oldberg after that Clement had dealt generously by me for
y sake; and when they were gone I bethought me what to
o, and thou knowest I can some skill with the fiddle and
ong, so I betook myself to that craft, both to earn somewhat,
nd that I might gather tidings and be little heeded; till with-
a awhile folk got to know me well, and would often send for
ae to their merry-makings, where they gave me fiddler's
ages, to wit, meat, drink, and money. So what with one
ning what with another I was rich enough to leave Goldburg
nd fall to my journey unto Utterbol; since I misdoubted me
om the first that the caytiff who had slain my brother was
e Lord thereof.

"But one day when I went into the market-place I found a

great stir and clutter there; some folk, both men and women screeching and fleeing, and some running to bows and other weapons. So I caught hold of one of the fleers, and asked him what was toward; and he cried out, 'Loose me! let me go! he is loose, he is loose!'

"'Who is loose, fool?' quoth I. 'The lion,' said he, and therewith in the extremity of his terror tore himself away from me and fled. By this time the others also had got some distance away from me, and I was left pretty much alone. So I went forth on a little, looking about me, and sure enough under one of the pillars of the cloister beneath the market-house (the great green pillar, if thou mindest it), lay crouched a huge yellow lion, on the carcase of a goat, which he had knocked down, but would not fall to eating of amidst all that cry and hubbub.

"Now belike one thing of me thou wottest not, to wit, that I have a gift that wild things love and will do my bidding. The house-mice will run over me as I lie awake looking on them; the small birds will perch on my shoulders without fear; the squirrels and hares will gambol about quite close to me as if I were but a tree; and, withal, the fiercest hound or mastiff is tame before me. Therefore I feared not this lion, and moreover, I looked to it that if I might tame him thoroughly he would both help me to live as a jongleur, and would be a sure ward to me.

"So I walked up towards him quietly, till he saw me and half rose up growling; but I went on still, and said to him in a peaceable voice: 'How now, yellow mane! what aileth thee? down with thee, and eat thy meat.' So he sat down to his quarry again, but growled still, and I went up close to him, and said to him: 'Eat in peace and safety, am I not here?' And therewith I held out my bare hand unclenched to him, and he smelt to it, and straightway began to be peaceable, and fell to tearing the goat, and devouring it, while I stood by speaking to him friendly.

"But presently I saw weapons glitter on the other side of the square place, and men with bended bows. The yellow king saw them also, and rose up again and stood growling; then I strove to quiet him, and said, 'These shall not harm thee.'

"Therewith the men cried out to me to come away, for they ould shoot: But I called out; 'Shoot not yet! but tell me, does y man own this beast?' 'Yea,' said one, 'I own him, and ppy am I that he doth not own me.' Said I, 'Wilt thou sell m?' 'Yea' said he, 'if thou livest another hour to tell down e money.' Said I, 'I am a tamer of wild beasts, and if thou ilt sell this one at such a price, I will rid thee of him.' The an yeasaid this, but kept well aloof with his fellows, who oked on, handling their weapons.

"Then I turned to my new-bought thrall and bade him come ith me, and he followed me like a dog to his cage, which was ard by; and I shut him in there, and laid down the money to s owner; and folk came round about, and wondered, and raised me. But I said: 'My masters, have ye naught of gifts for e tamer of beasts, and the deliverer of men?' Thereat they ughed: but they brought me money and other goods, till I d gotten far more than I had given for the lion.

"Howbeit the next day the officers of the Porte came and de me avoid the town of Goldburg, but gave me more money ithal. I was not loth thereto, but departed, riding a little horse at I had, and leading my lion by a chain, though when I was y he needed little chaining.

"So that without more ado I took the road to Utterbol, and heresoever I came, I had what was to be had that I would; either did any man fall on me, or on my lion. For though they ight have shot him or slain him with many spear-thrusts, yet esides that they feared him sorely, they feared me still more; eeming me some mighty sending from their Gods.

"Thus came I to Utterness, and found it poor and wretched, as forsooth, it yet is, but shall not be so for long). But the louse of Utterbol is exceeding fair and stately (as thou ightest have learned from others, my master,) and its ardens, and orchards, and acres, and meadows as goodly as ay be. Yea, a very paradise; yet the dwellers therein as if it ere hell, as I saw openly with mine own eyes.

"To be short, the fame of me and my beast had somehow one before me, and when I came to the House, I was dealt ith fairly, and had good entertainment; and this all the more, s the Lord was away for a while, and the life of folk not so

423

hard by a great way as it had been if he had been there: b
the Lady was there in the house, and on the morrow of m
coming by her command, I brought my lion before her win
dow and made him come and go, and fetch and carry at m
bidding, and when I had done my play she bade me up int
her bower, and bade me sit and had me served with win
while she asked me many questions as to my country an
friends, and whence and whither I was; and I answered he
with the very sooth, so far as the sooth was handy; and ther
was with her but one of her women, even thy friend Agatha
fair sir.

"Methought both that this Queen was a fair woman, an
that she looked kindly upon me, and at last she said, sighing
that she were well at ease if her baron were even such a ma
as I, whereas the said Lord was fierce and cruel, and yet
dastard withal. But the said Agatha turned on her, and chide
her, as one might with a child, and said: 'Hold thy peace of th
loves and thy hates before a very stranger! Or must I leave ye
more of my blood on the pavement of the White Pillar, for th
pleasure of thy loose tongue? Come out now, mountain
carle!'

"And she took me by the hand and led me out, and whe
we had passed the door and it was shut, she turned to me an
said: 'Thou, if I hear any word abroad of what my Lady ha
just spoken, I shall know that thou hast told it, and though I b
but a thrall, yea, and of late a mishandled one, yet am I c
might enough in Utterbol to compass thy destruction.'

"I laughed in her face and went my ways: and thereafter
saw many folk and showed them my beast, and soon learne
two things clearly.

"And first that the Lord and the Lady were now utterly a
variance. For a little before he had come home, and found
lack in his household—to wit, how a certain fair woman whon
he had but just got hold of, and whom he lusted after sorel
was fled away. And he laid the wyte thereof on his Lady, an
threatened her with death: and when he considered that h
durst not slay her, or torment her (for he was verily but
dastard), he made thy friend Agatha pay for her unde
pretence of wringing a true tale out of her.

"Now when I heard this story I said to myself that I should hear that other one of the slaying of my brother, and even so it befell. For I came across a man who told me when and how the Lord came by the said damsel (whom I knew at once could be none other than thou, Lady,) and how he had slain my brother to get her, even as doubtless thou knowest, Lord Ralph.

"But the second thing which I learned was that all folk at Utterbol, men and women, dreaded the home-coming of this tyrant; and that there was no man but would have deemed it a good deed to slay him. But, dastard as he was, use and wont, and the fear that withholdeth rebels, and the doubt that draweth back slaves, saved him; and they dreaded him moreover as a devil rather than a man. Forsooth one of the men there, who looked upon me friendly, who had had tidings of this evil beast drawing near, spake to me a word of warning, and said: 'Friend lion-master, take heed to thyself! For I fear for thee when the Lord cometh home and findeth thee here; lest he let poison thy lion and slay thee miserably afterward.'

"Well, in three days from that word home cometh the Lord with a rout of his spearmen, and some dozen of captives, whom he had taken. And the morrow of his coming, he, having heard of me, sent and bade me showing the wonder of the Man and the Lion; therefore in the bright morning I played with the lion under his window as I had done by the Queen. And after I had played some while, and he looking out of the window, he called to me and said: 'Canst thou lull thy lion to sleep, so that thou mayst leave him for a little? For I would fain have thee up here.'

"I yeasaid that, and chid the beast, and then sang to him till he lay down and slept like a hound weary with hunting. And then I went up into the Lord's chamber; and as it happed, all the while of my playing I had had my short-sword naked in my hand, and thus, I deem without noting it, yet as weird would, I came before the tyrant, where he sat with none anigh him save his Otter and another man-at-arms. But when I saw him, all the blood within me that was come of one mother with my brother's blood stirred within me, and I set my foot on the foot-pace of this murderer's chair, and hove up my short-

sword, and clave his skull, in front and with mine own hand
not as he wrought, not as he wrought with my brother.

"Then I turned about to Otter (who had his sword in his fi
when it was too late) till he should speak. Hah Otter, wh
didst thou say?"

Otter laughed: Quoth he, "I said: thus endeth the worst ma
in the world. Well done, lion-tamer! thou art no ill guest, an
hast paid on the nail for meat, drink and lodging. But wh
shall we do now? Then thou saidst; 'Well, I suppose thou wi
be for slaying me.' 'Nay,' said I, 'We will not slay thee; at lea
not for this, nor now, nor without terms.' Thou saids
'Perchance then thou wilt let me go free, since this man wa
ill-beloved: yea, and he owed me a life.' 'Nay, nay,' said I, 'no
so fast, good beast-lord.' 'Why not?' saidst thou, 'I can see o
thee that thou art a valiant man, and whereas thou hast bee
captain of the host, and the men-at-arms will lightly do th
bidding, why shouldest thou not sit in the place of this mar
and be Lord of Utterbol?'

" 'Nay nay,' said I, 'it will not do, hearken thou rather: Fc
here I give thee the choice of two things, either that thou b
Lord of Utterbol, or that we slay thee here and now. For w
be two men all-armed.'

"Thou didst seem to ponder it a while, and then saidst a
last: 'Well, I set not out on this journey with any such-lik
intent; yet will I not wrestle with weird. Only I forewarn the
that I shall change the days of Utterbol.'

" 'It will not be for the worst then,' quoth I. 'So now g
wake up thy lion, and lead him away to his den: and we wi
presently send him this carrion for a reward of his jonglery
'Gramercy, butcher,' saidst thou, 'I am not for thy flesh-mea
to-day. I was forewarned that the poor beast should b
poisoned at this man's home-coming, and so will he be if h
eat of this dastard; he will not outlive such a dinner.' Therea
we all laughed heartily."

"Yea," said Bull, "So I went to lead away the lion whe
thou hadst bidden me return in an hours' wearing, when a
should be ready for my Lordship. And thou wert not wors
than thy word, for when I came into that court again, ther
were all the men-at-arms assembled, and the free carles, an

426

the thralls; and the men-at-arms raised me on a shield, set a crowned helm on my head, and thrust a great sword into my hand, and hailed me by the name of the Bull of Utterbol, Lord of the Waste and the Wildwood, and the Mountain-side: and then thou, Otter, wert so simple as to kneel before me and name thyself my man, and take the girding on of sword at my hand. Then even as I was I went in to my Lady and told her the end of my tale, and in three minutes she lay in my arms, and in three days in my bed as my wedded wife. As to Agatha, when I had a little jeered her, I gave her rich gifts and good lands, and freedom, to boot her for her many stripes. And lo there, King's Son and Sweet Lady, the end of all my tale."

"Yea," quoth Otter, "saving this, that even already thou has raised up Utterbol from Hell to Earth, and yet meseemeth thou hast good-will to raise it higher."

Bull reddened at his word, and said: "Tush, man! praise the day when the sun has set." Then he turned to Ralph, and said: "Yet couldst thou at whiles put in a good word for me here and there amongst the folks that thou shalt pass through on thy ways home, I were fain to know that I had a well-speaking friend abroad." "We shall do no less," said Ralph; and Ursula spake in like wise.

So they talked together merrily a while longer, till night began to grow old, and then went to their chambers in all content and good-liking.

CHAPTER 6

They Ride From Vale Turris. Redhead Tells of Agatha

On the morrow when they arose, Ralph heard the sound of horses and the clashing of arms: he went to the window, and looked out, and saw how the spears stood up thick together at the Tower's foot, and knew that these were the men who were to be his fellows by the way. Their captain he saw, a big man all-armed in steel, but himseemed that he knew his face under his sallet, and presently saw that it was Redhead. He was glad thereof, and clad himself hastily, and went out a-doors, and went up to him and hailed him, and Redhead leapt off his horse, and cast his arms about Ralph, and made much of him, and said: "It is good for sore eyes to see thee, lord; and I am glad at heart that all went well with thee that time. Although, forsooth, there was guile behind it. Yet whereas I wotted nothing thereof, which I will pray thee to believe, and whereas thou hast the gain of all, I deem thou mayst pardon me."

Said Ralph: "Thou hast what pardon of me thou needest; so be content. For the rest, little need is there to ask if thou thrivest, for I behold thee glad and well honoured."

As they spoke came the Lord forth from the Tower, and said: "Come thou, Lord Ralph, and eat with us ere thou takest to the road; I mean with Otter and me. As for thee, Redhead, if aught of ill befall this King's Son under thy way-leading, look to it that thou shalt lose my good word with Agatha; yea, or gain my naysay herein; whereby thou shalt miss both fee and fair dame."

Redhead looked sheepishly on Ralph at that word, yet winked at him also, as if it pleased him to be jeered concerning his wooing; so that Ralph saw how the land lay, and that the guileful handmaid was not ill content with that big man. So he smiled kindly on him and nodded, and went back with Bull into the Tower. There they sat down all to meat together; and when they were done with their victual, Bull spake, and said to Ralph: "Fair King's Son, is this then the last sight of thee? wilt thou never come over the mountains again?" Said Ralph: "Who knoweth? I am young yet, and have drunk of the Water of the Well." Bull grew somewhat pensive and said: "Yea, thou meanest that thou mayest come back and find me no longer here. Yet if thou findest but my grave-mound, yet mayhappen thou shalt come on something said or sung of me, which shall please thee. For I will tell thee, that thou hast changed my conditions; how, I wot not."

"Thy word is good," said Ralph, "yet I meant not that; never should I come to Utterbol if I looked not to find thee living there." Bull smiled on him as though he loved him, and said: "This is well spoken; I shall look to see thee before I die."

Then said Ursula: "Lord of Utterbol, this also thou mayst think on, that it is no further from Utterbol to Upmeads than from Upmeads to Utterbol." The Lord laughed and said: "Sooth is that; and were but my Bull here, as I behold you I should be of mind to swear by him to come and see you at Upmeads ere ten years have worn."

Then she put forth her hand and said: "Swear by this!" So he took it and swore the oath; but the Sage of Swevenham said: "This oath thou shalt keep to the gain and not the loss both of thee and of thy friends of Upmeads."

Thus were they fain of each other, and Ralph saw how Bull's heart was grown big, and he rejoiced thereat. But anon he arose and said: "Now, Lord, we ask leave to depart, for the way is long, and mayhappen my kindred now lack a man's helping. Then Bull stood up and called for his horse, and Otter also, and they all went forth and gat a-horseback and rode away from Vale Turris, and Redhead rode behind them humbly, till it was noon and they made stay for meat. Then after they had broken bread together and drunk a cup, Bull and Otter kissed the wayfarers, and bade them farewell, and so rode back to Vale Turris, and Ralph and Ursula and the Sage tarried not but rode on their ways.

But anon Ralph called to Redhead, and bade him ride beside them that they might talk together, and he came up with them, and Ursula greeted him kindly, and they were merry one with another. And Ralph said to Redhead: "Friend captain, thou art exceeding in humility not to ride with the Lord or Captain Otter; save for chance-hap, I see not that thou art worser than they."

Redhead grinned, and said: "Well, as to Otter, that is all true; but as for Lord Bull it is another matter; I wot not but his kindred may be as good or better than any in these east parts. In any case, he hath his kin and long descent full often in his mouth, while I am but a gangrel body. Howbeit it is all one, whereas whatso he or Otter bid any man to do, he doeth it, but my bidding may be questioned at whiles. And look you, lord, times are not ill, so wherefore should I risk a change of days? Sooth to say, both these great lords have done well by me."

Ralph laughed: "And better will they do, as thou deemest; give thee Agatha, to wit?" "Yea, fair sir," quoth Redhead. "No great gift, that seemeth to me, for thy valiancy," said Ralph; "she is guileful enough and loose enough for a worse man than thee."

"Lord," said Redhead, "even of her thou shalt say what pleaseth thee; but no other man shall say of her what pleaseth me not. For all that is come and gone she is true and valiant, and none may say that she is not fair and sweet enough for a better man than me; and my great good luck it is that, as I hope, she looketh no further for a better."

Ursula said: "Is it so, perchance, that now she is free and hath naught to fear, she hath no need for guile?" "Hail to thee for thy word, lady," quoth Redhead; and then he was silent, glooming somewhat on Ralph.

But Ralph said: "Nay, my friend, I meant no harm, but I was wondering what had befallen to bring you two so close together."

"It was fear and pain, and the helping of each other that wrought it," said Redhead. Said Ursula: "Good Captain, how was it that she escaped the uttermost of evil at the tyrant's hands? since from all that I have heard, it must needs be that he laid the blame on her (working for her mistress) of my flight from Utterbol."

"Even so it was, lady," said Redhead; "but, as thou wottest belike, she had got it spread abroad that she was cunning in sorcery, and that her spell would not end when her life ended; nay, that he to whom her ghost should bear ill-will, and more especially such an one as might compass her death, should have but an ill time of it while he lived, which should not be long. This tale, which, sooth to say, I myself helped to spread, the Lord of Utterbol trowed in wholly, so cunningly was it told; so that, to make a long story short, he feared her, and feared her more dead than living. So that when he came home, and found thee gone, lady, he did indeed deem that thy flight was of Agatha's contrivance. And this the more because his

430

nephew (he whom thou didst beguile; I partly guess how) told him a made-up tale how all was done by the spells of Agatha. For this youth was of all men, not even saving his uncle, most full of malice; and he hated Agatha, and would have had her suffer the uttermost of torments and he to be standing by the while; howbeit his malice overshot itself, since his tale made her even more of a witch than the lord deemed before.

"Yea," said Ursula, "and what hath befallen that evil young man, Captain?" Said Redhead: "It is not known to many, lady; but two days before the slaying of his uncle, I met him in a wood a little way from Utterbol, and, the mood being on me I tied him neck and heels and cast him, with a stone round his neck, into a deep woodland pool hight the Ram's Bane, which is in that same wood. Well, as to my tale of Agatha. When the lord came home first, he sent for her, and his rage had so mastered his fear for a while that his best word was scourge and rack and faggot; but she was, outwardly, so calm and cold, smiling on him balefully, that he presently came to himself, a found that fear was in his belly, and that he might not do what he would with her; wherefore he looked to it that however she were used (which was ill enough, God wot!) she should keep the soul in her body. And at last the fear so mounted into his head that he made peace with her, and even craved forgiveness of her and gave her gifts. She answered him sweetly indeed, yet so as he (and all others who were bystanding, of whom I was one,) might well see that she deemed she owed him a day in harvest. As for me, he heeded me naught, and I lay low all I might. And in any wise we wore the time till the great day of deliverance."

Therewith dropped the talk about Agatha, when they had bidden him all luck in his life. Forsooth, they were fain of his words, and of his ways withal. For he was a valiant man, and brisk, and one who forgat no benefit, and was trusty as steel; merry-hearted withal, and kind and ready of speech despite his uplandish manners, which a life not a little rude had thrust on him.

CHAPTER 7

Of Their Riding the Waste, and of a Battle Thereon

They slept in no house that night nor for many nights after; for they were now fairly on the waste. They bore with them a light tent for Ursula's lodging benights, and the rest of them slept on the field as they might; or should they come to a thicket or shaw, they would lodge them there softly. Victual and drink failed them not, for they bore what they needed on sumpter-horses, and shot some venison on the way withal. They saw but few folk; for the most part naught save a fowler of the waste, or a peat-cutter, who stood to look on the men-at-arms going by, and made obeisance to the token of Utterbol.

But on a time, the fifth day of their journey, they saw, in the morning, spears not a few standing up against a thicket-side in the offing. Redhead looked under the sharp of his hand, and laughed as though he were glad, and said: "I know not clearly what these may be, but it looketh like war. Now, knight, this is best to do: hold with thee three of our best men, so that ye may safe guard the Lady, and I with the others will prick on and look into this."

"Nay," said Ralph, "thou mayst yet be apaid of a man's aid; and if there be strokes on sale in the cheaping-stead yonder, I will deal along with thee. Leave thy three men with the Lady, and let us on; we shall soon be back."

"Nay once more, dear lord," quoth Ursula, "I fear to be left alone of thee, and it is meet that thou free me from fear. I will ride with you, but three horse-lengths behind, so as not to hinder you. I have been worse bestead than this shall be."

"It is good," quoth Redhead, "let her ride with us: for why should she suffer the pain of fear in the lonely waste? But let her do on a hauberk over her coats, and steel coif over her head, for shaft and bolt will ofttimes go astray."

Even so they did, and rode forward, and presently they saw the spearmen that they were somewhat more than their company, and that they were well mounted on black horses and clad in black armour. Then they drew rein for awhile and Redhead scanned them again and said: "Yea, these are the men of the brother of thy hot wooer, Lady Ursula, whom I cooled in the Ram's Bane, but a man well nigh as old as his uncle, though he hath not made men tremble so sore, albeit he be far the better man, a good warrior, a wise leader, a reiver and lifter well wrought at all points. Well, 'tis not unlike that we shall have to speak to his men again, either out-going or home-coming: so we had best kill as many of these as we may now. Do on thy sallet, my lord; and thou, Michael-a-green, shake out the Bull; and thou, our Noise, blow a point of war, that they may be warned. God to aid! but they be ready and speedy!"

In sooth even as the pennon of the Bull ran down the wind, and the Utterbol horn was winded, the Black men-at-arms came on at a trot, and presently with a great screeching yell cast their spears into the rest, and spurred on all they might, while a half score of bowmen who had come out of the thicket bent their bows and fell a-shooting. But now the men of Utterbol spurred to meet the foe, and as Redhead cast his spear into the rest, he said to Ralph: "Glad am I that thy Lady is anear to see me, for now I worship her."

Therewith the two bands met, and whereas on neither side was the armour very stout, some men of either band were hurt or slain at once with spearthrust; though, save for Ralph, they did not run straight on each other; but fenced and foined with their spears deftly enough. As for Ralph, he smote a tall man full on the breast and pierced him through and through, and then pulled out the Upmeads blade and smote on the right hand and the left, so that none came anigh him willingly.

Shortly to say it, in five minutes' time the Black Riders were fleeing all over the field with them of Utterbol at their heels, and the bowmen ran back again into the wood. But one of the foemen as he fled cast a javelin at a venture, and who should be before it save Ursula, so that she reeled in her saddle, and would have fallen downright but for one of the Utterbol fellows who stayed her, and got her gently off her horse. This Ralph saw not, for he followed far in the chase, and was coming back somewhat slowly along with Redhead, who was hurt, but not sorely. So when he came up, and saw Ursula sitting on the grass with four or five men about her, he sickened for fear; but she rose up and came slowly and pale-faced to meet him, and said: "Fear not, beloved, for steel kept out steel: I have no scratch or point or edge on me." So therewith he kissed her, and embraced her, and was glad.

The Utterbol Riders had slain sixteen of their foemen; for they took none to mercy, and four of their band were slain outright, and six hurt, but not grievously. So they tarried awhile on the field of deed to rest them and tend their wounded men, and so rode on again heedfully.

But Redhead spake: "It is good to see thee tilting, King's Son. I doubt me I shall never learn thy downright thrust. Dost thou remember how sorry a job I made of it, when we met in the lists at Vale Turris that other day?"

"Yea, yea," said Ralph. "Thou were best let that flea stick on the wall. For to-day, at least, I have seen thee play at sharps deftly enough."

Quoth Redhead: "Lord, it is naught, a five minutes' scramble. That which trieth a man, is to fight and overcome, and straight have to fight with fresh foemen, and yet again, till ye long for dark night to cover you—yea, or even death."

"Warrior-like and wisely thou speakest," said Ralph; "and whoever thou servest thou shalt serve well. And now once more I would it were me."

Redhead shook his head at that word, and said: "I would it might be so; but it will not be so as now."

Forth on they rode, and slept in a wood that night, keeping good watch; but saw no more of the Black Riders for that time.

On a day thereafter when it was nigh evening, Ralph looked about, and saw a certain wood on the edge of a plain, and he stayed Ursula, and said: "Look round about, beloved; for this is the very field whereas I was betrayed into the hands of the

434

men of Utterbol." She smiled on him and said: "Let me light down then, that I may kiss the earth of that kind field, where thou wert not stayed over long, but even long enough that we might meet in the dark wood thereafter."

"Sweetling," said Ralph, "this mayst thou do and grieve no man, not even for a little. For lo you! the captain is staying the sumpter-beasts, and it is his mind, belike, that we shall sleep in yonder wood to-night." Therewith he lighted down and she in likewise: then he took her by the hand and led her on a few yards, and said: "Lo, beloved, this quicken-tree; hereby it was that the tent was pitched wherein I lay the night when I was taken."

She looked on him shyly and said: "Wilt thou not sleep here once more to-night?"

"Yea, well-beloved," said he, "I will bid them pitch thy tent on this same place, that I may smell the wild thyme again, as I did that other while."

So there on the field of his ancient grief they rested that night in all love and content.

CHAPTER 8

Of Goldburg Again, and the Queen Thereof

Next day they went forth through the country where-through Morfinn had led Ralph into captivity; and Redhead rode warily; for there were many passes which looked doubt-ful: but whether the ill men feared to meddle with them, or however it were, none waylaid them, and they all came safely to the gate of Goldburg, the towers whereof were full of folk looking forth on them. So they displayed their pennon, and rode into the street, where folk pressed about them in friendly wise; for the new Lord of Utterbol had made firm and fast peace with Goldburg. So they rode to the hostel, and gat them victual, and rested in peace that night. But Ralph wondered whether the Queen would send for him when she heard of his coming back again, and he hoped that she would let him be; for he was ashamed when he thought of her love for him, and how that he had clean forgotten her till he was close to Goldburg again.

But when morning was come Ralph spake to Redhead and asked him how he should do to wage men for the homeward journey on thence; and Redhead said: "I have already seen the Clerk of the Porte, and he will be here in an hour with the license for thee to wage men to go with thee to Cheaping Knowe. As for me, I must needs go see the King, and give him a letter sealed by my lord's hand; and when I come back from him, I will go round to the alehouses which be haunted of the men-at-arms to see after strong carles for thine avail. But to the King hast thou no need to go, save he send for thee, whereas thou art not come hither to chaffer, and he needeth not men of war."

Ralph stared at him and said: "The King, sayst thou? is there no Queen of Goldburg?" Said Redhead: "There is the King's wedded wife, but her they call not Queen, but Lady." "But the Queen that was," said Ralph, "where is she then?" "Yea truly," said Redhead, "a Queen sat alone as ruler here a while ago; but whether she died, or what befell her, I know nothing. I had little to do with Goldburg till our lord conquered Utterbol. Lo here the host! he may tell thee the tale thereof."

Therewith he departed, and left Ralph with the host, whom Ralph questioned of the story, for his heart was wrung lest such a fair woman and so friendly should have come to harm.

So the host sat down by Ralph and said: "My master, this is a tale which is grievous to us: for though the saints forbid I should say a word against my lord that is now, nor is there any need to, yet we deemed us happy to be under so dear a lady and so good and fair as she was. Well, she is gone so that we wot not whether she be living or dead. For so it is that in the early spring, somewhat more than a year ago that is, one morning when folk arose, the Queen's place was empty. Riding and running there was about and about, but none the more was she found. Forsooth as time wore, tales were told of what wise she left us, and why: but she was gone. Well, fair sir, many deemed that though her lineage was known by seeming, yet she was of the fairy, and needed neither steed nor chariot to go where she would. But her women and those that knew her best, deemed that whatso she were, she had slain herself, as they thought, for some unhappiness of love. For indeed she had long gone about sad and distraught, though she neither wept, nor would say one word of her sorrow, whatsoever it might be.

"But, fair sir, since thou art a stranger, and art presently departing from our city, I will tell thee a thing. To wit; one month or so after she had vanished away, I held talk with a certain old fisherman of our water, and he told me that on that same night of her vanishing, as he stood on the water-side handing the hawser of his barque, and the sail was all ready to to be sheeted home, there came along the shore a woman going very swiftly, who, glancing about her, as if to see that there was none looking on or prying, came up to him, and prayed him in a sweet voice for instant passage down the water. Wrapped she was in a dark cloak and a cowl over her head, but as she put forth her hand to give him gold, he saw even by the light of his lantern that it was exceeding fair, and that great gems flashed from the finger-rings, and that there was a great gold ring most precious on her arm.

"He yeasaid her asking, partly because of her gold, partly (as he told me) that he feared her, deeming her to be of the fairy. Then she stepped over his gangway of one board on to his boat, and as he held the lantern low down to light her, lest she should make a false step and fall into the water, he noted (quoth he) that a golden shoe all begemmed came out from under gown-hem and that the said hem was broidered thickly with pearl and jewels.

"Small was his barque, and he alone with the woman, and there was a wind in the March night, and the stream is swift betwixt the quays of our city; so that by night and cloud they made much way down the water, and at sunrise were sailing through the great wood which lieth hence a twenty leagues seaward. So when the sun was risen she stood up in the fore part of the boat, and bade him turn the barque toward the shore, and even as the bows ran upon the sand, she leapt out and let the thicket cover her; nor have any of Goldburg seen her since, or the Queen. But for my part I deem the woman to have been none other than the Queen. Seest thou then! she is gone: but the King Rainald her cousin reigns in her stead, a wise man, and a mighty, and no tyrant or skinner of the people."

Ralph heard and pondered, and was exceeding sorry, and more had he been but for the joyousness which came of the Water of the Well. Howbeit he might not amend it: for even were he to seek for the Queen and find her, it might well be worse than letting it be. For he knew (when he thought of her) that she loved him, and how would it be if she might not outwear her love, or endure the days of Goldburg, and he far away? This he said to himself, which he might not have said to any other soul.

CHAPTER 9

They Come to Cheaping Knowe Once More. Of the King Thereof

Toward evening comes Redhead, and tells Ralph how he hired him a dozen men-at-arms to follow him well-weaponed to Cheaping Knowe: withal he counselled him to take a good gift with him to that same town to buy the good will of the King there; who was a close-fist and a cruel lord.

Afterwards they sat together in the court of that fair house before good wine, Ralph and Ursula, and Redhead and the Sage of Swevenham, and spake of many things, and were merry and kind together. But on the morrow Redhead departed from Goldburg with his men, and he loth to depart, and they gave him farewell lovingly. Thereafter Ralph's new men came to him in the hostelry, and he feasted them and did well to them, so that they praised him much. Then he gat him victuals and sumpter-horses for the journey, and bought good store of bows and arrows withal. Furthermore he took heed to Redhead's word and bought a goodly gift of silver vessel and fine cloth for the King of Cheaping Knowe.

The day after he and his company departed from Gold-burg toward the mountains, which they passed unfought and unwaylaid: partly because they were a band of stout men, and partly because a little before there had been a great over-throw of the wild men of those mountains at the hands of the men of Goldburg and the Chapmen; so that now the moun-tain-men lay close, and troubled none that rode with any force.

On the way they failed not to pass by the place where they had erst found Bull Nosy slain: there they saw his howe, heaped up exceeding high, covered in with earth, whereon the grass was now beginning to grow, and with a great standing stone on the top thereof, whereon was graven the image of a bull, with a sword thereunder; whereby the wayfarers wotted that this had been done in his memory by his brother, the new Lord of Utterbol.

So they came down out of the mountains to Whiteness, where they had good entertainment, but tarried not save for one night, riding their ways betimes to Cheaping Knowe: and they came before the gate thereof safe and sound on the third day; and slept in the hostelry of the chapmen. On the morrow Ralph went up to the King's Castle with but three men unweaponed bearing the gift which he had got for the King. Albeit he sent not away his men-at-arms till he should know how the King was minded towards him.

As he went he saw in the streets sad tokens of the lord's cruel justice, as handless men, fettered, dragging themselves about, and folk hung up before chapmen's booths, and whip-ping-cheer, and the pillar, and such like. But whereas he might not help he would not heed, but came right to the Castle-gate, and entered easily when he had told his errand, for gift-bearing men are not oftenest withstood.

He was brought straightway into the great hall, where sat the King on his throne amidst the chiefs of the Porte, and his captains and sergeants, who were, so to say, his barons, though they were not barons of lineage, but masterful men who were wise to do his bidding.

As he went up the hall he saw a sort of poor caytiffs, women as well as men, led away from the high-place in chains by bailiffs and tipstaves; and he doubted not that these were for torments or maiming and death; and thought it were well might he do them some good.

Being come to the King, he made his obeisance to him, and craved his good will and leave to wage men-at-arms to bring him through the mountains.

The King was a tall man, a proper man of war; long-legged, black bearded, and fierce-eyed. Some word he had heard of Ralph's gift, therefore he was gracious to him; he spake and said: "Thou hast come across the mountains a long way, fair Sir; prithee on what errand?" Answered Ralph: "For no errand, lord, save to fare home to mine own land." "Where is thine own land?" said the King, stretching out his legs and lying back in his chair. "West-away, lord, many a mile," said Ralph. "Yea," quoth the King, "and how far didst thou go beyond the mountains? As far as Utterbol?" Said Ralph: "Yet further, but not to Utterbol." "Hah!" said the King, "who goeth beyond Utterbol must have a great errand; what was thine?"

Ralph thought for a moment, and deemed it best to say as little as he might concerning Ursula; so he answered, and his voice grew loud and bold: "I was minded to drink a draught of the WELL at the WORLD'S END, and even so I did." As he spake, he drew himself up, and his brows were knit a little, but his eyes sparkled from under them, and his cheeks were bright and rosy. He half drew the sword from the scabbard, and sent it back rattling, so that the sound of it went about the hall; he upreared his head and looked around him on this and that one of the warriors of the aliens, and he sniffed the air into his nostrils as he stood alone amongst them, and set his foot down hard on the floor of the King's hall, and his armour rattled upon him.

But the King sat bolt upright in his chair and stared Ralph's face; and the warriors and lords and merchants fell ack from Ralph and stood in an ordered rank on either side of him and bent their heads before him. None spoke till the King said in a hoarse voice, but lowly and wheedling: "Tell us, fair Sir, what is it that we can do to pleasure thee?"

"King," said Ralph, "I am not here to take gifts but to give them rather: yet since thou biddest me I will crave somewhat of thee, that thou mayst be the more content: and moreover the giving shall cost thee nothing: I crave of thee to give me life and limb and freedom for the poor folk whom I saw led down the hall by thy tipstaves, even now. Give me that or nothing." The King scowled, but he spake: "This is indeed a little gift of thee to take; yet to none else save thee had I given it."

Therewith he spake to a man beside him and said: "Go thou, set them free, and if any hurt hath befallen them thy life shall answer for it. Is it enough, fair Sir, and have we thy goodwill?" Ralph laughed for joy of his life and his might, and he answered: "King, this is the token of my goodwill; fear naught of me." And he turned to his men, and bade them bright forth the gift of Goldburg and open it before the King; and they did so. But when the King cast eyes on the wares his face was gladdened, for he was a greedy wolf, and whoso had been close to his mouth would have heard him mutter: "So mighty! yet so wealthy!" But he thanked Ralph aloud and in smooth words. And Ralph made obeisance to him again, and then turned and went his ways down the hall, and was glad at heart that he had become so mighty a man, for all fell back before him and looked on him with worship. Howbeit he had looked on the King closely and wisely, and deemed that he was both cruel and guileful, so that he rejoiced that he had spoken naught of Ursula, and he was minded to keep her within gates all the while they abode at Cheaping-Knowe.

When he came to the hostel he called his men-at-arms together and asked them how far they would follow him, and with one voice they said all that they would go with him whereso he would, so that it were not beyond reason. So they arrayed them for departure on the morrow, and were to ride out of gates about mid-morning. So wore the day to evening;

but ere the night was old came a man asking for Ralph, and one who would have a special alms of him, a poor man by seeming, and evilly clad. But when Ralph was alone with him, the poor man did him to wit that for all his seeming wretchedness he was but disguised, and was in sooth a man of worship, and one of the Porte. Quoth he: "I am of the King's Council, and I must needs tell thee a thing of the King: that though he was at the first overawed and cowed by the majesty of thee, a Friend of the Well, he presently came to himself, which was but ill; so that what for greed, what for fear even, he is minded to send men to waylay thee some three leagues from the town, on your way to the mountains, but ye shall easily escape his gin now I have had speech of thee; for ye may take a by-road and fetch a compass of some twelve miles, and get aback of the waylayers. Yet if ye escape this first ambush, unless ye are timely in riding early tomorrow it is not unlike that he shall send swift riders to catch up with you ere ye come to the mountains. Now I am come to warn thee hereof, partly because I would not have so fair a life spilt, which should yet do so well for the sons of Adam, and partly also because I would have reward of thee for my warning and my wayleading, for I shall show thee the way and the road."

Said Ralph: "Ask and fear not; for if I may trust thee I already owe thee a reward." "My name is Michael-a-dale," said the man, "and from Swevenham I came hither, and fain would I go thither, and little hope I have thereof save I go privily in some such band as thine, whereas the tyrant holdeth me on pain, as well I know, of an evil death."

"I grant thine asking, friend," said Ralph; "and now thou wert best go to thine house and truss what stuff thou mayst have with thee and come back hither in the grey of the morning."

The man shook his head and said: "Nay; here must I bide night-long, and go out of gates amongst thy men-at-arms and clad like one of them with iron enough about me to hide the fashion of me; it were nowise safe for me to go back into the town; for this tyrant wages many a spy: yea, forsooth, fear me by certain tokens that it is not all so certain that

442

have not been spied upon already, and that it is known that I have come to thee. And I will tell thee that by hook or by crook the King already knoweth somewhat of thee and of the woman who is in thy company."

Ralph flushed red at that word, and felt his heart bound: but even therewith came into them the Sage; and straightway Ralph took him apart and told him on what errand the man was come, and ask him if he deemed him trusty. Then the Sage went up to Michael and looked him hard in the face awhile, and then said: "Yea, honest he is unless the kindred of Michael of the Hatch of Swevenham have turned thieves in the third generation."

"Yea," said Michael, "and dost thou know the Hatch?"

"As I know mine own fingers," said the Sage; "and even so I knew it years and years before thou wert born." Therewith he told the new-comer what he was, and the two men of Swevenham made joy of each other. And Ralph was fain of them, and went into the chamber wherein sat Ursula, and told her how all things were going, and she said that she would be naught but glad to leave that town, which seemed to her like to Utterbol over again.

CHAPTER 10

An Adventure on the Way to the Mountains

On the morrow Ralph got his men together betimes and rode out a-gates, and was little afraid that any should meddle with him within the town or anigh it, and even so it turned out. But Michael rode in the company new clad, and with his head and face all hidden in a wide sallet. As for Ralph and Ursula, they were exceeding glad, and now that their heads were turned to the last great mountains, it seemed to them that they were verily going home, and they longed for the night, that they might be alone together, and talk of all these matters in each others' arms.

When they were out a-gates, they rode for two miles along the highway, heedlessly enough by seeming, and then, as Michael bade, turned suddenly into a deep and narrow lane, and forth on, as it led betwixt hazelled banks and coppices of small wood, skirting the side of the hills, so that it was late in the afternoon before they came into the Highway again, which was the only road leading into the passes of the mountains. Then said Michael that now by all likelihood they had beguiled the waylayers for that time; so they went on merrily till half the night was worn, when they shifted for lodging in a little oak-wood by the wayside. There they lay not long, but were afoot betimes in the morning, and rode swiftly daylong, and lay down at night on the wayside with the less dread because they were come so far without hurt.

But on the third day, somewhat after noon, when they were come up above the tilled upland and the land was rough and the ways steep, there lay before them a dark wood swallowing up the road. Thereabout Ralph deemed that he saw weapons glittering ahead, but was not sure, for as clear-sighted as he was. So he stayed his band, and had Ursula into the rearward, and bade all men look to their weapons, and then they went forward heedfully and in good order, and presently not only Ralph, but all of them could see men standing in the jaws of the pass with the wood on either side of them, and though at first they doubted if these were aught but mere strong-thieves, such as any wayfarers might come on, they had gone but a little further when Michael knew them for the riders of Cheaping Knowe. "Yea," said the Sage of Swevenham, "it is clear how it has been: when they found that we came not that first morning, they had an inkling of what had befallen, and went forward toward the mountains, and not back to Cheaping Knowe, and thus outwent us while we were fetching that compass to give them the go-by: wherefore I deem that some great man is with them, else had they gone back to town for new orders."

"Well," said Ralph, "then will they be too many for us; so now will I ride ahead and see if we may have peace." Said the Sage, "Yea, but be wary, for thou hast to do with the guileful."

Then Ralph rode on alone till he was come within hail of those waylayers. Then he thrust his sword into the sheath, and cried out: "Will any of the warriors in the wood speak with me; for I am the captain of the wayfarers?"

Then rode out from those men a very tall man, and two with him, one on either side, and he threw back the sallet from his face, and said: "Wayfarer, all we have weapons in our hands, and we so many that thou and thine will be in regard of us as the pips to the apple. Wherefore, yield ye!" Quoth Ralph: "Unto whom then shall I yield me?" Said the other: "To the men of the King of Cheaping Knowe." Then spake Ralph: "What will ye do with us when we are yolden? Shall we not pay ransom and go our ways?" "Yea," said the tall man, "and this is the ransom: that ye give up into my hands my dastard who hath bewrayed me, and the woman who wendeth in your company."

Ralph laughed; for by this time he knew the voice of the King, yea, and the face of him under his sallet. So he cried back in answer, and in such wise as if the words came rather from his luck than from his youth: "Ho, Sir King! beware, beware! lest thou tremble when thou seest the bare blade of the Friend of the Well more than thou trembledst erst, when the blade was hidden in the sheath before the throne of thine hall."

But the King cried out in a loud harsh voice. "Thou, young man, beware thou! and try not thy luck overmuch. We are as many as these trees, and thou canst not prevail over us. Go thy ways free, and leave me what thou canst not help leaving."

"Yea, fool," cried Ralph, "and what wilt thou do with these two?"

Said the King: "The traitor I will flay, and the woman I will bed."

Scarce were the words out of his mouth ere Ralph gave forth a great cry and drew his sword, set spurs to his horse, and galloped on up the road with all his band at his back, for they had drawn anigh amidst this talk. But or ever they

445

came on the foemen, they heard a great confused cry of onset mingled with affright, and lo! the King threw up his arms, and fell forward on his horse's neck with a great arrow through his throat.

Ralph drave on sword in hand, crying out, "Home, home to Upmeads!" and anon was amidst of the foe smiting on either hand. His men followed, shouting: "Ho, for the Friend of the Well!" And amongst the foemen, who were indeed very many, was huge dismay, so that they made but a sorry defence before the band of the wayfarers, who knew not what to make of it, till they noted that arrows and casting-spears were coming out of the wood on either side, which smote none of them, but many of the foemen. Short was the tale, for in a few minutes there were no men of the foe together save those that were fleeing down the road to Cheaping Knowe.

Ralph would not suffer his men to follow the chase, for he wotted not with whom he might have to deal besides the King's men. He drew his men together and looked round for Ursula, and saw that the Sage had brought her up anigh him, and there she sat a-horseback, pale and panting with the fear of death and joy of deliverance.

Now Ralph cried out from his saddle in a loud voice, and said: "Ho ye of the arrows of the wood! ye have saved me from my foemen; where be ye, and what be ye?" Came a loud voice from out of the wood on the right hand: "Children, tell the warrior whose sons ye be!" Straightway brake out a huge bellowing on either side of the road, as though the wood were all full of great neat.

Then cried out Ralph: "If ye be of the kindred of the Bull, ye will belike be my friends rather than my foes. Or have ye heard tell of Ralph of Upmeads? Now let your captain come forth and speak with me."

Scarce were the words out of his mouth ere a man came leaping forth from out the wood, and stood before Ralph in the twilight of the boughs, and Ralph noted of him that he was clad pretty much like to Bull Shockhead of past time, save that he had a great bull's head for a helm (which

446

afterwards Ralph found out was of iron and leather) and a great gold ring on his arm.

Then Ralph thrust his sword back into the sheath, and his folk handled their weapons peaceably, while Ralph hailed the new-comer as Lord or Duke of the Bulls.

"Belike," quoth the said chieftain, "thou wouldst wish to show me some token, whereby we may wot that thou art that Friend of the Well and of our kinsman concerning whom he sent us a message."

Then Ralph bethought him of the pouch with the knot of grass therein which Bull Shockhead had given him at Goldburg; so he drew it out, and gave it into the hand of the chieftain, who no sooner caught a glimpse thereof than he said: "Verily our brother's hand hath met thine when he gave thee this. Yet forsooth, now that I look on thee, I may say that scarce did I need token to tell me that thou wert the very man. For I can see thee, that thou art of great honour and worship, and thou didst ride boldly against the foemen when thou knewest not that we had waylaid thy waylayers. Now I wot that there is no need to ask thee whether thou wouldst get thee out of our mountains by the shortest road, yet wilt thou make it little longer, and somewhat safer, if ye will suffer us to lead thee by way of our dwelling." So Ralph yeasaid his bidding without more words.

As they spake thus together the road both above and below was become black with weaponed men, and some of Ralph's band looked on one another, as though they doubted their new friends somewhat. But the Sage of Swevenham spoke to them and bade them fear nought. "For," said he, "so far as we go, who are now their friends, there is no guile in these men." The Bull captain heard him and said: "Thou sayest sooth, old man; and I shall tell thee that scarce had a band like thine come safe through the mountains, save by great good luck, without the leave of us; for the fool with the crown that lieth there dead had of late days so stirred up the Folks of the Fells through his grimness and cruelty that we have been minded to stop everything bigger than a cur-dog that might seek to pass by us, for at least so long as yonder

447

rascal should live. But ye be welcome; so now let us to the road, for the day weareth."

So the tribesmen gat them into order, and their Duke went on the left side of Ralph, while Ursula rode on his right hand. The Duke and all his men were afoot, but they went easily and swiftly, as wolves trot. As for the slain of the waylayers, of whom there were some threescore, the Bull captain would do nought but let them lie on the road. "For," said he, "there be wolves and lynxes enough in the wood, and the ravens of the uplands, and the kites shall soon scent the carrion. They shall have burial soon enough. Neither will we meddle with it; nay, not so much as to hang the felon King's head at thy saddle-bow, lord."

By sunset they were out of the wood and on the side of a rough fell, so they went no further, but lighted fires at the edge of the thicket, and made merry round about them, singing their songs concerning the deeds of their folk, and jesting withal, but not foully; and they roasted venison of hart and hind at the fires, and they had with them wine, the more part whereof they had found in the slain King's carriages, and they made great feast to the wayfarers, and were exceeding fain of them; after their fashion, whereas if a man were their friend he could scarce be enough their friend, and if he were their foe, they could never be fierce enough with him.

CHAPTER 11

They Come Through the Mountains Into the Plain

On the morrow early they all fared on together, and thereafter they went for two days more till they came into a valley amidst of the mountains which was fair and lovely, and therein was the dwelling or town of this Folk of the

Fells. It was indeed no stronghold, save that it was not easy to find, and that the way thither was well defensible were foemen to try it. The houses thereof were artless, the chiefest of them like to the great barn of an abbey in our land, the others low and small; but the people, both men and women, haunted mostly the big house. As for the folk, they were for the more part like those whom they had met afore: strong men, but not high of stature, black-haired, with blue or grey eyes, cheerful of countenance, and of many words. Their women were mostly somewhat more than comely, smiling, kind of speech, but not suffering the caresses of aliens. They saw no thralls amongst them; and when Ralph asked hereof, how that might be, since they were men-catchers, they told him that when they took men and women, as oft they did, they always sold them for what they would bring to the plain-dwellers; or else slew them, or held them to ransom, but never brought them home to their stead. Howbeit, when they took children, as whiles befell, they sometimes brought them home, and made them very children of their Folk with many uncouth prayers and worship of their Gods, who were indeed, as they deemed, but forefathers of the Folk.

Now Ralph, he and his, being known for friends, these wild men could not make enough of them, and as it were, compelled them to abide there three days, feasting them, and making them all the cheer they might. And they showed the wayfarers their manner of hunting, both of the hart and the boar, and of wild bulls also. At first Ralph somewhat loathed all this (though he kept a pleasant countenance toward his host), for sorely he desired the fields of Upmeads and his father's house. But at last when the hunt was up in the mountains, and especially of the wild bulls, the heart and the might in him so arose that he enforced himself to do well, and the wild men wondered at his prowess, whereas he was untried in this manner of sports, and they deemed him one of the Gods, and said that their kinsman had done well to get him so good a friend. Both Ursula and the Sage withheld them from this hunting, and Ursula abode with the women, who told her much of their ways of life, and stories of old time; frank and free they were, and loved her much, and she was fain of such manly-minded women after the sleight and lies of the poor thralls of Utterbol.

On the fourth day the wayfarers made them ready and departed; and the chief of the Folk went with them with a chosen band of weaponed men, partly for the love of his guests, and partly that he might see the Goldburg men-at-arms safe back to the road unto the plain and the Midhouse of the Mountains, for they went now by other ways, which missed the said House. On this journey naught befell to tell of, and they all came down safe into the plain.

There the Goldburg men took their wage, and bidding farewell, turned back with the wild men, praising Ralph much for his frankness and open hand. As for the wild men, they exceeded in their sorrow for the parting, and many of them wept and howled as though they had seen him die before their faces. But all that came to an end, and presently their cheer was amended, and their merry speech and laughter came down from the pass unto the wayfarers' ears as each band rode its way.

CHAPTER 12

The Roads Sunder Again

Ralph and Ursula, with the Sage and Michael-a-dale went their ways, and all was smooth with them, and they saw but few folk, and those mild and lowly. At last, of an afternoon, they saw before them afar off the towers and pinnacles of Whitwall, and Ralph's heart rose within him, so that he scarce knew how to contain himself; but Ursula was shy and silent, and her colour came and went, as though some fear had hold of her. Now they two were riding on somewhat ahead of the others, so Ralph turned to Ursula, and asked what ailed her. She smiled on him and said: "A simple sickness. I am drawing nigh to thy home, and I am ashamed. Beyond the mountains, who knew what and whence I was? I was fair, and for a woman not unvaliant, and that was enough. But now when I am coming amongst the baronages and the lineages, what shall I do to hold up my head before the fools and the dastards of these high kindreds? And that all the more, my knight, because thou art changed since yester-year, and since we met on the want-way of the Wood Perilous, when I bade thee remember that thou wert a King's son and I a yeoman's daughter; for then thou wert but a lad, high-born and beautiful, but simple maybe, and untried; whereas now thou art meet to sit in the Kaiser's throne and rule the world from the Holy City."

He laughed gaily and said: "What! is it all so soon forgotten, our deeds beyond the Mountains? Belike because we had no minstrel to rhyme it for us. Or is it all but a dream? and has the last pass of the mountains changed all that for us? What then! hast thou never become my beloved, nor lain in one bed with me? Thou whom I looked to deliver from the shame and the torment of Utterbol, never didst thou free thyself without my helping, and meet me in the dark wood, and lead me to the Sage who rideth yonder behind us! No, nor didst thou ride fearless with me, leaving the world behind; nor didst thou comfort me when my heart went nigh to breaking in the wilderness! Nor thee did I deliver as I saw thee running naked from the jaws of death. Nor were we wedded in the wilderness far from our own folk. Nor didst thou deliver me from the venom of the Dry Tree. Yea verily, nor did we drink together of the Water of the Well! It is all but tales of Swevenham, a blue vapour hanging on the mountains yonder! So be it then! And here we ride together, deedless, a man and a maid of whom no tale may be told. What next then, and who shall sunder us?"

Therewith he drew his sword from the sheath, and tossed it into the air, and caught it by the hilts as it came down, and he cried out: "Hearken, Ursula! By my sword I swear it, that when I come home to the little land, if my father and my mother and all my kindred fall not down before thee and worship thee, then will I be a man without kindred, and I will turn my back on the land I love, and the House wherein I was born, and will win for thee and me a new kindred that all the world shall tell of. So help me Saint Nicholas, and all Hallows, and the Mother of God!"

She looked on him with exceeding love, and said: "Ah, beloved, how fair thou art! Is it not as I said, yea, and more, that now lieth the world at thy feet, if thou wilt stoop to pick it up? Believe me, sweet, all folk shall see this as I see it, and shall judge betwixt thee and me, and deem me naught."

"Beloved," he said, "thou dost not wholly know thyself; and I deem that the mirrors of steel serve thee but ill; and now must thou have somewhat else for a mirror, to wit, the uprising and increase of trouble concerning thee and thy fairness, and the strife of them that love thee overmuch, who shall strive to take thee from me; and then the blade that hath seen the Well at the World's End shall come out of his sheath and take me and thee from the hubbub, and into the quiet fields of my father's home, and then shalt thou be learned of thyself, when thou seest that thou art the desire of all hearts."

"Ah, the wisdom of thee," she said, "and thy valiancy, and I am become feeble and foolish before thee! What shall I do then?"

He said: "Many a time shall it be shown what thou shalt do; but here and now is the highway dry and long, and the plain meads and acres on either hand, and a glimmer of Whitwall afar off, and the little cloud of dust about us two in the late spring weather; and the Sage and Michael riding behind us, and smiting dust from the hard road. And now if this also be a dream, let it speedily begone, and let us wake up in the ancient House at Upmeads, which thou hast never seen—and thou and I in each other's arms."

CHAPTER 13

They Come to Whitwall Again

Herewith they were come to a little thorp where the way sundered, for the highway went on to Whitwall, and a byway turned off to Swevenham. Thereby was a poor hostel, where they stayed and rested for the night, because evening was at hand. So when those four had eaten and drunk there together, Ralph spoke and said: "Michael-a-dale, thou art for Swevenham to-morrow?" "Yea, lord," said Michael, "belike I shall yet find kindred there; and I call to thy mind that I craved of thee to lead me to Swevenham as payment for all, if I had done aught for thy service."

"Sooth is that," said Ralph, "thou shalt go with my good-will; and, as I deem, thou shalt not lack company betwixt here and Swevenham, whereas our dear friend here, the friend of thy father's father, is going the same road."

Then the Sage of Swevenham leaned across the board, and said: "What word hath come out of thy mouth, my son?" Said Ralph, smiling on him: "It is the last word which we have heard from thee of this matter, though verily it was spoken a while ago. What wilt thou add to it as now?" "This," quoth the Sage, "that I will leave thee no more till thou biddest me go from thee. Was this word needful?"

Ralph reached his hand to him and said: "It is well and more; but the road hence to Upmeads may yet be a rough one." "Yea," said the Sage, "yet shall we come thither all living, unless my sight now faileth."

Then Ursula rose up and came to the old man, and cast her arms about him and said: "Yea, father, come with us, and let thy wisdom bless our roof-tree. Wilt thou not teach our children wisdom; yea, maybe our children's children, since thou art a friend of the Well?"

"I know not of the teaching of wisdom," said the Sage; "but as to my going with thee, it shall be as I said e'en-now; and forsooth I looked for this bidding of thee to make naught of the word which I spoke ere yet I had learned wisdom of thee."

Therewith were they merry, and fain of each other, and the evening wore amidst great content.

But when morning was come they gat to horse, and Ralph spake to Michael and said: "Well, friend, now must thou ride alone to thy kindred, and may fair days befall thee in Swevenham. But if thou deem at any time that matters go not so well with thee as thou wouldst, then turn thine head to Upmeads, and try it there, and we shall further thee all we may."

Then came the Sage to Michael as he sat upon his horse, a stalwarth man of some forty winters, and said: "Michael-a-dale, reach me thine hand." So did he, and the Sage looked into the palm thereof, and said: "This man shall make old bones, and it is more like than not, King's son, that he shall seek to thee at Upmeads ere he die." Said Ralph: "His coming shall be a joy to us, how pleasant soever our life may be otherwise. Farewell, Michael! all good go with thee for thine wholesome redes."

So then Michael gave them farewell, and rode his ways to Swevenham, going hastily, as one who should hurry away from a grief.

But the three held on their way to Whitwall, and it was barely noon when they came to the gate thereof on a Saturday of latter May. It was a market-day, and the streets were thronged, and they looked on the folk and were fain of them, since they seemed to them to be something more than aliens. The folk also looked on them curiously, and deemed them goodly, both the old man and the two knights, for they thought no otherwise of Ursula than that she was a carle.

But now as they rode, slowly because of the crowd, up Petergate, they heard a cry of one beside them, as of a man astonished but joyful; so Ralph drew rein, and turned thither whence the cry came, and Ursula saw a man wide-shouldered, grey-haired, blue-eyed, and ruddy of countenance—a man warrior-like to look on, and girt with a long sword. Ralph lighted down from his horse, and met the man, who was coming toward him, cast his arms about his neck, and kissed him, and lo, it was Richard the Red. The people round about, when they saw it, clapped their hands, and crowded about the two crying out: "Hail to the friends long parted, and now united!" But Richard, whom most knew, cried out: "Make way, my masters! will ye sunder us again?" Then he said to Ralph: "Get into thy saddle, lad; for surely thou hast a tale to tell overlong for the open street."

Ralph did as he was bidden, and without more ado they went on all toward that hostelry where Ralph had erst borne the burden of grief. Richard walked by Ralph's side, and as he went he said: "Moreover, lad, I can see that thy tale is no ill one; therefore my heart is not wrung for thee or me, though I wait for it a while." Then again he said: "Thou doest well to hide her loveliness in war-weed even in this town of peace."

Ursula reddened, and Richard laughed and said: "Well, it is a fair rose which thou hast brought from east-away. There will be never another couple in these parts like you. Now I see the words on thy lips; so I tell thee that Blaise thy brother is alive and well and happy; which last word means that his coffer is both deep and full. Forsooth, he would make a poor bargain in buying any kingship that I wot of, so rich he is, yea, and mighty withal."

Said Ralph: "And how went the war with Walter the Black?"

Even as he spake his face changed, for he bethought him over closely of the past days, and his dream of the Lady of Abundance and of Dorothea, who rode by him now as Ursula. But Richard spake: "Short is the tale to tell. I slew him in shock of battle, and his men craved peace of the good town. Many were glad of his death, and few sorrowed for it; for, fair as his young body was, he was a cruel tyrant."

Therewith were they come to the hostel of the Lamb, which was the very same house wherein Ralph had abided aforetime; and as he entered it, it is not to be said but that inwardly his heart bled for the old sorrow. Ursula looked on him lovingly and blithely; and when they were within doors Richard turned to the Sage and said: "Hail to thee, reverend man! wert thou forty years older to behold, outworn and forgotten of death, I should have said that thou wert like to the Sage that dwelt alone amidst the mountains nigh to Swevenham when I was a little lad, and fearsome was the sight of thee unto me."

The Sage laughed and said: "Yea, somewhat like am I yet to myself of forty years ago. Good is thy memory, greybeard."

Then Richard shook his head, and spake under his breath: "Yea, then it was no dream or coloured cloud, and he hath drank of the waters, and so then hath my dear lord." Then he looked up bright-faced, and called on the serving-men, and bade one lead them into a fair chamber, and another go forth and provide a banquet to be brought in thither. So they went up into a goodly chamber high aloft; and Ursula went forth from it awhile, and came back presently clad in very fair woman's raiment, which Ralph had bought for her at Goldburg. Richard looked on her and nothing else for a while; then he walked about the chamber uneasily, now speaking with the Sage, now with Ursula, but never with Ralph. At last he spake to Ursula, and said: "Grant me a grace, lady, and be not wroth if I take thy man into the window yonder that I may talk with him privily while ye hold converse together, thou and the Sage of Swevenham."

She laughed merrily and said: "Sir nurse, take thy bantling and cosset him in whatso corner thou wilt, and I will turn away mine eyes from thy caresses."

So Richard took Ralph into a window, and sat down beside him and said: "Mayhappen I shall sadden thee by my question, but I mind me what our last talking together was about, and therefore I must needs ask thee this, was that other one fairer than this one is?"

Ralph knit his brows: "I wot not," quoth he, "since she is gone, that other one."

"Yea," said Richard, "but this I say, that she is without a blemish. Did ye drink of the Well together?"

"Yea, surely," said Ralph. Said Richard: "And is this woman of a good heart? Is she valiant?" "Yea, yea," said Ralph, flushing red.

"As valiant as was that other?" said Richard. Said Ralph: "How may I tell, unless they were tried in one way?" Yet Richard spake: "Are ye wedded?" "Even so," said Ralph.

"Dost thou deem her true?" said Richard. "Truer than myself," said Ralph, in a voice which was somewhat angry.

Quoth Richard: "Then is it better than well, and better than well; for now hast thou wedded into the World of living men, and not to a dream of the Land of Fairy."

Ralph sat silent a little, and as if he were swallowing somewhat; at last he said: "Old friend, I were well content if thou wert to speak such words no more; for it irks me, and woundeth my heart."

Said Richard: "Well, I will say no more thereof; be content therefore, for now I have said it, and thou needest not fear me, what I have to say thereon any more; and thou mayst well wot that I must needs have said somewhat of this."

Ralph nodded to him friendly, and even therewith came in the banquet, which was richly served, as for a King's son, and wine was poured forth of the best, and they feasted and were merry. And then Ralph told all the tale of his wanderings how it had betid, bringing in all that Ursula had told him of Utterbol; while as for her she put in no word of it. So that at last Ralph, being wishful to hear her tell somewhat, made more of some things than was really in them, so that she might set him right; but no word more she said for all that, but only smiled on him now and again, and sat blushing like a rose over her golden-flowered gown, while Richard looked on her and praised her in his heart exceedingly.

But when Ralph had done the story (which was long, so that by then it was over it had been dark night some while), Richard said: "Well, fosterling, thou hast seen much, and done much, and many would say that thou art a lucky man, and that more and much more lieth ready to thine hand. Whither now wilt thou wend, or what wilt thou do?"

Ralph's face reddened, as its wont had been when it was two years younger, at contention drawing nigh, and he answered: "Where then should I go save to the House of my Fathers, and the fields that fed them? What should I do but live amongst my people, warding them from evil, and loving them and giving them good counsel? For wherefore should I love them less than heretofore? Have they become dastards, and the fools of mankind?"

Quoth Richard: "They are no more fools than they were belike, nor less valiant. But thou art grown wiser and mightier by far; so that thou art another manner man than thou wert, and the Master of Masters maybe. To Upmeads wilt thou go; but wilt thou abide there? Upmeads is a fair land, but a narrow; one day is like another there, save when sorrow and harm is blent with it. The world is wide, and now I deem that thou holdest the glory thereof in the hollow of thine hand."

Then spake the Sage, and said: "Yea, Richard of Swevenham, and how knowest thou but that this sorrow and trouble have not now fallen upon Upmeads? And if that be so, upon whom should they call to their helping rather than him who can help them most, and is their very lord?" Said Richard: "It may be so, wise man, though as yet we have heard no tidings thereof. But if my lord goeth to their help, yet, when the trouble shall be over, will he not betake him thither where fresh deeds await him?"

"Nay, Richard," said the Sage, "art thou so little a friend of thy fosterling as not to know that when he hath brought back peace to the land, it will be so that both he shall need the people, and they him, so that if he go away for awhile, yet shall he soon come back? Yea, and so shall the little land, it may be, grow great."

Now had Ralph sat quiet while this talk was going on, and as if he heeded not, and his eyes were set as if he were beholding something far away. Then Richard spoke again after there had been silence awhile: "Wise man, thou sayest sooth; yea, and so it is, that though we here have heard no tale concerning war in Upmeads, yet, as it were, we have been feeling some stirring of the air about us; even as though matters were changing, great might undone, and weakness grown to strength. Who can say but our lord may find deeds to hand or ever he come to Upmeads?"

Ralph turned his head as one awaking from a dream, and he said: "When shall to-morrow be, that we may get us gone from Whitwall, we three, and turn our faces toward Upmeads?"

Said Richard: "Wilt thou not tarry a day or two, and talk with thine own mother's son and tell him of thine haps?"

"Yea," said Ralph, "and so would I, were it not that my father's trouble and my mother's grief draw me away."

"O tarry not," said Ursula; "nay, not for the passing of the night; but make this hour the sunrise, and begone by the clear of the moon. For lo! how he shineth through the window!"

Then she turned to Richard, and said: "O fosterer of my love, knowest thou not that as now he speaketh as a Friend of the Well, and wotteth more of far-off tidings than even this wise man of many years?"

Said Ralph: "She sayeth sooth, O Richard. Or how were it if the torch were even now drawing nigh to the High House of Upmeads: yea, or if the very House were shining as a dreary candle of the meadows, and reddening the waters of the ford! What do we here?"

Therewith he thrust the board from him, and arose and went to his harness, and fell to arming him, and he spake to Richard: "Now shall thine authority open to us the gates of the good town, though the night be growing old; we shall go our ways, dear friend, and mayhappen we shall meet again, and mayhappen not: and thou shalt tell my brother Blaise, who wotteth not of my coming hither, how things have gone with me, and how need hath drawn me hence. And bid him come see me at Upmeads, and to ride with a good band of proper men, for eschewing the dangers of the road."

Then spake Richard: "I shall tell Lord Blaise neither more nor less than thou mayst tell him thyself: for think it not that thou shalt go without me. As for Blaise, he may well spare me; for he is become a chief and Lord of the Porte; and the Porte hath now right good men-at-arms, and captains withal younger and defter than I be. But now suffer me to send a swain for my horse and arms, and another to the captain of the watch at West-gate Bar that he be ready to open to me and three of my friends, and to send me a let-pass for the occasion. So shall we go forth ere it be known that the brother of the Lord of the Porte is abiding at the Lamb. For verily I see that the Lady hath spoken truth; and it is like that she is forseeing, even as thou hast grown to be. And now I bethink me I might lightly get me a score of men to ride with us, whereas we may meet men worse than ourselves on the way."

Said Ralph: "All good go with thy words, Richard; yet gather not force: there may stout men be culled on the road; and if thou runnest or ridest about the town, we may yet be stayed by Blaise and his men. Wherefore now send for thine horse and arms, and bid the host here open his gates with little noise when we be ready; and we will presently ride out by the clear of the moon. But thou, beloved, shalt don thine armour no more, but shalt ride henceforth in thy woman's raiment, for the wild and the waste is well nigh over, and the way is but short after all these months of wandering; and I say that now shall all friends drift toward us, and they that shall rejoice to strike a stroke for my father's son, and the peaceful years of the Friend of the Well."

To those others, and chiefly to Ursula, it seemed that now he spoke strongly and joyously, like to a king and a captain of men. Richard did his bidding, and was swift in dealing with the messengers. But the Sage said: "Ralph, my son, since ye have lost one man-at-arms, and have gotten but this golden angel in his stead, I may better that. I prithee bid thy man Richard find me armour and weapons that I may amend the shard in thy company. Thou shalt find me no feeble man when we come to push of staves."

Ralph laughed, and bade Richard see to it; so he dealt with the host, and bought good war-gear of him, and a trenchant sword, and an axe withal; and when the Sage was armed he looked as doughty a warrior as need be. By this time was Richard's horse and war-gear come, and he armed him speedily and gave money to the host, and they rode therewith all four out of the hostel, and found the street empty and still, for the night was wearing. So rode they without tarrying into Westgate and came to the Bar, and speedily was the gate opened to them; and anon were they on the moonlit road outside of Whitwall.

CHAPTER 14

They Ride Away From Whitwall

But when they were well on the way, and riding a good pace by the clear of the moon, Richard spake to Ralph, and said: "Wither ride we now?" said Ralph: "Wither, save to Upmeads?" "Yea, yea," said Richard, "but by what road? shall we ride down to the ford of the Swelling Flood, and ride the beaten way, or take to the downland and the forest, and so again by the forest and downland and the forest once more, till we come to the Burg of the Four Friths?"

"Which way is the shorter?" said Ralph. "Forsooth," said Richard, "by the wildwood ye may ride shorter, if ye know it as I do." Quoth the Sage: "Yea, or as I do. Hear a wonder! that two men of Swevenham know the wilds more than twenty miles from their own thorp."

Said Ralph: "Well, wend we the shorter road; why make more words over it? Or what lion lieth on the path? Is it that we may find it hard to give the go-by to the Burg of the Four Friths?"

Said Richard: "Though the Burg be not very far from Whitwall, we hear but little tidings thence; our chapmen but seldom go there, and none cometh to us thence save such of our men as have strayed thither. Yet, as I said e'en now in the hostel, there is an air of tidings abroad, and one rumour sayeth, and none denieth it, that the old fierceness and stout headstrong mood of the Burg is broken down, and that men dwell there in peace and quiet."

Said the Sage: "In any case we have amongst us lore enough to hoodwink them if they be foes; so that we shall pass easily. Naught of this need we fear."

But Richard put his mouth close to Ralph's ear, and spake to him softly: "Shall we indeed go by that shorter road, whatever in days gone by may have befallen in places thereon, to which we must go a-nigh tomorrow?" Ralph answered softly in turn: "Yea, forsooth: for I were fain to try my heart, how strong it may be."

So they rode on, and turned off from the road that led down to the ford of the Swelling Flood, anigh which Ralph had fallen in with Blaise and Richard on the day after the woeful slaying, which had made an end of his joy for that time. But when they were amidst of the bushes and riding a deep ghyll of the waste, Richard said: "It is well that we are here: for now if Blaise send riders to bring us back courteously, they shall not follow us at once, but shall ride straight down to the ford, and even cross it in search of us." "Yea," said Ralph, "it is well in all wise."

So then they rode thence awhile till the moon grew low, and great, and red, and sank down away from them; and by then were they come to a shepherd's cot, empty of men, with naught therein save an old dog, and some victual, as bread and white cheese, and a well for drinking. So there they abode and rested that night.

CHAPTER 15

A Strange Meeting in the Wilderness

On the morrow betimes they got to the road again; the country at first, though it was scanty of tillage, was not unfurnished of sheep, being for the most part of swelling hills and downs well grassed, with here and there a deep cleft in them. They saw but few houses, and those small and poor. A few shepherds they fell in with, who were short of speech, after the manner of such men, but deemed a greeting not wholly thrown away on such goodly folk as those wayfarers.

So they rode till it was noon, and Richard talked more than his wont was, though his daily use it was to be of many words: nor did the Sage spare speech; but Ursula spoke little, nor heeded much what the others said, and Ralph deemed that she was paler than of wont, and her brows were knitted as if she were somewhat anxious. As for him, he was grave and calm, but of few words; and whiles when Richard was wordiest he looked on him steadily for a moment, whereat Richard changed countenance, and for a while stinted his speech, but not for long; while Ralph looked about him, inwardly striving to gather together the ends of unhappy thoughts that floated about him, and to note the land he was passing through, if indeed he had verily seen it aforetime, elsewhere than in some evil dream.

At last when they stopped to bait by some scrubby bushes at the foot of a wide hill-side, he took Richard apart, and said to him: "Old friend, and whither go we?" Said Richard: "As thou wottest, to the Burg of the Four Friths." "Yea," said Ralph, "but by what road?" Said Richard: "Youngling, is not thine heart, then, as strong as thou deemedst last night?" Ralph was silent a while, and then he said: "I know

463

what thou wouldst say; we are going by the shortest road to the Castle of Abundance."

He spake this out loud, but Richard nodded his head to him, as if he would say: "Yea, so it is; but hold thy peace." But Ralph knew that Ursula had come up behind him, and, still looking at Richard, he put his open hand aback toward her, and her hand fell into it. Then he turned about to her, and saw that her face was verily pale; so he put his hands on her shoulders and kissed her kindly; and she let her head fall on to his bosom and fell a-weeping, and the two elders turned away to the horses, and feigned to be busy with them.

Thus then they bided some minutes of time, and then all gat to horse again, and Ursula's face was cleared of the grief of fear, and the colour had come back to her cheeks and lips. But Ralph's face was stern and sorrowful to behold; howbeit, as they rode away he spake in a loud and seeming cheerful voice: "Still ever shorteneth more and more the way unto my Fathers' House: and withal I am wishful to see if it be indeed true that the men of the Burg have become mild and peaceful; and to know what hath befallen those doughty champions of the Dry Tree; and if perchance they have any will to hold us a tilting in courteous fashion."

Richard smiled on him, and said: "Thou holdest more then by the Dry Tree than by the Burg; though while agone we deemed the Champions worse men to meet in the wood than the Burgers."

"So it is," said Ralph; "but men are oft mis-said by them that know them not thoroughly: and now, if it were a good wish, O Sage of Swevenham, I were fain to fall in with the best of all those champions, a tall man and a proper, who, meseems, had good-will toward me, I know not why."

Quoth the Sage: "If thou canst not see the end of this wish fulfilled, no more can I. And yet, meseems something may follow it which is akin to grief: be content with things so done, my son."

Now Ralph holds his peace, and they speed on their way, Ursula riding close by Ralph's side, and caressing him with looks, and by touch also when she might; and after a while he fell to talking again, and ever in the same loud, cheerful voice. Till at last, in about another hour, they came in sight of the stream which ran down toward the Swelling Flood from that pool wherein erst the Lady of Abundance had bathed her before the murder. Hard looked Ralph on the stream, but howsoever his heart might ache with the memory of that passed grief, like as the body aches with the bruise of yesterday's blow, yet he changed countenance but little, and in his voice was the same cheery sound. But Ursula noted him, and how his eyes wandered, and how little he heeded the words of the others, and she knew what ailed him, for long ago he had told her all that tale, and so now her heart was troubled, and she looked on him and was silent.

Thus, then, a little before sunset, they came on that steep cliff with the cave therein, and the little green plain thereunder, and the rocky bank going down sheer into the water of the stream. Forsooth they came on it somewhat suddenly from out of the bushes of the valley; and there indeed not only the Sage and Richard, but Ursula also, were stayed by the sight as folk compelled; for all three knew what had befallen there. But Ralph, though he looked over his shoulder at it all, yet rode on steadily, and when he saw that the others lingered, he waved his hand and cried out as he rode: "On, friends, on! for the road shortens towards my Fathers' House." Then were they ashamed, and shook their reins to hasten after him.

But in that very nick of time there came forth one from amidst the bushes that edged the pool of the stream and strode dripping on to the shallow; a man brown and hairy, and naked, save for a green wreath about his middle. Tall he was above the stature of most men; awful of aspect, and his eyes glittered from his dark brown face amidst of his shock-head of the colour of rain-spoilt hay. He stood and looked while one might count five, and then without a word or cry rushed up from the water, straight on Ursula, who was riding first of the three lingerers, and in the twinkling of an eye tore her from off her horse; and she was in his grasp as the cushat in the claws of the kite. Then he cast her to earth, and stood over her, shaking a great club, but or ever he brought it down he turned his head over his shoulder toward the cliff

465

and the cave therein, and in that same moment first one blade and then another flashed about him, and he fell crashing down upon his back, smitten in the breast and the side by Richard and Ralph; and the wounds were deep and deadly.

Ralph heeded him no more, but drew Ursula away from him, and raised her up and laid her head upon his knee; and she had not quite swooned away, and forsooth had taken but little hurt; only she was dizzy with terror and the heaving up and casting down.

She looked up into Ralph's face, and smiled on him and said: "What hath been done to me, and why did he do it?"

His eyes were still wild with fear and wrath, as he answered: "O Beloved, Death and the foeman of old came forth from the cavern of the cliff. What did they there, Lord God? and he caught thee to slay thee; but him have I slain. Nevertheless, it is a terrible and evil place: let us go hence."

"Yea," she said, "let us go speedily!" Then she stood up, weak and tottering still, and Ralph arose and put his left arm about her to stay her; and lo, there before them was Richard kneeling over the wild-man, and the Sage was coming back from the river with his headpiece full of water; so Ralph cried out: "To horse, Richard, to horse! Hast thou not done slaying the woodman?"

But therewith came a weak and hoarse voice from the earth, and the wild-man spake. "Child of Upmeads, drive not on so hard: it will not be long. For thou and Richard the Red are naught lighthanded."

Ralph marvelled that the wild-man knew him and Richard, but the wild-man spake again: "Hearken, thou lover, thou young man!"

But therewith was the Sage come to him and kneeling beside him with the water, and he drank thereof, while Ralph said to him: "What is this woodman? and canst thou speak my Latin? What art thou?"

Then the wild-man when he had drunk raised him up a little, and said: "Young man, thou and Richard are deft leeches; ye have let me blood to a purpose, and have brought back to me my wits, which were wandering wide. Yet am I indeed where my fool's brains told me I was."

Then he lay back again, and turned his head as well as he could toward the cavern in the cliff. But Ralph deemed he had heard his voice before, and his heart was softened toward him, he knew not why; but he said: "Yea, but wherefore didst thou fall upon the Lady?" The wild-man strove with his weakness, and said angrily: "What did another woman there?" Then he said in a calmer but weaker voice: "Nay, my wits shall wander no more from me; we will make the journey together, I and my wits. But O, young man, this I will say if I can. Thou fleddest from her and forgattest her. I came to her and forgat all but her; yea, my very life I forgat."

Again he spoke, and his voice was weaker yet: "Kneel down by me, or I may not tell thee what I would; my voice dieth before me."

Then Ralph knelt down by him, for he began to have a deeming of what he was, and he put his face close to the dying man's, and said to him; "I am here, what wouldst thou?"

Said the wild-man very feebly: "I did not much for thee, time was; how might I, when I loved her so sorely? But I did a little. Believe it, and do so much for me that I may lie by her side when I am dead, who never lay by her living. For into the cave I durst go never."

Then Ralph knew him, that he was the tall champion whom he had met first at the churchyard gate of Netherton; so he said: "I know thee now, and I will promise to do thy will herein. I am sorry that I have slain thee; forgive it me."

A mocking smile came into the dying man's eyes, and he spake whispering: "Richard it was; not thou."

The smile spread over his face, he strove to turn more toward Ralph, and said in a very faint whisper: "The last time!"

No more he said, but gave up the ghost presently. The Sage rose up from his side and said: "Ye may now bury this man as he craved of thee, for he is dead. Thus hath thy wish been accomplished; for this was the great champion and duke of the men of the Dry Tree. Indeed it is a pity of him that he is dead, for as terrible as he was to his foes, he was no ill man."

Spake Richard: "Now is the riddle areded of the wild-man and the mighty giant that haunted these passes. We have played together or now, in days long past, he and I; and ever he came to his above. He was a wise man and a prudent that he should have become a wild-man. It is great pity of him."

But Ralph took his knight's cloak of red scarlet, and they lapped the wild-man therein, who had once been a champion beworshipped. But first Ursula sheared his hair and his beard, till the face of him came back again, grave, and somewhat mocking, as Ralph remembered it, time was. Then they bore him in the four corners across the stream, and up on to the lawn before the cliff; and Richard and the Sage bore him into the cave, and laid him down there beside the howe which Ralph had erewhile heaped over the Lady; and now over him also they heaped stones.

Meanwhile Ursula knelt at the mouth of the cave and wept; but Ralph turned him about and stood on the edge of the bank, and looked over the ripple of the stream on to the valley, where the moon was now beginning to cast shadows, till those two came out of the cave for the last time. Then Ralph turned to Ursula and raised her up and kissed her, and they went down all of them from that place of death and ill-hap, and gat to horse on the other side of the stream, and rode three miles further on by the glimmer of the moon, and lay down to rest amongst the bushes of the waste, with few words spoken between them.

CHAPTER 16

They Come to the Castle of Abundance Once More

When they rode on next morning Ralph was few-spoken, and seemed to heed little so long as they made good speed on the way: most of the talk was betwixt Richard and the Sage, Ralph but putting in a word when it would have seemed churlish to forbear.

So they went their ways through the wood till by then the sun was well westering they came out at the Water of the Oak, and Richard drew rein there, and spake: "Here is a fair place for a summer night's lodging, and I would warrant both good knight and fair lady have lain here aforetime, and wished the dark longer: shall we not rest here?"

Ralph stared at him astonished, and then anger grew in his face for a little, because, forsooth, as Richard and the Sage both wotted of the place of the slaying of the Lady, and he himself had every yard of the way in his mind as they went, it seemed but due that they should have known of this place also, what betid there: but it was not so, and the place was to Richard like any other lawn of the woodland.

But thought came back to Ralph in a moment, and he smiled at his own folly, howbeit he could not do to lie another night on that lawn with other folk than erst. So he said quietly: "Nay, friend, were we not better to make the most of this daylight? Seest thou it wants yet an hour of sunset?"

Richard nodded a yeasay, and the Sage said no word more; but Ursula cast her anxious look on Ralph as though she understood what was moving in him; and therewith those others rode away lightly, but Ralph turned slowly from the oak-tree, and might not forbear looking on to the short

469

sward round about, as if he hoped to see some token left behind. Then he lifted up his face as one awaking, shook his rein, and rode after the others down the long water.

So they turned from the water anon, and rode the woodland ways, and lay that night by a stream that ran west.

They arose betimes on the morrow, and whereas the Sage knew the woodland ways well, they made but a short journey of it to the Castle of Abundance, and came into the little plain but two hours after noon, where saving that the scythe had not yet wended the tall mowing grass in the crofts which the beasts and sheep were not pasturing, all was as on that other tide. The folk were at work in their gardens, or herding their cattle in the meads, and as aforetime they were merry of countenance and well-clad, fair and gentle to look on.

There were their pleasant cots, and the little white church, and the fair walls of the castle on its low mound, and the day bright and sunny, all as aforetime, and Ralph looked on it all, and made no countenance of being moved beyond his wont.

So they came out of the wood, and rode to the ford of the river, and the carles and queans came streaming from their garths and meads to meet them, and stood round wondering at them; but an old carle came from out the throng and went up to Ralph, and hailed him, and said: "Oh, Knight! and hast thou come back to us? and has thou brought us tidings of our Lady? Who is this fair woman that rideth with thee? Is it she?"

Spake Ralph: "Nay; go look on her closely, and tell me thy deeming of her."

So the carle went up to Ursula, and peered closely into her face, and took her hand and looked on it, and knelt down and took her foot out of the stirrup, and kissed it, and then came back to Ralph, and said: "Fair Sir, I wot not but it may be her sister; for yonder old wise man I have seen here erst with our heavenly Lady. But though this fair woman may be her sister, it is not she. So tell me what is become of her, for it is long since we have seen her; and what thou tellest us, that same shall we trow, even as if thou wert her angel. For I spake with thee, it is nigh two years agone, when

470

thou wert abiding the coming of our Lady in the castle yonder. But now I see of thee that thou art brighter-faced, and mightier of aspect than aforetime, and it is in my mind that the Lady of Abundance must have loved thee and holpen thee, and blessed thee with some great blessing."

Said Ralph: "Old man, canst thou feel sorrow, and canst thou bear it?" The carle shook his head. "I wot not," said he, "I fear thy words." Said Ralph: "It were naught to say less than the truth; and this is the very truth, that thou shalt never see thy Lady any more. I was the last living man that ever saw her alive."

Then he spake in a loud voice and said: "Lament, ye people! for the Lady of Abundance is dead; yet sure I am that she sendeth this message to you, Live in peace, and love ye the works of the earth."

But when they heard him, the old man covered up his face with the folds of his gown, and all that folk brake forth into weeping, and crying out: "Woe for us! the Lady of Abundance is dead!" and some of the younger men cast themselves down on to the earth, and wallowed, weeping and wailing: and there was no man there that seemed as if he knew which way to turn, or what to do; and their faces were foolish with sorrow. Yet forsooth it was rather the carles than the queans who made all this lamentation.

At last the old man spake: "Fair sir, ye have brought us heavy tidings, and we know not how to ask you to tell us more of the tale. Yet if thou might'st but tell us how the Lady died? Woe's me for the word!"

Said Ralph: "She was slain with the sword."

The old man drew himself up stiff and stark, the eyes of him glittered under his white hair, and wrath changed his face, and the other men-folk thronged them to hearken what more should be said.

But the elder spake again: "Tell me who it was that slew her, for surely shall I slay him, or die in the pain else."

Said Ralph: "Be content, thou mayst not slay him; he was a great and mighty man, a baron who bore a golden sun on a blue field. Thou mayst not slay him." "Yea," said the old man, "but I will, or he me."

"Live in peace," said Ralph, "for I slew him then and there."

The old man held his peace a while, and then he said: "I know the man, for he hath been here aforetime, and not so long ago. But if he be dead, he hath a brother yet, an exceeding mighty man: he will be coming here to vex us and minish us."

Said Ralph: "He will not stir from where he lies till Earth's bones be broken, for my sword lay in his body yesterday."

The old man stood silent again, and the other carles thronged him; but the woman stood aloof staring on Ralph. Then the elder came up to Ralph and knelt before him and kissed his feet; then he turned and called to him three of the others who were of the stoutest and most stalwarth, and he spake with them awhile, and then he came to Ralph again, and again knelt before him and said: "Lord, ye have come to us, and found us void of comfort, since we have lost our Lady. But we see in thee, that she hath loved thee and blessed thee, and thou hast slain her slayer and his kindred. And we see of thee also that thou art a good lord. O the comfort to us, therefore, if thou wouldest be our Lord! We will serve thee truly so far as we may: yea, even if thou be beset by foes, we will take bow and bill from the wall, and stand round about thee and fight for thee. Only thou must not ask us to go hence from this place: for we know naught but the Plain of Abundance, and the edges of the wood, and the Brethren of the House of the Thorn, who are not far hence. Now we pray thee by thy fathers not to naysay us, so sore as thou hast made our hearts. Also we see about thy neck the same-like pair of beads which our Lady was wont to bear, and we deem that ye were in one tale together."

Then was Ralph silent awhile, but the Sage spake to the elder: "Old man, how great is the loss of the Lady to you?" "Heavy loss, wise old man," said the carle, "as thou thyself mayst know, having known her."

"And what did she for you?" said the Sage. Said the elder: "We know that she was gracious to us; never did she lay tax or tale on us, and whiles she would give us of her store, and

472

that often, and abundantly. We deem also that every time when she came to us our increase became more plenteous, which is well seen by this, that since she hath ceased to come, the seasons have been niggard unto us."

The Sage smiled somewhat, and the old man went on: "But chiefly the blessing was to see her when she came to us: for verily it seemed that where she set her feet the grass grew greener, and that the flowers blossomed fairer where the shadow of her body fell." And therewith the old man fell a-weeping again.

The Sage held his peace, and Ralph still kept silence; and now of these men all the younger ones had their eyes upon Ursula.

After a while Ralph spake and said: "O elder, and ye folk of the People of Abundance, true it is that your Lady who is dead loved me, and it is through her that I am become a Friend of the Well. Now meseemeth though ye have lost your Lady, whom ye so loved and worshipped, God wot not without cause, yet I wot not why ye now cry out for a master, since ye dwell here in peace and quiet and all wealth, and the Fathers of the Thorn are here to do good to you. Yet, if ye will it in sooth, I will be called your Lord, in memory of your Lady whom ye shall not see again. And as time wears I will come and look on you and hearken to your needs: and if ye come to fear that any should fall upon you with the strong hand, then send ye a message to me, Ralph of Upmeads, down by the water, and I will come to you with such following as need be. And as for service, this only I lay upon you, that ye look to the Castle and keep it in good order, and ward it against thieves and runagates, and give guesting therein to any wandering knight or pilgrim, or honest goodman, who shall come to you. Now is all said, my masters, and I pray you let us depart in peace; for time presses."

Then all they (and this time women as well as men) cried out joyfully: "Hail to our lord! and long life to our helper." And the women withal drew nearer to him, and some came close up to him, as if they would touch him or kiss his hand, but by seeming durst not, but stood blushing before him, and he looked on them, smiling kindly.

But the old man laid his hand on his knee and said: "Lord, wouldst thou not light down and enter thy Castle; for none hath more right there now than thou. The Prior of the Thorn hath told us that there is no lineage of the Lady left to claim it; and none other might ever have claimed it save the Baron of Sunway, whom thou hast slain. And else would we have slain him, since he slew our Lady."

Ralph shook his head and said: "Nay, old friend, and new vassal, this we may not do: we must on speedily, for belike there is work for us to do nearer home."

"Yea, Lord," said the carle, "but at least light down and sit for a while under this fair oak-tree in the heat of the day, and eat a morsel with us, and drink a cup, that thy luck may abide with us when thou art gone."

Ralph would not naysay him; so he and all of them got off their horses, and sat down on the green grass under the oak: and that people gathered about and sat down by them, save that a many of the women went to their houses to fetch out the victual. Meanwhile the carles fell to speech freely with the wayfarers, and told them much concerning their little land, were it hearsay, or stark sooth: such as tales of the wights that dwelt in the wood, wodehouses, and elf-women, and dwarfs, and such like, and how fearful it were to deal with such creatures. Amongst other matters they told how a hermit, a holy man, had come to dwell in the wood, in a clearing but a little way thence toward the north-west. But when Ralph asked if he dwelt on the way to the ford of the Swelling Flood, they knew not what he meant; for the wood was to them as a wall.

Hereon the Sage held one of the younger men in talk, and taught him what he might of the way to the Burg of the Four Friths, so that they might verily send a messenger to Upmeads if need were. But the country youth said there was no need to think thereof, as no man of theirs would dare the journey through the wood, and that if they had need of a messenger, one of the Fathers of the Thorn would do their errand, whereas they were holy men, and knew the face of the world full well.

Now in this while the folk seemed to have gotten their courage again, and to be cheery, and to have lost their grief for the Lady: and of the maidens left about the oak were more than two or three very fair, who stood gazing at Ralph as if they were exceeding fain of him.

But amidst these things came back the women with the victual; to wit bread in baskets, and cheeses both fresh and old, and honey, and wood-strawberries, and eggs cooked diversely, and skewers of white wood with gobbets of roasted lamb's flesh, and salad good plenty. All these they bore first to Ralph and Ursula, and their two fellows, and then dealt them to their own folk: and they feasted and were merry in despite of that tale of evil tidings. They brought also bowls and pitchers of wine that was good and strong, and cider of their orchards, and called many a health to the new Lord and his kindred.

Thus then they abode a-feasting till the sun was westering and the shadows waxed about them, and then at last Ralph rose up and called to horse, and the other wayfarers arose also, and the horses were led up to them. Then the maidens, made bold by the joy of the feast, and being stirred to the heart by much beholding of this beloved Lord, cast off their shamefacedness and crowded about him, and kisssed his raiment and his hands: some even, though trembling, and more for love than fear, prayed him for kisses, and he, nothing loath, laughed merrily and laid his hands on their shoulders or took them by the chins, and set his lips to the sweetness of their cheeks and their lips, of those that asked and those that refrained; so that their hearts failed them for love of him, and when he was gone, they knew not how to go back to their houses, or the places that were familiar to them. Therewith he and his got into their saddles and rode away slowly, because of the thronging about them of that folk, who followed them to the edge of the wood, and even entered a little thereinto; and then stood gazing on Ralph and his fellows after they had spurred on and were riding down a glade of the woodland.

CHAPTER 17

They Fall in With That Hermit

So much had they tarried over this greeting and feasting, that though they had hoped to have come to the hermit's house that night, he of whom that folk had told them, it fell not so, whereas the day had aged so much ere they left the Plain of Abundance that it began to dusk before they had gone far, and they must needs stay and await the dawn there; so they dight their lodging as well as they might, and lay down and slept under the thick boughs.

Ralph woke about sunrise, and looking up saw a man standing over him, and deemed at first that it would be Richard or the Sage; but as his vision cleared, he saw that it was neither of them, but a new comer; a stout carle clad in russet, with a great staff in his hand and a short-sword girt to his side. Ralph sprang up, still not utterly awake, and cried out, "Who art thou, carle?" The man laughed, and said: "Yea, thou art still the same brisk lad, only filled out to something more warrior-like than of old. But it is unmeet to forget old friends. Why dost thou not hail me?"

"Because I know thee not, good fellow," said Ralph. But even as he spoke, he looked into the man's face again, and cried out: "By St. Nicholas! but it is Roger of the Ropewalk. But look you, fellow, if I have somewhat filled out, thou, who wast always black-muzzled, art now become as hairy as a wodehouse. What dost thou in the wilds?" Said Roger: "Did they not tell thee of a hermit new come to these shaws?" "Yea," said Ralph. "I am that holy man," quoth Roger, grinning; "not that I am so much of that, either. I have not come hither to pray or fast overmuch, but to rest my soul and be out of the way of men. For all things have changed since my Lady passed away."

He looked about, and saw Ursula just rising up from the ground and the Sage stirring, while Richard yet hugged his bracken bed, snoring. So he said: "And who be these, and why hast thou taken to the wildwood? Yea lad, I see of thee, that thou hast gotten another Lady; and if mine eyes do not fail me she is fair enough. But there be others as fair; while the like to our Lady that was, there is none such."

He fell silent a while, and Ralph turned about to the others, for by this time Richard also was awake, and said: "This man is the hermit of whom we were told."

Roger said: "Yea, I am the hermit and the holy man; and withal I have a thing to hear and a thing to tell. Ye were best to come with me, all of you, to my house in the woods; a poor one, forsooth, but there is somewhat of victual here, and we can tell and hearken therein well sheltered and at peace. So to horse, fair folk."

They would not be bidden twice, but mounted and went along with him, who led them by a thicket path about a mile, till they came to a lawn where-through ran a stream; and there was a little house in it, simple enough, of one hall, built with rough tree-limbs and reed thatch. He brought them in, and bade them sit on such stools or bundles of stuff as were there. But withal he brought out victual nowise ill, though it were but simple also, of venison of the wildwood, with some little deal of cakes baked on the hearth, and he poured for them also both milk and wine.

They were well content with the banquet, and when they were full, Roger said: "Now, my Lord, like as oft befalleth minstrels, ye have had your wages before your work. Fall to, then, and pay me the scot by telling me all that hath befallen you since (woe worth the while!) my Lady died, —I must needs say, for thy sake."

" 'All' is a big word," said Ralph, "but I will tell thee somewhat. Yet I bid thee take note that I and this ancient wise one, and my Lady withal, deem that I am drawn by my kindred to come to their help, and that time presses."

Roger scowled somewhat on Ursula; but he said: "Lord

and master, let not that fly trouble thy lip. For so I deem of it, that whatsoever time ye may lose by falling in with me, ye may gain twice as much again by hearkening my tale and the rede that shall go with it. And I do thee to wit that the telling of thy tale shall unfreeze mine; so tarry not, if ye be in haste to be gone, but let thy tongue wag."

Ralph smiled, and without more ado told him all that had befallen him; and of Swevenham and Utterbol, and of his captivity and flight; and of the meeting in the wood, and of the Sage (who there was), and of the journey to the Well, and what betid there and since, and of the death of the Champion of the Dry Tree.

But when he had made an end, Roger said: "There it is, then, as I said when she first spake to me of thee and bade me bring about that meeting with her, drawing thee first to the Burg and after to the Castle of Abundance, I have forgotten mostly by what lies; but I said to her that she had set her heart on a man over lucky, and that thou wouldst take her luck from her and make it thine. But now I will let all that pass, and will bid thee ask what thou wilt; and I promise thee that I will help thee to come thy ways to thy kindred, that thou mayst put forth thy luck in their behalf."

Said Ralph: "First of all, tell me what shall I do to pass unhindered through the Burg of the Four Friths?" Said Roger: "Thou shalt go in at one gate and out at the other, and none shall hinder thee."

Said Ralph: "And shall I have any hindrance from them of the Dry Tree?"

Roger made as if he were swallowing down something, and answered: "Nay, none."

"And the folk of Higham by the Way, and the Brethren and their Abbot?" said Ralph.

"I know but little of them," quoth Roger, "but I deem that they will make a push to have thee for captain; because they have had war on their hands of late. But this shall be at thine own will to say yea or nay to them. But for the rest on this side of the shepherds' country ye will pass by peaceful folk."

"Yea," said Ralph, "what then hath become of the pride

478

and cruelty of the Burg of the Four Friths, and the eagerness and fierceness of the Dry Tree?"

Quoth Roger: "This is the tale of it: After the champions of the Dry Tree had lost their queen and beloved, the Lady of Abundance, they were both restless and fierce, for the days of sorrow hung heavy on their hands. So on a time a great company of them had ado with the Burgers somewhat recklessly and came to the worse; wherefore some drew back into their fastness of the Scaur and the others still rode on, and further west than their wont had been; but warily when they had the Wood Perilous behind them, for they had learned wisdom again. Thus riding they had tidings of an host of the Burg of the Four Friths who were resting in a valley hard by with a great train of captives and beasts and other spoil: for they had been raising the fray against the Wheat-wearers, and had slain many carles there, and were bringing home to the Burg many young women and women-children, after their custom. So they of the Dry Tree advised them of these tidings, and deemed that it would ease the sorrow of their hearts for their Lady if they could deal with these sons of whores and make a mark upon the Burg: so they lay hid while the daylight lasted, and by night and cloud fell upon these fainéants of the Burg, and won them good cheap, as was like to be, though the Burg-dwellers were many the more. Whereof a many were slain, but many escaped and gat home to the Burg, even as will lightly happen even in the worst of overthrows, that not all, or even the more part be slain.

"Well, there were the champions and their prey, which was very great, and especially of women, of whom the more part were young and fair: for the women of the Wheat-wearers be goodly, and these had been picked out by the rutters of the Burg for their youth and strength and beauty. And whereas the men of the Dry Tree were scant of women at home, and sore-hearted because of our Lady, they forbore not these women, but fell to talking with them and loving them; howbeit in courteous and manly fashion, so that the women deemed themselves in heaven and were ready to do anything to please their lovers. So the end of it was that the

479

Champions sent messengers to Hampton and the Castle of the Scaur to tell what had betid, and they themselves took the road to the land of the Wheat-wearers, having those women with them not as captives but as free damsels.

"Now the road to the Wheat-wearing country was long, and on the way the damsels told their new men many things of their land and their unhappy wars with them of the Burg and the griefs and torments which they endured of them. And this amongst other things, that wherever they came, they slew all the males even to the sucking babe, but spared the women, even when they bore them not into captivity.

"'Whereof,' said these poor damsels, 'it cometh that our land is ill-furnished of carles, so that we women, high and low, go afield and do many things, as crafts and the like, which in other lands are done by carles.' In sooth it seemed of them that they were both of stouter fashion, and defter than women are wont to be. So the champions, part in jest, part in earnest, bade them do on the armour of the slain Burgers, and take their weapons, and fell to teaching them how to handle staff and sword and bow; and the women took heart from the valiant countenance of their new lovers, and deemed it all bitter earnest enough, and learned their part speedily; and yet none too soon. For when the fleers of the Burg came home the Porte lost no time, but sent out another host to follow after the Champions and their spoil; for they had learned that those men had not turned about to Hampton after their victory, but had gone on to the Wheat-wearers.

"So it befell that the host of the Burg came up with the Champions on the eve of a summer day when there were yet three hours of daylight. But whereas they had looked to have an easy bargain of their foemen, since they knew the Champions to be but a few, lo! there was the hillside covered with a goodly array of spears and glaives and shining helms. They marvelled; but now for very shame, and because they scarce could help it, they fell on, and before sunset were scattered to the winds again, and the fleers had to bear back the tale that the more part of their foes were women of the Wheat-wearers; but this time few were those that came back alive to

480

the Burg of the Four Friths; for the freed captives were hot and eager in the chase, casting aside their shields and hauberks that they might speed the better, and valuing their lives at naught if they might but slay a man or two of the tyrants before they died.

"Thus was the Burg wounded with its own sword: but the matter stopped not there: for when that victorious host of men and women came into the land of the Wheat-wearers, all men fled away in terror at first, thinking that it was a new onset of the men of the Burg; and that all the more, as so many of them bore their weapons and armour. But when they found out how matters had gone, then, as ye may deem, was the greatest joy and exultation, and carles and queans both ran to arms and bade their deliverers learn them all that belonged to war, and said that one thing should not be lacking, to wit, the gift of their bodies, that should either lie dead in the fields, or bear about henceforth the souls of free men. Nothing lothe, the Champions became their doctors and teachers of battle, and a great host was drawn together; and meanwhile the Champions had sent messengers again to Hampton telling them what was befallen, and asking for more men if they might be had. But the Burg-abiders were not like to sit down under their foil. Another host they sent against the Wheat-wearers, not so huge, as well arrayed and wise in war. The Champions espied its goings, and knew well that they had to deal with the best men of the Burg, and they met them in like wise; for they chose the very best of the men and the women, and pitched on a place whence they might ward them well, and abode the foemen there; who failed not to come upon them, stout and stern and cold, and well-learned in all feats of war.

"Long and bitter was the battle, and the Burgers were fierce without head-strong folly, and the Wheat-wearers deemed that if they blenched now, they had something worse than death to look to. But in the end when both sides were grown weary and worn out, and yet neither would flee, on a sudden came into the field the help from the Dry Tree, a valiant company of riders to whom battle was but game and play. Then indeed the men of the Burg gave back and drew out of the battle as best they might: yet were they little chased, save by the new-comers of the Dry Tree, for the others were over weary, and moreover the leaders had no mind to let the new-made warriors leave their vantage-ground lest the old and tried men-at-arms of the Burg should turn upon them and put them to the worse.

"Men looked for battle again the next day; but it fell not out so; for the host of the Burg saw that there was more to lose than to gain, so they drew back towards their own place. Neither did they waste the land much; for the riders of the Dry Tree followed hard at heel, and cut off all who tarried, or strayed from the main battle.

"When they were gone, then at last did the Wheat-wearers give themselves up to the joy of their deliverance and the pleasure of their new lives: and one of their old men that I have spoken with told me this; that before when they were little better than the thralls of the Burg, and durst scarce raise a hand against the foemen, the carles were but slow to love, and the queans, for all their fairness, cold and but little kind. However, now in the fields of the wheat-wearers themselves all this was changed, and men and maids took to arraying themselves gaily as occasion served, and there was singing and dancing on every green, and straying of couples amongst the greenery of the summer night; and in short the god of love was busy in the land, and made the eyes seem bright, and the lips sweet, and the bosom fair, and the arms sleek and the feet trim: so that every hour was full of allurement; and ever the nigher that war and peril was, the more delight had man and maid of each other's bodies.

"Well, within a while the Wheat-wearers were grown so full of hope that they bade the men of the Dry Tree lead them against the Burg of the Four Friths, and the Champions were ready thereto; because they wotted well, that, Hampton being disgarnished of men, the men of the Burg might fall on it; and even if they took it not, they would beset all ways and make riding a hard matter for their fellowship. So they fell to, wisely and deliberately, and led an host of the best of the carles with them, and bade the women keep their land surely, so that their host was not a great many. But so wisely they led them that they came before the Burg well-nigh unawares; and though it seemed little likely that they should take so strong a place, yet nought less befell. For the Burg-dwellers beset with cruelty and bitter anger cried out that now at last they would make an end of this cursed people, and the whoreson strong-thieves their friends: so they went out a-gates a great multitude, but in worser order than their wont was; and there befell that marvel which sometimes befalleth even to very valiant men, that now at the pinch all their valour flowed from them, and they fled before the spears had met, and in such evil order that the gates could not be shut, and their foemen entered with them slaying and slaying even as they would. So that in an hour's space the pride and the estate of the Burg of the Four Friths was utterly fallen. Huge was the slaughter; for the Wheat-wearers deemed they had many a grief whereof to avenge them; nor were the men of the Dry Tree either sluggards or saints to be careless of their foemen, or to be merciful in the battle: but at last the murder was stayed: and then the men of the Wheat-wearers went from house to house in the town to find the women of their folk who had been made thralls by the Burgers. There then was many a joyful meeting betwixt those poor women and the men of their kindred: all was forgotten now of the days of their thralldom, their toil and mocking and stripes; and within certain days all the sort of them came before the host clad in green raiment, and garlanded with flowers for the joy of their deliverance; and great feast was made to them.

"As for them of the Burg, the battle and chase over, no more were slain, save that certain of the great ones were made shorter by the head. But the Champions and the Wheat-wearers both, said that none of that bitter and cruel folk should abide any longer in the town; so that after a delay long enough for them to provide stuff for their wayfaring, they were all thrust out a-gates, rich and poor, old and young, man, woman and child. Proudly and with a stout countenance they went, for now was their valour come again to them. And it is like that we shall hear of them oft again; for though they had but a few weapons amongst them when they were driven out of their old home, and neither hauberk nor shield nor helm, yet so learned in war be they and so marvellous great of pride, that they will somehow get them weapons; and even armed but with headless staves, and cudgels of the thicket, woe betide the peaceful folk whom they shall first fall on. Yea, fair sir, the day shall come meseemeth when folk shall call on thee to lead the hunt after these famished wolves, and when thou dost so, call on me to tell thee tales of their doings which shall make thine heart hard, and thine hand heavy against them."

"Meantime," said Ralph, "what has betid to the Fellowship of the Dry Tree? for I see that thou hast some grief on thy mind because of them."

Roger kept silence a little and then he said: "I grieve because Hampton is no more a strong place of warriors; two or three carles and a dozen of women dwell now in the halls and chambers of the Scaur. Here on earth, all endeth. God send us to find the world without end!"

"What then," said Ralph, "have they then had another great overthrow, worse than that other?" "Nay," said Roger doggedly, "it is not so." "But where is the Fellowship?" said Ralph. "It is scattered abroad," quoth Roger. "For some of the Dry Tree had no heart to leave the women whom they had wooed in the Wheat-wearer's land: and some, and a great many, have taken their dears to dwell in the Burg of the Four Friths, whereas a many of the Wheat-wearers have gone to beget children on the old bondwomen of the Burgers; of whom there were some two thousand alive after the Burg was taken; besides that many women also came with the carles from their own land.

"So that now a mixed folk are dwelling in the Burg, partly of those women-thralls, partly of carles and queans come newly from the Wheat-wearers, partly of men of our Fellowship the more part of whom are wedded to queans of the Wheat-wearers, and partly of men, chapmen and craftsmen and others who have drifted into the town, having heard that there is no lack of wealth there, and many fair women unmated."

"Yea," said Ralph, "and is all this so ill?" Said Roger, "Meseems it is ill enough that there is no longer, rightly said,

484

a Fellowship of the Dry Tree, though the men be alive who were once of that fellowship." "Nay," said Ralph, "and why should they not make a new fellowship in the Burg, whereas they may well be peaceful, since they have come to their above of their foemen?"

"Yea," said Roger slowly, "that is sooth; and so is this, that there in the Burg they are a strong band, with a captain of their own, and much worshipped of the peaceful folk; and moreover, though they be not cruel to torment helpless folk, or hard to make an end of all joy to-day, lest they lose their joy to-morrow, they now array all men in good order within the Burg, so that it shall be no easier for a foeman to win that erst it was."

"What, man!" said Ralph, "then be of better cheer, and come thou with us, and may be the old steel of the champions may look on the sun down in Upmeads. Come thou with me, I say, and show me and my luck to some of thy fellows who are dwelling in the Burg, and it may be when thou hast told my tale to them, that some of them shall be content to leave their beds cold for a while, that they may come help a Friend of the Well in his need."

Roger sat silent as it he were pondering the matter, while Richard and the Sage, both of them, took up the word one after the other, and urged him to it.

At last he said: "Well, so be it for this adventure. Only I say not that I shall give up this hermitage and my holiness for ever. Come thou aside, wise man of Swevenham, and I shall tell thee wherefore." "Yea," said Ralph, laughing, "and when he hath told thee, tell me not again; for sure I am that he is right to go with us, and belike shall be wrong in his reason therefore."

Roger looked a little askance at him, and he went without doors with the Sage, and when they were out of earshot, he said to him: "Hearken, I would have gone with my lord at the first word, and have been fain thereof; but there is this woman that followeth him. At every turn she shall mind me of our Lady that was; and I shall loath her, and her fairness and the allurements of her body, because I see of her, that she it is that hath gotten my Lady's luck, and that but for her my Lady might yet have been alive."

Said the Sage: "Well quoth my lord that thou wouldst give me a fool's reason! What! dost not thou know, thou that knowest so much of the Lady of Abundance, that she it was who ordained this Ursula to be Ralph's bedmate, when she herself should be gone from him, were she dead or alive, and that she also should be a Friend of the Well, so that he might not lack a fellow his life long? But this thou sayest, not knowing the mind of our Lady, and how she loved him in her inmost heart."

Roger hung his head and spake not for a while, and then he said: "Well, wise man, I have said that I will go on this adventure, and I will smooth my tongue for this while at least, and for what may come hereafter, let it be. And now we were best get to horse; for what with meat and minstrelsy, we have worn away the day till it wants but a little of noon. Go tell thy lord that I am ready. Farewell peace, and welcome war and grudging!"

So the Sage went within, and came out with the others, and they mounted their horses anon, and Roger went ahead on foot, and led them through the thicket-ways without fumbling; and they lay down that night on the farther side of the Swelling Flood.

CHAPTER 18

A Change of Days in the Burg of the Four Friths

There is naught to tell of their ways till they came out of the thicket into the fields about the Burg of the Four Friths; and even there was a look of a bettering of men's lives; though forsooth the husbandmen there were much the same as had abided in the fields aforetime, whereas they were not for the most part freemen of the Burg, but aliens who did service in war and otherwise thereto. But, it being eventide, there were men and women and children, who had come out of gates, walking about and disporting themselves in the loveliness of early summer, and that in far merrier guise than they had durst do in the bygone days. Moreover, there was scarce a sword or spear to be seen amongst them, whereat Roger grudged somewhat, and Richard said: "Meseems this folk trusts the peace of the Burg overmuch, since, when all is told, unpeace is not so far from their borders."

But as they drew a little nigher Ralph pointed out to his fellows the gleam of helms and weapons on the walls, and they saw a watchman on each of the high towers of the south gate; and then quoth Roger: "Nay, the Burg will not be won so easily; and if a few fools get themselves slain outside it is no great matter."

Folk nowise let them come up to the gate unheeded, but gathered about them to look at the newcomers, but not so as to hinder them, and they could see that these summerers were goodly folk enough, and demeaned them as though they had but few troubles weighing on them. But the wayfarers were not unchallenged at the gate, for a stout man-at-arms stayed them and said: "Ye ride somewhat late, friends. What are ye?" Quoth Ralph: "We be peaceful wayfarers save to them that would fall on us, and we seek toward Upmeads." "Yea?" said the man, "belike ye shall find something less than peace betwixt here and Upmeads, for rumour goes that there are alien riders come into the lands of Higham, and for aught I know the said unpeace may spread further on. Well, if ye will go to the Flower de Luce and abide there this night, ye shall have a let-pass to-morn betimes."

Then Ralph spake a word in Roger's ear, and Roger nodded his head, and, throwing his cowl aback, went up to the man-at-arms and said: "Stephen a-Hurst, hast thou time for a word with an old friend?" "Yea, Roger," said the man, "is it verily thou? I deemed that thou hadst fled away from all of us to live in the wilds."

"So it was, lad," said Roger, "but times change from good

487

to bad and back again; and now am I of this good lord's company; and I shall tell thee, Stephen, that though he rideth but few to-day, yet merry shall he be that rideth with him to-morrow if unpeace be in the land. Lo you, Stephen, this is the Child of Upmeads, whom belike thou hast heard of; and if thou wilt take me into the chamber of thy tower, I will tell thee things of him that thou wottest not."

Stephen turned to Ralph and made obeisance to him and said: "Fair Sir, there are tales going about concerning thee, some whereof are strange enow, but none of them ill; and I deem by the look of thee that thou shalt be both a stark champion and a good lord; and I deem that it shall be my good luck, if I see more of thee, and much more. Now if thou wilt, pass on with thine other fellows to the Flower de Luce, and leave this my old fellow-in-arms with me, and he shall tell me of thy mind; for I see that thou wouldest have somewhat of us; and since, I doubt not by the looks of thee, that thou wilt not bid us aught unknightly, when we know thy will, we shall try to pleasure thee."

"Yea, Lord Ralph," said Roger, "thou mayest leave all the business with me, and I will come to thee not later than betimes to-morrow, and let thee wot how matters have sped. And methinks ye may hope to wend out-a-gates this time otherwise than thou didest before."

So Ralph gave him yeasay and thanked the man-at-arms and rode his ways with the others toward the Flower de Luce, and whereas the sun was but newly set, Ralph noted that the booths were gayer and the houses brighter and more fairly adorned than aforetimes. As for the folk, they were such that the streets seemed full of holiday makers, so joyous and well dight were they; and the women like to those fair thralls whom he had seen that other time, saving that they were not clad so wantonly, however gaily. They came into the great square, and there they saw that the masons and builders had begun on the master church to make it fairer and bigger; the people were sporting there as in the streets, and amongst them were some weaponed men, but the most part of these bore the token of the Dry Tree.

So they entered the Flower de Luce, and had good welcome there, as if they were come home to their own house; for when its people saw such a goodly old man in the Sage, and so stout and trim a knight as was Richard, and above all when they beheld the loveliness of Ralph and Ursula, they praised them open-mouthed, and could scarce make enough of them. And when they had had their meat and were rested, came two of the maids there and asked them if it were lawful to talk with them; and Ralph laughed and bade them sit by them, and eat a dainty morsel; and they took that blushing, for they were fair and young, and Ralph's face and the merry words of his mouth stirred the hearts within them: and forsooth it was not so much they that spake as Ursula and the Sage; for Ralph was somewhat few spoken, whereas he pondered concerning the coming days, and what he half deemed that he saw a-doing at Upmeads. But at last they found their tongues, and said how that already rumour was abroad that they were in the Burg who had drunk of the Water of the Well at the World's End; and said one: "It is indeed a fair sight to see you folk coming back in triumph; and so methinks will many deem if ye abide with us over to-morrow, and yet, Lady, for a while we are well-nigh as joyous as ye can be, whereas we have but newly come into new life also: some of us from very thralldom of the most grievous, and I am of those; and some of us in daily peril of it, like to my sister here. So mayhappen," said she, smiling, "none of us shall seek to the Well until we have worn our present bliss a little threadbare."

Ursula smiled on her, but the Sage said: "Mayhappen it is of no avail speaking of such things to a young and fair woman; but what would betide you if the old Burgers were to come back and win their walls again?" The maid who had been a thrall changed countenance at his word; but the other one said: "If the Burgers come back, they will find them upon the walls who have already chaced them. Thou mayst deem me slim and tender, old wise man; but such as mine arm is, it has upheaved the edges against the foe; and if it be a murder to slay a Burger, then am I worthy of the gallows." "Yea, yea," quoth Richard, laughing, "ye shall be double-manned then in this good town: ye may well win, unless the sight of you shall make the foe over fierce for the gain."

Said the Sage: "It is well, maiden, and if ye hold to that, and keep your carles in the same road, ye need not to fear the Burgers: and to say sooth, I have it in my mind, that before long ye shall have both war and victory."

Then Ralph seemed to wake up as from a dream, and he arose, and said: "Thou art in the right, Sage, and to mine eyes it seemeth that both thou and I shall be sharers in the war and the victory." And therewith he fell to striding up and down the hall, while the two maidens sat gazing on him with gleaming eyes and flushed cheeks.

But in a little while he came back to his seat and sat him down, and fell to talk with the women, and asked them of the town and the building therein, and the markets, whether they throve; and they and two or three of the townsmen or merchants answered all, and told him how fair their estate was, and how thriving was the lot of one and all with them. Therewith was Ralph well pleased, and they sat talking there in good fellowship till the night was somewhat worn, and all men fared to bed.

CHAPTER 19

Ralph Sees Hampton
and the Scaur

When it was morning Ralph arose and went into the hall of the hostelry, and even as he entered it the outside door opened, and in came Roger, and Richard with him (for he had been astir very early) and Roger, who was armed from head to foot and wore a coat of the Dry Tree, cried out: "Now, Lord, thou wert best do on thy war-gear, for thou shalt presently be captain of an host." "Yea, Roger," quoth Ralph, "and hast thou done well?" "Well enough," said Rich-

490

ard; "thine host shall not be a great one, but no man in it will be a blencher, for they be all champions of the Dry Tree."

"Yea," quoth Roger, "so it was that Stephen a-Hurst brought me to a company of my old fellows, and we went all of us together to the Captain of the Burg (e'en he of the Dry Tree, who in these latest days is made captain of all), and did him to wit that thou hadst a need; and whereas he, as all of us, had heard of the strokes that thou struckest in the wood that day when thy happiness first began, (woe worth the while!) he stickled not to give some of us leave to look on the hand-play with thee. But soft, my Lord! abound not in thanks as yet, till I tell thee. The said Captain hath gotten somewhat of the mind of a chapman by dwelling in a town, 'tis like (the saints forgive me for saying so!) and would strike a bargain with thee." "Yea," said Ralph, smiling, "I partly guess what like the bargain is; but say thou."

Said Roger: "I like not his bargain, not for thy sake but mine own; this it is, that we shall ride, all of us who are to be of thy fellowship, to the Castle of the Scaur to-day, and there thy Lady shall sit in the throne whereas in past days our Lady and Queen was wont to sit; and that thou shalt swear upon her head, that whensoever he biddeth thee come to the help of the Burg of the Four Friths and the tribes of the Wheat-wearers, thou shalt come in arms by the straightest road with such fellowship as thou mayst gather; and if thou wilt so do, we of the Dry Tree who go with thee on this journey are thine to save or to spend by flood or field, or castle wall, amidst the edges and the shafts and the fire-flaught. What sayest thou—thou who art lucky, and hast of late become wise? And I will tell thee, that though I hope it not, yet I would thou shouldst naysay it; for it will be hard for me to see another woman sitting in our Lady's seat: yea, to see her sitting there, who hath stolen her luck."

Said Ralph: "Now this proffer of the Captain's I call friendly and knightly, and I will gladly swear as he will; all the more as without any oath I should never fail him when-soever he may send for me. As for thee, Roger, ride with us if thou wilt, and thou shalt be welcome both in the company, and at the High House of Upmeads whenso we come there."

Then was Roger silent, but nowise abashed; and as they spoke they heard the tramp of horses and the clash of weapons, and they saw through the open door three men-at-arms riding up to the house; so Ralph went out to welcome them; they were armed full well in bright armour, and their coats were of the Dry Tree, and were tall men and warrior-like. They hailed Ralph as captain, and he gave them the sele of the day and bade come in and drink a cup; so did they, but they were scarce off their horses ere there came another three, and then six together, and so one after other till the hall of the Flower de Luce was full of the gleam of steel and clash of armour, and the lads held their horses without and were merry with the sight of the stalwart men-at-arms. Now cometh Ursula down from her chamber clad in her bravery; and when they saw her they set up a shout for joy of her, so that the rafters rang again; but she laughed for pleasure of them, and poured them out the wine, till they were merrier with the sight of her than with the good liquor.

Now Roger comes to Ralph and tells him that he deems his host hath come to the last man. Then Ralph armed him, and those two maidens brought him his horse, and they mount all of them and draw up in the Square; and Roger and Stephen a-Hurst array them, for they were chosen of them as leaders along with Ralph, and Richard, whom they all knew, at least by hearsay. Then Roger drew from his pouch a parchment, and read the roll of names, and there was no man lacking, and they were threescore save five, besides Roger and the way-farers, and never was a band of like number seen better; and Richard said softly unto Ralph: "If we had a few more of these, I should care little what foemen we should meet in Upmeads: soothly, my lord, they had as well have ridden into red Hell as into our green fields." "Fear not, Richard," said Ralph, "we shall have enough."

So then they rode out of the Square and through the streets to the North Gate, and much folk was abroad to look on them, and they blessed them as they went, both carles and queans; for the rumour was toward that there was riding a good and dear Lord and a Friend of the Well to get his own again from out of the hands of the aliens.

Herewith they ride a little trot through the Freedom of the Burg, and when they were clear of it they turned aside from the woodland highway whereon Ralph had erst ridden with Roger and followed the rides a good way till it was past noon, when they came into a very close thicket where there was but a narrow and winding way whereon two men might not ride abreast, and Roger said: "Now, if we were the old Burgers, and the Dry Tree still holding the Scaur, we should presently know what steel-point dinner meaneth; if the dead could rise out of their graves to greet their foemen, we should anon be a merry company here. But at last they learned the trick, and were wont to fetch a compass round about Grey Goose Thicket as it hight amongst us."

"Well," said Ralph, "but how if there by any waylaying us; the Burgers may be wiser still than thou deemest, and ye may have learned them more than thou art minded to think."

"Nay," said Roger, "I bade a half score turn aside by the thicket path on our left hands; that shall make all sure; but indeed I look for no lurkers as yet. In a month's time that may betide, but not yet; not yet. But tell me, fair Sir, have ye any deeming of where thou mayst get thee more folk who be not afraid of the hard hand-play? For Richard hath been telling me that there be tidings in the air."

Said Ralph: "If hope play me not false, I look to gather some stout carles of the Shepherd Country." "Yea," said Roger, "but I shall tell thee that they have been at whiles unfriends of the Dry Tree." Said Ralph: "I think they will be friends unto me." "Then it shall do well," said Roger, "for they be good in a fray."

So talked they as they rode, but ever Roger would give no heed to Ursula, but made as if he wotted not that she was there, though ever and anon Ralph would be turning back to speak to her and help her through the passes.

At last the thicket began to dwindle, and presently riding out of a little valley or long trench on to a ridge nearly bare of trees, they saw below them a fair green plain, and in the midst of it a great heap of grey rocks rising out of it like a reef out of the sea, and on the said reef, and climbing up as it were to the topmost of it, the white walls of a great castle, the crown whereof was a huge round tower. At the foot of the ridge was a thorp of white houses thatched with straw scattered over a good piece of the plain. The company drew rein on the ridge-top, and the Champions raised a great shout at the sight of their old strong-place; and Roger turned to Ralph and said: "Fair Sir, how deemest thou of the Castle of the Scaur?" but Richard broke in: "For my part, friend Roger, I deem that ye do like to people unlearned in war to leave the stronghold ungarnished of men. This is a fool's deed." "Nay, nay," said Roger, "we need not be over-hasty, while it is our chief business to order the mingled folk of the Wheat-wearers and others who dwell in the Burg as now."

Then spake Ralph: "Yet how wilt thou say but that the foemen whom we go to meet in Upmeads may be some of those very Burgers: hast thou heard whether they have found a new dwelling among some unhappy folk, or be still roving: maybe they shall deem Upmeads fair."

Spake Michael a-Hurst: "By thy leave, fair Sir, we have had a word of those riders and strong-thieves that they have fetched a far compass, and got them armour, and be come into the woodland north of the Wood Debateable. For like all strong-thieves, they love the wood."

Roger laughed: "Yea, as we did, friend Michael, when we were thieves; whereas now we be lords and gentlemen. But as to thy tidings, I set not much by them; for of the same message was this word that they had already fallen on Higham by the Way; and we know that this cannot be true; since though forsooth the Abbot has had unpeace on his hands, we know where his foemen came from, the West to wit, and the Banded Barons."

"Yea, yea," quoth the Sage, "but may not the Burgers have taken service with them?" "Yea, forsooth," quoth Roger, "but I deem not, or we had been surer thereof."

Thus they spake, and they lighted down all of them to breathe their horses, and Ursula spake with Ralph as they walked the greensward together a little apart, and said: "Sweetheart, I am afraid of to-day."

"Yea, dear," said he, "and wherefore?" She said: "It will be hard for me to enter that grim house yonder, and sit in the seat whence I was erewhile threatened by the evil hag with hair like a grey she-bear."

He made much of her and said: "Yet belike a Friend of the Well may overcome this also; and withal the hall shall be far other to-day when it was."

She looked about on the warriors as they lay on the grass or loitered by their horses; then she smiled, and her face lightened, and she reddened and cast down her eyes and said: "Yea, that is sooth; that day there were few men in the hall, and they old and evil of semblance. It was a band of women who took me in the thorp and brought me up into the Castle, and mishandled me there, and cast me into prison there; whereas these be good fellows, and frank and free of aspect. But O, my heart, look thou how fearful the piled-up rocks rise from the plain and the walls wind up amongst them; and that huge tower, the crown of all! Surely there is none more fearful in the world."

He kissed her and laughed merrily, and said: "Yea, sweetheart, and there will be another change in the folk of the hall when we come there this time, to wit, that thou shouldst not be alone therein, even were all these champions, and Richard and the Sage away from thee. Wilt thou tell me how that shall be?"

She turned to him and kissed him and caressed him, and then they turned back again toward their fellows, for by now they had walked together a good way along the ridge.

So then they gat to horse again and rode into the thorp, where men and women stood about to behold them, and made them humble reverence as they passed by. So rode they to the bailly of the Castle; and if that stronghold looked terrible from the ridge above, tenfold more terrible of aspect it was when the upper parts were hidden by the grey rocks, and they so huge and beetling, and though the sun was bright about them, and they in the midst of their friends, yet even Ralph felt somewhat of dread creep over him: yet he smiled cheerfully as Ursula turned an anxious face on him. They alighted from their horses in the bailly, for over steep for horse-hoofs was the walled way upward; and as they began to mount, even the merry Champions hushed their holiday clamour for awe of the huge stronghold, and Ralph took Ursula by the hand, and she sidled up to him, and said softly: "Yea, it was here they drave me up, those women, thrusting and smiting me; and some would have stripped off my raiment, but one who seemed the wisest, said, 'Nay, leave her till she come before the ancient Lady, for her gear may be a token of whence she is, and whither, if she be come as a spy.' So I escaped them for that moment. And now I wonder what we shall find in the hall when we come in thither. It is somewhat like to me, as when one gets up from bed in the dead night, when all is quiet and the moon is shining, and goes out of the chamber into the hall, and coming back, almost dreads to see some horror lying in one's place amid the familiar bedclothes."

And she grew paler as she spake. Then Ralph comforted her and trimmed his countenance to a look of mirth, but inwardly he was ill at ease.

So up they went and up, till they came to a level place whereon was built the chief hall and its chambers: there they stood awhile to breathe them before the door, which was rather low than great; and Ursula clung to Ralph and trembled, but Ralph spake in her ear: "Take heart, my sweet, or these men, and Roger in especial, will think the worse of thee; and thou a Friend of the Well. What! here is naught to hurt thee! this is naught beside the perils of the desert, and the slaves and the evil lord of Utterbol." "Yea," she said, "but meseemeth I loved thee not so sore as now I do. O friend, I am become a weak woman and unvaliant, and there is naught in me but love of thee, and love of life because of thee; nor dost thou know altogether what befell me in that hall."

But Ralph turned about and cried out in a loud, cheerful voice: "Let us enter, friends! and lo you, I will show the Champions of the Dry Tree the way into their own hall and high place." Therewith he thrust the door open, for it was not locked, and strode into the hall, still leading Ursula by the hand, and all the company followed him, the clash of their

496

armour resounding through the huge building. Though it was long, it was not so much that it was long as that it was broad, and exceeding high, so that in the dusk of it the great vault of the roof was dim and misty. There was no man therein, no halling on its walls, no benches nor boards, naught but the great standing table of stone on the dais, and the stone high-seat amidst of it: and the place did verily seem like the house and hall of a people that had died out in one hour because of their evil deeds.

They stood still a moment when they were all fairly within doors, and Roger thrust up to Ralph and said, but softly: "The woman is blenching, and all for naught; were it not for the oath, we had best have left her in the thorp: I fear me she will bring evil days on our old home with her shivering fear. How far otherwise came our Lady in hither when first she came amongst us, when the Duke of us found her in the wood after she had been thrust out from Sunway by the Baron whom thou slewest afterward. Our Duke brought her in hither wrapped up in his knight's scarlet cloak, and went up with her on to the dais; but when she came thither, she turned about and let her cloak fall to earth, and stood there barefoot in her smock, as she had been cast out into the wildwood, and she spread abroad her hands, and cried out in a loud voice as sweet as the May blackbird, 'May God bless this House and the abode of the valiant, and the shelter of the hapless.' "

Said Ursula (and her voice was firm and the colour come back to her cheeks now, while Ralph stood agaze and wondering): "Roger, thou lovest me little, meseemeth, though if I did less than I do, I should do against the will of thy Lady that was Queen in this hall. But tell me, Roger, where is gone that other one, the fearful she-bear of this crag, who sat in yonder stone high-seat, and roared at me and mocked me, and gave me over into the hands of her tormentors, who haled me away to the prison wherefrom thy very Lady delivered me?"

"Lady," said Roger, "the tale of her is short since the day thou sawest her herein. On the day when we first had the evil tidings of the slaying of my Lady we were sad at heart, and called to mind ancient transgressions against us; therefore we fell on the she-bear, as thou callest her, and her company of men and women, and some we slew and some we thrust forth; but as to her, I slew her not three feet from where thou standest now. A rumour there is that she walketh, and it may be so; yet in the summer noon ye need not look to see her."

Ralph said coldly: "Roger, let us be done with minstrels' tales; lead me to the place where the oath is to be sworn, for time presses."

Scarce were the words out of his mouth ere Roger strode foward and gat him on to the dais and went hastily to the wall behind the high-seat, whence he took down a very great horn, and set it to his lips and winded it loudly thrice, so that the great and high hall was full of its echoes. Richard started thereat and half drew his sword; but the Sage put his hand upon the hilts, and said: "It is naught, let the edges lie quiet." Ursula stared astonished, but now she quaked no more; Ralph changed not countenance a wit, and the champions of the Tree made as if naught had been done that they looked not for. But thereafter cried Roger from the dais: "This is the token that the men of the Dry Tree are met for matters of import; thus is the Mote hallowed. Come up hither, ye aliens, and ye also of the fellowship, that the oath may be sworn, and we may go our ways, even as the alien captain biddeth."

Then Ralph took Ursula's hand again, and went up the hall calmly and proudly, and the champions followed with Richard and the Sage. Ralph and Ursula went up on to the dais, and he set down Ursula in the stone high-seat, and even in the halldusk a right fair-coloured picture she looked therein; for she was clad in a goodly green gown broidered with flowers, and a green cloak with gold orphreys over it; her hair was spread abroad over her shoulders, and on her head was a garland of roses which the women of the Flower de Luce had given her; so there she sat with her fair face, whence now all the wrinkles of trouble and fear were smoothed out, looking like an image of the early summer-tide itself. And the champions looked on her and marvelled, and

498

one whispered to the other that it was their Lady of aforetime come back again; only Roger, who had now gone back to the rest of the fellowship, cast his eyes upon the ground, and muttered.

Now Ralph draws his sword, and lays it naked on the stone table, and he stood beside Ursula and said: "Champions of the Dry Tree, by the blade of Upmeads which lieth here before me, and by the head which I love best in the world, and is best worthy of love" (and herewith he laid his hand on Ursula's head), "I swear that whensoever the Captain of the Dry Tree calleth on me, whether I be eating or drinking, abed or standing on my feet, at peace or at war, glad or sorry, I shall do my utmost to come to his aid straightway with whatso force I may gather. Is this rightly sworn, Champions?"

Said Stephen a-Hurst: "It is sworn well and knightly, and now cometh our oath."

"Nay," said Ralph, "I had no mind to drive a bargain with you; your deeds shall prove you; and I fear not for your doughtiness."

Said Stephen: "Yea, Lord; but he bade us swear to thee. Reach me thy sword, I pray thee."

Then Ralph reached him his sword across the great stone table, and Stephen took it, and kissed the blade and the hilts; and then lifted up his voice and said: "By the hilts and the blade, by the point and the edge, we swear to follow the Lord Ralph of Upmeads for a year and a day, and to do his will in all wise. So help us God and Allhallows!"

And therewith he gave the sword to the others, and each man of them kissed it as he had.

But Ralph said: "Champions, for this oath I thank you all heartily. But it is not my meaning that I should hold you by me for a year, whereas I deem I shall do all that my kindred may need in three days' space from the first hour wherein we set foot in Upmeads."

Stephen smiled friendly at him and nodded, and said: "That may well be; but now to make a good end of this mote I will tell thee a thing; to wit, that our Captain, yea, and all we, are minded to try thee by this fray in Upmeads, now we know that thou hast become a Friend of the Well. And if thou turn out as we deem is likest, we will give thee this Castle of the Scaur, for thee and those that shall spring from thy loins; for we deem that some such man as thou will be the only one to hold it worthily, and in such wise as it may be a stronghold against tyrants and for the helping of peaceable folk; since forsooth, we of the Dry Tree have heard somewhat of the Well at the World's End, and trow in the might thereof."

He made an end; and Ralph kept silence and pondered the matter. But Roger lifted up his head and broke in, and said: "Yea, yea! that is it: we are all become men of peace, we riders of the Dry Tree!" And he laughed withal, but as one nowise best pleased.

But as Ralph was gathering his words together, and Ursula was looking up to him with trouble in her face again, came a man of the thorp rushing into the hall, and cried out: "O, my lords! there are weaponed men coming forth from the thicket. Save us, we pray you, for we are ill-weaponed and men of peace."

Roger laughed, and said: "Eh, good man! So ye want us back again? But my Lord Ralph, and thou Richard, and thou Stephen, come ye to the shot-window here, that giveth on to the forest. We are high up here, and we shall see all as clearly as in a good mirror. Hast thou shut the gates, carle?" "Yea, Lord Roger," quoth he, "and there are some fifty of us together down in the base-court."

Ralph and Richard and Stephen looked forth from the shot window, and saw verily a band of men riding down the bent into the thorp, and Ralph, who as aforesaid was far-sighted and clear-sighted, said: "Yea, it is strange: but without doubt these are riders of the Dry Tree; and they seem to me to be some ten-score. Thou Stephen, thou Roger, what is to hand? Is your Captain wont to give a gift and take it back . . . and somewhat more with it?" Stephen looked abashed at his word; and Roger hung his head again.

But therewith the Sage drew up to them and said: "Be not dismayed, Lord Ralph. What wert thou going to say to the Champions when this carle brake in?"

"This," said Ralph, "that I thanked the Dry Tree heartily for its gift, but that meseemed it naught wise to leave this stronghold disgarnished of men till I can come or send back from Upmeads."

Stephen's face cleared at the word, and he said: "I bid thee believe it, lord, that there is no treason in our Captain's heart; and that if there were I would fight against him and his men on thy behalf." And Roger, though in a somewhat surly voice, said the like.

Ralph thought a little, and then he said: "It is well; go we down and out of gates to meet them, that we may the sooner get on our way to Upmeads." And without more words he went up to Ursula and took her hand and went out of the hall, and down the rock-cut stair, and all they with him. And when they came into the Base-court, Ralph spoke to the carles of the thorp, who stood huddled together sore afeard, and said: "Throw open the gates. These riders who have so scared you are naught else than the Champions of the Dry Tree who are coming back to their stronghold that they may keep you sure against wicked tyrants who would oppress you."

The carles looked askance at one another, but straightway opened the gates, and Ralph and his company went forth, and abode the new-comers on a little green mound half a bowshot from the Castle. Ralph sat down on the grass and Ursula by him, and she said: "My heart tells me that these Champions are no traitors, however rough and fierce they have been, and still shall be if occasion serve. But O, sweetheart, how dear and sweet is this sunlit greensward after yonder grim hold. Surely, sweet, it shall never be our dwelling?"

"I wot not, beloved," said he; "must we not go and dwell where deeds shall lead us? and the hand of Weird is mighty. But lo thou, here are the newcomers to hand!"

So it was as he said, and presently the whole band came before them, and they were all of the Dry Tree, stout men and well weaponed, and they had ridden exceeding fast, so that their horses were somewhat spent. A tall man very gallantly armed, who rode at their head, leapt at once from his horse and came up to Ralph and hailed him, and Roger and Stephen both made obeisance to him. Ralph, who had risen up, hailed him in his turn, and the tall man said: "I am the Captain of the Dry Tree for lack of a better; art thou Ralph of Upmeads, fair sir?" "Even so," said Ralph.

Said the Captain: "Thou wilt marvel that I have ridden after thee on the spur; so here is the tale shortly. Your backs were not turned on the walls of the Burg an hour, ere three of my riders brought in to me a man who said, and gave me tokens of his word being true, that he had fallen in with a company of the old Burgers in the Wood Debateable, which belike thou wottest of."

"All we of Upmeads wot of it," said Ralph. "Well," said the Captain, "amongst these said Burgers, who were dwelling in the wildwood in summer content, the word went free that they would gather to them other bands of strong-thieves who haunt that wood, and go with them upon Upmeads, and from Upmeads, when they were waxen strong, they would fall upon Higham by the Way, and thence with yet more strength on their old dwelling of the Burg. Now whereas I know that thou art of Upmeads, and also what thou art, and what thou hast done, I have ridden after thee to tell thee what is toward. But if thou deemest I have brought thee all these riders it is not wholly so. For it was borne into my mind that our old stronghold was left bare of men, and I knew not what might betide; and that the more, as more than one man has told us how that another band of the disinherited Burgers have fallen upon Higham or the lands thereof, and Higham is no great way hence; so that some five score of these riders are to hold our Castle of the Scaur, and the rest are for thee to ride afield with. As for the others, thou hast been told already that the Scaur, and Hampton therewith is a gift from us to thee; for henceforward we be the lords of the Burg of the Four Friths, and that is more than enough for us."

Ralph thanked the Captain for this, and did him to wit that he would take the gift if he came back out the Upmeads fray alive: said he, "With thee and the Wheat-wearers in the Burg, and me in the Scaur, no strong-thief shall dare lift up his hand in these parts."

The Captain smiled, and Ralph went on: "And now I must needs ask thee for leave to depart; which is all the more needful, wheras thy men have over-ridden their horses, and we must needs go a soft pace till we come to Higham."

"Yea, art thou for Higham, fair sir?" said the Captain. "That is well; for ye may get men therefrom, and at the least it is like that ye shall hear tidings: as to my men and their horses, this hath been looked to. For five hundred good men of the Wheat-wearers, men who have not learned the feat of arms a-horseback, are coming through the woods hither to help ward thy castle, fair lord; they will be here in some three hours' space and will bring horses for thy five score men, therefore do ye but ride softly to Higham and if these sergeants catch up with you it is well, but if not, abide them at Higham."

"Thanks have thou for this once more," said Ralph; "and now I have no more word than this for thee; that I will come to thee at thy least word, and serve thee with all that I have, to my very life if need be. And yet I must say this, that I wot not why ye and these others are become to me, who am alien to you, as very brothers." Said the Captain: "There is this to be said of it, as was aforesaid, that all we count thy winning of the Well at the World's End as valiancy in thee, yea, and luck withal. But, moreover, she who was Our Lady would have had thee for her friend had she lived, and how then could we be less than friends to thee? Depart in peace, my friend, and we look to see thee again in a little while."

Therewith he kissed him, and bade farewell; and Ralph bade his band to horse, and they were in the saddle in a twinkling, and rode away from Hampton at a soft pace.

But as they went, Ralph turned to Ursula and said: "And now belike shall we see Bourton Abbas once more, and the house where first I saw thee. And O how sweet thou wert! And I was so happy and so young."

"Yea," she said, "and sorely I longed for thee, and now we have long been together, as it seemeth; and yet that long space shall be but a little while of our lives. But, my friend, as to Bourton Abbas, I misdoubt me of our seeing it; for there is a nigher road by the by-ways to Higham, which these

men know, and doubtless that way we shall wend; and I am
glad thereof; for I shall tell thee, that somewhat I fear that
thorp, lest it should lay hold of me, and wake me from a
dream."

"Yea," said Ralph, "but even then, belike thou shouldst
find me beside thee; as if I had fallen asleep in the ale-house,
and dreamed of the Well at the World's End, and then awoke
and seen the dear barefoot maiden busying her about her
house and its matters. That were naught so ill."

"Ah," she said, "look round on thy men, and think of the
might of war that is in them, and think of the deeds to come.
But O how I would that these next few days were worn away,
and we yet alive for a long while."

CHAPTER 20

They Come to the Gate of
Higham By the Way

It was as Ursula had deemed, and they made for Higham
by the shortest road, so that they came before the gate a
little before sunset: to the very gate they came not; for there
were strong barriers before it, and men-at-arms within them,
as though they were looking for an onfall. And amongst these
were bowmen who bended their bows on Ralph and his company. So Ralph stayed his men, and rode up to the barriers
with Richard and Stephen a-Hurst, all three of them bareheaded with their swords in the sheaths; and Stephen moreover bearing a white cloth on a truncheon. Then a knight of
the town, very bravely armed, came forth from the barriers
and went up to Ralph, and said: "Fair sir, art thou a knight?"
"Yea," said Ralph. Said the knight, "Who be ye?" "I hight
Ralph of Upmeads," said Ralph, "and these be my men: and
we pray thee for guesting in the town of my Lord Abbot to-
night, and leave to depart to-morrow betimes."

"O unhappy young man," said the knight, "meseems these men be not so much thine as thou art theirs; for they are of the Dry Tree, and bear their token openly. Wilt thou then lodge thy company of strong-thieves with honest men?"

Stephen a-Hurst laughed roughly at this word, but Ralph said mildly: "These men are indeed of the Dry Tree, but they are my men and under my rule, and they be riding on my errands, which be lawful."

The knight was silent a while and then he said: "Well, it may be so; but into this town they come not, for the tale of them is over long for honest men to hearken to."

Even as he spake, a man-at-arms somewhat evilly armed shoved through the barriers, thrusting aback certain of his fellows, and, coming up to Ralph, stood staring up into his face with the tears starting into his eyes. Ralph looked a moment, and then reached down his arms to embrace him, and kissed his face; for lo! it was his own brother Hugh. Withal he whispered in his ear: "Get thee behind us, Hugh, if thou wilt come with us, lad." So Hugh passed on quietly toward the band, while Ralph turned to the knight again, who said to him, "Who is that man?" "He is mine own brother," said Ralph. "Be he the brother of whom he will," said the knight, "he was none the less our sworn man. Ye fools," said he, turning toward the men in the barrier, "why did ye not slay him?" "He slipped out," said they, "before we wotted what he was about." Said the knight, "Where were your bows, then?"

Said a man: "They were pressing so hard on the barrier, that we could not draw a bowstring. Besides, how might we shoot him without hitting thee, belike?"

The knight turned toward Ralph, grown wroth and surly, and that the more he saw Stephen and Richard grinning; he said: "Fair sir, ye have strengthened the old saw that saith, Tell me what thy friends are, and I will tell thee what thou art. Thou hast stolen our man with not a word on it."

"Fair sir," said Ralph, "meseemeth thou makest more words than enough about it. Shall I buy my brother of thee, then? I have a good few pieces in my pouch." The captain shook his head angrily.

"Well," said Ralph, "how can I please thee, fair sir?"

Quoth the knight: "Thou canst please me best by turning thy horses' heads away from Higham, all the sort of you." He stepped back toward the barriers, and then came forward again, and said: "Look you, man-at-arms, I warn thee that I trust thee not, and deem that thou liest. Now have I mind to issue out and fall upon you: for ye shall be evil guests in my Lord Abbot's lands."

Now at last Ralph waxed somewhat wroth, and he said: "Come out then, if you will, and we shall meet you man for man; there is yet light on this lily lea, and we will do so much for thee, churl though thou be."

But as he spoke, came the sounds of horns, and lo, over the bent showed the points of spears, and then all those five-score of the Dry Tree whom the captain had sent after Ralph came pouring down the bent. The knight looked on them under the sharp of his hand, till he saw the Dry Tree on their coats also, and then he turned and gat him hastily into the barriers; and when he was amongst his own men he fell to roaring out a defiance to Ralph, and a bolt flew forth, and two or three shafts, but hurt no one. Richard and Stephen drew their swords, but Ralph cried out: "Come away, friends, tarry not to bicker with these fools, who are afraid of they know not what: it is but lying under the naked heaven to-night instead of under the rafters, but we have all lodged thus a many times: and we shall be nigher to our journey's end to-morrow when we wake up."

Therewith he turned his horse with Richard and Stephen and came to his own men. There was much laughter and jeering at the Abbot's men amidst of the Dry Tree, both of those who had ridden with Ralph, and the new-comers; but they arrayed them to ride further in good order, and presently were skirting the walls of Higham out of bow-shot, and making for the Down country by the clear of the moon. The sergeants had gotten a horse for Hugh, and by Ralph's bidding he rode beside him as they went their ways, and the two brethren talked together lovingly.

CHAPTER 21

Talk Between Those
Two Brethren

Ralph asked Hugh first if he wotted aught of Gregory their brother. Hugh laughed and pointed to Higham, and said: "He is yonder." "What," said Ralph, "in the Abbot's host?" "Yea," said Hugh, laughing again, "but in his spiritual, not his worldly host: he is turned monk, brother; that is, he is already a novice, and will be a brother of the Abbey in six months' space." Said Ralph: "And Launcelot Long-tongue, thy squire, how hath he sped?" Said Hugh: "He is yonder also, but in the worldly host, not the spiritual: he is a sergeant of theirs, and somewhat of a catch for them, for he is no ill man-at-arms, as thou wottest, and besides he adorneth everything with words, so that men hearken to him gladly."

"But tell me," said Ralph, "how it befalleth that the Abbot's men of war be so churlish, and chary of the inside of their town; what have they to fear? Is not the Lord Abbot still a mighty man?" Hugh shook his head: "There hath been a change of days at Higham; though I say not but that the knights are over careful, and much over fearful." "What has the change been?" said Ralph. Hugh said: "In time past my Lord Abbot was indeed a mighty man, and both this town of Higham was well garnished of men-at-arms, and also many of his manors had castles and strong-houses on them, and the yeomen were ready to run to their weapons whenso the gathering was blown. In short, Higham was as mighty as it was wealthy; and the Abbot's men had naught to do with any, save with thy friends here who bear the Tree Leafless; all else feared those holy walls and the well-blessed men who warded them. But the Dry Tree feared, as men said, neither man nor devil (and I hope it may be so still since they are

507

become thy friends), and they would whiles lift in the Abbot's lands when they had no merrier business on hand, and not seldom came to their above in their dealings with his men. But all things come to an end; for, as I am told, some year and a half ago, the Abbot had debate with the Westland Barons, who both were and are ill men to deal with, being both hungry and doughty. The quarrel grew till my Lord must needs defy them, and to make a long tale short, he himself in worldly armour led his host against them, and they met some twenty miles to the west in the field of the Wry Bridge, and there was Holy Church overthrown; and the Abbot, who is as valiant a man as ever sang mass, though not over-wise in war, would not flee, and as none would slay him, might they help it, they had to lead him away, and he sits to this day in their strongest castle, the Red Mount west-away. Well, he being gone, and many of his wisest warriors slain, the rest ran into gates again; but when the Westlanders beset Higham and thought to have it good cheap, the monks and their men warded it not so ill but that the Westlanders broke their teeth over it. Forsooth, they turned away thence and took most of the castles and stronghouses of the Abbot's lands; burned some and put garrisons into others, and drave away a mighty spoil of chattels and men and women, so that the lands of Higham are half ruined; and thereby the monks, though they be stout enough within their walls, will not suffer their men to ride abroad. Whereby, being cooped up in a narrow place, and with no deeds to hand to cheer their hearts withal, they are grown sour and churlish."

"But, brother," said Ralph, "howsoever churlish they may be, and howso timorous, I cannot see why they should shut their gates in our faces, a little band, when there is no foe anear them."

"Ralph," said Hugh, "thou must think of this once more, that the Dry Tree is no good let-pass to flourish in honest men's faces; specialiter if they be monks. Amongst the brothers of Higham the tale goes that those Champions have made covenant with the devil to come to their above whensoever they be not more than one to five. Nay, moreover, it is

508

said that there be very devils amongst them; some in the likeness of carles, and some (God help us) dressed up in women's flesh; and fair flesh also, meseemeth. Also to-day they say in Higham that no otherwise might they ever have overcome the stark and cruel carles of the Burg of the Four Friths and chased them out of their town, as we know they have done. Hah! what sayest thou?"

"I say, Hugh," quoth Ralph angrily, "that thou art a fool to go about with a budget of slanderous old wives' tales." Hugh laughed. "Be not so wroth, little lord, or I shall be asking thee tales of marvels also. But hearken. I shall smooth out thy frowns with a smile when thou hast heard this: this folk are not only afeard of their old enemies, the devil-led men, but also they fear those whom the devil-led men have driven out of house and home, to wit, the Burgers. Yet again they fear the Burgers yet more, because they have beaten some of the very foes of Higham, to wit, the Westland Barons; for they have taken from them some of their strongholds, and are deemed to be gathering force."

Ralph pondered a while, and then he said: "Brother, hast thou any tidings of Upmeads, or that these Burgers have gone down thither?" "God forbid!" said Hugh. "Nay, I have had no tidings of Upmeads since I was fool enough to leave it."

"What! brother," said Ralph, "thou hast not thriven then?"

"I have had ups and downs," said Hugh, "but the ups have been one rung of the ladder, and the downs three—or more. Three months I sat in prison for getting me a broken head in a quarrel that concerned me not. Six months was I besieged in a town whither naught led me but ill-luck. Two days I wore in running thence, having scaled the wall and swam the ditch in the night. Three months I served squire to a knight who gave me the business of watching his wife of whom he was jealous; and to help me out of the weariness of his house I must needs make love myself to the said wife, who sooth to say was perchance worth it. Thence again I went by night and cloud. Ten months I wore away at the edge of the wildwood, and sometimes in it, with a sort of fellows who taught me many things, but not how to keep my hands from

509

other men's goods when I was hungry. There was I taken with some five others by certain sergeants of Higham, whom the warriors of the town had sent out cautiously to see if they might catch a few men for their ranks. Well, they gave me the choice of the gallows-tree or service for the Church, and so, my choice made, there have I been ever since, till I saw thy face this evening, fair sir."

"Well, brother," said Ralph, "all that shall be amended, and thou shalt back to Upmeads with me. Yet wert thou to amend thyself somewhat, it might not be ill."

Quoth Hugh: "It shall be tried, brother. But may I ask thee somewhat?" Said Ralph: "Ask on." "Fair Sir," said Hugh, "thou seemedst grown into a pretty man when I saw thee e'en-now before this twilight made us all alike; but the men at thy back are not wont to be led by men who have not earned a warrior's name, yet they follow thee: how cometh that about? Again, before the twilight gathered I saw the woman that rideth anigh us (who is now but a shadow) how fair and gentle she is: indeed there is no marvel in her following thee (though if she be an earl's daughter she is a fair getting for an imp of Upmeads), for thou art a well shapen lad, little lord, and carriest a sweet tongue in thy mouth. But tell me, what is she?"

"Brother," said Ralph kindly, "she is my wife."

"I kiss her hands," said Hugh; "but of what lineage is she?"

"She is my wife," said Ralph. Said Hugh: "That is, forsooth, a high dignity." Said Ralph: "Thou sayest sooth, though in mockery thou speakest, which is scarce kind to thine own mother's son: but learn, brother, that I am become a Friend of the Well, and were meet to wed with the daughters of the best of the Kings: yet is this one meeter to wed with me than the highest of the Queens; for she also is a Friend of the Well. Moreover, thou sayest it that the champions of the Dry Tree, who would think but little of an earl for a leader, are eager to follow me: and if thou still doubt what this may mean, abide, till in two days or three thou see me before the foeman. Then shalt thou tell me how much

510

changed I am from the stripling whom thou knewest in Upmeads a little while ago."

Then was Hugh somewhat abashed, and he said: "I crave thy pardon, brother, but never had I a well filed tongue, and belike it hath grown no smoother amid the hard haps which have befallen me of late. Besides it was dull in there, and I must needs try to win a little mirth out of kith and kin."

"So be it, lad," quoth Ralph kindly, "thou didst ask and I told, and all is said."

"Yet forsooth," said Hugh, "thou hast given me marvel for marvel, brother." "Even so," said Ralph, "and hereafter I will tell thee more when we sit safe by the wine at Upmeads."

Now cometh back one of the fore-riders and draweth rein by Ralph and saith that they are hard on a little thorp under the hanging of the hill that was the beginning of the Down country on that road. So Ralph bade make stay there and rest the night over, and seek new tidings on the morrow; and the man told Ralph that the folk of the thorp were fleeing fast at the tidings of their company, and that it were best that he and some half score should ride sharply into the thorp, so that it might not be quite bare of victuals when they came to their night's lodging. Ralph bids him so do, but to heed well that he hurt no man, or let fire get into any house or roof; so he takes his knot of men and rides off on the spur, and Ralph and the main of them come on quietly; and when they came into the street of the thorp, lo there by the cross a big fire lighted, and the elders standing thereby cap in hand, and a score of stout carles with weapons in their hands. Then the chief man came up to Ralph and greeted him and said: "Lord, when we heard that an armed company was at hand we deemed no less than that the riders of the Burg were upon us, and deemed that there was nought for it but to flee each as far and as fast as he might. But now we have heard that thou art a good lord seeking his own with the help of worthy champions, and a foeman to those devils of the Burg, we bid thee look upon us and all we have as thine, lord, and take kindly such guesting as we may give thee."

The old man's voice quavered a little as he looked on the stark shapes of the Dry Tree; but Ralph looked kindly on him, and said: "Yea, my master, we will but ask for a covering for our heads, and what victual thou mayst easily spare us in return for good silver, and thou shalt have our thanks withal. But who be these stout lads with staves and bucklers, or whither will they to-night?"

Thereat a tall young man with a spear in his hand and girt with a short sword came forth and said boldly: "Lord, we be a few who thought when we heard that the Burg-devils were at hand that we might as well die in the field giving stroke for stroke, as be hauled off and drop to pieces under the hands of their tormentors; and now thou hast come, we have little will to abide behind, but were fain to follow thee, and do thee what good we can: and after thou hast come to thine above, when we go back to our kin thou mayst give us a gift if it please thee: but we deem that no great matter if thou but give us leave to have the comfort of thee and thy Champions for a while in these hard days."

When he had done speaking there rose up from the Champions a hum as of praise, and Ralph was well-pleased withal, deeming it a good omen; so he said: "Fear not, good fellows, that I shall forget you when we have overcome the foemen, and meanwhile we will live and die together. But thou, ancient man, show our sergeants where our riders shall lie to-night, and what they shall do with their horses."

So the elders marshalled the little host to their abodes for that night, lodging the more part of them in a big barn on the western outskirt of the thorp. The elder who led them thither, brought them victual and good drink, and said to them: "Lords, ye were best to keep a good watch to-night because it is on this side that we may look for an onfall from the foemen if they be abroad to-night; and sooth to say that is one cause we have bestowed you here, deeming that ye would not grudge us the solace of knowing that your valiant bodies were betwixt us and them, for we be a poor unwalled people."

Stephen to whom he spake laughed at his word, and said: "Heart-up, carle! within these few days we shall build up a better wall than ye may have of stone and lime; and that is the overthrow of our foemen in the open field."

So there was kindness and good fellowship betwixt the thorp-dwellers and the riders, and the country folk told those others many tales of the evil deeds of the Burg-devils, as they called them; but they could not tell them for certain whether they had gone down into Upmeads.

As to Ralph and Ursula they, with Richard and Roger, were lodged in the headman's house, and had good feast there, and he also talked over the where-abouts of the Burgers with the thorp-dwellers, but might have no certain tidings. So he and Ursula and his fellows went to bed and slept peacefully for the first hours of the night.

CHAPTER 22

An Old Acquaintance Comes From the Down Country to See Ralph

But an hour after midnight Ralph arose, as his purpose was, and called Richard, and they took their swords and went forth and about the thorp and around its outskirts, and found naught worse than their own watch any where; so they came back again to their quarters and found Roger standing at the door, who said to Ralph: "Lord, here is a man who would see thee." "What like is he?" said Ralph. Said Roger, "He is an old man, but a tough one; however, I have got his weapons from him." "Bring him in," said Ralph, "and he shall have his say."

So they all went into the chamber together and there was light therein; but the man said to Ralph: "Art thou the Captain of the men-at-arms, lord?" "Yea," said Ralph. Said the man, "I were as lief have these others away." "So be it," said Ralph; "depart for a little while, friends." So they went, but Ursula lay in the bed, which was in a nook in the wall; the man looked about the chamber and said: "Is there any one in the bed?" "Yea," said Ralph, "my wife, good fellow; shall

513

she go also?" "Nay," said the carle, "we shall do as we are now. So I will begin my tale."

Ralph looked on him and deemed he had seen him before, but could not altogether call his visage to mind; so he held his peace and the man went on.

"I am of the folk of the shepherds of the Downs: we be not a many by count of noses, but each one of us who is come to man's years, and many who be past them, as I myself, can handle weapons at a pinch. Now some deal we have been harried and have suffered by these wretches who have eaten into the bowels of this land; that is to say, they have lifted our sheep, and slain some of us who withstood them: but whereas our houses be uncostly and that we move about easily from one hill-side to another, it is like that we should have deemed it wisest to have borne this trouble, like others of wind and weather, without seeking new remedy, but that there have been tokens on earth and in the heavens, whereof it is too long to tell thee, lord, at present, which have stirred up our scattered folk to meet together in arms. Moreover, the blood of our young men is up, because the Burg-devils have taken some of our women, and have mishandled them grievously and shamefully, so that naught will keep point and edge from seeking the war-clash. Futhermore, there is an old tale which hath now come up again, That some time when our folk shall be in great need, there shall come to our helping one from afar, whose home is anigh; a stripling and a great man; a runaway, and the conqueror of many: then, say they, shall the point and the edge bring the red water down on the dear dales; whereby we understand that the blood of men shall be shed there, and naught to our shame or dishonour. Again I mind me of a rhyme concerning this which sayeth:

> The Dry Tree shall be seen
> On the green earth, and green
> The Well-spring shall arise
> For the hope of the wise.
> They are one which were twain,
> The Tree bloometh again,

And the Well-spring hath come
From the waste to the home.

Well, lord, thou shalt tell me presently if this hath aught to
do with thee: for indeed I saw the Dry Tree, which hath
scared us so many a time, beaten on thy sergeants' coats;
but now I will go on and make an end of my story."

Ralph nodded to him kindly, for now he remembered the
carle, though he had seen him but that once when he rode
the Greenway across the downs to Higham. The old man
looked up at him as if he too had an inkling of old acquaintance with Ralph, but went on presently:

"There is a woman who dwells alone with none to help
her, anigh to Saint Ann's Chapel; a woman not very old; for
she is of mine own age, and time was we have had many a
fair play in the ingles of the downs in the July weather—not
very old, I say, but wondrous wise, as I know better than
most men; for oft, even when she was young, would she
foretell things to come to me, and ever it fell out according
to her spaedom. To the said woman I sought to-day in the
morning, not to win any wisdom of her, but to talk over
remembrances of old days; but when I came into her house,
lo, there was my carline walking up and down the floor, and
she turned round upon me like the young woman of past
days, and stamped her foot and cried out: 'What does the
sluggard dallying about women's chambers when the time is
come for the deliverance?'

"I let her talk, and spake no word lest I should spoil her
story, and she went on:

" 'Take thy staff, lad, for thou art stout as well as merry,
and go adown to the thorps at the feet of the downs toward
Higham; keep thee well from the Burg-devils, and go from
stead to stead till thou comest on a captain of men-at-arms
who is lord over a company of green-coats, green-coats of
the Dry Tree—a young lord, fair-faced, and kind-faced, and
mighty, and not to be conquered, and the blessing of the folk
and the leader of the Shepherds, and the foe of their foeman
and the well-beloved of Bear-father. Go night and day, sit
not down to eat, stand not to drink; heed none that crieth

after thee for deliverance, but go, go, go till thou hast found him. Meseems I see him riding toward Higham, but those dastards will not open gate to him, of that be sure. He shall pass on and lie to-night, it may be at Mileham, it may be at Milton, it may be at Garton; at one of those thorps shall ye find him. And when ye have found him thus bespeak him: O bright Friend of the Well, turn not aside to fall on the Burgers in this land, either at Foxworth Castle, or the Longford, or the Nineways Garth: all that thou mayest do hereafter, thou or thy champions. There be Burgers otherwhere, housed in no strong castle, but wending the road toward the fair greensward of Upmeads. If thou delay to go look on them, then shall thy work be to begin again amid sorrow of heart and loss that may not be remedied.' Hast thou heard me, lord?"

"Yea, verily," said Ralph, "and at sunrise shall we be in the saddle to ride straight to Upmeads. For I know thee, friend."

"Hold a while," said the carle, "for meseemeth I know thee also. But this withal she said: 'But hearken, Giles, hearken a while, for I see him clearly, and the men that he rideth with, and the men that are following to his aid, fierce and fell are they; but so withal are the foemen that await them, and his are few, howsoever fierce. Therefore bid him this also. Haste, haste, haste! But haste not overmuch, lest thou speed the worse: in Bear Castle I see a mote of our folk, and thee amidst of it with thy champions, and I see the staves of the Shepherds rising round thee like a wood. In Wulstead I see a valiant man with sword by side and sallet on head, and with him sitteth a tall man-at-arms grizzle-headed and red-bearded, big-boned and mighty; they sit at the wine in a fair chamber, and a well-looking dame serveth them; and there are weaponed men no few about the streets. Wilt thou pass by friends, and old friends? Now ride on, Green Coats! stride forth, Shepherds! staves on your shoulders, Wool-wards! and there goes the host over the hills into Upmeads, and the Burg-devils will have come from the Wood Debateable to find graves by the fair river. And then do thy will, O Friend of the Well.' "

516

The carle took a breath, and then he said: "Lord, this is the say I was charged with, and if thou understandest it, well; but if it be dark to thee, I may make it clear if thou ask me aught."

Ralph pondered a while, and then he said: "Is it known of others than thy spaewife that the Burgers be in Upmeads?" "Nay, lord," said the carle, "and this also I say to thee, that I deem what she said that they be not in Upmeads yet, and but drawing thitherward, as I deem from the Wood Debateable."

Ralph arose from his seat and strode up and down the chamber a while; then he went to bed, and stood over Ursula, who lay twixt sleeping and waking, for she was weary; then he came back to the carle, and said to him: "Good friend, I thank thee, and this is what I shall do: when daylight is broad (and lo, the dawn beginning!) I shall gather my men, and ride the shortest way, which thou shalt show me, to Bear Castle, and there I shall give the token of the four fires which erewhile a good man of the Shepherds bade me if I were in need. And it seems to me that there shall the mote be hallowed, though it may be not before nightfall. But the mote done, we shall wend, the whole host of us, be we few or many, down to Wulstead, where we shall fall in with my friend Clement Chapman, and hear tidings. Thence shall we wend the dear ways I know into the land where I was born and the folk amongst whom I shall die. And so let St. Nicholas and All Hallows do as they will with us. Deemest thou, friend, that this is the meaning of thy wise shefriend?"

The carle's eyes glittered, and he rose up and stood close by Ralph, and said: "Even so she meant; and now I seem to see that but few of thy riders shall be lacking when they turn their heads away from Upmeads towards the strongplaces of the Burg-devils that are hereabouts. But tell me, Captain of the host, is that victual and bread that I see on the board?"

Ralph laughed: "Fall to, friend, and eat thy fill; and here is wine withal. Thou needest not to fear it. Wert thou any the worse of the wine that Thirly poured into thee that other day?"

"Nay, nay, master," said the carle between his mouthfuls, "but mickle the better, as I shall be after this: all luck to thee! Yet see I that I need not wish thee luck, since that is thine already. Sooth to say, I deemed I knew thee when I first set eyes on thee again. I looked not to see thee more; though I spoke to thee words at that time which came from my heart, almost without my will. Though it is but a little while ago, thou hast changed much since then, and hast got another sort of look in the eyes than then they had. Nay, nay," said he laughing, "not when thou lookest on me so frankly and kindly; that is like thy look when we passed Thirly about. Yea, I see the fashion of it: one look is for thy friends, another for thy foes. God be praised for both. And now I am full, I will go look on thy wife."

So he went up to the bed and stood over Ursula, while she, who was not fully awake, smiled up into his face. The old man smiled back at her and bent down and kissed her mouth, and said: "I ask thy pardon, lady, and thine, my lord, if I be too free, but such is our custom of the Downs; and sooth to say thy face is one that even a old man should not fail to kiss if occasion serve, so that he may go to paradise with the taste thereof on his lips."

"We are nowise hurt by thy love, friend," said Ursula; "God make thy latter days of life sweet to thee!"

CHAPTER 23

They Ride to Bear Castle

But while they spake thus and were merry, the dawn had wellnigh passed into daylight. Then Ralph bade old Giles sleep for an hour, and went forth and called Roger and Richard and went to the great barn. There he bade the watch wake up Stephen and all men, and they gat to horse as speedily as they might, and were on the road ere the sun was fully up. The spearmen of the thorp did not fail them, and numbered twenty and three all told. Giles had a horse given him and rode the way by Ralph.

They rode up and down the hills and dales, but went across country and not by the Greenway, for thuswise the road was shorter.

But when they had gone some two leagues, and were nigh on top of a certain low green ridge, they deemed that they heard men's voices anigh and the clash of arms; and it must be said that by Ralph's rede they journeyed somewhat silently. So Ralph, who was riding first with Giles, bid all stay and let the crown of the ridge cover them. So did they, and Giles gat off his horse and crept on to the top of the ridge till he could see down to the dale below. Presently he came down again the old face of him puckered with mirth, and said softly to Ralph: "Did I not say thou wert lucky? here is the first fruits thereof. Ride over the ridge, lord, at once, and ye shall have what there is of them as safe as a sheep in a penfold."

So Ralph drew sword and beckoned his men up, and they all handled their weapons and rode over the brow, and tarried not one moment there, not even to cry their cries; for down in the bottom were a sort of men, two score and six (as they counted them afterward) sitting or lying about a cooking fire, or loitering here and there, with their horses standing behind them, and they mostly unhelmed. The Champions knew them at once for men of their old foes, and there was scarce time for a word ere the full half of them had passed by the sword of the Dry Tree; then Ralph cried out to spare the rest, unless they offered to run; so the foemen cast down their weapons and stood still, and were presently brought before Ralph, who sat on the grass amidst of the ring of the Champions. He looked on them a while and remembered the favour of those whom he had seen erewhile in the Burg; but ere he could speak Giles said softly in his ear: "These be of the Burg, forsooth, as ye may see by their dogs' faces; but they be not clad nor armed as those whom we have met heretofore. Ask them whence they be, lord."

Ralph spake and said: "Whence and whither are ye, ye manslayers?" But no man of them answered. Then said Ralph: "Pass these murderers by the edge of the sword, Stephen; unless some one of them will save his life and the life of his fellows by speaking."

As he spake, one of the youngest of the men hung down his head a little, and then raised it up: "Wilt thou spare our lives if I speak?" "Yea," said Ralph. "Wilt thou swear it by the edge of the blade?" said the man. Ralph drew forth his sword and said: "Lo then! I swear it." The man nodded his head, and said: "Few words are best; and whereas I wot not if my words will avail thee aught, and since they will save our lives, I will tell thee truly. We are men of the Burg whom these green-coated thieves drave out of the Burg on an unlucky day. Well, some of us, of whom I was one, fetched a compass and crossed the water that runneth through Upmeads by the Red Bridge, and so gat us into the Wood Debateable through the Uplands. There we struck a bargain with the main band of strong-thieves of the wood, that we and they together would get us a new home in Upmeads, which is a fat and pleasant land. So we got us ready; but the Woodmen told us that the Upmeads carles, though they be not many, are strong and dauntless, and since we now had pleasant life before us, with good thralls to work for us, and with plenty of fair women for our bed-mates, we deemed it best to have the most numbers we might, so that we might over-whelm the said carles at one blow, and get as few of ourselves slain as might be. Now we knew that another band of us had entered the lands of the Abbot of Higham, and had taken hold of some of his castles; wherefore the captains considered and thought, and sent us to give bidding to our folk south here to march at once toward us in Upmeads, that our bands might meet there, and scatter all before us. There is our story, lord."

Ralph knitted his brow, and said: "Tell me (and thy life lieth on thy giving true answers), do thy folk in these strongholds know of your purpose of falling upon Upmeads?" "Nay," said the Burger. Said Ralph: "And will they know otherwise if ye do them not to wit?" "Nay," again said the man. Said Ralph: "Are thy folk already in Upmeads?" "Nay," said the captive, "but by this time they will be on the road thither." "How many all told?" said Ralph. The man reddened and stammered: "A thousand— two—two thousand—A thousand, lord," said he. "Get thy sword ready, Stephen," said Ralph. "How many, on thy life, Burger?" "Two thousand, lord," said the man. "And how many do ye look to have from Higham-land?" Said the Burger, "Somewhat more than a thousand." Withal he looked uneasily at his fellows, some of whom were scowling on him felly. "Tell me now," said Ralph, "where be the other bands of the Burgers?"

Ere the captive could speak, he who stood next him snatched an unsheathed knife from the girdle of one of the Dry Tree, and quick as lightning thrust it into his fellow's belly, so that he fell dead at once amongst them. Then Stephen, who had his sword naked in his hand, straightway hewed down the slayer, and swords came out of the scabbards everywhere; and it went but a little but that all the Burgers were slain at once. But Ralph cried out: "Put up your swords, Champions! Stephen slew yonder man for slaying his fellow, who was under my ward, and that was but his due. But I have given life to these others, and so it must be held to. Tie their hands behind them and let us on to Bear Castle. For this tide brooks no delay."

So they gat to horse, and the footmen from Garton mounted the horses of the slain Burgers, and had the charge of guarding the twenty that were left. So they rode off all of them toward Bear Castle, and shortly to say it, came within sight of its rampart two hours before noon. Sooner had they came thither; but divers times they caught up with small companies of weaponed men, whose heads were turned the same way; and Giles told Ralph each time that they were of the Shepherd-folk going to the mote. But now when they were come so nigh to the castle they saw a very stream of men setting that way, and winding up the hill to the rampart. And Giles said: "It is not to be doubted but that Martha hath sent round the war-brand, and thou wilt presently have an host that will meet thy foemen without delay; and what there lacks in number shall be made good by thy luck, which once again was shown by our falling in with that company e'en now."

"Yea truly," said Ralph, "but wilt thou now tell me how I shall guide myself amongst thy folk, and if they will grant me the aid I ask?"

"Look, look," said Giles, "already some one hath made clear thine asking to our folk; and hearken! up there they are naming the ancient Father of our Race, without whom we may do nought, even with the blessed saints to aid. There then is thine answer, lord."

Indeed as he spoke came down on the wind the voice of a chant, sung by many folk, the words whereof he well remembered: SMITE ASIDE THE AXE, O BEAR-FATHER. And therewith rose up into the air a column of smoke intermingled with fire from each of the four corners of that stronghold of the Ancient Folk. Ralph rejoiced when he saw it, and the heart rose within him and fluttered in his bosom, and Ursula, who rode close behind him, looked up into his face well pleased and happy.

Thus rode they up the bent and over the turf bridge into the plain of the garth, and whatso of people were there flocked about to behold the new-come warriors; sooth to say, there were but some two hundreds, who looked but few indeed in the great square place, but more were streaming in every minute. Giles led him and his men into the north-east corner of the castle, and there they gat off their horses and lay down on the grass awaiting what should betide.

CHAPTER 24

The Folkmote of the Shepherds

In about an hour all the folk within the castle began to set toward the ingle wherein lay Ralph and his fellows, and then all rose up, while the folk of the Shepherds took their places on the slopes of the earth walls, but on the top hard by the fire, which was still burning, stood up an old hoar man with a beard exceeding long; he had a sallet on his head, and held a guisarme in his hand. All men held their peace when they saw him standing there; and straightway he proclaimed the hallowing of the Mote in such form of words as was due amongst that folk, and which were somewhat long to tell here. Then was silence again for a little, and then the old man spake: "Few words are best to-day, neighbours; for wherefore are we met together? There arose a hum of assent from the Shepherds as he spoke and men clashed their weapons together; but none said any clear word. Then spake the old man: "We be met together because we have trouble on hand, and because there is a helper to hand, of whom the words of the wise and tales of old have told us; and because as he shall help us, so shall we help him, since indeed our trouble is his also: now, neighbours, shall I say the word for you which ye would say to this young man, who is nevertheless old in wisdom, and true-hearted and kind?"

Then came the hum of yeasay again, the clashing of weapons, and the old man spake again: "Ralph of Upmeads, there thou standest, wilt thou help us against the tyrants, as we shall help thee?"

"Yea," said Ralph. Said the Elder: "Wilt thou be our Captain, if we do according to thy bidding? For thou needest not fear our failing thee."

"Yea verily," said Ralph.

Said the Elder: "Ralph of Upmeads, wilt thou be our Captain as an alien and a hireling, or as a brother?"

"As a brother," quoth Ralph.

"Come up here then, Captain of our folk, and take my hand in thine, and swear by our fathers and thine to be a true brother of us, and take this ancient staff of war in thine hand. And, ye kindred of the Shepherds, bear witness of his swearing. Yea and ye also, O neighbours of the Dry Tree!"

So Ralph went up on the wall-top and took the Elder's hand, and took from him the ancient guisarme, which was inlaid with gold letters of old time; and he swore in a loud voice to be a true brother of the Shepherd-folk, and raised the weapon aloft and shook it strongly, and all the Folk cried, "Hail our brother!" and the Champions shouted gladly withal, and great joy there was in that ingle of the ancient work.

Then spake the Elder and said: "Ye champions of the Dry Tree, will ye wend with us under the Captain our brother against his foemen and ours?"

Then stood forth Stephen a-Hurst and said, "Master shepherd, for nought else are we come hither."

Said the Elder: "Will ye come with us as friends or as hirelings? for in any case we would have you by our sides, and not in face of us; and though we be shepherds, and unhoused, or ill-housed, yet have we wherewithal to wage you, as ye know well enough, who have whiles lifted our gear."

Then Stephen laughed and said: "True it is that we have whiles driven prey in your country, yea, and had some hard knocks therein; but all that was in playing the game of war, and now since we are to fight side by side, we will be paid by our foes and not by our friends; so neither hair nor wool will we have of yours, whatever we may have of the Burgers; and it is like that we shall be good friends of yours hence-forward."

Once more all they that were there shouted. But once more the Elder spoke and said: "Is any man now wishful to speak?" None answered till a big and burly man rose up and said: "Nay, Tall Thomas, thou hast said and done all that need was, and I deem that time presses; wherefore my mind is that we now break up this mote, and that after we have eaten a morsel we get ourselves into due array and take to the road. Now let any man speak against this if he will."

None gainsaid him; nay, all seemed well-pleased. So the Elder proclaimed the breaking up of the mote, and they went from out the hallowed place and sat down in the dyke on the outside of the rampart and behind the country which stretched out all lovely and blue before them, for the day was bright and fair. There then certain women brought victual and drink to them, and served the strangers first.

So when they had eaten and drunk, Ralph bade the Shepherds array them duly, and appointed them leaders of tens and hundreds with the help of Giles, who was now clad in a hauberk and mail-coif and looked a proper man-at-arms. Then they told over their company, and numbered of the Dry Tree one hundred and fifty champions, outtaken Stephen and Roger; of the men of Garton were twenty and two, and of the Shepherds three hundred and seventy and seven stout carles, some eighty of whom had bows, and the rest glaives and spears and other staff-weapons. There was not much armour of defence amongst them, but they were one and all stark carles and doughty.

So when they were told over and made five hundred and fifty and four, they gat them into array for the road; and Ralph went afoot with no armour but his sallet, and a light coat of fence which he had gotten him in the Burg. He would have had Ursula ride on her palfrey with the Sage, but she would not, and held it for mirth and pleasure that she should go afoot through the land, now she was so nigh come home to her lord's house; so she went forth by Ralph's side with her broidered gown trussed through her girdle so that the trimness of her feet drew the eyes of all men to them. As for Richard, he took a half score of the champions, and they rode on ahead to see that all was clear before the main host; which he might well do, as he knew the country so well.

CHAPTER 25

They Come to Wulstead

Thus went they, and nought befell them to tell of till they came anigh the gates of Wulstead hard on sunset. The gates, it has been said; for whereas Ralph left Wulstead a town unwalled, he now found it fenced with pales, and with two towers strongly framed of timber, one on either side the gate, and on the battlements of the said towers they saw spears glittering; before the gate they saw a barrier of big beams also, and the gleaming of armour therein. Ralph was glad when he saw that they meant some defence; for though Wulstead was not in the lands of Upmeads, yet it was always a friendly neighbour, and he looked to eke out his host therein.

Wulstead standeth on a little hill or swelling of the earth, and the road that the company of Ralph took went up to the gate across the plain meadows, which had but here and there a tree upon them, so that the going of the company was beheld clearly from the gate; as was well seen, because anon came the sound of the blowing of great horns, and the spears thickened in the towers. Then Ralph stayed his company two bowshots from the barriers, while he himself, with his sword in his sheath, took Ursula's hand and set forth an easy pace toward the gate. Some of his company, and specially Roger and Stephen, would have letted him; but he laughed and said, "Why, lads, why? these be friends." "Yea," quoth Roger, "but an arrow knoweth no kindred nor well-willers: have a care, lord." Said the Sage of Swevenham: "Ye speak but after the folly of men of war; the hands and the eyes that be behind the bows have other hands and eyes behind them which shall not suffer that a Friend of the Well shall be hurt."

So Ralph and Ursula went forth, and came within a stone's cast of the barrier, when Ralph lifted up his voice and said: "Is there a captain of the townsfolk within the timber there?" A cheery voice answered him: "Yea, yea, lad; spare thy breath; I am coming to thee."

And therewith a man came from out the barrier and did off his headpiece and ran straight toward Ralph, who saw at once that it was Clement Chapman; he made no more ado, but coming up to Ralph fell to clipping him in his arms, while the tears ran down his face. Then he stood aloof and gazed upon him speechless a little while, and then spake: "Hail, and a hundred times hail! but now I look on thee I see what hath betid, and that thou art too noble and high that I should have cast mine arms about thee. But now as for this one, I will be better mannered with her."

Therewith he knelt down before Ursula, and kissed her feet, but reverently. And she stooped down and raised him up, with a merry countenance kissed his face, and stroked his cheeks with her hand and said: "Hail, friend of my lord! Was it not rather thou than he who delivered me from the pain and shame of Utterbol, whereas thou didst bring him safe through the mountains unto Goldburg? And but for that there had been no Well, either for him or for me."

But Clement stood with his head hanging down, and his face reddening. Till Ralph said to him: "Hail, friend! many a time we thought of this meeting when we were far away and hard bestead; but this is better than all we thought of. But now, Clement, hold up thine head and be a stout man of war, for thou seest that we are not alone."

Said Clement: "Yea, fair lord, and timely ye come, both thou and thy company; and now that I have my speech again which joy hath taken away from me at the first, I shall tell thee this, that if ye go further than the good town ye shall be met and fought withal by men who are over-many and over-fierce for us." "Yea," said Ralph, "and how many be they?" Quoth Clement: "How many men may be amongst them I wot not, but I deem there be some two thousand devils."

Now Ralph reddened, and he took Clement by the shoul-

der, and said: "Tell me, Clement, are they yet in Upmeads?"
"Sooth to say," said Clement, "by this while they may be
therein; but this morn it was yet free of them; but when thou
art home in our house, thy gossip shall belike tell thee much
more than I can; for she is foreseeing, and hath told us
much in this matter also that hath come to pass." Then spake
Ralph: "Where are my father and my mother; and shall I go
after them at once without resting, through the dark night
and all?"

Said Clement, and therewith his face brightened: "Nay,
thou needest go no further to look for them than the House
of Black Canons within our walls: there are they dwelling in
all honour and dignity these two days past." "What!" said
Ralph, "have they fled from Upmeads, and left the High
House empty? I pray thee, Clement, bring me to them as
speedily as may be."

"Verily," said Clement, "they have fled, with many another, women and children and old men, who should but hinder
the carles who have abided behind. Nicholas Longshanks is
the leader of them down there, and the High House is their
stronghold in a way; though forsooth their stout heads and
strong hands are better defence."

Here Ralph brake in: "Sweetling Ursula, though thy feet
have worn a many miles to-day, I bid thee hasten back to the
company and tell Richard that it is as I said, to wit, that
friends, and good guesting await them; so let them hasten
hither and come within gates at once. For as for me, I have
sworn it that I will not go one step back till I have seen my
father and mother in their house of Upmeads. Is it well said,
Clement?" "Yea, forsooth," said Clement; but he could not
take his eyes off Ursula's loveliness, as she kilted her skirts
and ran her ways like one of Diana's ladies in the wildwood.
At last he said, "Thou shalt wot, fair sir, that ye will have a
little band to go with thee from us of Wulstead; forsooth we
had gone to-morrow morn in any case, but since thou art here,
all is well." Even as he spake a great shout broke out from the
company as Ursula had given her message, and then came the
tramp of men and horses and the clash of weapons as they set
forward; and Clement looked and beheld how first of all the

array came Ursula, bearing the hallowed staff in her hand; for her heart also was set on what was to come. Then cried out Clement: "Happy art thou, lord, and happy shalt thou be, and who shall withstand thee? Lo! what a war-duke it is! and what a leader that marches with fate in her hands before thine host!"

Therewith were they all joined together, and Ursula gave the guisarme into Ralph's hand, and with his other hand he took hers, and the bar of the barrier was lifted and the gates thrown open, and they all streamed into the street, the champions coming last and towering over the footmen as they sat, big men on their big horses, as if they were very bodyguards of the God of War.

CHAPTER 26

Ralph Sees His Father and Mother Again

Thus came they into the market-place of Wulstead nigh to Clement's house, and there the company stood in ordered ranks. Ralph looked round about half expecting to see his gossip standing in the door; but Clement smiled and said: "Thou art looking round for thy gossip, fair sir; but she is upon the north gate in war-gear; for we be too few in Wulstead to spare so clean-limbed and strong-armed a dame from our muster; but she shall be here against thou comest back from the Austin Canons, wither forsooth thou mayst go at once if thou wilt let me be master in the matter of lodging." Said Ralph, smiling: "Well, King of Wulstead, since thou givest leave I will e'en take it, nor needest thou give me any guide to the House of St. Austin, for I know it well. Sweetheart," said he, turning to Ursula, "what sayest thou: wilt thou come with me, or abide till to-morrow, when I shall show thee to my kinsmen?" "Nay," she said, "I will with thee at once, my lord, if thou wilt be kind and take me; for meseemeth I also have a word to say to thy father, and the mother that bore thee."

"And thou, Hugh," said Ralph, "what sayest thou?" "Why, brother," said Hugh, "I think my blessing will abide the morrow's morn, for I have nought so fair and dear to show our father and mother as thou hast. Also to-morrow thou wilt have more to do; since thou art a captain, and I but a single varlet." And he smiled a little sourly on Ralph; who heeded it little, but took Ursula's hand and went his way with her.

It was but a few minutes for them to come to the House of the Canons, which was well walled toward the fields at the west of the town, so that it was its chief defence of that side. It was a fair house with a church but just finished, and Ralph could see down the street its new white pinnacles and the cross on its eastern gable rising over the ridge of the dortoir. They came to the gate, and round about it were standing men-at-arms not a few, who seemed doughty enough at first sight; but when Ralph looked on them he knew some of them, that they were old men, and somewhat past warlike deeds, for in sooth they were carles of Upmeads. Him they knew not, for he had somewhat cast down the visor of his helm; but they looked eagerly on the fair lady and the goodly knight.

So Ralph spake to the porter and bade him show him where was King Peter of Upmeads and his Lady wife; and the porter made him obeisance and told him that they were in the church, wherein was service toward; and bade him enter. So they went in and entered the church, and it was somewhat dim, because the sun was set, and there were many pictures, and knots of flowers in the glass of the windows.

So they went halfway down the nave, and stood together there; and the whole church was full of the music that the minstrels were making in the rood-loft, and most heavenly sweet it was; and as Ralph stood there his heart heaved with hope and love and the sweetness of his youth; and he looked at Ursula, and she hung her head, and he saw that her shoulders were shaken with sobs; but he knew that it was with her as with him, so he spake no word to her.

Now when his eyes cleared and he was used to the twilight of the church, he looked toward the choir, and saw near to the Jesus altar a man and a woman standing together even as they were standing, and they were somewhat stricken in years. So presently he knew that this would be his father and mother; so he stood still and waited till the service should be over; and by then it was done the twilight was growing fast in the church, and the sacristan was lighting a lamp here and there in some of the chapels, and the aisles of the choir.

So King Peter and his wife turned and came slowly down the nave, and when they were come anigh, Ralph spake aloud, and said: "Hail, King Peter of Upmeads!" And the old man stopped and said unto him: "Yea, forsooth, my name is Peter, and my business is to be a king, or a kinglet rather; and once it seemed no such hard craft; but now it all goes otherwise, and belike my craft has left me; even as it fares with a leech when folk are either too well or too ill to need his leech-craft."

Then he looked at Ralph and at Ursula, and said: "Either my eyes are worse than I deemed yesterday, or thou art young, and a gallant knight, and she that is standing by thee is young, and fair. Ah, lad! time was when I would have bid thee come home, thou and thy sweetling, to my house with me, and abide there in ease and feastfully; but now the best rede I can give thee is to get thee gone from the land, for there is all unpeace in it. And yet, forsooth, friend, I know not where to send thee to seek for peace, since Upmeads hath failed us."

While he spoke, and Ralph was sore moved by the sound of his voice, and his speech wherein kindness and mocking was so blended, the Dame of Upmeads came to Ralph and laid her hand on his arm, and said in a pleasant voice, for she was soft-hearted and soft-spoken both: "Will not the fair young warrior and his mate do so much for an old man and his wife, who have heard not tidings of their best beloved son for two years well nigh, as to come with them to their chamber, and answer a little question or two as to the parts of the world they have seen of late?"

Ralph nodded yeasay and began to move toward the porch, the Dame of Upmeads sticking close to him all the time, and King Peter following after and saying: "Yea, young man, thou mayst think the worse of me for hanging about here amongst the monks, when e'en now, for all I know, the battle is pitched in Upmeads; but Nicholas and all of them would have it so—Yea, and all my sons are away, fair sir; though of the eldest, who meseems was born with a long head, we hear that he is thriving, and hath grown great."

As he spake they were come into the porch, and passed into the open air, where it was still light; then the Dame turned round on Ralph and caught him by the two arms and cried out and cast her arms about his neck; and when she could sunder herself a little from him, she said: "O Ralph, I deemed that I knew thy voice, but I durst not halse thee till I knew it was mine own flesh and blood, lest I should have died for grief to think it was thee when it was not. O son, how fair thou art! Now do off thy sallet that I may see thee, thy face and thy curly head."

So did he, smiling as one who loved her, and again she fell to kissing and clipping him. Then his father came up and thrust her aside gently and embraced him also, and said: "Tell me, son, what thou are become? Thou art grown much of a man since thou stolest thyself away from me. Is there aught behind this goodly raiment of thine? And this fair lady, hath she stolen thee away from thy foes to bring thee home to us?"

Ralph laughed and said: "No less than that, father; I will tell thee all presently; but this first, that I am the captain of a goodly company of men-at-arms; and"——"Ah, son, sweetheart," said his mother, "and thou wilt be going away from us again to seek more fame: and yet, as I look on thee thou seemest to have grown great enough already. I deem thou wilt not leave us."

"Mother, my dear," said Ralph, "to-morrow morn we shall go down to battle in Upmeads, and the day after I shall come hither again, and bring you back to the High House with all honour and glory. But look, mother," and he took Ursula's hand, "here is a daughter and a darling that I have brought back to thee, for this is my wedded wife."

Then Ursula looked beseechingly at the Dame, who took her in her arms and clipped her and kissed her, and said, "Welcome, daughter; for I feel thy body that thou lovest me."

Then said King Peter; "Forsooth, son, she is a sweet and dainty creature. If there be a fairer than her, I wot not; but none so fair have mine eyes looked on. Tell me whose daughter she is, and of what lineage?" And therewith he took her hand and kissed her.

But Ursula said: "I am come of no earl or baron. I am a yeoman's daughter, and both my father and my mother are dead, and I have no nigh kin save one brother who loveth me not, and would heed it little if he never saw my face again. Now I tell thee this: that if my lord biddeth me go from him, I will depart; but for the bidding of none else will I leave him."

King Peter laughed and said: "Never will I bid thee depart." Then he took her hand and said: "Sweetling, fair daughter, what is thy name?" "Ursula," she said. Said he: "Ursula, thy palms are harder than be the hands of the dainty dames of the cities, but there is no churls' blood in thee meseemeth. What is thy kindred of the yeoman?" She said: "We be come of the Geirings of old time: it may be that the spear is broken, and the banner torn; but we forget not our forefathers, though we labour afield, and the barons and the earls call us churls. It is told amongst us that that word is but another way of saying earl, and that it meaneth a man."

Then spoke Ralph: "Father and mother both, I may well thank thee and bless thee that your eyes look upon this half of me with kind eyes. And now I shall tell thee that for this woman, her heart is greater than a king's or a leader of folk. And meseemeth her palms have hardened with the labour of delivering me from many troubles."

Then the Dame of Upmeads put her arms about Ursula's

neck again, and bade her all welcome once more, with sweet words of darling and dear, and well-beloved daughter.

But King Peter said: "Son, thou hast not told me what thou are become; and true it is that thou hast the look of a great one."

Said Ralph: "Father and King, I have become the Lord of the Little Land of Abundance, the sworn brother of the Champions of the Dry Tree, the Lord of the Castle of the Scaur, the brother and Warduke of the Shepherds; and to-morrow shall I be the Conqueror of the robbers and the devils of the Burg. And this be not enough for me, hearken! I and my wife both, yea and she leading me, have drunk of the Well at the World's End, and have become Friends thereof."

And he looked at his father with looks of love, and his father drew nigh to him again, and embraced him once more, and stroked his cheeks and kissed him as if he had become a child again: "O son," said he, "whatsoever thou dost, that thou dost full well. And lo, one while when I look on thee thou art my dear and sweet child, as thou wert years agone, and I love thee dearly and finely; and another while thou art a great and mighty man, and I fear thee; so much greater thou seemest than we poor upland folk."

Then smiled Ralph for love and happiness, and he said: "Father, I am thy child in the house and at the board, and that is for thine helping. And I am thy champion and the fierce warrior afield, and that also is for thine helping. Be of good cheer; for thine house shall not wane, but wax." And all those four were full of joy and their hearts were raised aloft.

But as they spake thus came a lay-brother and bent the knee before King Peter and bade him and the Dame of Upmeads to supper in the name of the Prior, and the Captain and the Lady therewith; for indeed the rumour of the coming of an host for the helping of the countryside had gotten into that House, and the Prior and the brethren sorely desired to look upon the Captain, not knowing him for Ralph of Upmeads. So into the Hall they went together, and there the holy fathers made them great feast and joy; and King Peter might not refrain him, but told the Prior how this was his son come back from far lands, with the goodly Lady he had won to wife therein; and the Prior and all the fathers made much of Ralph, and rejoiced in their hearts when they saw how goodly a man of war he had gotten to be. And the Prior would lead him on to tell him of the marvels he had seen in the far parts of the world; but Ralph said but little thereon, whereas his thought was set on the days that lay even before his feet; yet some deal he told him of the uncouth manners of the lands beyond Whitwall, and at last he said: "Father, when the battles be over here, and there is peace on our lands again, I will ask thee to give me guesting for a night, that I may tell thee all the tale of what hath befallen me since the last summer day when I rode through Wulstead; but now I ask leave of thee to depart, for I have many things to do this even, as behoveth a captain, before I sleep for an hour or two. And if it be thy will, I would leave the Lady my wife with my mother here at least till morrow morn."

So the Prior gave him leave, loth though he were, and Ralph kissed his father and mother, and they blessed him. But Ursula said to him softly: "It is my meaning to go with thee down into Upmeads to-morrow; for who knoweth what may befall thee." Then he smiled upon her and went his ways down the hall and out-a-gates, while all men looked on him and did him worship.

CHAPTER 27

Ralph Holds Converse With Katherine His Gossip

Ralph went straight from St. Austin's to Clement's house, and found much people about the door thereof, what of the townsmen, what of the men of his own host. He passed through these, and found Clement in his chamber, and with him a half score of such company as was without, and amongst them Roger and the Sage; but Stephen and Richard both were amongst their men doing what was needful. All men arose when Ralph entered; but he looked around, and could see nought of his gossip amongst them. Then he sat down by Clement and asked if he had any fresh tidings; and Clement did him to wit that there had come in a carle from out of Upmeads, who had told them by sure tokens that the foe were come into the Upmeads-land at noon that day, and between then and sunset had skirmished with Nicholas and them that were holding the High House, but had gotten nought thereby. This man, said Clement, being both bold and of good sleight had mingled with the foe; and had heard the talk of them, and he said that they had no inkling of the Shepherds or the Dry Tree coming against them; but they looked to have aid from their own folk from the lands of Higham; wherefore they made a mock of the defence of the Upmeads' men; and said that since, when they were all joined together in Upmeads, they might enter where they would without the loss of a half-score men, therefore they would risk nought now; nor would they burn either the High House or the other steadings, since, said they, they were minded to keep them sound and whole for their own.

These tidings seemed good to Ralph; so he took a cup of wine and pledged the company, and said: "My masters, such of you as list to sleep long to-night had best be abed presently, for I warn you that the trumpets will blow for departure before the sun riseth to-morrow; and he that faileth to see to-morrow's battle will be sorry for his lack all his life long."

When he had thus spoken they all cried hail to him, and anon arose and went their ways. Then Ralph bade Clement come with him that he might visit the quarters of his men-at-arms, and see that all the leaders knew of the muster, and of the order of departing on the morrow; and Clement arose and went with him.

As they were on the way Ralph asked Clement what ailed his gossip Katherine that she had not come to meet him already; and Clement laughed and said: "Nought, nought; she is somewhat shamefaced to meet thee first amongst a many folk, and she not able belike to refrain her kisses and caresses to thee. Fear not, she is in her bower-aloft, and we shall find her there when we come back from our errand; fear not! she will not sleep till she hath had her arms about thee." "Good is that," said Ralph; "I had looked to see her ere now; but when we meet apart from folk, something we shall be able to say to each other, which belike neither she nor I had liked to leave unsaid till we meet again."

So came they to the chief quarters of the fighting men, and Ralph had all the leaders called to him, and he spake to them of how they should do on the morrow, both footmen and horsemen, whatwise they should stand together, and how they should fall on; and he told them all as clearly as if he were already in the field with the foe before him; so that they wondered at him, so young in years, being so old in the wisdom of war. Withal they saw of him that he had no doubt but that they should come to their above on the morrow; and all men, not only of the tried men-at-arms of the Dry Tree, but they of the Shepherds also, even those of them who had never stricken a stroke in anger, were of high heart and feared not what should befall.

So when all this business was over, they turned about and came their ways home to Clement's house again.

They saw lights in the chamber or ever they entered, and when they came to the door, lo! there within was Katherine walking up and down the floor as if she knew not how to contain herself. She turned and saw Ralph at the door, and she cried aloud and ran towards him with arms outspread. But when she drew nigh to him and beheld him closely, she withheld her, and falling down on her knees before him took his hand and fell to kissing it and weeping and crying out, "O my lord, my lord, thou art come again to us!" But Ralph stooped down to her, and lifted her up, and embraced her, and kissed her on the cheeks and the mouth, and led her to the settle and sat down beside her and put his arm about her; and Clement looked on smiling, and sat him down over against them.

Then spake Katherine: "O my lord! how great and masterful hast thou grown; never did I hope to see thee come back so mighty a man." And again she wept for joy; but Ralph kissed her again, and she said, laughing through her tears: "Master Clement, this lord and warrior hath brought back with him something that I have not seen; and belike he hath had one fair woman in his arms, or more it may be, since I saw him last. For though he but kisses me as his gossip and foster-mother, yet are his kisses closer and kinder than they were aforetime."

Said Clement: "Sooth is the Sage's guess; yet verily, fair sir, I have told her somewhat of thy journeys, so far as I knew of them."

Said Katherine: "Dear lord and gossip, wilt thou not tell me more thereof now?"

"What!" said Ralph; "shall I not sleep to-night?"

"Dear gossip," she said, "thou art over-mighty to need sleep. And ah! I had forgotten in the joy of our meeting that to-morrow thou goest to battle; and how if thou come not again?"

"Fear nought," said Ralph; "art thou not somewhat fore-seeing? Dost thou not know that to-morrow or the day after I shall come back unhurt and victorious; and then shall both thou and Clement come to Upmeads and abide there as long as ye will; and then shall I tell thee a many tales of my wanderings; and Ursula my beloved, she also shall tell thee."

Katherine reddened somewhat, but she said: "Would I might kiss her feet, dear lord. But now, I pray thee, tell me somewhat, now at once."

"So shall it be," said Ralph, "since thou wilt have it, dear gossip; but when I have done I shall ask thee to tell me somewhat, whereof hath long been wonder in my mind; and meseemeth that by the time we are both done with tales, I shall needs be putting on my helm again.—Nay, again I tell thee it is but a show of battle that I go to!"

So then he went and sat by Clement's side, and began and told over as shortly as might be the tidings of his journeys. And oft she wept for pity thereat.

But when he was done and he had sat beholding her, and saw how goodly a woman she was, and how straight and well knit of body, he said: "Gossip, I wonder now, if thou also hast drunk of the Well; for thou art too fair and goodly to be

538

of the age that we call thee. How is this? Also tell me how thou camest by this pair of beads that seem to have led me to the Well at the World's End? For as I said e'en now, I have long marvelled how thou hadst them and where."

"Fair sir," said Clement, "as for her drinking of the Well at the World's End, it is not so; but this is a good woman, and a valiant, and of great wisdom; and such women wear well, even as a well-wrought piece of armour that hath borne many strokes of the craftsman's hand, and hath in it some deal of his very mind and the wisdom of him. But now let her tell thee her tale (which forsooth I know not), for night is growing old."

CHAPTER 28

Dame Katherine Tells of the Pair of Beads, and Whence She Had Them

Katherine cast friendly looks on them and said: "Gossip, and thou, Clement, I will make a clean breast of it once for all. In the days when I was first wedded to Master Clement yonder, he found his bed cold without me, for he was a hot lover; therefore would he often have me with him on his journeys, how hard soever or perilous the way might be. Yea, Clement, thou lookest the sooth, though thou sayest it not, I was nought loth thereto, partly because I would not grieve thee, my man; but partly, and belike mostly, because I was wishful to see the ways of the world even at the risk of being thrust out of the world. So it befell us on a time to make a journey together, a journey exceeding long, in the company of certain chapmen, whereof some, and not a few, died on the way. But we lived, and came into the eastern parts of the earth to a city right ancient, and fulfilled of marvels, which hight Sarras the Holy. There saw we wonders whereof were it overlong to tell of here; but one while I will tell thee, my lord. But this I must needs say, that I heard tell of a woman dwelling there, who was not old by seeming, but had in her the wisdom of ten lives, and the longing gat hold of me to see her and learn wisdom of her. So I entreated many who were called wise, some with prayers, and some with gifts also, to help me to speech of her; but I gat nothing either by praying or giving; they that would have helped me could not, and they that could would not. So, what between one thing and another, the longing to see the Wise Woman grew as it were into a madness in me. Amidst of which we fell in with a merchant exceeding wise in ancient lore, who looked at me (though Clement knew it not) with eyes of love. Of this man I asked concerning the Wise Woman, and he seeing my desire, strove to use it merchant-like, and would deal with me and have in payment for his learning a gift which I had nought to do to give. Howbeit madness and my desire for speech with the Wise Woman got the better of me, and I promised to give no less than he would, trusting to beguile him after I had got my desire, and be quit of him. So he led me to the woman and went his ways. She dwelt all by herself in a nook of an ancient ruined palace, erst the house of the ancientest of all the kings of Sarras. When I came to her, I saw nought dreadful or ugsome about her: she was cheerful of countenance and courteous of demeanour, and greeted me kindly as one neighbour in the street of Wulstead might do to another. I saw her, that she was by seeming a woman of some forty winters, trim and well-fashioned of body, nowise big, but slender, of dark red hair and brown eyes somewhat small.

"Now, she said to me, 'I have looked for thee a while; now thou art come, thou shalt tell me what thou needest, and thy needs will I fulfil. Yet needs must thou do a thing for me in return, and maybe thou wilt deem it a great thing. Yet whereas thou has struck a bargain before thou camest hither, if I undo that for thee, the bargain with me may be nought so burdensome. How sayest thou?'

"Well, I saw now that I was in the trap, for ill had it been in those days had Clement come to know that I had done amiss; for he was a jealous lover, and a violent man."

540

Clement smiled hereat, but said nought, and Katherine went on: "Trap or no trap, if I were eager before, I was over-eager now; so when she bade me swear to do her will, I swore it without tarrying.

"Then she said: 'Sit down before me, and I will teach thee wisdom.' What did she teach me? say ye. Well, if I told you belike ye would be none the wiser; but so much she told me, that my heart swelled with joy of the wisdom which I garnered. Say thou, Clement, if I have been the worser woman to thee, or thy friends, or mine."

"Nay, goodwife," said Clement, "I have nought against thee."

Katherine laughed and went on:

"At last the Wise Woman said, 'Now that thou hast of me all that may avail thee, comes the other part of our bargain, wherein I shall take and thou shalt give.'

"Quoth I, 'That is but fair, and thou shalt find me true to thee.' She said, 'If thou be not, I shall know it, and shall amend it in such wise that it shall cost thee much.'

"Then she looked on me long and keenly, and said afterward: 'Forsooth I should forbear laying this charge upon thee if I did not deem that thou wouldst be no less than true. But now I will try it, whereas I deem that the days of my life henceforward shall not be many; and many days would it take me to find a woman as little foolish as thee and as little false, and thereto as fairly fashioned.'

"Therewith she put her hand to her neck, and took thence the self-same pair of beads which I gave to thee, dear gossip, and which (praise be to All Hallows!) thou hast borne ever since; and she said: 'Now hearken! Thou shalt take this pair of beads, and do with them as I bid thee. Swear again thereto.' So I swore by All Angels; and she said again: 'This pair of beads shall one day lead a man unto the Well at the World's End, but no woman; forsooth, if a woman have them of a woman, or the like of them, (for there be others,) they may serve her for a token; but will be no talisman or leading-stone to her; and this I tell thee lest thou seek to the Well on the strength of them. For I bid thee give them to a man that thou lovest—that thou lovest well, when he is in most need; only he shall not be of thine own blood. This is all that I lay upon thee; and if thou do it, thou shalt thrive, and if thou do it not, thou shalt come to harm. And I will tell thee now that this meeting betwixt us is not by chance-hap, but of my bringing about; for I have laboured to draw thee to me, knowing that thou alone of women would avail me herein. Now shalt thou go home to thine hostel, and take this for a token of my sooth-saying. The wise merchant who led thee unto me is abiding thine homecoming that he may have of thee that which thou promisedst to him. If then thou find him at thine hostel, and he take thee by the hand and lead thee to bed, whereas Clement is away till to-morrow even, then shalt thou call me a vain word-spinner and a liar; but if when thou comest home there, the folk there say to thee merchant Valerius is ridden away hastily, being called afar on a message of life and death, then shalt thou trow in me as a wise woman. Herewith depart, and I bid thee farewell.'

"So I went my ways to my hostel trembling, and at the door I met the chamberlain, who said to me, 'Lady, the merchant Valerius hath been here seeking thee, and he said that he would abide thy coming; but amidst of his abiding cometh a man who would speak to him privily; whereof it came that he called for his horse and bade me tell thee, Lady, that he was summoned on a matter of life and death, and would return to kiss thine hands in five days' space.'

"So I wotted that the woman had spoken sooth, and was wise and foreseeing, and something of a dread of her came upon me. But the next even back cometh Clement, and the day after we rode away from Sarras the Holy, and Valerius I saw never again. And as to the beads, there is nought to tell of them till they came into thine hands; and something tells me that it was the will of the Wise Woman that to no other hands they should come."

Here Katherine made an end, and both the men sat pondering her tale a little. As for Ralph, he deemed it certain that the Wise Woman of Sarras would be none other than she who had taught lore to the Lady of Abundance; but why she should have meant the beads for him he wotted not. Again he wondered how it was that the Lady of Abundance

542

hould have given the beads to Ursula, and whether she knew hat they had no might to lead her to the Well at the World's End. And yet further he wondered how it was that Ursula, unholpen by the talisman, should have done so much to bring him to the Well; yea, and how she was the first to see it while he slept. But his heart told him that whereas he was seeking the Well with her, she must needs come thither with him, unless they were both cast away; withal Katherine looked at him and said: "Yea, dear lord, I wot what thou art thinking of; but couldest thou have left her, when thou hadst once found her again, Well or no Well?" "Sooth is that," said Ralph, "yet for all that she hath done without help of talisman or witchcraft is she the more worshipful and the dearer."

Then speech came into Clement's mouth, and he said: "Wife, it is as I said before, when thy gossip had just departed from us. It was meet enough that thou shouldst have loved him better than me; but now it is even less to be undone than ever, when he has come back bringing with him a woman so valiant and lovely as is my Lady Ursula. So thou must e'en take the life that fate hath sent thee." Katherine laughed through her tears, and said: "Withal, goodman, I have been no bad wife to thee. And moreover, look thou, gossip dear: when I was wandering about with Clement amongst many perils, when our need seemed sorest, then would I think to give the beads to Clement; but so soon as I began to speak to him of the Well at the World's End he would belittle the tale of it, and would bid me look to it if it were not so, that where the world endeth the clouds begin."

As she spoke, Ralph lifted up his hand and pointed to the window, and said: "Friends, as we were speaking of all these marvels we were forgetting the need of Upmeads and the day of battle; and lo now! how the dawn is widening and the candles fading."

Scarce were the words out of his mouth, when on the quietness of the beginning of day brake out the sound of four trumpets, which were sounding in the four quarters of the town, and blowing men to the gathering. Then rose up both Ralph and Clement and took their weapons, and they kissed

543

Katherine and went soberly out-a-doors into the market
place, where already weaponed men were streaming in to the
muster.

CHAPTER 29

They Go Down to Battle
in Upmeads

Before it was light were all men come into the market
place, and Ralph and Richard and Clement and Stephen
a-Hurst fell to and arrayed them duly; and now, what with
the company which Ralph had led into Wulstead, what with
the men of the town, and them that had fled from Upmeads
(though these last were mostly old men and lads), they were
a thousand and four score and three. Ralph would go afoot
as he went yesterday; but today he bore in his hand the
ancient staff of war, the gold-written guisarme; and he went
amongst the Shepherds, with whom were joined the feeble
folk of Upmeads, men whom he had known of old and who
knew him, and it was as if their hearts had caught fire from
his high heart, and that whatever their past days had been to
them, this day at least should be glorious. Withal anon come
Ursula from St. Austin's with the Sage of Swevenham, whose
face was full smiling and cheerful. Ursula wore that day a
hauberk under her gown, and was helmed with a sallet; and
because of her armour she rode upon a little horse. Ralph
gave her into the warding of the Sage, who was armed at all
points, and looked a valiant man of war. But Ralph's brother, Hugh, had gotten him a horse, and had fallen into the
company of the Champions, saying that he deemed they
would go further forth than a sort of sheep-tending churls
and the runaways of Upmeads.

As for Ralph, he walked up and down the ranks of the
stout men of the Down-country, and saw how they had but

little armour for defence, though their weapons for cutting and thrusting looked fell and handy. So presently he turned about to Giles, who, as aforesaid, bore a long hauberk, and said: "Friend, the walk we are on to-day is a long one for carrying burdens, and an hour after sunrise it will be hot. Wilt thou not do with thy raiment as I do?" And therewith he did off his hauberk and his other armour save his sallet. "This is good," said he, "for the sun to shine on, so that I may be seen from far; but these other matters are good for folk who fight a-horseback or on a wall; we striders have no need of them."

Then arose great shouting from the Shepherds, and men stretched out the hand to him and called hail on his valiant heart.

Amidst of which cries Giles muttered, but so as Ralph might hear him: "It is all down hill to Upmeads; I shall take off my iron-coat coming back again." So Ralph clapped him on the shoulder and bade him come back whole and well in any case. "Yea, and so shalt thou come back," said he.

Then the horns blew for departure, and they went their ways out of the market-place, and out into the fields through the new wooden wall of Wulstead. Richard led the way with a half score of the Champions, but he rode but a little way before Ralph, who marched at the head of the Shepherds.

So they went in the fresh morning over the old familiar fields, and strange it seemed to Ralph that he was leading an host into the little land of Upmeads. Speedily they went, though in good order, and it was but a little after sunrise when they were wending toward the brow of the little hill whence they would look down into the fair meads whose image Ralph had seen on so many days of peril and weariness.

And now Richard and his fore-riders had come up on to the brow and sat there on their horses clear against the sky; and Ralph saw how Richard drew his sword from the scabbard and waved it over his head, and he and his men shouted; then the whole host set up a great shout, and hastened up the bent, but with the end of their shout and the sound of the tramp of their feet and the rattle of their war-gear was mingled a confused noise of cries a way off, and the blowing of horns, and as Ralph and his company came crowding up on to the brow, he looked down and saw the happy meadows black with weaponed men, and armour gleaming in the clear morning, and the points of weapons casting back the low sun's rays and glittering like the sparks in a dying fire of straw. Then again he looked, and lo! the High House rising over the meadows unburned and unhurt, and the banner of the fruited tree hanging forth from the topmost tower thereof.

Then he felt a hand come on to his cheek, and lo, Ursula beside him, her cheeks flushed and her eyes glittering; and she cried out: "O thine home, my beloved, thine home!" And he turned to her and said; "Yea, presently, sweetheart!" "Ah," she said, "will it be long? and they so many!" "And we so mighty!" said Ralph. "Nay, it will be but a little while. Wise man of Swevenham, see to it that my beloved is anigh me to-day, for where I am, there will be safety."

The Sage nodded yeasay and smiled.

Then Ralph looked along the ridge to right and left of him, and saw that all the host had come up and had a sight of the foemen; on the right stood the Shepherds staring down into the meadow and laughing for the joy of battle and the rage of the oppressed. On the left sat the Champions of the Dry Tree on their horses, and they also were tossing up their weapons and roaring like lions for the prey; and down below the black crowd had drawn together into ordered ranks, and still the clamour and rude roaring of the warriors arose thence, and beat against the hill's brow.

Now so fierce and ready were the men of Ralph's company that it was a near thing but that they, and the Shepherds in especial, did not rush tumultuously down the hill all breathless and in ill order. But Ralph cried out to Richard to go left, and Giles to go right, and stay the onset for a while; and to bid the leaders come to him where he stood. Then the tumult amidst his folk lulled, and Stephen a-Hurst and Roger and three others of the Dry Tree came to him, and Giles brought three of the Shepherds, and there was Clement and a fellow of his. So when they were come and standing in a ring round Ralph, he said to them:

"Brothers in arms, ye see that our foes are all in array to meet us, having had belike some spy in Wulstead, who hath brought them the tale of what was toward. Albeit methinks that this irks not either you nor me; for otherwise we might have found them straggling, and scattered far and wide, which would have made our labour the greater. Now ye can see with your eyes that they are many more than we be, even were Nicholas to issue out of the High House against them, as doubtless he will do if need be. Brethren, though they be so many, yet my heart tells me that we shall overcome them; yet if we leave our strength and come down to them, both our toil shall be greater, and some of us, belike many, shall be slain; and evil should I deem it if but a score of my friends should lose their lives on this joyous day when at last I see Upmeads again after many troubles. Wherefore my rede is that we abide their onset on the hillside here; and needs must they fall on us, whereas we have Wulstead and friends behind us, and they nought but Nicholas and the bows and bills of the High House. But if any have aught to say against it let him speak, but be speedy; for already I see a stir in their array, and I deem that they will send men to challenge us to come down to them."

Then spake Stephen a-Hurst: "I, and we all meseemeth, deem that thou art in the right, Captain; though sooth to say, when we first set eyes on these dogs again, the blood so stirred in us that we were like to let all go and ride down on them."

Said Richard: "Thou biddest us wisdom of war; let them have the hill against them." Said Clement: "Yea, for they are well learned and well armed; another sort of folk to those wild men whom we otherthrew in the mountains."

And in like wise said they all.

Then spake Stephen again: "Lord, since thou wilt fight afoot with our friends of the Shepherds, we of the Dry Tree are minded to fare in like wise and to forego our horses; but if thou gainsay it——"

"Champion," said Ralph, "I do gainsay it. Thou seest how many of them be horsed, and withal ye it is who must hold

547

the chase of them; for I will that no man of them shall escape."

They laughed joyously at his word, and then he said: "Go now, and give your leaders of scores and tens the word that I have said, and come back speedily for a little while; for now I see three men sundering them from their battle, and one beareth a white cloth at the end of his spear; these shall be the challengers."

So they did after his bidding, and by then they had come back to Ralph those three men were at the foot of the hill, which was but low. Then Ralph said to his captains: "Stand before me, so that I be not seen of them until one of you hath made answer, 'Speak of this to our leader and captain.'" Even so they did; and presently those three came so nigh that they could see the whites of their eyes. They were all three well armed, but the foremost of them was clad in white steel from head to foot, so that he looked like a steel image, all but his face, which was pale and sallow and grim. He and his two fellows, when they were right nigh, rode slowly all along the front of Ralph's battles thrice, and none spake aught to them, and they gave no word to any; but when they came over against the captains who stood before Ralph for the fourth time, they reined up and faced them, and the leader put back his sallet and spake in a great and rough voice:

"Ye men! we have heard these three hours that ye were coming, wherefore we have drawn out into the meads which we have taken, that ye might see how many and how valiant we be, and might fear us. Wherefore now, ye broken reivers of the Dry Tree, ye silly shepherds of silly sheep, ye weavers and apprentices of Wulstead, and if there by any more, ye fools! we give you two choices this morn. Either come down to us into the meadow yonder, that we may slay you with less labour, or else, which will be the better for you, give up to us the Upmeads thralls who be with you, and then turn your faces and go back to your houses, and abide there till we come and pull you out of them, which may be some while yet. Hah! what say ye, fools?"

Then spake Clement and said: "Ye messengers of the

robbers and oppressors, why make ye this roaring to the common people and the sergeants? Why speak ye not with our Captain?"

Cried out the challenger, "Where then is the Captain of the Fools? is he hidden? can he hear my word?"

Scarce was it out of his mouth ere the captains fell away to right and left, and there, standing by himself, was Ralph, holding the ancient lettered war-staff; his head was bare, for now he had done off his sallet, and the sun and the wind played in his bright hair; glorious was his face, and his grey eyes gleamed with wrath and mastery as he spake in a clear voice, and there was silence all along the ranks to hearken him:

"O messenger of the robbers! I am the captain of this folk. I see that the voice hath died away within the jaws of you; but it matters not, for I have heard thy windy talk, and this is the answer: we will neither depart, nor come down to you, but will abide our death by your hands here on this hill-side. Go with this answer."

The man stared wild at Ralph while he was speaking, and seemed to stagger in his saddle; then he let his sallet fall over his face, and, turning his horse about, rode swiftly, he and his two fellows, down the hill and away to the battle of the Burgers. None followed or cried after him; for now had a great longing and expectation fallen upon Ralph's folk, and they abode what shall befall with little noise. They noted so soon as the messenger was gotten to the main of the foemen that there was a stir amongst them, and they were ordering their ranks to move against the hill. And withal they saw men all armed coming from out the High House, who went down to the Bridge and abode there. Upmeads-water ran through the meadows betwixt the hill and the High House, as hath been said afore; but as it winded along, one reach of it went nigh to the House, and made wellnigh a quarter of a circle about it before it turned to run down the meadows to the eastward; and at this nighest point was there a wide bridge well builded of stone.

The Burg-devils heeded not the men at the Bridge, but, being all arrayed, made but short tarrying (and that belike only to hear the tale of their messenger) ere they came in two battles straight across the meadow. They on their right were all riders, and these faced the Champions of the Dry Tree, but a great battle of footmen came against the Shepherds and the rest of Ralph's footmen, but in their rearward was a company of well-horsed men-at-arms; and all of them were well armed and went right orderly and warrior-like.

It was but some fifteen minutes ere they were come to the foot of the hill, and they fell to mounting it with laughter and mockery, but Ralph's men held their peace. The horsemen were somewhat speedier than those on foot, though they rode but at a foot's pace, and when they were about halfway up the hill and were faltering a little (for it was somewhat steep, though nought high), the Champions of the Dry Tree could forbear them no longer, but set up a huge roar, and rode at them, so that they all went down the hill together, but the Champions were lost amidst of the huge mass of the foemen.

But Ralph was left at the very left end of his folk, and the foemen came up the hill speedily with much noise and many foul mocks as aforesaid, and they were many and many more than Ralph's folk, and now that the Champions were gone, could have enfolded them at either end; but no man of the company blenched or faltered, only here and there one spake soft to his neighbour, and here and there one laughed the battle-laugh.

Now at the hanging of the hill, whenas either side could see the whites of the foemen's eyes, the robbers stayed a little to gather breath; and in that nick of time Ralph strode forth into the midst between the two lines and up on to a little mound on the hill-side (which well he knew), and he lifted up the ancient guisarme, and cried on high: "Home now! Home to Upmeads!"

Then befell a marvel, for even as all eyes of the foemen were turned on him, straightway their shouts and jeering and laughter fell dead, and then gave place to shrieks and wailing, as all they who beheld him cast down their weapons and fled wildly down the hill, overturning whatever stood in their way, till the whole mass of them was broken to pieces, and the hill was covered with nought but cravens and the light-footed Shepherds slaughtering them in the chase.

But Ralph called Clement to him and they drew a stalworth band together, and, heeding nought the chase of the runaways, they fell on those who had the Champions in their midst, and fell to smiting down men on either hand; and every man who looked on Ralph crouched and cowered before him, casting down his weapons and throwing up his hands. Shortly to say it, when these horsemen felt this new onset, and looking round saw their men fleeing hither and thither over the green fields of Upmeads, smitten by the Shepherds and leaping into the deep pools of the river, they turned and fled, every man who could keep his saddle, and made for the Bridge, the Dry Tree thundering at their backs. But even as they came within bowshot, a great flight of arrows came from the further side of the water, and the banner of the Fruitful Tree came forth from the bridge-end with Nicholas and his tried men-at-arms behind it; and then indeed great and grim was the murder, and the proud men of the Burg grovelled on the ground and prayed for mercy till neither the Champions nor the men of Nicholas could smite helpless men any longer.

Now had Ralph held his hand from the chase, and he was sitting on a mound amidst of the meadow under an ancient thorn, and beside him sat the Sage of Swevenham and Ursula. And she was grown pale now and looked somewhat scared, and she spake in a trembling voice to Ralph, and said: "Alas friend! that this should be so grim! When we hear the owls a-nighttime about the High House, shall we not deem at whiles that it is the ghosts of this dreadful battle and slaughter wandering about our fair fields?" But Ralph spake sternly and wrathfully as he sat there bareheaded and all unarmed save for the ancient glaive: "Why did they not slay me then? Better the ghosts of robbers in our fields by night, than the over-burdened hapless thrall by day, and the scourged woman, and ruined child. These things they sought for us and have found death on the way—let it be!"

He laughed as he spake; but then the grief of the end of battle came upon him and he trembled and shook, and great tears burst from his eyes and rolled down his cheeks, and he became stark and hard-faced.

Then Ursula took his hands and caressed them, and kissed his face, and fell a-talking to him of how they rode the pass to the Valley of Sweet Chestnuts; and in a while his heart and his mind came back to him as it did that other time of which she spake, and he kissed her in turn, and began to tell her of his old chamber in the turret of the High House.

And now there come riding across the field two warriors. They draw rein by the mound, and one lights down, and lo! it is Long Nicholas; and he took Ralph in his arms, and kissed him and wept over him for all his grizzled beard and his gaunt limbs; but few words he had for him, save this: "My little Lord, was it thou that was the wise captain to-day, or this stout lifter and reiver?" But the other man was Stephen a-Hurst, who laughed and said: "Nay, Nicholas, I was the fool, and this stripling the wise warrior. But, Lord Ralph, thou wilt pardon me, I hope, but we could not kill them all, for they would not fight in any wise; what shall we do with them?" Ralph knit his brows and thought a little; then he said: "How many hast thou taken?" Said Stephen: "Some two hundred alive." "Well," quoth Ralph; "strip them of all armour and weapons, and let a score of thy riders drive them back the way they came into the Debateable Wood. But give them this last word from me, that or long I shall clear the said wood of all strong-thieves."

Stephen departed on that errand; and presently comes Giles and another of the Shepherds with a like tale, and had a like answer.

Now amidst all these deeds it yet lacked an hour of noon. So presently Ralph arose and took Richard apart for a while and spoke with him a little, and then came back to Ursula and took her by the hand, and said: "Beloved, Richard shall take thee now to a pleasant abode this side the water; for I grudge that thou shouldst enter the High House without me; and as for me I must needs ride back to Wulstead to bring hither my father and mother, as I promised to do after the battle. In good sooth, I deemed it would have lasted longer." Said Ursula: "Dear friend, this is even what I should have bidden thee myself. Depart speedily, that thou mayst be back the sooner; for sórely do I long to enter thine house, beloved." Then Ralph turned to Nicholas, and said: "Our host is not so great but that thou mayst victual it well; yet I deem it is little less than when we left Wulstead early this morning."

"True is that, little lord," said Nicholas. "Hear a wonder amongst battles: of thy Shepherds and the other footmen is not one slain, and but some five hurt. The Champions have lost three men slain outright, and some fifteen hurt; of whom is thy brother Hugh, but not sorely." "Better than well is thy story then," said Ralph. "Now let them bring me a horse." So when he was horsed, he kissed Ursula and went his ways. And she abode his coming back at Richard's house anigh the water.

CHAPTER 30

Ralph Brings His Father and Mother to Upmeads

Short was the road back again to Wulstead, and whereas the day was not very old when Ralph came there, he failed not to stop at Clement's house, and came into the chamber where sat Dame Katherine in pensive wise nigh to the window, with her open hands in her lap. Quoth Ralph: "Rejoice, gossip! for neither is Clement hurt, nor I, and all is done that should be done." She moved her but little, but the tears came into her eyes and rolled down her cheeks. "What, gossip?" quoth Ralph; "these be scarce tears of joy; what aileth thee?" "Nay," said Katherine, "indeed I am joyful of thy tidings, though sooth to say I looked for none other. But, dear lord and gossip, forgive me my tears on the day of thy triumph; for if they be not wholly of joy, so also are they not wholly of sorrow. But love and the passing of the days are bitter-sweet within my heart to-day. Later on thou shalt see few faces more cheerful and merry in the hall at Upmeads than this of thy gossip's. So be merry now, and go fetch thy father and thy mother, and rejoice their hearts that thou hast been even better than thy word to them. Farewell, gossip; but look to see me at Upmeads before many days are past; for I know thee what thou art; and that the days will presently find deeds for thee, and thou wilt be riding into peril, and coming safe from out of it. Farewell!"

So he departed and rode to the House of St. Austin, and the folk gathered so about him in the street that at the gate of the Priory he had to turn about and speak to them; and he said: "Good people, rejoice! there are no more foemen of Wulstead anigh you now; and take this word of me, that I will see to it in time to come that ye live in peace and quiet here."

Folk shouted for joy, and the fathers who were standing within the gate heard his word and rejoiced, and some of them ran off to tell King Peter that his son was come back victorious already; so that by then he had dismounted at the Guest-house door, lo! there was the King and his wife with him, and both they alboun for departure. And when they saw him King Peter cried out: "There is no need to say a word, my son; unless thou wouldst tell the tale to the holy father Prior, who, as ye see, has e'en now come out to us."

Said Ralph: "Father and mother, I pray your blessing, and also the blessing of the father Prior here; and the tale is short enough: that we have overthrown them and slain the more part, and the others are now being driven like a herd of swine into their stronghold of the Wood Debateable, where, forsooth, I shall be ere the world is one month older. And in the doing of all this have but three of our men been slain and a few hurt, amongst whom is thy son Hugh, but not sorely."

"O yea, son," said his mother, "he shall do well enough. But now with thy leave, holy Prior, we will depart, so that we may sleep in the High House to-night, and feel that my dear son's hand is over us to ward us."

Then Ralph knelt before them, and King Peter and his wife blessed their son when they had kissed and embraced each other, and they wept for joy of him. The Prior also, who was old, and a worthy prelate, and an ancient friend of King Peter, might not refrain his tears at the joy of his friends as he gave Ralph his blessing. And then, when Ralph had risen up and the horses were come, he said to him: "One thing thou art not to forget, young conqueror, to wit, that thou art to come here early one day, and tell me all thy tale at full length."

"Yea, Prior," said Ralph, "or there is the High House of Upmeads for thee to use as thine own, and a rest for thee of three or four days while thou hearkenest the tale; for it may need that."

"Hearken," said King Peter softly to the Dame, "how he reckons it all his own; my day is done, my dear." He spake smiling, and she said: "Soothly he is waxen masterful, and well it becometh the dear youngling."

Now they get to horse and ride their ways, while all folk blessed them. The two old folk rode fast and pressed their nags whatever Ralph might do to give them pastime of words; so they came into the plain field of Upmeads two hours before sunset; and King Peter said: "Now I account it that I have had one day more of my life than was my due, and thou, son, hast added it to the others whereas thou didst not promise to bring me hither till morrow."

Ralph led them round by the ford, so that they might not come across the corpses of the robbers; but already were the Upmeads carles at work digging trenches wherein to bury them.

So Ralph led his father and his mother to the gate of the garth of High House; then he got off his horse and helped them down, and as he so dealt with his father, he said to him: "Thou art springy and limber yet, father; maybe thou wilt put on thine helm this year to ride the Debateable Wood with me."

The old man laughed and said: "Maybe, son; but as now it is time for thee to enter under our roof-tree once more."

"Nay," said Ralph, "but go ye in and sit in the high-seat and abide me. For did I not go straight back to you from the field of battle; and can I suffer it that any other hand than mine should lead my wife into the hall and up to the high-seat of my fathers; and therefore I go to fetch her from the house of Richard the Red where she is abiding me; but presently I shall lead her in, and do ye then with us what ye will."

Therewith he turned about and rode his ways to Richard's house, which was but a half-mile thence. But his father and mother laughed when he was gone, and King Peter said: "There again! thou seest, wife, it is he that commands and we that obey."

"O happy hour that so it is!" said the Lady, "and happy now shall be the wearing of our days."

So they entered the garth and came into the house, and were welcomed with all joy by Nicholas, and told him all that Ralph had said, and bade him array the house as he best might; for there was much folk about the High House, though the Upmeads carles and queans had taken the more part of the host to their houses, which they had delivered from the fire and sword, and they made much of them there with a good heart.

CHAPTER 31

Ralph Brings Ursula Home
to the High House

Ralph speedily came to Richard's house and entered the chamber, and found Ursula alone therein, clad in the daintiest of her woman's gear of the web of Goldburg. She rose up to meet him, and he took her in his arms, and said: "Now is come the very ending of our journey that we so often longed for; and all will be ready by then we come to the High House."

"Ah," she said, as she clung to him, "but they were happy

days the days of our journey; and to-morrow begins a new life."

"Nay," he said, "but rather this even; shall it be loathly to thee, lady?"

She said: "There will be many people whom I knew not yesterday." "There will be but me," he said, "when the night hath been dark for a little."

She kissed him and said nought. And therewithal came some of Richard's folk, for it was his house, and led with them a white palfrey for Ursula's riding, dight all gay and goodly.

"Come then," said Ralph, "thou needest not to fear the ancient house, for it is kind and lovely, and my father and my mother thou hast seen already, and they love thee. Come then, lest the hall be grown too dusk for men to see thy fairness." "Yea, yea," she said, "but first here is a garland I made for thee, and one also for me, while I was abiding thee after the battle, and my love and my hope is woven into it. And she set it on his head, and said, "O thou art fair, and I did well to meet thee in the dark wood." Then he kissed her dearly on the mouth and led her forth, and none went with them, and they mounted and went their ways.

But Ralph said: "I deem that we should ride the meadow to the bridge, because that way lies the great door of the hall, and if I know my father and Nicholas they will look for us that way. Dost thou yet fear these dead men, sweetheart, whom our folk slew this morning?" "Nay," she said, "it has been a long time since the morning, and they, and their fierieness which has so burned out, are now to me as a tale that hath been told. It is the living that I am going to, and I hope to do well by them."

Came they then to the bridge-end and there was no man there, nought but the kine that were wandering about over the dewy grass of eventide. Then they rode over the bridge and through the orchard, and still there was no man, and all gates were open wide. So they came into the base-court of the house, and it also was empty of folk; and they came to the great doors of the hall and they were open wide, and they could see through them that the hall was full of folk, and therein by the light of the low sun that streamed in at the shot-window at the other end they saw the faces of men and the gleam of steel and gold.

So they lighted down from their horses, and took hand in hand and entered bright-faced and calm, and goodly beyond the goodliness of men; then indeed all that folk burst forth into glad cries, and tossed up their weapons, and many wept for joy.

As they went slowly up the long hall (and it was thirty fathom of length) Ralph looked cheerfully and friendly from side to side, and beheld the faces of the Shepherds and the Champions, and the men of Wulstead, and his own folk; and all they cried hail to him and the lovely and valiant Lady. Then he looked up to the high-seat, and saw that his father's throne was empty, and his mother's also; but behind the throne stood a knight all armed in bright armour holding the banner of Upmeads; but his father and mother stood on the edge of the daïs to meet him and Ursula; and when they came up thither these old folk embraced them and kissed them and led them up to the table. Then Ralph bade Ursula sit by his mother, and made him ready to sit by his father in all love and duty. But King Peter stayed him and said: "Nay, dear son, not there, but here shalt thou sit, thou saviour of Upmeads and conqueror of the hearts of men; this is a little land, but therein shall be none above thee." And therewith he set Ralph down in the throne, and Ralph, turning to his left hand, saw that it was Ursula, and not his mother, who sat beside him. But at the sight of these two in the throne the glad cries and shouts shook the very timbers of the roof, and the sun sank under while yet they cried hail to the King of Upmeads.

Then were the lights brought and the supper, and all men fell to feast, and plenteous was the wine in the hall; and sure since first men met to eat together none have been merrier than they.

But now when men had well eaten, and the great cup called the River of Upmeads was brought in, the cupbearers, being so bidden before, brought it last of all to King Peter, and he stood up with the River in his hand and spoke aloud,

nd said: "Lords and warriors, and good people all, here I do
ou to wit, that it is not because my son Ralph has come
ome to-day and wrought us a great deliverance, and that
ny love hath overcome me; it is not for this cause that I
ave set him in my throne this even; but because I see and
erceive that of all the kindred he is meetest to sit therein so
ong as he liveth; unless perchance this lovely and valiant
voman should bear him a son even better than himself—and
o may it be. Therefore I do you all to wit that this man is
he King of Upmeads, and this woman is his Lady and
Queen; and so deem I of his prowess, and his wisdom, and
indliness, that I trow he shall be lord and servant of other
ands than Upmeads, and shall draw the good towns and the
indreds and worthy good lords into peace and might and
vell-being, such as they have not known heretofore. Now
vithin three days shall mass be sung in the choir of St.
Laurence, and then shall King Ralph swear on the gospels
uch oaths as ye wot of, to guard his people, and help the
needy, and oppress no man, even as I have sworn it. And I
ay to you, that if I have kept the oath to my power, yet
hall he keep it better, as he is mightier than I.

"Furthermore, when he hath sworn, then shall the vassals
wear to him according to ancient custom, to be true to him
nd hardy in all due service. But so please you I will not
bide till then, but will kneel to him and to his Lady and
Queen here and now."

Even so he did, and took Ralph's hand in his and swore
ervice to him such as was due; and he knelt to Ursula also,
nd bade her all thanks for what she had done in the helping
f his son; and they raised him up and made much of him
nd of Ralph's mother; and great was the joy of all folk in
he hall.

So the feast went on a while till the night grew old, and
olk must fare bedward. Then King Peter and his wife
rought Ralph and Ursula to the chamber of the solar, the
ingly chamber, which was well and goodly dight with hang-
ngs and a fair and glorious bed, and was newly decked with
uch fair flowers as the summer might furnish; and at the
hreshold King Peter stayed them and said: "Kinsman, and

thou, dear friend, this is become your due chamber an
resting-place while ye live in the world, and this night of a
others it shall be a chamber of love; for ye are, as it wer«
new wedded, since now first ye are come amongst the kir
dred as lover and beloved; and thou, Ursula, art now at la§
the bride of this ancient house; now tell me, doth it not loo
friendly and kindly on thee?"

"O yea, yea," she said. "Come thou, my man and m
darling and let us be alone in the master-chamber of thi
ancient House."

Then Ralph drew her unto him; and the old man blesse
them and prayed for goodly offspring for them, that th
House of Upmeads might long endure.

And thus were they two left alone amidst the love an
hope of the kindred, as erst they lay alone in the desert.

CHAPTER 32

Yet a Few Words Concerning
Ralph of Upmeads

Certain it is that Ralph failed not of his promise to th
good Prior of St. Austin's at Wulstead, but went to see hir
speedily, and told him all the tale of his wanderings as close!
as he might, and hid naught from him; which, as ye ma
wot, was more than one day's work or two or three. An«
ever when Ralph thus spoke was a brother of the Hous
sitting with the Prior, which brother was a learned and wis
man and very speedy and deft with his pen. Wherefore it ha
been deemed not unlike that from this monk's writing ha
come the more part of the tale above told. And if it be so, i
is well.

Furthermore, it is told of Ralph of Upmeads that he rule«
over his lands in right and might, and suffered no oppressio
within them, and delivered other lands and good towns whe

hey fell under tyrants and oppressors; and for as kind a man
s he was in hall and at hearth, in the field he was a warrior
o wise and dreadful, that oft forsooth the very sound of his
ame and rumour of his coming stayed the march of hosts
nd the ravage of fair lands; and no lord was ever more
eloved. Till his deathday he held the Castle of the Scaur,
nd cleansed the Wood Perilous of all strong-thieves and
eivers, so that no high-street of a good town was safer than
ts glades and its byways. The new folk of the Burg of the
ʾour Friths made him their lord and captain, and the Cham-
ions of the Dry Tree obeyed him in all honour so long as
ny of them lasted. He rode to Higham and offered himself
s captain to the abbot thereof, and drave out the tyrants
nd oppressors thence, and gave back peace to the Frank of
Higham. Ever was he true captain and brother to the Shep-
erd-folk, and in many battles they followed him; and were
here any scarcity or ill hap amongst them, he helped them to
· uttermost of his power. The Wood Debateable also he
leared of foul robbers and reivers, and rooted out the last of
he Burg-devils, and delivered three good towns beyond the
wood from the cruelty of the oppressor.

Once in every year he and Ursula his wife visited the Land
of Abundance, and he went into the castle there as into a
holy place, and worshipped the memory of the Lady whom
he had loved so dearly. With all the friends of his quest he
was kind and well-beloved.

In about two years from the day when he rode home,
came to him the Lord Bull of Utterbol with a chosen band,
of whom were both Otter and Redhead. That very day they
came he was about putting his foot in the stirrup to ride
against the foemen; so Bull and his men would not go into
the High House to eat, but drank a cup where they stood,
and turned and rode with him straightway, and did him right
manly service in battle; and went back with him afterwards
to Upmeads, and abode with him there in feasting and
joyance for two months' wearing. And thrice in the years
that followed, when his lands at home seemed safest and
most at peace, Ralph took a chosen band, and Ursula with
them, and Clement withal, and journeyed through the wastes

and the mountains to Utterbol, and passed joyous days with his old thrall of war, Bull Nosy, now become a very mighty man and the warder of the peace of the Uttermost lands.

Clement and Katherine came oft to the High House, and Katherine exceeding often; and she loved and cherished Ursula and lived long in health of body and peace of mind.

All the days that Ralph of Upmeads lived, he was the goodliest of men, and no man to look on him had known it when he grew old; and when he changed his life, an exceeding ancient man, he was to all men's eyes in the very blossom of his age.

As to Ursula his wife, she was ever as valiant and true as when they met in the dark night amidst of the Eastland wood. Eight goodly children she bore him, and saw four generations of her kindred wax up; but even as it was with Ralph, never was she less goodly of body. nay rather, but fairer than when first she came to Upmeads; and the day whereon any man saw her was a day of joyful feast to him, a day to be remembered for ever. On one day they two died and were laid together in one tomb in the choir of St Laurence of Upmeads. AND HERE ENDS THE TALE OF THE WELL AT THE WORLD'S END.